Barbara
DELINSKY

Tess
GERRITSEN

Linda
HOWARD

IMPULSE

TORONTO • NEW YORK • LONDON
AMSTERDAM • PARIS • SYDNEY • HAMBURG
STOCKHOLM • ATHENS • TOKYO • MILAN • MADRID
PRAGUE • WARSAW • BUDAPEST • AUCKLAND

ISBN 0-373-83432-2

IMPULSE

This edition published by arrangement with Harlequin Books S.A.

Visit us at www.romance.net

Printed in U.S.A.

CONTENTS

A Single Rose

Barbara
DELINSKY

Chapter One

VICTORIA LESSER TOOK A BREAK from the conversation to sit back and silently enjoy the two couples with her. They were a striking foursome. Neil Hersey, with his dark hair and close-cropped beard, was a perfect foil for his fair and petite wife, Deirdre, but the perfection of the match didn't stop at their looks. Deirdre's quick spirit complimented Neil's more studied approach to life. In the nineteen months of their marriage, they'd both grown personally and professionally.

As had the Rodenhisers. Though married a mere six months, they'd been together for nearly fifteen. Leah, with her glossy raven pageboy and bangs and the large round glasses perched on her nose, had found the ideal mate in Garrick, who gave her the confidence to live out her dreams. Garrick, sandy-haired, tall, and bearded like Neil, had finally tasted the richness of life that he'd previously assumed existed only in a scriptwriter's happy ending.

Glancing from one face to the next as the conversation flowed around her, Victoria congratulated herself on bringing the four together. It had been less of a brainstorm, of course, than her original matchmaking endeavors, but it was making for a lively and lovely evening.

Feeling momentarily superfluous, she let her gaze meander among the elegantly dressed patrons of the restaurant. She spotted several familiar faces on the far side of the room, and when her attention returned to her own party, she met Deirdre's eye. "Recognize them, Dee?"

Deirdre nodded and spoke in a hushed voice to her husband. "The Fitzpatricks and the Grants. They were at the lawn party Mother gave last fall."

Neil's wry grin was a flash of white cutting through his beard. His voice was low and smooth. "I'm not sure I remember the Fitzpatricks or the Grants, but I do remember that party. We were leaving Benji with a baby-sitter, and almost didn't get away. He was three months old and in one hell of a mood." He sent a lopsided grin across the table. "He takes after his mother in that respect."

Deirdre rolled her eyes. "Don't believe a word he says."

"Just tell me it gets better," Leah Rodenhiser begged. "You heard what Amanda gave us tonight."

Victoria, who had never had a child of her own and adored even the baby's wail, answered with the gentle voice of authority. "Of course it gets better. Amanda was just frightened. My apartment is strange and new to her. So is the baby-sitter. I left this number, but we haven't gotten a frantic call yet, have we?"

"I think you're about to get a frantic call from across the room," came a gravelly warning from Garrick. "They've spotted you, Victoria."

"Oh dear."

"Go on over," Deirdre urged softly. "If you don't, they'll come here. Spare us that joy. We'll talk babies until you get back."

Victoria, who knew all too well Deirdre's aversion to many of her mother's friends, shot her a chiding glance. But the glance quickly mellowed, and touched each of her guests in turn. "You don't mind?"

Leah grinned and answered for them all. "Go. We're traveling sub rosa."

"Sub rosa?"

"Incognito." Beneath the table she felt Garrick squeeze her hand. Once a well-known television star, he cherished his privacy. Basically shy herself, Leah protected it well.

"Are you sure you can manage without me?" Victoria quipped, standing when Neil drew out her chair. "Talk babies. I dare you." Her mischievous tone faded away as she headed off to greet her friends.

Four pairs of eyes watched her go, each pair as affectionate as the next. Victoria held a special place in their hearts, and they weren't about to talk babies when there were more immediate things to be said.

"She is a wonder," Leah sighed. "Little did I know what a gem I'd encountered when I ran into her that day in the library."

Neil was more facetious. "We didn't think she was such a gem when she stranded us on her island up in Maine. I don't think I've ever been as furious with anyone before."

"You were pretty furious with *me* before that day was out," Deirdre reminded him.

His grin grew devilish. "You asked for it. Lord, I wasn't prepared for you." He shifted his gaze to Leah and Garrick. "She was unbelievably bitchy. Had her leg in a cast and a mouth—"

Deirdre hissed him into silence, but couldn't resist reminiscing on her own. "It was just as well there weren't any neighbors. We'd have driven them crazy. We yelled at each other for days."

"While Leah and I were silent," Garrick said. "We were isolated in my cabin together, barely talking. I'm not sure which way is worse."

"Amazing how both worked out," Leah mused.

Deirdre nodded. "I'll second that."

"We owe Victoria one," Neil said.

"Two," Garrick amended.

Deirdre twirled the swizzle stick in her spritzer. "It's a tall order. The woman has just about everything she wants and needs."

Leah frowned. "There has to be something we can do in return for all she's given us."

"She needs a man."

Deirdre was quick to refute her husband's contention. "Come on, Neil. She has all the men she wants. And you know she'll never remarry. Arthur was the one and only love of her life."

Garrick exchanged a glance with Neil. "That doesn't mean we can't treat her to some fun."

Leah studied her husband. "I'm not sure I care for that mischievous gleam in your eye. Victoria is my friend. I won't have you—"

"She's my friend, too," he interrupted innocently. "Would I do anything to harm her?"

Neil was on Garrick's wavelength all the way. "The idea is to do something for her that she wouldn't dream up by herself."

"But she does just about everything she wants to," Deirdre pointed out. "She lives in luxury, dabbles in ballet, ceramics, the cello. She travels. She has the house in Southampton...." Her eyes brightened. "We could rent a yacht, hire a crew and put them at her disposal for a week. She'd be able to go off alone or invite friends along."

Garrick absently chafed his mustache with a finger. "Too conventional."

"How about a stint with Outward Bound?" Leah suggested. "There are groups formed specifically for women over forty."

Neil shot Garrick a look. "Not quite what I had in mind."

Deirdre had caught and correctly interpreted the look. "You have a one-track mind. Believe me, we'd be hard put to find a man with enough spunk for Victoria. Can you think of anyone suitable at Joyce?" Joyce Enterprises was Deirdre's family's corporation. Upon their marriage, Neil had taken it over and brought it from stagnation to productivity to expansion. Of the many new people he'd hired—or clients and associates of the company—Deirdre couldn't think of a single male who would be challenge enough for Victoria.

Neil's silence was ample show of agreement.

"It would be fun," Leah declared, "to turn the tables on Victoria."

"Someone good-looking," Deirdre said, warming to the idea.

Leah nodded. "And bright. We want a match here."

Neil rubbed his bearded jaw. "He'll have to be financially comfortable if he can afford to go in for adventure."

"Adventure," Garrick murmured. "That's the key."

Deirdre's brows lifted toward Neil. "Flash?" Flash Jensen was a neighbor of theirs in the central Connecticut suburb where they lived. A venture capitalist and a divorcé, he was always on the lookout for novel ways to spend his time.

Neil shook his head. "Flash is a little *too* much."

Leah chuckled. "We could always fix her up with one of Garrick's trapper friends. She'd die."

Garrick nodded, but he was considering another possibility. "There's a fellow I've met. One of my professors." Earlier he'd explained to the Herseys that he was working toward a Latin degree at Dartmouth. "Samson may well...fit the bill."

"Samson?" Leah echoed in mild puzzlement. She knew who he was, but nothing of what Garrick had told her in the past put the man forward as a viable candidate.

"He's a widower, and he's the right age."

Deirdre sat straighter. "Samson. From the name alone, I love him."

"That's because you've always had this thing about full heads of hair," Neil muttered in her ear. He'd never quite forgotten their earliest days together, when, among other things, she'd made fun of his widow's peak.

Deirdre hadn't forgotten either. As self-confident as Neil was, he had his sensitivities, and his hairline was one of them. "Forget hair," she whispered back. "Think strength. You have it even without the hair."

"You're putting your foot in deeper," he grumbled.

"I think you're right." Hastily she turned to Garrick, who'd been having a quiet discussion with Leah during the Herseys' private sparring. "Tell us about Samson."

Garrick was more than willing. "His name is Samson VanBaar. Leah thinks he's too conservative, but that's because she doesn't know him the way I do."

"He smokes a pipe," Leah informed them dryly.

"But that's all part of the image, love. Tweed jacket, pipe, tattered briefcase—he does it for effect. Tongue-in-cheek. A private joke."

"Weird private joke," was Leah's retort, but her tone had softened. "Do you really think he'd be right for Victoria?"

"If we're talking adventure, yes. He's good-looking and bright. He's independently wealthy. And he loves doing the unconventional." When Leah remained skeptical, he elaborated. "He's a private person, shy in some ways. He takes his little trips for his own pleasure, and they have nothing to do with the university. I had to coax him to talk, but once he got going, his stories were fascinating."

Deirdre sat forward, propping her chin in her hand. "We're listening."

"How does dog-sledding across the Yukon sound?"

"Challenging."

"How about a stint as a snake charmer in Bombay?"

"Not bad, if you're into snakes."

"Try living with the Wabians in Papua New Guinea."

"That does sound a little like Victoria," Leah had to admit. "When I first met her, she was boning up on the Maori of New Zealand."

Neil rubbed his hands together. "Okay. Let's see what we've got. A, the guy is okay in terms of age and marital status. B, he's good-looking and reasonably well-off. C, he's a respected member of the academic community." At the slight question in his voice, Garrick nodded. "And D, he's an adventurer." He took a slow breath. "So how do we go about arranging an adventure that Victoria could join him in?"

"I believe," Garrick said with a smug gleam in his eye, "it's already arranged. Samson VanBaar will be leaving next month for Colombia, from which point he'll sail across the Caribbean to Costa Rica in search of buried treasure."

"Buried treasure!"

"Gold?"

"He has a map," Garrick went on, his voice lower, almost secretive. "It's old and faded—"

"You've seen it?"

"You bet, and it looked authentic enough to me. Samson is convinced that it leads to a cache on the Costa Rican coast."

"It's so absurd, it's exciting!"

"Could be a wild goose chase. On the other hand—"

"Victoria would love it!"

"She very well might," Garrick concluded.

Neil was weighing the pros and cons. "Even if nothing comes of it in terms of a treasure, it'd certainly be a fun—how long?"

"I think he's allowed himself two weeks."

"Two weeks." Deirdre mulled it over. "Could be disastrous if they can't stand each other."

"She threw *us* together for two weeks, and we couldn't stand each other."

"It wasn't that we couldn't stand each other, Neil. We just had other things on our minds."

"We couldn't stand each other."

"Well, maybe at the beginning, but even then we couldn't keep our hands off each other."

Garrick coughed.

Leah rushed in to fill the momentary silence. "She threw us together for an *indefinite* period of time."

"Not that she planned it that way. She didn't count on mud season."

"That's beside the point. She sat by while I gave up my loft and put my furniture into storage. Then she sent me off to live in a cabin that had burned to the ground three months before. She knew I wouldn't have anywhere to go but your place, and those first few days were pretty tense...." Her words trailed off. Remembering the nights, she shot Garrick a shy glance and blushed.

Deirdre came to her aid. "There's one significant difference here, I believe. Victoria got us together in Maine; she got you two together in New Hampshire. Costa Rica—that's a little farther afield, and definitely foreign soil."

"It's a democratic country," Garrick pointed out, "and a peaceful one."

"Right next door to Nicaragua?" Leah asked in dismay, pushing her glasses higher on her nose as she turned to Neil. "Do you know anything about Costa Rica?"

"She *is* peaceful. Garrick's right about that. She's managed to stay out of her neighbors' turmoil. And she happens to be the wealthiest country in Central America."

"Then Victoria would be relatively safe?"

Garrick nodded.

"From Samson?" Deirdre asked. "Is he an honest sort of man?"

"Completely."

"Gentle?"

"Infinitely."

"Law abiding?"

"A Latin professor on tenure at one of the Ivies?" was Garrick's answer-by-way-of-a-question.

Neil stopped chewing on the inside of his cheek. "Is he, in any way, shape or manner, a lecher?"

"I've never heard any complaints," Garrick said. "Victoria can handle him. She's one together lady."

Having no argument there, Neil put the matter to an impromptu vote. "Are we in agreement that two weeks with Samson VanBaar won't kill her?"

Three heads nodded in unison.

"I'll speak with Samson and make the arrangements," Garrick offered. "I can't see that he'd have any objection to bringing one more person along on the trip, but we'd better not say anything to Victoria until I've checked it out."

"It'll be a surprise."

"She won't be able to refuse."

"She'll never know what hit her."

Garrick's lips twitched. "That'd be poetic justice, don't you think? After what she did to us—" His voice rose and he broke into his best show-stopping smile as the object of their discussion returned. "Hel-lo, Victoria!"

. . .

FIVE DAYS AFTER THAT DINNER in New York, Victoria received a bulky registered letter from New Hampshire. Opening it, she unfolded the first piece of paper she encountered.

"Dear Victoria," she read in Garrick's classic scrawl. "A simple thank you couldn't possibly convey our gratitude for all you've done. Hence, the enclosures. You'll find a round-trip ticket to Colombia, plus detailed instruction on where to go once you're there. You'll be taking part in a hunt for buried treasure led by one of my professors, a fascinating gentleman named Samson VanBaar. We happen to know you have no other plans for the last two weeks in July, and if you try to call us to weasel your way out, we won't be in. Samson is expecting you on the fourteenth. Have a wonderful time! All our love, Garrick and Leah and Deirdre and Neil."

Bemused, Victoria sank into the Louis XVI chair just inside the living-room arch. A treasure hunt? She set aside the plane tickets and read through the instructions and itinerary Garrick had seen fit to send.

New York to Miami to Barranquilla by plane. Accommodations in Barranquilla at El Prado, where Samson VanBaar would make contact. Brief drive from Barranquilla to Puerto Colombia. Puerto Colombia to Costa Rica—*Costa Rica*—by sail. Exploration of the Caribbean coast of Costa Rica as designated by Samson VanBaar's treasure map. Return by sail to Colombia and by plane to New York. Expect much sun, occasional rain. Dress accordingly.

The instructions joined the letter and tickets on her lap. She couldn't believe it! She'd known they had something up their sleeves when she'd returned to the table that night and seen smugness in their eyes.

They'd been sly; she had to hand it to them. They'd waited until the arrangements were made before presenting her with the fait accompli. Oh, yes, she could graciously refuse, but they knew she wouldn't. *She* knew she wouldn't. She'd never gone in search of buried treasure before, and though she certainly had no need for treasure, the prospect of the search was too much to resist!

Other things had been swirling around in those scheming minds of theirs as well. She knew because she'd been there herself. And because she'd been there, she knew it had something to do with Samson VanBaar. Were they actually fixing her up?

She'd sent Deirdre and Neil to the island in Maine after receiving separate, desperate calls begging for a place of solitude. She'd sent Leah to New Hampshire, to a cabin that didn't exist, knowing Leah would have no recourse but to seek out Garrick, her nearest neighbor on the mountain. What would Victoria find when she arrived in Colombia?

If Samson VanBaar was one of Garrick's professors, he had to be responsible. He might be wonderful. Or he might be forty years old and too young for her, or old and stuffy and too dry for her. One of Garrick's professors. A Latin professor. Definitely old and stuffy and dry. Perhaps simply the organizer of the expedition. In which case the Herseys and the Rodenhisers had someone else in mind. Someone else in the group?

There were many questions and far too few answers, but Victoria did know one thing. She had already blocked out the last two weeks in July for a treasure hunt. It was an opportunity, a challenge, an adventure. Regardless of her friends' wily intentions, she knew she could handle herself.

AS THAT DAY ZIPPED BY and the next began, Victoria couldn't help but think more and more about the trip. She had to admit that there was something irresistibly romantic about a sail through the Caribbean and a treasure hunt. Perhaps this Samson VanBaar would turn out to be a pirate at heart. Or perhaps one of the other group members would be the pirate.

That night, unable to shake a particularly whimsical thought, she settled in the chintz-covered chaise in the sitting area of her bedroom and put through a call to her niece.

"Hi there, Shaye!"

"Victoria?" Shaye Burke hadn't called Victoria "aunt" in years. Victoria was a dear friend with whom she'd weathered many a storm. "It's so good to hear your voice!"

"Yours, sweetheart, is sounding foreign. Do you have something against dialing the phone?"

Duly chastised, Shaye sank onto the tall stool by the kitchen phone and spoke with a fair amount of contrition. "I'm sorry, Victoria. Work's been hectic. By the time I get home my mind is addled."

"Did you just get in?"

"Mmm. We're in the process of installing a new system. It's time consuming, not to mention energy consuming." Shaye headed the computer department of a law firm in Philadelphia that specialized in corporate work. Victoria was familiar enough with such firms to know that computerization had become critical to their productivity.

"And the bulk of the responsibility is on your shoulders, I'd guess."

Shaye nodded, too tired to realize that Victoria couldn't see the gesture. "Not that I'm complaining. The new machines are incredible. Once we're fully on-line, we'll be able to do that much more that much more quickly."

"When will that be?"

"Hopefully by the end of next week. I'll have to work this weekend, but that's nothing new."

"Ahh, Shaye, where's your private life?"

"What's a private life?" Shaye returned with mock innocence.

Victoria saw nothing remotely amusing in the matter. "Private life is that time you spend away from work. It's critical, sweetheart. If you're not careful, you'll burn out before you're thirty."

"Then I'd better get on the stick. Four more months and I'll be there."

"I'm serious, Shaye. You work too hard and play too little."

Suddenly Shaye was serious, too. "I've played, Victoria. You know that better than anyone. I had six years of playing and the results were dreadful."

"You were a child then."

"I was twenty-three when I finally woke up. It was a pretty prolonged childhood, if you ask me."

"I'm not asking you, I'm telling you. What you did then was an irresponsible kind of playing. We've discussed this before, so I'm not breaking any new ground. When I use the word 'playing' now, I'm talking about something quite different. I'm talking about reading a good book, or going shopping just for the fun of it, or watching a fluff movie. I'm talking about spending time with friends."

Shaye knew what she was getting at. "I date."

"Oh yes. You've told me about those exciting times. Three hours talking shop with a lawyer from another firm. Another firm—that is daring. Of course, the fellow was nearly my age and probably arthritic."

Shaye chuckled. "We can't all reach fifty-three and be as agile as you."

"But you *can*. It's all in the mind. That lawyer's mind was no doubt ready for retirement five years ago. And your stock-broker friend doesn't sound much better. Does he give you good leads, at least?"

"It'd be illegal for me to act on an inside tip. You know that."

Victoria did know it. She also knew that her niece gave wide berth to anything vaguely questionable, let alone illegal. Shaye Burke had become a disgustingly respectable pillar of society. "Okay. Forget about stock tips. Let's talk fun. Do you have fun with him?"

"He's pleasant."

"So is the dentist. Have you been with anyone lately who's fun?"

"Uh-huh. Shannon."

"Shannon's your sister!" Victoria knew how close the two were; they'd always been so. Shaye, the elder by four years, felt personally responsible for Shannon. "She doesn't count. Who else?"

"Judy."

Victoria gave an inward groan. Judy Webber was a lawyer in Shaye's firm. The two women had become friends. If occasional weekend barbecues with Judy, her husband and their two teen-aged daughters comprised Shaye's attempts at relaxation, she was in pretty bad shape.

"How is Judy?" Victoria asked politely.

"Fine. She and Bob are heading for Nova Scotia next week. She's looking forward to it."

"That does sound nice. In fact, that's one of the reasons I called."

"To hear about Judy and Bob and Nova Scotia?"

"To talk to you about *your* vacation plans. I need two weeks of your time, sweetheart. The last two weeks in July."

"Two weeks? Victoria, I can't take off in July."

"Why not?"

"Because I'm scheduled for vacation in August."

"Schedules can be changed."

"But I've already made reservations."

"Where?"

"In the Berkshires. I've rented a cottage."

"Alone?"

"Of course alone. How else will I manage to do the reading and shopping and whatever else you claim I've been missing?"

"Knowing the way you've worked yourself to the bone, you'll probably spend the two weeks sleeping."

"And what more peaceful a place to sleep than in the country?"

"Sleeping is boring. You don't accomplish anything when you sleep."

"We're not all like you," Shaye pointed out gently. "You may be able to get by on five hours of sleep a night, but I need eight."

"And you don't usually get them because you work every night, then get up with the sun the next day to return to the office."

Shaye didn't even try to refute her aunt's claim. All she could do was rationalize. "I have six people under me—six people I'm responsible for. The hours are worth it because the results are good. I take pride in my work. And I'm paid well for my time."

"You must be building up quite some kitty in the bank, because I don't see you spending much of that money on yourself."

"I do. I live well."

"You're about to live better," Victoria stated firmly. "Two weeks in July. As my companion."

Shaye laughed. "Your companion? That's a new one."

"This trip is."

"What trip?"

"We're going to Colombia, you and I, and then on to Costa Rica."

"You aren't serious."

"Very. We're going on a treasure hunt."

Shaye stared at the receiver before returning it to her ear. "Want to run that by me again?"

"A treasure hunt, Shaye. We'll fly to Barranquilla, spend the night in a luxury hotel, drive to Puerto Colombia and then sail in style across the Caribbean. You can do all the sleeping you want on the boat. By the time we reach Costa Rica you'll be refreshed and ready to dig for pirates' gold.''

Shaye made no attempt to muffle her moan. ''Oh, Victoria, where did you dream this one up?''

''I didn't dream it up. It was handed to me on a silver platter. The expedition is being led by a friend of a friend, a professor from Dartmouth who even has a map.''

''Pirates' gold?'' Shaye echoed skeptically.

Victoria waved a negligent hand in the air. ''Well, I don't actually know what the treasure consists of, but it sounds like a fun time, don't you think?''

''I think it sounds—''

''Absurd. I knew you would, but believe me, sweetheart, this is a guaranteed adventure.''

''For you. But why *me*?''

''Because I need you along for protection.''

''Come again?''

''I need you for protection.''

Shaye's laugh was even fuller this time. ''The day you need protection will be the day they put you in the ground, and even then, I suspect they'll be preparing for outrageous happenings at the pearly gates. Try another one.''

Anticipating resistance, Victoria had thought of every possible argument. This one was her most powerful, so she repeated it a third time, adding a note of desperation to her voice. ''I need your protection, Shaye. This trip was arranged for me by some friends, and I'm sure they have mischief in mind.''

''And you'd drag me along to suffer their mischief? No way, Victoria. I'm not in the market for mischief.''

''They're trying to fix me up. I know they are. Their hearts are in the right place, but I don't need fixing up. I don't want it.'' She lowered her voice. ''You, of all people, ought to understand.''

Shaye understood all too well. Closing her eyes, she tried to recall the many times people had tried—the many times Victoria herself had tried—to fix her up with men who were sure to be the answer to her prayers. What they failed to realize was that Shaye's prayers were different from most other people's.

''All I'm asking,'' Victoria went on in the same deliberately urgent tone, ''is that you act as a buffer. If I have you with me, I won't be quite so available to some aging lothario.''

"What if they're fixing you up with a younger guy? It's done all the time."

Then he's all yours, sweetheart. "No. My friends wouldn't do that. At least," she added after sincere pause, "I don't think they would."

Shaye began, one by one, to remove the pins that had held her thick auburn hair in a twist since dawn. "I can't believe you're asking this of me," she said.

Victoria wasn't about to be touched by the weariness in her voice. "Have I ever asked much else?"

"No."

"And think of what you'll be getting out of the trip yourself. A luxurious sail through the Caribbean. Plenty of sun and clean air. We can spend a couple of extra days in Barranquilla if you want."

"Victoria, I don't even know if I can arrange for those two weeks, let alone a couple of extra days."

"You can arrange it. I have faith."

"You always have faith. That's the trouble. Now your faith is directed at some pirate stash. For years and years people have been digging for pirate treasure. Do you honestly believe anything's left to be found?"

"The point of the trip isn't the treasure, it's the hunt. And for you it will be the rest and the sun and—"

"The clean air. I know."

"Then you'll come?"

"I don't know if I can."

"You have to. I've already made the arrangements." It was a little white lie, but Victoria felt it was justified. She'd simply call Samson VanBaar and tell him one more person would be joining them. What was another person? Shaye ate like a bird, and if there was a shortage of sleeping space, Victoria herself would scrunch up on the floor.

"You're forcing me into this," Shaye accused, but her voice held an inkling of surrender.

"That's right."

"If I say no, you'll probably call the senior partner of my firm first thing tomorrow."

"I hadn't thought of that, but it's not a bad idea."

Shaye screwed up her face. "Isn't there *anyone* else you can bring along in my place?"

"No one I'd rather be with."

"That's emotional blackmail."

"So be it."

"Oh, Victoria..."

"Is that a yes?"

For several minutes, Shaye said nothing. She didn't want to traipse off in search of treasure. She didn't want to take two weeks in July, rather than the two weeks she'd planned on in August. She didn't want to have to spend her vacation acting as a buffer, when so much of her time at work was spent doing that.

But Victoria was near and dear to her. Victoria had stood by her, compassionate and forgiving when she'd nearly made a mess of her life. Victoria understood her, as precious few others did.

"Are we on?" came the gentle voice from New York.

From Philadelphia came a sigh, then a soft-spoken, if resigned, "We're on."

Later that night, as Shaye worked a brush through the thick fall of her hair, she realized that she'd given in for two basic reasons. The first was the she adored Victoria. Time spent with her never failed to be uplifting.

The second was that, in spite of all she might say to the contrary, the thought of spending two weeks in a rented cottage in the Berkshires had a vague air of loneliness to it.

VICTORIA, MEANWHILE, basked in her triumph without the slightest twinge of guilt. Shaye needed rest, and she'd get it. She needed a change of scenery, and she'd get that too. Adventure was built into the itinerary, and along the way if a man materialized who could make her niece laugh the way she'd done once upon a time, so much the better.

A spunky doctoral candidate would do the trick. Or a fun-loving assistant professor. Samson VanBaar had to be bringing a few interesting people along on the trip, didn't he?

She glanced at the temple clock atop a nearby chest. Was ten too late to call? Definitely not. One could learn a lot about a man by phoning him at night.

Without another thought, she contacted information for Hanover, New Hampshire, then punched out his home number. The phone rang twice before a rather bland, not terribly young female voice came on the line. ''Hello,'' it said. ''You have reached the residence of Samson VanBaar. The professor is not in at the moment. If you'd care to leave a message, he will be glad to return your call. Please wait for the sound of the tone.''

Victoria thought quickly as she waited. Nothing learned here; the man could be asleep or he could be out. But perhaps it was for the best that she was dealing with a machine. She could leave her message without giving him a chance to refuse her request on the spot.

The tone sounded.

''This is Victoria Lesser calling from New York. Garrick Rodenhiser has arranged for me to join your expedition to Costa Rica, but there has been a minor change in my plans. My niece, Shaye Burke, will be accompanying me. She is twenty-nine, attractive, intelligent and hardworking. I'll personally arrange for her flight to and from Colombia, and, of course, I'll pay all additional costs. Assuming you have no problem with this plan, Shaye and I will see you in Barranquilla on the fourteenth of July.''

Pleased with herself, she hung up the phone.

Four days later, she received a cryptic note typed on a plain postcard. The postmark read, ''Hanover, NH,'' and the note read, very simply, ''Received your message and have made appropriate arrangements. Until the fourteenth—VanBaar.''

Though it held no clue to the man himself, at least he hadn't banned Shaye from the trip, and for that she was grateful. Shaye had called the night before to say she'd managed to clear the two weeks with her firm, and Victoria had already contacted both the Costa Rican Embassy in New York regarding visas and her travel agent regarding a second set of airline tickets.

They were going on a treasure hunt. No matter what resulted in the realm of romance, Victoria was sure of one thing: come hell or high water, she and Shaye were going to have a time to remember.

Chapter Two

THE FOURTEENTH OF JULY was not one of Shaye's better days. Having worked late at the office the night before to clear her desk, then rushing home to pack for the trip, she'd gotten only four hours' sleep before rising to shower, dress and catch an early train into New York to meet Victoria. Their plane was forty-five minutes late leaving Kennedy and the flight was a turbulent one, though Shaye suspected that a certain amount of the turbulence she experienced was internal. She had a headache and her stomach wouldn't settle. It didn't help that they nearly missed their transfer in Miami, and when they finally landed in Barranquilla, their luggage took forever to appear. She was cursing the Colombian heat by the time they reached their hotel, and after waiting an additional uncomfortable hour for their room to be ready, she discovered that she'd gotten her period.

"Why me?" she moaned softly as she curled into a chair.

Victoria came to the rescue with aspirin and water. "Here, sweetheart. Swallow these down, then take a nap. You'll feel better after you've had some sleep."

Not about to argue, when all she wanted was an escape from her misery, Shaye dutifully swallowed the aspirin, then undressed, sponged off the heat of the trip, drew back the covers of one of the two double beds in the room and slid between the sheets. She was asleep within minutes.

It was evening when a gentle touch on her shoulder awakened her. Momentarily disoriented, she peered around the room, then up at Victoria.

"You missed the zoo."

"Huh?"

"And you didn't even know I'd gone. Shame on you. But I'm back, and I thought I'd get a bite to eat. Want anything?"

Shaye began to struggle up, but Victoria easily pressed her back to the bed.

"No, no, sweetheart. I'll bring it here. You need rest far more than you need to sit in a restaurant."

Shaye was finally getting her bearings. "But...your professor. Aren't we supposed to meet him?"

Settling on the edge of the bed, Victoria shook her head. "He sent a message saying he'll be tied up stocking the boat for a good part of the night. We're to meet him there tomorrow morning at nine."

"Where's there?"

"A small marina in Puerto Colombia, about fifteen miles east of here. The boat is called the *Golden Echo*."

"The *Golden Echo*. Appropriate."

Victoria gave an impish grin. "I thought so, too. Pirates' gold. Echoes of the past. It's probably just a coincidence, since I assume the boat is rented."

"Don't assume it. If VanBaar does this sort of thing often, he could well own the boat." She hesitated, then ventured cautiously, "He does do this sort of thing often, doesn't he?"

"I really don't know."

"How large is the boat?"

"I don't know that either."

"How large is our group?"

Victoria raised both brows, pressed her lips together in a sheepish kind of way and shrugged.

"Victoria," Shaye wailed, fully awake now and wishing she weren't, "don't you ask questions before you jump into things?"

"What do I need to ask? I know that Samson VanBaar is Garrick's friend, and I trust Garrick."

"You dragged me along because you *didn't* trust him."

"I didn't trust that he wouldn't try to foist me off on some unsuspecting man, but that's a lesser issue here. The greater issue is the trip itself. Garrick would never pull any punches in the overall scheme of things."

Shaye tugged at a hairpin that was digging into her scalp. "Exactly what *do* you know about this trip?"

"Just what I've told you."

"Which is precious little."

"Come on, sweetheart. The details will come. They'll unfold like a lovely surprise."

"I hate surprises."

"Mmm. You like to know what's happening before it happens. That's the computerized you.'' Her gaze dropped briefly to the tiny mark at the top of Shaye's breast, a small shadow beneath the lace edging of her bra. ''But there's another side, Shaye, and this trip's going to bring it out. You'll learn to accept it and control it. It's really not such a bad thing when taken in moderation.''

''Victoria...''

''Look at it this way. You're with me. I'll be your protector, just as you'll be mine.''

''How can you protect me from something you can't anticipate?''

''Oh, I can anticipate.'' She tipped up her head and fixed a dreamy gaze on the wall. ''I'm anticipating that boat. It'll be a beauty. Long and sleek, with polished brass fittings and crisp white sails. We'll have a lovely stateroom to share. The food will be superb, the martinis nice and dry...''

''You hope.''

''And why not? Look around. I wouldn't exactly call this room a hovel.''

''No, but it could well be the equivalent of a last meal for the condemned.''

Victoria clucked her tongue. ''Such pessimism in one so young.''

Shaye shifted onto her side. She was achy all over. ''Right about now, I feel ninety years old.''

''When you're ninety, you won't have to worry about monthly cramps. When you're fifty, for that matter.'' She grinned. ''I rather like my age.''

''What's not to like about sixteen?''

''Now, now, do I sound that irresponsible?''

''Carefree may be a better word, or starry-eyed, or naive. Victoria, for all you know the *Golden Echo* may be a leaky tub and Samson VanBaar a blundering idiot.''

Victoria schooled her expression to one of total maturity. ''I've thought a lot about that. Samson won't be an idiot. Maybe an absentminded professor, or a man bent on living out his childhood dreams.'' She took a quick breath. ''He could be fun.''

''He could be impossible.''

''But there will be others aboard.''

''Mmm. A bunch of his students, all around twenty and so full of themselves that they'll be obnoxious.''

"You were pretty full of yourself at that age," she reminded her niece, smoothing a stray wisp of hair from Shaye's pale cheek.

"And obnoxious."

"You didn't think so at the time."

"Neither will they."

But Victoria's eyes had grown thoughtful again. "I don't think there'll be many students. Garrick wouldn't have signed me on as a dorm mother. No, I'd guess that we'll be encountering adults, people very much like us looking for a break from routine."

"Since when do you have a routine you need a break from?"

"Not me. You. You need the break. I don't need anything, but my friends wanted to give me a good time, and that's exactly what I intend to have." She pushed herself gracefully from the bed. "Starting now. I'm famished. What'll it be—a doggie bag from the restaurant or room service later?"

Shaye tucked up her knees and closed her eyes. "Sleep. Tomorrow will be soon enough for superb food and nice dry martinis."

THE TWO WOMEN HAD NO TROUBLE finding the *Golden Echo* the next morning. She was berthed at the end of the pier and very definitely stood apart from the other craft they'd passed.

"Oh Lord," Shaye muttered.

Victoria was as wide-eyed as her niece. "Maybe we have the wrong one."

"The name board says *Golden Echo*."

"Maybe I got the name wrong."

"Maybe you got the trip wrong."

They stood with their elbows linked and their heads close together as, eyes transfixed on the boat before them, they whispered back and forth.

"She isn't exactly a tub," Victoria offered meekly.

"She's a pirate ship—"

"In miniature."

"Looks like she's been through one too many battles. Or one too few. She should have sunk long ago."

"Maybe not," Victoria argued, desperately searching for something positive to say. "She looks sturdy enough."

"Like a white elephant."

"But she's clean."

"Mmm. The chipped paint's been neatly scraped away. Lord, I don't believe I've seen anything as boxy since the Tall Ships passed through during the Bicentennial."

"They were impressive."

"*They* were."

"So's this—"

"If you close your eyes and pretend you're living in the eighteenth century."

Victoria didn't close her eyes, but she was squinting hard. "You have to admit that she has a certain...character."

"Mmm. Decrepit."

"She takes three sails. That should be pretty."

Her enthusiasm was lost on Shaye, who was eyeing in dismay the ragged bundles of canvas lashed to the rigging. "Three crisp...white...sails."

"Okay, they may not be crisp and white. What does it matter, if they're strong?"

"Are they?"

"If Samson VanBaar is any kind of friend to Garrick—and if Garrick is any kind of friend to me—they are."

Shaye moaned. "And to think that I could have been in the Berkshires, lazing around without a care in the world."

"You'll be able to laze around here."

"I don't see any deck chairs."

"But it's a nice broad deck."

"It looks splintery."

"So we'll lie on towels."

"Did you bring some?"

"Of course not. They'll have towels aboard."

"Like they have polished brass fittings?" Shaye sighed. "Well, you were right in a way."

"What way was that?" Victoria asked, at a momentary loss.

"We are going in style. Of course, it's not exactly *our* style—for that matter, I'm not sure whose style it is." Her voice hardened. "You may be crazy enough to give it a try, but I'm not."

She started to pivot away, intending to take the first cab back to Barranquilla, but Victoria clamped her elbow tighter and dragged her forward. "Excuse me," she was calling, shading her eyes from the sun with her free hand. "We're looking for Samson VanBaar."

Keeping step with her aunt through no will of her own, Shaye forced herself to focus on the figure that had just emerged from the bowels of the boat. "It gets worse," she moaned, then whispered a hoarse, "What *is* he?"

"I'm VanBaar," came the returning call. "Mrs. Lesser, Miss Burke?" With a sweep of his arm, he motioned them forward. "We've been expecting you."

Nothing they'd imagined had prepared either Shaye or Victoria for Samson VanBaar. In his mid to late fifties, he was remarkably tall and solid. His well-trimmed salt-and-pepper hair, very possibly combed in a dignified manner short days before, tumbled carelessly around his head, forming a reckless frame for a face that was faintly sunburned, though inarguably sweet.

What was arguable was his costume, and it could only be called that. He wore a billowy white shirt tucked into a pair of narrow black pants, which were tucked into knee-high leather boots. A wide black belt slanted low across his hips, and if it lacked the scabbard for a dagger or a sword, the effect was the same.

"He forgot the eye patch," Shaye warbled hysterically.

"Shh! He's darling!" Victoria whispered under her breath. Smiling broadly—and never once releasing Shaye, who, she knew, would head in the opposite direction given the first opportunity—she started up the gangplank. At the top, she put her free hand in the one Samson offered and stepped onto the deck. "It's a delight to meet you at last, Professor VanBaar. I'm Victoria Lesser, and this is my niece, Shaye Burke."

Shaye was too busy silently cursing her relationship with Victoria to say much of anything, but she managed a feeble smile in return for the open one the professor gave her.

"Welcome to the *Golden Echo*," he said, quietly now that they were close. "I trust you had no problem finding us."

"No, no," Victoria answered brightly. "None at all." She made a grand visual sweep of the boat, trying to see as little as possible while still conveying her point. "This is charming!"

Shaye nearly choked. When Victoria gave a tight, warning squeeze to her elbow before abruptly releasing it, she tipped back her head, closed her eyes and drew in an exaggerated lungful of Caribbean air. It was certainly better than having to look at the boat, and though Samson VanBaar was attractive enough, the insides of her eyelids were more reassuring than his getup.

"I felt that the *Golden Echo* would be more in keeping with the spirit of this trip than a modern yacht would be," he explained. "She's a little on the aged side, but I've been told she's trusty."

Shaye opened one eye. "You haven't sailed her yet?"

Almost imperceptibly he ducked his head, but the tiny movement was enough to suggest guilt. "I've sailed ones like her, but I just flew in yesterday myself, and the bulk of my time between then and now had been spent buying supplies. I hope you understood why I couldn't properly welcome you in Barranquilla last night."

"Of course," Victoria reassured him gently. "It worked out just as well, actually. We were both tired after the flight."

"You slept well?"

"Very well."

"Good." He ran a forefinger along the corner of his mouth, as though unsure of what to say next. Then his eyes brightened. "Your bags." He quickly spotted them on the pier. "Let me bring them aboard, then I'll give you the Cook's tour."

He'd no sooner descended the gangplank when Shaye whirled on Victoria. "The Cook's tour?" she whispered wildly. "Is he the cook or are we?"

"Don't fret," Victoria whispered back with confidence, "there's a cook."

"Like there's a lovely stateroom for us to share? Do you have any idea what's down there?"

"Nope. That's what the Cook's tour is for."

"Aren't you worried?"

"Of course not. This is an adventure."

"The boat is a wreck!"

"She's trusty."

"So says the professor who's staging Halloween three months early."

Victoria's eyes followed Samson's progress. "And I thought he'd be stuffy. He's precious!"

"Good. Since you like him so well, you won't need my protection after all. I'll just take my bag and head back—"

"You will not! You're staying!"

"Victoria, there'll be lots of other people..." The words died on her lips. Her head remained still while her eyes moved from one end of the empty deck to the other. She listened. "Where are they? It's too quiet. We were ten minutes late, ourselves. Where are the others?''

Victoria was asking herself the same question. Her plan was contingent on there being other treasure seekers, specifically of the young and good-looking male variety. True, in terms of rest alone, the trip would be good for Shaye, and Victoria always enjoyed her niece's company. But matching her up with a man—it had worked so well with Deirdre, then Leah... Where *were* the men?

Concealing her concern behind a gracious smile, she turned to VanBaar, who had rejoined them with a suitcase in either hand. ''We don't expect you wait on us. Please. Just tell us what to do.'' She reached for her bag, but Samson drew it out of her reach.

''Chivalry is a dying art. You'll have plenty to do as time goes on, but for now, I think I can manage two bags.''

Chivalry? Shaye thought, amused. *Plenty to do?* she thought, appalled.

Victoria was thinking about the good-looking young men she didn't see. ''Is this standard service given to all the members of your group?'' she ventured, half teasing, half chiding, and subtly fishing for information.

''No, ma'am. We men fend for ourselves. You and your niece are the only women along.''

Swell, Shaye groused silently, *just swell.*

Victoria couldn't have been more delighted. ''How many others are there, Professor VanBaar?''

He blushed. ''Samson, please.''

She smiled. ''Samson, then. How many of us will there be in all?''

''Four.''

''Four?'' the women echoed in unison.

''That's right.'' Setting the bags by his booted feet, he scratched the back of his head. ''Didn't Garrick explain the situation?''

Victoria gave a delicate little cough. ''I'm afraid he didn't go quite that far.''

''That was negligent of him,'' Samson said, but he didn't seem upset, and Victoria saw a tiny twinkle in his eye. ''Let me explain. Originally there were to be just two of us, myself and an old college buddy with whom I often travel in the summer.

When Garrick called me about your joining us, I saw no problem. Unfortunately, my friend had to cancel at the last minute, so I hoodwinked my nephew into taking up the slack." He stole a glance at Shaye's dismayed expression. "It takes two to comfortably man the boat, and since I didn't know whether either of you were sailors—"

"We're not," Shaye burst out. "I don't know about my aunt, but I get seasick."

"Ignore her, Samson. She's only teasing."

"*Violently* seasick."

"Not to worry," Samson assured her in the same kind tone that made it hard to hold a grudge. "I have medicine for seasickness, though I doubt you'll need it. We shouldn't run into heavy seas."

At that moment, Shaye would have paid a pirate's ransom to be by her lonesome in the Berkshires. A foursome—Victoria and Samson, Samson's nephew and her. It was too cozy, too convenient. Suddenly something smacked of a setup. Could Samson have done it? Or Garrick? Or... She skewered her aunt with an accusatory glare.

Victoria had her eyes glued to Samson. "I'm sure we'll be fine." She took a deep breath and straightened her shoulders. "Now then, I believe you said something about a tour?"

NOAH VANBAAR WAS nearly as disgusted as Shaye. Arms crossed over his chest and one knee bent up as he lounged on a hardwood bench within earshot of the three above, he struggled in vain to contain his frustration. He'd had other plans for his summer vacation, but when his uncle had called, claiming that Barney was sick and there was no one else who could help him sail, he'd been indulgent.

Samson and he were the only two surviving members of the VanBaar family, but even if sentimentality hadn't been a factor, Noah was fond enough of his uncle to take pity. He knew how much Samson looked forward to his little jaunts. He also knew that Samson was an expert sailor and more than capable of handling the boat himself, but that for safety's sake he needed another pair of hands along. If Noah's refusal meant that Samson had to cancel his trip, there was no real choice to be made.

Naturally, his uncle had waited until last night to inform him that they wouldn't be sailing alone. Naturally, he had waited until this morning to inform him that the pair joining them would be female.

Noah didn't want one woman along, much less two. Not that he had anything against women in general, but on this trip, they would be in the way. He'd planned to relax, to take a break from the tension that was part and parcel of his work. He'd planned to have one of the two cabins on the boat to himself, to sleep to his heart's content, to dress as he pleased, shave when and if he pleased, swim in the buff, and, in short, let it all hang out.

The presence of women didn't figure into his personal game plan. They were bound to screw things up. A widow and her niece. Charming. Samson was already carrying their bags. If they thought *he* was going to wait on them, they had another think coming!

Actually, he mused, the aunt didn't sound so bad. She had a pleasant voice, sounded lively without being obnoxious, and to her further credit, had protested Samson's playing bellboy. He wondered what she looked like and whether Samson would be enthralled. He hoped not, because then he'd be stuck with the niece, who sounded far less lively and more obnoxious than her aunt.

It was obvious that the niece wasn't thrilled with the looks of the sloop. What had she expected? The *Brittania*? If so, he decided as his eyes skimmed the gloomy interior of the *Golden Echo*, she was in for an even ruder awakening than she'd already had.

Not that the boat bothered him; he'd sailed in far worse. This time around, though, he could have asked for more space. This time around he'd have preferred the *Brittania*, himself. At least then he'd have been able to steer clear of the women.

Though he didn't move an inch, he grew instinctively alert when he heard footsteps approaching the gangway. Samson was in the lead, his booted feet appearing several seconds before the two suitcases. "The *Golden Echo* was refurbished ten years ago," he was saying, his voice growing louder as his head came into view. "The galley is quite modern and the cabins comfortable—ah, Noah, right where I left you." Stepping aside, he set down the bags to give an assisting hand to each of the women in turn.

Noah didn't have to marvel at his uncle's style. Though a bit eccentric at times, Samson was a gentleman through and through, which was fine as long as he didn't expect the same standard from his nephew. Noah spent his working life straddling the lines between gentleman, diplomat and czar; he intended to spend his vacation answering to no one but himself.

"Noah, I'd like you to meet Victoria Lesser," Samson said. He knew better than to ask his nephew to rise. Noah was intimidating enough when seated; standing he was formidable. Given the dark mood he was in at the moment, intimidation was the lesser of the evils.

Noah nodded toward Victoria, careful to conceal the slight surprise he felt. Victoria had not only sounded lively, she looked lively. What had Samson said—that she was in her early fifties? She didn't look a day over forty. She wore a bright yellow, oversize shirt, a pair of white slacks with the cuffs rolled to midcalf, and sneakers, and her features were every bit as youthful. Her hair was an attractive walnut shade and thick, loosely arranged into a high, short ponytail that left gentle wisps to frame the delicate structure of her face. Her skin was flawless, firm-toned and lightly made up, if at all. Her eyes twinkled, and her smile was genuine.

"It's a pleasure to meet you, Noah," she said every bit as sincerely. "Thank you for letting us join you on this trip. I've done many things in my day, but I've never been on a treasure hunt before. It sounds as though it'll be fun."

Lured by the subtle melody of her voice, Noah almost believed her. Then he shifted his gaze to the young woman who'd followed her down the steps and took back the thought.

"Shaye Burke," Samson was saying by way of introduction, "Noah VanBaar."

Again Noah nodded his head, this time a trifle more stiffly. Shaye Burke was a looker; he had to give her that. Slightly taller than her aunt, she was every bit as slender. Her white jeans were pencil thin, her blousy, peach-colored T-shirt rolled at the sleeves and knotted chicly at the waist. Her skin, too, was flawless, but it was pale; she'd skillfully applied makeup to cover shadows beneath her eyes and add faint color to her cheeks.

Any similarities to her aunt had already ended. Shaye's deep auburn hair was anchored at the nape of her neck in a sedate twist from which not a strand escaped. The younger woman's lips were set, her nose marked with tension, and the eyes that met his held a shadow of rebellion.

She didn't want to be here. It was written all over her face. Adding that to the comments he'd overheard earlier, he begrudged her presence more than ever. If Shaye Burke did anything to spoil his uncle's adventure, he vowed, he would personally even the score.

Samson, who'd sensed the instant animosity between Noah and Shaye, spoke up quickly. "If you ladies will come this way, I'll show you to your cabin. Once we've deposited your things there, we can walk around more freely."

Short of turning and fleeing, Shaye had no choice but to follow Victoria, who followed Samson through the narrow passageway. Her shoulders were ramrod straight, held that way by the force of a certain man's gaze piercing her back.

Noah. Noah and Samson. The VanBaar family, she decided, had a thing about biblical names. But her image of *that* Noah was one of kindness; *this* Noah struck her as being quite different. Sitting in the shadows as he'd been, she hadn't been able to see much beyond gloom and a glower. She knew one thing, though: She hadn't expected to have to protect her aunt, but if Noah VanBaar so much as dared do anything to dampen Victoria's spirits, he'd have to answer to her.

SAMSON LED VICTORIA AND SHAYE to the cabin they'd be sharing, then backtracked to show them the salon, the galley and the captain's quarters in turn. Noah was nowhere in sight during the backtracking, and Shaye was grateful for that. There was precious little else to be grateful for.

"We do have our own bathroom," Victoria pointed out when they'd returned to their cabin to unpack. She lowered herself to Shaye's side of the double bed that occupied three quarters of the small cabin's space. "I know that it's not quite what we expected, but if we clear our minds of those other expectations, we'll do fine."

Shaye's lips twisted wryly. "Grin and bear it?"

"Make the most of it." She jabbed at the bedding with a delicate fist. "The mattress feels solid enough." Her eye roamed the trapezoid-shaped room. "And we could have been stuck with a V-berth."

"This bed is bolted to the wall. I thought Samson said it'd be a calm trip."

"This one will be, but we have no idea what other waters the *Golden Echo* has sailed."

"If only she were somewhere else—without us."

"Shaye..."

"And where do we go to relax?"

"The salon."

"For privacy?" She was thinking of the dagger-edged gaze that had followed her earlier, and wasn't sure whether she'd be able to endure it as a constant.

Victoria's mind was still on the salon. "There are comfortable chairs, a sofa—"

"And a distinctly musty smell."

"That's the smell of the sea. It adds atmosphere."

Shaye snorted. "That kind of atmosphere I can do without." She knew she was being unfair; after all, the cottage she'd booked in the Berkshires very probably had its own musty smell, and she normally wasn't that fussy. But her bad mood seemed to feed on itself and on every tiny fault she could find with the boat.

"Come on, sweetheart," Victoria coaxed as she rose to open her suitcase. "We'll have fun. I promise."

Shaye's discouraged gaze wandered around the cabin, finally alighting on the row of evenly spaced, slit-like windows. "At least there are portholes. Clever, actually. They're built into the carving of the hull. I didn't notice them from the dock."

"And they're open. The air's circulating. And it's relatively bright."

"All the better to see the simplicity of the decor," Shaye added tongue-in-cheek. She watched her aunt unpack in silence for several minutes before tipping her head to the side and venturing a wary, "Victoria?"

"Uh-huh?"

"How much did you really know about all this?"

Victoria stacked several pairs of shorts in a pile, then straightened. "About all what?"

"This trip."

"Haven't we discussed this before?"

"But something's beginning to smell."

"I told you," Victoria responded innocently. "It's the sea."

"Not smell as in brine. Smell as in rat. Did you have any idea at all that there'd be just four of us?"

"Of course not."

"It never occurred to you that Samson would be 'precious' and that I'd be left with his nephew?"

Victoria gave a negligent shrug and set the shorts in the nearby locker. "You heard what Samson said. Noah's joining us was a last-minute decision. I mentioned this trip to you nearly a month ago."

But Shaye remained skeptical. "Samson didn't say exactly how 'last-minute' the decision was. Are you sure you're not trying to pair me up with Noah?"

"Would I do that—"

"She asks a little too innocently. You did it with Deirdre Joyce."

"I thought you approved."

"In that case I did—do. Neil Hersey is a wonderful man." Shaye had never forgotten that it was Neil, with his legal ability and compassion, who had come to the rescue when Shannon had been arrested.

Victoria was grateful that Shaye knew nothing of her role in bringing Garrick and Leah together. The less credence given the word *matchmaker*, the better, she decided. "Noah VanBaar may be every bit as wonderful."

Shaye coughed comically. "Try again."

"He may be!"

"Then you did do it on purpose?"

Victoria felt only a smidgen of guilt as she propped her hands on her hips in a stance of exasperation. "Really, Shaye. How could I have done it on purpose when I had no idea Noah would be along?"

"Then you intended to fix me up with Samson's old-fart friend?"

"I did not! I truly, truly expected that we'd be only two more members of a larger group."

Sensing a certain truth to that part of Victoria's story at least, Shaye sighed. "If only there *were* a larger group—"

"So you could fade into the woodwork? I wouldn't have let you do that even if there were fifty others on board this boat." She lifted a pair of slacks and nonchalantly shook them out. "What did you think of Noah, by the way?"

"I thought he was rude, by the way. He could have stood up

when we were introduced. He could have said something. Do you realize the man didn't utter a single word?"

"Neither did you at that point."

"That's because I chose silence over saying something unpleasant."

"Maybe that's what he was doing. Maybe he's as tired as you are. Maybe he, too, had other plans before Samson called him."

"I wish he'd stuck to his guns."

"Like you did?"

Bowing her head, Shaye pressed the throbbing spot between her eyes. "I gave in because you're my aunt and my friend and because I love you."

Draping an arm around Shaye's shoulders, Victoria hugged her close. "You know how much that means to me, sweetheart. And it may be that Noah feels the same about Samson. Cheer up. He won't be so bad. How can he be, with an uncle like that?"

WHEN VICTORIA LEFT to go on deck, Shaye stayed behind to unpack. But there was only so much unpacking to do, and only so much to look at within the close cabin walls. She realized she was stalling, and that annoyed her, then hardened her. If Noah VanBaar thought he could cower her with his dark and brooding looks, he was in for a surprise.

Emboldened, she made her way topside to find Samson drawing up the gangplank. A powerboat hovered at the bow of the *Golden Echo*, prepared to tow her clear of the pier. At Samson's call, Noah cast off the lines, the powerboat accelerated and they were off.

When the other three gathered at the bow, Shaye took refuge at the stern. Mounting the few steps to the ancient version of a cockpit, she bypassed the large wooden wheel to rest against the transom and watch the shore slowly but steadily recede.

It was actually a fine day for a sail, she had to admit. The breeze feathered her face, cooling what might otherwise have been heated rays of the sun. But she felt a wistfulness as her gaze encompassed more and more of the Colombian shore. Given her druthers, she'd have stayed in Barranquilla and waited for Victoria's return. No, she insisted, given her druthers, she'd be working in Philadelphia, patiently waiting for her August break.

But that was neither here nor there. She was on the *Golden Echo*, soon to be well into the Caribbean, and there was no point bemoaning her fate. She had to see the bright side, as Victoria was doing. She'd brought books along, and she'd spotted cushions in the salon that could be used as padding in lieu of a deck chair. And if she worked to keep her presence as inconspicuous as possible, she knew she'd do all right.

"Having second thoughts?"

The low, taunting baritone came from behind her. She didn't have the slightest doubt as to whose voice it was.

"What's to have second thoughts about?" she asked quietly. "This is my vacation. I'm looking forward to it."

"Are you always uptight when you're looking forward to something?"

"I'm not uptight."

He moved forward until he, too, leaned against the wood. "No?"

Shaye was peripherally aware of his largeness and did her best to ignore it. "No."

"Then why are your knuckles white on that rail?"

"Because if the boat lurches, I don't want to be thrown."

"She's called a sloop, and she doesn't lurch."

"Sway, tilt, heel—whatever the term is."

"Not a sailor, I take it?"

"I've sailed."

"Sunfish? Catboat?"

"Actually, I've spent time on twelve-meters, but as a guest, not a student of nautical terminology."

"A twelve-meter is a far cry from the *Golden Echo*."

"Do tell."

"You're not pleased with her?"

"She's fine," Shaye answered diplomatically.

"But not up to your usual standards?"

"I didn't say that."

"You're thinking it. Tell me, if you're used to something faster and sleeker, what are you doing here?"

Shaye bit off the sharp retort that was on the tip of her tongue and instead answered calmly, "As I said, I'm on vacation."

"Why here?"

"Because my aunt invited me to join her."

"And you were thrilled to accept?"

She did turn to him then and immediately wished she hadn't. He towered over her, a good six-four to her own five-six, and there was an air of menace about him. She took a deep breath to regain her poise, then spoke slowly and as evenly as possible.

"No, I was not thrilled to accept. Sailing off in the facsimile of a pirate ship on a wild goose chase for a treasure that probably doesn't exist is not high on my list of ways I'd like to spend my vacation."

Noah's gaze was hard as he studied her face. She was a beauty, but cool, very cool. Her features were set in rigid lines, her hazel eyes cutting. Had he seen any warmth, any softening, he would have eased off. But he was annoyed as hell that she was along, and to have her match his stare with such boldness was just what he needed to goad him on.

"That was what I figured." His eyes narrowed. "Now listen here, and listen good. If you repeat any of those pithy comments within earshot of my uncle, you'll regret it."

The blatant threat took Shaye by surprise. She'd assumed Noah to be rude; she hadn't expected him to be openly hostile. "Excuse me?"

"You heard."

"Heard, but don't believe. What makes you think I'd say anything to your uncle?"

"I know your type."

"How could you possibly—"

"You expected a luxury yacht, not a wreck of a boat. You expected a lovely stateroom, not a small, plain cabin. You expected a captain and a cook, not a professor who's staging Halloween three months early."

Shaye's blood began a slow boil. "You were eavesdropping!"

His eyes remained steady, a chilling gray, and the dark spikes of hair that fell over his brow, seeming to defy the wind, added to the aura of threat that was belied by the complacency of his voice. "I was sitting below while you and your aunt chatted on deck."

"So you listened."

"The temptation was too great. In case you haven't realized it yet, we'll be practically on top of each other for the next two weeks. I wanted to know what I was in for." His gaze dropped to her hands. "I'd ease up if I were you. Those nails of yours will leave marks on the wood."

Shaye's fingernails weren't overly long, though they were neatly filed and wore a coat of clear polish. Instead of arguing, she took yet another deep breath and squared her shoulders. "Thank you for making your feelings clear."

"Just issuing a friendly little warning."

"Friendly?"

"We-e-e-ll, maybe that is stretching it a little. You're too stiff-backed and fussy for my tastes."

Shaye's temper flared. "You have to be one of the most arrogant individuals I've ever had the misfortune to meet. You don't know me at all. You have no idea what I do, what I like or what I want. But I'll tell you one thing, I don't take to little warnings the likes of which you just issued."

"Consider it offered nonetheless."

"And you can consider it rejected." Eyes blazing, she made a slow and deliberate sweep from his thick, dark hair over his faded black T-shirt and worn khaki shorts, down long, hair-roughened legs to his solid bare feet. "I don't need you telling me what to do. I can handle myself and in good taste, which is a sight more than I can say for you." Every bit as deliberately as she'd raked his form, and with as much indifference to his presence as she could muster, she returned her gaze to the shrinking port.

"I'd watch it, if I were you. I'm not in the mood to be crossed."

"Another threat?" she asked, keeping her eyes fixed on the shore. "And what will you do if I choose to ignore it?"

"I'll be your shadow for the next two weeks. I could make things unpleasant, you know."

"I have the distinct feeling you'll do that anyway." Turning, she set off smoothly for the bow.

Chapter Three

VICTORIA SQUINTED UP at Samson. "How much farther will we be towed?"

"Not much. We're nearly clear of the smaller boats, and the wind is picking up nicely."

Shaye joined them in time to catch his answer. "What happens if it dies once we're free?"

Samson grinned. "Then we'll lie on the deck and bask in the sun until it decides to come back to life."

She had visions of lying in the sun and basking for days, and the visions weren't enticing. Still smarting from her set-to with Noah, she feared that if they were becalmed she'd go stark, raving mad. "Given a reasonable wind, how long will it take to reach Costa Rica?"

"Given a reasonable wind, four days. The *Golden Echo* wasn't built for speed."

"What was she built for?" Shaye asked, her curiosity offset by a hint of aspersion.

"Effect," came Noah's tight reply as he took up a position beside her.

Her shadow. Was it starting already? Tipping up her head, she challenged him with a stare. "Explain, please."

Noah directed raised brows toward his uncle, who in his own shy way was a storyteller. But Samson shook his head, pivoted on his heel and headed aft, calling over his shoulder, "It's all yours. I have to see to the sails."

Noah would have offered his assistance if it hadn't been for two things. First, Samson would have refused: he took pride in his sailing skill and preferred, whenever possible, to do things himself. Second, Noah wanted to stay by Shaye. He knew that he annoyed her, and he intended to take advantage of that fact. It was some solace, albeit perverse, to have her aboard.

"The *Golden Echo* was modeled after an early eighteenth century Colonial sloop," he began, broadening his gaze to include

Victoria in the tale. "She was built in the 1920s by a man named Horgan, a sailor and a patriot, who saw in her lines a classic beauty that was being lost in the sleeker, more modern craft. Horgan wanted to enjoy her, but he also wanted to make a statement."

"He did that," Shaye retorted, then asked on impulse, "Where did he sail her?"

"Up and down the East Coast at first."

"For pleasure?"

Noah's eyes bore into her. "Some people do it that way."

Victoria, who'd been watching the two as she leaned back against the rail, asked gently, "Did he parade her?"

"I'm sure he did," Noah answered, softening faintly with the shift of his gaze, "though I doubt there was as much general interest in a vessel like this then as there is today. From what Samson learned, Horgan made several Atlantic crossings before he finally berthed the *Golden Echo* in Bermuda. When his own family lost interest and he grew too ill to sail her alone, he began renting her out. She was sold as part of his estate in the mid-sixties."

"That leaves twenty years unaccounted for," Shaye prompted.

"I'm getting there." But he took his time, leisurely looking amidship to check on his uncle's progress. By the time he resumed, Shaye was glaring out to sea. "The new owners, a couple by the name of Payne, expanded on the charter business. For a time, they worked summers out of Boston, where the *Golden Echo* was in demand for private parties and small charity functions. Eventually they decided that the season was too limited, so they moved south."

"Why aren't they with us now?" Shaye asked without turning her head.

"Because there isn't room. Besides, they have a number of other boats to manage. The business is headquartered in Jamaica."

"Why are we in Colombia?"

"Because that's where the last charter ended. It's a little like Hertz—"

"Noah!" came Samson's buoyant shout. "Set us free!"

With a steadying hand on the bowsprit, Noah folded himself

over the prow, reaching low to release the heavy steel clip that had held the powerboat's line to the *Golden Echo*.

The powerboat instantly surged ahead, then swung into a broad U-turn. Its driver, a Colombian with swarthy skin and a mile-wide white grin, saluted as he passed. A grinning Victoria waved back, moving aft to maintain the contact.

Shaye was unaware of her departure. She hadn't even seen the Colombian. Rather, her eyes were glued to the spot where Noah had released the clip. The large, rusty ring spoke for itself, but what evoked an odd blend of astonishment and amusement was the fact that it protruded from the navel of a scantily clad lady. That the lady was time-worn and peeling served only to accentuate her partial nudity.

"That's the figurehead," Noah informed her, crossing his arms over his chest.

"I know what it is," she answered, instantly losing grasp of whatever amusement she'd felt. "I just hadn't seen her earlier."

"Does her state of undress embarrass you?"

"I've seen breasts before."

Insolent eyes scanned the front of her T-shirt. "I should hope so."

Shaye kept her arms at her sides when they desperately wanted to cover her chest. She was far from the prude that Noah had apparently decided she was, but while she'd learned to control her desires, there was something about the way he was looking at her that set off little sparks inside. She felt nearly as bare-breasted as the lady on the bow and not nearly as wooden—which was something she sought to remedy by turning the tables on Noah.

"Does she excite you?"

"Who?"

Shaye tossed her head toward the bow, then watched as he bent sideways.

"She's not bad," he decided, straightening. "A little stern-faced for my tastes. Like you."

"Your tastes are probably as pathetic as old Horgan's. If he were building a boat like this today and dared to put a thing like that at the bow, he'd have women's groups picketing the pier."

Noah drew himself to his full height and glared down at her. "If there's one thing I can't stand it's a militant feminist."

She glared right back. "And if there's one thing *I* can't stand, it's a presumptuous male. You're just itching for a fight, aren't you?"

"Damn right."

"Why?"

"Why not?"

"The way I see it," she said, taking a deep breath for patience, "either you're annoyed that I've come along or you didn't want to be here in the first place."

His hair was blowing freely now. "Oh, I would have been happy enough sailing off with Samson. He's undemanding. I'd have gotten the R and R I need."

"Then it's me. Why do I annoy you?"

"You're a woman, and you're prissy."

Unable to help herself, Shaye laughed. *"Prissy?"* Then some vague instinct told her that prissy was precisely the way to be with this man. "Prissy." She cleared her throat. "Yes, well, I do believe in exercising a certain decorum."

"I'm sure you give new meaning to the word."

Shaye was about to say that Noah probably didn't know the *first* meaning of the word when the sound of unfurling canvas caught her ear. She looked up in time to see the mainsail fill with wind, then down to see Samson securing the lines.

"Shouldn't you give him a hand?"

"He doesn't need it."

"Then why are you here at all?"

Noah's smile might have held humor but didn't. "To give you a hard time. Why else?" With that, he sauntered off.

Aware that he'd had the last word this time around, Shaye watched him until he disappeared into the companionway. Then she turned back to the bow and closed her eyes. His image remained, a vivid echo in her mind of tousled dark hair, a broad chest, lean hips and endless legs. He was attractive; she had to give him that. But the attraction ended with the physical. He was unremittingly disagreeable.

And exhausting. It had been a long time since she'd sparred with anyone as she was sparring with him. Not that she didn't have occasional differences with people at work, but that was something else, something professional. In her private life she'd grown to love peace. She avoided abrasive people and chose friends who were conventional and comfortable. She dated the least threatening of men, indulging their occasional need to assert themselves over choice of restaurants or theaters because, through it all, she was in control. Not even her parents, with their parochial views, could rile her.

But Noah VanBaar had done just that. She wasn't sure how they'd become enemies so quickly. Was it his fault? Hers? Had she really seemed prissy?

A helpless smile broke across her face. Prissy. Wouldn't André and the guys from the garret—wherever they were today—die laughing if they heard that! Her parents, on the other hand, wouldn't die laughing. They'd choke a little, then breathe sighs of relief, then launch into a discourse on her age and the merits of marriage.

Prissy. It wasn't such a bad thing to be around Noah. If he hated prissiness so much, he'd leave her alone, which was all she really wanted, wasn't it?

Buoyed by her private pep talk, she sought out Victoria, who was chatting with Samson as he hauled up the first of two jibs. Indeed, it was Samson she addressed. "Would you like any help?"

Deftly lashing the line to its cleat, he stood back to watch the sail catch the wind. "Nope. All's under control." He darted them a quick glance. "Have you ladies had breakfast yet?"

"Victoria, has, but I, uh, slept a little later."

"You'll find fresh eggs and bacon in the icebox. Better eat and enjoy before they spoil."

Fresh eggs and bacon sounded just fine to Shaye, even if the word *icebox* was a little antiquated. Somehow, though, coming from Samson it didn't seem strange. Without pausing to reflect on the improvement in her attitude toward him, she asked, "How about you? Can I bring you something?"

"Ah no," he sighed, patting his belt. "I had a full breakfast earlier."

"How about coffee?"

"Now that's a thought. If you make it strong and add cream and two sugars, I could be sorely tempted."

Shaye smiled and turned to her aunt. "Anything for you?"

"Thanks, sweetheart, but I'm fine."

"See you in a bit, then." Still smiling, she entered the companionway, trotted down the steps and turned into the galley. There her smile faded. Noah was sprawled on the built-in settee that formed a shallow U behind the small table. He'd been alerted by the pad of her sneakers and was waiting, fork in hand, chewing thoughtfully.

"Well, well," he drawled as soon as he'd swallowed, "if it isn't the iron maiden."

"I though you'd already eaten."

"Samson has, but I don't make a habit of getting up at dawn like he does."

She was looking at his plate, which still held healthy portions of scrambled eggs and bacon, plus a muffin and a half, and a huge wedge of melon. "Think you have enough?"

"I hope so. I'm going to need all the strength I can get."

"To sit back and watch Samson sail?"

"To fight with you."

Determined not to let him irk her—or to let him interfere with her breakfast—she went to the refrigerator. "It's not really worth the effort, you know."

"I'll be the judge of that."

She shrugged and reached for two eggs and the packet of bacon. After setting them on the stove, she opened one cabinet, then the second in search of a pan.

"In the sink," Noah informed her.

She took in the contents of the sink at a disdainful glance. "And filthy. Thanks."

"You're welcome."

Automatically she reached for the tap, only to find there was none.

"Try the foot pump. You won't get water any other way. Not that you really need it. Why not just wipe out the pan with a paper towel and use it again?"

"That's disgusting."

"Not really. You're having the same thing I had."

"But there's an inch of bacon fat in this pan."

"Drain it."

There was a subtle command in his voice that drew her head around. "I take it we're conserving water."

"You take it right."

She pressed her lips together, then nodded slowly as she considered her options. She could pump up the water in a show of defiance, but if water was indeed in short supply, she'd be biting off her nose to spite her face. Bathing was going to be enough of a challenge; a little water spared now would make her feel less guilty for any she used later.

Very carefully she drained the pan, then swabbed it out with a paper towel and set it on the stove to heat.

"Need any help?" he taunted.

"I can crack an egg."

"Better put on the bacon first. It takes longer."

"I know that."

"Then you'd better start separating the bacon. The pan will be hot and you'll be wasting propane."

"Are you always a tightwad?"

"Only when I'm with a spendthrift."

"You don't know what you're talking about."

"So educate me."

But Shaye wasn't about to do any such thing. It suited her purpose to keep Noah in the dark, just as it suited her purpose to leisurely place one rasher of bacon, then another in the pan. While they cooked, she rummaged through the supplies until she located the coffee, then set a pot on to perk.

"I'm impressed," Noah said around a mouthful of food. "I didn't think you had it in you."

She'd been acutely aware of his eyes at her back, and despite good intentions, her temper was rising. "Shows how much you know," she snapped.

"Then you don't have a cook back in wherever?"

"I don't have a cook."

"How about a husband?"

Without turning, she raised her left hand, fingers rigidly splayed and decidedly bare.

"The absence of a ring doesn't mean anything. Militant feminists often—"

"I am not a militant feminist!" Gripping the handle of the frying pan, she forked the bacon onto its uncooked side. Slowly and silently she counted to ten. With measured movements, she reached for an egg.

It came down hard on the edge of the pan. The yoke broke. The white spilled over the rim.

Repairing the damage as best she could, she more carefully cracked the second egg, then stood, spatula in hand, waiting for both to cook.

"I thought you said you could crack an egg."

She didn't respond to the jibe.

"Got anything planned for an encore?"

She clamped her lips together.

"You could always flip an egg onto the floor."

"Why don't you shut up and eat?"

"I'm done."

Eyes wide, she turned to see that his plate, piled high short moments before, was now empty. "You're incredible."

He grinned broadly. "I know."

Her gaze climbed to his face, lured there by a strange force, one that refused to release her. Even after the slash of white teeth had disappeared, she stared, seeing a boyishness that was totally at odds with the man.

Unable to rationalize the discrepancy, she tore herself away and whirled back to the stove. The tiny whispers deep in her stomach could be put down to hunger, and the faint tremor in her hands as she transferred the eggs and bacon to a dish could be fatigue. But *boyishness*, in *Noah*?

A warning rang in her mind at the same moment she felt a pervasive warmth stretch from the crown of her head to her heels.

"Like I said," Noah murmured in her ear, "I'll need all my strength."

One arm reached to her left and deposited his dish, utensils clattering, in the sink. The other reached to her right and shifted the frying pan to the cold burner. The overall effect was one of imprisonment.

"Do you mind?" she muttered as she held herself stiffly against the stove.

He didn't move. Only his nose shifted, brushing the upper curve of her ear. "You smell good. Don't you sweat like the rest of us?"

Shaye felt a paradoxical dampness in the palms of her hands, at the backs of her knees, in the gentle hollow between her breasts, and was infinitely grateful that he couldn't possibly know. "Would you please move back?" she asked as evenly as she could.

"Have you ever been married?"

"I'd like to eat my eggs before they dry up."

"Got a boyfriend?"

"If you're looking for something to do, you could take a cup of coffee to your uncle."

"You never get those sweet little urges the rest of us get?"

Swinging back her elbow, she made sharp contact with his ribs. In the next instant she was free.

"That was dirty," he accused, rubbing the injured spot as she spun around.

"That was just for starters." Her hands were balled at her sides, and she was shaking. "I don't like to be crowded. Do you think you can get that simple fact through your skull, or is it too much to take in on a full stomach?"

Noah's hand stilled against his lean middle, and he studied her for a long minute. "I think I make you nervous."

"Angry. You make me angry."

"And nervous." He was back to taunting. "You're flushed."

"Anger."

Silkily he lowered his eyes to her left breast. "That, too?"

She refused to believe that he could see the quick quiver of her heart, though she couldn't deny the rapidity of her breathing. Even more adamantly she refused to believe that the tiny ripples of heat surging through her represented anything but fury. "That, too."

His gaze dropped lower, charting her midriff, caressing the bunching of jersey at her waist, arriving at last at her hips. His brow furrowed. He seemed confused yet oddly spellbound. Then, as though suddenly regaining the direction he'd lost, he snapped his eyes back to her face. "Too bad," he said, his lips hardening. "You've got the goods. It's a shame you can't put them to better use."

Shaye opened her mouth to protest his insolence, but he had already turned and was stalking away. "You left your dirty things in the sink!" she yelled.

He didn't answer. His tall frame blended with the shadow of the companionway, then disappeared into the blinding light above.

SOME TIME LATER, bearing cups of coffee for Samson and herself, Shaye returned to the deck. Samson stood at the helm, looking utterly content. He accepted the coffee with a smile, but Shaye didn't stay to talk. He was in his own world. He didn't need company.

Besides, Noah sat nearby. His long legs formed an open circle around a coil of rope and, while his hands were busily occupied, he watched her every move.

So she proceeded on toward the bow, where Victoria leaned against the bulwark gazing out to sea.

"Pretty, isn't it?"

Shaye nodded. The Colombian coast was a dark ridge on the horizon behind. Ahead was open sea. Far in the distance a cargo ship headed for Barranquilla or Cartagena. Less far a trawler chugged along, no doubt from one of the fishing villages along the coast.

Her fancy was caught, though, by a third, smaller craft, a yacht winging through the waters like a slender white dove. Peaceful, Shaye thought. Ahh, what she'd give for a little of that peace.

"Everything okay?" Victoria asked.

"Just fine."

"You look a little piqued."

"I'm tired."

"Not feeling seasick?"

Shaye shot her the wry twist of a grin. "Not quite."

"Have you ever been seasick?"

"Nope."

"Mmm." Victoria shook back her head and tipped it up to the sky. "In spite of everything, you have to admit that this is nice." When Shaye didn't respond, she went on. "It doesn't really matter what boat you're on, the air is the same, the sky, the waves." She slitted one eye toward Shaye. "Still want to go back?"

"It's a little late for that, don't you think?"

"But if you could, would you?"

Shaye dragged in a long, deep breath, then released it in a sigh. "No, Victoria, I wouldn't go back. But that doesn't mean this is going to be easy."

"What happened in the galley?"

Shaye took a deliberately lengthy sip of her coffee. "Nothing."

"Are you sure?"

"I'm sure."

"You sound a little tense."

"Blame that on fatigue, too." Or on anger. Or on frustration. Or, in a nutshell, on Noah VanBaar.

"But it's not even noon."

"It feels like midnight to me. I may go to bed pretty soon."

"But we've just begun to sail!"

"And we'll be sailing for the next four days straight, so there'll be plenty of time for me to take it all in."

"Oh, Shaye..."

"If I were in the Berkshires, I'd still be in bed."

"Bo-ring."

"Maybe so, but this is my vacation, isn't it? If I don't catch up on my sleep now, I never will. Weren't you the one who said I could do it on the boat?"

Victoria yielded with grace. "Okay. Sleep. Why don't you drag some cushions up here and do it in the sun?"

Because Noah is on deck and there's no way *I could sleep knowing that.* "That much sun I don't need."

"Then, the shade. You can sleep in the shade of the sails."

But Shaye was shaking her head. "No, I think I'll try that bed of ours." Her lips twisted. "Give it a test run." She took another swallow of coffee.

Victoria leaned closer. "Running away from him won't help, y'know. You have to let him know that he doesn't scare you."

"He doesn't scare me."

"He can't take his eyes off you."

"Uh-huh."

"It's true. He's been watching you since you came on deck."

"He's worried that I'm going to spoil Samson's trip by saying something ugly."

"He said that?"

"In no uncertain terms."

"What else did he say?" Victoria said, and Shaye realized she'd fallen into the trap. But it wasn't too late to extricate herself. She didn't want to discuss Noah with Victoria, who would, no doubt, play the devil's advocate. Shaye wasn't ready to believe *anything* good about Noah.

So she offered a cryptic, "Not much."

Victoria had turned around so that her back was to the bulwark. Quite conveniently, she had a view of the rest of the boat. "He's very good-looking."

"If you say so," Shaye answered indifferently.

"He appears to be good with his hands."

"I wouldn't know about that."

"Do you have any idea what he does for a living?"

"Nope."

"Aren't you curious?"

"Nope."

"Then you're hopeless," Victoria decided, tossing her hands in the air and walking away.

"Traitor," Shaye muttered under her breath. "I'm only here because of you, and are you grateful? Of course not. You won't be satisfied until I'm falling all over that man, but I can assure you that won't happen. He and I have nothing in common. Nothing at all."

THEY DID, as it turned out. Noah was as tired as Shaye. He'd flown in the day before from New York via Atlanta, where he'd had a brief business meeting, and rather than going to a hotel in Barranquilla, he'd come directly to the *Golden Echo* to help Samson prepare for the trip.

Though he'd never have admitted it aloud, Shaye hadn't been far off the mark when she'd called the boat a wreck. Oh, she was seaworthy; he'd checked for signs of leakage when he'd first come aboard and had found none. The little things were what needed attention—lines to be spliced, water pumps to be primed, hurricane lamps to be cleaned—all of which should by rights have been done before the *Golden Echo* left Jamaica on her previous charter. But that was water over the dam. He didn't mind the work. What he needed now, though, was rest.

"I'm turning in for a while," he told Samson, who was quite happily guarding the helm. "If you need me for anything, give a yell."

The older man kept his eyes on the sea. "Do me a favor and check on Shaye? She went below a little while ago. I hope she's not sick."

Noah knew perfectly well that she'd gone below. He wouldn't have said that she'd looked particularly sick, since she'd seemed pale to him from the start.

"I'd ask Victoria to do it," Samson was saying, "but I hate to disturb her." She was relaxing on the foredeck, taking obvious pleasure in both the sun and the breeze. "Since you're going below anyway..."

"I'll check."

But only because Samson had asked. Left to his own devices, Noah would have let Shaye suffer on her own. His encounter with her in the galley had left him feeling at odds with himself, and though that had been several hours before, he hadn't been able to completely shake the feeling. All he wanted was to strip down and go to sleep without thought of the woman. But Samson had asked...

She wasn't in the galley or the salon, and since she certainly wouldn't be in the captain's quarters, he made for her cabin. The door was shut. He stood for a minute, head bowed, hands on his hips. Then he knocked very lightly on the wood. When there was no answer, he eased open the door.

The sight before him took him totally by surprise. Shaye had pulled back the covers and was lying on her side on the bare sheets, sound asleep. She wore a huge white T-shirt that barely grazed her upper thighs. Her legs were slightly bent, long and slender. But what stunned him most was her hair. It fanned behind her on the pillow, a thick, wavy train of auburn that caught the light off the portholes and glowed.

Fascinated, he took one step closer, then another. She seemed like another woman entirely when she was relaxed. There was gentleness in her loosely resting fingers, softness in her curving body, vulnerability in the slight part of her lips and in the faint sheen of perspiration that made her skin gleam. And in her hair? Spirit. Oh, yes. There it was—promise of the same fire he'd caught from time to time in her eyes.

Unable to resist, he hunkered down by the side of the bed. Her lashes were like dark flames above her cheekbones. Free now of tension, her nose looked small and pert. Her cheeks were the lightest shade of a very natural pink that should have clashed with her hair but didn't. And that hair—he wondered if it were as soft as it looked, or as hot. His fingers curled into his palms, resisting the urge to touch, and he forced his eyes away.

It was a major mistake. The thin T-shirt, while gathered loosely in front, clung to her slender side and the gentle flare of her hip, leaving just enough to the imagination to make him ache. And edging beneath the hem of the shirt was a slash of the softest, sweetest apricot-colored silk. His gaze jumped convulsively to the far side of the bed, where she'd left the clothes she'd discarded. There, lying atop the slacks and T-shirt she'd been wearing earlier, was a lacy bra of the same apricot hue.

With a hard swallow, he flicked his gaze back to her face. Stern, stiff-backed and fussy—was that the image she chose to convey to the world? Her underthings told a different story, one that was enhanced by her sleeping form. It was interesting, he mused, interesting and puzzling.

Image making was his business. He enjoyed it, was good at it. Moreover, knowing precisely what went into the shaping of public images, he prided himself on being able to see through them. He hadn't managed to this time, though, and he wondered why. Was Shaye that good, or had his perceptiveness been muddled?

He suspected it was a little of both, and there was meager comfort in the thought. If Shaye was that good, she was far stronger and more complex than he'd imagined. If his perceptiveness had been muddled, it was either because he was tired...or because she did something to his mind.

He feared it was the latter. He'd been ornery because he hadn't wanted her along, but that orneriness had been out of proportion. He didn't normally goad people the way he had her. But Shaye—she brought out the rawest of his instincts.

In every respect. Looking at her now, all soft and enticing, he felt the heat rise in his body as it hadn't done in years. How could he possibly be attracted to as prickly a woman? Was it her softness his body sensed and responded to? Or her hidden fire?

His insides tensed in a different way when her lashes fluttered, then it was too late to escape. Not that he would have, he told himself. He'd never run from a woman, and he wasn't about to now. But he'd be damned if he'd let her know how she affected him. Retrieving his mask of insolence, he met her startled gaze.

Shaye didn't move a muscle. She simply stared at him. "What are you doing here?"

"Checking on you. Samson thought you might be sick."

"I'm not."

"Not *violently* seasick?"

"... No."

His gaze idly scored her body. "Did you lie about anything else?"

Why, she asked herself, did he sound as though he knew

something he shouldn't? Victoria would never have betrayed her. And there was no way he could see through her T-shirt, though she almost imagined he had. She'd have given anything to reach for the sheet and cover herself, but she refused to give him the satisfaction of knowing that his wandering eye made her nervous. "No," she finally answered.

"Mmm."

"What is that supposed to mean?"

"That you're a contradiction," he said without hesitation.

He'd obviously been thinking about her—or crouching here, watching her—for some time. The last thought made her doubly nervous, and the explanation he offered didn't help.

"Cactus-prickly when you're awake, sweet woman when you're asleep. It makes me wonder which is the real you."

"You'll never know," she informed him. Her poise was fragile; there was something debilitating about lying on a bed near Noah, wearing not much more than an old T-shirt.

His gray eyes glittered. "It'd be a challenge for me to find out. Mmm, maybe I'll make it my goal. I'll have two full weeks with not much else to do."

Shaye didn't like the sound of that at all. "And what about the treasure you're supposedly seeking?" she demanded.

"Samson's doing the seeking. As far as I'm concerned, there are many different kinds of treasure." He surveyed her body more lazily. "Could be that the one you're hiding is worth more than the one my uncle seeks."

"As though I could hide anything this way," she mumbled.

"Precisely."

"Look, I was sleeping. I happen to be exhausted. Do you think you could find a tiny bit of compassion within that stone-hard soul of yours to leave me be?"

He grinned, wondering what she'd have said if she'd known something else had been close to stone-hard moments before. No doubt she'd have used far more potent words to describe his character. Come to think of it, he wondered how many of those potent words she knew.

"You're really very appealing like this," he said softly. "Much more approachable than before. I like your hair."

"Go away."

"I hadn't realized it was so long. Or so thick. The color comes alive when you let it down like that. Why do you bother to tack it up?"

"To avoid comments like the ones you just made."

"I'd think you'd be flattered."

"I'm not."

"You don't like me," he said with a pout.

"Now you're getting there."

"Is it something I said, something I did?"

She squeezed her eyes shut for a minute, then, unable to bear the feeling of exposure any longer, bolted up and reached for the sheet.

Noah looked as though he'd lost his best friend. "What did you do that for? I wouldn't have touched you."

There was touching and there was touching. He could touch her with his hands, or with his eyes. Or he could touch her with the innocent little expressions he sent her way from time to time. She knew not to trust those little expressions, but, still, they did something to her. Far better that he should be growling and scowling.

"It's your eyes," she accused as she pressed her back to the wall. "I don't like them."

This time his innocence seemed more genuine. "What's wrong with my eyes?"

"They creep."

"They explore," he corrected, "and when they find something they like, they take a closer look." He shrugged. "Can you blame them? Your legs are stunning."

She quickly tucked her legs under her. "Please. Just leave and let me sleep."

Since the path had been cleared for him, he hopped up and sat on the bed.

"Noah..." she warned.

"That's the first time you've called me by name. I like it when you say it, though you could soften the tone a little."

"Leave this cabin now!"

He made himself more comfortable, extending an arm, propping his weight on his palm. "You never answered me when I asked about boyfriends. Do you have any back home? Where is home, by the way?"

"Philadelphia," she growled. "There, you've gotten some information. Now you can leave."

"A little more. I want a little more. Is there a boyfriend?"

In a bid for dignity, she drew herself up as straight as she could. Unfortunately he was sitting on the sheet, which ended up stretched taut. And even with the extra inches she felt dwarfed. Why did he have to be so *big*? Why couldn't he be of average height like her lawyer friend, or the stockbroker? For that matter, why couldn't he be malleable, like they were? They'd have left the instant she'd asked *if* they ever made it to her room at all.

"Boyfriends?" he prompted.

"That's none of your business."

"I'll tell you about me if you tell me about you," he cajoled.

"I don't want to know about you."

Bemused, he tipped his dark head to the side. "Wouldn't it be easier if you knew what you faced?"

"I'm not facing anything," she argued, but there was a note of desperation in her voice.

"Two weeks, Shaye. We're going to be together for two long weeks."

"Miss Burke, to you."

For a split second he looked chastised, then spoiled it with a helpless spurt of laughter.

"All right," she grumbled quickly. "Call me Shaye."

"Shaye." He tempered his grin. "Do you have any boyfriends?"

She knew she'd lost a little ground on the Miss Burke bit, which even to her own ears had sounded inane. But she was supposed to be prissy. And as far as boyfriends were concerned, a few white lies wouldn't hurt.

"I don't date."

His eyes widened. "You've got to be kidding."

"No."

"With a body like yours?"

"For your information, there's more to life than sex." She wondered if she was sounding *too* prissy. She didn't want to overdo it.

"Really?"

"I'm too busy to date. I have a very demanding job, and I love it. My life is complete."

He shook his head. "Whew! You're something else." He didn't believe her for a minute, but if she wanted to play games, he could match her. "I have a demanding job myself, but I couldn't make it through life without steady helpings of sex. Women's liberation has its up side, in that sense."

"Then what are you doing on this trip?" she asked through gritted teeth. "How could you drag yourself away from all those warm beds and passionate arms?"

"And legs," he added quickly. "Don't forget legs. I'm a leg man, remember?"

She was getting nowhere, she realized. He looked as though he had no intention of budging, and she didn't think she had the physical strength to make him. "Please," she said, deliberately wilting a little, "I really am tired. I don't want to fight you, and I don't want to be on guard every minute of this trip. If you just leave me alone, I'll stay out of your way."

"Please, Noah."

"Please, Noah."

Her meekness was too much, he decided. When she was meek, there was no fire in her eyes, and he rather liked that fire. "Well, I have learned something new about you."

"What's that?"

His eyes slid over the moistness of her skin. "You sweat."

"Of course I sweat! It's damn hot in here!"

He grinned. So much for meekness. "The question," he ventured in a deep, smooth voice, "is whether you smell as good like this as you did before." He leaned closer.

Shaye put up here hands to hold him off, losing her grip on the sheet in the process. But she'd been right; she was no match for his strength. Her palms were ineffective levers against his chest, and despite her efforts, she felt his face against her neck.

His nose nuzzled her. His lips slid to the underside of her jaw. He opened his mouth and dragged it across her cheek to her ear.

And all the while, Shaye was dying a thousand little deaths because she liked the feel of his mouth on her, she liked it!

"Even...better," he whispered hoarsely. His lips nipped at her earlobe, and the hoarse whisper came again. "You smell... even better."

Her eyes were shut and her breathing had grown erratic. "Please, stop," she gasped brokenly. "Please, Noah..."

He was dizzy with pleasure at the contact, and would have gone on nuzzling her forever had he not caught the trace of fear in her voice. He hadn't heard that before, not fear, and he knew instinctively that there was nothing put on about it. Slowly and with a certain amount of puzzlement, he drew back and searched her eyes. They were wide with fear, yes, but with other things as well. And he knew then, without a doubt, what he was going to do.

He'd leave her now, but he'd be true to his word. He'd spend the next two weeks shadowing her, learning what made her tick. She might in fact be the prissy lady she wanted him to believe she was. Or she might be the woman of passion he suspected she was. In either case, he stirred her. That was what he read in her eyes, and though he wasn't sure why, it was what he wanted.

"Go back to sleep," he said gently as he rose from the bed. He was halfway to the door when he heard her snort.

"Fat chance of that! Can I really believe you won't invade my privacy again? And if I were to fall asleep, I'd have nightmares. Hmph. So much for a lovely vacation. Stuck on a stinking pirate ship with a man who thinks he's God's gift to women—"

Noah closed the door on the last of her tirade and, smiling, sauntered off through the salon.

Chapter Four

"*AHH, mes belles amies. Notre dîner nous attend sur le pont. Suivez-moi, s'il vous plaît.*"

Shaye, who'd been curled in an easy chair in the salon, darted a disbelieving glance at Victoria before refocusing her eyes on Samson. She'd known he'd been busily working in the galley and that he'd refused their offers of help. But she hadn't expected to be called to the table in flawless French—he was a professor of *Latin*, wasn't he?—much less by a man sporting a bright red, side-knotted silk scarf and a cockily set black beret.

Victoria thought he was precious; eccentric was the word Shaye would choose. But he was harmless, certainly more so than his nephew, she mused, and at the moment she was in need of a little comic relief.

It had been a long afternoon. She hadn't been able to fall back to sleep after Noah had left her cabin, though she'd tried her best. After cursing the sheets, the mattress, the heat and everything else in the room, she'd dressed, reknotted her hair and gone on deck.

Noah hadn't been there—he was sleeping, Samson told her, which had irritated her no end. *He* was sleeping, after he'd ruined her own! She'd seethed for a while, then been gently, gradually, helplessly lulled by the rocking of the boat into a better frame of mind.

And now Samson had called them to dinner. The table, it turned out, was a low, folding one covered by a checkered cloth, and the seats were cushions they carried up from the salon. Noah had lowered the jibs and secured the wheel, dashing Shaye's hope that he'd be too busy sailing to join them. To make matters worse, he crossed his long legs and fluidly lowered himself to the cushion immediately on her left.

The meal consisted of a hearty bouillabaisse, served with a Muscadet wine, crusty French bread and, for dessert, a raspberry tart topped with thick whipped cream. Other than complimenting the chef on his work, Shaye mostly stayed out of the conversation, which involved Samson and Victoria and the other unlikely trips each had taken.

Noah, too, was quiet, but his eyes were like living things reaching out, touching her, daring her to reveal something of herself as Victoria and Samson were doing. Since she had no intention of conforming, she remained quiet and ignored his gaze as best she could.

Samson, bless him, was more than willing to accept help with the cleanup, and Shaye was grateful for the escape. By the time she finished in the galley, she was feeling better.

Armed with a cup of coffee and a book, she settled in the salon. Hurricane lamps provided the light, casting a warm golden glow that she had to admit was atmospheric. In fact, she had to admit that the *Golden Echo* wasn't all that bad. Sails unfurled and full once again, the sloop sliced gently through the waves. A crosswind whispered from porthole to porthole, comfortably ventilating the salon. The mustiness that had bothered Shaye earlier seemed to have disappeared, though perhaps, she reflected, she'd simply grown accustomed to it.

She was well fed. She was comfortable. She was peacefully reading her book. Would a vacation in the Berkshires have been any different? *It's all in the mind, Shaye.* Isn't that what Victoria would say? *He can only be a threat if you allow it, whereas if you put him from mind, he doesn't exist.*

For a time it worked. She flew through the first hundred pages of her book, finally putting it down when her lids began to droop. Victoria was still on deck. Samson had turned in some time before, intending to sleep until two, when he would relieve Noah at the helm.

Intending to sleep far longer than that, Shaye went to bed herself. When she awoke, though, it wasn't ten in the morning as she'd planned. It was three and very dark, and she was feeling incredibly warm all over.

A fever? Not quite. She'd awakened from a dream of Noah. A nightmare? she asked herself, as she lay flat on her back taking slow, easy breaths to calm her quivering body. Only in hindsight. At the time, it had been an excitingly erotic dream. Even now her skin was damp in response.

It isn't fair, she railed, silently. She could push him from her thoughts when she was awake, but how could she control the demon inside while she slept? And what breed of demon was it that caused her to dream erotic dreams about *any* man? She'd lived wildly and passionately for a time, and the life-style left much to be desired. She'd sworn off it. She'd outgrown it. She was perfectly content with what she had now.

Could that demon be telling her something?

Uncomfortable with the direction of her thoughts, she carefully rose from the bed so as not to awaken Victoria, dragged a knee-length sweatshirt over her T-shirt and padded silently to the door.

All was quiet save the slap of the waves against the hull and the sough of the breeze. She passed through the salon and the narrow passageway, sending a disdainful glance toward the door of the captain's cabin, where Noah would no doubt be sleeping by now, and carefully climbed the companionway.

On deck she dropped her head back and let the breeze take her unfettered hair as it would. The sea air felt good against her skin, and the sweatshirt was just loose enough, just warm enough to keep her comfortable. Almost reluctantly she straightened her head and opened her eyes, intending to tell Samson that she would be standing at the bow for a bit.

Only it wasn't Samson at the helm. Though the transom's hanging lamp left his face in shadows, the large frame rakishly planted behind the wheel could belong to no one but Noah.

The image struck her, then, with devastating force. He didn't need a billowing shirt, tight pants, boots and a cross belt. He didn't need anything beyond gently clinging shorts and a windbreaker that was barely zipped. He had the rest—thick hair blowing, broad shoulders set, strong hands on the wheel, bare feet widespread and rooted to the deck. Looking more like a descendant of Fletcher Christian than the nephew of Samson VanBaar, he was a rebel if ever there was one. And his prize? Her peace of mind...for starters.

"Welcome," he said with unexpected civility. "You wouldn't by chance care to take the helm for a minute while I go get a cup of coffee?"

She certainly wouldn't have allowed herself to turn tail and run once he'd seen her, but she felt impelled to explain her presence. The last thing she wanted was for him to think she was seeking him out. "I thought this was Samson's shift."

"He's exhausted. I decided to let him sleep a while longer."

"You seem tired yourself," she heard herself say. He certainly didn't *sound* like a rebel just then.

He shrugged. "I'll sleep later."

Nodding, she looked away. Something had happened. It was as though the intimacy they'd shared in her dream had softened her. Or was it his fatigue, which softened *him*? Or the gently gusting night air? Or the hypnotic motion of the sloop? Or the fact that starlit nights in the Caribbean were made, in the broadest sense, for love, not war?

Whatever, she turned and started back down the companionway.

"Don't go," he said quickly.

"I'll bring up some coffee."

It was an easy task to reheat what was in the pot. When she returned a few minutes later carrying two mugs, Noah accepted his with a quiet, "Thank you."

Nodding, Shaye stepped back to lean against the transom. For a time, neither spoke. Noah's eyes were ahead, Shaye's were directed northward.

Philadelphia seemed very far away, and it occurred to her that she didn't miss it. Nor, she realized, did she regret the fact that she wasn't heading for the Berkshires. Come light of day, she might miss both, but right now, she felt peaceful. Sated. As though...as though her dream had filled some need that she'd repressed. She felt as though she'd just made love with Noah, as though they were now enjoying the companionable afterglow.

"Couldn't sleep?" he asked quietly.

"I, uh, it must have been the rest I had earlier."

"That'll do it sometimes."

They relapsed into silence. Shaye sipped her coffee. Noah did the same, then set the mug down and consulted his compass.

"I was wondering about that," she ventured. "I didn't see any navigational equipment when Samson showed us around."

"I'm not sure what was available when Horgan built the sloop in the twenties, but I assume he felt—and the Paynes must have agreed—that fancy dials would have been sacrilegious." He made a slight adjustment to the wheel, then beckoned to her. "Hold it for a second?"

Setting the mug by her feet, she grasped the wooden wheel with both hands while he moved forward to adjust the sails.

When he returned, though, it was to take the place she'd left at the transom, slightly behind her, slightly to the right.

"So you use a compass?"

"And a sextant. My uncle's the expert with that."

"Is there a specific point we're aiming at?"

Noah took a healthy swallow of his coffee. "He has coordinates, if that's what you mean."

"For the treasure?"

"Uh-huh."

She was looking ahead, holding the wheel steady, assuming that Noah would correct her if she did something wrong. "He hasn't said much about that."

"He's a great one for prioritizing. First, the sail. Then the treasure."

She felt a nudge at her elbow and turned to find him holding out her mug. She took it and lifted it, but rather than drinking, she brushed her lips back and forth against the rim. "It's strange..."

"What?"

"That Samson should be a Latin professor and yet have such a proclivity for adventure. Not that I'm being critical. I just find it...curious."

"Not really," Noah said. He paused for a minute, deciding how best to explain. "It's a matter of having balance in one's life. Samson has his teaching, which is stable, and his adventures, which are a little more risqué. But there's a link between the two. For example, he sees the same beauty in Latin that he sees in this sloop. They're both ancient—forefathers of other languages, other boats. They both have an innate beauty, a romanticism. Samson is a romantic."

"I hadn't noticed," Shaye teased.

Belatedly, Noah chuckled. "Mmm. He must seem a little bizarre to you."

"No. He's really very sweet."

"He stages Halloween year-round."

She wondered if she'd ever live down that particular comment, but since Noah didn't seem to be angry anymore, there was no point in defending herself. "So I gather," she said with a little grin.

Noah was content with that. "Samson has always believed in doing what he loves. He loves teaching." Reaching out, he rescued a blowing strand of her hair from her mouth and tucked it behind her ear. ''He takes delight in making the language come alive for his students. And he does it. I've sat in on some of his classes. In his own quiet way, he is hilarious.''

Shaye could believe it. ''His stories are something else.''

''You were listening?''

She shot him a quick glance. ''Tonight? Of course I was.''

''I wasn't sure. You were very quiet.''

She wasn't about to say that listening hard to Samson had kept her mind off *him*. ''Why interrupt something good when you have nothing better to add? It's really a shame that Samson doesn't write about his adventures. They'd make wonderful reading.''

''They do.''

''Magazine articles?'' she asked with some excitement, immediately conjuring up images of a beautiful *National Geographic* spread.

''Books.''

''No kidding!''

''How do you think he pays for these little adventures?''

''I really hadn't thought about it.'' She frowned. ''He didn't say anything tonight about writing.''

''He's an understated man. He downplays it.''

''Can he do that? Isn't there a certain amount of notoriety that comes with being a published author?''

Noah leaned forward and lowered his voice to a conspiratorial level. ''Not if you publish under another name.'' He leaned back again.

''Ahh. So that's how he does it.''

''Mmm.'' He took another drink. ''But don't tell him I told you.''

She grinned. ''Can I ask him where he learned to cook?''

''Cooking he'll discuss any day. It's one of his passions.''

Passions. The word stuck in Shaye's mind, turning slowly, a many-faceted diamond with sides of brilliance, darkness, joy and grief.

She shook her hair back, freeing it for the caress of the wind. ''You and he seem to be very close. Do you live in Hanover?''

It was a minute before Noah heard the question. He was fascinated by the little movement she'd made. It had been totally unaffected but beguiling. Bare-legged as she was, and with that gorgeous mane of hair—soft, oh yes, soft—blowing behind her, she didn't look anything like the prissy little lady he'd accused her of being.

He closed his eyes for a second and shook off both images, leaving in their place the same gentle ambiance that had existed before. Did he live near Samson in Hanover? "No. But we see each other regularly. There's just him and me. All the others are gone. We have a mutual-admiration society, so it works out well."

"All the others—you mean, your parents?"

"And Samson's wife. Samson and Gena never had children of their own, and since Samson and my father had no other siblings, I was pretty much shared between them."

She smiled. "That must have been fun."

"It was."

She thought about her own childhood, the time she'd spent with her parents. Fun wasn't a word she'd ever used to describe those days. "Was your father as much of a character as Samson?"

"No. He was more serious. Dividing my time between the two men gave a balance to my life, too."

It was the second time he'd spoken of balance, and she wondered if he'd done it deliberately. Her life was far from balanced. Work was her vocation, her avocation, the sole outlet for her energies. Victoria argued that there was more to life, and Shaye smiled and nodded and gave examples of the men she dated and the friends she saw. But apart from her friendship with her sister, the others were largely token friendships. And she knew why. To maintain a steady keel in her life, she chose to be with people who wouldn't rock the boat. Unfortunately, those people were uninspiring. They left her feeling alone and frustrated. Her only antidote was work.

But Noah couldn't possibly know all that, could he?

Feeling strangely empty, she took a large gulp of her coffee, then set the mug down and grasped the wheel more firmly. But neither the solidity of the hard wood nor the warm brew settling in her stomach could counter the chill she was feeling. Unconsciously, she rubbed one bare foot over the other.

In the next instant a third foot covered hers, a larger, warmer one. And then a human shield slipped behind her, protecting her back, her hips, her legs from elements that came from far beyond the Caribbean.

Noah had surrounded her this way in the galley, but the sense of imprisonment was far different now. It was gentle, protective and welcome.

She closed her eyes when she felt his face in her hair, and whispered, "Why are you being so nice?"

His voice was muffled. "Maybe because I'm too tired to fight."

"Then the secret is keeping you tired?"

"The secret," he said as his lips touched her ear, "is keeping your hair down and your legs bare and your mouth sweet. I think something happens when you screw back your hair and cinch yourself into your clothes. Everything tightens up. Your features stiffen and your tongue goes tart."

"It does not!" she cried, but without conviction. She couldn't believe how wonderful she felt, and she wasn't about to deny it any more than she could think to end it. When his face slid to her neck, she relaxed her head against his shoulder.

"I won't argue," he murmured thickly. "Not now."

"You're too tired."

"Too content."

He was pressing open-mouthed kisses to the side of her neck, inching his way lower to the spot where her sweatshirt began. She felt a trembling start at her toes and spread upward, and she grasped the wheel tighter, though she wasn't about to move.

He shifted behind her, spreading his legs to cradle her at the same time his hands fell to her thighs and began to work their way upward.

"Noah..." she whispered.

"So soft..." His fingers were splayed, thumbs dragging up along the crease where her thighs met her hips, tracing her pelvic bones, etching a path over her waist and ribs. Then his fingers came together to cup her breasts, and she went wild inside. She arched into his hands, while her head came around, mouth open, tongue trapped against his jaw.

She was melting. Every bone in her body, every muscle, every inch of flesh seemed to lose definition and gather into a single yearning mass. Had she missed this so, this wonderful sense of anticipatory fulfillment? Had she ever experienced it before?

He was roughly caressing her breasts, but it wasn't enough,

and her mouth, with hungry nips at his chin, told him so. Then her mouth was being covered, eaten, devoured, and she was taking from him, taste for taste, bite for bite.

Totally oblivious to her role at the helm she wound her arms backward, around Noah. Her hands slid up and down the backs of his thighs, finally clasping his buttocks, urging his masculine heat closer to the spot that suddenly and vividly ached.

"Oh God," he gasped, dragging his mouth from hers. He wrapped quivering arms tightly around her waist and breathed raggedly as his pelvis moved against her. "Ahh..."

More hungry than ever, Shaye tried to turn. She wanted to wrap her arms around his neck, to feed again from his mouth, to drape her leg over his and feel his strength where she craved it so. But he wouldn't have it. He squeezed her hard to hold her still, and the movement was enough to restore the first fragments of reason. When he felt that she'd regained a modicum of control, he eased up his hold, but he didn't release her.

With several more gusts of wind, their breathing, their pulse rates, began to slow.

Shaye was stunned. It wasn't so much what had happened but the force with which it had happened that shocked her most. She didn't know what to say.

Noah did, speaking gently and low. "Has it been a long time?"

She'd returned a hand to the wheel, though her fingers were boneless. "Yes," she whispered.

"It took you by surprise?"

Another whispered, "Yes."

"Will you be sorry in the morning?"

"Probably."

He released her then, but without anger. When he reached for the wheel, she stepped aside. "Go below...please?" he asked gruffly.

She knew what he was doing, and she was grateful. He was alerting her to the fact that if she stayed she might have even more to be sorry for in the morning. She'd felt his arousal; she'd actively fed it. She had to accept her share of responsibility for what had happened, just as she had to respect the pleading note in his voice. He was human. He wanted her. And he was asking her not to want him back...at least, not tonight.

Without saying a word, she climbed down the companionway. At the bottom, she gasped, a helpless little cry.

"I frightened you," Samson said. "I'm sorry. You seemed very deep in thought."

She was, but her heart was pounding at thoughts that had taken a sudden turn. *What if Samson had awakened earlier and come up on deck during…during…*

"I should have been up a while ago," he was saying. "Noah must be exhausted. I'm glad he wasn't alone all that time."

Shaye wasn't sure whether to be glad or not. As she made her silent way to the cabin, then stole back into bed, she wasn't sure of much—other than that she'd be furious with herself later.

SHE WAS FURIOUS. She didn't sleep well, but kept waking up to recall what had happened, to toss and turn for a while, then bury her face in the pillow and plead for the escape of sleep. Mercifully, Victoria was gone from the cabin by seven, which meant that Shaye could do her agonizing in peace.

She slept. She awoke. She slept again, then awoke again. The cycle repeated itself until nearly noon, when she gave up one battle to face the next.

Noah was in the galley. All she wanted was a cup of coffee, but even that wasn't going to be easy.

"Sleep well?" he asked in a tone that gave nothing away.

"Not particularly."

"Bad dreams?"

"It was what was *between* the dreams that was bad," she muttered, pouring coffee into a cup with hands that shook.

"Are you always this cheerful in the morning?"

"Always."

"If you'd woken up in bed with me, it might have been different."

Bracing herself against the stove, she squeezed her eyes shut and made it to the count of eight before his next sally came.

"I'll bet you're dynamite in bed."

She went on counting.

"You were dynamite on the deck."

She cringed. "Don't remind me."

"Are you schizophrenic?"

At that, she turned and stared. "Excuse me?"

"Do you have two distinct personalities?"

"Of course not!"

"Then why are you so crabby this morning when you were so sweet last night?" He gave her a thorough once-over, then decided, "It *has* to be the clothes. You're wearing shorts, but they must be binding somewhere." Her T-shirt was big enough for *him* to swim in, so it couldn't be that. "And your hair. Safely secured once again. Does it make you *feel* secure when it's pinned back like that?"

She grabbed her coffee and made for the salon.

He was right behind her. "Careful. You're spilling."

She whirled on him, only to gasp when several drops of coffee hit his shirt.

He jumped back. "Damn it, that's hot!"

She hadn't intended to splatter him. Without thinking, she reached out to repair the damage.

He pushed her hand away. "It's all right."

"Are you burned?" she asked weakly.

"I'll live."

"The coffee will stain if you don't rinse it out."

"This shirt has seen a lot worse."

Eying the T-shirt, Shaye had to agree. She guessed that it had been navy once upon a time, but no longer. It was ragged at the hem and armholes, and it dipped tiredly at the neck, but damn if it didn't make him look roguish!

Sighing unsteadily, she moved more carefully into the salon and sank into a chair. Her head fell back and she closed her eyes. She felt Noah take the seat opposite her.

"Why are you doing this to me?" she whispered.

He didn't have to think about it, when he'd done nothing else for the past few hours. "You intrigue me."

It wasn't the answer she wanted. "I didn't think you were intrigued by cactus prickly women."

"Ahh, but are you really cactus prickly? That's the question."

"I'm prissy."

"Really?"

"You said it yourself."

"Maybe I was wrong."

"You weren't."

"Could've fooled me last night."

Eyes still closed, she scrunched up her face. "Do you think we could forget about last night?"

"Jeeez, I hope not. Last night was really something."

She moaned his name in protest, but he turned even that to his advantage.

"You did that last night and I liked it. You wanted me. Was that so terrible?"

Her eyes shot open and she met his gaze head-on. "I do not want you."

"You did then."

"I was too tired to know what I was doing."

He was sitting forward, fingers loosely linked between spread knees. "That's just the point. Your defenses were down. Maybe that's the real you."

"The real me," she stated as unequivocably as she could, "is what you see here and now." She had to make him believe it. She had to make *herself* believe it. "I live a very sane, very structured, very controlled existence."

"What fun's that?"

"It's what I choose. You may say its boring, but it's what *I* choose!"

"Is that why you burst into flames in my arms?"

She was getting nowhere. She'd known from the moment she'd left the deck so early this morning that she was in trouble, and Noah wasn't helping. But then, she hadn't really expected he would. So she closed her eyes again and tuned him out.

"You were hungry."

She said nothing.

He upped the pressure. "Sex starved."

Still silence.

He pursed his lips. "You can't seduce Samson because he has his eye on your aunt, so that leaves only me."

"I wouldn't know how to seduce a man if I tried," she mumbled. It fit in with the image of prissiness, but it was also the truth. She'd never had to seduce a man. Sex had been free and easy in the circles she'd run in. Perhaps that was why it had held so little meaning for her. Last night—this morning—had been different. She was still trying to understand how.

"I told you. All you have to do is bare those legs, shake out that hair and say something sweet." He shifted and grimaced. "Lord, you're only one-third of the way there, and I'm getting hard."

Her eyes flew open. "You're crude."

He considered that. "Crude connotes a raw condition. Mmm, that's pretty much the same thing as being hard."

She bolted from the chair and stormed toward her cabin.

"You can't hide there all day, y'know!" he called after her.

"I have no intention of hiding here," she yelled back. "I'm getting a book—" she snatched it from her suitcase, which, standing on end, served as a makeshift nightstand "—and I'm going on deck." She slammed past Noah back through the salon, then momentarily reversed direction to grab a cushion from the sofa.

"You can't escape me there," he warned.

"No," she snapped as she marched down the alley toward the companionway, "but with other people around, you might watch your tongue."

He was on her heels. "I'd rather watch yours. I liked what it did to me last night."

"This morning." She stomped up the steps. "It was this morning, and I can guarantee it won't happen again."

"Don't do that," he pleaded, once again the little boy with the man's mind and body. "You really turned me on—"

"Shh!" She whipped her head around to give him a final glare, then with poise emerged topside, smiled and said, "Good morning, Samson."

NOAH STOOD AT THE WHEEL, his legs braced apart, his fingers curled tightly around the handles. Steering the *Golden Echo* didn't take much effort, but it gave him a semblance of control. He needed that. He wasn't sure why, but he did.

Shifting his gaze from the ocean, he homed in on Shaye. She was propped on a cushion against the bulwark in the shade of the sails, reading. Her knees were bent, her eyes never left the page. Not a single, solitary strand of hair escaped its bonds to blow free in the breeze.

Prickly. God, was she prickly! She was the image of primness, but he knew there was another side. *He* knew it. She refused to admit it. And the more he goaded her, the more prickly she became.

He was no stranger to women. Granted, he wasn't quite the roué he'd told Shaye he was, but his work brought him into contact with women all the time. He'd known charming ones, spunky ones, aggressive and ambitious ones. Shaye was as beautiful as any of them—or, he amended, she was when she let go. She'd done it last night, but it had been dark then. He wanted to see her do it now. If she freed her hair from its knot, relaxed her body, tossed back her head and smiled, he knew he'd take her image to his grave.

But she wouldn't do that. She wouldn't give him the satisfaction. He recalled the times when they'd bickered, when she'd bitten back retorts, taken deep breaths, done everything in her power to ignore his taunts. Sometimes she'd lost control and had lashed back in turn, but even then she'd been quick to regain herself.

What had she said—that she lived a structured and controlled existence? Beyond that he didn't know much, other than that she was from Philadelphia and that she had neither a husband nor a cook. He did know that she was aware of him physically. She couldn't deny what had happened right here, on this very spot, less than twelve hours before.

Nor could he deny it. He knew he was asking for trouble tangling with a woman who clearly had a hang-up with sex. But sex wasn't all he wanted. She intrigued him; he hadn't lied about that. He felt a desperate need to understand her, and that meant getting to know her. And *that* meant breaking through the invisible wall she'd built.

As he saw it, there were two ways to go about it. The first, the more civil way, was to simply approach her and strike up conversation. Of course, it would take a while to build her trust, and if she resisted him he might run out of time.

The second, the more underhanded way, was to keep coming at her as he'd been doing. She wouldn't like it, but he might well be able to wear her down. Since she was vulnerable to him on a physical level, he could prey on that—even if it meant prying out one little bit of personal information at a time.

He had to get those bits of information. Without them, he couldn't form a composite of her, and without that, he wouldn't be able to figure out why in the hell he was interested in the first place!

"HOW'S IT GOING, ladies?"

Shaye looked up from her book to see Noah approach. So he'd finally turned the sailing over to Samson. She had to admit, albeit begrudgingly, that he was doing his share.

"I should ask you the same question," Victoria said, smiling up in welcome. "Are we making good progress?"

Noah looked out over the bow toward the western horizon. "Not bad. If the trade winds keep smiling and we continue to make five knots an hour, we'll reach Costa Rica right on schedule."

Shaye was relieved to hear that.

Victoria wasn't so sure. "I'm enjoying the sail," she said, stretching lazily. "I could take this for another month."

Noah chuckled, then turned to Shaye. "How about you? Think you could take it for another month?"

Had it not been for that knowing little glint in his eye, Shaye might have smiled and nodded. Instead, she boldly returned his gaze and said, "Not on your life. I have to be back at work."

He hunkered down before her, balancing on the balls of his feet. "But if you were to stretch your imagination a little and pretend that work wasn't there, could you sail on and on?"

She crinkled her nose. "Nah. I'm a landlubber at heart. Give me a little cottage in the Berkshires and I'd be in heaven."

"Not heaven, sweetheart," Victoria scoffed. "You'd be in solitary confinement."

"Is that what she usually does for her vacations?" Noah asked.

"What I usually do—"

"That's what she would have been doing this year if I hadn't suggested she come with me."

"Suggested! That's—"

"I can understand what she sees in it," Noah interrupted blithely, ignoring both Shaye and her attempts to speak. "I have my own place in southern Vermont. I don't usually make it there for more than a few days at a stretch, but those few days are wonderful. There's nothing like time spent alone in a peaceful setting to replenish one's energies."

Victoria disagreed. "No, no. Time spent with someone special—that's different. But alone?"

"You spent time alone," Shaye argued hurriedly before someone cut her off.

"Naturally. I can't be with people all the time. But to choose to go off alone—just for the sake of being alone—for days at a time isn't healthy. It says something about your life, if you need that kind of escape."

"We all need escapes from habit," Noah reasoned, "don't we, Shaye?"

He'd tagged on the last in an intimate tone, leaving no doubt in Shaye's mind that he was referring to what had happened between them beneath the stars.

"Victoria is right. Certain kinds of escape are unhealthy."

"But, hot damn, they're fun," he countered in that same low tone.

Victoria looked from one to the other. "Am I missing something?"

"You missed it but good," Noah said with a grin. His eyes were fixed on Shaye. "We had quite a time of it last night—"

"Noah—"

"You did? Shaye, you didn't *tell* me."

Shaye couldn't believe what was happening. "What Noah means is that we had a little disagreement—"

"Only after the fact. It wasn't a disagreement at the time."

Turning to Victoria, Shaye affected a confident drawl. "He gets confused. Poor thing, he's so used to being ornery that it doesn't faze him."

"What happened last night?"

"Nothing hap—"

"You stole out while I was asleep, clever girl." She turned to Noah. "I hope she didn't shock you."

"As a matter of fact—"

"Please!" Shaye cried. "Stop it, both of you!" In her torment she shifted her legs, the better to brace herself.

Noah's gaze shifted too.

She snapped her knees together.

With an almost imperceptible sigh of regret, he dipped his head to the side. "Your niece has beautiful hair, Victoria. It's thick and rich like yours, but the color—where did she get the color?"

"Her father is a flaming redhead. When Shaye was a child—"

"That's enough, Victoria."

Victoria ignored her. "When she was a child, hers was nearly as red as his."

"Does she get her temper from him, too?"

"What do *you* think?"

"Victoria, if you—"

"I think she does," Noah decided with a grin that turned wry. "I'm not sure if I should thank him or curse him."

"You should leave him out of this," Shaye cried.

"Now, now, Shaye," Victoria soothed, "no need to get upset."

Noah added, "I want to know about him. You're much too closemouthed, Shaye. In all the talking we've done, you've barely said a word about yourself."

"Shame on you, Shaye," Victoria chided. "You act as though you have something to hide."

It was a challenge, well intended but a challenge nonetheless. If Shaye denied that she had anything to hide, she'd have to answer Noah's questions. If she came right out and said that she *did* have something to hide, he'd be all the more curious. For a long minute she glared at her aunt, then at Noah, but she still didn't know what to do.

At last Noah took pity. At least, he mused mischievously, he was willing to defer the discussion of her parents until later. But he wasn't about to miss out on another golden opportunity.

In a single fluid movement, he was sitting by her side against the bulwark. "What say we go for a swim later?"

She didn't answer at first. Her right side was tingling—her arm, her hip, everywhere his body touched. She cleared her throat and looked straight ahead. "Be my guest."

"I said 'we.'"

"Thanks, but I don't care to be left in the water while the boat sails on ahead." Implied was that she wouldn't mind if *he* was left behind.

He ruled out that possibility. "We'll lower the sails and drift. The *Golden Echo* won't go anywhere, and we can play." With one finger he blotted the dampness from her upper lip. "It'll be fun."

She was afraid to move. "I'll watch."

"But the water will feel great." He pried his back from the bulwark. "My shirt's sticking. You'd think the breeze would help."

"You're too hot for your own good."

"I don't know about that," he said in a sultry tone, "but I am hot." Without another word, he leaned forward and peeled off his shirt.

Shaye nearly died. She'd never seen a back as strong and as

well formed, and when he relaxed against the bulwark again, the sight of his broad, leanly muscled chest was nearly more than she could bear. She swallowed down a moan.

"Did you say something?" he queried innocently.

"No, no."

"Your voice sounds strange. Higher than usual."

"It's the altitude. We must be climbing."

"We're at sea level."

"Oh. Mmm. That's right."

Without warning he stole her hand, linked their fingers together and placed them on his bare thigh. Then he looked at Victoria. "Maybe you'd like to join us for that swim."

Victoria grinned. "I'd like that."

"'Course, if you come, I'll have to behave."

Shaye grunted. "Like you're doing now?" She tried to pull her hand away but only succeeded in getting a better feel of his warm, hair-roughened thigh.

He feigned hurt. "I'm behaving."

"You're half-naked."

"I'm also half-dressed. Would you rather I'd left on my shirt and taken off my shorts?"

Victoria laughed. He was outrageous! And still he went on, this time turning injured eyes her way.

"I beg your pardon, Victoria. Are you suggesting that I have something to be ashamed of?"

Unable to help herself, she was laughing again. "Of course not. I—"

"This is no laughing matter! You wound my pride!"

"No, no, Noah," she managed to gasp. "I didn't intend—"

"But the damage is done," he said with such an aggrieved expression that she burst into another peal of laughter, which only made him square his chin more. "I can guarantee you that I'm fully equipped."

"I'm sure—"

"You don't believe me," he said in a flurry. He looked at Shaye. "You don't believe me either." He dropped his hand. "Well, I'll show you both!" He had the drawstring of his shorts undone and his thumbs tucked under the waistband before Shaye pressed a frantic hand to his belly.

"Don't," she whispered. "Please?"

Never in his life had Noah seen as beseeching a look. Her

hand was burning a hole in him, but she seemed not to notice. She was near tears.

In that moment he lost his taste for the game. "I was only teasing," he said gently.

She looked at him for a minute longer, her eyes searching his face, moving from one feature to another. Her lower lip trembled.

Then she was up like a shot, running aft along the deck and disappearing down the companionway.

He started after her, but Victoria caught his hand. "Let her be for a while. She has to work some things out for herself."

"I don't want to hurt her."

"I know that. I trust you. Your uncle is a talker once he gets going. He's proud of you, and with good reason."

Noah frowned. "When did he do all this talking?" His eyes widened. "While we were on deck last night?"

"While *we* were on deck this *morning*," she answered, grinning mischievously. "You and Shaye sleep late. Samson and I wake up early."

"Ahh," Noah said, but his frown returned. "I'm trying to understand Shaye, but it's tough. She doesn't like to talk about herself."

"She's trained herself to be that way."

He wanted to ask why, just as he wanted to ask Victoria about all those other things Shaye wouldn't talk about. But it wasn't Victoria's place to talk. What was happening here was between Shaye and him. Sweet as she was, Victoria wasn't part of it, and he refused to put her in the position of betraying her niece.

"She'll tell you in time," Victoria said.

"How can you be sure?"

"I know, that's all. Be patient."

Thrusting a hand through his hair, he realized that he had no other choice. With a sigh, he scooped up his shirt and started off.

"Noah?"

He turned.

She dropped a deliberate glance to his shorts, which, without benefit of the drawstring, had fallen precariously low on his hips.

"Oh." He tied the string almost absently, then continued on.

So comfortable with his body, Victoria mused. *So comfortable with his sexuality. If only he could teach Shaye to be that way....*

Chapter Five

NOAH WAS RIGHT, Shaye knew. She couldn't hide in her cabin forever. It had been childish of her to run off that way, but at the time she'd been unable to cope with the feelings rushing through her. Noah had been so close, so bare, so provocative, and she was so drawn to him on a physical level that it frightened her to tears.

Brash and irreverent, impulsive and uninhibited, he was on the surface everything she tried to avoid. What was beneath the surface, though, was an enigma. She didn't know much about him—what he did for a living, whether he was attached in any manner to a woman, where his deepest needs and innermost values lay. She wanted to label him as all bad, but she couldn't. He was incredibly devoted to Samson and unfailingly kind to Victoria, and that had to account for something.

So. Here she sat—eyes moist, palms clammy, feeling perfectly juvenile. A reluctant smile played along her lips. Was this the adolescence she'd never had? She'd matured with such lightning speed that she'd never had time to feel growing pains—as good a term as any to describe what she was feeling now. She was being forced to reevaluate her wants and needs. And it was painful.

But nothing was accomplished sitting here. She wasn't an adolescent with the luxury of wallowing for hours in self-pity. Her wisest move, it seemed, would be to pull herself together, rejoin the others and try to regain a little of her self-esteem. She would sort things out in time.

Changing into a bathing suit, she unknotted her hair, brushed it out, then caught it up into a ponytail at her crown. After splashing her face with water, she belted on a short terry-cloth robe and left the cabin.

Noah was waiting in the salon, sitting in one of the chairs. She stopped on the threshold and eyed him uncertainly. He didn't comment on her outfit, or on her bare legs, or on her hair.

In fact, he seemed almost as uncertain as she, which was just the slightest bit bolstering.

"You said something about going swimming," she reminded him softly.

He sat still for another minute, his face an amalgam of confusion, hesitation and hope. "You want to?" he cautiously asked.

She nodded.

With the blink of an eye, his grin returned, "You're on." He stood and headed for his cabin. "Stay put. I'll just change into trunks and we'll be ready."

"But the sails—"

"Tell Samson to take them in. He'll be game; he loves to swim. And tell Victoria to change, too. She wanted to come."

The door of the aft cabin closed. Shaye watched it for a minute, then walked quietly past and started up the companionway. She wondered about the way he'd been sitting in the salon, about the uncertainty she'd read on his face. That was a side of him she'd never seen, one she hadn't thought existed. It was a far cry from the smugness—or arrogance or annoyance—he usually granted her, and even his returning confidence was somehow different and more manageable. If only she knew what was going on in his head…

Noah hung a rope ladder off the port quarter and let Shaye climb down first. She went about halfway before jumping. In the very first instant submerged, she realized by contrast how hot and grubby she'd felt before. Her sense of exhilaration was nearly as great as her sense of refreshment.

Ducking under a second time, she came up with her head back and a smile on her face. She opened her eyes in time to see Noah balance on the transom for an instant before soaring up, out, then down, slicing neatly into the waves. Feeling incredibly light, she treaded water until he appeared by her side.

"Not bad," she said, complimenting his dive.

"Not bad, yourself," he said, complimenting her smile. Then he took off, stroking strongly around the *Golden Echo*'s stern, then along her starboard side. Shaye followed a bit more slowly, but he was waiting for her at the bow before starting down the port side.

Completing the lap, he turned to her with a grin. "You're a

good swimmer. It must be that suit you're wearing. It covers up enough of your body. Is it covering up a flotation device, too?''

She rolled her eyes. ''Fifteen minutes.''

''Fifteen minutes, what?''

''That's how long you made it without a snippy comment. But now you've blown it, and by insulting my suit, no less! There is nothing wrong with this suit.'' It was, in fact, a designer maillot that she'd paid dearly for.

He sank beneath the surface for a minute, tossing his hair back with a flourish when he came up. ''I was hoping to see more of your body. I was hoping for a bikini.''

''Sorry,'' she said, then turned and swam off.

He'd caught up to her in a minute. ''You are not sorry. You take perverse pleasure in teasing me.''

''Look who's talking!''

''But you're so teasable,'' he argued, eyes twinkling. ''You rise to my taunts.''

''No more,'' she decided and propelled herself backward.

He negated the distance with a single stroke. ''Wanna test that out?''

''Sure.'' She turned sideways and tipped up her nose in an attempt to look imperturbable. It was a little absurd given the steady movement of her arms and legs, but she did her best.

Noah went underwater.

She waited, eventually darting a sidelong glance to where he'd gone down, then waited again, certain that any minute she'd feel a tug at her leg. When she felt so such thing, she glanced to the other side.

No Noah. No bubbles. Nothing but gentle waves.

Vaguely concerned, she made a complete turn. When she saw no sign of him, she submerged for an underwater look.

Nothing!

''Noah?'' she called, reaching the surface again. ''Noah!''

Samson's head appeared over the side of the boat. ''Problem, Shaye?''

Her heart was thudding. ''It's Noah! He went under and I can't find him!''

Samson cocked his head toward the opposite side of the boat. ''Try over here,'' he said and disappeared.

Performing a convulsive breast stroke, Shaye sped to the port side, to find Noah riding the waves on his back, eyes closed, basking in the sun.

"You bastard!" she screamed, furiously batting water his way. "You terrified me!"

His serenity ruined by her splashing, he advanced on her, turning his face one way then the other against her wet attack. Then he cinched an arm around her waist and drew her against him, effectively stopping the barrage.

"Y'see?" he gloated. "It worked."

"That was a totally stupid thing to do!" she cried, tightly clutching his shoulders. "And irresponsible! What if something really had happened to you? I'm not a trained lifesaver. I couldn't have helped! And think of *me*. I could have gone under looking for you and stayed there too long. You would never have known I was drowning, because you were out of sight, on the far side of the boat, playing your silly little game."

"Samson was keeping an eye on you."

"That's not the point!" She narrowed her eyes. "Next time I won't even bother to look. You know what happened to the little boy who cried wolf?"

"But I'm not a little boy."

She snorted.

His arm tightened. "Wrap your legs around my waist."

"Are you kidding?"

"I'll keep us afloat."

"I don't trust you."

"You don't trust yourself."

He was right. "You're wrong."

"Nuh-uh." His lips twitched. "You don't want to wrap your legs around me because that would put you flush against my—hey, stop that!"

She'd found that he was ticklish, and in the nick of time. Within seconds they were both underwater, but at least she was free, and when she resurfaced, Noah was waiting. What ensued then was a good, old-fashioned, rollicking water fight that was broken up at length by Samson's, "Children! Children!"

The water settled some around them as they looked up.

"Bath time," he called. He was lowering a small basket that contained soap and shampoo.

Shaye looked at Noah; Noah looked at Shaye.

"Do you think he's trying to tell us something?" he asked.

"Diplomatically," she answered.

He wrinkled his nose. "Was I that bad?"

"Was *I*?"

"Maybe we canceled each other out."

"So we didn't notice?"

"Yeah." He scowled. "Hell, it's only been three days."

"Three? That's disgusting!"

His eyes widened in accusation. "It has to have been just as long for you."

"Two. Only two, and I've been—"

"Are you going to wash or not?" came the call from above. "We're dying to swim, but we don't want to go in until you get out!"

Shaye looked at Noah in horror. "Is it that bad that they don't want to be near us even in water?"

He laughed and swam toward the basket. "For safety, Shaye. One of us should be on the boat at any given time, and since no one should swim alone, it makes sense to divide it up, two and two." He drew a bright yellow container from the basket and squirted liberal jets of its contents on his arms, hands and neck.

"Joy?" she asked, swimming closer.

He tossed her the plastic bottle. "It's one of the few detergents that bubbles in salt water," he explained as he scrubbed his arms, offering proof. "Go on. It does the trick."

She followed his lead and, scissoring steadily with her legs, had soon lathered her arms, shoulders and neck. Noah took the bottle from the basket again and filled his palm, then set to work beneath the waterline. Shaye took her time rinsing her arms.

His eyes grew teasing. "I'm doing my chest. How about you?"

"I'm getting there," she managed, but she was feeling suddenly awkward. She darted a self-conscious glance upward and was relieved to see no sign of Samson.

"You'll need more soap." He tossed his head toward the basket.

She took the bottle, directed a stream of the thick liquid into her hand and replaced the bottle. Then she stared at her palm, wondering how to start.

"Don't turn around," he said. "I want to watch."

"I'm sure."

"Come on. We're in the shadow of the boat. The water's too dark to see anything."

It wasn't what he could see that she feared. It was what he could picture. She knew what *she* was picturing as his shoulders rotated, hands out of sight but very obviously on that broad and virile chest.

"You'd better hurry, Shaye. Samson won't wait forever."

"Okay, okay." With hurried movements, she rubbed her hands together, then thrust them under her suit.

"You could lower the suit. It'd help."

"This is fine." Eyes averted, she soaped her breasts as quickly as she could.

"Look at me while you do that," he commanded softly.

She shot him a glance that was supposed to be quelling, but when her eyes locked with his, she couldn't look away. There was nothing remotely quelling in her gaze then; it mirrored the desire in his. Sudden, startling, explosive. They were separated by a mere arm's length, which, given the expanse of the Caribbean, seemed positively intimate.

Her hands worked over and around her breasts while his hands worked over and around his chest, but it was his fingers she seemed to feel on her sensitive skin, his harder flesh beneath her fingers. When he moved his hands to his lower back, she followed suit and the tingling increased, touching her vertebrae, sizzling down to the base of her spine.

Her lips were parted; her breath rushed past in shallow pants. Her legs continued to scissor, though hypnotically. She was in Noah's thrall, held there by the dark, smoldering charcoal of his eyes and by the force of her own vivid imagination.

The curve of his shoulders indicated that his hands had returned to his front and moved lower. She gulped in a short breath, but her shoulders were also curving, her hands moving forward, then lower.

His eyes held hers, neither mocking nor dropping in an attempt to breach the sea's modest veil. The waves rose and fell around and with them, like a mentor, teaching them the movement, rewarding them with gentle supplementary caresses.

But supplementary caresses were the last things they needed. Shaye felt as though she were vibrating from the inside out, and Noah's muscles were tense, straining for the release that he wouldn't allow himself.

When he closed his eyes for an instant, the spell broke. Two sets of arms joined trembling legs in treading water, and it was a minute more before either of them could speak.

Noah's lips twisted into a self-mocking grin. "You are one hell of a lady to make love with," he said gruffly. "Com'ere."

Shaye gave several rapid shakes of her head.

"I want to do your hair."

"My hair's okay."

He was fishing a bottle of shampoo from the basket when Victoria's voice came over the side. "Aren't you two done *yet*?"

"Be right up," Shaye gasped. She turned to start for the ladder, but a gentle tug on her ponytail brought her right back to Noah. The water worked against her then, denying her the leverage to escape him. And his fingers were already in her hair, easing the thick elastic band from its place. "Please don't, Noah," she begged.

His voice was close to her ear. "Indulge me this, after what you denied me just now."

"Denied you? I didn't deny you a thing!"

"You didn't give me what I *really* wanted...."

She wasn't about to touch that one. So she faced him and held out a hand, palm up. "The shampoo?"

"Right here," he said, pressing his gloppy hand on the top of her head and instantly starting to scrub.

She squeezed her eyes shut. "I'll do it, Noah."

"Too late," he said with an audible grin, then paused. "I've never washed a woman's hair before. Am I doing it right?"

His fingers were everywhere, gathering even the longest strands into the cloud of lather, massaging her scalp, stimulating nerve ends she hadn't known about. Was he doing it right? Was he ever!

She tried to think of something to say, but it was as though his fingers had penetrated her skull and were impeding the workings of her brain. Her eyes were still closed, but in ecstasy now. Her head had fallen back a little as he worked his thumbs along her hairline. She was unaware that her breasts were pushing against his chest, or that her legs had floated around his hips and she was riding him gently in the waves, because those were but small eddies in the overall vortex of pleasure.

His fingers were suddenly still, cupping her head, and his voice was gruff as he pressed his lips to her brow. "Maybe this wasn't such a good idea after all. Better rinse and let me do mine. If our time isn't up, my self-control is."

Shaye opened her eyes then. They widened when she realized how she was holding Noah. "Oh Lord," she whispered and quickly let go. With frantic little movements, she sculled away.

"You're a hussy, Shaye Burke!" Noah taunted. He poured shampoo directly from the bottle onto his head.

She sank underwater and shook her own. When she resurfaced, he was scrubbing his hair, but wore a grin that was naughty.

"A hussy and a tease!"

"You are a corrupter!" she cried back.

"Me? I was washing your hair! You were the one who tried to make something more of it!"

Tipping her head to the right to finger-comb water through her hair, she glared at him. "That's exactly how you're going to look in ten years, Noah—all white-haired and prune-faced." She tipped her head to the left and rinsed the long tresses further. "*No* woman's going to want to look at you then!"

"So I'd better catch someone now, hmm? Take out an insurance policy?" He submerged, raking the soap from his hair with his fingers.

"I dare say the premiums would be too high," she called the minute he'd resurfaced.

"Are you selling?"

"To you? No way!" She headed for the ladder. "You are a sneaky, no-good...seducer of innocent women."

Noah caught her on the second rung, encircling her hips with one strong arm. He said nothing until she looked down at him, then asked quietly and without jest, "Are you innocent?"

She could take the question different ways, she knew, but if she were honest the answer would be the same. No, she wasn't innocent in what had just happened, because no one had told her to wrap herself so snugly around him. No, she hadn't been innocent last night. He hadn't asked her to go wild in his arms. And she wasn't innocent in that broadest sense; she'd lost her virginity half a lifetime ago.

Sad eyes conveyed her answer, but she said nothing. Noah held a frightening power over her already. That power would surely increase if she confirmed how truly less than innocent she was.

His gaze dropped over her gleaming shoulders and down her bare back to the edge of her suit. His hand slid lower, over the flare of her bottom to her thigh. When he gave her a gentle boost, she climbed the ladder, then crossed the deck to the bow, knowing Noah would remain at the stern to serve as lifeguard to Samson and Victoria.

She needed to be alone. The past weighed too heavily on her to allow for even the most banal of conversation.

SHAYE HAD BEGUN TO REBEL at the age of thirteen, when her father's fierce temper and her mother's conventionalism first crowded in on her budding adolescence. Life to that point had been placid, a sedate cycle revolving around school and church. But she had suddenly developed from a redheaded little girl into an eye-catching teenager, and even if she hadn't seen the change in herself, it would have been impossible for her to mistake the admiring male looks that came her way.

Those looks promised excitement, something she'd never experienced, and she thrived on them, since they compensated for the more dismissing ones she'd received before. Her father was a factory hand, and though he worked hard, the socio-economic class in which the Burkes were trapped was on the lower end of the scale. Donald Burke had been proud to buy the small, two-bedroom cottage in which they lived, because it was on the right side of the tracks, if barely. Unfortunately, the tracks delineated the school districts, which put Shaye and Shannon in classes with far more privileged children.

Gaining the attention of some of the most attractive boys around was a heady experience for Shaye. For the first time she was able to compete with girls she'd envied, girls whose lives where less structured and more frivolous. For the first time she was able to partake in that frivolity—as the guest of the very boys those girls covetously eyed.

In theory, Anne Burke wouldn't have objected to the attention her daughter received. She idolized her husband and was perfectly comfortable with their life, which was not unlike the one she'd known herself as a child. But she'd seen how well her sister, Victoria, had done in marrying Arthur Lesser, and she had no objection to her daughter aiming high.

What she objected to was the fact that Shaye was only thirteen and that the boys of whom she was enamored were sixteen and seventeen. They were dangerous ages, ages of discovery, and Anne Burke didn't want her daughter used. So she set strict limits on Shaye's social life, and when Shaye argued, as any normal teenager would, Donald Burke was there to enforce the law.

Perhaps, Shaye had often mused later, if they'd been a little more flexible she'd have managed—or if she'd been more manageable, they'd have flexed. But by the time she was fifteen, she felt totally at odds with her parents' conventionality, and her response was to flaunt it in any way she could. She stole out to a party at Jimmy Danforth's house, when she was supposedly studying at the library. She cut classes to go joyriding with Brett Hagen in the Mustang his parents had given him for his eighteenth birthday. She told her parents she was baby-sitting, when the baby in question was a dog that belonged to Alexander Bigelow.

Three days before her sixteenth birthday, she made love with Ben Parker on the floor of his parents' wine cellar. She'd known precisely what she was doing and why. She'd given her innocence to Ben because it was fun and exciting and a little bit dangerous—and because it was the last thing her parents wanted her to do.

She was her own person, she'd decided. If her parents were happy with their lives, that was fine, but she resented the dogma of hard work and self-restraint that they imposed on her. Discovering that she could have a wonderful time—and get away with it—was self-perpetuating.

She played her way through high school. Reasonably bright, she maintained a B average without much effort—a good thing, since she didn't have much time to spare from her social life. Fights with her parents were long and drawn out, until true communication became almost nonexistent. That didn't bother Shaye. She knew what she wanted to do, and she did it. She applied to NYU, was accepted on scholarship, and finally escaped her parents' watchful eyes.

New York was as much fun as she'd hoped. She liked her classes, but she liked even more the freedom she had and the people she met. And she adored Victoria, whom she saw regularly. In hindsight, Shaye knew that keeping in such close touch with her aunt represented a need for family ties. At the time she only knew Victoria understood her as her parents never had.

Victoria was as different from her sister, Anne, as night from day. While Anne chose to take the more traveled highways through life, Victoria took the back roads that led to greater beauty and pleasure. The one thing they shared was their devotion to their husbands, but since each had married a man to suit her tastes, their differences had grown more marked as time went on.

Shaye identified with Victoria. It wasn't that she yearned to be wealthy; wealth, or the lack of it, had never played as prominently in her mind as had adventure. But Victoria *did* things. She acted on her impulses, rather than putting them off for a day far in the future. And if she subtly cautioned Shaye to exercise moderation, Shaye put it down to the loyalty Victoria felt toward Anne.

Despite Victoria's subtle words of caution, Shaye had a ball. In February of her freshman year she hitchhiked with Graham Hauk to New Orleans for Mardi Gras. That summer she took a house in Provincetown with five friends, all of whom were working, as she was, in local restaurants. Much of her sophomore year was spent at the off-campus apartment of Josh Milgram, her latest love and a graduate student of philosophy, who had a group of ever-present and fascinating, if bizarre, friends.

She spent the summer before her junior year selling computer equipment in Washington. She'd secured the job principally on her interview, during which she'd demonstrated both an aptitude for handling the equipment and an aptitude for selling herself. She loved Washington. Sharing an apartment with two friends from school, she had regular working hours, which left plenty of time for play.

It was during that summer that Shannon joined her, and Shaye couldn't have been more delighted. She'd always felt that Shannon was being stifled at home. More than once she'd urged her sister to break out, but it was only by dint of a summer-school program held at American University for high school students that Shannon made it.

Proud of her sister, Shaye introduced her to all her friends. At summer's end, she sent Shannon back home reasonably assured that she was awakened to the pleasures of life.

Shaye whizzed through her junior year seeing Tom, Peter and Gene, but the real fun came in her senior year when she met André. André—né Andrew, but he'd decided that that name was too plebeian—was a perpetual student of art. He had a small garret in Soho, where Shaye spent most of her time, and a revolving group of friends and followers who offered never-ending novelty. André and Shaye were a couple, but in the loosest sense of the word. André was far from possessive, and Shaye was far from committed. She adored André for his eccentricity; his painting was as eclectic as his lovemaking. But she adored Christopher's brashness and Jamal's wild imagination and Stefan's incredible irreverence.

She was treading a fine line in her personal life, though at the time she didn't see it. Graduating from college, she took a position in the computer department of an insurance company, and if her friends teased her about such a staid job, she merely laughed, took a puff of the nearest pipe and did something totally outrageous to show where her heart lay.

She was one year out of college and living at the garret with André and his friends when the folly of her life-style hit home.

"FRÄULEIN?"

Shaye's head shot up, her thoughts boomeranging back to the present. Her eyes focused on Samson, who was wearing a black tuxedo jacket with tails and, beneath it, a white apron tied at the waist and falling to mid-calf.

"*Darf ich Sie bitten, an unserem* Dinner *teilzunehmen? Wir sind bereit; bitte sagen Sie nicht nein.*"

It was a minute before comprehension came. She didn't speak German, but a pattern was emerging, reinforced by the sight of Victoria and Noah already settling at the table on the other end of the deck.

She didn't know how long she'd been sitting so lost in thought—an hour, perhaps two—but she was grateful for the rescue. Smiling, she took the hand Samson graciously offered, realizing only after she'd risen that she was still wearing her bathing suit.

"Let me change first," she said softly.

"You don't need to."

But she'd be asking for trouble from Noah if she appeared at dinner so minimally covered. "I'll be quick."

Hurrying below, she discarded the suit and drew on a one-piece shorts outfit. She'd reached the companionway before realizing that her hair was still down. Deciding that it was too late to pin it up, she finger-combed it back from her face and continued to the deck.

Dinner was sauerbraten, red cabbage and strudel. It was accompanied by a sturdy red Ingelheimer whose mildly sedative effect helped Shaye handle both the lingering shadow of her reminiscing and Noah's very large, very virile and observant presence.

Actually, he behaved himself admirably, or so he decided. He didn't make any comments about Shaye's free-flowing hair, though he was dying to. Even more, he was dying to touch it. Clean and shining, it seemed thicker than ever, as though its life had been released by the sea and the breeze. Nor did he comment on her smile, which was coming more frequently. He wondered if it was the wine, or whether the afternoon swim had eased a certain tension from her. Somehow he doubted the latter, after the words they'd exchanged in the water. But she'd spent a good long time since then at the bow, and he wondered if what she'd been thinking about was responsible for the softening of her mood.

He'd watched her but she hadn't known it. She'd been lost in a world of her own. Even now, sitting over the last of the wine, she faded in and out from time to time. During those "out" phases her expression was mellow, vaguely sad—as it had been on the rope ladder when he'd asked about her innocence.

He was more curious about her than ever, but he could bide his time. Sunset was upon them. Soon it would be dark. Perhaps if her mellow mood continued, he'd be able to pry some information from her without a fight.

After dinner Shaye returned to her perch at the bow. She took a cushion with her, and though she'd fetched a book, she didn't bother to open it. Instead, she propped herself comfortably and studied the sky.

To the west were the deepening orange colors of the waning day, above that the purples of early night. As she watched, the purples spread and darkened, until the last of the sun's rays had been swallowed up.

She took one deep breath, then another. Her body felt clean and relaxed, and if her mind wasn't in quite that perfect a state, it was close. There were things to be considered, but not now, not when the Caribbean night was so beautiful.

Victoria was with Samson at the helm. They clearly enjoyed

each other, and, deep down inside, Shaye was pleased. Samson was an interesting man. He had the style and spirit to make Victoria's trip an adventure even without the treasure no one had spoken of yet.

Shifting herself and the cushion so that she was lying down, she crossed her ankles, folded her hands on her middle and closed her eyes. So different from home, she mused. She couldn't remember the last time she'd lain down like this and just...listened. What was there to listen to in her Philadelphia apartment? Traffic? The siren of a police car or an ambulance? Peals of laughter from a party at one of the other apartments?

None of that here. Just the rhythmic thrust of the waves against the hull and the periodic flap of a sail. There was something to be said for going on a treasure hunt after all.

Her brow creased lightly. Noah had said that there were different types of treasures to be sought, and he was right. He seemed to be right about a lot of things. She had to define the treasure *she* was seeking. Was it a job well done in Philadelphia? Career advancement? Perhaps movement to a broader, more prestigious position?

After all she'd thought about that afternoon, she had to smile. Her life now was the antithesis of what it had been seven, eight, nine years before. If someone had told her then what she'd be doing in subsequent years, she'd have thought him mad.

But even back then, without conscious planning, she'd made provisions for a more stable life. She'd completed her education and had established herself in a lucrative field. Had her subconscious known something?

The question was whether the life she now had would stand her in good stead for the next thirty years. If so, if she was as self-contained and complete a being as she'd thought, why did Noah VanBaar make her ache? Did her subconscious know something else?

Eyes still closed, she grew alert. He was here now. She hadn't heard him approach, but she knew he was near. There was something hovering, newly coagulating in her mind...a sense of familiarity, a scent. Noah. Smelling of the sun and the sea, of musk and man.

She opened her eyes and met his curious gaze. He was squatting an arm's length away, a dimly-glowing lantern hanging from his fingers.

"I wasn't sure if you were sleeping."

"I wasn't."

"You've been lying here a long time."

And still she didn't move; she felt too comfortable. "It's peaceful." Was that a hint that he should leave? She was trying to decide if she wanted him to when he reached up, hooked the lantern on the bowsprit, then sat down and stretched out his legs. She'd known he wouldn't ask to join her; that wasn't his style. In a way she was glad he hadn't. She'd been spared having to make the choice.

Resting his head back, he sighed. "We're almost halfway there. From the looks of the clouds in the east, we may get a push."

"Clouds?" She peered eastward. "I don't see a thing."

"Mmm. No moon, no stars."

"Oh, dear. A storm?"

He shrugged. "Who knows? Maybe rain, maybe wind, maybe nothing. Storm clouds can veer off. They can dissipate. Weather at sea is fickle."

Sliding an arm behind her head, she studied him. "You must sail a lot."

"Not so much now. I used to though. Samson got me hooked when I was a kid. I spent several summers crewing on windjammers off the coast of Maine."

"Sounds like fun."

"It was. I love the ocean, especially when it's wild. I could sit for hours and watch the waves thrash about."

"You should have a place on the coast, rather than in Vermont."

"Nah. Watching the ocean in a storm is inspirational, not restful. When I leave the city on weekends, I need rest."

"The city—New York?"

He nodded.

"What do you do?"

"Are you sure you want to know?"

"Why wouldn't I?"

"Because knowing about me will bring us closer, and I had the impression that you wanted to stay as far from me as possible."

"True. But tell me anyway."

"Why?"

"Because I'm curious."

He considered that. "I suppose it's as good a reason as any. Of course," he tilted his head and his voice turned whimsical, "it would be nicer if you'd said that you've changed your mind about staying away, or that you want to know about the man who's swept you off your feet, or—" his voice dropped "—that you're as interested in exploring my mind as you are in exploring my body."

Her skin tingled and she was grateful that the lantern was more a beacon to other ships than an illuminator of theirs. The dark was her protector, when she felt oddly exposed. "Just tell me," she grumbled, then added a taunting, "unless you have something to hide."

That was all Noah needed to hear. "I'm a political pollster."

"A political—"

"Pollster. When a guy decides to make a run for political office, he hires me to keep tabs on his status among the electorate."

"Interesting," she said and meant it.

"I think so. Actually, I started out doing only polling, but the business has evolved into something akin to public relations."

"In what sense?"

Encouraged that she wanted to hear more, Noah explained. "John Doe comes to me and says that he's running for office. I do my research, ferreting out his opponent's strengths and weaknesses, plus the characteristics of the constituency. Between us we determine the image we want to project, the kind of image that will go across with the voters—"

"But isn't that cheating? If you tailor-make the candidate to the voters, what about issues? Isn't John Doe compromising himself?"

"Not at all. He doesn't alter his stand; he merely alters the way that stand is put across. One or another of his positions may be more popular among the voters, so we focus on those and push the others into the background. The key is to get the man elected, at which point he can bring other issues forward."

"Clever, if a little devious."

"That's the way the game is played. His opponent does it; why shouldn't he? It's most useful on matters that have little to do with the issues."

"Such as...?"

"Age. Marital status. Religion, ethnic background, prior political experience. Again, it's a question of playing something up or down, depending on the bias of the voters."

Shaye frowned. "Sounds to me like there's a very fine line between your job and an ad agency's."

"Sure is, and that's who takes over from me. Ad agencies, media consultants—they're the ones who put together the specifics of the campaign itself."

"And your job is done at that point?"

He shook his head. "We keep polling right up to, sometimes beyond, the campaign. Obviously, some candidates have more money to pay for our services than others. By the same token, some political offices require more ongoing work than others."

She could easily guess which offices those would be and was duly impressed. "I suppose that's good for you. Otherwise you'd have a pretty seasonal job."

"Seasonal it isn't," he drawled. "I use the word 'political' in the broadest sense. We do polling for lobbyists, for public interest groups, for hospitals and real estate developers and educational institutions."

"When you say 'we,' who do you mean?"

"I have a full-time staff of ninety people, with several hundred part-timers on call."

"But you're the leader?"

"It's my baby, yes."

"You started it from scratch?"

"Planted the seed and nurtured it," he said with an inflection of intimacy that made her blush. He didn't follow up, though, but leaned forward and rubbed his back before returning to his original position.

"You must feel proud."

"I do."

"There must be a lot of pressure."

He nodded.

"But it's rewarding?"

"Very." He sat forward again and flexed his back muscles, then grumbled crossly, "This boat leaves much to be desired by way of comfort. I've never heard of a boat with a deck this size and no deck chairs."

She was hard put not to laugh, clearly recalling the discussion she'd had with Victoria when they'd first boarded the sloop, a discussion Noah had overheard and mocked. "You don't like the *Golden Echo*?" she asked sweetly.

He heard the jibe in her tone and couldn't let it go unanswered. In the blink of an eye, he'd closed the distance between them, displaced her from the cushion and drawn her to him so that her back was against his chest.

Chapter Six

SHAYE TRIED TO WIGGLE AWAY, but Noah hooked his legs around hers. When she continued to squirm, he made a low, sexy sound. ''Ooh, that feels good. A little more pressure... there...lower.''

Abruptly she went still. ''This is not a good idea, Noah.''

''My back sure feels a hell of a lot better.''

''Mine doesn't.''

''That's because you've got a rod up it—'' He caught himself and backed off. ''Uh, no, that came out the wrong way. What I meant was that you've stiffened up. If you relax and let me cushion you, you'll be as comfortable as you were before.''

That was what Shaye feared, but the temptation was great. It was a peaceful night and she'd been interested in what he'd been saying. Would it hurt to relax a little?

''Better,'' he said with a sigh when he felt her body soften to his. Though his legs fell away, his arms remained loosely around her waist. He'd thrown on a shirt after dinner, but it was unbuttoned. Her hair formed a thick pillow on his chest, with wayward strands teasing his throat and chin.

Having made the decision to stay in his arms, Shaye was surprisingly content. ''Have you ever been married?''

''Where did that come from?''

''I was thinking about your work. You said there was pressure, and I assume the hours are long. I was curious.''

Curious, again. Okay. ''No. I've never been married.''

''Do you dislike women?''

''Where did *that* come from?''

''One of the first things you said you didn't like about me was that I was a woman.''

''Ah. That was because I hadn't known there were going to be women along on this trip until a few minutes before you and your aunt arrived.''

''And it bothered you?''

"At the time."

"Why?"

"Because I wanted to get away from it all. Before Samson drafted me I'd planned to spend two weeks alone in Normandy."

"Normandy." She slid her head sideways and looked up at him. "A château?"

"A small one."

She righted her head. "Small one, big one...it sounds lovely."

"It would have been, but this isn't so bad."

"Would you have done anything differently if Victoria and I hadn't been along?"

"A few things."

"Like...?"

"Shaving. I wouldn't have bothered."

"You don't have to shave for our sakes. Be my guest. Grow a beard."

He'd been hoping she'd thank him; after all, stubble looked grubby, and then there was the matter of kissing. But she wouldn't consider that. Not Shaye.

"I don't want to grow a beard," he grumbled. "I just didn't want to have to shave unless I felt like it."

"So don't." She paused. "What else would you have done if we weren't along?"

"Swam in the nude. Sunbathed in the nude. *Sailed* in the nude," he added just for spite.

Forgetting that she was supposed to be prissy, she grinned. "That would be a sight."

"Oh God, are we onto that again? Why is it that everyone's always insulting my manhood?"

She shaped her hands to his wrists and gave a squeeze. "I'm just teasing...though I don't believe I've ever seen a naked pirate before."

"This is not a pirate ship," was his arch response.

"Then, a naked patriot."

"Have you ever seen any man naked?"

Her grin was hidden. He should only know. "I saw *American Gigolo*. There were some pretty explicit scenes."

He tightened his arms in mock punishment. "A real man. In the flesh. Have you ever seen one up close and all over?"

"I walked in on my father once when I was little."

He sighed. "I'm not talking about—"

"I've learned to keep my eyes shut since then."

Which told him absolutely nothing. So he put that particular subject on hold and tried one he thought she'd find simpler to answer. "What kind of work do you do?"

She hesitated, then echoed his own earlier question. "Are you sure you want to know?"

"Why wouldn't I?"

"Because you won't like the answer."

"Why not?"

"Because it fits my personality to a tee."

"You're the headmistress of an all-girls school?"

"Nope."

"A warden at a penitentiary?"

She shook her head.

"I give up. What do you do?"

Again she hesitated, then confessed, "I work with computers."

"That figures."

"I told you you wouldn't like it."

"I didn't say I didn't like it, just that it figures. You work with machines. Very structured and controlled." He lowered his voice. "Do they turn you on?"

"Shows how much you know about computers. Noah, you have to turn *them* on or they don't do a thing."

She was teasing, and he loved it. He wasn't quite sure why she was in such good humor, but he wasn't about to upset the applecart by saying something lewd. "Once you turn them on, what do you do with them?"

"Same thing you do. Program them to store information and spit it back up on command."

"Your command?"

"Or one of my assistants'."

"Then you're the one in charge?"

"Of the department, yes."

"Where is the department?"

"In a law firm."

"A law firm in Philadelphia." Her head bobbed against his chest. He loved that, too—the undulating silk of her hair against his bare skin. "So—" he cleared his throat "—what kind of information are we dealing with here?"

"Client files, financial projections, accounts receivable, attorney profitability reports, balance sheets." She reeled them off, pausing only at the end for a breath. "Increasingly we're using the computers for the preparation of documents. And we're plugged into LEXIS."

"What's LEXIS?"

"A national computer program for research. By typing certain codes into the computer, our lawyers can find cases or law review articles that they need for briefs. It saves hours of work in the library."

"I'm impressed."

She swiveled and met his gaze. "By LEXIS?"

"By you. You really know what you're talking about."

"You didn't think I would?"

"It's not that," he said. "But you sound so...so on top of the whole thing."

"How do you think I got where I am?"

"I don't know. How did you?" His voice dropped to a teasing drawl. He couldn't resist; she was so damned sexy peering up at him that way. "Did you wow all those computer guys with your body?"

She stared at him for a minute, then faced forward. "Exactly."

"Come on," he soothed, brushing her ear with his mouth. "I know you wouldn't do that. Tell me how you got hooked up with computers."

"I took computer courses in college."

"And that was it? A few courses and, pow, you're the head of a department?"

"Of course not. I worked summers, then worked after graduation, and by the time the opening came at the law firm, I had the credentials and was there."

"How large is the firm?"

"Seventy-five lawyers."

"General practice?"

"Corporate."

"Ahh. Big money-getters."

"Lucky for me. If they weren't, they'd never be able to support a computer department the size of ours, and my job would be neither as interesting nor as challenging."

"Are they nice?"

"The lawyers? Some I like better than others."

"Do they treat you well?"

"I'm not complaining."

"But you do love your work."

"Yes."

"Any long-range ambitions?"

"I don't know. I'm thinking about that. I've risen pretty fast in a field that's steadily changing."

"Personnel-wise?"

"Equipment-wise. Personnel-wise, too, I guess. A lot of people jumped on the bandwagon when computers first got big, but time has weeded out the men from the boys."

"Or the women from the girls."

"Mmm."

He nudged her foot with his. "What about marriage? Or pregnancy? Does that weed out the women from the girls?"

"Not as much as it used to. The firm is generous when it comes to maternity leave. Many of the women, lawyers included, have taken time off, then returned. In my department, word processing is done round the clock. Women can choose their shifts to accommodate child-care arrangements."

"Is that what you'll do?"

"I hadn't thought I was pregnant," she remarked blithely.

"Do you want to be?"

"I like what I'm doing now."

"Cuddling?"

"Heading the computer department."

He bent his knees and brought his legs in closer. "But someday. Do you want to have kids?"

"I haven't really thought about it."

"Come on. Every woman thinks about it."

"I've been too busy."

"To do it?"

"To think about doing it."

He dipped his head, bringing his lips into warm intimacy with her cheek. "I'll give you a baby."

She shifted, turning onto her side so she could better see his expression. "You're crazy, do you know that?"

"Not really."

"Give me a baby—why in the world would you say something like that? In case you don't know it, a baby takes after both its parents. I've been bugging you since I stepped foot on this sloop. How would you like to have a baby that bugged you from the day it was born?"

He shrugged. "There's bugging, and there's bugging." Her hand was using his chest for leverage; he covered it with his own. "You have certain qualities that I'd want in a child of mine."

"Like what?"

It was a minute before he answered. "Beauty."

She shot a quick glance skyward. "Spare me."

"Intelligence."

"That's a given." She tipped up her chin. "What else?" When he was quiet, she gave him a lopsided grin. "Run out of things already?"

It wasn't that he'd run out, just that he was having trouble concentrating. She was so soft in his arms, her face so pert as it tilted toward his, her legs smooth as they tangled with his, her hip firm as it pressed his groin.

"There's...there's spunk."

"Spunk?"

"Sure. Seven times out of ten you have answers for my jibes."

"Only seven?"

Almost imperceptibly, he moved her hand on his chest. He closed his eyes for a minute and swallowed hard. "Maybe eight."

"But I'm stern-faced and prissy," she said, shifting slightly. "Is that what you want your children to inherit?"

He'd closed his eyes again, and when he opened them, he was smiling ever so gently, ever so wryly, and his warning came ever so softly. "You're playing with fire."

"I...what?"

"Your legs brush mine, your hair torments me." His voice began to sizzle. "You move those hips and I'm on fire, and your hand on my skin gives me such pleasure.... Can't you feel what's happening?"

Her stunned eyes dropped to her hand. It was partially covered by his, but her fingers were buried in the soft, curling hairs on his chest. As she watched, they began to tingle, then throb above the beat of his heart.

"A little to your right," he whispered huskily. "Move them."

She swallowed. Her fingers straightened and inched forward until a single digit came to rest atop a clearly erect nipple.

He moaned and moved his hips.

Her eyes flew to his face.

"Shocked?" he asked thickly. "Didn't you know? Am I the only one suffering?"

"I...we were talking...I was comfortable." The words seemed feeble, but they were the truth. She couldn't remember when she'd ever been with a man this way, just talking, enjoying the physical closeness for something other than sex. "I'm sorry...."

But she didn't move away. Her senses were awakening to him with incredible speed. All the little things that had hovered just beyond sexual awareness—the sole of his foot against her instep, the brush of his hair-spattered legs against her calves and thighs, the solidity of his flesh beneath her hand, his enveloping male scent, the cradle of his body, the swelling virility between his legs—all came into vivid focus. And his voice, his voice, honing her awareness like scintillating sand...

"I'd like to make love to you, Shaye. I'd like to open that little thing you're wearing and touch you all over, taste you all over. I think I could bury myself in your body and never miss the world again. Would you let me do that?"

The rising breeze cooled her face, but she could barely breathe, much less think. "I...we can't."

"We can." He had one arm across her back in support while his hand caressed her hip. The other hand tipped up her face. "Kiss me, Shaye. Now."

Say no. Push him away. Tell him you don't want this. She had the answers but no motivation, and when his mouth closed over hers, she could do nothing but savor its purposeful movement. Caressing, sucking, stroking—he was a man who kissed long and well. He was also a man who demanded a response.

"Open your mouth," he ordered in an uncompromising growl. "Do it the way I like it."

Shaye wasn't quite sure how he liked it, but the break in his kiss had left her hungry. This time when he seized them, her lips were parted. As they had the night before, they erupted into a fever against his, building the heat so high that she had to use her tongue as a coolant. But that didn't work, either, because Noah's own response increased the friction. Her breath came quickly, and her entire body was trembling by the time he dragged his lips away.

"Ahh, you do it right," he said on a groan.

Gasping softly, she pressed her forehead to his jaw. She felt his hand on her neck, but she was too weak to object, and in a second that hand was inside her blouse, taking the full weight of her breast. Her small cry was lifted and carried away by the wind.

"This is what I want," he whispered. His long fingers kneaded her, then drew a large arc on her engorged flesh. The top snap of her blouse released at the pressure of his wrist, but she barely heard it. His palm was passing over her nipple once, then again, and his fingers settled more broadly when his thumb took command.

"Look at me, Shaye."

Through passion-glazed eyes, she looked.

His voice was a rasping whisper. "This is what I'd do for starters." As he held her gaze, he dragged his thumb directly across her turgid nipple. He repeated the motion. "Do you feel it inside?"

"Oh yes," she whispered back. The thrumming still echoed in her core. Her legs stirred restlessly. "Do it again."

A tiny whimper came from the back of her throat when he did, but then he was whispering again. "I'd touch the other one like that, too. And then I'd take it in my mouth...." Another snap popped and he lowered his head. She took handfuls of his hair and held on when his thumb was replaced by the heat of his mouth, the wetness of his tongue, the gentle but volatile raking of his teeth.

Nothing had ever felt so exciting and so right. Shaye had spent the past six years of her life denying that the two—exciting and right—could be compatible, but she couldn't deny what she felt now. As his mouth drew her swelling breast deeper and deeper into its hot, wet hold, she knew both peace and yearning. She wanted him to tell her what he'd do next, and she wanted him to do it. She ached to do all kinds of wild things in return. And still there was that sense of rightness, and it confused her.

"Noah... Noah, Samson..."

"Can't see. Shh."

She wanted, but she didn't. The feel of Noah's mouth firmly latched to her burning flesh was a dangerous Eden. She didn't trust herself and her judgement of rightness, and she couldn't trust Noah to understand what she felt. She was in deep water and sinking fast. If she didn't haul herself up soon, she'd be lost.

Tugging at his hair, she pulled him away with a moan. "We have to stop."

"Samson's way back at the stern," Noah argued hoarsely. "The sails are between us and him, and it's dark."

But Shaye was already sliding from his lap. He watched her scramble against the bow, clutching the lapels of her blouse with one hand, holding her middle with the other. His body was throbbing and his breathing unsteady. He hiked his knees up and wrapped his arms around them. "It's not just Samson," he stated.

"No."

"Is it me?"

"No."

"Then it's you."

She said nothing, just continued to look at him. The wind had picked up, blowing her hair around her face. She was almost grateful for the shield.

Her insides were in knots. She felt as though she'd been standing on the brink of either utter glory or total disaster—only she didn't know which. If he took her back in his arms, coaxed the least bit, pushed the least bit, she'd give in. Her nipple was still damp where he'd suckled; both breasts—her entire body—tingled. She'd never in her life felt as strong a craving for more, and she didn't understand why.

But common sense cried for self-control. Self-control! Was it so much to ask? Shaye wondered. When she'd been younger, she'd thought that by doing her own thing when and where she wanted, she was controlling her life. In fact, the opposite had been the case. For years she'd been out of control, acting irresponsibly with little thought for the consequences of her actions.

Now she was older and wiser. Responsibility had closed in on her, weighing her down at times, uplifting her at others. Perhaps it was an obsession, but self-control had been a passion in and of itself.

"What is it, Shaye?" Noah asked. "You're not an eighteen-year-old virgin."

She'd never been an eighteen-year-old virgin, and that was part of the problem. She'd given in too soon, too fast, too far.

"Have you been hurt...abused?"

"No!"

"But you're afraid."

"I just want to stop."

"You're afraid."

"Think what you will."

"But it doesn't make sense!" he burst out in frustration. "One minute you want me, the next you don't."

"I know."

"Well? Are you going to explain?" The demands of his body had died. He stretched out his legs in a show of indolence he was far from feeling. The wind was whipping at his shirt, but when he folded his arms over his chest, it was more because he felt exposed to Shaye's whims than to those of the weather. He wasn't used to the feeling of exposure and didn't like it.

"I can't explain. It's just...just me."

"Have you ever been involved with a man?"

"I've never been in love."

"That wasn't the question. Have you ever had a relationship with a man?"

"Certainly—just as you have."

"Sexually. Have you ever been involved sexually with a man?"

"You pointed out—" she began, then repeated herself in a voice loud enough to breach the wind "—you pointed out that I'm not an eighteen-year-old virgin."

He sighed, but the sound was instantly whisked away. "Shaye, you know what I'm getting at."

"I've been involved with many men, but never deeply," she blurted out, then wondered why she had. At the time she'd thought herself deeply involved with Josh...or André...or Christopher. But "deep" meant something very different now. It was almost...almost the way she was beginning to think herself involved with Noah, and that stunned her.

"Have you ever lived with a man?"

It was a minute before she could answer. "I, uh, lived in a kind of communal setup for a while," she hedged, and even that was pushing it a little. The garret had been André's; the others had simply crashed there for a time. She'd spent seven months with Josh, who'd eventually run off—with her blessing—to follow the Maharishi. She'd lived with other men for brief periods; she'd quickly gotten restless.

"Communal setups can mean either constant sex or no sex at all. Which was it?"

"I'm prissy. Which do you think?"

"I'm beginning to think this prissy bit is a cop-out. I'm beginning to think you're not one bit prissy. At least, that's what your fiery little body leads me to suspect."

She shrugged.

"Damn it, don't do that," he snapped. The sloop seemed to echo his frustration with a sudden roll. "I'm trying to get information. Shrugging tells me nothing."

"I don't like being the butt of your polling."

He rubbed the tight muscles at the back of his neck. "Was it that obvious?"

"Now that I know what you do for a living, yes."

The flapping of canvas high above suddenly grabbed their attention. Noah sprang to his feet. "It's about to rain. Do you have a slicker?"

Shaye, too, had risen. She'd snapped up her blouse and was holding her hair off her face with both hands. "A poncho." She swayed toward the bulwark when the boat took a lunge.

"Better get it," he said as he started toward the stern. She was right behind him. "Better still, get below. This deck in a storm is no place for a woman."

Shaye was about to make a derisive retort when Noah started shouting to Samson. And at the moment the first large drops of rain hit the deck. Having no desire to get drenched, she made straight for the companionway.

For several hours, she remained in the salon with Victoria while the *Golden Echo* bucked the waves with something less than grace. The men had run below in turns to get rain gear, and Shaye's repeated offers of help had been refused. She noticed that Victoria wasn't offering. In fact, Victoria was very quiet.

"Are you feeling all right?"

"I'm fine," Victoria said softly. "Or I will be once the wind dies down."

"That could be hours from now."

The expression on Victoria's face would have been priceless if she hadn't been so pale. "Don't remind me."

"Why don't you lie down in the cabin?"

"I'm afraid that might be worse." She scowled. "This tub isn't the best thing to be on in weather like this."

"So it's a tub now, is it?" Shaye said with a teasing smile. "You didn't think so before."

"Before I wasn't being jostled. And the portholes were open then." Victoria fanned herself. "It's hot as Hades here."

"Would you rather the waves poured in?"

"No, no. Not that."

"Are you scared?"

"Are you?"

Shaye was, a little. But the storm was a diversion. It gave her something to think about besides Noah and herself. Even now, with little effort, she could feel his arms around her and his tongue on her breast. She felt the same yearning she had then, the same confusion, the same fear. She'd come so close to giving in....

But she couldn't think about that. There was the storm to consider, one danger exchanged for another. She did trust that Samson and Noah knew what they were doing. She wondered if they were frightened—but didn't really want to know.

So she pasted a crooked grin on her face and said to Victoria, "I'm sure we'll pull through fine. Look at the experience as exciting. It's not everyone who gets tossed over the high seas in an ancient colonial sloop."

"Cute," Victoria said, then gingerly pushed herself from the sofa. "On second thought, I will lie down."

Concerned, Shaye started out of her chair. "Can I do anything to help?"

But Victoria pressed her shoulder down as she passed. "If death is imminent, I'll call."

SHAYE DIDN'T WAIT for the call. She checked on Victoria every few minutes, trying to talk her out of her preoccupation with her insides. But with each visit, Victoria felt less like talking. By the third visit, she'd lost the contents of her stomach and was looking like death warmed over.

"Let me get you something."

Victoria moaned. "Leave me be."

"But I feel helpless."

"It'll pass."

"My helplessness?"

"My seasickness."

"What about my guilt?" Shaye asked in a meek stab at humor. "I was the one who joked about getting violently seasick."

"Tss. You're making it worse."

"Samson said he had medicine."

"Don't bother Samson. He has enough on his hands."

Shaye rose from the bed. "I'm getting his medicine."

"They'll think I'm a sissy."

"God forbid."

"Shaye, I'm fine—"

"You will be," she said as she left the cabin. Shimmying into her poncho, she climbed the companionway. She paused only to raise her hood and duck her head in preparation for the rain before pushing open the hatch. The wind instantly whipped the hood back and her hair was soaked before she'd reached the helm, where Samson stood wearing bright yellow oilskins and a sou'wester, looking for all the world like a seasoned Gloucester fisherman.

"Whatcha doin' up heah, geul?" he yelled in an accent to match.

The rain was coming down in sheets while the wind whipped everything in sight, but still Shaye laughed. His role playing conveyed a confidence that was contagious. "You're too much, Samson!"

"Best enjoy ev'ry minute!" he declared in a voice that challenged the storm.

Shaye tugged up her hood to deflect the rain from her face while she looked around. The sea was a mass of whitecaps. The jibs were down, the mainsail reefed. In essence, Samson was doing little more than holding the keel steady while they rode out the storm.

"Has Noah gone overboard?" she yelled.

"Not likely!"

She was about to ask where he was when the boat heaved and veered to port. Steadying herself as best she could, she shouted, "Are we in danger?"

He straightened the wheel and shouted back, "Nope!"

"How long do you think it'll keep up?"

"Mebbe an hour. Mebbe five."

"Victoria won't be terribly pleased to hear that."

"She'll prob'ly be hopin' it las' ten," he roared with an appreciative smile.

"I don't think so, Samson. She's sick!"

While the storm didn't faze him, that bit of news did. For the first time, he seemed concerned. The accent vanished. "Her stomach's acting up?"

Shaye nodded vigorously. "You said something about medicine?"

"In the locker by the galley. Noah may have it, though."

"Where *is* Noah?"

"In bed."

"What's he doing in bed when—oh, no, he's sick?"

"And not pleased about it at all! He wanted to stay on deck, but when he started to reel on his feet, I ordered him down."

Shaye had no way of knowing that the same concern she'd seen on Samson's face moments before now registered on her own. Noah sick? He was so large, so strong. She couldn't picture him being brought down by anything, much less *mal de mer*.

Actually, though, the more she thought about it, the more she saw a touch of humor in it. Or poetic justice.

"I didn't see him come in," she said more to herself than to Samson. "It must have been while I was with Victoria."

At the reminder of her aunt, she turned quickly back to the hatch. Once below, she peeled off the soaking poncho and checked the locker for Samson's medicine. It was there. Either Noah wasn't all that sick or he was too proud to take anything.

Victoria wasn't too proud. When Shaye lifted her head and pressed the pill between her lips, she sipped enough water to get it down, then sank weakly back to the pillow. Pill bottle in hand, Shaye returned to the locker. She paused before opening it, though, eyes moving helplessly toward the captain's quarters. Then, without asking herself why or to what end, she took the few steps necessary and quietly opened the door.

A trail of sodden clothes led to the bed, and on that bed lay Noah. He was sprawled on his stomach atop the bare sheets, one arm thrown over his head. The faint glow from the lamp showed the sheen of sweat that covered his body. He was naked.

Feeling not humor but a well of compassion that she'd never have dreamed she'd feel for the man, she quietly approached and knelt down by the bed. "Noah?" she asked softly.

He moaned and turned his face away.

"Have you taken something?"

He grunted.

Compassion turned to tenderness. She reached out and stroked his hair. It was wet from the rain, but his neck was clammy. "Victoria's sick. I just gave her some of Samson's medicine. If I get water, will you take some, too?"

He groaned. "Let me die in peace."

"You're not going to die."

He made a throaty sound of agreement. "I won't be so lucky."

"If you die, who'll be left to give me a hard time?"

There was a short silence from Noah, then a terse, "Get the pill."

Shaye brought water and held his head while he managed to swallow the pill. Then she sponged his back with a damp cloth.

"It's not helping," he mumbled. Though his head was turned her way, his eyes remained closed.

"Give it time."

"I haven't got time. I'm already in hell."

"Serves you right for living the life of a sinner."

He moaned, then grumbled, "What would you know about the life of a sinner?"

"You'd be surprised," she answered lightly, continuing to bathe him.

At length he dragged open an eye. "Why aren't *you* sick?"

"I'm just not."

"Are you scared."

"No."

"You should be. We're about to be swallowed by a great white whale."

"Does delirium come with seasickness?"

He gave up the effort of keeping that one eye open, pulled the pillow between his chest and the sheet and moaned again.

"Does that help?" she asked.

"What?"

"Moaning."

"Yes." A minute later he turned onto his side and curled into a ball, with the pillow pressed to his stomach. "God, I feel awful."

He looked it. His face was an ashen contrast to his dark hair, and tight lines rimmed his nose and mouth.

"Are you going to be sick?" she said.

"I *am* sick."

"Are you going to throw up?"

"Already have. Twice."

"That should have helped."

He grunted.

"It's really a shame. After Samson went to such efforts with the sauerbraten—"

"Shut up, Shaye," he gasped, then gave another moan.

"The storm should be over sometime tomorrow."

"If you can't say something nice..."

"I thought the storm was pretty exciting. I've never seen waves quite like that."

This time his moan had more feeling. Shaye said nothing more as she smoothed the cloth over his skin a final time. Then, brushing the damp hair from his brow, she asked, "Will you be okay?"

"Fine."

"I should get back to Victoria."

"Go."

"Can I check on you later?"

"Only if you're into autopsies."

She smiled. He was the fallen warrior, but there was something endearing about him. "I'll steel myself," she said, then quietly rose from his bedside and left the cabin.

She didn't steel herself for an autopsy, of course. She checked on Victoria, who'd settled some, then went to sleep to dream dreams of a long-legged, lean-hipped man whose body had to be the most beautiful she'd ever seen in her life.

Chapter Seven

THE STORM HAD DIED by morning. Shaye awoke to find Victoria on deck with Noah, who'd sent Samson below for a well-earned rest.

"Well, well, if it isn't our own Florence Nightingale," Noah remarked as she approached the helm.

The last time he'd said something like that, Shaye mused, he'd called her an iron maiden. She didn't particularly care for either image, but at least she didn't hear sarcasm this time.

She had wondered how he'd greet her after the state she'd last seen him in. Some men would have been embarrassed. Others, particularly those with a macho bent—and Noah did have a touch of that—would have been defensive. But Noah seemed neither defensive nor embarrassed. He'd bounced right back to his confident self. She should have known he would.

"You're both looking chipper," she said.

Victoria smiled. "Thanks to you."

Noah seconded that. "She really is a marvel. Has an unturnable stomach and an unrivaled bedside manner."

"Mmmm. She does have a way of coaxing down medicine."

"And bathing sweaty bodies."

Victoria gaped at him. "She bathed you? I didn't get a bath!"

"I guess she can't resist a naked man."

"Naked?" She turned to Shaye, but the twinkle in her eyes took something from the horror of her expression. "Shaye, how could you?"

Before Shaye could utter a word, Noah was wailing, "There you go again—suggesting that my body's distasteful! What is it with you women?"

"I didn't suggest anything of the sort," Shaye said smoothly, and turned to Victoria. "He actually has a stunning body—a sweet little birthmark on his right hip and the cutest pair of buns you'd ever hope to see."

"I didn't think you noticed," Noah drawled to Shaye, then said to Victoria, "but don't worry. I kept the best parts hidden."

Shaye didn't answer that. She'd seen the "best parts" too, and they'd been as impressive as the rest. But she wasn't about to play the worldly woman so far that she totally cancelled out the prissy one. So she tipped back her head, to find the sky a brilliant blue. "No clouds in sight, and we're making headway again. Did we lose much ground during the storm?"

"A little," Noah answered, indulgently accepting the change in subject, "but we're back on course."

"Good." She rubbed her hands together. "Anyone want breakfast?"

Noah and Victoria exchanged a glance, then answered in unison, "Me."

"You're cooking for all of us?" Noah asked.

"I'm feeling benevolent."

He snagged her around the shoulders and drew her to his side. "Domestic instincts coming to the fore?"

"No. I'm just hungry."

"So am I."

She sent him a withering look.

He didn't wither. "Just think," he murmured for her ears alone, "how nice it would be to have breakfast together in bed."

"I never eat breakfast in bed."

"If I were still sick, would you have brought it to me there?"

"If you were still sick, you wouldn't have wanted it."

"What if my stomach was fine but my knees were so weak that I couldn't get up?"

"That'd be the day."

"You were very gentle last night. No one's taken the time to bathe me like that since I was a child."

She knew he was playing on her soft side, but before she should could come up with suitably repressive words, he spoke again.

"So you liked what you saw?"

"Oh yes. The storm was breathtaking."

"*Me*. My *body*."

"Oh, that. Well, it wasn't quite as exciting as the sea."

"Catch me tonight, and I'll show you exciting."

"Is another storm brewing?" she asked, being purposely obtuse.

Noah wasn't buying. "You bet," he said with a naughty grin.

Shaye quickly escaped from his clutches and went below to fix breakfast. Throughout the morning, though, she thought of Noah, of his body and its potential for excitement. The more she thought, the more agitated she grew.

She tried to understand what it was about him that turned her on. He was cocky and quick-tongued. He could be presumptuous and abrasive. He was, in his own way, a rebel. There were so many things not to like. Still, he turned her on.

Always before she'd been safe, and it wasn't merely a question of dating bland men. She encountered men at work, men in the supermarket, men in the bookstore, the hardware store, the laundry. She'd never given any of them a second glance.

Granted, she'd had no choice with Noah. She was stuck on a boat with him, and in such close quarters second glances were hard to avoid, particularly when the man in question made his presence felt at every turn.

Not only was she looking twice, she was also fantasizing. With vivid clarity she recalled how he'd looked naked. She hadn't been thinking lascivious thoughts at the time, but since then her imagination had worked overtime. Everything about him was manly, with a capital *M*—the bunching muscles of his back, the prominent veins in his forearms, the tapering of his torso, his neat, firm bottom, the sprinkling of dark hair on the backs of his thighs. And in front—she could go on and on, starting with the day's growth of beard on his face and ending with the heaviness of his sex.

If the attraction were purely physical, she could probably hold him off. But increasingly she thought of other things—his sense of humor, his intelligence, his daring, his disregard for convention—and she felt deeply threatened. Last night hadn't helped. What she'd felt when he'd been sick, when he'd needed her and she'd been there for him, came dangerously close to affection. She'd never experienced the overwhelming urge to care for a man before.

So why was it wrong? In principle, she had nothing against involvement. She supposed that some day she'd like to fall in love, just as some day she'd like to have children. She hadn't planned on falling in love now, though, when her career was in full swing. And she hadn't planned on falling in love with a man like Noah.

Not that she was in love with him, she cautioned herself quickly. But still...

The problem was that Noah wasn't meek. He wasn't conservative or conventional. She couldn't control him—or herself when she was with him. He was wrong for her.

Had she been in Philadelphia, she'd have run in the opposite direction. But she wasn't in Philadelphia. She was stuck on a boat in the middle of the Caribbean with Noah, and she was vulnerable. In his arms, she was lost—and she fell into his arms easily!

She'd just have to be on her guard, she decided. That was all there was to it.

THE AFTERNOON BROUGHT a torment of its own. Where the night before the wind had picked up, gusted, then positively raged, today it faded, sputtered, then died.

Shaye was sitting on deck reading when the sails began to pucker. She looked up at the mast, then at Victoria, who was sitting in blissful ignorance nearby, then down at her book again. But the sails grew increasingly limp, and at the moment of total deflation, she didn't need the unusual calm of the sea to tell her what had happened.

Noah sauntered by, nonchalantly lowering and lashing the sails.

"How long?" she asked.

He shrugged. "Maybe an hour or two. We'll see."

An hour or two didn't sound so bad. The part she didn't like was the "maybe." If their idle drifting lasted for eight hours, or sixteen, or God forbid, twenty-four...

"You look alarmed," he commented, tossing her a glance as he worked.

"No, no. I'm fine."

"View it as a traffic jam. If you were in the city, chances are you'd be on your way somewhere. But you wouldn't be able to move, so you'd be frustrated, and you'd be sick from exhaust fumes. Here you have none of that." He took a long, loud breath that expanded his chest magnificently. "Fresh air. Bright sun. Clear water. What more could you ask?"

Shaye could have asked for the wind to fill the sails and set them on their way again. The sooner they reached Costa Rica, the sooner they'd return to Colombia and the sooner she'd go home. One virile man with a magnificent chest was pushing her resolve.

"I couldn't ask for anything more," she said.

"Sing it."

"Excuse me?"

"The song. You know—" Noah jumped into a widespread stance, leaned back, extended both arms and did his best Ethel Merman imitation: "I got rhythm, I got music..."

She covered her face with a hand. "We did that in junior high. I believe the last line is, '*Who* could ask for anything more?'"

"Close enough."

She peered through her fingers. "Were you in the glee club?"

"Through high school. Then I was in an *a cappella* group in college. We traveled all over the place. It was really fun." His face suddenly dropped.

"What?"

"Well, it was fun for a while."

"What happened?"

He hesitated, then shrugged. "I resigned."

"Why did you do that?"

"I, uh, actually there were three of us. We got into a little trouble."

"What kind of trouble?"

He returned to his work. "It was nothing."

"What kind of trouble?"

He secured the last fold of the mainsail to the boom, then mumbled, "We went on a drinking binge in Munich. The administrators decided we weren't suitable representatives of the school."

"You didn't resign. You were kicked out."

"No, we resigned."

"It was either that or be kicked out."

He ran a hand through his hair. "You don't have to put it so bluntly."

"But that was what it boiled down to, wasn't it? You should be ashamed of yourself, Noah."

Victoria, who'd remained on the periphery of the discussion to that point, felt impelled to join in. "Aren't you being a little hard on the man, Shaye? You were in college once. You know what college kids do. They're young and having fun. They outgrow it."

"Thank you, Victoria," Noah said.

Shaye echoed his very words, but with a different inflection. She picked up her book again.

Having nothing better to do, Noah stretched out on his back in the sun. Within thirty seconds, he bobbed up to remove his shirt. Then he lay back again, folding his arms beneath his head. "I'll bet Shaye never did anything wrong in school. The model student. Hmmmm?"

Shaye didn't answer.

Victoria pressed a single finger to her lips, holding in words that were aching to spill out. Shaye shot her a warning look. The finger stayed where it was, which was both a good sign and a bad sign.

"Did you study all the time?" Noah asked.

"I studied."

"What did you do for fun?"

"Oh, this and that." She glanced toward the stern. "Where's Samson?"

"I believe he's cooking," Victoria answered, dropping her finger at last.

"What's it going to be tonight?"

Noah smirked. "Now, if he told us, it wouldn't be a surprise, and that's half the fun."

"I hate surprises."

"You hate fun. What a boring person."

"Noah," Victoria chided.

But Shaye could stand up for herself. "It's okay. I have a strong back."

"Stiff," Noah corrected in an absent tone. His eyes were closed, his body relaxed. "Stiff back. But not all the time. When I take you in my arms—"

Shaye cut him off. "Does Samson always cook foreign?"

He grinned and answered only after a meaningful pause. "Not always. He does a wicked Southern-fried chicken."

"What does he wear then?"

"I'm not telling."

She glared at him for a minute, but his eyes were still closed so he didn't see. "You wouldn't," she muttered, and returned to her book. She couldn't concentrate, of course. Not with Noah stretched out nearby. The occasional glances she darted his way brought new things to her attention—the pattern of hair swirling over his chest, the bolder tufts beneath his arms, the small indentation of his navel.

She looked back at her book, turned one page, waited several minutes, turned another. Then she set the book down in disgust. "How long have we been sitting?"

"Half an hour."

"And still no wind."

"It'll come."

"Why doesn't this boat have an engine? Nowadays every boat has an engine."

"The *Golden Echo* wasn't built 'nowadays.'"

"But she was refurbished. She has a stove and a refrigerator. Why doesn't she have an engine?"

Noah shrugged. "The Paynes must be purists."

With a snort, she picked up her book, turned several more pages, then sighed and lifted her ponytail from her neck. "Is it ever hot!"

Noah opened a lazy eye and surveyed the shorts and T-shirt she wore. "Feel free to strip."

Sending him a scowl, she pushed herself up, stalked to the companionway and went below.

He looked innocently at Victoria. "Did I say something wrong?"

Victoria didn't know whether to scold or laugh. She compromised by slanting him a chiding grin before she, too, rose.

"Hey," he called as she started off, "don't you leave me, too!"

"I'm going to visit with your uncle. It can't be much hotter down there than it is up here, and at least there's some shade."

Noah lay where he was for several minutes, then sat up and studied the horizon. He gave a voluminous sigh and pasted a jaunty smile on his face. This was what he wanted, wasn't it? Peace and quiet. The deck all to himself. He could relax if he wanted, sing if he wanted, do somersaults if he wanted.

So why did he feel restless?

Because he was hot and bothered and the damn sun wasn't helping. Abruptly dropping the smile, he surged to his feet, reached for the rope ladder, hung it from the starboard quarter, kicked off his shorts and dove into the sea. He'd done two laps around the boat when he overtook Shaye. He was as startled as she was.

"What are you doing here?" she gasped. "I thought I was alone."

"Who do you think put the ladder out?" he snapped. "And if you thought you were alone, why in the hell were you swimming? You're not supposed to swim alone."

"You were."

"That's different."

"How so?"

"I'm a man and I'm stronger."

"What a chauvinistic thing to say!"

"But it's true."

"It's absurd, and, besides, it's a moot point. You don't exactly need strength in a bathtub like this. If there were waves, there'd be a wind, and if there were a wind, we wouldn't be stuck out here floating in the middle of nowhere!"

"Always the logical answer. Y'know, Shaye, you're too rational for your own good. Ease up, will ya?"

She gave him a dirty look and started to swim around him, but he caught her arm and held it. "Let go," she ordered. "I want to swim."

"Need the exercise?"

"Yes."

"Feeling as restless as I am?"

"Yes."

"How about reckless?" he asked, his eyes growing darker.

Shaye recognized that deepening gray. His eyes went like that when he was on the verge of either mischief or passion. She didn't know which it was now, but she did know that with his hair slicked back and his lashes wet, nearly black and unfairly long, he looked positively demonic. Either that or sexy. Was she feeling reckless? "No," she stated firmly.

"Do you *ever* feel reckless?"

She shook her head.

"Not even when I take you in my arms?" He did it then, and she knew better than to try to escape. After all, he was stronger then she. "Why do I frighten you?"

"You don't."

He tipped his head to the side and gave her a reproving look.

"You don't," she repeated, but more quietly. As though to prove it—to them both—she put her hands on his shoulders.

"Are you afraid of sex?"

"I'm not a virgin."

"I know. We've been over that one before. I'm not asking whether you've done it, just whether you're afraid of it."

She was afraid of *him*, at that moment, because his mouth was so close, his lips firm and mobile. She couldn't seem to take her eyes from them. The lower was slightly fuller than its mate and distinctly sensual. Both were wet.

"Shaye?"

She wrenched her gaze to his eyes. "I'm not afraid of sex."

"Are you afraid of commitment?"

"No."

"Then why haven't you married?"

"I thought that was clear. I've been busy."

"If the right man had come along, you'd have married."

"How do you know that?"

"You ooze certain values. There's a softness to you that wouldn't be there if you were a hard-bitten career woman all the way. I have to assume that the right man just hasn't come along."

"I said that I don't date."

"You also said that you'd been involved with many men."

"But not recently. And if I don't date now, how can I possibly meet the right man?"

You don't have to date to meet men, Noah thought. *You could meet one during a vacation in the Caribbean.* "With your looks—come on, baby, with your looks the right man would make sure you dated. Him. Exclusively."

Baby. It was a stereotypically offensive endearment, yet the way he said it made her tingle. "What are you trying to prove, Noah?"

"I'm working on the theory that you turn away from men who threaten your very sane, very structured, very controlled existence. Just like you turn away from me."

"And now that you have me analyzed, you can let me go."

His arms tightened. "Hit a raw cord, did I?"

She slid her hands to his elbows and tried to push. "Not raw, nonexistent." Her teeth were gritted. "Let me go, Noah."

"I can make your body hum, but still you fight me. Why won't you let me make love to you, Shaye?"

"Because—" she was still pushing "—I don't want to."

"It'd be so easy. We could do it right here. Right now."

Her limbs were shaking, but it wasn't from the effort of trying to free herself. His tone was tender, his words electric. The combination was devastating. "Don't do this to me," she begged.

"What would I be doing that's so wrong? Is it wrong to feel drawn to someone? I do feel drawn to you, Shaye, sour moods and all."

She didn't want to hear this. Closing her eyes, she gave a firm shake of her head. "Don't say another word."

"I respect your work and your dedication to it. I respect what you feel for your aunt. I respect and admire your independence, but I want to know more about where it comes from. At the slightest mention of your family or your past, you clam up."

"I have two parents with whom I don't get along and a sister with whom I do. There. Are you satisfied?" She tried to propel herself away from him, but he wasn't letting go. She only succeeded in tangling her legs with his, which were warm, strong and very bare.

"Why don't you get along with your parents?"

"Noah, I'm getting tired. I'd like to go back on the boat."

"I'm not tired. I'll hold you. You know how."

She turned her head to the side and let out an exasperated breath. "Will you let me go?"

"No."

"I'll scream."

"Go ahead. There's no one to hear but Samson and Victoria, and they trust me." He pressed a warm kiss to her cheek, then asked gently, "Why do you do this to yourself? Why do you fight?"

His gentleness was her undoing. Suddenly tired of the whole thing, she dropped her chin to his shoulder. "Oh Lord, sometimes I wonder." Her arms slipped around him, and she felt his hands on the backs of her thighs, spreading them. In as natural a movement as she'd ever made, she wrapped her legs around his waist. "You're not wearing a suit," she murmured. "Why not?"

"I was in a rush to get in the water and there was no one around."

"Oh Noah."

He was nuzzling her ear. "What is it, hon?"

"I really am tired. I'm not used to constant sparring. I'm not good at it."

"Could've fooled me."

"All I wanted was a peaceful vacation in the Berkshires."

"Things don't always work out the way we plan. Good sometimes comes from the unexpected."

The lazy frog kick he was doing kept them bobbing gently on the sea's surface. Beneath the surface the bobbing was more erotic—the tiniest glide of their bodies against one another, a teasing, a soft simulation. Her suit was thin. She clearly felt his sex. But while her body craved the contact, she felt too spent to carry though.

"I'm so tired," she murmured, tightening her arms around him simply for the comfort of his strength.

"Things are warring inside?"

"Yes."

"Maybe if we talk it out you'll feel better."

She sighed sadly against his neck. "I don't know. For so long I've drummed certain things into my head...." Her voice trailed off.

He was stroking her back. "I'm listening."

But she couldn't go on. There were too many thoughts, too much confusion, and as comfortable as she was with him just then, she was deathly afraid of saying something she'd later regret.

"Hey," he breathed. He took her head in his hands and raised it to find her eyes brimming with tears. "Ah-h-h, Shaye," he whispered hoarsely, "don't do that. Don't torment yourself so."

She could only shut her eyes and shake her head, then cling more tightly when he hugged her again.

"I guess I've come on pretty strong."

She nodded against his neck.

"That wasn't very nice of me."

She shook her head.

"I'm really not a bad guy when you get to know me."

She was coming to see that, and it was part of the problem. Brashness she could withstand, as she could irreverence and impulsiveness. But mix any of those with gentleness, and she was in trouble.

"Come on," he said softly. His hands left her back and broke into a broad breast stroke. "Let's go back on board."

She made no effort to help him swim, and when they reached the ladder she was almost sorry to let go of him. It had been so nice holding on and being held without other threats. But she did let go and climbed the ladder, then stood on the deck pressing a towel to her face.

She heard Noah's wet feet on the wood behind her. She heard the swish of material that told her he was pulling on his shorts. For a fleeting instant she wondered whether he ever bothered with underwear, then his voice came quietly.

"Why don't you stretch out in the sun to dry? It looks like we're not going anywhere yet."

Dragging the towel slowly down her face, she nodded. Moments later, she was lying on her stomach in the sun. She cleared her mind of all but her immediate surroundings—the warmth of the sun feeling good now on her wet skin, the utter silence of the air, the gentle sway of the boat as it drifted. Noah sat nearby, but he did nothing to disturb her other than to ask if she wanted a cool drink, then fetch it when she said yes.

She knew that there were other things he could have done and said, such as stretching out beside her, offering to spread lotion on her back, suggesting that she lower the straps of her suit to avoid getting marks. He could have prodded her, pried into her thoughts, forced her to think about those things she was trying so hard to avoid.

But he did none of those things. He seemed to respect the fact that she needed a break from the battle if she was to regain her strength for the skirmishes ahead.

Late in the afternoon, Victoria joined them on deck, followed a few minutes after that by Samson. Conversation was light and for the most part flowed around Shaye. When the others decided to swim, she took her turn and savored the coolness but remained subdued, and after climbing back on board she went below to change for dinner.

When all four had gathered back on deck, Samson declared, "*Nu, yesly vnyesyosh stol, Noah, ee vee pryekrasnie zhenshchina vnyes yote pagooshkee, prig at oveem yest.*"

"*Myehdlyeenyehyeh, pahzhahloostah,*" Victoria requested.

Straightening the red tunic over his shorts and shirt, Samson repeated his instructions, but more slowly this time. He accompanied them with hand motions, for which Victoria was grateful. Her course in conversational Russian had only gone so far, and she was rusty.

By the time she was ready to interpret, the others had gotten the drift of Samson's request. Noah set up the table, while Shaye and Victoria brought cushions from the salon. Samson then proceeded to serve a dinner of *kulebiaka* and salad, and with a free-flowing vodka punch, the meal was lively.

Still, Shaye was more quiet than usual. She listened to the others joke about experiences they'd had, following particularly closely when Noah spoke. She learned that he'd taken Spanish through college, that he'd spent a semester in Madrid, that he'd spent the year following graduation working on a cattle ranch in Argentina. She also learned that, while there, he'd been nicknamed the Playboy of the Pampas, and though he'd been annoyed when Samson had let that little jewel slip, he hadn't denied it.

They lingered for a long time over coffee. With no wind, there was nowhere to go and no work to do. At length Samson went below deck, reappearing moments later wearing a tricorne. Then, with one of the hurricane lamps supplementing the silver light of the moon, he produced his treasure map.

Not even Shaye could resist its lure. She sat forward with the others to study the weathered piece of paper-thin parchment. "Where did you get it?" she asked.

"I was on Montserrat last winter and befriended an old British chap, who'd found it in an old desk in the villa he'd bought there fifteen years before. We'd been discussing the lore of the pirates in these parts when he brought out the map."

Victoria leaned closer to peer at the markings. "When was it supposed to have been drawn?"

"In the mid eighteen hundreds. My friend—Fitzsimmons was his name—theorized that the crew of a pirate ship stashed its booty and left, planning to return at a later, safer time."

"Only they never made it?"

"We don't know that for sure, but it's doubtful, since the map was well hidden and intact. The desk in which Fitzsimmons found it was traced back to a man named Angus Cummins, and Englishman who settled on Montserrat in the 1860s. No one seems to have known much about Cummins other than that he was a shady character, usually drunk and alone. My own research showed him to have been quartermaster on an English vessel that was shadowed by trouble. In 1859, during one of its last voyages to the Caribbean, the captain died at sea. When the boat returned to England, there were rumors of piracy and murder, but the crew stood as one and nothing was ever proven."

Victoria expelled a breath. "Murder!"

Samson shrugged. "We'll never know, but given this," he tapped the map, "there's reason to suspect that the crew was involved in piracy."

"But if that's true, why didn't Cummins—or one of the others—ever return for the treasure?" Shaye asked.

"Cummins may have been the only one with the map. As quartermaster, he was in a position of power second only to the captain. My guess is that he left England under dubious circumstances, stationed himself on Montserrat in the hope of one day crossing the Caribbean to retrieve the treasure, but never quite found the wherewithal to do it."

Assuming the accuracy of Samson's research, Noah agreed with his guess. He was skeptical, though, about the treasure still existing. "People have been searching for gold along the Costa Rican coast since Columbus dubbed the country the 'rich coast,' but the only riches discovered were bananas. If there were anything else hidden there, wouldn't it have been long since plundered?"

Feeling an odd sense of vindication, Shaye glanced at Victoria. She'd expressed a similar sentiment when Victoria had first called her about the trip.

But Samson was undaunted. "They didn't have the map." He held up a hand. "Now, I'm not saying that the treasure's there. I've checked with the Costa Rican authorities and they have no record of anyone reporting a stash being found in the area where we're headed. But that doesn't mean the treasure hasn't been stolen. Cummins may have gone back for it, then lived out his life in frustration when he realized he couldn't return to England a wealthy man. It's possible, too, that only his small portion of the take was hidden. Then again, the map may have been a fraud from the start."

Shaye leaned closer. "It looks authentic enough."

"Oh, it's authentic. At least, it was drawn during the right time period. I had it examined by experts who attested to that."

"Then how could it be fraudulent?" Victoria asked.

"Cummins may have drawn the map on a whim. He may have drawn it to indicate the spot where he'd put a treasure if he ever had one."

"You mean, there may never have been any treasure to begin with?"

"There's always that possibility." He smiled. "For the sake of adventure, though—and until we prove otherwise—we'll assume the treasure's there."

Shaye was grateful that she'd had a few drinks with dinner. Though the coffee had lessened the vodka's effects, her senses were still numbed. Had they not been, she feared she'd have said something blunt, and she didn't want to dampen Samson's enthusiasm any more than she wanted to evoke Noah's ire. "Are we talking gold?" she asked carefully.

"Most likely. Artifacts would be found in an undersea wreckage. I doubt that a man who planted a treasure with the intention of retrieving it in his lifetime would want anything but gold."

Noah was studying the map. "This spot is between Parismina and Limón?"

Samson cleared his throat, pushed the tricorne back on his head and got down to business. "That's right." His finger traced the pen scratchings. "The Costa Rican coast is lowland. Between the Nicaraguan border at the north and Puerto Limón, which lies about midway to Panama at the south, much of that lowland is swampy."

"Swampy?" Shaye cried in dismay.

"Not to worry. We're heading for a sandy spot just north of Puerto Limón, a small bay, almost a lagoon. It should be lovely."

She hoped he was right. "And once we get there…?"

"Once we get there, we look for the rose."

Shaye bit her lip. She shot a glance at Victoria, then lowered her eyes to her lap.

Victoria was as dismayed as Shaye but had the advantage of being the quintessential diplomat. "An orchid I could believe," she began softly. "Orchids are the national flower. Roses, though, are not indigenous to Central America. Is it possible that a rose Cummins planted would still be alive?"

Noah chuckled as he looked from Shaye's face to Victoria's. "Tell them, Samson. They're dying."

Samson, too, was smiling. "The rose is a rock, possibly a

boulder. Cummins must have taken one look at it and associated its shape with the flowers he knew from home. The treasure, if it exists, will be found in a series of paces measured from the rock.''

Dual sighs of relief came from the women, causing Noah to chuckle again. But while Samson elaborated on the specifics of those paces, Shaye's thoughts lingered on the rock.

The rose. Was it pure coincidence...or an omen? She had a rose of her own, and it symbolized all she'd once been and done. She hid it carefully; no more than a handful of people had ever seen it. It was her personal scarlet letter, and she was far from proud of its existence.

She'd never been a superstitious person, but at that moment, she wanted nothing at all to do with the Costa Rican rose.

Chapter Eight

NOAH AWOKE AT EIGHT on the fourth day of the trip and lay in bed for a long time. After spending most of the night on deck, manning the sails when the wind picked up shortly after one, he'd expected to sleep later. But Shaye had invaded his dream world as much as she was invading his thoughts now that he was awake.

A change had come over her in the water yesterday, and it hadn't been a momentary thing. She'd been distracted for most of the afternoon and thoughtful for much of the evening.

Was it surrender? Not quite. She hadn't come to him that night on deck to declare her devotion and beg him to make love to her. But she did seem to have conceded to an inner turmoil. She seemed to have realized that it wouldn't just go away, that it had to be faced.

He wished he knew what was at the root of that inner turmoil, but she guarded it closely. He wasn't dumb; he knew when to push a subject and when to back off. Not that he really thought of her as a "subject." He was too personally involved for that. But his feel for people had gotten him where he was professionally, and he was counting on it now.

She'd opened up a bit before she'd gone to bed. He'd produced a deck of cards and they'd played several games of gin, and during this she'd mentioned that she and her sister, Shannon, had played gin when they'd been kids. It was one of the few things her parents had thought harmless, she'd said wryly, and when he'd teased her, she'd admitted that her parents were strict. She obviously resented that, yet from what he could see she was nearly as strict with herself as they'd been with her.

Wouldn't she have rebelled? That was what often happened to the offspring of strict parents. Or perhaps she had rebelled and been subsequently swamped by guilt. Ingrained values were hard to shake.

She was a passionate woman. He didn't doubt that for a minute. The way she'd come alive to him on those few occasions when she'd stepped out of her self-imposed mold had been telling. She had a fire inside, all right. The question was whether she'd allow it to burn.

He wasn't about to let it go out, though he was biding his time just now. He'd found her weakness and knew that when he played it soft and gentle she was more vulnerable. Yes, he was impatient; soft and gentle hadn't traditionally been strong points in his character. But then, he'd never met a woman quite like Shaye—or felt quite as compulsively drawn to one before.

He had to admit, with some surprise, that behaving softly and gently toward Shaye wasn't as much of a hardship as he might have expected. She responded well to it. Of course, that didn't mean that his loins didn't ache. He felt an utterly primal urge to make her his. But he wanted far more than a meaningless roll in the hay—or on the deck, or in a cabin, as the case might be.

Hell, where could they do it? His cabin was Samson's, too, and Shaye shared hers with Victoria. The deck was neither comfortable nor private. There was always the water, but he wanted leverage, not to mention access to certain parts of her body without fear of drowning. On the other hand, a sandy beach on the Costa Rican coast…

Allowing for the time they'd lost during the storm and then being becalmed, they had two days' sailing ahead before they reached their destination. Two days in which to soften her up. He'd have to work on it, he decided as he sprang from the bed and reached for a pair of shorts. He'd have to work on it, starting with a soft and gentle morning talk.

He went on deck to find Victoria and Samson but no sign of Shaye. And since he was reserving all his softness and gentleness for her, his impatience found vent in the demand, "Where is she?"

Samson tried to conceal a grin and didn't quite make it. "I haven't seen her yet this morning."

"I think she's still sleeping," Victoria added innocently. "It was after two before she finally dozed off."

A scowling Noah left them and crossed to the bow.

"Now how would you know that?" Samson drawled softly. "You were asleep yourself by eleven."

Victoria didn't ask him how *he'd* known *that*. While Noah and Shaye had been playing cards on deck, Samson had walked her to her cabin, then sat talking with her until she'd fallen asleep. She was normally a night owl, but knowing Samson relieved Noah at the helm between three and four, she'd wanted to be up soon after. Watching the sunrise with him was a memorable experience.

"Actually," she whispered, "I don't know it for sure, but I could feel her tossing and turning. And it won't do any harm to let Noah know she's losing sleep over him."

"Is that what she's doing?"

"I believe so."

He narrowed one eye. "Are you matchmaking?"

She narrowed an eye right back at him. "No more than you."

He lowered his head in that same subtle gesture of guilt that Victoria and Shaye had seen the first day. "I wasn't matchmaking, exactly," he hedged. "But when you called to say that your niece was coming along and that she was twenty-nine, attractive, intelligent and hardworking—well, I couldn't help but think of Noah."

"So you *did* get him to come after I called."

"Barney was ticked off."

"But other than what I said, you knew nothing about Shaye."

"I knew Noah. He needed a break, and not at an isolated château in Normandy. He needs a woman. He's the proverbial man who has everything...except that. Besides," he added with a roguish smile, "Garrick had told me about you, and I knew that if the niece took after the aunt in any small way..."

Victoria reached up to kiss him lightly. "You're a very sweet man. Have I told you that lately?"

"I don't mind hearing it again."

"You're a very sweet man. Thank you for the compliment...and for bringing Noah along. He and Shaye are right for each other. I just know it."

At that moment, Noah swung by en route to the companionway. "Enjoy yourselves, folks."

"Where are you off to?" Samson asked.

"Breakfast," was all Noah said before he disappeared.

It was a brainstorm, he mused as he quickly whipped up pancake batter. She was still in bed, and she hadn't eaten since dinner, and since he was hungry and she was bound to be hungry... Very innocent, he decided, it would all be very innocent. He'd simply carry in breakfast, wake her gently, and they'd eat.

As he spooned batter onto the griddle, he recalled his initial fear that she'd expect to be waited on. But he wasn't waiting on her, at least not in the sense of pandering to a woman who refused to do for herself. She'd proven more than willing to pitch in. She'd even made him breakfast yesterday. So now he was returning the favor. Only with a sightly different twist.

A short time later, balancing the tray that Samson always used to cart food to the deck, he went to her cabin. When a light knock at the door produced no response, he quietly opened it and slipped inside. Then he stood there for a minute, stunned as always by the sight of her in bed. She was on her stomach this time, dark red hair spilling around her head, more vivid than ever against the white linens. Where the sheet left off at mid-back, her T-shirt took over in covering her completely. Still she was alluring. All white and red, primness and fire. God, was she alluring!

He quietly set the tray down by the side of the bed and perched on its edge. "Shaye?" he whispered. His hand hovered over her shoulder for a minute before lowering and squeezing lightly. "Shaye?"

She stirred, turning her head his way. Her eyes were still closed. Lock by lock, he stroked her hair back from her face.

She barely opened her mouth, and the words were slurred. "Something smells good."

"Pancakes and apple butter. I thought maybe you'd join me."

She was quiet for such a long time that he wondered if she'd fallen back to sleep. Then she murmured, "I never eat breakfast in bed."

"Are you turning down room service?"

Again a pause. Her eyes remained closed. "No."

He swallowed down a tiny sigh of relief. "Would you rather sleep a little longer?"

She yawned and struggled to open one eye. "What time is it?"

"Nine-thirty."

With a moan, she turned away. "I didn't get to bed until two."

"Get to bed" versus "doze off." Two very different connotations. "Get to bed" meant she could have been reading; he'd been on deck, so he hadn't seen whether she'd stayed in the salon for a while. "Doze off," the phrase Victoria had used, suggested that she'd tried to sleep but that her thoughts had kept her awake. He hoped it was the latter, but he wasn't about to ask. For someone who usually woke up crabby, she was in a relatively civil mood.

"Are you falling asleep on me?" he whispered.

She shook her head against the pillow.

"Just taking it slow?"

She didn't move. At length she said, "I'm trying to decide whether or not to be angry. You woke me up."

The fact that she didn't sound at all angry gave Noah hope. "I'll leave if you want. I'm hungry enough to eat both helpings."

She turned over then, pushed herself up until she was sitting against the wall, straightened the sheet across her hips and patted her lap.

With a smile he reached for the tray.

Few words were exchanged as they ate. She glanced at him from time to time, thinking how considerate it had been of him to bring her breakfast, and how good he looked even before he'd shaved, and how well he wore an unbuttoned shirt. He glanced at her from time to time, thinking how the shadows beneath her eyes had faded, and how becoming her light tan was, and how disheveled and sexy she looked.

From time to time their glances meshed, held for a second or two, broke away.

When Shaye had finished the last of her pancakes she said, "You're nearly as good a cook as Samson."

"Breakfast is my specialty."

"Between you and your uncle, you could run a restaurant."

"I have enough to do already, thank you."

She sat very still for a minute. "We're moving."

"Have been since one this morning."

She hadn't realized that and wondered how she could have been so caught up in her thoughts that she hadn't noticed.

"Want to go on deck?" Noah asked.

"I'll have to get dressed first."

"You do that while I take care of these," he said, indicating the dishes. "I'll meet you up there in, say, ten minutes?"

"Okay," she agreed quietly and watched him leave.

Ten minutes later they were standing side by side at the bow.

She raised her face and closed her eyes. "Mmm, that feels good."

Noah didn't comment on the fact that she'd left her hair down, or that it was positively dancing in the breeze, or that it was tempting him nearly beyond reason. Instead he took a deep breath and asked casually, "Where do you live in Philly? An apartment?"

"Condominium. It's in a renovated building not far from the historic area."

"Is your family in Philly, too?"

"Uh-uh. Connecticut."

He turned around to lean back against the bulwark. The sails were full. He studied them, wondering if he dared ask more. Before he had a chance to decide either way, she asked, "How about you? A condo in the city?"

"Yup."

"What's your place like in Vermont?"

"Contemporary rustic."

She laughed softly. "That's honest. Most people would pride themselves on saying rustic, when in fact they have every modern amenity imaginable."

A short time later, after they'd watched a school of fish swim by, she asked, "Do you ski?"

"Sure do. You?"

"I tried a few times in college, but I never really went at it seriously."

He wanted to say that she could use his place anytime, that he'd teach her how to ski, that the most fun was après-ski, with a warm fire, a hot toddy and a bear rug before the hearth. Instead he asked what she'd been reading the day before.

Eventually they brought cushions up and made themselves more comfortable. Their talk was sporadic, never touching on deep issues, but even the trivia that emerged was enlightening.

Shaye learned that Noah was an avid Mets fan, that he want to games whenever he could spare the time, which wasn't often enough, and that he'd even became friends with a few of the players. Once he'd been mistaken for a bona fide member of the team by a small-town reporter, who interviewed him outside the locker room after a game. She learned that when he watched television, it was usually a program of the public information or documentary type. He had certain favorite restaurants he returned to often, the most notable of which was a no-name dive on the Lower East Side that had filthy floors, grumpy waiters and the best guacamole north of Chihuahua. She learned that he hated shopping, loved dressing up on Halloween—which, he assured her, came only once a year at his office—and fantasized about buying a Harley and biking across the country.

Noah learned that Shaye talked to her plants and that she generally hated to cook but could do it well when inspired. He learned that she'd always loved to read and belonged to a book group, that she wanted to take up aerobics but didn't have the time, that she liked Foreigner, Survivor, and Chicago but never went to live rock concerts.

The day passed with surprising speed. Shaye wasn't quite sure whether the new Noah, the one who was companionable rather than seductive, was the real Noah. But since he'd offered her a respite from the torment he'd previously inflected, she wasn't about to raise the issue aloud.

Her subconscious wasn't quite as obedient. No sooner had she gone to bed that night than the sensual Noah popped up in her dreams, only it was worse, now, because the man who excited her physically was the same one she'd begun to respect. She awoke in a frenzy, torn apart and sweaty, and immediately put the blame on the Vietnamese dinner Samson had prepared that night. By the next morning, though, that excuse had worn thin. One look at Noah, freshly shaved and wearing nothing but a low-slung pair of shorts, stirred her blood.

She fought it all day, but to no avail. They were together nearly constantly, and though he didn't fall back on either double entendres or provocative observations, his eyes held the dark sexuality that expressed her own deepest thoughts. She was acutely, viscerally, passionately aware of him.

While they ate breakfast, which he consumed in bulk and with enthusiasm, she was entranced by his mouth. It was mobile and firm, yet sensual. She couldn't help but recall how aggressively it had consumed her own, and when her eyes met his for a fleeting moment, she knew he was remembering the same.

Later she sat with him on deck while he cleaned the hurricane lamps, his long, lean fingers working the cloth over brass. She was mesmerized by those fingers and finally had to tear her eyes away, but the memory of them working her breasts with agile intimacy caused a rush of warmth to spread beneath her skin.

Noah didn't comment on the blush or on the sudden shift of her gaze, but when she dared look back at him, she caught a starkly hungry expression.

Later still, when he relieved Samson at the helm, she relaxed against the transom—or she'd intended to relax, until Noah's bold stance commanded her attention. He had a beautiful body and he held it well, shoulders back, head up. Whether standing with his legs spread or with his ankles crossed or with his weight on one hip, he oozed self-confidence. And when he walked, as he did to occasionally adjust the sails, he oozed masculinity. She wondered what it was about tight-hipped men who moved with nothing more than the subtlest shift of their bottoms—whether it was the economy of movement that made a woman greedy, or the pelvic understatement that was overwhelmingly suggestive, or simply the fact that between waist and thigh men were built so differently from women.

Of course, she couldn't remember ever having taken much notice of men's bottoms before, not even in the old days. So it had to be Noah.

Self-confident, sexy, every move natural and spontaneous. He wasn't a preener. Not one of his motions seemed tutored. His body was simply...his body. And his very indifference to it made him all the more attractive to Shaye.

And all *that* was before she got down to the details. The roughened skin on his elbows...the compact lobes of his ears...the symmetry of his upper back, the gleam of sun-bronzed skin over flexing muscles...the shallow dip at his hipline just before his shorts cut off the view... So many things she wanted to touch, so many things that touched her even without actual physical contact.

Like his chest. Noah's chest inspired wanton behavior. She wanted to feel its varying textures, to touch her finger to a smooth spot, a hairy spot, a firm spot, a soft spot. His nipples were small in that male kind of way, but that didn't mean there was anything less intimate about them. The more she looked, the more intimately she was moved.

In the end, though, it was his eyes, always his eyes that touched her most deeply. To say that his eyes stripped her naked was too physical a description. They delved far deeper, burrowing beneath her skin and touching hidden quarters that no man, *no* man had ever touched. With each look she felt his thoughts, and she knew that he wanted her.

So the sexual tension built. What had rippled in the morning was simmering by noon and smoldering three hours later. The air between them grew positively charged, but they could no more have left each other's sides than they could have denied that the charge existed.

Then, shortly before five, a low shadow materialized on the distant horizon.

"Land, ho!" Noah shouted from the bow, grateful to relieve his tension with the hearty yell.

Shaye was at his elbow. "Costa Rica?"

"It had better be," he said, "or we're in trouble."

She knew he wasn't referring to an accidental landing in another country. They needed a diversion, and they needed one fast.

"What happens now?" Victoria asked, joining them.

Noah and Shaye exchanged a quick, hot look. "Now," he said, "we try to find out exactly where we are."

Samson was already doing that, working with binoculars, a compass, and the charts and notes he'd made. "We're pretty much on target," he finally announced to his waiting audience. "Assuming that the cargo ships we've seen are heading for either Limón or Moin, all we need to do is to sail a little north. Once we're in closer, I'll know more."

It took a while, for the wind lessened the closer they got, but they gradually worked their way in the right direction. Shaye, who'd begun the trip with a minimum of enthusiasm for Costa Rica, couldn't deny the country's tropical beauty. Spectral mountains provided a distant backdrop for the lush jungle growth that grew more delineated as they neared the shore. The graceful fronds of tall palms arched over small stretches of sandy beach. Thicker mangroves and vines populated swampier sections.

They approached a small bay, and three pairs of eyes sought Samson's. But he shook his head. "The configuration is wrong."

"Perhaps it's changed with time?" Shaye asked.

"Not that much," was his answer. So they sailed on.

After a time they neared another sandy area. Low outcroppings of rock lay at either end, curving out to give a lagoon effect. "Could be," Samson said. "It's broad enough in the middle, flat enough from front to back.... Could be," he repeated, this time with enthusiasm. "I won't know for sure until can take a reading with the sextant, and it looks like the stars will be elusive for a while."

Those three pairs of eyes joined him in scanning the cloud cover that was fast moving in.

Recalling how sick she'd been on the second night of the trip, Victoria asked with a touch of horror, "Another storm?"

"Probably nothing more than rain," Noah guessed, then asked Samson, "Should we go in and drop anchor?"

"That's our best bet."

By the time the *Golden Echo* was anchored about two hundred yards from shore, night had fallen. The four gathered in the salon, with an air of great expectancy.

"This is frustrating," Victoria decided. "To be here and not really know whether we are, in fact, here...."

"Patience," Samson urged with a smile. "We'll know soon enough. We've made good time, and I've allowed five days to search for the treasure. That's far more than we should need once we reach the right lagoon. Even if this one isn't it, we can't be far."

Shaye's eyes met Noah's for a minute before slanting away.

Victoria's eyes were on Samson. "How does the Costa Rican government take to treasure hunts like ours?"

"I filed the proper papers and was granted a permit. The government has a right to half of anything we recover."

Victoria knew by this time that Samson had as little need of gold as she did. "What will you do with it?"

"The treasure? Of the half that's left, only a quarter will be mine." His gaze skipped meaningfully from one face to another.

"I don't want any treasure," Shaye said quickly. It had never occurred to her that she'd receive a thing, and picturing the rose-shaped rock, she felt vehement about it.

"Count me out, too," Noah said forcefully. He looked at Shaye, and his eyes grew smoky. *There are many different kinds of treasure....*

"I'm bequeathing my portion to you," Victoria informed Samson. "Lord only knows I pay enough in taxes now." She settled more comfortably onto the sofa. "What will you do with it?"

Samson gave a quick shrug. "Give it to charity—four times as much as I'd originally planned."

Victoria grinned. "I like that idea. What do you think, Shaye?"

Shaye's head popped up. She'd been studying her knotted hands, wishing that they could somehow take the tension from inside her and wring it away. "Excuse me?"

"Charity. Samson plans to give our treasure to charity."

"I like that idea."

Victoria laughed. "That was what I said."

"Oh."

"How about you, Noah?" Samson asked. "Any objections?"

Hearing his name, Noah tore his gaze from Shaye. "To you and Victoria splitting the treasure?"

Samson sighed. "To my giving the entire thing to charity."

"I like that idea," Noah said, then frowned when both Samson and Victoria laughed. He'd obviously missed something, but he didn't know what it was. He did know that he was the brunt of the joke. Then again, Shaye wasn't laughing.

Victoria took pity on him and turned to Samson with what she hoped was a suitably serious expression. "What's for dinner tonight?"

"Bologna sandwiches."

"Bologna sandwiches?"

"That's right."

Neither Noah nor Shaye showed the slightest reaction to his announcement. They were alternately looking at each other, looking at the floor, looking at Samson or Victoria for the sake of politeness. They saw little, heard even less.

"So you finally got tired of cooking," Victoria declared with relief. "You're human, after all."

Arching a brow her way, Samson grabbed her hand, pulled her from the sofa and made a beeline for the galley, muttering under his breath, "I could probably open a can of dog food and neither of them would notice."

He was right. Neither Noah nor Shaye commented on the artlessness of the menu, though both drank their share of the Chianti Samson decanted.

Shaye tried, really she did, to concentrate on the dinner conversation, but her thoughts and senses were too filled with Noah to allow space for much else.

Noah tried every bit as hard to interject a word here or there to suggest he was paying attention, but more often than not the word was inappropriate, several sentences too late or offered in a totally wrong inflection.

They roused a bit when it began to rain and everything had to be carried below deck in a rush, but the alternate arrangements had them sitting close together in the galley. Not only was sane thought all the harder, but the tension between them rose to a fevered pitch.

"Why don't we adjourn to the salon and finish the wine?" Samson suggested at last. "There's no reason why Chianti won't go with Ding-Dongs."

"You didn't bring Ding-Dongs," Victoria chided.

"I certainly did. Next to chocolate mousse, Ding-Dongs are my favorite dessert."

Neither Noah nor Shaye had a word to say about Ding-Dongs, but they came to when Samson and Victoria rose to leave. "I'll clean up," they offered in unison, then eyed each other.

Shaye said, "You go on into the salon with the others. I'll take care of this."

Noah said, "There isn't much. I don't mind. You go relax."

"I've been relaxing all day. I'd like to do something."

"And I feel guilty because my uncle has been the major cook. The least I can do is clean up."

"Noah, I'll do it." She started stacking dirty plates.

He had the four wineglasses gathered, a finger in each. "*I'll* do it."

"We wanted those glasses," Samson remarked.

Noah sent him a confused look. "I thought we were done."

"I had suggested that we finish the wine in the salon."

"Oh." He looked down at the glasses. "But they're mixed up now. I don't know whose is whose."

"Obviously," said Samson, whereupon Noah turned on Shaye.

"If you hadn't been so stubborn, this wouldn't have happened."

"Me, stubborn? You were the one who was being difficult."

"How can you say that someone offering to do the dirty work is being difficult?"

"*I* offered to do the dirty work *first*."

"Then *you* were the one who was difficult, when all I wanted was to relieve you of the chore."

"But I didn't *want* to be relieved—"

Victoria cut her off with a loud declaration. "We'll take clean glasses." She did just that and led Samson from the galley.

Shaye attacked the dishes with a vengeance.

"Take it easy on the water," Noah snapped. "There's no need to run more than you need."

"I need *some*, if you want the plates clean."

"Of course I want the plates clean, but you could be economical."

She thrust a dripping plate his way. "Dry this."

"You're very good at giving orders. Is that what you do all day at work?"

"At least I don't get any back talk there."

"I'm sure they wouldn't dare or you'd boot them out. I assume," he drawled, "that you have the power to hire or fire."

"In my department, I certainly do. Lawyers know nothing about computers or the people who use them."

He held up the plate he'd been drying and asked with cloying sweetness, "Is this shiny enough for Her Highness?"

She simply glared at him and handed him another, then started on the next with a double dose of elbow grease.

"You're gonna break that plate if you're not careful."

She ignored him. "And you're a fine one to talk. You're the head of your own company—a power trip if there ever was one. I'll bet *you* run a tight ship. A regular Captain Bligh."

"I have high standards, as well I should. My name's on top. I get the blame when someone flubs up."

"And the same isn't true for me? Don't you think the lawyers get on *my* back when documents come out screwed up?"

"What I want to know," he snarled, "is if they ever get you *on* your back."

The glass she'd been scrubbing came close to breaking against the sink. "You have the filthiest mind I've ever been exposed to!"

"And who's been fueling it? Little looks here, darting glances there. I'm not made of stone, for Christ's sake!"

She'd rinsed off the glass she'd nearly broken and was onto another. "Could've fooled me. Your eyes are as lecherous as your mind. You sit there making me squirm, and what do you expect me to do—whistle 'Dixie'?"

"You couldn't whistle if you tried. Your lips are too stiff."

"It's a lucky thing they are. Anything but a stiff lip around you would result in a physical attack."

"I have never physically attacked a woman in my life! But I'm beginning to wonder about you and that past you try so hard to hide. It comes out, y'know. I can see it in your eyes. You've had sex, and you've had it but good. What was it—with a married guy? Or a highly visible guy you're determined to protect?"

"You're out in left field, Noah." She thrust a handful of forks and knives at him, then, having run out of things to wash, went at the sink itself.

"I think it was with a married guy. You fell in love, gave him everything and only after the fact learned that he wasn't yours for the taking."

"Dream on." She began to wipe down the table with a fury.

"Either that, or you're totally repressed. Your parents instilled the fear of God in you and you're afraid to do a damn thing. But the urges are there. You live them vicariously through sexy rock ballads, but you don't have the guts to recognize what you need."

"And you know what that is, I suppose?"

"Damn right I do. You need a man and lots of good, old-fashioned loving. You may like to think of yourself as a prim and proper old maid, but I've seen your true colors. They're hot and vibrant and dripping with passion."

She turned to him, hands on her hips, nostrils flaring. "What I need is none of your business. I sure don't need *you*."

"You need a man who's forceful. I fight you, and I'd wager that's a hell of a lot more than any other man has ever done."

"Power trip, ego trip—they're one and the same with you, aren't they?" Throwing the damp rag into the sink, she whirled around and stalked out of the galley. A second later she was back, glowering at Noah while she reached for a clean wineglass.

Snatching up his own, he followed her. He filled it as soon as she'd set down the bottle, then took his place in the same chair he'd had before dinner.

"We were talking about pirates," Victoria said. She and Samson sat on the sofa, hard-pressed to ignore the foul moods the newcomers were in. ‘‘Samson’s done a lot of reading. He says that many of the stereotypes are wrong.’’

‘‘In what way?’’ Shaye demanded.

Noah grunted. ‘‘They were frustrated men, stuck on a boat without a willing woman to ease their aches.’’

‘‘Not every man is fixated on his libido,’’ she snapped, then turned to Samson. ‘‘Tell me about pirates.’’

‘‘Pirates turn you on, huh?’’

‘‘Keep quiet, Noah. You were saying, Samson...’’

‘‘I was saying that when one begins to study the age of piracy, one learns some interesting things. For example, pirates rarely flew the skull and crossbones. They rarely made anyone walk the plank. They rarely marooned a man.’’

Noah snorted. ‘‘And when they did, they left him a pistol so that he could put an end to his misery. That’s compassion for you.’’

‘‘I’m not trying to idealize the buccaneer, simply to point out that he was more than a blood-thirsty ruffian with no respect for life. Pirates had their own kind of code.’’

‘‘Nonpolitical anarchy,’’ was Noah’s wry retort.

‘‘It worked for them,’’ Samson said. ‘‘They chose their captains at will and could dismiss them as easily.’’

‘‘Dismiss or execute?’’

‘‘Noah, let the man talk.’’

Noah slid lower in his chair. His brows formed a dark shelf over his eyes, but he said nothing.

‘‘They did execute their captains on occasion,’’ Samson conceded, ‘‘but only when those captains mistreated them. You have to understand that most of the men who crewed on pirate ships had known the brunt of poverty, or religious or political persecution at home. Fair treatment was one of the few benefits of piracy.’’

‘‘But what about the gold they captured?’’ Shaye asked. ‘‘Didn’t they benefit from that?’’

Noah looked her in the eye. ‘‘They blew it on women in the first port they hit. I hope to hell the doxies were worth it.’’

‘‘You’ll never know, will you?’’ she asked sweetly.

He glared at her. She glared right back. Then he bolted from his chair and stormed toward the companionway.

‘‘Where are you going?’’

‘‘Out.’’

"But it's raining!"

"Good!"

Shaye dragged her gaze back to the salon. She looked first at Victoria, then at Samson. "He's impossible!"

Samson contemplated that for a minute, then went on in his customary gentle voice, "The popular image is that pirates were irreligious plunderers who had a wonderful time for themselves, but it wasn't so. They were unhappy men. With each voyage, their hopes of returning home dimmed. It didn't matter that home wasn't wonderful. Home was familiar. It had to have been frustrating."

Shaye dropped her gaze to her hands. Victoria took up the slack and continued talking with Samson, but it wasn't until Noah reappeared that Shaye raised her eyes.

He was soaking wet and impatient. "Come on," he said, grabbing her hand.

"What—"

"We'll be back," he called over his shoulder as he led her toward the companionway.

"Hold on a minute." She tugged back on her hand. "I'm not going up there."

But he refused to let go, and he wasn't stopping. "You won't melt." He pushed the hatch open and had pulled her through before she could do anything about it.

Chapter Nine

THE RAIN was a warm, steady shower, drenching Shaye within seconds. "Noah, this is crazy!"

He loomed over her, the outline of his face glistening in the light of the lamp that hung at the stern. "We're going ashore."

"But it's pouring!"

Plowing his fingers into her hair, he took her mouth in a kiss that was as fevered as the tension had been earlier, as hungry as he'd felt all day, as wild as he'd ever been at his boldest moments. By the time he raised his head, Shaye was reeling.

"We're going ashore," he repeated hoarsely.

The night was dark and stormy, but that meager light from the stern clearly illuminated the intent on his face and the desire in his eyes. At that moment, she knew precisely what he had in mind. And she knew at that moment that she wouldn't refuse him. The flame within her was too hot to be denied. It blotted out everything but a basic, driving need.

"How?" she whispered shakily.

"The dingy." Snatching up a huge flashlight, he aimed it over the side of the boat, where the small rubber lifeboat he'd just inflated bobbed in the rain. Then he swung onto the rope ladder and started down. Midway, he waited for Shaye. When she was just above him, he lowered himself into the raft. As soon as she was safely settled, he began to row quickly toward shore.

With a trembling hand, Shaye tossed back her dripping hair. She didn't know whether what she was doing was right, but she knew that she had no choice. The darkness abetted her primal need; it erased reality, leaving only the urgency of the moment. Her entire body shook in anticipation of the intimacy she was about to share with Noah. Her eyes were locked on his large dark form throughout the brief trip, receiving an unbroken message that sizzled through the rainy night.

The dingy touched shore with a quivering bump. Noah jumped out seconds before Shaye, made a brief survey of the beach with the light, then dropped it and, in a single flowing movement, whipped the boat onto the sand and reached for her.

She was made for his arms, fitting them perfectly. Her hands went into his wet hair as her open mouth met his. Tension, hunger, fierceness—the combined effect was galvanic. His tongue plunged deeply. She nipped it, sucked it, played it wildly with her own.

With a groan, Noah set frenzied fingers to work tugging the soaked T-shirt from her body. But he was unwilling to release her mouth for an instant, so he abandoned it at her shoulders and dug his fingers under the waistband of her shorts. She helped him in the tugging, her lips passionate beneath his all the while. As soon as the soggy cotton passed her knees, she kicked free of the shorts and turned her efforts to Noah's. They'd barely hit the sand when he dropped his hands to her thighs and lifted her onto his waiting heat.

At the bold impaling, Shaye cried out.

"It's okay, baby," he soothed, panting. "It's okay."

She gasped his name and clung to his neck. "I feel so full..."

"You're hot and tight around me. Ahh, you feel good!" His fingers dug into her bottom, holding her bonded to him as he sank to his knees. "Have I hurt you?" he asked between nips at her mouth.

"No. Oh, no."

"I was afraid you'd change your mind, and I couldn't last another minute without being inside." His hands had risen to cover her breasts, stroking her through silk, then hastily releasing the front catch of her bra and seeking out her naked flesh.

Again she cried out. His fingers were everywhere, circling her, kneading her, daubing her nipples with raindrops. She was in a lagoon. She couldn't see the lagoon or the jungle, but she knew it was paradise, she just knew it, and with less thought than Eve she gave in to temptation.

Her hands began a greedy exploration under his shirt, over his waist, across his buttocks, up and down his thighs. He wasn't moving inside her, but she could feel every inch of him against her moist sheath, and the solid stimulation was breathtaking. Whispering his name, she tried to move her hips. But he followed the movement with his own, preventing even the slightest withdrawal.

"You're mine now," he said with the tightness of self-restraint. "We'll take it slow."

She raked her teeth against his jaw. "I want to feel you move."

"Soon, baby. Soon."

His mouth plundered hers. His thumbs began a slow, sliding rotation of her nipples. Live currents snapped and sizzled so hotly inside her that she almost feared she'd be electrocuted in the rain. Noah was grounding her, she told herself, yet still she burned. She caught at his hair and kissed him more deeply. She drew her nails across his shoulders, then dug them in and tried to move again, but he wouldn't have it.

"Noah..."

He worked her T-shirt over her head and pushed the bra straps from her shoulders, leaving her naked in the night but hot, so hot against him. "Soon," he murmured thickly. "Soon." The last was breathed against her breast moments before he sucked her in.

For a minute all she could do was hold his head. Her own was thrown back, her eyes were closed, and the rain was as gentle, as persistent and seductive as his ever-moving tongue. With the visual deprivation imposed by the night, her senses grew that much sharper. She felt everything he did with vivid clarity, and the knot of need inside her grew tighter.

Shaye wondered where he got his self-control and vowed to break it. While her mouth grew more seductive, her hands taunted his chest. Short, wet hairs slid between her marauding fingers and his nipples grew hard. She undulated her middle, then, when he clutched her there to hold her still, her hips. She felt him quiver insider her, and, encouraged, repeated the motion.

But through it all there was something more. Instead of simply snapping his control, she wanted to give him a pleasure so hot and intense that he'd be branded every bit as deeply as she was. Bent on that, she reached low and stroked that part of him that hung so heavily between his thighs.

The bold caress was his undoing. Making a low, guttural sound, he tumbled her down to the sand. Bowing his back, he withdrew, then thrust upward with a force that thrilled her. She'd been right to want movement, for the friction, the sliding pressure was exquisite. But Noah had been right, too, for the wait had enhanced both her desire and appreciation.

He set a masterful rhythm that varied with their needs. Faster or slower, she met him and matched him, each arching stroke stretching the heavenly torment into an ever-tautening fine wire.

The tension snapped with a final, agonizingly deep thrust. Implosion and explosion, simultaneous and mind shattering, sent blind cries slicing through the beat of the rain. Soft gasps followed, an occasional whimper from Shaye, a moan from Noah. They clung tightly to each other until they were totally limp, and then the rain began to soothe their bodies, cleansing, cooling and replenishing.

When Noah had regained a modicum of strength, he maneuvered them both into the kneeling position from which they'd fallen. He wasn't ready to leave Shaye, and given the renewed strength of her hold, he suspected he'd have been unable to if he tried. It was gratifying, the perfect denouement to what had been a heartrending experience.

He spread his hands over her bare back, able to savor now the delight of her shape as he hadn't had the patience to do earlier. "I knew it would be like that," he murmured. "We're like tinder, Shaye. All it takes is a single match and we go up." He gave a throaty laugh. "I'm still up."

She could feel that. Oh, she could feel it, and she was astonished to find that corresponding parts of her were similarly alert. "You're a powerful lover," she whispered. It was an understatement, but she didn't think the words existed to adequately describe what she'd felt.

"I could say the same about you," he whispered back. He was thinking that he didn't care how many other lovers she'd had or who had first awakened her to the fiery art of passion, but he didn't say so. It wasn't that he didn't want to know, because that jealous male part of him did, but he didn't want to disturb the precious peace that existed between them. So he asked, "Do you mind the rain?"

"No. There's something erotic about it."

"There's something erotic about this whole setting. I wish to hell I could see it."

Resting her cheek on his shoulder, she chuckled. She knew what he meant. But then, she needed the darkness. She didn't want to see herself, and she didn't want Noah to see her. There was still the matter of the small mark on her breast; she had no idea how she would explain it, whether she wanted to, what the ramifications would be. Too much thought at too sensitive at time...she was still into feeling, rather than thinking.

"Take off your shirt," she whispered, then slid her hands to his waist to hold their bodies together while he complied. When he was as naked as she, she wrapped her arms around his neck, bringing her breasts into contact with his chest for the very first time.

The feeling was heavenly. She moved gently against him. He sucked in a shaky breath, and when she felt him swell inside her, her muscles automatically tightened.

"Ohh, baby..."

"You can feel that?" She smiled when his groan clearly indicated that he could, but then he was kissing her smile away and touching her in ways that reduced her to quivering jelly. She sighed when he released her mouth, only to gasp when he slid a hand between their bodies and began an ultra-sensitive stroking. It wasn't long before she reached a second fierce climax.

She was panting against his shoulder, her hands grasping his chest, thumbs on his nipples, when he went tense, uttered a strangled cry and pushed more deeply into her. She felt the spasms that shook him, felt his warmth flowing into her and knew an incredible joy.

"Ahh, Shaye," he whispered when he could finally speak, "you're amazing."

She basked in the glow of his words. She'd heard similar ones before, but never spoken with quite the same awe, and that meant the world to her. Pressing her face to his neck, she nestled into his arms. It was apparently the right thing to do, for he held her closely and seemed as satisfied as she with the silence.

At length, though, it occurred to her that a rainy Eden had its drawbacks. She wanted a bed. She wanted to lie down beside Noah in the darkness, to breathe in his undiluted scent, to hear the unaccompanied beat of his heart. She wanted to rest in his arms, just rest. She was suddenly very tired.

"I think we'd better go back," he murmured into her hair.

She wondered if he'd read her mind. His voice sounded as tired as she felt. More than that, it contained a note of sadness that she understood; no matter how they looked at it, there wasn't a bed for them to share.

She let him help her to her feet and together they retrieved their clothing. As though afraid of breaking the spell further, Noah didn't turn on the flashlight. He set the dingy in the water, helped Shaye inside, then climbed in and more slowly rowed back to the *Golden Echo*. As had been the case during the trip to shore, her eyes held him the entire way back. This time, though, rather than the heat of desire, she felt something even deeper and more tender. Shaye wasn't about to put a name to it any more than she was ready to face what it entailed. She simply wanted it to go on and on.

After securing the dingy to the stern of the sloop, they climbed back on deck. Holding Shaye's hand firmly in his, Noah cast a despairing glance at the rain that continued to pour. Then he guided her down the companionway and closed the hatch.

"Want to change into dry things and sit in the salon for a little while?" he asked softly.

She nodded, but still she didn't move. Their fingers were interlaced; she tightened hers. She feared that even the briefest parting would allow for an unwelcome intrusion.

Noah raised her hand and gently kissed each of her fingers, then lowered his head and gently kissed her mouth. "Go," he whispered against her lips. "I'll be waiting for you."

Determined to change as quickly as possible, she whirled around and promptly stumbled. She'd have fallen to the floor had not Noah caught her. While he held her to his side, he frowned at the cause of her near-accident. A large bundle and one about half its size were stacked in the passageway by the aft cabin.

"My duffel bags?" he asked softly. His confused gaze shifted to Shaye before returning to the bundles. "Packed?" He stared at them a minute longer, then, with dawning awareness, broke into a lopsided grin. "I'll be damned...."

Shaye left his side long enough to check out the forward cabin. It was empty. "They must both be in your cabin," she whispered, draping an arm around his neck in delight.

"Looks that way."

"But...how did they know?"

"Maybe they had the dingy bugged."

"Impossible."

"Then they're simply very wise people."

"Or very selfish."

"Hell, they deserve pleasure, too. On the other hand, maybe they meant this as punishment for the way I behaved earlier."

"You could be right."

He scowled. "That's not what you were supposed to say."

Her eyes turned innocent, while her heart positively brimmed. "What was I supposed to say?"

"That I was only being ornery out of frustration." His whisper grew softer. "Are you going to make me sleep on the couch?"

She gave a quick shake of her head.

"I can share your bed?"

She nodded as quickly.

"Because you feel sorry for me?"

"Because I want you with me."

His smile was so warm then, so filled with satisfaction that she knew a hundred-fold return on her honesty. He didn't make a smug comment on her primness, or lack thereof. He didn't accuse her of being wanton. He just smiled, and another bit of the retaining wall surrounding her defenses fell away.

Without a word, he scooped up his bags and followed her to the forward cabin. Once side, he dropped his things and took her in his arms. He didn't kiss her. He didn't caress her. He simply held her.

"Shall I light the lamp?" he asked quietly.

"No."

"I'd like to get out of these wet things."

"Me, too."

"Got a towel?"

She nodded, and when he released her, went to get it. He'd shed his shorts and shirt by the time she returned with the towel, and by the time she'd wrestled her way out of her own things, he was ready to dry her. There was nothing seductive in his touch; it was infinitely gentle and made her feel more special than she'd ever felt before. The feeling remained when they curled next to each other in bed, and it was so strong and gave her such confidence that she probably would have answered any question he'd asked just then.

He only asked one thing. "Comfortable?"

"Mmm."

He was quiet for a time before he spoke. "There is such pleasure in this. Just lying here. Close."

"I know," she whispered and softly kissed his chest.

"I just want to hold you."

"Me, too."

"I want you with me when I wake up."

"I will be."

"You can kick me if I snore."

She yawned. "Okay."

"If Samson wakes us at five to go digging for his damned treasure, I'll wring his neck."

"I'll help you."

"On the other hand," he added, his voice beginning to slur, "maybe they'll sleep late themselves."

"Or maybe they'll take pity on us."

"Fat chance..."

"Mmm..."

ALL THINGS WERE relative. The knock on the door didn't come until eight the next morning, but Shaye and Noah weren't ready for it even then. They'd been awake on and off during the night and were dragged out of a sound sleep by Samson's subsequent shout.

"We've been waiting for two hours! Can you give us an ETA?"

"That's Expected Time of Arising," Victoria called.

After bolting upright in alarm, Noah collapsed, burying his face in Shaye's hair. "Make them go away," he whispered.

"Noon!" she shouted to the two beyond the door.

"Noon?" Victoria echoed. "That's obscene!"

Samson agreed. "If you think we're going to wait until noon to go ashore, think again!"

"Go ashore," Shaye suggested, tugging the sheet higher. "I'll just sleep a little longer."

"But I need Noah's help," Samson argued.

"He's on shore. I left him there last night."

"What do you mean, you left him there?"

"He was behaving like a jackass." She twisted over Noah to muffle his snicker. "What choice did I have? And it's a good thing I did leave him there. Exactly where did you expect him to sleep?"

There was silence on the other side of the door, so she went on. "That was a fine stunt you two pulled—behaving like a pair of oversexed teenagers.'' Noah nuzzled her collarbone. She slid to her side again and wrapped her arms around his neck. ''What kind of an example is that to set? I have to say that I was a little shocked—''

Her words were cut off by the abrupt opening of the door. Victoria stood with one hand on the knob, the other on her hip. Samson was close behind her. Their eyes went from Shaye to the outline of bodies beneath the sheet.

''I am assuming,'' Victoria said drolly, ''that Noah is hidden somewhere under that mane of hair. Either that, or you've grown an extra body, a pair of very long legs and a dark beard.''

''Tell her to go away,'' came Noah's muffled voice.

''Go away,'' Shaye said.

''ETA?'' Samson prodded.

''Noon.''

Victoria made a face. ''Nine.''

''Eleven.''

''Ten,'' said Samson. ''Ten, and not a minute later.'' He raised his voice. ''Do you hear me, Noah?''

Noah groaned. ''I hear.''

''Good. Ten o'clock. Topside.'' His hand covered Victoria's as he pulled the door shut.

Closing her eyes, Shaye slid lower to lay her head on Noah's chest. He wrapped an arm around her back and murmured, ''I'd like to stay here all day.''

''Mmm.''

''Sleep well?''

''Mmm.''

''Shaye?'' He began to toy with her hair.

''Mmm?''

''That little mark on your breast. What is it?''

Her eyes came open and for several seconds she barely breathed. ''Nothing,'' she said at last.

''It isn't nothing. It looks like a tattoo.''

She was silent.

''Let me see.''

She held him tighter.

''Shaye, let me see.'' Taking her shoulders, he set her to the side. His eyes didn't immediately lower, though, but held hers. ''You didn't really hope to hide it forever, did you?'' he asked gently. ''I've touched and tasted every part of you. There's pleasure to be had from looking, too.''

She bit her lip, but she knew that she wouldn't deny him. If he'd sounded smug or lecherous, she'd have been able to put up a fight. But against gentleness she was helpless.

Very carefully he eased the sheet away. He sat up and pushed it lower, then leaned back on his elbow while his eyes began at her toes and worked their way upward. His hand followed, skimming her calves and her thighs, brushing lightly over auburn curls before tracing her hip bones and belly to her waist.

His hand was growing less steady. He swallowed once and took a deep breath. ''Your body is lovely,'' he whispered as his eyes crept higher. He touched her ribs, then slowly, slowly outlined her breasts.

She'd been lying on her left side. Gently rolling her to her back, he brought a single forefinger to touch the small mark that lay just above her pounding heart.

''A rose,'' he breathed. It was less than half the size of his smallest fingernail, delicately etched in black and red. His gaze was riveted to it. ''When did you get it?''

''A lifetime ago,'' she whispered brokenly.

''Why?''

''It...I...on a whim. A stupid whim.''

''You don't like it?''

She shook her head, close to tears. ''But I can't make it go away.''

Lowering his head, he kissed it lightly, then dabbed it with the tip of his tongue. ''It's you,'' he whispered.

''No!''

''Yes. Something hidden. A secret side.''

She was clenching her fists. ''Please cover it up,'' she begged.

He did, but with his mouth rather than with the sheet, and at the same time he covered the rest of her body with his. ''You are beautiful, tattoo and all. You make me burn.'' Holding the brunt of his weight on his forearms, he moved sensuously over her.

Shaye, too, burned. She'd lost track of the number of times they'd made love during the night, but still she wanted him. There was something about the way she felt when he made love to her—a sense of richness and completion. When he possessed her, she felt whole. When she was with him, she felt alive.

It didn't make sense that she should feel that way, when what she'd found with Noah was a moment out of time, when he was everything she'd sworn she didn't want, when he was everything she feared. But it wasn't the time to try to make sense of things. Not with his lips closing over hers and his hand caressing her breast. Not with their legs tangling and their stomachs rubbing. Not with his sex growing larger by the minute against her thigh.

Raising her knees to better cradle him, she responded ardently to his kisses. She loved the firmness of his lips and their mobility, just as she loved the feel of his skin beneath her fingers. His back was a broad mass of ropy muscles, his hips more narrow and smooth. The heat his body exuded generated an answering heat. His natural male scent was enhanced by that of passion.

Slowly and carefully, he entered her. When their bodies were fully joined, his back arched, his weight on his palms, he looked down at her and searched her eyes. "I want to see this, too," he said hoarsely. His breathing was unsteady. The muscles of his arms trembled. He was working so hard to rein in the same desires that buzzed through her, and he was doing so much better a job of it than she, that she broke into a sheepish smile.

Carefully he brought her up onto his lap, then, hugging her to him, inched his way backward until he'd reached the edge of the bed. When he slid off to kneel on the floor, she tightened the twist of her ankles at the small of his back. Not once was the penetration broken.

Shaye couldn't believe what happened then. Where another man would have simply begun to move while he watched, Noah cupped her face and kissed her deeply. He worshipped her mouth, her cheeks, her chin. He plumped up her breasts with his hands and devoured them as adoringly. And only when she was thinking she'd die from the searing bliss did he lower his gaze. Hers followed.

He withdrew and slowly reentered. A long, low moan slipped from his throat. His head fell back, eyes momentarily closed against the enormity of sensation.

Needing grounding of her own, Shaye looped her arms around his neck and dropped her forehead to his shoulder. She was panting softly. Her insides were on fire. She was stunned by the depth of emotion she felt, the profoundness of what they were doing, the overwhelming sense of rightness.

His cheek came down next to hers. He pulled back his hips, slowly pushed forward, pulled back, pushed forward. Every movement was controlled and deeply, deeply arousing.

When Shaye began to fear that she'd reach her limit before him, she unlocked her ankles and moved her thighs against his hips. Unable to resist, Noah ran his palms the length of her legs. The feel of the smooth, firm silk was too much. He made a low, throaty sound and within seconds surged into a throbbing climax. Only then did she allow herself the same release.

He whispered her name over and over until their bodies had begun to quieten. Then he framed her face with his hands and tipped it up. "I love you, Shaye." He sealed the vow with a long, sweet kiss, and when he held her back again, there were tears in her eyes. "There are more secrets. I know that. But I do love you. Secrets and all. I don't care where you've been or what you've done. I love you."

She didn't return the words, but held him in tight, trembling arms. *Do I love him? Can I love him? Will I be asking for trouble if I love him? I can't control him. I can't control myself when I'm with him. If love is forever, can it possibly work?*

THE ACTIVITY that followed offered Shaye a welcome escape from her thoughts. She and Noah dressed, ate a fast breakfast, then joined Victoria and Samson on deck. Though the rain had stopped, the sky remained heavily overcast. Ever the optimist, Samson said it was for the best, that without the sun, they'd be cooler.

Shaye wondered about that. It was hot and sticky anyway. One glance at Noah told her he felt the same, and she noted that Samson had even passed up his pirate outfit in favor of more practical shorts and T-shirt. He wore his tricorne, though. She couldn't begrudge him that.

Since there had, as yet, been no stars by which to measure their position, Samson was left with making a sight judgment. Having carefully studied the small bay from the deck of the sloop, he'd already decided that it compared favorably with the one on his map. When he questioned Noah and Shaye about what they'd seen when they'd been ashore the night before, they looked at each other sheepishly. He didn't pursue the issue.

Loading the dingy with shovels and a pick, they left the

Golden Echo securely anchored and rowed to shore. As soon as they'd safely beached the raft, Samson pulled out his map.

"Okay, let's look for the rose."

Shaye winced. Noah sent her a wink that made her feel a little better. Then he, too, turned his attention to the map. "According to this, the rock should be near the center of the back of the lagoon and not too far from shore."

Samson nodded distractedly. His gaze alternated between the map and the beach before them. "That's what the map suggests, though I dare say it wasn't drawn to scale." He refolded and pocketed the fragile paper. "Let's take a look."

The spot where they were headed was a short distance along the beach. After allowing Samson and Victoria a comfortable lead, Noah took Shaye's hand and they set off.

"Excited?" he asked.

"Certainly."

He cast her a sidelong glance. "Is that a little dryness I detect in your tone?"

"Me? Dryness?"

"Mmm. Do you believe we'll find a treasure?"

"Of course we'll find a treasure," she said. Her eyes were on Samson's figure striding confidently ahead.

"Forget about my uncle. What do *you* think?"

"Honestly?" She paused. "I doubt it."

"Are you in a betting mood?"

"You think there is a treasure?"

"Honestly? I doubt it."

"Then why bet?"

"'Cause it's fun. You say no. I say yes. Whoever wins... whoever wins..."

She was smiling. "Go on. I want to know. What will you bet?"

"How about a pair of Mets tickets?"

"Boo-hiss."

"How about a weekend in the country?"

"Not bad." She pursed her lips. "What country?"

He chuckled. She'd deftly ruled out his place in Vermont. "Say Canada—the Gaspé Peninsula?"

"Getting warm."

"England—Cornwall?"

"Getting warmer."

"France?"

"A small château in Normandy?" At his nod, she grinned. "You're on."

He studied her upturned face. "You look happy. Feeling that confident you'll win?"

"No. But win or lose I get to visit Normandy."

He threw back his head with an exaggerated, "Ahh," and made no mention of the fact that according to the terms of the bet, win or lose, she'd be visiting Normandy with *him*. For a weekend? No way. It'd be a full week or two if he had his say.

Draping an arm around her shoulder, he held her to his side. Their hips bumped as they walked. She suspected he was purposely doing it and, in the spirit of fun, she bumped him right back. They were nearly into an all-out-kick-and-dodge match when Samson's applause cut into their play.

"Bravo! Nice footwork there, Shaye. Noah, your legs are too long. Better quit while you're ahead." Turning his back on them, he propped his hands on his hips and studied the shoreline. "This is our starting point."

"Quit while I'm ahead," Noah muttered under his breath as he looked around. There wasn't a rock in sight. He lowered his head toward Shaye's. "Seaweed, driftwood, sand and palm trees. That's it."

"Ahh, but beyond the palm trees—"

"More palm trees."

"And a wealth of other trees and shrubs—"

"And monkeys and parrots and alligators—"

"Alligators! Are you kidding?"

"Would I kid you about something like that?"

"Victoria," Shaye cried plaintively, "you didn't tell me there'd be alligators!"

"No problem, sweetheart," Victoria said breezily. "Just watch where you step."

Samson started toward the palms and gestured for them to follow. Within ten minutes it was clear that they were going to have to broaden the search. They'd seen quite a few rocks among the foliage, but nothing of significant size and nothing remotely resembling a rose.

"Let's fan out. Shaye, you and Noah head south. Victoria and I will head north. Don't go farther inland then we are now, and head back out to the beach in, say—'' he checked his watch ''—half an hour. Okay?''

''Okay,'' Shaye and Noah answered together. They stood watching as Samson and Victoria started off.

Noah raked damp spikes of hair from his forehead. ''Man, it's warm in here.''

''Do you want to take off your shirt?''

''And get bitten alive?'' He swatted something by his ear. ''Was there any insect repellent in the dingy?''

''I think Samson had some in his pocket.''

''Lots of good it'll do us there,'' he grumbled, then did an about-face to study the area Samson had assigned them. ''Wish we had a machete.''

''It's not that dense.'' She took a quick breath. ''Noah, wouldn't alligators prefer a wetter area?''

''There are marshes just a little bit inland.'' He was studying the jungle growth. ''I think if we work back and forth diagonally we'll be able to cover the most space in the least time.''

''Is it alligators that bite, or crocodiles?''

''Crocs, I think.'' He rubbed his hands together, clearly working up enthusiasm. ''Okay. L-l-l-l-l-let's hit it!''

Shaye stayed slightly behind Noah on the assumption that he'd scare away anything crawling in their path. She kept a lookout on either side, more than once catching herself when her eyes skimmed right past a rock formation simply because it didn't have a scaly back, a long tail, four squat legs and an ominous snout.

They followed a zigzag pattern, working slowly from jungle to shore and back. Soon after the third shore turn, they stopped short.

''It is a large rock,'' Shaye said cautiously.

''Would you go so far as to call it a boulder?''

''Depends how you define boulder. But it does have odd markings. Do you think it resembles a rose?''

Noah tipped his head and, squinted. ''With a stretch of the imagination.''

''Mmm. Let's look around a little more.''

They completed that zig and the next zag and found a number of rocks that could, by that same stretch of the imagination, be said to resemble a rose. None were as large, though, and none stood alone as the first had.

"That has to be it," Noah decided.

Against her better judgment, Shaye felt a glimmer of excitement. "Let's tell the others." They started back. When they cleared the palms, they saw Samson and Victoria heading their way.

"We found it!" Shaye cried.

Victoria stopped short. "*We* found it!"

"Oh boy," Noah murmured.

Samson beamed. It looked as though they had a double puzzle on their hands, which was going to make the adventure that much more exciting.

Chapter Ten

THE FOUR TREKKED from one rock to the other. ''Either could be it,'' Victoria decided.

''Or neither,'' said Shaye.

Noah mopped his face on the sleeve of his T-shirt. ''If you ask me, there are half a dozen other rocks here that could fit the bill.'' He received three dirty looks so quickly that he held up a hand. ''Okay. Okay. I'll admit that these two are more distinctive than the others.'' He frowned at the rock. ''What do you think, Samson—could the markings be man-made?''

''They could be, but I don't think they are. Even allowing for lousy artistry and the effects of time, something man-made would be more exact. These are just irregular enough to look authentic.''

''Which leaves the major problem of choosing between the two rocks,'' Shaye reminded them. ''Does the map give any clue?''

Samson removed the map from his shirt pocket and extended it to her. She unfolded it and studied it. Victoria peered in from her right side, Noah hung over her left shoulder.

After a short time, Shaye and Victoria looked at each other in dismay. ''You were right before,'' Victoria told Noah. ''According to the map, the rose is smack in the middle of the back stretch of beach. But there wasn't any rose-shaped rock there. It has to be one of these two.''

''But which one?'' Shaye asked.

''Which looks more like a rose?''

''I don't know, so we're back to square one.''

Victoria held up a finger. ''I want to look at the other rock.'' Grabbing Shaye's arm, she propelled her through the jungle to the second rock.

Samson and Noah didn't move. They waited until the women returned, then Noah asked, ''Okay, ladies, which rock will it be?''

"This one—"

"That one—"

He dug into his shorts pocket. "I'll flip a coin."

"You can't flip a coin on something as crucial," Victoria cried.

Shaye agreed.

"I don't have a coin anyway," Noah said and turned to Samson. "Got a coin?"

Samson produced a jackknife. "We'll let it fall. The slant of the handle will determine which rock we go with."

"A jackknife—"

"Is worse than a coin!"

The women were overruled. Samson flipped the knife. They went with the southern rock, the one Shaye and Noah had found and, coincidentally, the one Shaye thought looked more like a rose.

Putting defeat behind her, Victoria read off instructions from the map. "Seventeen paces due west."

"How long is a 'pace'?" Shaye asked.

"An average stride. Noah, you walk it off."

"Noah's stride can't be average. Samson, you walk it off."

"Samson is nearly as tall as Noah," Victoria pointed out. "Shaye you do it. Just stretch your stride a little."

With the others supervising, Shaye accepted and consulted the compass, marked off fifteen paces due west, then stopped.

"You need two more," Noah said.

"Two more paces will take me into the middle of that bromeliad colony. What do the instructions say from there, Victoria?"

"Twenty paces due south."

"Twenty paces due south," Shaye murmured, making estimates as she positioned herself on the south side of the bromeliads. "Say we're two paces south now. Three...four... five..."

Her progress was broken from time to time by another bit of the forest that was impenetrable, but she finally managed to reach twenty. Victoria, Samson and Noah were by her side.

"What now?" she asked.

"Southeast twenty-one paces," Victoria read.

"This is really pretty inexact—"

"Twenty-one paces," Noah coaxed. "Walk 'em off."

Compass in hand, she started walking. Victoria counted, while Samson followed the progress with an indulgent smile on his face. In the same manner they worked their way through additional twists and turns.

"What next?" Shaye finally asked.

"Nothing," Victoria said. "That's it. A big X on the map. You're standing on the treasure."

Shaye looked at the hard-packed sand beneath her feet. "It could be here, or here." She pointed three feet to the right. "Or even over there. Now, if we had some kind of metal detector, we might be in business."

"No metal detector," Samson said. "That would be cheating."

"But treasure hunters always use metal detectors," Shaye argued.

"We don't have one," Noah said in a tone that settled the matter. If there was no metal detector, there was no metal detector.

Shaye pointed straight down and raised skeptical eyes to Noah, who gave a firm nod.

A quick trip to the dingy produced the digging equipment and a knapsack that Victoria had filled with sandwiches and cans of soda earlier that morning. The soda had gone a little warm, but none of them complained. It was thirst quenching. The sandwiches were energizing. The insect repellent was better late than never.

They started digging in pairs, trading off every few minutes. There were diversions—a trio of spider monkeys swinging through the nearby trees, the chatter of a distant parrot—and the occasional reward of a quick swim in the bay. But by three in the afternoon, they had a large, deep hole and no treasure.

They'd initially dug down three feet, then another, then had widened the hole until it was nearly five feet in diameter. Now Noah stood at its center with his arms propped on the shovel handle. He looked hot and tired.

Shaye, who'd stopped digging several minutes before, sat on the edge of the hole. Victoria was beside her, and Samson stood behind them with a pensive look on his face.

"How much deeper do we go before we give up?" Shaye asked softly. She felt every bit as hot and tired as Noah looked.

"It has to be here," Victoria said. "Maybe we marked it out wrong."

"It *doesn't* have to be here," Shaye reminded her. "We knew there was the possibility the map was a sham."

Noah leaned against their side of the pit. He pushed his hair back with his forearm, smudging grime with the sweat. "I've dug the pick in another foot and hit nothing. I doubt a pirate would have buried anything deeper than this."

"If only we knew what we were looking for," Victoria mused. "Large box, small box, tiny leather pouch..."

Shaye sighed. "It's like trying to find a needle in a haystack, and you don't even know which haystack to look in."

"The other rock," said Noah. "It has to be that. We picked the wrong one to start pacing from." He hoisted himself from the hole. "Y'know, whoever drew up this map was either a jokester, a romantic or an imbecile."

Shaye was right beside him, followed by Victoria and Samson, as he strode quickly toward the other rock. "What do you mean?"

"The directions. They were given in paces west, south, southeast, etc., when we would have reached the same spot by one set of paces heading due south. When I first saw the map, I assumed there were natural barriers to go around, but we didn't find any." He'd reached the second rock and was studying the map. Then he closed his eyes and made some mathematical calculations.

"How many paces due south?" Samson asked.

"Let's try sixty-five."

He stood back while Shaye marked sixty-five paces due south. When she finished counting, she was standing directly before the first rock. She looked up at the others.

Victoria was the only one who seemed to share her surprise. "Let's walk it off the original way," she suggested.

So Shaye went back, walked through the directions again, and wound up in the same spot, directly before the second rock. "He was a jokester," she decided in dismay.

Samson scratched the back of his head. "He has made things interesting."

"Interesting?" Victoria echoed, then grinned. "Mmm, I suppose he's done that." She shifted her gaze from Samson to Noah, who was striding off. "Where are you going?"

"To get the shovels."

"We're not going to do this now, are we?"

"Why not?"

Shaye ran after him, looping her elbow through his when she caught up. "Isn't it a little late in the day to start something new?"

"It's only four."

"But we've been digging all day."

"All afternoon," he corrected.

"The treasure's not going anywhere."

His eyes twinkled. "I'm curious to see if it's there."

"But wouldn't it be smarter to start again fresh tomorrow morning?"

Having arrived back at the first hole, he scooped up the pick and shovels. Then he leaned in close to Shaye and whispered, "But if we finish this up tonight, we can do whatever we want tomorrow."

She took in a shaky breath and whispered back, "But aren't you tired?"

"Are you?"

"Yes. And it looks like it might rain any minute."

"Then we'll have to work quickly," he said with a mischievous grin and started back toward the rock.

As it happened, Noah did most of the work. Shaye made a show of assisting, silently reasoning that she was young and strong. But the digging she'd done earlier had taken its toll. She was tired. She had blisters. To make matters worse, the hole was only three feet deep and wide when it started to drizzle.

"Leave it," Shaye urged.

Samson agreed. "She's right, Noah. We can finish in the morning."

"No way," he grunted, setting to work with greater determination. "Another eighteen inches either way." He hoisted a shovelful of wet sand and tossed it aside with another grunt. "That's all we need."

"We can do it tomorrow—"

"And have the rain wash the sand—" another toss, another grunt "—back into this hole during the night? Just a little more now—give me forty-five minutes." Another shovelful hit the pile. "If I haven't struck anything by then, I'll quit."

The rain grew heavier. When Shaye eased into the hole and

started to shovel again, Noah set her bodily back up on the edge. Likewise, when Samson tried to give a hand, Noah insisted that he could work more freely on his own.

They were all soaked, but no one complained. The rain offered relief from the heat. Unfortunately, though, it made Noah's work harder. Each shovelful of sand was wetter and heavier than the one before, and, if anything, he seemed bent on making this hole bigger than the last. He was obviously tiring. And neither the shovel nor the pick, which he periodically used, were turning up anything remotely resembling hidden treasure.

Then it happened. Shaye was watching Noah work under the edge of the large rock, wondering what would happen if the rain lessened the stability of the sand, when suddenly that side of the hole began to crumble.

"Noah!" she cried, but the rock was already sliding. Through eyes wide with horror, she saw Noah twist to the side and try to scramble away without success. He gave a deep cry of pain as the lower half of his right leg was pinned beneath the rock. In a second, Shaye had shimmied down into the narrow space left and was pushing against the rock, as were Samson and Victoria from above.

It wouldn't budge.

"Oh God," Shaye whispered. She took a quick look at Noah's ashen face and pushed harder, but the rock had sunk snugly in the hole with precious little space for maneuvering.

Samson, too, was pale, but he kept calm. "Let me take your place, Shaye. You and Victoria scoot up against the side, put your feet flat against the rock and push as hard as you can when I say so."

They hurried into position. He gave the word. They pushed. Nothing happened.

"Again," he ordered. "Now!"

Nothing happened that time or, when they'd slightly altered position, the next. Even Noah tried then, though he wasn't at the best angle—or in the best condition—to help. Despite the varied attempts they made, the rock didn't move.

Samson shook his head. "We can't get leverage. If we could only raise it the tiniest bit, even for a few seconds, you could pull free. A broom handle would snap. We could try a palm—"

Noah gave a rough shake of his head and muttered, "Too thick."

"Not at the top, but it's too weak there. We need metal."

"We don't have metal," Noah said tightly. The lower part of his leg was numb, but pain was shooting through his thigh. In an attempt to ease the pressure, he turned and sank sideways on the sand.

Shaye's heart was pounding. She couldn't take her eyes off him. "There has to be something on the *Golden Echo* we can use," she said frantically, then tacked on an even more frantic, "isn't there?"

Noah groped for her hand, but it was Samson to whom he spoke. "There's nothing on the boat. You'll have to go for help."

Samson had reached the same conclusion and was already on his feet and motioning for Victoria. "We'll make a quick trip to the boat for supplies. You'll stay here, Shaye?"

"Yes!"

With a nod, he was gone.

Shaye turned back to Noah. He was resting his head against the side of the hole. She combed the wet hair from his forehead. "How do you feel?"

He was breathing heavily. "Not great."

"Think it's broken?"

"Yup."

"I should have seen it coming. I should have been able to warn you."

"My fault. I was careless. Too tired." The word broke into a gasp. "I usually do better—"

She put a finger to his lips. "Shh. Save your strength."

He grabbed her hand. "Stay close."

She slid into the narrow space facing him and tucked his hand beneath her chin. For a long time neither of them spoke. The rain continued to fall. Noah closed his eyes against the pain that he could feel more clearly now below his knee.

Shaye alternately watched him and the shore. "Where are they?" she demanded finally in a tight, panicky whisper.

Noah didn't answer. It was fast getting dark. The rain continued to fall.

Samson and Victoria returned at last with a replenished knapsack, rain ponchos and two lanterns. Then Samson knelt with a hand on Noah's shoulder. "We'll be back as soon as we can. There are painkillers in the sack. Don't be a hero, and whatever you do, don't try to tug that leg free now or you'll make the damage worse."

Noah, who'd already figured that out, simply nodded.

"Hurry," Shaye whispered, hugging both Victoria and Samson before they left. "Hurry." Moments later, she watched them push off in the dingy, then she sank down beside Noah and put her hand to his cheek. "Can I get you anything?"

He shook his head.

"Food?"

Again he shook his head.

"Drink?"

"Later."

She didn't bother to ask if he wanted the poncho. She knew that he wouldn't. In spite of the rain, the night was warm. It did occur to her, though, that they'd feel more comfortable if they were leaning against rubber rather than grit. Popping up, she spread the ponchos over the side of the hole. Noah shifted and helped, then sank back against them with his head tipped up to the rain. Very gently, she washed the lingering grime from his face with her fingers, then slid back to his side and watched him silently.

His facial muscles twitched, then rested. His brow furrowed, then relaxed. Then he swore under his breath.

"The leg?"

"God, it hurts."

"Damn the rose. I had a feeling. I knew it would be bad luck."

"No. My own stupid fault. I was so determined to dig, so determined to find that treasure."

"It was the bet—"

"Uh-uh. I just wanted to get it done. But I should have anticipated the problem. Take the ground out from under a rock and it's gonna fall."

"You didn't take much out. I had to have been the rain."

"I should have seen it coming."

"*I* should have. I was the one sitting there watching. If I'd been able to give you a few more seconds' warning..."

Noah curved his hand around the back of her neck and brought her face to his throat. "Not your fault." He kissed her temple and left his mouth there. "I'm glad you're with me."

She lifted her face and kissed him. "I just wish there were something I could do to make you more comfortable."

"How about...that drink..."

She quickly dug into the knapsack, extracted first a can of Coke, then, more satisfactorily, a bottle of wine. Tugging out the cork, she handed it to him. "Want a sandwich with it?"

He tipped the bottle and took several healthy swallows. "And dilute the effects? No way?"

"You want to get smashing drunk?"

He took another drink. "Not smashing. Just mildly." He closed his eyes again, and the expression of pain that crossed his face tore right through Shaye.

"Is it getting worse?" she whispered fearfully.

He said nothing for a minute, but seemed to be gritting his teeth. Then he took a shaky breath and opened his eyes. "Talk to me."

"About what?"

"You."

"Me? There's nothing much to say—"

"I want to hear about the past. I want to hear about all the things you've sidestepped before."

"I haven't—"

"You have."

She searched his eyes, seeing things that went beyond the physical pain he was experiencing. "Why does it matter?"

"Because I love you."

She put her fingertips to his mouth, caressing his lips moments before she leaned forward and kissed them. "I didn't expect you in my life, Noah," she breathed brokenly, then kissed him again.

"Tell me what you feel."

"Frightened. Confused." She sought out his lips again, craving their drugging effect.

He gave himself up to her kiss, but as soon as it ended, the pain was back. "Talk to me."

She carried his hand to her mouth and kissed his knuckles.

"My leg hurts like hell, Shaye. If you want to help, you can give me something to think about beside the fact that it's probably broken in at least three places."

"Don't say that—"

"Not to mention scraped raw."

"Noah—"

"I may well be lame for life."

"Don't even think that!"

"Tell me you wouldn't care."

"If you were lame? Of course, I'd care! The thought of your being in pain—"

"Tell me that you wouldn't care if I were lame, that you'd love me anyway."

"I'd love you if *both* legs were lame! What a stupid thing to ask."

"Not stupid," he said quietly, soberly, almost grimly. "Not stupid at all. Do you love me, Shaye?"

Shocked, she looked at him.

"Do you?" he prodded.

She bit her lip. "Yes."

"You haven't thought about it before now?"

"I've tried not to."

"But you do love me?"

She frowned. "If loving a person means that you like him even when you hate him, that you think about him all the time, that you hurt when he's hurt—" she took a tremulous breath "—the answer is yes."

"Ahh, baby," he said with a groan that held equal parts relief and pain. He drew her in close and held her as tightly as his awkward sideways position would allow.

"I love you," she whispered against his chest, "do love you."

His arms tightened. He winced, then groaned, then mumbled, "Talk to me. Talk to me, Shaye. Please?"

There seemed no point in holding back. With the confession he'd drawn from her, Noah had broken down the last of her defenses. He knew her. He knew what made her tick. He knew what pleased her, hurt her, drove her wild. Revealing the details of her past to him was little more than a formality.

Closing her eyes, Shaye began to talk. She told him about her childhood and the teenage years when she'd grown progressively wild. She told him about going off to college, about being free and irresponsible and believing that she had the world on a string. She told him about the boys and the men, the trips, the adventures, the apartments and the garret. Once started, she spilled it all. She wanted Noah to know everything.

For the most part, he listened quietly. Once or twice he made ceremony of wiping the rain from his face, but she suspected he was covering up a wince. At those times she stopped, offered him aspirin, and finally plied him with more wine, which was all the painkilling he'd accept. And she went on talking.

Only when she was near the end did she falter. She grew still, eyes downcast, hands tightly clenched.

"What happened then?" he prodded in a voice weakened by pain. "You were with André when you got a call from Shannon, and...?"

She raked her teeth over her lower lip.

"Shaye?"

She took a broken breath. "She was in trouble. She'd been hanging around a pal of André's named Geoff, and when he introduced her to another guy, a friend of his, she didn't think anything of it. The friend turned out to be from the vice squad. Poor Shannon. She was nineteen at the time, not nearly sophisticated enough to protect herself from the Geoffs of the world. He was picked up on a dozen charges. She was arrested for possession of cocaine. She never knew what hit her."

"And you blamed yourself."

"I was at fault. I'd introduced her to André, André had introduced her to Geoff. I should have checked Geoff out myself." She waved a hand impatiently. "But it was more than that. The whole *scene* was wrong. Rebellion for the sake of rebellion, adventure of the sake of adventure, sex for the sake of sex—very little that went deeper, and nothing at all that resulted in personal growth. For six years I did that." She was shaking all over. "Blame myself? Not only was I responsible for what happened to Shannon, by rights, I should have been the one arrested!"

"Shh," Noah whispered against her temple. "It's okay."

"It's not!"

"What finally happened to Shannon?"

Shaye took several quick breaths to calm herself. "Victoria came to the rescue. She introduced us to a lawyer friend who introduced us to another lawyer friend, and between the two of them, Shannon got off with a suspended sentence and probation. She went on for a degree in communications and has a terrific job now in Hartford."

He shifted, and swallowed down a moan. The pain in his leg

was excruciating. He had to keep his mind off it. "Sounds like she got off lighter than you did," he said tightly.

"Lighter?"

"You sentenced yourself to a lifetime of hard labor."

"No. I just decided to become very sane and sensible."

"Where do I fit into sane and sensible?"

She smoothed wet hair back from her forehead with the flat of her hand. "I don't know."

"Do you see me as being sane and sensible?"

"In some respects, yes. In others, no."

"And the 'no's' frighten you."

She nodded.

"Why?"

"Because I can't control them. Because you can be spontaneous and impulsive and irreverent, and that's everything I once was that nearly ended tragically!"

"But you like it when I'm that way. That's part of the attraction."

"I know," she wailed.

"And it's not bad. Look at it rationally, Shaye. You're nearly thirty now. Your entire outlook on life has matured since the days when you were wild." He caught in a breath, squeezed his eyes shut, finally went on in a raspy voice. "But you haven't found a man to love because the men you allow yourself to see don't excite you. You'd never have allowed yourself to see me if we'd met back in civilization, would you?"

"No."

"But there's nothing wrong with what we share! Okay, so we go nuts together in bed. Is that harmful? If it's just the two of us, and we're consenting adults, and we get up in the morning perfectly sane and sensible. Where's the harm?" His voice had risen steadily in pitch, and he was breathing raggedly by the time he finished.

"Oh God, Noah," she whispered. "What can I do—"

"Talk. Just talk."

She did, trying her best to tune out his pain. "I hear what you're saying. It makes perfect sense. But then I get to worrying and even the sensible seems precarious."

"You trust me?"

"I...yes."

"And love me?"

She nodded.

"Nothing is precarious. I'll protect you."

"But I have to be responsible, myself. That was one of the first things I learned from Shannon's fiasco."

"Ahh, Shaye, Shaye..." He tightened his arm around her shoulder and pressed his cheek to her wet hair. "You've gone to extremes. You don't have to be on guard every minute. There are times to let go and times not to." He stopped, garnering his strength. "Where's the lightness in your life, the sunshine, the frivolity? We all need that sometimes. Not all the time, just sometimes. There has to be a balance—don't you see?" His words had grown more and more strained. He loosened his hold on her and took a long drink of wine.

Shaye looked up, eyes wide. She stroked the side of his face with the backs of her fingers. "Don't talk so much, Noah. Please. It must be taking something out of you."

"It's the only thing that's helping. No, that's not true. The wine helps. And you. Your being here. Marry me, Shaye. I want you to marry me."

"I—"

"It looks like the trip is going to be cut short. We have to face the future."

"But—"

"I love you, Shaye. I didn't plan to fall in love. I've never really been in love before in my life. But I do love you."

"But these are such...bizarre circumstances. How can you possibly know what your feelings will be back in the real world?"

"I know my feelings," he said with a burst of strength. "I know what's been wrong with my life, what's been missing in the women I've known. You have everything I want. You're dignified and poised and intelligent. You're witty and gentle. You're compassionate and loyal. You're gorgeous. And you're spectacular in my arms. I meant it when I said I wanted you to mother my children. I do want that, Shaye. But I want you first and foremost for *me*." He punctuated the last with a loud, involuntary groan, followed by a pithy oath.

Shaye was on her knees in a minute, cradling his dripping face with both hands. "Let me get the codeine."

He shook his head. "Wine." He lifted the bottle and swallowed as much as he could.

"Where are they?" she cried, looking out to sea.

"They've just left. Won't be back until morning."

"Morning! Why morning?"

"It's a lee coast. We lucked out yesterday. It'll take them a while to reach Limón—"

"Isn't Moin closer?"

"No resources. Samson may try it, but by the time he locates a rescue team—"

"He has to do something before morning. You're in pain."

"Make that agony."

"This is no time for joking, Noah."

"I'm not."

"Oh. Oh God, isn't there anything I can do?"

"Say you'll marry me."

"I'll marry you."

"Ahh. Feels better already." He pried his head from the poncho. "Is there another bottle of wine?"

She reached for the bottle he held and saw that it was nearly empty. With relief, she found two more bottles in the knapsack. Opening one, she gave it to Noah in exchange for the first, the contents of which she proceeded to indulge in herself.

Had she just agreed to marry Noah?

She took another drink.

He drew her against his chest and encircled her with his arms, leaving the wine bottle to dangle against her side. "I need to hold on," he said, his voice husky with pain.

"Hold on," she whispered. "Hold on."

They sat like that for a while. Shaye heard the rain and the lap of the sea on the shore, but mostly she heard Noah's heart, beating erratically beneath her ear.

"I'm well-respected in the community," he muttered out of the blue. "I give to charity. I pay my taxes. Okay, so I do the unexpected from time to time, but I've never done anything illegal or immoral."

Gently, soothingly, she stroked his ribs, working at the tension in the surrounding muscles.

"I'll buy us a place midway between Manhattan and Philly, so you won't have to leave your job."

She kissed his collarbone.

"In fact," he rushed on, "you don't have to work at all if you don't want to. I'm loaded."

She laughed.

"I am," he protested.

"I believe you," she said, still smiling, thinking how incredibly much she did love him.

He took a shuddering breath, then another drink of wine. "I want the whole thing—the house, the kids, the dog, the station wagon."

"You do?"

"Don't you?"

"Yes, but I didn't think you would."

"Too conventional?"

"No, no. Very stable."

He closed a fist around her ponytail, pressed her head to his throat and moaned, "This isn't how it was supposed to be. There's nothing romantic in this. It's *sick*. My damn leg's caught under a rock. I can't move. I can't sweep you off your feet and carry you to bed, or bend you back over my arm and kiss you senseless. I'm not sure I can even get it up—that's how much everything down there hurts!"

Shaye knew he was in severe pain. She knew he was feeling frustrated. She couldn't do anything about either, so she decided to use humor. "The Playboy of the Pampas—impotent?"

"Not impotent—temporarily sidelined. You'll still marry me, won't you?"

"I'll still marry you." She took a deep breath and looked around. "It is a waste, though. We did so well in the rain last night, just think of what we could have done tonight." She moved her lips against his jaw, her voice an intimate whisper. "I'd like to make love in the water. Not deep water—shallow, just a few feet out from shore. Do you remember how it was when we were swimming? Only this time neither of us would have suits on, and there'd be a sandy floor for maneuvering, but the tide would wash around us. I'd wrap my legs around you—"

Noah interrupted her with a feral growl. "Enough. You've made your point."

"I have?"

He tried to shift to a more comfortable position, which was nearly impossible, given the circumstances.

Shaye felt instantly contrite. "Can I help?" she whispered, dropping her hand to his swollen sex.

He covered it and pressed it close for a minute, then raised it to his chest. "I think I'll take a rain check."

He took another drink, then held the bottle to her lips while she did the same. The sounds of the rain and the sea and the jungle night surrounded them, and for a time they sat in silence. Then Shaye asked, "The lanterns will keep the alligators away, won't they?"

He nodded.

"Hungry?"

He shook his head.

"Is there any chance of this hole flooding?"

He shook his head again.

"Do you have Blue Cross-Blue Shield?"

"Through the nose." A little while later, he said, "Maybe you're pregnant."

"No."

"Are you taking the pill?"

"No. But my period just ended. Last night was about as safe a time as any could be."

He considered that, then said, "No wonder you felt so lousy at the start of the trip."

She snorted. "You should have seen me when we first got to the hotel in Barranquilla."

"Don't use anything."

"What?"

"When we make love. I like knowing that there's a chance..."

"You really do want children."

"Very much. If you want to wait, though. I'll understand."

But the more she thought about it, the more Shaye liked the idea of growing big with Noah's child. She smiled into the night.

"You are going to marry me, aren't you?" he asked.

"I've said I would."

"What if you change your mind?"

"I won't."

"What if you have second thoughts when we get back home?"

"I won't."

"Why not?"

"I can't answer that now. Ask me again later."

He did, several times during the course of the night, but it wasn't until a pair of helicopters closed noisily in on the beach the following morning that Shaye had an answer for him.

She'd been with Noah throughout the night, had suffered with him and worried for him, had done what little she could to make him comfortable. She'd forced him to eat half a sandwich for the sake of his strength and had limited her own intake of wine to leave more for him. She'd sponged him off when the rain stopped and the air grew thick and heavy. She'd batted mosquitoes from his skin and had held his hand tightly when he'd twisted in pain.

The night had been hell. She never wanted to live through another like it. But she knew she wouldn't have been anywhere else in the world that night, and that was what she told Noah when the sheer relief of his impending rescue loosened her thoughts.

"You have the ability to make me happy, sad, excited, frustrated, angry, aroused and confused—but through it all I feel incredibly alive."

She combed her fingers through his hair. "You have the spirit and the sense of adventure I had before, only you've channeled it right." Affectionately she brushed some sand off his neck. "I want you to help me do that. Make my life full. Be my friend and protector." She kissed his forehead. "And lover. I want all that and more." She shot a glance at the crew bounding from the chopper, then tacked on, "Think you can handle it?"

He was a mess—dirty, sweaty, with one leg crushed beneath a boulder—but the look he sent her was eloquent in promise and love. She knew that she'd never, never forget it.

Epilogue

"TWO HELICOPTERS?" Deirdre asked.

Victoria nodded. "One for the medics, the other for the fellows who raised the rock."

Leah winced. "Noah must have been out of his mind with pain by that time."

"He was out of it with something—whether pain or wine, I'll never know. The doctors in Limón did a preliminary patch-up job while Samson arranged for our transportation home. Noah's had surgery twice in the six weeks we've been back. He's scheduled to go in for a final procedure next week."

"Is the prognosis good?"

"Excellent, thank God. But even if it weren't, Noah's a fighter." She sighed. "He's quite a man."

Deirdre curled her legs beneath her on the chaise. It was the last day in August, a rare cool, dry, sunny summer day in New York, and Victoria's rooftop garden was the place to be. "When did they get married?"

Victoria smiled. "Four days after we got back. It was beautiful. Very simple. A judge, their closest friends and relatives." Her eyes grew misty. "Shaye was radiant. I know they say that about all brides, but she was. She positively glowed. And when Noah...presented her with...that single rose..."

Leah handed her a tissue, which Victoria waved around, as though it didn't occur to her to wipe her tears.

"When he gave her the rose, he said...he said—" her voice dropped to a tremulous whisper "—so softly and gently that I wouldn't have heard if I hadn't been standing right there..."

Both women were waiting wide-eyed. Deirdre leaned forward and asked urgently, "What did he say?"

Victoria sniffled. "He said, 'One rose. Just one. Pure, fresh and new. And it's in our hands.'" She took in a shuddering breath. "It was so...beautiful..." She pressed the tissue to her trembling lip.

Leah didn't understand the deeper significance of Noah's words any more than Deirdre did, but the romance of it was still there. She sighed loudly, then burst into a helpless smile. "Victoria Lesser strikes again." She was delighted with Victoria's latest story. She'd had no idea what to expect when Victoria had invited her down for a visit, and now she couldn't wait to get back to tell Garrick. But there was still more she wanted to know. "What about you and Samson?"

Victoria took a minute to collect herself. "Yes?"

"I thought you liked him. You said that in spite of the accident the trip was wonderful."

"It was."

"Well?" Deirdre prompted. "Is that all you have to say—just that it was wonderful? Neil will spend the entire night cross-examining me if I don't have anything better to give him when I get home."

Gracefully pushing herself from her chair, Victoria breezed across the garden to pluck a dried petal from a hanging begonia. "It'd serve you right," she said airily, "after what the four of you did."

"It was poetic justice," Deirdre argued.

Leah agreed. "Just deserts."

"A taste of your own medicine."

"*Lex talionis.*" When Victoria turned to arch a brow her way, Leah translated. "The law of retribution. But all with the best of intentions." She paused. "So. Were our good intentions in vain?"

Victoria hesitated for a long moment. Her gaze skipped from Leah's face to Deirdre's. Then she slanted them both a mischievous grin. "I won't remarry, you know."

"We know," Deirdre said.

"He was...very nice."

Leah held her breath. "And...?"

"And we've decided to make a return visit to Costa Rica next summer to find out for sure whether that treasure does exist. Noah and Shaye weren't thrilled with that thought; they're hung up on the idea of going to some château in Normandy. So we'll just have to put together another group. In the meantime, Samson thought he'd do a bicycle tour of the Rhineland and asked if I'd like to go along."

"Where does he get the time?" Deirdre asked. "I thought he taught."

"Vacations, sweetheart. Vacations." Her eyes twinkled and her cheeks grew pink. "And weekends. There are lovely things that can be done on weekends." Turning her back on the two younger women, she busied herself hand pruning a small dogwood. "I was thinking that I'd drive north next month. The foliage is beautiful when it turns. Samson has invited me to stay with him in Hanover, claims he makes a mean apple cider. Now, theoretically, making apple cider should be as boring as sin. But then, theoretically, Latin professors should be as boring as sin, too, and Samson isn't. I guess I'll have to give his apple cider a shot...."

Keeper of the Bride

Tess
GERRITSEN

Chapter One

The wedding was off. Cancelled. Canned. Kaput.

Nina Cormier sat staring at herself in the church dressing room mirror and wondered why she couldn't seem to cry. She knew the pain was there, deep and terrible beneath the numbness, but she didn't feel it. Not yet. She could only sit dry-eyed, staring at her reflection. The picture-perfect image of a bride. Her veil floated in gossamer wisps about her face. The bodice of her ivory satin dress, embroidered with seed pearls, hung fetchingly off-shoulder. Her long black hair was gathered into a soft chignon. Everyone who'd seen her that morning in the dressing room—her mother, her sister Wendy, her stepmother Daniella—had declared her a beautiful bride.

And she *would* have been. Had the groom bothered to show up.

He didn't even have the courage to break the news to her in person. After six months of planning and dreaming, she'd received his note just twenty minutes before the ceremony. Via the best man, no less.

Nina,
I need time to think about this. I'm sorry, I really am. I'm leaving town for a few days. I'll call you.
Robert

She forced herself to read the note again.

I need time.... I need time....

How much time does a man need? she wondered.

A year ago, she'd moved in with Dr. Robert Bledsoe. It's the only way to know if we're compatible, he'd told her. Marriage was such a major commitment, a permanent commitment, and he didn't want to make a mistake. At 41, Robert had known his share of disastrous relationships. He was determined not to make any more mistakes. He wanted to be sure that Nina was the one he'd been waiting for all his life.

She'd been certain Robert was the man *she'd* been waiting for. So certain that, on the very day he'd suggested they live together, she'd gone straight home and packed her bags....

"Nina? Nina, open the door!" It was her sister Wendy, rattling the knob. "Please let me in."

Nina dropped her head in her hands. "I don't want to see anyone right now."

"You need to be with someone."

"I just want to be alone."

"Look, the guests have all gone home. The church is empty. It's just me out here."

"I don't want to talk to anyone. Just go home, will you? Please, just go."

There was a long silence outside the door. Then Wendy said, "If I leave now, how're you going to get home? You'll need a ride."

"Then I'll call a cab. Or Reverend Sullivan can drive me. I need some time to think."

"You're sure you don't want to talk?"

"I'm sure. I'll call you later, okay?"

"If that's what you really want." Wendy paused, then added, with a note of venom that penetrated even through the oak door, "Robert's a jerk, you know. I might as well tell you. I've always thought he was."

Nina didn't answer. She sat at the dressing table, her head in her hands, wanting to cry, but unable to squeeze out a single tear. She heard Wendy's footsteps fade away, then heard only the silence of the empty church. Still no tears would come. She couldn't think about Robert right now. Instead, her mind seemed to focus stubbornly on the practical aspects of a cancelled wedding. The catered reception and all that uneaten food. The gifts she had to return. The nonrefundable airline tickets to St. John Island. Maybe she should go on that honeymoon anyway and forget Dr. Robert Bledsoe. She'd go by herself, just her and her bikini. Out of this whole heartbreaking affair, at least she'd come out with a tan.

Slowly she raised her head and once again looked at her reflection in the mirror. Not such a beautiful bride after all, she thought. Her lipstick was smeared and her chignon was coming apart. She was turning into a wreck.

With sudden rage she reached up and yanked off the veil. Hairpins flew in every direction, releasing a rebellious tumble of black hair. To hell with the veil; she tossed it in the trash can. She snatched up her bouquet of white lilies and pink sweetheart roses and slam-dunked it into the trash can as well. That felt good. Her anger was like some new and potent fuel flooding her veins. It propelled her to her feet.

She walked out of the church dressing room, the train of her gown dragging behind her, and entered the nave.

The pews were deserted. Garlands of white carnations draped the aisles, and the altar was adorned with airy sprays of pink roses and baby's breath. The stage had been beautifully set for a wedding that would never take place. But the lovely results of the florist's hard work was scarcely noticed by Nina as she strode past the altar and started up the aisle. Her attention was focused straight ahead on the front door. On escape. Even the concerned voice of Reverend Sullivan calling to her didn't slow her down. She walked past all the floral reminders of the day's fiasco and pushed through the double doors.

There, on the church steps, she halted. The July sunshine glared in her eyes, and she was suddenly, painfully aware of how conspicuous she must be, a lone woman in a wedding gown, trying to wave down a taxi. Only then, as she stood trapped in the brightness of afternoon, did she feel the first sting of tears.

Oh, no. Lord, no. She was going to break down and cry right here on the steps. In full view of every damn car driving past on Forest Avenue.

"Nina? Nina, dear."

She turned. Reverend Sullivan was standing on the step above her, a look of worry on his kind face.

"Is there anything I can do? Anything at all?" he asked. "If you'd like, we could go inside and talk."

Miserably she shook her head. "I want to get away from here. Please, I just want to get away."

"Of course. Of course." Gently, he took her arm. "I'll drive you home."

Reverend Sullivan led her down the steps and around the side of the building, to the staff parking lot. She gathered up her train, which by now was soiled from all that dragging, and climbed into his car. There she sat with all the satin piled high on her lap.

Reverend Sullivan slid in behind the wheel. The heat was stifling inside the car, but he didn't start the engine. Instead they sat for a moment in awkward silence.

"I know it's hard to understand what possible purpose the Lord may have for all this," he said quietly. "But surely there's a reason, Nina. It may not be apparent to you at the moment. In fact, it may seem to you that the Lord has turned His back."

"Robert's the one who turned his back," she said. Sniffling, she snatched up a clean corner of her train and wiped her face. "Turned his back and ran like hell."

"Ambivalence is common for bridegrooms. I'm sure Dr. Bledsoe felt this was a big step for him—"

"A big step for *him?* I suppose marriage is just a stroll in the park for me?"

"No, no, you misunderstand me."

"Oh, please." She gave a muffled sob. "Just take me home."

Shaking his head, he put the key in the ignition. "I only wanted to explain to you, dear, in my own clumsy way, that this isn't the end of the world. It's the nature of life. Fate is always throwing surprises at us, Nina. Crises we never expect. Things that seem to pop right out of the blue."

A deafening boom suddenly shook the church building. The explosion shattered the stained glass windows, and a hail of multicolored glass shards flew across the parking lot. Torn hymn books and fragments of church pews tumbled onto the blacktop.

As the white smoke slowly cleared, Nina saw a dusting of flower petals drift gently down from the sky and settle on the windshield right in front of Reverend Sullivan's shocked eyes.

"Right out of the blue," she murmured. "You couldn't have said it better."

"YOU TWO, WITHOUT A DOUBT, are the biggest screwups of the year."

Portland police detective Sam Navarro, sitting directly across the table from the obviously upset Norm Liddell, didn't bat an eyelash. There were five of them sitting in the station conference room, and Sam wasn't about to give this prima donna D.A. the satisfaction of watching him flinch in public. Nor was Sam going to refute the charges, because they *had* screwed up. He and Gillis had screwed up big time, and now a cop was dead. An idiot cop, but a cop all the same. One of their own.

"In our defense," spoke up Sam's partner Gordon Gillis, "we never gave Marty Pickett permission to approach the site. We had no idea he'd crossed the police line—"

"You were in charge of the bomb scene," said Liddell. "That makes you responsible."

"Now, wait a minute," said Gillis. "Officer Pickett has to bear some of the blame."

"Pickett was just a rookie."

"He should've been following procedure. If he'd—"

"Shut up, Gillis," said Sam.

Gillis looked at his partner. "Sam, I'm only trying to defend our position."

"Won't do us a damn bit of good. Since we're obviously the designated fall guys." Sam leaned back in his chair and eyed Liddell across the conference table. "What do you want, Mr. D.A.? A public flogging? Our resignations?"

"No one's asking for your resignations," cut in Chief Abe Coopersmith. "And this discussion is getting us nowhere."

"*Some* disciplinary action is called for," said Liddell. "We have a dead police officer—"

"Don't you think I know that?" snapped Coopersmith. "*I'm* the one who had to answer to the widow. Not to mention all those bloodsucking reporters. Don't give me this *us* and *we* crap, Mr. D.A. It was one of *ours* who fell. A cop. *Not* a lawyer."

Sam looked in surprise at his chief. This was a new experience, having Coopersmith on his side. The Abe Coopersmith he knew was a man of few words, few of them complimentary. It was because Liddell was rubbing them all the wrong way. When under fire, cops always stuck together.

"Let's get back to the business at hand, okay?" said Coopersmith. "We have a bomber in town. And our first fatality. What do we know so far?" He looked at Sam, who was head of the newly re-formed Bomb Task Force. "Navarro?"

"Not a hell of a lot," admitted Sam. He opened a file folder and took out a sheaf of papers. He distributed copies to the other four men around the table—Liddell, Chief Coopersmith, Gillis, and Ernie Takeda, the explosives expert from the Maine State Crime Lab. "The first blast occurred around 2:15 a.m. The second blast around 2:30 a.m. It was the second one that pretty much levelled the R. S. Hancock warehouse. It also caused minor damage to two adjoining buildings. The night watchman was the one who found the first device. He noticed signs of breaking and entering, so he searched the building. The bomb was left on a desk in one of the offices. He put in the call at 1:30 a.m. Gillis got there around 1:50, I was there at 2:00 a.m. We had the blast area cordoned off and the top-vent container truck had just arrived when the first one went off. Then, fifteen minutes later—before we could search the building—the second device exploded. Killing Officer Pickett." Sam glanced at Liddell, but this time the D.A. chose to keep his mouth shut. "The dynamite was Dupont label."

There was a brief silence in the room. Then Coopersmith said, "Not the same Dupont lot number as those two bombs last year?"

"It's very likely," said Sam. "Since that missing lot number's the only reported large dynamite theft we've had up here in years."

"But the Spectre bombings were solved a year ago," said Liddell. "And we know Vincent Spectre's dead. So who's making *these* bombs?"

"We may be dealing with a Spectre apprentice. Someone who not only picked up the master's technique, but also has access to the master's dynamite supply. Which, I point out, we never located."

"You haven't confirmed the dynamite's from the same stolen lot number," said Liddell. "Maybe this has no connection at all with the Spectre bombings."

"I'm afraid we have other evidence," said Sam. "And you're not going to like it." He glanced at Ernie Takeda. "Go ahead, Ernie."

Takeda, never comfortable with public speaking, kept his gaze focused on the lab report in front of him. "Based on materials we gathered at the site," he said, "we can make a preliminary guess as to the makeup of the device. We believe the electrical action fuse was set off by an electronic delay circuit. This in turn ignited the dynamite via Prima detonating cord. The sticks were bundled together with two-inch-wide green electrical tape." Takeda cleared his throat and finally looked up. "It's the identical delay circuit that the late Vincent Spectre used in his bombings last year."

Liddell looked at Sam. "The same circuitry, the same dynamite lot? What the hell's going on?"

"Obviously," said Gillis, "Vincent Spectre passed on a few of his skills before he died. Now we've got a second generation bomber on our hands."

"What we still have to piece together," said Sam, "is the psychological profile of this newcomer. Spectre's bombings were coldbloodedly financial. He was hired to do the jobs and he did them, *bam, bam, bam.* Efficient. Effective. This new bomber has to set a pattern."

"What you're saying," said Liddell, "is that you expect him to hit again."

Sam nodded wearily. "Unfortunately, that's exactly what I'm saying."

There was a knock on the door. A patrolwoman stuck her head into the conference room. "Excuse me, but there's a call for Navarro and Gillis."

"I'll take it," said Gillis. He rose heavily to his feet and went to the conference wall phone.

Liddell was still focused on Sam. "So this is all that Portland's finest can come up with? We wait for *another* bombing so that we can establish a *pattern?* And then maybe, just *maybe,* we'll have an idea of what the hell we're doing?"

"A bombing, Mr. Liddell," said Sam calmly, "is an act of cowardice. It's violence in the absence of the perpetrator. I repeat the word—*absence.* We have no ID, no fingerprints, no witnesses to the planting, no—"

"Chief," cut in Gillis. He hung up the phone. "They've just reported another one."

"What?" said Coopersmith.

Sam had already shot to his feet and was moving for the door.

"What was it this time?" called Liddell. "Another warehouse?"

"No," said Gillis. "A church."

THE COPS ALREADY had the area cordoned off by the time Sam and Gillis arrived at the Good Shepherd Church. A crowd was gathered up and down the street. Three patrol cars, two fire trucks and an ambulance were parked haphazardly along Forest Avenue. The bomb disposal truck and its boiler-shaped carrier in the flatbed stood idly near the church's front entrance—or what was left of the front entrance. The door had been blown clear off its hinges and had come to rest at the bottom of the front steps. Broken glass was everywhere. The wind scattered torn pages of hymn books like dead leaves along the sidewalk. Gillis swore. "This was a big one."

As they approached the police line, the officer in charge turned to them with a look of relief. "Navarro! Glad you could make it to the party."

"Any casualties?" asked Sam.

"None, as far as we know. The church was unoccupied at the time. Pure luck. There was a wedding scheduled for two, but it was cancelled at the last minute."

"Whose wedding?"

"Some doctor's. The bride's sitting over there in the patrol car. She and the minister witnessed the blast from the parking lot."

"I'll talk to her later," said Sam. "Don't let her leave. Or the minister, either. I'm going to check the building for a second device."

"Better you than me."

Sam donned body armor, made of overlapping steel plates encased in nylon. He also carried a protective mask, to be worn in case a second bomb was identified. A bomb tech, similarly garbed, stood by the front door awaiting orders to enter the building. Gillis would wait outside near the truck; his role this time around was to fetch tools and get the bomb carrier ready.

"Okay," Sam said to the technician. "Let's go."

They stepped through the gaping front entrance.

The first thing Sam noticed was the smell—strong and faintly sweet. Dynamite, he thought. He recognized the odor of its aftermath. The force of the blast had caused the pews at the rear to topple backward. At the front, near the altar, the pews had been reduced to splinters. All the stained glass panels were broken, and where the windows faced south, hazy sunlight shone in through the empty frames.

Without a word between them, Sam and the tech automatically split up and moved along opposite sides of the nave. The site would be more thoroughly searched later; this time around, their focus was only on locating any second bombs. The death of Marty Pickett still weighed heavily on Sam's conscience, and he wasn't about to let any other officers enter this building until he had cleared it.

Moving in parallel, the two men paced the nave, their eyes alert for anything resembling an explosive device. All the debris made it a slow search. As they moved forward, the damage visibly worsened, and the odor of exploded dynamite grew stronger. Getting closer, he thought. The bomb was planted somewhere around here....

In front of the altar, at a spot where the first row of pews would have stood, they found the crater. It was about three feet across and shallow; the blast had ripped through the carpet and pad, but had barely chipped the concrete slab below. A shallow crater was characteristic of a low-velocity blast—again, compatible with dynamite.

They would take a closer look at it later. They continued their search. They finished with the nave and progressed to the hallways, the dressing rooms, the restrooms. No bombs. They went into the annex and surveyed the church offices, the meeting rooms, the Sunday school classroom. No bombs. They exited through a rear door and searched the entire outside wall. No bombs.

Satisfied at last, Sam returned to the police line, where Gillis was waiting. There he took off the body armor. "Building's clean," Sam said. "We got the searchers assembled?"

Gillis gestured to the six men waiting near the bomb carrier truck. There were two patrolmen and four crime lab techs, each one clutching empty evidence bags. "They're just waiting for the word."

"Let's get the photographer in there first, then send the team in. The crater's up front, around the first row of pews on the right."

"Dynamite?"

Sam nodded. "If I can trust my nose." He turned and eyed the crowd of gawkers. "I'm going to talk to the witnesses. Where's the minister?"

"They just took him off to the ER. Chest pains. All that stress."

Sam gave an exasperated sigh. "Did anyone talk to him?"

"Patrolman did. We have his statement."

"Okay," said Sam. "I guess that leaves me with the bride."

"She's still waiting in the patrol car. Her name's Nina Cormier."

"Cormier. Gotcha." Sam ducked under the yellow police line and worked his way through the gathering of onlookers. Scanning the official vehicles, he spotted a silhouette in the front passenger seat of one of the cars. The woman didn't move as he approached; she was staring straight ahead like some wedding store mannequin. He leaned forward and tapped on the window.

The woman turned. Wide dark eyes stared at him through the glass. Despite the smudged mascara, the softly rounded feminine face was undeniably pretty. Sam motioned to her to roll down the window. She complied.

"Miss Cormier? I'm Detective Sam Navarro, Portland police."

"I want to go home," she said. "I've talked to so many cops already. Please, can't I just go home?"

"First I have to ask you a few questions."

"A few?"

"All right," he admitted. "It's more like a lot of questions."

She gave a sigh. Only then did he see the weariness in her face. "If I answer all your questions, Detective," she said, "will you let me go home?"

"I promise."

"Do you keep your promises?"

He nodded soberly. "Always."

She looked down at her hands, clasped in her lap. "Right," she muttered. "Men and their promises."

"Excuse me?"

"Oh, never mind."

He circled around the car, opened the door, and slid in behind the wheel. The woman next to him said nothing; she just sat there in resigned silence. She seemed almost swallowed up by those frothy layers of white satin. Her hairdo was coming undone and silky strands of black hair hung loose about her shoulders. Not at all the happy picture of a bride, he thought. She seemed stunned, and very much alone.

Where the hell was the groom?

Stifling an instinctive rush of sympathy, he reached for his notebook and flipped it open to a blank page. "Can I have your full name and address?"

The answer came out in a bare whisper. "Nina Margaret Cormier, 318 Ocean View Drive."

He wrote it down. Then he looked at her. She was still staring straight down at her lap. Not at him. "Okay, Miss Cormier," he said. "Why don't you tell me exactly what happened?"

SHE WANTED TO GO HOME. She had been sitting in this patrol car for an hour and a half now, had talked to three different cops, had answered all their questions. Her wedding was a shambles, she'd barely escaped with her life, and those people out there on the street kept staring at her as though she were some sort of sideshow freak.

And this man, this cop with all the warmth of a codfish, expected her to go through it again?

"Miss Cormier," he sighed. "The sooner we get this over with, the sooner you can leave. What, exactly, happened?"

"It blew up," she said. "Can I go home?"

"What do you mean by blew up?"

"There was a loud boom. Lots of smoke and broken windows. I'd say it was your typical exploding building."

"You mentioned smoke. What color was the smoke?"

"What?"

"Was it black? White?"

"Does it matter?"

"Just answer the question, please."

She gave an exasperated sigh. "It was white, I think."

"You think?"

"All right. I'm sure." She turned to look at him. For the first time she really focused on his face. If he'd been smiling, if there'd been even a trace of warmth, it would have been a pleasant enough face to look at. He was in his late thirties. He had dark brown hair that was about two weeks overdue for a trim. His face was thin, his teeth were perfect, and his deep set green eyes had the penetrating gaze one expected of a romantic lead movie cop. Only this was no movie cop. This was an honest-to-goodness cop with a badge, and he wasn't in the least bit charming. He was studying her with a completely detached air, as though sizing up her reliability as a witness.

She gazed back at him, thinking, *Here I am, the rejected bride. He's probably wondering what's wrong with me. What terrible flaws I possess that led to my being stood up at the altar.*

She buried her fists in the white satin mounded on her lap. "I'm sure the smoke was white," she said tightly. "For whatever difference that makes."

"It makes a difference. It indicates a relative absence of carbon."

"Oh. I see." Whatever that told him.

"Were there any flames?"

"No. No flames."

"Did you smell anything?"

"You mean like gas?"

"Anything at all?"

She frowned. "Not that I remember. But I was outside the building."

"Where, exactly?"

"Reverend Sullivan and I were sitting in his car. In the parking lot around the side. So I wouldn't have smelled the gas. Anyway, natural gas is odorless. Isn't it?"

"It can be difficult to detect."

"So it doesn't mean anything. That I didn't smell it."

"Did you see anyone near the building prior to the explosion?"

"There was Reverend Sullivan. And some of my family. But they all left earlier."

"What about strangers? Anyone you don't know?"

"No one was inside when it happened."

"I'm referring to the time *prior* to the explosion, Miss Cormier."

"Prior?"

"Did you see anyone who shouldn't have been there?"

She stared at him. He gazed back at her, green eyes absolutely steady. "You mean—are you thinking—"

He didn't say anything.

"It wasn't a gas leak?" she said softly.

"No," he said. "It was a bomb."

She sank back, her breath escaping in a single shocked rush. Not an accident, she thought. Not an accident at all....

"Miss Cormier?"

Wordlessly she looked at him. Something about the way he was watching her, that flat, emotionless gaze of his, made her frightened.

"I'm sorry to have to ask you this next question," he said. "But you understand, it's something I have to pursue."

She swallowed. "What...what question?"

"Do you know of anyone who might want you dead?"

Chapter Two

"This is crazy," she said. "This is absolutely nuts."
"I have to explore the possibility."
"*What* possibility? That the bomb was meant for *me?*"
"Your wedding was scheduled for two o'clock. The bomb went off at 2:40. It exploded near the front row of pews. Near the altar. There's no doubt in my mind, judging by the obvious force of the blast, that you and your entire wedding party would have been killed. Or, at the very least, seriously maimed. This *is* a bomb we're talking about, Miss Cormier. Not a gas leak. Not an accident. A bomb. It was meant to kill someone. What I have to find out is, who was the target?"
She didn't answer. The possibilities were too horrible to even contemplate.
"Who was in your wedding party?" he asked.
She swallowed. "There was…there was…"
"You and Reverend Sullivan. Who else?"
"Robert—my fiancé. And my sister Wendy. And Jeremy Wall, the best man…."
"Anyone else?"
"My father was going to give me away. And there was a flower girl and a ring bearer…"
"I'm only interested in the adults. Let's start with you."
Numbly she shook her head. "It—it wasn't me. It couldn't be me."
"Why couldn't it?"
"It's impossible."
"How can you be sure?"
"Because no one would want me dead!"
Her sharp cry seemed to take him by surprise. For a moment he was silent. Outside, on the street, a uniformed cop turned and glanced at them. Sam responded with an *everything's fine* wave of the hand, and the cop turned away again.
Nina sat clutching the rumpled hem of her gown. This man

was horrid. Sam Spade without a trace of human warmth. Though it was getting hot in the car, she found herself shivering, chilled by the lack of obvious emotion displayed by the man sitting beside her.

"Can we explore this a little more?" he said.

She said nothing.

"Do you have any ex-boyfriends, Miss Cormier? Anyone who might be unhappy about your marriage?"

"No," she whispered.

"No ex-boyfriends at all?"

"Not—not in the last year."

"Is that how long you've been with your fiancé? A year?"

"Yes."

"His full name and address, please."

"Robert David Bledsoe, M.D., 318 Ocean View Drive."

"Same address?"

"We've been living together."

"Why was the wedding cancelled?"

"You'd have to ask Robert."

"So it was his decision? To call off the wedding?"

"As the expression goes, he left me at the altar."

"Do you know why?"

She gave a bitter laugh. "I've come to the earth-shattering conclusion, Detective, that the minds of men are a complete mystery to me."

"He gave you no warning at all?"

"It was just as unexpected as that..." She swallowed. "As that bomb. If that's what it was."

"What time was the wedding called off?"

"About one-thirty. I'd already arrived at the church, wedding gown and all. Then Jeremy—Robert's best man—showed up with the note. Robert didn't even have the nerve to tell me himself." She shook her head in disgust.

"What did the note say?"

"That he needed more time. And he was leaving town for a while. That's all."

"Is it possible Robert had any reason to—"

"No, it's *not* possible!" She looked him straight in the eye. "You're asking if Robert had something to do with it. Aren't you?"

"I keep an open mind, Miss Cormier."

"Robert's not capable of violence. For God's sake, he's a doctor!"

"All right. For the moment, we'll let that go. Let's look at other possibilities. I take it you're employed?"

"I'm a nurse at Maine Medical Center."

"Which department?"

"Emergency room."

"Any problems at work? Any conflicts with the rest of the staff?"

"No. We get along fine."

"Any threats? From your patients, for instance?"

She made a sound of exasperation. "Detective, wouldn't I know if I had enemies?"

"Not necessarily."

"You're trying your damn best to make me feel paranoid."

"I'm asking you to step back from yourself. Examine your personal life. Think of all the people who might not like you."

Nina sank back in the seat. *All the people who might not like me.* She thought of her family. Her older sister Wendy, with whom she'd never been close. Her mother Lydia, married to her wealthy snob of a husband. Her father George, now on his fourth wife, a blond trophy bride who considered her husband's off-spring a nuisance. It was one big, dysfunctional family, but there were certainly no murderers among them.

She shook her head. "No one, Detective. There's no one."

After a moment he sighed and closed his notebook. "All right, Miss Cormier. I guess that's all for now."

"For now?"

"I'll probably have other questions. After I talk to the rest of the wedding party." He opened the car door, got out, and pushed the door shut. Through the open window he said, "If you think of anything, anything at all, give me a call." He scribbled in his notebook and handed her the torn page with his name, Detective Samuel I. Navarro, and a phone number. "It's my direct line," he said. "I can also be reached twenty-four hours a day through the police switchboard."

"Then...I can go home now?"

"Yes." He started to walk away.

"Detective Navarro?"

He turned back to her. She had not realized how tall he was. Now, seeing his lean frame at its full height, she wondered how he'd ever fit in the seat beside her. "Is there something else, Miss Cormier?" he asked.

"You said I could leave."

"That's right."

"I don't have a ride." She nodded toward the bombed-out church. "Or a phone either. Do you think you could give my mother a call? To come get me?"

"Your mother?" He glanced around, obviously anxious to palm off this latest annoyance. Finally, with a look of resignation, he circled around to her side of the car and opened the door. "Come on. We can go in my car. I'll drive you."

"Look, I was only asking you to make a call."

"It's no trouble." He extended his hand to help her out. "I'd have to go by your mother's house anyway."

"My mother's house? Why?"

"She was at the wedding. I'll need to talk to her, too. Might as well kill two birds with one stone."

What a gallant way to put it, she thought.

He was still reaching out to her. She ignored his outstretched hand. It was a struggle getting out of the car, since her train had wrapped itself around her legs, and she had to kick herself free of the hem. By the time she'd finally extricated herself from the car, he was regarding her with a look of amusement. She snatched up her train and whisked past him in a noisy rustle of satin.

"Uh, Miss Cormier?"

"What?" she snapped over her shoulder.

"My car's in the other direction."

She halted, her cheeks flushing. Mr. Detective was actually smiling now, a full-blown ate-the-canary grin.

"It's the blue Taurus," he pointed out. "The door's unlocked. I'll be right with you." He turned and headed away, toward the gathering of cops.

Nina flounced over to the blue Taurus. There she peered in disgust through the window. She was supposed to ride in *this* car? With that mess? She opened the door. A paper cup tumbled out. On the passenger floor was a crumpled McDonald's bag, more coffee cups, and a two-day-old *Portland Press Herald.* The back seat was buried under more newspapers, file folders, a briefcase, a suit jacket, and—of all things—a baseball mitt.

She scooped up the debris from the passenger side, tossed it into the back, and climbed in. She only hoped the seat was clean.

Detective Cold Fish was walking toward the car. He looked hot and harassed. His shirtsleeves were rolled up now, his tie yanked loose. Even as he tried to leave the scene, cops were pulling him aside to ask questions.

At last he slid in behind the wheel and slammed the door. "Okay, where does your mother live?" he asked.

"Cape Elizabeth. Look, I can see you're busy—"

"My partner's holding the fort. I'll drop you off, talk to your mother, and swing by the hospital to see Reverend Sullivan."

"Great. That way you can kill *three* birds with one stone."

"I do believe in efficiency."

They drove in silence. She saw no point in trying to dredge up polite talk. Politeness would go right over this man's head. Instead, she looked out the window and thought morosely about the wedding reception and all those finger sandwiches waiting for guests who'd never arrive. She'd have to call and ask for the food to be delivered to a soup kitchen before it all spoiled. And then there were the gifts, dozens of them, piled up at home. Correction—*Robert's* home. It had never really been *her* home. She had only been living there, a tenant. It had been her idea to pay half the mortgage. Robert used to point out how much he respected her independence, her insistence on a separate identity. In any good relationship, he'd say, privilege as well as responsibility was a fifty-fifty split. That's how they'd worked it from the start. First he'd paid for a date, then she had. In fact, she'd insisted, to show him that she was her own woman.

Now it all seemed so stupid.

I was never my own woman, she thought. I was always dreaming, longing for the day I'd be Mrs. Robert Bledsoe. It's what her family had hoped for, what her mother had expected of her: to marry well. They'd never understood Nina's going to nursing school, except as a way to meet a potential mate. A doctor. She'd met one, all right.

And all it's gotten me is a bunch of gifts I have to return, a wedding gown I can't return, and a day I'll never, ever live down.

It was the humiliation that shook her the most. Not the fact that Robert had walked out. Not even the fact that she could have died in the wreckage of that church. The explosion itself seemed unreal to her, as remote as some TV melodramas. As remote as this man sitting beside her.

"You're handling this very well," he said.

Startled that Detective Cold Fish had spoken, she looked at him. "Excuse me?"

"You're taking this very calmly. Calmer than most."

"I don't know how else to take it."

"After a bombing, hysteria would not be out of line."

"I'm an ER nurse, Detective. I don't do hysteria."

"Still, this had to be a shock for you. There could well be an emotional aftermath."

"You're saying this is the calm before the storm?"

"Something like that." He glanced at her, his gaze meeting hers. Just as quickly, he looked back at the road and the connection was gone. "Why wasn't your family with you at the church?"

"I sent them all home."

"I would think you'd want them around for support, at least."

She looked out the window. "My family's not exactly the supportive type. And I guess I just...needed to be alone. When an animal gets hurt, Detective, it goes off by itself to lick its wounds. That's what I needed to do...." She blinked away an unexpected film of tears and fell silent.

"I know you don't feel much like talking right now," he said. "But maybe you can answer this question for me. Can you think of anyone else who might've been a target? Reverend Sullivan, for instance?"

She shook her head. "He's the last person anyone would hurt."

"It was his church building. He would've been near the blast center."

"Reverend Sullivan's the sweetest man in the world! Every winter, he's handing out blankets on the street. Or scrounging up beds at the shelter. In the ER, when we see patients who have no home to go to, he's the one we call."

"I'm not questioning his character. I'm just asking about enemies."

"He has no enemies," she said flatly.

"What about the rest of the wedding party? Could any of them have been targets?"

"I can't imagine—"

"The best man, Jeremy Wall. Tell me about him."

"Jeremy? There's not much to say. He went to medical school with Robert. He's a doctor at Maine Med. A radiologist."

"Married?"

"Single. A confirmed bachelor."

"What about your sister, Wendy? She was your maid of honor?"

"Matron of honor. She's a happy homemaker."

"Any enemies?"

"Not unless there's someone out there who resents perfection."

"Meaning?"

"Let's just say she's the dream daughter every parent hopes for."

"As opposed to you?"

Nina gave a shrug. "How'd you guess?"

"All right, so that leaves one major player. The one who, coincidentally, decided not to show up at all."

Nina stared straight ahead. *What can I tell him about Robert,* she thought, *when I myself am completely in the dark?*

To her relief, he didn't pursue that line of questioning. Perhaps he'd realized how far he'd pushed her. How close to the emotional edge she was already tottering. As they drove the winding road into Cape Elizabeth, she felt her calm facade at last begin to crumble. Hadn't he warned her about it? The emotional aftermath. The pain creeping through the numbness. She had held together well, had weathered two devastating shocks with little more than a few spilt tears. Now her hands were beginning to shake, and she found that every breath she took was a struggle not to sob.

When at last they pulled up in front of her mother's house, Nina was barely holding herself together. She didn't wait for Sam to circle around and open her door. She pushed it open herself and scrambled out in a sloppy tangle of wedding gown. By the time he walked up the front steps, she was already leaning desperately on the doorbell, silently begging her mother to let her in before she fell apart completely.

The door swung open. Lydia, still elegantly coiffed and gowned, stood staring at her dishevelled daughter. "Nina? Oh, my poor Nina." She opened her arms.

Automatically Nina fell into her mother's embrace. So hungry was she for a hug, she didn't immediately register the fact that Lydia had drawn back to avoid wrinkling her green silk dress. But she did register her mother's first question.

"Have you heard from Robert yet?"

Nina stiffened. *Oh please,* she thought. *Please don't do this to me.*

"I'm sure this can all be worked out," said Lydia. "If you'd just sit down with Robert and have an honest discussion about what's bothering him—"

Nina pulled away. "I'm not going to sit down with Robert," she said. "And as for an honest discussion, I'm not sure we ever had one."

"Now, darling, it's natural to be angry—"

"But aren't you angry, Mother? Can't you be angry *for* me?"

"Well, yes. But I can't see tossing Robert aside just because—"

The sudden clearing of a male throat made Lydia glance up at Sam, who was standing outside the doorway.

"I'm Detective Navarro, Portland Police," he said. "You're Mrs. Cormier?"

"The name's now Warrenton." Lydia frowned at him. "What is this all about? What do the police have to do with this?"

"There was an incident at the church, ma'am. We're investigating.

"An incident?"

"The church was bombed."

Lydia stared at him. "You're not serious."

"I'm very serious. It went off at 2:45 this afternoon. Luckily no one was hurt. But if the wedding had been held..."

Lydia paled to a sickly white. She took a step back, her voice failing her.

"Mrs. Warrenton," said Sam, "I need to ask you a few questions."

Nina didn't stay to listen. She had heard too many questions already. She climbed upstairs to the spare bedroom, where she had left her suitcase—the suitcase she'd packed for St. John Island. Inside were her bathing suits and sundresses and tanning lotion. Everything she'd thought she needed for a week in paradise.

She took off the wedding dress and carefully draped it over an armchair where it lay white and lifeless. Useless. She looked at the contents of her suitcase, at the broken dreams packed neatly between layers of tissue paper. That's when the last vestiges of control failed her. Dressed only in her underwear, she sat down on the bed. Alone, in silence, she finally allowed the grief to sweep over her.

And she wept.

LYDIA WARRENTON was nothing like her daughter. Sam had seen it the moment the older woman opened the front door. Flawlessly made up, elegantly coiffed, her slender frame shown to full advantage by the green gown, Lydia looked like no mother of the bride he'd ever seen. There was a physical resemblance, of course. Both Lydia and Nina had the same black hair, the same dark, thickly lashed eyes. But while Nina had a softness about her, a vulnerability, Lydia was standoffish, as though surrounded by some protective force field that would zap anyone who ventured too close. She was definitely a looker, not only thin but also rich, judging by the room he was now standing in.

The house was a veritable museum of antiques. He had noticed a Mercedes parked in the driveway. And the living room, into which he'd just been ushered, had a spectacular ocean view. A million-dollar view. Lydia sat down primly on a brocade sofa and motioned him toward a wing chair. The needlepoint fabric was so pristine-looking he had the urge to inspect his clothes before sinking onto the cushion.

"A bomb," murmured Lydia, shaking her head. "I just can't believe it. Who would bomb a church?"

"It's not the first bombing we've had in town."

She looked at him, bewildered. "You mean the warehouse? The one last week? I read that had something to do with organized crime."

"That was the theory."

"This was a church. How can they possibly be connected?"

"We don't see the link either, Mrs. Warrenton. We're trying to find out if there is one. Maybe you can help us. Do you know of any reason someone would want to bomb the Good Shepherd Church?"

"I know nothing about that church. It's not one I attend. It was my daughter's choice to get married there."

"You sound as if you don't approve."

She shrugged. "Nina has her own odd way of doing things.

I'd have chosen a more...established institution. And a longer guest list. But that's Nina. She wanted to keep it small and simple."

Simple was definitely not Lydia Warrenton's style, thought Sam, gazing around the room.

"So to answer your question, Detective, I can't think of any reason to bomb Good Shepherd."

"What time did you leave the church?"

"A little after two. When it became apparent there wasn't anything I could do for Nina."

"While you were waiting, did you happen to notice anyone who shouldn't have been there?"

"There were just the people you'd expect. The florists, the minister. The wedding party."

"Names?"

"There was me. My daughter Wendy. The best man—I don't remember his name. My ex-husband, George, and his latest wife."

"Latest."

She sniffed. "Daniella. His fourth so far."

"What about your husband?"

She paused. "Edward was delayed. His plane was two hours late leaving Chicago."

"So he hadn't even reached town yet?"

"No. But he planned to attend the reception."

Again, Sam glanced around the room, at the antiques. The view. "May I ask what your husband does for a living, Mrs. Warrenton?"

"He's president of Ridley-Warrenton."

"The logging company?"

"That's right."

That explained the house and the Mercedes, thought Sam. Ridley-Warrenton was one of the largest landowners in northern Maine. Their forest products, from raw lumber to fine paper, were shipped around the world.

His next question was unavoidable. "Mrs. Warrenton," he asked, "does your husband have any enemies?"

Her response surprised him. She laughed. "Anyone with money has enemies, Detective."

"Can you name anyone in particular?"

"You'd have to ask Edward."

"I will," said Sam, rising to his feet. "As soon as your husband's back in town, could you have him give me a call?"

"My husband's a busy man."

"So am I, ma'am," he answered. With a curt nod, he turned and left the house.

In the driveway, he sat in his Taurus for a moment, gazing up at the mansion. It was, without a doubt, one of the most impressive homes he'd ever been in. Not that he was all that familiar with mansions. Samuel Navarro was the son of a Boston cop who was himself the son of a Boston cop. At the age of twelve, he'd moved to Portland with his newly widowed mother. Nothing came easy for them, a fact of life which his mother resignedly accepted.

Sam had not been so accepting. His adolescence consisted of five long years of rebellion. Fistfights in the school yard. Sneaking cigarettes in the bathroom. Loitering with the rough-and-tumble crowd that hung out in Monument Square. There'd been no mansions in his childhood.

He started the car and drove away. The investigation was just beginning; he and Gillis had a long night ahead of them. There was still the minister to interview, as well as the florist, the best man, the matron of honor, and the groom.

Most of all, the groom.

Dr. Robert Bledsoe, after all, was the one who'd called off the wedding. His decision, by accident or design, had saved the lives of dozens of people. That struck Sam as just a little bit too fortunate. Had Bledsoe received some kind of warning? Had he been the intended target?

Was that the real reason he'd left his bride at the altar?

Nina Cormier's image came vividly back to mind. Hers wasn't a face he'd be likely to forget. It was more than just those big brown eyes, that kissable mouth. It was her pride that impressed him the most. The sort of pride that kept her chin up, her jaw squared, even as the tears were falling. For that he admired her. No whining, no self-pity. The woman had been humiliated, abandoned, and almost blown to smithereens. Yet she'd had enough spunk left to give Sam an occasional what-for. He found that both irritating and amusing. For a woman who'd probably grown up with everything handed to her on a silver platter, she was a tough little survivor.

Today she'd been handed a heaping dish of crow, and she'd eaten it just fine, thank you. Without a whimper.

Surprising, surprising woman.

He could hardly wait to hear what Dr. Robert Bledsoe had to say about her.

IT WAS AFTER five o'clock when Nina finally emerged from her mother's guest bedroom. Calm, composed, she was now wearing jeans and a T-shirt. She'd left her wedding dress hanging in the closet; she didn't even want to look at it again. Too many bad memories had attached themselves like burrs to the fabric.

Downstairs she found her mother sitting alone in the living room, nursing a highball. Detective Navarro was gone. Lydia raised the drink to her lips, and by the clinking of ice cubes in the glass, Nina could tell that Lydia's hands were shaking.

"Mother?" said Nina.

At the sound of her daughter's voice, Lydia's head jerked up. "You startled me."

"I think I'll be leaving now. Are you all right?"

"Yes. Yes, of course." Lydia gave a shudder. Then she added, almost as an afterthought, "How about you?"

"I'll be okay. I just need some time. Away from Robert."

Mother and daughter looked at each other for a moment, neither one speaking, neither one knowing what to say. This was the way things had always been between them. Nina had grown up hungry for affection. Her mother had always been too self-absorbed to grant it. And this was the result: the silence of two women who scarcely knew or understood each other. The distance between them couldn't be measured by years, but by universes.

Nina watched her mother take another deep swallow of her drink. "How did it go?" she asked. "With you and that detective?"

Lydia shrugged. "What's there to say? He asked questions, I answered them."

"Did he tell you anything? About who might have done it?"

"No. He was tight as a clam. Not much in the way of charm."

Nina couldn't disagree. She'd known ice cubes that were warmer than Sam Navarro. But then, the man was just doing his job. He wasn't paid to be charming.

"You can stay for dinner, if you'd like," said Lydia. "Why don't you? I'll have the cook—"

"That's all right, Mother. Thank you, anyway."

Lydia looked up at her. "It's because of Edward, isn't it?"

"No, Mother. Really."

"That's why you hardly ever visit. Because of him. I wish you *could* get to like him." Lydia sighed and looked down at her drink. "He's been very good to me, very generous. You have to grant him that much."

When Nina thought of her stepfather, *generous* was not the first adjective that came to mind. No, *ruthless* would be the word she'd choose. Ruthless and controlling. She didn't want to talk about Edward Warrenton.

She turned and started toward the door. "I have to get home and pack my things. Since it's obvious I'll be moving out."

"Couldn't you and Robert patch things up somehow?"

"After today?" Nina shook her head.

"If you just tried harder? Maybe it's something you could talk about. Something you could change."

"Mother. Please."

Lydia sank back. "Anyway," she said, "you *are* invited to dinner. For what it's worth."

"Maybe some other time," Nina said softly. "Bye, Mother."

She heard no answer as she walked out the front door.

Her Honda was parked at the side of the house, where she'd left it that morning. The morning of what should have been her wedding. How proudly Lydia had smiled at her as they'd sat together in the limousine! It was the way a mother *should* look at her daughter. The way Lydia never had before.

And probably never would again.

That ride to the church, the smiles, the laughter, seemed a lifetime away. She started the Honda and pulled out of her mother's driveway.

In a daze she drove south, toward Hunts Point. Toward Robert's house. What had been *their* house. The road was winding, and she was functioning on automatic pilot, steering without thought along the curves. What if Robert hadn't really left town? she thought. What if he's home? What would they say to each other?

Try: goodbye.

She gripped the steering wheel and thought of all the things she'd *like* to tell him. All the ways she felt used and betrayed. *A whole year* kept going through her head. *One whole bloody year of my life.*

Only as she swung past Smugglers Cove did she happen to glance in the rearview mirror. A black Ford was behind her. The same Ford that had been there a few miles back, near Delano Park. At any other time, she would have thought nothing of it. But today, after the possibilities Detective Navarro had raised...

She shook off a vague sense of uneasiness and kept driving. She turned onto Ocean House Drive.

The Ford did too. There was no reason for alarm. Ocean House Drive was, after all, a main road in the neighborhood. Another driver might very well have reason to turn onto it as well.

Just to ease her anxiety, she took the left turnoff, toward Peabbles Point. It was a lonely road, not heavily traveled. Here's where she and the Ford would surely part company.

The Ford took the same turnoff.

Now she was getting frightened.

She pressed the accelerator. The Honda gained speed. At fifty miles per hour, she knew she was taking the curves too fast, but she was determined to lose the Ford. Only she wasn't losing him. He had sped up, too. In fact, he was gaining on her.

With a sudden burst of speed, the Ford roared up right beside her. They were neck and neck, taking the curves in parallel.

He's trying to run me off the road! she thought.

She glanced sideways, but all she could see through the other car's tinted window was the driver's silhouette. *Why are you doing this?* she wanted to scream at him. *Why?*

The Ford suddenly swerved toward her. The thump of the other car's impact almost sent the Honda spinning out of control. Nina fought to keep her car on course.

Her fingers clamped more tightly around the wheel. Damn this lunatic! She had to shake him off.

She hit the brakes.

The Ford shot ahead—only momentarily. It quickly slowed as well and was back beside her, swerving, bumping.

She managed another sideways glance. To her surprise, the Ford's passenger window had been rolled down. She caught a glimpse of the driver—a male. Dark hair. Sunglasses.

In the next instant her gaze shot forward to the road, which crested fifty yards ahead.

Another car had just cleared the crest and was barreling straight toward the Ford.

Tires screeched. Nina felt one last violent thump, felt the sting of shattering glass against her face. Then suddenly she was soaring sideways.

She never lost consciousness. Even as the Honda flew off the road. Even as it tumbled over and over across shrubbery and saplings.

It came to a rest, upright, against a maple tree.

Though fully awake, Nina could not move for a moment. She was too stunned to feel pain, or even fear. All she felt was amazement that she was still alive.

Then, gradually, an awareness of discomfort seeped through the layers of shock. Her chest hurt, and her shoulder. It was the seat belt. It had saved her life, but it had also bruised her ribs.

Groaning, she pressed the belt release and felt herself collapse forward, against the steering wheel.

"Hey! Hey, lady!"

Nina turned to see a face anxiously peering through the window. It was an elderly man. He yanked open her door. "Are you all right?" he asked.

"I'm—I think so."

"I'd better call an ambulance."

"No, I'm fine. Really, I am." She took a deep breath. Her chest was sore, but that seemed to be her only injury. With the old man's help, she climbed out of the car. Though a little unsteady, she was able to stand. She was shocked by the damage.

Her car was a mess. The driver's door had been bashed in, the window was shattered, and the front fender was peeled off entirely.

She turned and glanced toward the road. "There was another car," she said. "A black one—"

"You mean that damn fool who tried to pass you?"

"Where is it?"

"Took off. You oughta report that fella. Probably drunk as a skunk."

Drunk? Nina didn't think so. Shivering, she hugged herself and stared at the road, but she saw no sign of another car.

The black Ford had vanished.

Chapter Three

Gordon Gillis looked up from his burger and fries. "Anything interesting?" he asked.

"Not a damn thing." Sam hung his jacket up on the coatrack and sank into a chair behind his desk, where he sat wearily rubbing his face.

"How's the minister doing?"

"Fine, so far. Doctors doubt it's a heart attack. But they'll keep him in for a day, just to be sure."

"He didn't have any ideas about the bombing?"

"Claims he has no enemies. And everyone I talked to seems to agree that Reverend Sullivan is a certifiable saint." Groaning, Sam leaned back. "How 'bout you?"

Gillis peeled off the hamburger wrapper and began to eat as he talked. "I interviewed the best man, the matron of honor and the florist. No one saw anything."

"What about the church janitor?"

"We're still trying to locate him. His wife says he usually gets home around six. I'll send Cooley over to talk to him."

"According to Reverend Sullivan, the janitor opens the front doors at 7:00 a.m. And the doors stay open all day. So anyone could've walked in and left a package."

"What about the night before?" asked Gillis. "What time did he lock the doors?"

"The church secretary usually locks up. She's a part-timer. Would've done it around 6:00 p.m. Unfortunately, she left for vacation this morning. Visiting family in Massachusetts. We're still trying to get hold of..." He paused.

Gillis's telephone was ringing. Gillis turned to answer it. "Yeah, what's up?"

Sam watched as his partner scribbled something on a notepad, then passed it across the desk. *Trundy Point Road* was written on the paper.

A moment later, Gillis said, "We'll be there," and hung up. He was frowning.

"What is it?" asked Sam.

"Report just came in from one of the mobile units. It's about the bride. The one at the church today."

"Nina Cormier?"

"Her car just went off the road near Trundy Point."

Sam sat up straight in alarm. "Is she all right?"

"She's fine. They wouldn't have called us at all, but she insisted they notify us."

"For an accident? Why?"

"She says it wasn't an accident. She says someone tried to run her off the road."

HER RIBS HURT, her shoulder was sore, and her face had a few cuts from flying glass. But at least her head was perfectly clear. Clear enough for her to recognize the man stepping out of that familiar blue Taurus that had just pulled up at the scene. It was that sullen detective, Sam Navarro. He didn't even glance in her direction.

Through the gathering dusk, Nina watched as he spoke to a patrolman. They conversed for a few moments. Then, together, the two men tramped through the underbrush to view the remains of her car. As Sam paced a slow circle around the battered Honda, Nina was reminded of a stalking cat. He moved with an easy, feline grace, his gaze focused in complete concentration. At one point he stopped and crouched to look at something on the ground. Then he rose to his feet and peered more closely at the driver's window. Or what was left of the window. He prodded the broken glass, then opened the door and climbed into the front seat. What on earth was he looking for? She could see his dark hair bobbing in and out of view. Now he seemed to be crawling all over the interior, and into the back seat. It was a good thing she had nothing to hide in there. She had no doubt that the sharp-eyed Detective Navarro could spot contraband a mile away.

At last he reemerged from her car, his hair tousled, his trousers wrinkled. He spoke again to the patrolman. Then he turned and looked in her direction.

And began to walk toward her.

At once she felt her pulse quickening. Something about this

man both fascinated and frightened her. It was more than just his physical presence, which was impressive enough. It was also the way he looked at her, with a gaze that was completely neutral. That inscrutability unnerved her. Most men seemed to find Nina attractive, and they would at least make an attempt to be friendly.

This man seemed to regard her as just another homicide victim in the making. Worth his intellectual interest, but that was all.

She straightened her back and met his gaze without wavering as he approached.

"Are you all right?" he asked.

"A few bruises. A few cuts. That's all."

"You're sure you don't want to go to the ER? I can drive you."

"I'm fine. I'm a nurse, so I think I'd know."

"They say doctors and nurses make the worst patients. I'll drive you to the hospital. Just to be sure."

She gave a disbelieving laugh. "That sounds like an order."

"As a matter of fact, it is."

"Detective, I really think I'd know if I was..."

She was talking to his back. The man had actually turned his *back* to her. He was already walking away, toward his car. *"Detective!"* she called.

He glanced over his shoulder. "Yes?"

"I don't— This isn't—" She sighed. "Oh, never mind," she muttered, and followed him to his car. There was no point arguing with the man. He'd just turn his back on her again. As she slid into the passenger seat, she felt a sharp stab of pain in her chest. Maybe he was right after all. She knew it could take hours, or even days, for injuries to manifest themselves. She hated to admit it, but Mr. Personality was probably right about this trip to the ER.

She was too uncomfortable to say much as they drove to the hospital. It was Sam who finally broke the silence.

"So, can you tell me what happened?" he asked.

"I already gave a statement. It's all in the police report. Someone ran me off the road."

"Yes, a black Ford, male driver. Maine license plate."

"Then you've been told the details."

"The other witness said he thought it was a drunk driver trying to pass you on the hill. He didn't think it was deliberate."

She shook her head. "I don't know what to think anymore."

"When did you first see the Ford?"

"Somewhere around Smugglers Cove, I guess. I noticed that it seemed to be following me."

"Was it weaving? Show any signs of driver impairment?"

"No. It was just...following me."

"Could it have been behind you earlier?"

"I'm not sure."

"Is it possible it was there when you left your mother's house?"

She frowned at him. He wasn't looking at her, but was staring straight ahead. The tenor of his questions had taken a subtle change of course. He had started out sounding noncommittal. Maybe even skeptical. But this last question told her he was considering a possibility other than a drunk driver. A possibility that left her suddenly chilled.

"Are you suggesting he was waiting for me?"

"I'm just exploring the possibilities."

"The other policeman thought it was a drunk driver."

"He has his opinion."

"What's your opinion?"

He didn't answer. He just kept driving in that maddeningly calm way of his. Did the man ever show any emotion? Once, just once, she'd like to see something get under that thick skin of his.

"Detective Navarro," she said. "I pay taxes. I pay your salary. I think I deserve more than just a brush-off."

"Oh. The old civil servant line."

"I'll use whatever line it takes to get an answer out of you!"

"I'm not sure you want to hear my answer."

"Why wouldn't I?"

"I made a brief inspection of your car. What I found there backs up quite a bit of what you just told me. There were black paint chips on the driver's side, indicating that the vehicle that rammed yours was, indeed, black."

"So I'm not color blind."

"I also noticed that the driver's window was shattered. And that the breakage was in a starburst pattern. Not what I'd expect for a rollover accident."

"That's because the window was already broken when I went off the road."

"How do you know?"

"I remember I felt flying glass. That's how I cut my face. When the glass hit me. That was *before* I rolled over."

"Are you sure?" He glanced at her. "Absolutely sure?"

"Yes. Does it make a difference?"

He let out a breath. "It makes a lot of difference," he said softly. "It also goes along with what I found in your car."

"*In* my car?" Perplexed, she shook her head. "What, exactly, did you find?"

"It was in the right passenger door—the door that was jammed against the tree. The metal was pretty crumpled; that's why the other cops didn't notice it. But I knew it was there somewhere. And I found it."

"Found what?"

"A bullet hole."

Nina felt the blood drain from her face. She couldn't speak; she could only sit in shocked silence, her world rocked by the impact of his words.

He continued talking, his tone matter-of-fact. Chillingly so. *He's not human,* she thought. *He's a machine. A robot.*

"The bullet must have hit your window," he said, "just to the rear of your head. That's why the glass shattered. Then the bullet passed at a slightly forward angle, missed you completely, and made a hole in the plastic molding of the opposite door, where it's probably still lodged. It'll be retrieved. By tonight, we'll know the caliber. And possibly the make of the gun. What I still don't know—what *you'll* have to tell me—is why someone's trying to kill you."

She shook her head. "It's a mistake."

"This guy's going to a lot of trouble. He's bombed a church. Tailed you. Shot at you. There's no mistake."

"There has to be!"

"Think of every possible person who might want to hurt you. Think, Nina."

"I told you, I don't have any enemies!"

"You must have."

"I don't! I don't...." She gave a sob and clutched her head in her hands. "I don't," she whispered.

After a long silence he said, gently, "I'm sorry. I know how hard it is to accept—"

"You *don't* know." She raised her head and looked at him.

"You have no idea, Detective. I've always thought people liked me. Or—at least—they didn't *hate* me. I try so hard to get along with everyone. And now you're telling me there's someone out there—someone who wants to..." She swallowed and stared ahead, at the darkening road.

Sam let the silence stretch on between them. He knew she was in too fragile a state right now to press her with more questions. And he suspected she was hurting more, both physically and emotionally, than she was letting on. Judging by the condition of her car, her body had taken a brutal beating this afternoon.

In the ER, he paced the waiting room while Nina was examined by the doctor on duty. A few X rays later, she emerged looking even more pale than when she'd entered. It was reality sinking in, he thought. The danger was genuine, and she couldn't deny it any longer.

Back in his car, she sat in numb silence. He kept glancing sideways at her, waiting for her to burst into tears, into hysteria, but she remained unnervingly quiet. It concerned him. This wasn't healthy.

He said, "You shouldn't be alone tonight. Is there somewhere you can go?"

Her response was barely a shrug.

"Your mother's?" he suggested. "I'll take you home to pack a suitcase and—"

"No. Not my mother's," she murmured.

"Why not?"

"I...don't want to make things...uncomfortable for her."

"For *her?*" He frowned. "Pardon me for asking this, but isn't that what mothers are for? To pick us up and dust us off?"

"My mother's marriage isn't...the most supportive one around."

"She can't welcome her own daughter home?"

"It's not her home, Detective. It's her husband's. And he doesn't approve of me. To be honest, the feeling's mutual." She gazed straight ahead, and in that moment, she struck him as so very brave. And so very alone.

"Since the day they got married, Edward Warrenton has controlled every detail of my mother's life. He bullies her, and she takes it without a whimper. Because his money makes it all worthwhile for her. I just couldn't stand watching it any longer. So one day I told him off."

"Sounds like that's exactly what you should have done."

"It didn't do a thing for family harmony. I'm sure that's why he went on that business trip to Chicago. So he could conveniently skip my wedding." Sighing, she tilted her head back against the headrest. "I know I shouldn't be annoyed with my mother, but I am. I'm annoyed that she's never stood up to him."

"Okay. So I don't take you to your mother's house. What about dear old dad? Do you two get along?"

She gave a nod. A small one. "I suppose I could stay with him."

"Good. Because there's no way I'm going to let you be alone tonight." The sentence was scarcely out of his mouth when he realized he shouldn't have said it. It sounded too much as if he cared, as if feeling were getting mixed up with duty. He was too good a cop, too cautious a cop, to let that happen.

He could feel her surprised gaze through the darkness of the car.

In a tone colder than he'd intended, he said, "You may be my only link to this bombing. I need you alive and well for the investigation."

"Oh. Of course." She looked straight ahead again. And she didn't say another word until they'd reached her house on Ocean View Drive.

As soon as he'd parked, she started to get out of the car. He reached for her arm and pulled her back inside. "Wait."

"What is it?"

"Just sit for a minute." He glanced up and down the road, scanning for other cars, other people. Anything at all suspicious. The street was deserted.

"Okay," he said. He got out and circled around to open her door. "Pack one suitcase. That's all we have time for."

"I wasn't planning to bring along the furniture."

"I'm just trying to keep this short and sweet. If someone's really looking for you, this is where they'll come. So let's not hang around, all right?"

That remark, meant to emphasize the danger, had its intended effect. She scooted out of the car and up the front walk in hyperspeed. He had to convince her to wait on the porch while he made a quick search of the house.

A moment later he poked his head out the door. ''All clear.''

While she packed a suitcase, Sam wandered about the living room. It was an old but spacious house, tastefully furnished, with a view of the sea. Just the sort of house one would expect a doctor to live in. He went over to the grand piano—a Steinway—and tapped out a few notes. ''Who plays the piano?'' he called out.

''Robert,'' came the answer from the bedroom. ''Afraid I have a tin ear.''

He focused on a framed photograph set on the piano. It was a shot of a couple, smiling. Nina and some blond, blue-eyed man. Undoubtedly Robert Bledsoe. The guy, it seemed, had everything: looks, money and a medical degree. And the woman. A woman he no longer wanted. Sam crossed the room to a display of diplomas, hanging on the wall. All of them Robert Bledsoe's. Groton prep. B.A. Dartmouth. M.D. Harvard. Dr. Bledsoe was Ivy League all the way. He was every mother's dream son-in-law. No wonder Lydia Warrenton had urged her daughter to patch things up.

The phone rang, the sound so abrupt and startling, Sam felt an instant rush of adrenaline.

''Should I get it?'' Nina asked. She was standing in the doorway, her face drawn and tense.

He nodded. ''Answer it.''

She crossed to the telephone. After a second's hesitation, she picked up the receiver. He moved right beside her, listening, as she said, ''Hello?''

No one answered.

''Hello?'' Nina repeated. ''Who is this? *Hello?*''

There was a click. Then, a moment later, the dial tone.

Nina looked up at Sam. She was standing so close to him, her hair, like black silk, brushed his face. He found himself staring straight into those wide eyes of hers, found himself reacting to her nearness with an unexpected surge of male longing.

This isn't supposed to happen. I can't let it happen.

He took a step back, just to put space between them. Even though they were now standing a good three feet apart, he could still feel the attraction. Not far enough apart, he thought. This woman was getting in the way of his thinking clearly, logically. And that was dangerous.

He looked down and suddenly noticed the telephone answering machine was blinking. He said, "You have messages."

"Pardon?"

"Your answering machine. It's recorded three messages."

Dazedly she looked down at the machine. Automatically she pressed the Play button.

There were three beeps, followed by three silences, and then dial tones.

Seemingly paralyzed, she stared at the machine. "Why?" she whispered. "Why do they call and hang up?"

"To see if you're home."

The implication of his statement at once struck her full force. She flinched away from the phone as if it had burned her. "I have to get out of here," she said, and hurried back into the bedroom.

He followed her. She was tossing clothes into a suitcase, not bothering to fold anything. Slacks and blouses and lingerie in one disorganized pile.

"Just the essentials," he said. "Let's leave."

"Yes. Yes, you're right." She whirled around and ran into the bathroom. He heard her rattling in the cabinets, collecting toiletries. A moment later she reemerged with a bulging makeup bag, which she tossed in the suitcase.

He closed and latched it for her. "Let's go."

In the car, she sat silent and huddled against the seat as he drove. He kept checking the rearview mirror, to see if they were being followed, but he saw no other headlights. No signs of pursuit.

"Relax, we're okay," he said. "I'll just get you to your dad's house, and you'll be fine."

"And then what?" she said softly. "How long do I hide there? For weeks, months?"

"As long as it takes for us to crack this case."

She shook her head, a sad gesture of bewilderment. "It doesn't make sense. None of this makes sense."

"Maybe it'll become clear when we talk to your fiancé. Do you have any idea where he might be?"

"It seems that I'm the last person Robert wanted to confide in..." Hugging herself, she stared out the window. "His note said he was leaving town for a while. I guess he just needed to get away. From me..."

"From you? Or from someone else?"

She shook her head. "There's so much I don't know. So much he never bothered to tell me. God, I wish I understood. I could handle this. I could handle anything. If only I understood."

What kind of man is Robert Bledsoe? Sam wondered. What kind of man would walk away from this woman? Leave her alone to face the danger left in his wake?

"Whoever made that hang-up call may pay a visit to your house," he said. "I'd like to keep an eye on it. See who turns up."

She nodded. "Yes. Of course."

"May I have access?"

"You mean...get inside?"

"If our suspect shows up, he may try to break in. I'd like to be waiting for him."

She stared at him. "You could get yourself killed."

"Believe me, Miss Cormier, I'm not the heroic type. I don't take chances."

"But if he does show up—"

"I'll be ready." He flashed her a quick grin for reassurance. She didn't look reassured. If anything, she looked more frightened than ever.

For me? he wondered. And that, inexplicably, lifted his spirits. Terrific. Next thing he knew, he'd be putting his neck in a noose, and all because of a pair of big brown eyes. This was just the kind of situation cops were warned to avoid: assuming the role of hero to some fetching female. It got men killed.

It could get *him* killed.

"You shouldn't do this by yourself," she said.

"I won't be alone. I'll have backup."

"You're sure?"

"Yeah, I'm sure."

"You promise? You won't take any chances?"

"What are you, my mother?" he snapped in exasperation.

She took her keys out of her purse and slapped them on the dashboard. "No, I'm not your mother," she retorted. "But you're the cop in charge. And I need you alive and well to crack this case."

He deserved that. She'd been concerned about his safety, and he'd responded with sarcasm. He didn't even know why. All he knew was, whenever he looked in her eyes, he had the overwhelming urge to turn tail and run. Before he was trapped.

Moments later, they drove past the wrought iron gates of her father's driveway. Nina didn't even wait for Sam to open her door. She got out of the car and started up the stone steps. Sam followed, carrying her suitcase. And ogling the house. It was huge—even more impressive than Lydia Warrenton's home, and it had the Rolls-Royce of security systems. Tonight, at least, Nina should be safe.

The doorbell chimed like a church bell; he could hear it echoing through what must be dozens of rooms. The door was opened by a blonde—and what a blonde! Not much older than thirty, she was wearing a shiny spandex leotard that hugged every taut curve. A healthy sweat sheened her face, and from some other room came the thumpy music of an exercise video.

"Hello, Daniella," Nina said quietly.

Daniella assumed a look of sympathy that struck Sam as too automatic to be genuine. "Oh Nina, I'm so *sorry* about what happened today! Wendy called and told us about the church. Was anyone hurt?"

"No. No, thank God." Nina paused, as though afraid to ask the next question. "Do you think I could spend the night with you?"

The expression of sympathy faded. Daniella looked askance at the suitcase Sam was carrying. "I, uh...let me talk to your Dad. He's in the hot tub right now and—"

"Nina has no choice. She has to stay the night," said Sam. He stepped past Daniella, into the house. "It's not safe for her to be alone."

Daniella's gaze shifted to Sam, and he saw the vague spark of interest in those flat blue eyes. "I'm afraid I didn't catch your name," she said.

"This is Detective Navarro," said Nina. "He's with the Portland Bomb Squad. And this," she said to Sam, "is Daniella Cormier. My, uh...father's wife."

Stepmother was the appropriate term, but this stunning blonde didn't look like anybody's mother. And the look she was giving *him* was anything but maternal.

Daniella tilted her head, a gesture he recognized as both inquisitive and flirtatious. "So, you're a cop?"

"Yes, ma'am."

"Bomb Squad? Is that really what you think happened at the church? A bomb?"

"I'm not free to talk about it," he said. "Not while the investigation's underway." Smoothly he turned to Nina. "If you're okay for the night, I'll be leaving. Be sure to close those driveway gates. And activate the burglar alarm. I'll check back with you in the morning."

As he gave a nod of goodbye, his gaze locked with Nina's. It was only the briefest of looks, but once again he was taken by surprise at his instinctive response to this woman. It was an attraction so powerful he felt himself at once struggling to pull away.

He did. With a curt good-night, he walked out the front door.

Outside, in the darkness, he stood for a moment surveying the house. It seemed secure enough. With two other people inside, Nina should be safe. Still, he wondered whether those particular two people would be of much help in a crisis. A father soaking in a hot tub and a spandex-and-hormones stepmother didn't exactly inspire feelings of confidence. Nina, at least, was an intelligent woman; he knew she would be alert for signs of danger.

He drove back to Robert Bledsoe's house on Ocean View Drive and left the car on a side street around the corner.

With Nina's keys, he let himself in the front door and called Gillis to arrange for a surveillance team to patrol the area. Then he closed all the curtains and settled down to wait. It was nine o'clock.

At nine-thirty, he was already restless. He paced the living room, then roamed the kitchen, the dining room, the hallway. Any stalker watching the house would expect lights to go on and off in different rooms, at different times. Maybe their man was just waiting for the residents to go to bed.

Sam turned off the living room lights and went into the bedroom.

Nina had left the top dresser drawer hanging open. Sam, pacing the carpet, kept walking back and forth past that open drawer with its tempting glimpse of lingerie. Something black and silky lay on top, and one corner trailed partway out of the drawer. He couldn't resist the impulse. He halted by the dresser, picked up the item of lingerie, and held it up.

It was a short little spaghetti-strap thing, edged with lace, and designed to show a lot. An awful lot. He tossed it back in and slammed the drawer shut.

He was getting distracted again. This shouldn't be happening. Something about Nina Cormier, and his reaction to her, had him behaving like a damn rookie.

Before, in the line of duty, he'd brushed up against other women, including the occasional stunner. Women like that spandex bimbo, Daniella Cormier, Nina's stepmother. He'd managed to keep his trousers zipped up and his head firmly screwed on. It was both a matter of self-control as well as self-preservation. The women he met on the job were usually in some sort of trouble, and it was too easy for them to consider Sam their white knight, the masculine answer to all their problems.

It was a fantasy that never lasted. Sooner or later the knight gets stripped of his armor and they'd see him for what he really was: just a cop. Not rich, not brilliant. Not much of anything, in fact, to recommend him.

It had happened to him once. Just once. She'd been an aspiring actress trying to escape an abusive boyfriend; he'd been a rookie assigned to watch over her. The chemistry was right. The situation was right. But the girl was all wrong. For a few heady weeks, he'd been in love, had thought *she* was in love.

Then she'd dropped Sam like a hot potato.

He'd learned a hard but lasting lesson: romance and police work did not mix. He had never again crossed that line while on the job, and he wasn't about to do it with Nina Cormier, either.

He turned away from the dresser and was crossing to the opposite end of the room when he heard a thump.

It came from somewhere near the front of the house.

Instantly he killed the bedroom lights and reached for his gun. He eased into the hallway. At the doorway to the living room he halted, his gaze quickly sweeping the darkness.

The streetlight shone in dimly through the windows. He saw no movement in the room, no suspicious shadows.

There was a scraping sound, a soft jingle. It came from the front porch.

Sam shifted his aim to the front door. He was crouched and ready to fire as the door swung open. The silhouette of a man loomed against the backlight of the streetlamp.

"Police!" Sam yelled. *"Freeze!"*

Chapter Four

The silhouette froze.

"Hands up," ordered Sam. "Come on, *hands up!*"

Both hands shot up. "Don't hurt me!" came a terrified plea.

Sam edged over to the light switch and flipped it on. The sudden glare left both men blinking. Sam took one look at the man standing in front of him and cursed.

Footsteps pounded up the porch steps and two uniformed cops burst through the doorway, pistols drawn. "We got him covered, Navarro!" one of them yelled.

"You're right on time," muttered Sam in disgust. "Forget it. This isn't the guy." He holstered his gun and looked at the tall blond man, who was still wearing a look of terror on his face. "I'm Detective Sam Navarro, Portland Police. I presume you're Dr. Robert Bledsoe?"

Nervously Robert cleared his throat. "Yeah, that's me. What's going on? Why are you people in my house?"

"Where've you been all day, Dr. Bledsoe?"

"I've been—uh, may I put my hands down?"

"Of course."

Robert lowered his hands and glanced cautiously over his shoulder at the two cops standing behind him. "Do they, uh, really need to keep pointing those guns at me?"

"You two can leave," Sam said to the cops. "I'm all right here."

"What about the surveillance?" one of them asked. "Want to call it off?"

"I doubt anything's coming down tonight. But hang around the neighborhood. Just until morning."

The two cops left. Sam said, again, "Where've you been, Dr. Bledsoe?"

With two guns no longer pointed at his back, Robert's terror had given way to righteous anger. He glared at Sam. "First, you tell me why you're in my house! What is this, a police state?

Cops breaking in and threatening homeowners? You have no authority to be trespassing on my property. I'll have your ass in a sling if you don't produce a search warrant right now!"

"I don't have a warrant."

"You don't?" Robert gave an unpleasantly triumphant laugh. "You entered my house without a warrant? You break in here and threaten me with your macho cop act?"

"I didn't break in," Sam told him calmly. "I let myself in the front door."

"Oh, sure."

Sam pulled out Nina's keys and held them up in front of Robert. "With these."

"Those—those keys belong to my fiancée! How did you get them?"

"She lent them to me."

"She *what?*" Robert's voice had risen to a yelp of anger. "Where is Nina? She had no right to hand over the keys to my house."

"Correction, Doctor. Nina Cormier was living here with you. That makes her a legal resident of this house. It gives her the right to authorize police entry, which she did." Sam eyed the man squarely. "Now, I'll ask the question a third time. Where have you been, Doctor?"

"Away," snapped Robert.

"Could you be more specific?"

"All right, I went to Boston. I needed to get out of town for a while."

"Why?"

"What is this, an interrogation? I don't have to talk to you! In fact I *shouldn't* talk to you until I call my lawyer." He turned to the telephone and picked up the receiver.

"You don't need a lawyer. Unless you've committed a crime."

"A crime?" Robert spun around and stared at him. "Are you accusing me of something?"

"I'm not accusing you of anything. But I do need answers. Are you aware of what happened in the church today?"

Robert replaced the receiver. Soberly he nodded. "I...I heard there was some sort of explosion. It was on the news. That's why I came back early. I was worried someone might've been hurt."

"Luckily, no one was. The church was empty at the time it happened."

Robert gave a sigh of relief. "Thank God," he said softly. He stood with his hand still on the phone, as though debating whether to pick it up again. "Do the police—do you—know what caused it?"

"Yes. It was a bomb."

Robert's chin jerked up. He stared at Sam. Slowly he sank into the nearest chair. "All I'd heard was—the radio said—it was an explosion. There was nothing about a bomb."

"We haven't made a public statement yet."

Robert looked up at him. "Why the hell would anyone bomb a church?"

"That's what we're trying to find out. If the wedding had taken place, dozens of people might be dead right now. Nina told me you're the one who called it off. Why did you?"

"I just couldn't go through with it." Robert dropped his head in his hands. "I wasn't ready to get married."

"So your reason was entirely personal?"

"What else would it be?" Robert suddenly looked up with an expression of stunned comprehension. "Oh, my God. You didn't think the bomb had something to do with *me?*"

"It did cross my mind. Consider the circumstances. You cancelled the wedding without warning. And then you skipped town. Of course we wondered about your motives. Whether you'd received some kind of threat and decided to run."

"No, that's not at all what happened. I called it off because I didn't want to get married."

"Mind telling me why?"

Robert's face tightened. "Yes, as a matter of fact," he answered. Abruptly he rose from the chair and strode over to the liquor cabinet. There he poured himself a shot of Scotch and stood gulping it, not looking at Sam.

"I've met your fiancée," stated Sam. "She seems like a nice woman. Bright, attractive." *I'm sure as hell attracted to her,* he couldn't help adding to himself.

"You're asking why I left her at the altar, aren't you?" said Robert.

"Why did you?"

Robert finished off his drink and poured himself another.

"Did you two have an argument?"

"No."

"What was it, Dr. Bledsoe? Cold feet? Boredom?" Sam paused. "Another woman?"

Robert turned and glared at him. "This is none of your damn business. Get out of my house."

"If you insist. But I'll be talking to you again." Sam crossed to the front door, then stopped and turned back. "Do you know anyone who'd want to hurt your fiancée?"

"No."

"Anyone who'd want her dead?"

"What a ridiculous question."

"Someone tried to run her car off the road this afternoon."

Robert jerked around and stared at him. He looked genuinely startled. "*Nina?* Who did?"

"That's what I'm trying to find out. It may or may not be connected to the bombing. Do you have any idea at all what's going on? Who might try to hurt her?"

There was a split second's hesitation before Robert answered. "No. No one I can think of. Where is she?"

"She's in a safe place for tonight. But she can't stay in hiding forever. So if you think of anything, give me a call. If you still care about her."

Robert didn't say anything.

Sam turned and left the house.

Driving home, he used his car phone to dial Gillis. His partner, predictably, was still at his desk. "The bridegroom's back in town," Sam told him. "He claims he has no idea why the church was bombed."

"Why am I not surprised?" Gillis drawled.

"Anything new turn up?"

"Yeah. We're missing a janitor."

"What?"

"The church janitor. The one who unlocked the building this morning. We've been trying to track him down all evening. He never got home tonight."

Sam felt his pulse give a little gallop of excitement. "Interesting."

"We've already got an APB out. The man's name is Jimmy Brogan. And he has a record. Petty theft four years ago and two OUI's, that kind of stuff. Nothing major. I sent Cooley out to talk to the wife and check the house."

"Does Brogan have any explosives experience?"

"Not that we can determine. The wife swears up and down that he's clean. And he's always home for dinner."

"Give me more, Gillis. Give me more."

"That's all I have to give, unless you want me to slit open a vein. Right now I'm bushed and I'm going home."

"Okay, call it a day. I'll see you in the morning."

All the way home, Sam's mind was churning with facts. A cancelled wedding. A missing church janitor. An assassin in a black Ford.

And a bomb.

Where did Nina Cormier fit in this crazy thicket of events?

It was eleven-thirty when he finally arrived home. He let himself in the front door, stepped into the house, and turned on the lights. The familiar clutter greeted him. What a god-awful mess. One of these days he'd have to clean up the place. Or maybe he should just move; that'd be easier.

He walked through the living room, picking up dirty laundry and dishes as he went. He left the dishes in the kitchen sink, threw the laundry in the washing machine, and started the wash cycle. A Saturday night, and the swinging bachelor does his laundry. Wow. He stood in his kitchen, listening to the machine rumble, thinking about all the things he could do to make this house more of a home. Furniture, maybe? It was a good, sound little house, but he kept comparing it to Robert Bledsoe's house with its Steinway piano, the sort of house any woman would be delighted to call home.

Hell, Sam wouldn't know what to do with a woman even if one was crazy enough to move in with him. He'd been a bachelor too long, alone too long. There'd been the occasional woman, of course, but none of them had ever lasted. Too often, he had to admit, the fault lay with him. Or with his work. They couldn't understand why any man in his right mind would actually choose to stay with this insane job of bombs and bombers. They took it as a personal affront that he wouldn't quit the job and chose *them* instead.

Maybe he'd just never found a woman who made him *want* to quit.

And this is the result, he thought, gazing wearily at the basket of unfolded clothes. The swinging bachelor life.

He left the washing machine to finish its cycle and headed off to bed.

As usual, alone.

THE LIGHTS WERE ON at 318 Ocean View Drive. Someone was home. The Cormier woman? Robert Bledsoe? Or both of them?

Driving slowly past the house in his green Jeep Cherokee, he took a good long look at the house. He noted the dense shrubbery near the windows, the shadow of pine and birch trees ringing both edges of the property. Plenty of cover. Plenty of concealment.

Then he noticed the unmarked car parked a block away. It was backlit by a streetlamp, and he could see the silhouettes of two men sitting inside. *Police,* he thought. They were watching the house.

Tonight was not the time to do it.

He rounded the corner and drove on.

This matter could wait. It was only a bit of cleanup, a loose end that he could attend to in his spare time.

He had other, more important work to complete, and only a week in which to do it.

He drove on, toward the city.

AT 9:00 a.m., the guards came to escort Billy "The Snowman" Binford from his jail cell.

His attorney, Albert Darien, was waiting for him. Through the Plexiglas partition separating the two men, Billy could see Darien's grim expression and he knew that the news was not good. Billy sat down opposite his attorney. The guard wasn't standing close enough to catch their conversation, but Billy knew better than to speak freely. That stuff about attorney-client confidentiality was a bunch of bull. If the feds or the D.A. wanted you bad enough, they'd plant a bug on anyone, even your priest. It was outrageous, how they'd violate a citizen's rights.

"Hello, Billy," said Darien through the speaker phone. "How're they treating you?"

"Like a sultan. How the hell d'you *think* they're treating me? You gotta get me a few favors, Darien. A private TV. I'd like a private TV."

"Billy, we got problems."

Billy didn't like the tone of Darien's voice. "What problems?" he asked.

"Liddell's not even going to discuss a plea bargain. He's set on taking this to trial. Any other D.A.'d save himself the trouble, but I think Liddell's using you as a stepping stone to Blaine House."

"Liddell's running for governor?"

"He hasn't announced it. But if he puts you away, he'll be golden. And Billy, to be honest, he's got more than enough to put you away."

Billy leaned forward and glared through the Plexiglas at his attorney. "That's what I pay *you* for. So what the hell're you doing about the situation?"

"They've got too much. Hobart's turned state's witness."

"Hobart's a sleazeball. It'll be a piece of cake to discredit him."

"They've got your shipping records. It's all on paper, Billy."

"Okay, then let's try again with a plea bargain. Anything. Just keep my time in here short."

"I told you, Liddell's nixed a plea bargain."

Billy paused. Softly he said, "Liddell can be taken care of."

Darien stared at him. "What do you mean?"

"You just get me a deal. Don't worry about Liddell. I'm taking care of—"

"I don't want to know about it." Darien sat back, his hands suddenly shaking. "I don't want to know a damn thing, okay?"

"You don't have to. I got it covered."

"Just don't get me involved."

"All I want from you, Darien, is to keep this from going to trial. And get me out of here soon. You got that?"

"Yeah. Yeah." Darien glanced nervously at the guard, who wasn't paying the least bit of attention to their conversation. "I'll try."

"Just watch," said Billy. A cocky grin spread on his lips. "Next week, things'll be different. D.A.'s office will be happy to talk plea bargain."

"Why? What happens next week?"

"You don't want to know."

Darien exhaled a deep sigh and nodded. "You're right," he muttered. "I don't want to know."

NINA AWAKENED to the bass thump of aerobics dance music. Downstairs, she found Daniella stretched out on the polished oak floor of the exercise room. This morning Daniella was garbed in a shiny pink leotard, and her sleek legs knifed effortlessly through the air with every beat of the music. Nina stood watching in fascination for a moment, mesmerized by that display of taut muscles. Daniella worked hard at her body. In fact, she did little else. Since her marriage to George Cormier, Daniella's only goal in life seemed to be physical perfection.

The music ended. Daniella sprang to her feet with an easy grace. As she turned to reach for a towel, she noticed Nina standing in the doorway. "Oh. Good morning."

"Morning," said Nina. "I guess I overslept. Has Dad already left for work?"

"You know how he is. Likes to get started at the crack of dawn." With the towel, Daniella whisked away a delicate sheen of perspiration. A discomforting silence stretched between them. It always did. It was more than just the awkwardness of their relationship, the bizarre reality that this golden goddess was technically Nina's stepmother. It was also the fact that, except for their connection through George Cormier, the two women had absolutely nothing in common.

And never had that seemed more apparent to Nina than at this moment, as she stood gazing at the perfect face of this perfect blonde.

Daniella climbed onto an exercise bike and began pedaling away. Over the whir of the wheel, she said, "George had some board meeting. He'll be home for dinner. Oh, and you got two phone calls this morning. One was from that policeman. You know, the cute one."

"Detective Navarro?"

"Yeah. He was checking up on you."

So he's worried about me, thought Nina, feeling an unexpected lifting of her spirits. He'd cared enough to make sure she was alive and well. Then again, maybe he was just checking to make sure he didn't have a new corpse on his hands.

Yes, that was the likely reason he'd called.

Feeling suddenly glum, Nina turned to leave the room, then stopped. "What about the second call?" she asked. "You said there were two."

"Oh, right." Daniella, still pumping away, looked serenely over the handlebars. "The other call was from Robert."

Nina stared at her in shocked silence. "Robert called?"

"He wanted to know if you were here."

"Where is *he?*"

"At home."

Nina shook her head in disbelief. "You might have told me earlier."

"You were sound asleep. I didn't see the point of waking you." Daniella leaned into the handlebars and began to pedal with singleminded concentration. "Besides, he'll call back later."

I'm not waiting till later, thought Nina. *I want answers now. And I want them face-to-face.*

Heart thudding, she left the house. She borrowed her father's Mercedes to drive to Ocean View Drive. He'd never miss it; after all, he kept a spare Jaguar and a BMW in the garage.

By the time she pulled into Robert's driveway, she was shaking from both anger and dread. What on earth was she going to say to him?

What was he going to say to *her?*

She climbed the porch steps and rang the doorbell. She didn't have her house keys. Sam Navarro did. Anyway, this wasn't her house any longer. It never had been.

The door swung open and Robert stood looking at her in surprise. He was wearing running shorts and a T-shirt, and his face had the healthy flush of recent exercise. Not exactly the picture of a man pining for his fiancée.

"Uh, Nina," he said. "I—I was worried about you."

"Somehow I have a hard time believing that."

"I even called your father's house—"

"What happened, Robert?" Her breath rushed out in a bewildered sigh. "Why did you walk out on me?"

He looked away. That alone told her how far apart they'd drifted. "It's not easy to explain."

"It wasn't easy for me, either. Telling everyone to go home. Not knowing why it fell apart. You could have told me. A week before. A *day* before. Instead you leave me there, holding the damn bouquet! Wondering if it was all *my* fault. Something *I* did wrong."

"It wasn't you, Nina."

"What was it, then?"

He didn't answer. He just kept looking away, unwilling to face her. Maybe afraid to face her.

"I lived with you for a whole year," she said with sad wonder. "And I don't have the faintest idea who you are." With a stifled sob, she pushed past him, into the house, and headed straight for the bedroom.

"What are you doing?" he yelled.

"Packing the rest of my things. And getting the hell out of your life."

"Nina, there's no need to be uncivilized about this. We tried to make it. It just didn't work out. Why can't we still be friends?"

"Is that what we are? Friends?"

"I like to think so. I don't see why we can't be."

She shook her head and laughed. A bitter sound. "*Friends* don't twist the knife after they stab you." She stalked into the bedroom and began yanking open drawers. She pulled out clothes and tossed them on the bed. She was beyond caring about neatness; all she wanted was to get out of this house and never see it again. Or him again. Up until a moment ago, she'd thought it still possible to salvage their relationship, to pick up the pieces and work toward some sort of life together. Now she knew there wasn't a chance of it. She didn't want *him*. She couldn't even recall what it was about Robert Bledsoe that had attracted her. His looks, his medical degree—those were things she'd considered nice but not that important. No, what she'd seen in Robert—or imagined she'd seen—was intelligence and wit and caring. He'd shown her all those things.

What an act.

Robert was watching her with a look of wounded nobility. As if this was all her fault. She ignored him and went to the closet, raked out an armful of dresses, and dumped them on the bed. The pile was so high it was starting to topple.

"Does it all have to be done right now?" he asked.

"Yes."

"There aren't enough suitcases."

"Then I'll use trash bags. And I need to take my books, too."

"Today? But you've got tons of them!"

"This week I've got tons of time. Since I skipped the honeymoon."

"You're being unreasonable. Look, I know you're angry. You have a right to be. But don't go flying off the damn handle."

"I'll fly off the handle if I *want* to!" she yelled.

The sound of a throat being cleared made them both turn in surprise. Sam Navarro stood in the bedroom doorway, looking at them with an expression of quiet bemusement.

"Don't you cops *ever* bother to knock?" snapped Robert.

"I did knock," said Sam. "No one answered. And you left the front door wide open."

"You're trespassing," said Robert. "*Again* without a warrant."

"He doesn't need a warrant," said Nina.

"The law says he does."

"Not if I invite him in!"

"You didn't invite him in. He *walked* in."

"The door was open," said Sam. "I was concerned." He looked at Nina. "That wasn't smart, Miss Cormier, driving here alone. You should have told me you were leaving your father's house."

"What am I, your prisoner?" she muttered and crossed back to the closet for another armload of clothes. "How did you track me down, anyway?"

"I called your stepmother right after you left the house. She thought you'd be here."

"Well, I am. And I happen to be busy."

"Yeah," muttered Robert. "She's really good at being busy."

Nina spun around to confront her ex-fiancé. "What's that supposed to mean?"

"I'm not the only one to blame in all this! It takes two people to screw up a relationship."

"I didn't leave *you* at the church!"

"No, but you left me. Every night, for months on end."

"What? *What?*"

"Every damn night, I was here on my own! I would have enjoyed coming home to a nice meal. But you were never here."

"They needed me on the evening shift. I couldn't change that!"

"You could've quit."

"Quit my *job?* To do what? Play happy homemaker to a man who couldn't even decide if he wanted to marry me?"

"If you loved me, you would have."

"Oh, my God. I can't believe you're turning this into my fault. I didn't *love* you enough."

Sam said, "Nina, I need to talk to you."

"Not now!" Nina and Robert both snapped at him.

Robert said to her, "I just think you should know I had my reasons for not going through with it. A guy has only so much patience. And then it's natural to start looking elsewhere."

"Elsewhere?" She stared at him with new comprehension. Softly she said, "So there was someone else."

"What do you think?"

"Do I know her?"

"It hardly makes a difference now."

"It does to *me.* When did you meet her?"

He looked away. "A while ago."

"How long?"

"Look, this is irrelevant—"

"For six months, we planned that wedding. Both of us. And you never bothered to tell me the minor detail that you were seeing another woman?"

"It's clear to me you're not rational at the moment. Until you are, I'm not discussing this." Robert turned and left the room.

"Not *rational?*" she yelled. "I'm more rational now than I was six months ago!"

She was answered by the thud of the front door as it slammed shut.

Another woman, she thought. *I never knew. I never even suspected.*

Suddenly feeling sick to her stomach, she sank down on the bed. The pile of clothes tumbled onto the floor, but she didn't even notice. Nor did she realize that she was crying, that the tears were dribbling down her cheeks and onto her shirt. She was both sick and numb at the same time, and oblivious to everything but her own pain.

She scarcely noticed that Sam had sat down beside her. "He's not worth it, Nina," he soothed quietly. "He's not worth grieving over."

Only when his hand closed warmly over hers did she look up. She found his gaze focused steadily on her face. "I'm not grieving," she said.

Gently he brushed his fingers across her cheek, which was wet with tears. "I think you are."

"I'm not. I'm *not.*" She gave a sob and sagged against him, burying her face in his shirt. "I'm not," she whispered against his chest.

Only vaguely did she sense his arms folding around her back, gathering her against him. Suddenly those arms were holding her close, wrapping tightly around her. He didn't say a thing. As always, the laconic cop. But she felt his breath warming her hair, felt his lips brush the top of her head, and she heard the quickening of his heartbeat.

Just as she felt the quickening of her own.

It means nothing, she thought. He was being kind to her. Comforting her the way he would any hurt citizen. It was what she did every day in the ER. It was her job. It was his job.

Oh, but this felt so good.

It took a ruthless act of pure will to pull out of his arms. When she looked up, she found his expression calm, his green eyes unreadable. No passion, no desire. Just the public servant, in full control of his emotions.

Quickly she wiped away her tears. She felt stupid now, embarrassed by what he'd just witnessed between her and Robert. He knew it all, every humiliating detail, and she could scarcely bear to look him in the eye.

She stood up and began to gather the fallen clothes from the floor.

"You want to talk about it?" he asked.

"No."

"I think you need to. The man you loved leaves you for another woman. That must hurt pretty bad."

"Okay, I *do* need to talk about it!" She threw a handful of clothes on the bed and looked at him. "But not with some stone-faced cop who couldn't care less!"

There was a long silence. Though he looked at her without a flicker of emotion, she sensed that she'd just delivered a body blow. And he was too proud to show it.

She shook her head. "I'm sorry. Oh God, Navarro, I'm so sorry. You didn't deserve that."

"Actually," he said, "I think I did."

"You're just doing your job. And then I go and lash out at you." Thoroughly disgusted with herself, she sat down beside him on the bed. "I was just taking it out on you. I'm so—so angry at myself for letting him make me feel guilty."

"Why guilty?"

"That's the crazy part about it! I don't know why I should feel guilty! He makes it sound as if I neglected him. But I could never quit my job, even for him. I love my job."

"He's a doctor. He must've had long hours as well. Nights, weekends."

"He worked a lot of weekends."

"Did you complain?"

"Of course not. That's his job."

"Well?" He regarded her with a raised eyebrow.

"Oh." She sighed. "The old double standard."

"Exactly. I wouldn't expect my wife to quit a job she loved, just to make dinner and wait on me every night."

She stared down at her hands, clasped in her lap. "You wouldn't?"

"That's not love. That's possession."

"I think your wife's a very lucky woman," she said softly.

"I was only speaking theoretically."

She frowned at him. "You mean...it was just a theoretical wife?"

He nodded.

So he wasn't married. That piece of information made her flush with a strange and unexpected gladness. What on earth was the matter with her?

She looked away, afraid that he might see the confusion in her eyes. "You, uh, said you needed to talk to me."

"It's about the case."

"It must be pretty important if you went to all the trouble of tracking me down."

"I'm afraid we have a new development. Not a pleasant one."

She went very still. "Something's happened?"

"Tell me what you know about the church janitor."

She shook her head in bewilderment. "I don't know him at all. I don't even know his name."

"His name was Jimmy Brogan. We spent all yesterday evening trying to track Brogan down. We know he unlocked the church door yesterday. That he was in and out of the building all morning. But no one seems to know where he went after the explosion. We know he didn't turn up at the neighborhood bar where he usually goes every afternoon."

"You said *was.* That his name *was* Jimmy Brogan. Does that mean..."

Sam nodded. "We found his body this morning. He was in his car, parked in a field in Scarborough. He died from a gunshot wound to the head. The gun was in the car with him. It had his fingerprints on it."

"A suicide?" she asked softly.

"That's the way it looks."

She was silent, too shocked to say a thing.

"We're still waiting for the crime lab report. There are a number of details that bother me. It feels too neat, too packaged. It ties up every single loose end we've got."

"Including the bombing?"

"Including the bombing. There were several items in the car trunk that would seem to link Brogan to the bomb. Detonating cord. Green electrical tape. It's all pretty convincing evidence."

"You don't sound convinced."

"The problem is, Brogan had no explosives experience that we know of. Also, we can't come up with a motive for any bombing. Or for the attack on you. Can you help us out?"

She shook her head. "I don't know anything about the man."

"Are you familiar with the name Brogan?"

"No."

"He was familiar with *you.* There was a slip of paper with your address in his car."

She stared at him. His gaze was impenetrable. It frightened her, how little she could read in his eyes. How deeply the man was buried inside the cop. "Why would he have my address?" she asked.

"You must have some link to him."

"I don't know anyone named Brogan."

"Why would he try to kill you? Run you off the road?"

"How do you know *he* did it?"

"Because of his car. The one we found his body in."

She swallowed hard. "It was black?"

He nodded. "A black Ford."

Chapter Five

Sam drove her to the morgue. Neither one of them said much. He was being guarded about what information he told her, and she was too chilled to ask for the details. All the way there, she kept thinking, *Who was Jimmy Brogan and why did he want to kill me?*

In the morgue, Sam maintained a firm grip on her arm as they walked the corridor to the cold room. He was right beside her when the attendant led them to the bank of body drawers. As the drawer was pulled out she involuntarily flinched. Sam's arm came around her waist, a steady support against the terrible sight she was about to face.

"It ain't pretty," said the attendant. "Are you ready?"

Nina nodded.

He pulled aside the shroud and stepped back.

As an ER nurse, Nina had seen more than her share of grisly sights. This was by far the worst. She took one look at the man's face—what was left of it—and quickly turned away. "I don't know him," she whispered.

"Are you sure?" Sam asked.

She nodded and suddenly felt herself swaying. At once he was supporting her, his arm guiding her away from the drawers. Away from the cold room.

In the coroner's office she sat nursing a cup of hot tea while Sam talked on the phone to his partner. Only vaguely did she register his conversation. His tone was as matter-of-fact as always, betraying no hint of the horror he'd just witnessed.

"...doesn't recognize him. Or the name either. Are you sure we don't have an alias?" Sam was saying.

Nina cupped the tea in both hands but didn't sip. Her stomach was still too queasy. On the desk beside her was the file for Jimmy Brogan, open to the ID information sheet. Most of what she saw there didn't stir any memories. Not his address nor the name of his wife. Only the name of the employer was familiar:

the Good Shepherd Church. She wondered if Father Sullivan had been told, wondered how he was faring in the hospital. It would be a double shock to the elderly man. First, the bombing of his church, and then the death of the janitor. She should visit him today and make sure he was doing all right...

"Thanks, Gillis. I'll be back at three. Yeah, set it up, will you?" Sam hung up and turned to her. Seeing her face, he frowned in concern. "You all right?"

"I'm fine." She shuddered and clutched the mug more tightly.

"You don't look fine. I think you need some recovery time. Come on." He offered his hand. "It's lunchtime. There's a café up the street."

"You can think about lunch?"

"I make it a point never to skip a chance at a meal. Or would you rather I take you home?"

"Anything," she said, rising from the chair. "Just get me out of this place."

NINA PICKED LISTLESSLY at a salad while Sam wolfed down a hamburger.

"I don't know how you do it," she said. "How you go straight from the morgue to a big lunch."

"Necessity." He shrugged. "In this job, a guy can get skinny real fast."

"You must see so many awful things as a cop."

"You're an ER nurse. I would think you've seen your share."

"Yes. But they usually come to us still alive."

He wiped his hands on a napkin and slid his empty plate aside. "True. If it's a bomb, by the time I get to the scene, we're lucky to find anyone alive. If we find much of them at all."

"How do you live with it? How do you stand a job like yours?"

"The challenge."

"Really, Navarro. How do you deal with the horror?"

"My name's Sam, okay? And as for how I deal with it, it's more a question of *why* I do it. The truth is, the challenge is a lot of it. People who make bombs are a unique breed of criminal. They're not like the guy who holds up your neighborhood liquor store. Bombers are craftier. A few of them are truly geniuses. But they're also cowards. Killers at a distance. It's that combination that makes those guys especially dangerous. And it makes my job all the more satisfying when I can nail them."

"So you actually enjoy it."

"*Enjoy* isn't the right word. It's more that I can't set the puzzle aside. I keep looking at the pieces and turning them around. Trying to understand the sort of mind that could do such a thing." He shook his head. "Maybe that makes me just as much a monster. That I find it so satisfying to match wits with these guys."

"Or maybe it means you're an outstanding cop."

He laughed. "Either that or I'm as screwy as the bombers are."

She gazed across the table at his smiling face and suddenly wondered why she'd ever considered those eyes of his so forbidding. One laugh and Sam Navarro transformed from a cop into an actual human being. And a very attractive man.

I'm not going to let this happen, she thought with sudden determination. *It would be such a mistake to rebound from Robert, straight into some crazy infatuation with a cop.*

She forced herself to look away, at anything but his face, and ended up focusing on his hands. At the long, tanned fingers. She said, "If Brogan was the bomber, then I guess I have nothing to worry about now."

"If he was the bomber."

"The evidence seems pretty strong. Why don't you sound convinced?"

"I can't explain it. It's just...a feeling. Instinct, I guess. That's why I still want you to be careful."

She lifted her gaze to meet his and found his smile was gone. The cop was back.

"You don't think it's over yet," she said.

"No. I don't."

SAM DROVE NINA BACK to Ocean View Drive, helped her load up the Mercedes with a few armloads of books and clothes, and made sure she was safely on her way back to her father's house.

Then he returned to the station.

At three o'clock, they held a catch-up meeting. Sam, Gillis, Tanaka from the crime lab, and a third detective on the Bomb Task Force, Francis Cooley, were in attendance. Everyone laid their puzzle pieces on the table.

Cooley spoke first. "I've checked and rechecked the records on Jimmy Brogan. There's no alias for the guy. That's his real name. Forty-five years old, born and raised in South Portland, minor criminal record. Married ten years, no kids. He was hired by Reverend Sullivan eight years ago. Worked as a janitor and handyman around the church. Never any problems, except for a few times when he showed up late and hung over after falling off the wagon. No military service, no education beyond the eleventh grade. Wife says he was dyslexic. I just can't see this guy putting together a bomb."

"Did Mrs. Brogan have any idea why Nina Cormier's address was in his car?" Sam asked.

"Nope. She'd never heard the name before. And she said the handwriting wasn't her husband's."

"Were they having any marital troubles?"

"Happy as clams, from what she told me. She's pretty devastated."

"So we've got a happily married, uneducated, dyslexic janitor as our prime suspect?"

"Afraid so, Navarro."

Sam shook his head. "This gets worse every minute." He looked at Tanaka. "Eddie, give us some answers. Please."

Tanaka, nervous as usual, cleared his throat. "You're not going to like what I have."

"Hit me anyway."

"Okay. First, the gun in the car was reported stolen a year ago from its registered owner in Miami. We don't know how Brogan got the gun. His wife says he didn't know the first thing about firearms. Second, Brogan's car *was* the black Ford that forced Miss Cormier's Honda off the road. Paint chips match, both ways. Third, the items in the trunk are the same elements used in the church bombing. Two-inch-wide green electrical tape. Identical detonator cord."

"That's Vincent Spectre's signature," said Gillis. "Green electrical tape."

"Which means we're probably dealing with an apprentice of Spectre's. Now here's something else you're not going to like. We just got back the preliminary report from the coroner. The corpse had no traces of gunpowder on his hand. Now, that's not necessarily conclusive, since powder can rub off, but it does argue against a self-inflicted wound. What clinches it, though, is the skull fracture.''

''What?'' Sam and Gillis said it simultaneously.

''A depressed skull fracture, right parietal bone. Because of all the tissue damage from the bullet wound, it wasn't immediately obvious. But it did show up on X ray. Jimmy Brogan was hit on the head. *Before* he was shot.''

The silence in the room stretched for a good ten seconds. Then Gillis said, ''And I almost bought it. Lock, stock and barrel.''

''He's good,'' said Sam. ''But not good enough.'' He looked at Cooley. ''I want more on Brogan. I want you and your team to get the names of every friend, every acquaintance Brogan had. Talk to them all. It looks like our janitor got mixed up with the wrong guy. Maybe someone knows something, saw something.''

''Won't the boys in Homicide be beating those bushes?''

''We'll beat 'em as well. They may miss something. And don't get into any turf battles, okay? We're not trying to steal their glory. We just want the bomber.''

Cooley sighed and rose to his feet. ''Guess it's back to the ol' widow Brogan.''

''Gillis,'' said Sam, ''I need you to talk to the best man and the matron of honor again. See if they have any links to Brogan. Or recognize his photo. I'll go back to the hospital and talk to Reverend Sullivan. And I'll talk to Dr. Bledsoe as well.''

''What about the bride?'' asked Gillis.

''I've pressed the questions a couple times already. She denies knowing anything about him.''

''She seems to be the center of it all.''

''I know. And she hasn't the foggiest idea why. But maybe her ex-bridegroom does.''

The meeting broke up and everyone headed off to their respective tasks. It would take teamwork to find this bomber, and although he had good people working with him, Sam knew they were stretched thin. Since that rookie cop's death in the warehouse blast a week ago, Homicide had stepped into the investigation, and they were sucking up men and resources like crazy. As far as Homicide was concerned, the Bomb Task Force was little more than a squad of ''techies''—the guys you called in when you didn't want your own head blown off.

The boys in Homicide were smart enough.

But the boys in Bombs were smarter.

That's why Sam himself drove out to Maine Medical Center to reinterview Reverend Sullivan. This latest information on Jimmy Brogan's death had opened up a whole new range of possibilities. Perhaps Brogan had been a completely innocent patsy. Perhaps he'd witnessed something—and had mentioned it to the minister.

At the hospital, Sam learned that Reverend Sullivan had been transferred out of Intensive Care that morning. A heart attack had been ruled out, and Sullivan was now on a regular ward.

When Sam walked in the man's room, he found the minister sitting up in bed, looking glum. There was a visitor there already—Dick Yeats of Homicide. Not one of Sam's favorite people.

"Hey, Navarro," said Yeats in that cocky tone of his. "No need to spin your wheels here. We're on the Brogan case."

"I'd like to talk to Reverend Sullivan myself."

"He doesn't know anything helpful."

"Nevertheless," said Sam, "I'd like to ask my own questions."

"Suit yourself," Yeats said as he headed out the door. "Seems to me, though, that you boys in Bombs could make better use of your time if you'd let Homicide do its job."

Sam turned to the elderly minister, who was looking very unhappy about talking to yet another cop.

"I'm sorry, Reverend," said Sam. "But I'm afraid I'm going to have to ask you some more questions."

Reverend Sullivan sighed, the weariness evident in his lined face. "I can't tell you more than I already have."

"You've been told about Brogan's death?"

"Yes. That policeman—that Homicide person—"

"Detective Yeats."

"He was far more graphic than necessary. I didn't need all the...details."

Sam sat down in a chair. The minister's color was better today, but he still looked frail. The events of the last twenty-four hours must be devastating for him. First the destruction of his church building, and then the violent death of his handyman. Sam hated to flog the old man with yet more questions, but he had no choice.

Unfortunately, he could elicit no new answers. Reverend Sullivan knew nothing about Jimmy Brogan's private life. Nor could he think of a single reason why Brogan, or anyone else for that matter, would attack the Good Shepherd Church. There had been minor incidents, of course. A few acts of vandalism and petty theft. That's why he had started locking the church doors at night, a move that grieved him deeply as he felt churches should be open to those in need, day or night. But the insurance company had insisted, and so Reverend Sullivan had instructed his staff to lock up every evening at 6:00 p.m., and reopen every morning at 7:00 a.m.

"And there've been no acts of vandalism since?" asked Sam.

"None whatsoever," affirmed the minister. "That is, until the bomb."

This was a dead end, thought Sam. Yeats was right. He was just spinning his wheels.

As he rose to leave, there was a knock on the door. A heavyset woman poked her head in the room.

"Reverend Sullivan?" she said. "Is this a good time to visit?"

The gloom on the minister's face instantly transformed to a look of relief. Thankfulness. "Helen! I'm so glad you're back! Did you hear what happened?"

"On the television, this morning. As soon as I saw it, I packed my things and started straight back for home." The woman, carrying a bundle of carnations, crossed to the bed and gave Reverend Sullivan a tearful hug. "I just saw the church. I drove right past it. Oh, what a mess."

"You don't know the worst of it," said Reverend Sullivan. He swallowed. "Jimmy's dead."

"Dear God." Helen pulled back in horror. "Was it...in the explosion?"

"No. They're saying he shot himself. I didn't even know he had a gun."

Helen took an unsteady step backward. At once Sam grasped her ample arm and guided her into the chair from which he'd just risen. She sat quivering, her face white with shock.

"Excuse me, ma'am," said Sam gently. "I'm Detective Navarro, Portland Police. May I ask your full name?"

She swallowed. "Helen Whipple."

"You're the church secretary?"

She looked up at him with dazed eyes. "Yes. Yes."

"We've been trying to contact you, Miss Whipple."

"I was—I was at my sister's house. In Amherst." She sat twisting her hands together, shaking her head. "I can't believe this. I saw Jimmy only yesterday. I can't believe he's gone."

"You saw Brogan? What time?"

"It was in the morning. Just before I left town." She began digging in her purse, desperately fishing for tissues. "I stopped in to pay a few bills before I left."

"Did you two speak?"

"Naturally. Jimmy's such..." She gave a soft sob. "*Was* such...a friendly man. He was always coming up to the office to chat. Since I was leaving on vacation, and Reverend Sullivan wasn't in yet. I asked Jimmy to do a few things for me."

"What things?"

"Oh, there was so much confusion. The wedding, you know. The florist kept popping in to use the phone. The men's bathroom sink was leaking and we needed some plumbing done quick. I had to give Jimmy some last minute instructions. Everything from where to put the wedding gifts to which plumber to call. I was so relieved when Reverend Sullivan arrived, and I could leave."

"Excuse me, ma'am," Sam cut in. "You said something about wedding gifts."

"Yes. It's a nuisance, how some people have gifts delivered to the church instead of the bride's home."

"How many gifts arrived at the church?"

"There was only one. Jimmy—oh, poor Jimmy. It's so unfair. A wife and all..."

Sam fought to maintain his patience. "What about the gift?"

"Oh. That. Jimmy said a man brought it by. He showed it to me. Very nicely wrapped, with all these pretty silver bells and foil ribbons."

"Mrs. Whipple," Sam interrupted again. "What happened to that gift?"

"Oh, I don't know. I told Jimmy to give it to the bride's mother. I assume that's what he did."

"But the bride's mother hadn't arrived yet, right? So what would Jimmy do with it?"

Helplessly Helen Whipple shrugged her shoulders. "I suppose he'd leave it where she'd be sure to find it. In the front pew."

The front pew. The center of the blast.

Sam said, sharply, "Who was the gift addressed to?"

"The bride and groom, of course."

"Dr. Bledsoe and his fiancée?"

"Yes. That was on the card. Dr. and Mrs. Robert Bledsoe."

IT WAS STARTING to come together now, Sam thought as he got back in his car. The method of delivery. The time of planting. But the target wasn't quite clear yet. Was Nina Cormier or Robert Bledsoe supposed to die? Or was it both of them?

Nina, he knew, had no answers, no knowledge of any enemies. She couldn't help him.

So Sam drove to Ocean View Drive, to Robert Bledsoe's house. This time Bledsoe was damn well going to answer some questions, the first two being: Who was the other woman he'd been seeing, and was she jealous enough to sabotage her lover's wedding—and kill off a dozen people in the process?

Two blocks before he got there, he knew something was wrong. There were police lights flashing ahead and spectators gathered on the sidewalks.

Sam parked the car and quickly pushed his way through the crowd. At the edge of Bledsoe's driveway, a yellow police tape had been strung between wooden stakes. He flashed his badge to the patrolman standing guard and stepped across the line.

Homicide Detective Dick Yeats greeted him in the driveway with his usual I'm-in-charge tone of superiority.

"Hello again, Navarro. We have it all under control."

"You have *what* under control? What happened?"

Yeats nodded toward the BMW in the driveway.

Slowly Sam circled around the rear bumper. Only then did he see the blood. It was all over the steering wheel and the front seat. A small pool of it had congealed on the driveway pavement.

"Robert Bledsoe," said Yeats. "Shot once in the temple. The ambulance just left. He's still alive, but I don't expect he'll make it. He'd just pulled into his driveway and was getting out of his car. There's a sack of groceries in the trunk. Ice cream barely melted. The neighbor saw a green Jeep take off, just before she noticed Bledsoe's body. She thinks it was a man behind the wheel, but she didn't see his face."

"A man?" Sam's head snapped up. "Dark hair?"

"Yeah."

"Oh, God." Sam turned and started toward his car. *Nina,* he thought, and suddenly he was running. A dark-haired man had forced Nina off the road. Now Bledsoe was dead. Was Nina next?

Sam heard Yeats yell, "Navarro!" By then, he was already scrambling into his car. He made a screeching U-turn and headed away from Ocean View Drive.

He drove with his emergency lights flashing all the way to George Cormier's house.

It seemed he was ringing the bell forever before anyone answered the door. Finally it swung open and Daniella appeared, her flawless face arranged in a smile. "Why, hello, Detective."

"Where's Nina?" he demanded, pushing past her into the house.

"She's upstairs. Why?"

"I need to talk to her. *Now.*" He started for the stairway, then halted when he heard footsteps creak on the landing above. Glancing up, he saw Nina standing on the steps, her hair a tumble of black silk.

She's okay, he thought with relief. *She's still okay.*

She was dressed casually in jeans and a T-shirt, and she had a purse slung over her shoulder, as if she were just about to leave the house.

As she came down the stairs, she brought with her the elusive fragrance of soap and shampoo. Nina's scent, he thought with a pleasurable thrill of recognition. Since when had he committed her fragrance to memory?

By the time she reached the bottom step, she was frowning at him. "Has something happened?" she asked.

"Then no one's called you?"

"About what?"

"Robert."

She went very still, her dark eyes focused with sudden intensity on his face. He could see the questions in her eyes, and knew she was too afraid to ask them.

He reached for her hand. It was cold. "You'd better come with me."

"Where?"

"The hospital. That's where they took him." Gently he led her to the door.

"Wait!" called Daniella.

Sam glanced back. Daniella stood frozen, staring after them in panic. "What about Robert? What happened?"

"He's been shot. It happened a short while ago, just outside his house. I'm afraid it doesn't look good."

Daniella took a step backward, as though slapped. It was her reaction, that expression of horror in her eyes, that told Sam what he needed to know. *So she was the other woman,* he thought. *This blonde with her sculpted body and her perfect face.*

He could feel Nina's arm trembling in his grasp. He turned her toward the door. "We'd better go," he said. "There may not be much time."

Chapter Six

They spent the next four hours in a hospital waiting room.

Though Nina wasn't part of the medical team now battling to save Robert's life, she could picture only too vividly what was going on at that moment in the trauma suite. The massive infusions of blood and saline. The scramble to control the patient's bleeding, to keep his pressure up, his heart beating. She knew it all well because, at other times, on other patients, she had been part of the team. Now she was relegated to this useless task of waiting and worrying. Though her relationship with Robert was irrevocably broken, though she hadn't forgiven him for the way he'd betrayed her, she certainly didn't want him hurt.

Or dead.

It was only Sam's presence that kept her calm and sane during that long evening. Other cops came and went. As the hours stretched on, only Sam stayed next to her on the couch, his hand clasping hers in a silent gesture of support. She could see that he was tired, but he didn't leave her. He stayed right beside her as the night wore on toward ten o'clock.

And he was there when the neurosurgeon came out to inform them that Robert had died on the operating table.

Nina took the blow in numb silence. She was too stunned to shed any tears, to say much more than "Thank you for trying." She scarcely realized Sam had his arm around her. Only when she sagged against him did she feel his support, steadying her.

"I'm going to take you home," he said softly. "There's nothing more you can do here."

Mutely she nodded. He helped her to her feet and guided her toward the exit. They were halfway across the room when a voice called, "Miss Cormier? I need to ask you some more questions."

Nina turned and looked at the rodent-faced man who'd just spoken to her. She couldn't remember his name, but she knew he was a cop; he'd been in and out of the waiting room all evening. Now he was studying her closely, and she didn't like the look in his eyes.

"Not now, Yeats," said Sam, nudging her to the exit. "It's a bad time."

"It's the best time to ask questions," said the other cop. "Right after the event."

"She's already told me she knew nothing about it."

"She hasn't told *me.*" Yeats turned his gaze back to Nina. "Miss Cormier, I'm with Homicide. Your fiancé never regained consciousness, so we couldn't question him. That's why I need to talk to you. Where were you this afternoon?"

Bewildered, Nina shook her head. "I was at my father's house. I didn't know about it until..."

"Until I told her," filled in Sam.

"*You* did, Navarro?"

"I went straight from the crime scene to her father's house. Nina was there. You can ask Daniella Cormier to confirm it."

"I will." Yeats's gaze was still fixed on Nina. "I understand you and Dr. Bledsoe just called off the engagement. And you were in the process of moving out of his house."

Softly Nina said, "Yes."

"I imagine you must have been pretty hurt. Did you ever consider, oh...getting back at him?"

Horrified by his implication, she gave a violent shake of her head. "You don't really think that—that I had something to do with this?"

"Did you?"

Sam stepped between them. "That's enough, Yeats."

"What are you, Navarro? Her lawyer?"

"She doesn't have to answer these questions."

"Yes, she does. Maybe not tonight. But she does have to answer questions."

Sam took Nina's arm and propelled her toward the exit.

"Watch it, Navarro!" Yeats yelled as they left the room. "You're on thin ice!"

Though Sam didn't answer, Nina could sense his fury just by the way he gripped her arm all the way to the parking lot.

When they were back in his car, she said, quietly, "Thank you, Sam."

"For what?"

"For getting me away from that awful man."

"Eventually, you *will* have to talk to him. Yeats may be a pain in the butt, but he has a job to do."

And so do you, she thought with a twinge of sadness. She turned to look out the window. He was the cop again, always the cop, trying to solve the puzzle. She was merely one of the pieces.

"You're going to have to talk to him tomorrow," said Sam. "Just a warning—he can be a tough interrogator."

"There's nothing I have to tell him. I was at my father's house. You know that. And Daniella will confirm it."

"No one can knock your alibi. But murder doesn't have to be done in person. Killers can be hired."

She turned to him with a look of disbelief. "You don't think I'd—"

"I'm just saying that's the logic Yeats will use. When someone gets murdered, the number one suspect is always the spouse or lover. You and Bledsoe just broke up. And it happened in the most public and painful way possible. It doesn't take a giant leap of logic to come up with murderous intent on your part."

"I'm not a murderer. You know I'm not!"

He didn't answer. He just went on driving as though he had not registered a word.

"Navarro, did you hear me? I'm not a murderer!"

"I heard you."

"Then why aren't you saying anything?"

"Because I think something else just came up."

Only then did she notice that he was frowning at the rearview mirror. He picked up his car phone and dialed. "Gillis?" he said. "Do me a favor. Find out if Yeats has a tail on Nina Cormier. Yeah, right now. I'm in the car. Call me back." He hung up.

Nina turned and looked out the rear window, at a pair of headlights behind them. "Is someone following us?"

"I'm not sure. I do know that car pulled out behind ours when we left the hospital. And it's been there ever since."

"Your buddy in Homicide must really think I'm dangerous if he's having me followed."

"He's just keeping tabs on his suspect."

Me, she thought, and sank back against the seat, grateful that the darkness hid her face. *Am I your suspect as well?*

He drove calmly, making no sudden moves to alarm whoever

was in the car behind them. In that tense stillness, the ringing of the phone was startling.

He picked up the receiver. "Navarro." There was a pause, then he said, "You're sure?" Again he glanced in the mirror. "I'm at Congress and Braeburn, heading west. There's a dark truck—looks like a Jeep Cherokee—right behind me. I'll swing around, make a pass by Houlton. If you can be ready and waiting, we'll sandwich this guy. Don't scare him off. For now, just move in close enough to get a good look. Okay, I'm making my turn now. I'll be there in five minutes." He hung up and shot Nina a tense glance. "You pick up what's happening?"

"What *is* happening?"

"That's not a cop behind us."

She looked back at the headlights. Not a cop. "Then who is it?"

"We're going to find out. Now listen good. In a minute I'll want you down near the floor. Not yet—I don't want to make him suspicious. But when Gillis pulls in behind him, things could get exciting. Are you ready for this?"

"I don't think I have much of a choice..."

He made his turn. Not too fast—a casual change of direction to make it seem as if he'd just decided on a different route.

The other car made the turn as well.

Sam turned again, back onto Congress Street. They were headed east now, going back the way they'd come. The pair of headlights was still behind them. At 10:30 on a Sunday, traffic was light and it was easy to spot their pursuer.

"There's Gillis," Sam stated. "Right on schedule." He nodded at the blue Toyota idling near the curb. They drove past it.

A moment later, the Toyota pulled into traffic, right behind the Jeep.

"Perp sandwich," said Sam with a note of triumph. They were coming on a traffic light, just turning yellow. Purposely he slowed down, to keep the other two cars on his tail.

Without warning, the Cherokee suddenly screeched around them and sped straight through the intersection just as the light turned red.

Sam uttered an oath and hit the accelerator. They, too, lurched through the intersection just as a pickup truck barreled in from a side street. Sam swerved around it and took off after the sedan.

A block ahead, the Cherokee screeched around a corner.

"This guy's smart," muttered Sam. "He knew we were moving in on him."

"Watch out!" cried Nina as a car pulled out of a parking space, right in front of them.

Sam leaned on his horn and shot past.

This is crazy, she thought. *I'm riding with a maniac cop at the wheel.*

They spun around the corner into an alley. Nina, clutching the dashboard, caught a dizzying view of trash cans and Dumpsters as they raced through.

At the other end of the alley, Sam screeched to a halt.

There was no sign of the Cherokee. In either direction.

Gillis's Toyota squealed to a stop just behind them. "Which way?" they heard Gillis call.

"I don't know!" Sam yelled back. "I'll head east."

He turned right. Nina glanced back and saw Gillis turn left, in the other direction. A two-pronged search. Surely one of them would spot the quarry.

Four blocks later, there was still no sign of the Cherokee. Sam reached for the car phone and dialed Gillis.

"No luck here," he said. "How about you?" At the answer, he gave a grunt of disappointment. "Okay. At least you got the license number. I'll check back with you later." He hung up.

"So he did catch the number?" Nina asked.

"Massachusetts plate. APB's going out now. With any luck, they'll pick him up." He glanced at Nina. "I'm not so sure you should go back to your father's house."

Their gazes locked. What she saw, in his eyes, confirmed her fears.

"You think he was following me," she said softly.

"What I want to know is, why? There's something weird going on here, something that involves both you and Robert. You must have *some* idea what it is."

She shook her head. "It's a mistake," she whispered. "It must be."

"Someone's gone to a lot of trouble to ensure your deaths. I don't think he—or she—would mistake the target."

"She? Do you really think..."

"As I said before, murder needn't be done in person. It can be bought and paid for. And that could be what we're dealing with. I'm more and more certain of it. A professional."

Nina was shaking now, unable to answer him. Unable to argue. The man next to her was talking so matter-of-factly. *His* life didn't hang in the balance.

"I know it's hard to accept any of this yet," he added. "But in your case, denial could be fatal. So let me lay it out for you. The brutal facts. Robert's already dead. And you could be next."

But I'm not worth killing! she thought. *I'm no threat to anyone.*

"We can't pin the blame on Jimmy Brogan," said Sam. "I think he's the innocent in all this. He saw something he shouldn't have, so he was disposed of. And then his death was set up to look like a suicide, to throw us off the track. Deflect our bomb investigation. Our killer's very clever. And very specific about his targets." He glanced at her, and she heard, in his voice, pure, passionless logic. "There's something else I learned today," he told her. "The morning of your wedding, a gift was delivered to the church. Jimmy Brogan may have seen the man who left it. We think Brogan put the parcel somewhere near the front pews. Right near the blast center. The gift was addressed specifically to you and Robert." He paused, as though daring her to argue that away.

She couldn't. The information was coming too fast, and she was having trouble dealing with the terrifying implications.

"Help me out, Nina," he urged. "Give me a name. A motive."

"I told you," she said, her voice breaking to a sob. "I don't know!"

"Robert admitted there was another woman. Do you know who that might be?"

She was hugging herself, huddling into a self-protective ball against the seat. "No."

"Did it ever seem to you that Daniella and Robert were particularly close?"

Nina went still. *Daniella?* Her father's wife? She thought back over the past six months. Remembered the evenings she and Robert had spent at her father's house. All the invitations, the dinners. She'd been pleased that her fiancé had been so quickly accepted by her father and Daniella, pleased that, for once, harmony had been achieved in the Cormier family. Daniella, who'd never been particularly warm toward her stepdaughter, had suddenly started including Nina and Robert in every social function.

Daniella and Robert.

"That's another reason," he said, "why I don't think you should go back to your father's house tonight."

She turned to him. "You think Daniella..."

"We'll be questioning her again."

"But why would she kill Robert? If she loved him?"

"Jealousy? If she couldn't have him, no one could?"

"But he'd already broken off our engagement! It was over between us!"

"Was it really?"

Though the question was asked softly, she sensed at once an underlying tension in his voice.

She said, "You were there, Sam. You heard our argument. He didn't love me. Sometimes I think he never did." Her head dropped. "For him it was definitely over."

"And for you?"

Tears pricked her eyes. All evening she'd managed not to cry, not to fall apart. During those endless hours in the hospital waiting room, she'd withdrawn so completely into numbness that when they'd told her Robert was dead, she'd registered that fact in some distant corner of her mind, but she hadn't *felt* it. Not the shock, nor the grief. She knew she *should* be grieving. No matter how much Robert had hurt her, how bitterly their affair had ended, he was still the man with whom she'd spent the last year of her life.

Now it all seemed like a different life. Not hers. Not Robert's. Just a dream, with no basis in reality.

She began to cry. Softly. Wearily. Not tears of grief, but tears of exhaustion.

Sam said nothing. He just kept driving while the woman beside him shed soundless tears. There was plenty he *wanted* to say. He wanted to point out that Robert Bledsoe had been a first-class rat, that he was scarcely worth grieving over. But women in love weren't creatures you could deal with on a logical level. And he was sure she did love Bledsoe; it was the obvious explanation for those tears.

He tightened his grip on the steering wheel as frustration surged through him. Frustration at his own inability to comfort her, to assuage her grief. The Roberts of the world didn't deserve any woman's tears. Yet they were the men whom women always seemed to cry over. The golden boys. He glanced at Nina, huddled against the door, and he felt a rush of sympathy. And something more, something that surprised him. Longing.

At once he quelled the feeling. It was yet another sign that he should not be in this situation. It was fine for a cop to sympathize, but when the feelings crossed that invisible line into more dangerous emotions, it was time to pull back.

But I can't pull back. Not tonight. Not until I make sure she's safe.

Without looking at her, he said, "You can't go to your father's. Or your mother's for that matter—her house isn't secure. No alarm system, no gate. And it's too easy for the killer to find you."

"I—I signed a lease on a new apartment today. It doesn't have any furniture yet, but—"

"I assume Daniella knows about it?"

She paused, then replied, "Yes. She does."

"Then that's out. What about friends?"

"They all have children. If they knew a killer was trying to find me..." She took a deep breath. "I'll go to a hotel."

He glanced at her and saw that her spine was suddenly stiff and straight. And he knew she was fighting to put on a brave front. That's all it was, a front. God, what was he supposed to do now? She was scared and she had a right to be. They were both exhausted. He couldn't just dump her at some hotel at this hour. Nor could he leave her alone. Whoever was stalking her had done an efficient job of dispatching both Jimmy Brogan and Robert Bledsoe. For such a killer, tracking down Nina would be no trouble at all.

The turnoff to Route 1 north was just ahead. He took it.

Twenty minutes later they were driving past thick stands of trees. Here the houses were few and far between, all the lots heavily forested. It was the trees that had first attracted Sam to this neighborhood. As a boy, first in Boston, then in Portland, he'd always lived in the heart of the city. He'd grown up around concrete and asphalt, but he'd always felt the lure of the woods. Every summer, he'd head north to fish at his lakeside camp.

The rest of the year, he had to be content with his home in this quiet neighborhood of birch and pine.

He turned onto his private dirt road, which wound a short way into the woods before widening into his gravel driveway. Only as he turned off the engine and looked at his house did the first doubts assail him. The place wasn't much to brag about. It was just a two-bedroom cottage of precut cedar hammered together three summers ago. And as for the interior, he wasn't exactly certain how presentable he'd left it.

Oh, well. There was no changing plans now.

He got out and circled around to open her door. She stepped out, her gaze fixed in bewilderment on the small house in the woods.

"Where are we?" she asked.

"A safe place. Safer than a hotel anyway." He gestured toward the front porch. "It's just for tonight. Until we can make other arrangements."

"Who lives here?"

"I do."

If that fact disturbed her, she didn't show it. Maybe she was too tired and frightened to care. In silence she waited while he unlocked the door. He stepped inside after her and turned on the lights.

At his first glimpse of the living room, he gave a silent prayer of thanks. No clothes on the couch, no dirty dishes on the coffee table. Not that the place was pristine. With newspapers scattered about and dust bunnies in the corners, the room had that unmistakable look of a sloppy bachelor. But at least it wasn't a major disaster area. A minor one, maybe.

He locked the door and turned the dead bolt.

She was just standing there, looking dazed. Maybe by the condition of his house? He touched her shoulder and she flinched.

"You okay?" he asked.

"I'm fine."

"You don't look so fine."

In fact she looked pretty pitiful, her eyes red from crying, her cheeks a bloodless white. He had the sudden urge to take her face in his hands and warm it with his touch. Not a good idea. He was turning into a sucker for women in distress, and this woman was most certainly in distress.

Instead he turned and went into the spare bedroom. One glance at the mess and he nixed that idea. It was no place to put up a guest. Or an enemy, for that matter. There was only one solution. He'd sleep on the couch and let her have his room.

Sheets. Oh Lord, did he have any clean sheets?

Frantically he rummaged in the linen closet and found a fresh set. He was on top of things after all. Turning, he found himself face-to-face with Nina.

She held out her arms for the sheets. "I'll make up the couch."

"These are for the bed. I'm putting you in my room."

"No, Sam. I feel guilty enough as it is. Let me take the couch."

Something in the way she looked at him—that upward tilt of her chin—told him she'd had enough of playing the object of pity.

He gave her the sheets and added a blanket. "It's a lumpy couch. You don't mind?"

"I've taken a lot of lumps lately. I'll hardly notice a few more."

Almost a joke. That was good. She was pulling herself together—an act of will he found impressive.

While she made up the couch, he went to the kitchen and called Gillis at home.

"We got the info on that Massachusetts plate," Gillis told him. "It was stolen two weeks ago. APB hasn't netted the Cherokee yet. Man, this guy's quick."

"And dangerous."

"You think he's our bomber?"

"Our shooter, too. It's all tangled together, Gillis. It has to be."

"How does last week's warehouse bombing fit in? We figured that was a mob hit."

"Yeah. A nasty message to Billy Binford's rivals."

"Binford's in jail. His future's not looking so bright. Why would he order a church bombed?"

"The church wasn't the target, Gillis. I'm almost certain the target was Bledsoe or Nina Cormier. Or both."

"How does that tie in with Binford?"

"I don't know. Nina's never heard of Binford." Sam rubbed his face and felt the stubble of beard. God, he was tired. Too tired to figure anything out tonight. He said, "There's one other angle we haven't ruled out. The old crime of passion. You interviewed Daniella Cormier."

"Yeah. Right after the bombing. What a looker."

"You pick up anything odd about her?"

"What do you mean?"

"Anything that didn't sit right? Her reactions, her answers?"

"Not that I recall. She seemed appropriately stunned. What are you thinking?"

"I'm thinking Homicide should get their boys over there to question her tonight."

"I'll pass that message along to Yeats. What's your hunch?"

"She and Robert Bledsoe had a little thing going on the side."

"And she blew up the church out of jealousy?" Gillis laughed. "She didn't seem the type."

"Remember what they say about the female of the species."

"Yeah, but I can't imagine that gorgeous blonde—"

"Watch the hormones, Gillis."

His partner snorted. "If anyone better watch his hormones, it's you."

That's what I keep telling myself, thought Sam as he hung up. He paused for a moment in the kitchen, giving himself the same old lecture he'd given himself a dozen times since meeting Nina. *I'm a cop, I'm here to serve and protect. Not seduce.*

Not fall in love.

He went into the living room. At his first sight of Nina, he felt his resolve crumble. She was standing at the window, peering out at the darkness. He'd hung no curtains; here in the woods, he'd never felt the need for them. But now he realized just how open and vulnerable she was. And that worried him—more than he cared to admit.

He said, "I'd feel better if you came away from those windows."

She turned, a startled look in her eyes. "You don't think someone could have followed us?"

"No. But I'd like you to stay away from the windows all the same."

Shuddering, she moved to the couch and sat down. She'd already made the couch into a bed, and only now did he realize how tattered the blanket was. Tattered furniture, tattered linens. Those were details that had never bothered him before. So many things about his life as a bachelor had not bothered him, simply because he'd never stopped to think how much better, sweeter, his life could be. Only now, as he saw Nina sitting on his couch, did it occur to him how stark the room was. It was only the presence of this woman that gave it any life. Any warmth.

Too soon, she'd be gone again.

The sooner the better, he told himself. Before she grew on him. Before she slipped too deeply into his life.

He paced over to the fireplace, paced back toward the kitchen door, his feet restless, his instincts telling him to say something.

"You must be hungry," he said.

She shook her head. "I can't think about food. I can't think about anything except..."

"Robert?"

She lowered her head and didn't answer. Was she crying again? She had a right to. But she just sat very still and silent, as though struggling to hold her emotions in check.

He sat down in the chair across from her. "Tell me about Robert," he prompted. "Tell me everything you know about him."

She took a shaky breath, then said softly, "I don't know what to say. We lived together a year. And now I feel as if I never knew him at all."

"You met at work?"

She nodded. "The Emergency Room. Evening shift. I'd been working there for three years. Then Robert joined the ER staff. He was a good doctor. One of the best I'd ever worked with. And he was so fun to talk to. He'd traveled everywhere, done everything. I remember how surprised I was to learn he wasn't married."

"Never?"

"Never. He told me he was holding out for the best. That he just hadn't found the woman he wanted to spend his life with."

"At forty-one, he must've been more than a little picky."

Her glance held a trace of amusement. "*You're* not married, Detective. Does that make you more than a little picky?"

"Guilty as charged. But then, I haven't really been looking."

"Not interested?"

"Not enough time for romance. It's the nature of the job."

She gave a sigh. "No, it's the nature of the beast. Men don't really want to be married."

"Did I say that?"

"It's something I've finally figured out after years of spinsterhood."

"We're all rats, that kind of thing? Let's get back to one

specific rat. Robert. You were telling me you two met in the ER. Was it love at first sight?''

She leaned back, and he could clearly see the remembered pain on her face. ''No. No, it wasn't. At least, not for me. I thought he was attractive, of course.''

Of course, thought Sam with an undeniable twinge of cynicism.

''But when he asked me out, that first time, I didn't really think it would go anywhere. It wasn't until I introduced him to my mother that I began to realize what a catch he was. Mom was thrilled with Robert. All these years, I'd been dating guys she considered losers. And here I show up with a doctor. It was more than she'd ever expected of me, and she was already hearing wedding bells.''

''What about your father?''

''I think he was just plain relieved I was dating someone who wouldn't marry me for *his* money. That's always been Dad's preoccupation. His money. And his wives. Or rather, whichever wife he happens to be married to at the time.''

Sam shook his head. ''After what you've seen of your parents' marriages, I'm surprised you wanted to take the plunge at all.''

''But that's exactly why I *did* want to be married!'' She looked at him. ''To make it *work.* I never had that stability in my family. My parents were divorced when I was eight, and after that it was a steady parade of stepmothers and mother's boyfriends. I didn't want to live my own life that way.'' Sighing, she looked down at her ringless left hand. ''Now I wonder if it's just another urban myth. A stable marriage.''

''My parents had one. A good one.''

''Had?''

''Before my dad died. He was a cop, in Boston. Didn't make it to his twentieth year on the force.'' Now Sam was the one who wasn't looking at *her.* He was gazing, instead, at some distant point in the room, avoiding her look of sympathy. He didn't feel he particularly needed her sympathy. One's parents died, and one went on with life. There was no other choice.

''After my dad died, Mom and I moved to Portland,'' he continued. ''She wanted a safer town. A town where she wouldn't have to worry about her kid being shot on the street.'' He gave a rueful smile. ''She wasn't too happy when I became a cop.''

"Why did you become a cop?"

"I guess it was in the genes. Why did you become a nurse?"

"It was definitely *not* in the genes." She sat back, thinking it over for a moment. "I guess I wanted that one-on-one sense of helping someone. I like the contact. The touching. That was important to me, that it be hands-on. Not some vague idea of service to humanity." She gave a wry smile. "You said your mother didn't want you to be a cop. Well, my mother wasn't too happy about *my* career choice, either."

"What does she have against nursing?"

"Nothing. Just that it's not an appropriate profession for her daughter. She thinks of it as manual labor, something other women do. I was expected to marry well, entertain with flair, and help humanity by hosting benefits. That's why she was so happy about my engagement. She thought I was finally on the right track. She was actually*...proud* of me for the first time."

"That's not why you wanted to marry Robert, was it? To please your mother?"

"I don't know." She looked at him with genuine puzzlement. "I don't know anymore."

"What about love? You must have loved him."

"How can I be sure of anything? I've just found out he was seeing someone else. And now it seems as if I were caught up in some fantasy. In love with a man I made up." She leaned back and closed her eyes. "I don't want to talk about him anymore."

"It's important you tell me everything you know. That you consider all the possible reasons someone wanted him dead. A man doesn't just walk up to a stranger and shoot him in the head. The killer had a reason."

"Maybe he didn't. Maybe he was crazy. Or high on drugs. Robert could have been in the wrong place at the wrong time."

"You don't really believe that. Do you?"

She paused. Then, softly, she said, "No, I guess I don't."

He watched her for a moment, thinking how very vulnerable she looked. Had he been any other man, he would be taking her in his arms, offering her comfort and warmth.

Suddenly he felt disgusted with himself. This was the wrong time to be pressing for answers, the wrong time to be doing the cop act. Yet that act was the only thing that kept him comfortably at a distance. It protected him, insulated him. From her.

He rose from the chair. "I think we both need to get some sleep."

Her response was a silent nod.

"If you need anything, my room's at the end of the hall. Sure you wouldn't rather take my bed? Give me the couch?"

"I'll be fine here. Good night."

That was his cue to retreat. He did.

In his bedroom, he paced between the closet and the dresser, unbuttoning his shirt. He felt more restless than tired, his brain moving a mile a minute. In the last two days, a church had been bombed, a man shot to death, and a woman run off the road in an apparent murder attempt. He felt certain it was all linked, perhaps even linked to that warehouse bombing a week ago, but he couldn't see the connection. Maybe he was too dense. Maybe his brain was too drunk on hormones to think straight.

It was all her fault. He didn't need or want this complication. But he couldn't seem to think about this case without lingering on thoughts of her.

And now she was in his house.

He hadn't had a woman sleeping under his roof since…well, it was longer than he cared to admit. His last fling had amounted to little more than a few weeks of lust with a woman he'd met at some party. Then, by mutual agreement, it was over. No complications, no broken hearts.

Not much satisfaction, either.

These days, what satisfaction he got came from the challenge of his work. That was one thing he could count on: the world would never run out of perps.

He turned off the lights and stretched out on the bed, but still he wasn't ready to sleep. He thought of Nina, just down the hall. Thought of what a mismatch they'd be together. And how horrified her mother would be if a cop started squiring around her daughter. If a cop even had a chance.

What a mistake, bringing her here. Lately it seemed he was making a lot of mistakes. He wasn't going to compound this one by falling in love or lust or whatever it was he felt himself teetering toward.

Tomorrow, he thought, *she's out of here.*

And I'm back in control.

Chapter Seven

Nina knew she ought to be crying, but she couldn't. In darkness she lay on the couch and thought about those months she'd lived with Robert. The months she'd thought of as stepping stones to their marriage. When had it fallen apart? When had he stopped telling her the truth? She should have noticed the signs. The avoided looks, the silences.

She remembered that two weeks ago, he'd suggested the wedding be postponed. She'd assumed it was merely bridegroom jitters. By then, the arrangements were all made, the date set in stone.

How trapped he must have felt.

Oh Robert. If only you'd come out and told me.

She could have dealt with the truth. The pain, the rejection. She was strong enough and adult enough. What she couldn't deal with was the fact that, all these months, she'd been living with a man she scarcely knew.

Now she'd never know what he really felt about her. His death had cut off any chance she had to make peace with him.

At last she did fall asleep, but the couch was lumpy and the dreams kept waking her up.

Dreams not of Robert, but of Sam Navarro.

He was standing before her, silent and unsmiling. She saw no emotion in his eyes, just that flat, unreadable gaze of a stranger. He reached out to her, as though to take her hand. But when she looked down, there were handcuffs circling her wrists.

"You're guilty," he said. And he kept repeating the word. *Guilty. Guilty.*

She awakened with tears in her eyes. Never had she felt so alone. And she *was* alone, reduced to the pitiful state of seeking refuge in the home of a cop who cared nothing at all about her. Who considered her little more than an added responsibility. An added bother.

It was a flicker of shadow across the window that drew her

attention. She would not have noticed it at all, save for the fact it had passed just to the right of her, a patch of darkness moving across her line of vision. Suddenly her heart was thudding. She stared at the curtainless squares of moonlight, watching for signs of movement.

There it was again. A shadow, flitting past.

In an instant she was off the couch and running blindly up the hallway to Sam's room. She didn't stop to knock, but pushed right inside.

''Sam?'' she whispered. He didn't answer. Frantic to wake him, she reached down to give him a shake, and her hands met warm, bare flesh. ''Sam?''

At her touch, he awoke with such a violent start she jerked away in fright. ''What?'' he said. ''What is it?''

''I think there's someone outside!''

At once he seemed to snap fully awake. He rolled off the bed and grabbed his trousers from a chair. ''Stay here,'' he whispered. ''Don't leave the room.''

''What are you going to do?''

She was answered by a metallic click. A gun. Of course he had a gun. He was a cop.

''Just stay here,'' he ordered, and slipped out of the room.

She wasn't crazy; she wasn't going to go wandering around a dark house when there was a cop with a loaded gun nearby. Chilled and shivering, she stood by the door and listened. She heard Sam's footsteps creak down the hall toward the living room. Then there was silence, a silence so deep it made every breath she took seem like a roar. Surely he hadn't left the house? He wouldn't go outside, would he?

The creak of returning footsteps made her back away from the door. She scurried to the far side of the bed. At the first glimpse of a figure entering the room, she ducked behind the mattress. Only when she heard Sam say, ''Nina?'' did she dare raise her head.

''Here,'' she whispered, suddenly feeling ridiculous as she emerged from her hiding place.

''There's no one out there.''

''But I saw someone. Something.''

''It could have been a deer. An owl flying past.'' He set his gun down on the nightstand. The solid clunk of metal on wood made her flinch. She hated guns. She wasn't sure she wanted to be anywhere near a man who owned one. Tonight, though, she didn't have a choice.

"Nina, I know you're scared. You have a right to be. But I've checked, and there's no one out there." He reached toward her. At the first touch of his hand on her arm, he gave a murmur of alarm. "You're freezing."

"I'm scared. Oh God, Sam. I'm so scared..."

He took her by the shoulders. By now she was shaking so hard she could barely form any words. Awkwardly, he drew her against him, and she settled, trembling, against his chest. If only he'd hold her. If only he'd put his arms around her. When at last he did, it was like being welcomed home. Enclosed in warmth and safety. This was not the man she'd dreamed about, not the cold, unsmiling cop. This was a man who held her and murmured comforting sounds. A man whose face nuzzled her hair, whose lips, even now, were lowering toward hers.

The kiss was gentle. Sweet. Not the sort of kiss she ever imagined Sam Navarro capable of. Certainly she never imagined being hugged by him, comforted by him. But here she was, in his arms, and she had never felt so protected.

He coaxed her, still shivering, to the bed. He pulled the covers over them both. Again, he kissed her. Again the kiss was gently undemanding. The heat of the bed, of their bodies, banished her chill. And she became aware of so many other things: the scent of his bare skin, the bristly plane of his chest. And most of all, the touch of his lips, lingering against hers.

They had their arms wrapped around each other now, and their legs were slowly twining together. The kiss had gone beyond sweetness, beyond comfort. This was transforming to lust, pure and simple, and she was responding with such a rush of eagerness it astonished her. Her lips parted, welcoming the thrust of his tongue. Through the tangle of sheets, the barrier of her clothes, she felt the undeniable evidence of his arousal burgeoning against her.

She had not meant for this to happen, had not expected this to happen. But as their kiss deepened, as his hand slid hungrily down the curve of her waist, the flare of her hips, she knew that this had been inevitable. That for all his cool, unreadable looks, Sam Navarro harbored more passion than any man she'd ever known.

He regained control first. Without warning, he broke off the kiss. She heard his breathing, harsh and rapid, in the darkness.

"Sam?" she whispered.

He pulled away from her and sat up on the side of the bed. She watched his silhouette in the darkness, running his hands through his hair. "God," he murmured. "What am I doing?"

She reached out toward the dark expanse of his back. As her fingers brushed his skin, she felt his shudder of pleasure. He wanted her—that much she was certain of. But he was right, this was a mistake, and they both knew it. She'd been afraid and in need of a protector. He was a man alone, in need of no one, but still a man with needs. It was natural they'd seek each other's arms for comfort, however temporary it might be.

Staring at him now, at the shadow huddled at the side of the bed, she knew she still wanted him. The longing was so intense it was a physical ache.

She said, "It's not so awful, is it? What just happened between us?"

"I'm not getting sucked into this again. I can't."

"It doesn't have to mean anything, Sam. Not if you don't want it to."

"Is that how you see it? Quick and meaningless?"

"No. No, that's not at all what I said."

"But that's how it'd end up." He gave a snort of self-disgust. "This is the classic trap, you know. I want to keep you safe. You want a white knight. It's good only as long as that lasts. And then it falls apart." He rose from the bed and moved to the door. "I'll sleep on the couch."

He left the room.

She lay alone in his bed, trying to sort out the confusing whirl of emotions. Nothing made sense to her. Nothing was under her control. She tried to remember a time when her life was in perfect order. It was before Robert. Before she'd let herself get caught up in those fantasies of the perfect marriage. That was where she'd gone wrong. Believing in fantasies.

Her reality was growing up in a broken home, living with a succession of faceless stepparents, having a mother and father who despised each other. Until she'd met Robert, she hadn't expected to marry at all. She'd been content enough with her life, her job. That's what had always sustained her: her work.

She could go back to that. She *would* go back to that.

That dream of a happy marriage, that fantasy, was dead.

SAM WAS UP AT DAWN. The couch had been even more uncomfortable than he'd expected. His sleep had been fitful, his shoulder ached, and at 7:00 a.m., he was unfit for human companionship. So when the phone rang, he was hard-pressed to answer with a civil "Hello."

"Navarro, you've got some explaining to do," said Abe Coopersmith.

Sam sighed. "Good morning, Chief."

"I just got an earful from Yeats in Homicide. I shouldn't have to tell you this, Sam. Back off the Cormier woman."

"You're right. You shouldn't have to tell me. But you did."

"Anything going on between you two?"

"I felt she was in danger. So I stepped in."

"Where is she right now?"

Sam paused. He couldn't avoid this question; he had to answer it. "She's here," he admitted. "My house."

"Damn."

"Someone was following us last night. I didn't think it was prudent to leave her alone. Or unprotected."

"So you brought her to *your* house? Where, exactly, did you happen to park your common sense?"

I don't know, thought Sam. *I lost track of it when I looked into Nina Cormier's big brown eyes.*

"Don't tell me you two are involved. Please don't tell me that," said Coopersmith.

"We're not involved."

"I hope to God you're not. Because Yeats wants her in here for questioning."

"For Robert Bledsoe's murder? Yeats is fishing. She doesn't know anything about it."

"He wants to question her. Bring her in. One hour."

"She has an airtight alibi—"

"*Bring her in,* Navarro." Coopersmith hung up.

There was no way around this. Much as he hated to do it, he'd have to hand Nina over to the boys in Homicide. Their questioning might be brutal, but they had their job to do. As a cop, he could hardly stand in their way.

He went up the hall to the bedroom door and knocked. When

she didn't answer, he cautiously cracked open the door and peeked inside.

She was sound asleep, her hair spread across the pillow in a luxurious fan of black. Just the sight of her, lying so peacefully in his bed, in his house, sent a rush of yearning through him. It was so intense he had to grip the doorknob just to steady himself. Only when it had passed, when he had ruthlessly suppressed it, did he dare enter the room.

She awakened with one gentle shake of the shoulder. Dazed by sleep, she looked at him with an expression of utter vulnerability, and he cleared his throat just to keep his voice steady.

"You'll have to get up," he told her. "The detectives in Homicide want to see you downtown."

"When?"

"One hour. You have time to take a shower. I've already got coffee made."

She didn't say anything. She just looked at him with an expression of bewilderment. And no wonder. Last night they had held each other like lovers.

This morning, he was behaving like a stranger.

This was a mistake, coming into her room. Approaching the bed. At once he put distance between them and went to the door. "I'm sure it'll just be routine questions," he said. "But if you feel you need a lawyer—"

"Why should I need a lawyer?"

"It's not a bad idea."

"I don't need one. I didn't do anything." Her gaze was direct and defiant. He'd only been trying to protect her rights, but she had taken his suggestion the wrong way, had interpreted it as an accusation.

He didn't have the patience right now to set her straight. "They'll be waiting for us" was all he said, and he left the room.

While she showered, he tried to scrounge together a breakfast, but could come up with only frozen French bread and a months-old box of cornflakes. Both the pantry and the refrigerator looked pretty pathetic; bachelorhood was showing, and he wasn't at all proud of it.

In disgust, he went outside to fetch the newspaper, which had been delivered to its usual spot at the end of the driveway. He was walking back toward the house when he abruptly halted and stared at the ground.

There was a footprint.

Or, rather, a series of footprints. They tracked through the soft dirt, past the living room window, and headed off among the trees. A man's shoes, thick soled. Size eleven at least.

He glanced toward the house and thought about what the man who'd made those prints could have seen last night, through the windows. Only darkness? Or had he seen Nina, a moving target as she walked around the living room?

He went to his car, parked near the front porch. Slowly, methodically, he examined it from bumper to bumper. He found no signs of tampering.

Maybe I'm paranoid. Maybe those footprints mean nothing.

He went back inside, into the kitchen, and found Nina finishing up her cup of coffee. Her face was flushed, her hair still damp from the shower. At her first look at him, she frowned. "Is something wrong?" she asked.

"No, everything's fine." He carried his cup to the sink. There he looked out the window and thought about how isolated this house was. How open those windows were to the sight of a gunman.

He turned to her and said, "I think it's time to leave."

I SHOULD HAVE TAKEN Sam's advice. I should have hired a lawyer.

That was the thought that now crossed Nina's mind as she sat in an office at the police station and faced the three Homicide detectives seated across the table from her. They were polite enough, but she sensed their barely restrained eagerness. Detective Yeats in particular made her think of an attack dog—leashed, but only for the moment.

She glanced at Sam, hoping for moral support. He gave her none. Throughout the questioning, he hadn't even looked at her. He stood at the window, his shoulders rigid, his gaze focused outside. He'd brought her here, and now he was abandoning her. The cop, of course, had his duty to perform. And at this moment, he was playing the cop role to the hilt.

She said to Yeats, "I've told you everything I know. There's nothing else I can think of."

"You were his fiancée. If anyone would know, you would."

"I don't. I wasn't even there. If you'd just talk to Daniella—"

"We have. She confirms your alibi," Yeats admitted.

"Then why do you keep asking me these questions?"

"Because murder doesn't have to be done in person," one of the other cops said.

Now Yeats leaned forward, his gaze sympathetic, his voice quietly coaxing. "It must have been pretty humiliating for you," he persisted. "To be left at the altar. To have the whole world know he didn't want you."

She said nothing.

"Here's a man you trusted. A man you loved. And for weeks, maybe months, he was cheating on you. Probably laughing at you behind your back. A man like that doesn't deserve a woman like you. But you loved him anyway. And all you got for it was pain."

She lowered her head. She still didn't speak.

"Come on, Nina. Didn't you want to hurt him back? Just a little?"

"Not—not that way," she whispered.

"Even when you found out he was seeing someone else? Even when you learned it was your own stepmother?"

She looked up sharply at Yeats.

"It's true. We spoke to Daniella and she admitted it. They'd been meeting on the sly for some time. While you were at work. You didn't know?"

Nina swallowed. In silence she shook her head.

"I think maybe you *did* know. Maybe you found out on your own. Maybe he told you."

"No."

"And how did it make you feel? Hurt? Angry?"

"I didn't know."

"Angry enough to strike back? To find someone who'd strike back *for* you?"

"I didn't know!"

"That's simply not believable, Nina. You expect us to accept your word that you knew nothing about it?"

"I didn't!"

"You *did.* You—"

"That's *enough.*" It was Sam's voice that cut in. "What the hell do you think you're doing, Yeats?"

"My job," Yeats shot back.

"You're badgering her. Interrogating without benefit of counsel."

"Why should she need a lawyer? She claims she's innocent."

"She *is* innocent."

Yeats glanced smugly at the other Homicide detectives. "I think it's pretty obvious, Navarro, that you no longer belong on this investigation."

"You don't have the authority."

"Abe Coopersmith's given me the authority."

"Yeats, I don't give a flying—"

Sam's retort was cut off by the beeping of his pocket pager. Irritably he pressed the Silence button. "I'm not through here," he snapped. Then he turned and left the room.

Yeats turned back to Nina. "Now, Miss Cormier," he said. All trace of sympathy was gone from his expression. In its place was the razor-tooth smile of a pit bull. "Let's get back to the questions."

THE PAGE WAS FROM Ernie Takeda in the crime lab, and the code on the beeper readout told Sam it was an urgent message. He made the call from his own desk.

It took a few dialings to get through; the line was busy. When the usually low-key Takeda finally answered, there was an uncharacteristic tone of excitement in his voice.

"We've got something for you, Sam," said Takeda. "Something that'll make you happy."

"Okay. Make me happy."

"It's a fingerprint. A partial, from one of the device fragments from the warehouse bomb. It could be enough to ID our bomber. I've sent the print off to NCIC. It'll take a few days to run it through the system. So be patient. And let's hope our bomber is on file somewhere."

"You're right, Ernie. You've made me a happy man."

"Oh, one more thing. About that church bomb."

"Yes?"

"Based on the debris, I'd say the device had some sort of gift wrapping around it. Also, since it had no timing elements, my guess is, it was designed to be triggered on opening. But it went off prematurely. Probably a short circuit of some kind."

"You mentioned gift wrapping."

"Yeah. Silver-and-white paper."

Wedding wrap, thought Sam, remembering the gift that had been delivered that morning to the church. If the bomb was meant to explode on opening, then there was no longer any doubt who the intended victims were.

But why kill Nina? he wondered as he headed back to the conference room. Could this whole mess be attributed to another woman's jealousy? Daniella Cormier had a motive, but would she have gone so far as to hire a bomber?

What was he missing here?

He opened the office door and halted. The three homicide detectives were still sitting at the table. Nina wasn't. She was gone.

"Where is she?" Sam asked.

Yeats shrugged. "She left."

"What?"

"She got fed up with our questions, so she walked out."

"You *let* her leave?"

"We haven't charged her with anything. Are you saying we should have, Navarro?"

Sam's reply was unrepeatable. With a sudden sense of anxiety, he left Yeats and headed out the front entrance of police headquarters. He stood on the sidewalk, looking up and down the street.

Nina was nowhere in sight.

Someone's trying to kill her, he thought as he headed for his car. *I have to reach her first.*

From his car phone, he called Nina's father's house. She wasn't there. He called Robert Bledsoe's house. No answer. He called Lydia Warrenton's house. Nina wasn't there either.

On a hunch, he drove to Lydia's Cape Elizabeth home anyway. People in distress often flee home for comfort, he reasoned. Eventually, Nina might wind up at her mother's.

He found Lydia at home. But no Nina—not yet, at least.

"I haven't spoken to her since yesterday morning," said Lydia, ushering Sam into the seaview room. "I'm not sure she *would* come here."

"Do you know where she might go?" Sam asked. "Someone she might turn to?"

Lydia shook her head. "I'm afraid my daughter and I aren't very close. We never were. The truth is, she wasn't the easiest child."

"What do you mean, Mrs. Warrenton?"

Lydia seated herself on the white couch. Her silk pantsuit was a startling slash of purple against the pale cushions. "What I mean to say—I know it sounds awful—is that Nina was something of a disappointment to me. We offered her so many opportunities. To study abroad, for instance. At a boarding school in Switzerland. Her sister Wendy went and benefited wonderfully. But Nina refused to go. She insisted on staying home. Then there were the other things. The boys she brought home. The ridiculous outfits she'd wear. She could be doing so much with her life, but she never achieved much."

"She earned a nursing degree."

Lydia gave a shrug. "So do thousands of other girls."

"She's not any other girl, Mrs. Warrenton. She's your daughter."

"That's why I expected more. Her sister speaks three languages and plays the piano and cello. She's married to an attorney who's in line for a judicial seat. While Nina..." Lydia sighed. "I can't imagine how sisters could be so different."

"Maybe the real difference," said Sam, rising to his feet, "was in how you loved them." He turned and walked out of the room.

"Mr. Navarro!" he heard Lydia call as he reached the front door.

He looked back. She was standing in the hallway, a woman of such perfectly groomed elegance that she didn't seem real or alive. Or touchable.

Not like Nina at all.

"I think you have entirely the wrong idea about me and my daughter," Lydia said.

"Does it really matter what I think?"

"I just want you to understand that I did the best I could, under the circumstances."

"Under the circumstances," replied Sam, "so did she." And he left the house.

Back in his car, he debated which way to head next. Another round of phone calls came up empty. Where the hell was she?

The only place he hadn't checked was her new apartment. She'd told him it was on Taylor Street. There was probably no phone in yet; he'd have to drive there to check it out.

On his way over, he kept thinking about what Lydia Warrenton had just told him. He thought about what it must have been like for Nina to grow up the black sheep, the unfavored child. Always doing the wrong thing, never meeting Mommy's approval. Sam had been fortunate to have a mother who'd instilled in him a sense of his own competence.

I understand now, he thought, *why you wanted to marry Robert.* Marrying Robert Bledsoe was the one sure way to gain her mother's approval. And even that had collapsed in failure.

By the time he pulled up at Nina's new apartment building, he was angry. At Lydia, at George Cormier and his parade of wives, at the entire Cormier family for its battering of a little girl's sense of self-worth.

He knocked harder at the apartment door than he had to.

There was no response. She wasn't here, either.

Where are you, Nina?

He was about to leave when he impulsively gave the knob a turn. It was unlocked.

He pushed the door open. ''Nina?'' he called.

Then his gaze focused on the wire. It was almost invisible, a tiny line of silver that traced along the doorframe and threaded toward the ceiling.

Oh, my God...

In one fluid movement he pivoted away and dived sideways, down the hallway.

The force of the explosion blasted straight through the open door and ripped through the wall in a flying cloud of wood and plaster.

Deafened, stunned by the blast, Sam lay facedown in the hallway as debris rained onto his back.

Chapter Eight

"Man, oh man," said Gillis. "You sure did bring down the house."

They were standing outside, behind the yellow police line, waiting for the rest of the search team to assemble. The apartment house—what was left of it—had been cleared of any second devices, and now it was Ernie Takeda's show. Takeda was, at that moment, diagramming the search grid, handing out evidence bags, and assigning his lab crew to their individual tasks.

Sam already knew what they'd find. Residue of Dupont label dynamite. Scraps of green two-inch-wide electrical tape. And Prima detonating cord. The same three components as the church bomb and the warehouse bomb.

And every other bomb put together by the late Vincent Spectre.

Who's your heir apparent, Spectre? Sam wondered. *To whom did you bequeath your tricks of the trade? And why is Nina Cormier the target?*

Just trying to reason it through made his head pound. He was still covered in dust, his cheek was bruised and swollen, and he could barely hear out of his left ear. But he had nothing to complain about. He was alive.

Nina would not have been so fortunate.

"I've got to find her," he said. "Before he does."

"We've checked with the family again," said Gillis. "Father, mother, sister. She hasn't turned up anywhere."

"Where the hell could she have gone?" Sam began to pace along the police line, his worry turning to agitation. "She walks out of headquarters, maybe she catches a cab or a bus. Then what? What would she do?"

"Whenever my wife gets mad, she goes shopping," Gillis offered helpfully.

"I'm going to call the family again." Sam turned to his car. "Maybe she's finally shown up somewhere."

He was about to reach inside the Taurus for the car phone when he froze, his gaze focused on the edge of the crowd. A small, dark-haired figure stood at the far end of the street. Even from that distance, Sam could read the fear, the shock, in her pale face.

"Nina," he murmured. At once he began to move toward her, began to push, then shove his way through the crowd. "Nina!"

She caught sight of him, struggling to reach her. Now she was moving as well, frantically plunging into the gathering of onlookers. They found each other, fell into each other's embrace. And at that moment, there was no one else in the world for Sam, no one but the woman he was holding. She felt so very precious in his arms, so easily taken from him.

With a sudden start, he became acutely aware of the crowd. All these people, pressing in on them. "I'm getting you out of here," he said. Hugging her close to his side, he guided her toward his car. The whole time, he was scanning faces, watching for any sudden movements.

Only when he'd bundled her safely into the Taurus did he allow himself a deep breath of relief.

"Gillis!" he called. "You're in charge here!"

"Where you going?"

"I'm taking her somewhere safe."

"But—"

Sam didn't finish the conversation. He steered the car out of the crowd and they drove away.

Drove north.

Nina was staring at him. At the bruise on his cheek, the plaster dust coating his hair. "My God, Sam," she murmured. "You've been hurt—"

"A little deaf in one ear, but otherwise I'm okay." He glanced at her and saw that she didn't quite believe him. "I ducked out just before it blew. It was a five-second delay detonator. Set off by opening the door." He paused, then added quietly, "It was meant for you."

She said nothing. She didn't have to; he could read the comprehension in her gaze. This bombing was no mistake, no random attack. She was the target and she could no longer deny it.

"We're chasing down every lead we have," he said. "Yeats is going to question Daniella again, but I think that's a dead end. We did get a partial fingerprint off the warehouse bomb, and we're waiting for an ID. Until then, we've just got to keep you alive. And that means you have to cooperate. Do exactly what I tell you to do." He gave an exasperated sigh and clutched the steering wheel tighter. "That was *not* smart, Nina. What you did today."

"I was angry. I needed to get away from all you cops."

"So you storm out of headquarters? Without telling me where you're going?"

"You threw me to the wolves, Sam. I expected Yeats to clap the handcuffs on me. And you delivered me to him."

"I had no choice. One way or the other, he was going to question you."

"Yeats thinks I'm guilty. And since *he* was so sure of it, I thought...I thought you must have your doubts as well."

"I have no doubts," he said, his voice absolutely steady. "Not about you. And after this latest bomb, I don't think Yeats'll have any doubts either. You're the target."

The turnoff to Route 95—the Interstate—was just ahead. Sam took it.

"Where are we going?" she asked.

"I'm getting you out of town. Portland isn't a safe place for you. So I have another spot in mind. A fishing camp on Coleman Pond. I've had it for a few years. You'll be roughing it there, but you can stay as long as you need to."

"You won't be staying with me?"

"I have a job to do, Nina. It's the only way we'll get the answers. If I do my job."

"Of course, you're right." And she looked straight ahead at the road. "I forget sometimes," she said softly, "that you're a cop."

ACROSS THE STREET from the police line, he stood in the thick of the crowd, watching the bomb investigators scurry about with their evidence bags and their notebooks. Judging by the shattered glass, the debris in the street, the blast had been quite impressive. But of course he'd planned it that way.

Too bad Nina Cormier was still alive.

He'd spotted her just moments before, being escorted through the crowd by Detective Sam Navarro. He'd recognized Navarro at once. For years he'd followed the man's career, had read every news article ever written about the Bomb Squad. He knew about Gordon Gillis and Ernie Takeda as well. It was his business to know. They were the enemy, and a good soldier must know his enemy.

Navarro helped the woman into a car. He seemed unusually protective—not like Navarro at all, to be succumbing to romance on the job. Cops like him were supposed to be professionals. What had happened to the quality of civil servants these days?

Navarro and the woman drove away.

There was no point trying to follow them; another opportunity would arise.

Right now he had a job to do. And only two days in which to finish it.

He gave his gloves a little tug. And he walked away, unnoticed, through the crowd.

BILLY "THE SHOWMAN" Binford was happy today. He was even grinning at his attorney, seated on the other side of the Plexiglas barrier.

"It's gonna be all right, Darien," said Billy. "I got everything taken care of. You just get ready to negotiate that plea bargain. And get me out of here, quick."

Darien shook his head. "I told you, Liddell's not in a mood to cut any deals. He's out to score big with your conviction."

"Darien, Darien. You got no faith."

"What I got is a good grip on reality. Liddell's aiming for a higher office. For that, he's got to put you away."

"He won't be putting anyone away. Not after Saturday."

"What?"

"You didn't hear me say nothing, okay? I didn't say nothing. Just believe me, Liddell won't be a problem."

"I don't want to know. Don't tell me about it."

Billy regarded his attorney with a look of both pity and amusement. "You know what? You're like that monkey with his paws over his ears. Hear no evil. That's you."

"Yeah," Darien agreed. And he nodded miserably. "That's me exactly."

A FIRE CRACKLED in the hearth, but Nina felt chilled to the bone. Outside, dusk had deepened, and the last light was fading behind the dense silhouettes of pine trees. The cry of a loon echoed, ghostlike, across the lake. She'd never been afraid of the woods, or the darkness, or of being alone. Tonight, though, she *was* afraid, and she didn't want Sam to leave.

She also knew he had to.

He came tramping back into the cottage, carrying an armload of firewood, and began to stack it by the hearth. "This should do you for a few days," he said. "I just spoke to Henry Pearl and his wife. Their camp's up the road. They said they'd check up on you a few times a day. I've known them for years, so I know you can count on them. If you need anything at all, just knock on their door."

He finished stacking the wood and clapped the dirt from his hands. With his shirtsleeves rolled up and sawdust clinging to his trousers, he looked more like a woodsman than a city cop. He threw another birch log on the fire and the flames shot up in a crackle of sparks. He turned to look at her, his expression hidden against the backlight of fire.

"You'll be safe here, Nina. I wouldn't leave you alone if I had even the slightest doubt."

She nodded. And smiled. "I'll be fine."

"There's a fishing pole and tackle box in the kitchen, if you feel like wrestling with a trout. And feel free to wear anything you find in the closet. None of it'll fit, but at least you'll be warm. Henry's wife'll drop by some, uh, women's wear tomorrow." He paused and laughed. "Those probably won't fit either. Since she's twice *my* size."

"I'll manage, Sam. Don't worry about me."

There was a long silence. They both knew there was nothing more to say, but he didn't move. He glanced around the room, as though reluctant to leave. Almost as reluctant as she was to see him go.

"It's a long drive back to the city," she said. "You should eat before you go. Can I interest you in dinner? Say, a gourmet repast of macaroni and cheese?"

He grinned. "Make it anything else and I'll say yes."

In the kitchen, they rummaged through the groceries they'd bought at a supermarket on the way. Mushroom omelets, a loaf of French bread, and a bottle of wine soon graced the tiny camp table. Electricity had not yet made it to this part of the lake, so they ate by the light of a hurricane lamp. Outside, dusk gave way to a darkness alive with the chirp of crickets.

She gazed across the table at him, watching the way his face gleamed in the lantern light. She kept focusing on that bruise on his cheek, thinking about how close he'd come to dying that afternoon. But that was exactly the sort of work he did, the sort of risk he took all the time. Bombs. Death. It was insane, and she didn't know why any man in his right mind would take those risks. *Crazy cop,* she thought. *And I must be just as insane, because I think I'm falling for this guy.*

She took a sip of wine, the whole time intensely, almost painfully aware of his presence. And of her attraction toward him, an attraction so strong she was having trouble remembering to eat.

She had to remind herself that he was just doing his job, that to him, she was nothing more than a piece of the puzzle he was trying to solve, but she couldn't help picturing other meals, other nights they might spend together. Here, on the lake. Candlelight, laughter. Children. She thought he'd be good with children. He'd be patient and kind, just as he was with her.

How would I know that? I'm dreaming. Fantasizing again.

She reached across to pour him more wine.

He put his hand over the glass. "I have to be driving back."

"Oh. Of course." Nervously she set the bottle down again. She folded and refolded her napkin. For a whole minute they didn't speak, didn't look at each other. At least, she didn't look at him.

But when she finally raised her eyes, she saw that he was watching her. Not the way a cop looks at a witness, at a piece of a puzzle.

He was watching her the way a man watches a woman he wants.

He said, quickly, "I should leave now—"

"I know."

"—before it gets too late."

"It's still early."

"They'll need me, back in the city."

She bit her lip and said nothing. Of course he was right. The city did need him. Everyone needed him. She was just one detail that required attending to. Now she was safely tucked away and he could go back to his real business, his real concerns.

But he didn't seem at all eager to leave. He hadn't moved from the chair, hadn't broken eye contact. She was the one who looked away, who nervously snatched up her wineglass.

She was startled when he reached over and gently caught her hand. Without a word he took the glass and set it down. He raised her hand, palm side up, and pressed a kiss, ever so light, to her wrist. The lingering of lips, the tickle of his breath, was the sweetest torture. If he could wreak such havoc kissing that one square inch of skin, what could he do with the rest of her?

She closed her eyes and gave a small, soft moan. "I don't want you to leave," she whispered.

"It's a bad idea. For me to stay."

"Why?"

"Because of this." He kissed her wrist again. "And this." His lips skimmed up her arm, his beard delightfully rough against her sensitive skin. "It's a mistake. You know it. I know it."

"I make mistakes all the time," she replied. "I don't always regret them."

His gaze lifted to hers. He saw both her fear and her fearlessness. She was hiding nothing now, letting him read all. Her hunger was too powerful to hide.

He rose from the table. So did she.

He pulled her toward him, cupped her face in his hands, and pressed his lips to hers. The kiss, sweet with the taste of wine and desire, left her legs unsteady. She swayed against him, her arms reaching up to clutch his shoulders. Before she could catch her breath, he was kissing her again, deeper. As their mouths joined, so did their bodies. His hands slid down her waist, to her hips. He didn't need to pull her against him; she could already feel him, hard and aroused. And that excited her even more.

"If we're going to stop," he breathed, "it had better be now...."

She responded with a kiss that drowned out any more words between them. Their bodies did all the talking, all the communicating.

They were tugging at each other's clothes, feverish for the touch of bare skin. First her sweater came off, then his shirt. They kissed their way into the next room, where the fire had quieted to a warm glow. Still kissing her, he pulled the afghan off the couch and let it fall onto the floor by the hearth.

Facing each other, they knelt before the dying fire. His bare shoulders gleamed in the flickering light. She was eager, starved for his touch, but he moved slowly, savoring every moment, every new experience of her. He watched with longing as she unhooked her bra and shrugged the straps off her shoulders. When he reached out to cup her breast, to tug at her nipple, she let her head sag back with a moan. His touch was ever so gentle, yet it left her feeling weak. Conquered. He tipped her back and lowered her onto the afghan.

Her body was pure liquid now, melting under his touch. He unzipped her jeans, eased them off her hips. Her underwear slid off with the hiss of silk. She lay unshielded to his gaze now, her skin rosy in the firelight.

"I've had so many dreams about you," he whispered as his hand slid exploringly down her belly, toward the dark triangle of hair. "Last night, when you were in my house, I dreamed of holding you. Touching you just the way I am now. But when I woke up, I told myself it could never happen. That it was all fantasy. All longing. And here we are..." He bent forward, his kiss tender on her lips. "I shouldn't be doing this."

"I want you to. I want us to."

"I want it just as much. More. But I'm afraid we're going to regret it."

"Then we'll regret it later. Tonight, let's just be you and me. Let's pretend there's nothing else, no one else."

He kissed her again. And this time his hand slipped between her thighs, his finger dipping into her wetness, sliding deep into her warmth. She groaned, helpless with delight. He slid another finger in, and felt her trembling, tightening around him. She was ready, so ready for him, but he wanted to take his time, to make this last.

He withdrew his hand, just long enough to remove the rest of his clothes. As he knelt beside her, she couldn't help drawing in a sharp breath of admiration. What a beautiful man he was. Not just his body, but his soul. She could see it in his eyes: the caring, the warmth. Before it had been hidden from her, concealed behind that tough-cop mask of his. Now he was hiding nothing. Revealing everything.

As she was revealing everything to him.

She was too lost in pleasure to feel any modesty, any shame. She lay back, whimpering, as his fingers found her again, withdrew, teased, plunged back in. Already she was slick with sweat and desire, her hips arching against him.

"Please," she murmured. "Oh, Sam. I—"

He kissed her, cutting off any protest. And he continued his torment, his fingers dipping, sliding, until she was wound so tight she thought she'd shatter.

Only then, only as she reached the very edge, did he take away his hand, fit his hips to hers, and thrust deep inside her.

She gripped him, crying out as he swept her, and himself, toward climax. And when it came, when she felt herself tumbling into that wondrous free fall, they clung to each other and they tumbled together, to a soft and ever-so-gentle landing.

She fell asleep, warm and safe, in his arms.

It was later, much later, when she awakened in the deepest chill of night.

The fire had died out. Although she was cocooned in the afghan, she found herself shivering.

And alone.

Hugging the afghan to her shoulders, she went into the kitchen and peered out the window. By the light of the moon, she could see that Sam's car was gone. He had returned to the city.

Already I miss him, she thought. Already his absence was like a deep, dark gulf in her life.

She went into the bedroom, climbed under the blankets, and tried to stop shivering, but she could not. When Sam had left, he had taken with him all the warmth. All the joy.

It scared her, how much she felt his absence. She was not going to fall in love with him; she could not afford to. What they'd experienced tonight was pleasure. The enjoyment of each other's bodies. As a lover, he was superb.

But as a man to love, he was clearly wrong for her.

No wonder he'd stolen away like a thief in the night. He'd known it was a mistake, just as she did. At this moment, he was probably regretting what they'd done.

She burrowed deeper under the blankets and waited for sleep, for dawn—whichever came first. Anything to ease the ache of Sam's departure.

But the night, cold and lonely, stretched on.

IT WAS A MISTAKE. A stupid, crazy mistake.

All the way back to Portland, on the drive down that long, dark highway, Sam kept asking himself how he could have let it happen.

No, he *knew* how it happened. The attraction between them was just too strong. It had been pulling them together from the first day they'd met. He'd fought it, had never stopped reminding himself that he was a cop, and she was an important element in his investigation. Good cops did not fall into this trap.

He used to think he was a good cop. Now he knew he was far too human, that Nina was a temptation he couldn't resist, and that the whole investigation would probably suffer because he'd lost his sense of objectivity.

All because she'd come to mean too much to him.

Not only would the investigation suffer, *he* would as well, and he had only himself to blame. Nina was scared and vulnerable; naturally she'd turn to her protector for comfort. He should have kept her at arm's length, should have kept his own urges in check. Instead he'd succumbed, and now she was all he could think about.

He gripped the steering wheel and forced himself to focus on the road. On the case.

By 1:00 a.m., he was back in the city. By 1:30, he was at his desk, catching up on the preliminary reports from Ernie Takeda. As he'd expected, the bomb in Nina's apartment was similar to the devices that blew up the church and the warehouse. The difference between the three was in the method of detonation. The warehouse device had had a simple timer. The church device was a package bomb, designed to explode on opening. Nina's apartment had been wired to blow after the door opened. This bomber was a versatile fellow. He could trigger a blast in any number of ways. He varied his device according to the situation, and that made him both clever and extremely dangerous.

He went home at 5:00 a.m., caught a few hours of sleep, and was back at headquarters for an eight o'clock meeting.

With three bombings in two weeks, the pressure was on, and the tension showed in the faces around the conference table. Gillis looked beat, Chief Coopersmith was testy, and even the normally unemotional Ernie Takeda was showing flashes of irritation. Part of that irritation was due to the presence of two federal agents from Alcohol, Tobacco and Firearms. Both the men from ATF wore expressions of big-time experts visiting Hicksville.

But the most annoying source of irritation was the presence

of their esteemed D.A. and perpetual pain in the neck, Norm Liddell.

Liddell was waving the morning edition of the *New York Times*. "Look at the headline," he said. "'Portland, Maine, the new bombing capital?' New York's saying that about us? *Us?*" He threw the newspaper down on the table. "What the hell is going on in this town? Who *is* this bomber?"

"We can give you a likely psychological profile," said one of the ATF agents. "He's a white male, intelligent—"

"I already know he's intelligent!" snapped Liddell. "A hell of a lot more intelligent than we are. I don't want some psychological profile. I want to know who he *is*. Does anyone have any idea about his identity?"

There was a silence at the table. Then Sam said, "We know who he's trying to kill."

"You mean the Cormier woman?" Liddell snorted. "So far, no one's come up with a single good reason why she's the target."

"But we know she is. She's our one link to the bomber."

"What about the warehouse bomb?" said Coopersmith. "How's that connect to Nina Cormier?"

Sam paused. "That I don't know," he admitted.

"I'd lay ten-to-one odds that Billy Binford's people ordered that warehouse bombing," said Liddell. "It was a logical move on his part. Scare off a prosecution witness. Does the Cormier woman have any connection to Binford?"

"All she knows about him is what she's read in the newspapers," said Sam. "There's no link."

"What about her family? Are they linked at all to Binford?"

"No link there, either," spoke up Gillis. "We've checked into the finances of the whole family. Nina Cormier's father, mother, stepfather, stepmother. No connection to Binford. Her ex-fiancé was just as clean."

Liddell sat back. "Something's coming. I can feel it. Binford's got something big planned."

"How do you know?" asked Coopersmith.

"I have sources." Liddell shook his head in disgust. "Here I finally get The Snowman behind bars, and he's still pulling strings, still making mincemeat of the court system. I'm convinced that warehouse bomb was an intimidation tactic. He's trying to scare all my witnesses. If I don't get a conviction, he'll be a free man in a few months. And he'll be scaring them in person."

"But chances are good you'll get that conviction," Coopersmith reassured him. "You've got credible witnesses, financial records. And you've drawn a law-and-order judge."

"Even so," countered Liddell, "Binford's not finished maneuvering. He's got something up his sleeve. I just wish I knew what it was." He looked at Sam. "Where are you hiding Nina Cormier?"

"A safe place," said Sam.

"You keeping it top secret or something?"

"Under the circumstances, I'd prefer to keep it known only to myself and Gillis. If you have questions to ask her, I can ask them for you."

"I just want to know what her connection is to these bombings. Why The Snowman wants her dead."

"Maybe this has nothing to do with Binford," suggested Sam. "He's in jail, and there's another party involved here. The bomber."

"Right. So find him for me," snapped Liddell. "Before Portland gets known as the American Beirut." He rose from his chair, his signal that the meeting was over. "Binford goes to trial in a month. I don't want my witnesses scared off by any more bombs. So *get* this guy, before he destroys my case." With that, Liddell stalked out.

"Man, election year is hell," muttered Gillis.

As the others filed out of the room, Coopersmith said, "Navarro, a word with you."

Sam waited, knowing full well what was coming. Coopersmith shut the door and turned to look at him.

"You and Nina Cormier. What's going on?"

"She needs protection. So I'm looking out for her."

"Is that all you're doing?"

Sam let out a weary sigh. "I...may be more involved than I should be."

"That's what I figured." Coopersmith shook his head. "You're too smart for this, Sam. This is the sort of mistake rookies make. Not you."

"I know."

"It could put you both in a dangerous situation. I ought to yank you off the case."

"I need to stay on it."

"Because of the woman?"

"Because I want to nail this guy. I'm *going* to nail him."

"Fine. Just keep your distance from Nina Cormier. I shouldn't have to tell you this. This kind of thing happens, someone always gets hurt. Right now she thinks you're John Wayne. But when this is all over, she's gonna see you're human like the rest of us. Don't set yourself up for this, Sam. She's got looks, she's got a daddy with lots of money. She doesn't want a cop."

I know he's right, thought Sam. *I know it from personal experience. Someone's going to get hurt. And it'll be me.*

The conference room door suddenly swung open and an excited Ernie Takeda stuck his head in the room. "You're not gonna believe this," he said, waving a sheet of fax paper.

"What is it?" asked Coopersmith.

"From NCIC. They just identified that fingerprint off the bomb fragment."

"And?"

"It's a match. With Vincent Spectre."

"That's impossible!" exclaimed Sam. He snatched the sheet from Ernie's grasp and stared at the faxed report. What he read there left no doubt that the ID was definite.

"There has to be a mistake," said Coopersmith. "They found his body. Spectre's been dead and buried for months."

Sam looked up. "Obviously not," he growled.

Chapter Nine

The rowboat was old and well used, but the hull was sound. At least, it didn't leak as Nina rowed it out into the lake. It was late afternoon and a pair of loons were paddling lazily through the water, neither one alarmed by the presence of a lone rower. The day was utter stillness, utter peace, as warm as a summer day should be.

Nina guided the boat to the center of the pond, where sunlight rippled on the water, and there she let the boat drift. As it turned lazy circles, she lay back and stared up at the sky. She saw birds winging overhead, saw a dragonfly hover, iridescent in the slanting light.

And then she heard a voice, calling her name.

She sat up so sharply the boat rocked. She saw him then, standing at the water's edge, waving to her.

As she rowed the boat back to shore, her heart was galloping, more from anticipation than exertion. Why had he returned so soon? Last night he'd left without a word of goodbye, the way a man leaves a woman he never intends to see again.

Now here he was, standing silent and still on the shore, his gaze as unreadable as ever. She couldn't figure him out. She'd never be able to figure him out. He was a man designed to drive her crazy, and as she glided across the last yards of water, she could already feel that lovely insanity take hold of her. It required all her willpower to suppress it.

She tossed him the painter rope. He hauled the rowboat up onto the shore and helped her step out. Just the pressure of his hand grasping her arm gave her a thrill of delight. But one look at his face quelled any hopes that he was here as a lover. This was the cop, impersonal, businesslike. Not at all the man who'd held her in his arms.

"There's been a new development," he said.

Just as coolly, she met his gaze. "What development?"

"We think we know who the bomber is. I want you to take a look at some photographs."

On the couch by the fireplace—the same fireplace that had warmed them when they'd made love the night before—Nina sat flipping through a book of mug shots. The hearth was now cold, and so was she, both in body and in spirit. Sam sat a good foot away, not touching her, not saying a word. But he was watching her expectantly, waiting for some sign that she recognized a face in that book.

She forced herself to concentrate on the photos. One by one she scanned the faces, carefully taking in the features of each man pictured there. She reached the last page. Shaking her head, she closed the cover.

"I don't recognize anyone," she declared.

"Are you certain?"

"I'm certain. Why? Who am I supposed to recognize?"

His disappointment was apparent. He opened the book to the fourth page and handed it back to her. "Look at this face. Third one down, first column. Have you ever seen this man?"

She spent a long time studying the photo. Then she said, "No. I don't know him."

With a sigh of frustration, Sam sank back against the couch. "This doesn't make any sense at all."

Nina was still focused on the photograph. The man in the picture appeared to be in his forties, with sandy hair, blue eyes, and hollow, almost gaunt, cheeks. It was the eyes that held her attention. They stared straight at her, a look of intimidation that burned, lifelike, from a mere two-dimensional image. Nina gave an involuntary shiver.

"Who is he?" she asked.

"His name is—or was—Vincent Spectre. He's five foot eleven, 180 pounds, forty-six years old. At least, that's what he would be now. If he's still alive."

"You mean you don't know if he is?"

"We thought he was dead."

"You're not sure?"

"Not any longer." Sam rose from the couch. It was getting chilly in the cabin; he crouched at the hearth and began to arrange kindling in the fireplace.

"For twelve years," he said, "Vincent Spectre was an army demolitions expert. Then he got booted out of the service. Dishonorable discharge, petty theft. It didn't take him long to launch a second career. He became what we call a specialist. Big bangs, big bucks. Hired himself out to anyone who'd pay for his expertise. He worked for terrorist governments. For the mob. For crime bosses all over the country.

"For years he raked in the money. Then his luck ran out. He was recognized on a bank security camera. Arrested, convicted, served only a year. Then he escaped."

Sam struck a match and lit the kindling. It caught fire in a crackle of sparks and flames. He lay a log on top and turned to look at her.

"Six months ago," he continued, "Spectre's remains were found in the rubble after one of his bombs blew up a warehouse. That is, authorities *thought* it was his body. Now we think it might have been someone else's. And Spectre's still alive."

"How do you know that?"

"Because his fingerprint just turned up. On a fragment of the warehouse bomb."

She stared at him. "You think he also blew up the church?"

"Almost certainly. Vincent Spectre's trying to kill you."

"But I don't know any Vincent Spectre! I've never even heard his name before!"

"And you don't recognize his photo."

"No."

Sam stood up. Behind him, the flames were now crackling, consuming the log. "We've shown Spectre's photo to the rest of your family. They don't recognize him, either."

"It must be a mistake. Even if the man's alive, he has no reason to kill me."

"Someone else could have hired him."

"You've already explored that. And all you came up with was Daniella."

"That's still a possibility. She denies it, of course. And she passed the polygraph test."

"She let you hook her up to a *polygraph?*"

"She consented. So we did it."

Nina shook her head in amazement. "She must have been royally ticked off."

"As a matter of fact, I think she rather enjoyed giving the performance. She turned every male head in the department."

"Yes, she's good at that. She certainly turned my father's head. And Robert's, too," Nina added softly.

Sam was moving around the room now, pacing a slow circle around the couch. "So we're back to the question of Vincent Spectre," he said. "And what his connection is to you. Or Robert."

"I told you, I've never heard his name before. I don't remember Robert ever mentioning the name, either."

Sam paced around the couch, returned to stand by the fireplace. Against the background of flames, his face was unreadable. "Spectre *is* alive. And he built a bomb intended for you and Robert. Why?"

She looked down again at the photo of Vincent Spectre. Try as she might, she could conjure up no memory of that face. The eyes, perhaps, seemed vaguely familiar. That stare was one she might have seen before. But not the face.

"Tell me more about him," she suggested.

Sam went to the couch and sat down beside her. Not quite close enough to touch her, but close enough to make her very aware of his presence.

"Vincent Spectre was born and raised in California. Joined the army at age nineteen. Quickly showed an aptitude for explosives work, and was trained in demolitions. Saw action in Grenada and Panama. That's where he lost his finger—trying to disarm a terrorist explosive. At that point, he could have retired on disability but—"

"Wait. Did you just say he was missing a finger?"

"That's right."

"Which hand?"

"The left. Why?"

Nina went very still. Thinking, remembering. A missing finger. Why did that image seem so vividly familiar?

Softly she said, "Was it the left middle finger?"

Frowning, Sam reached for his briefcase and took out a file folder. He flipped through the papers contained inside. "Yes," he said. "It was the middle finger."

"No stump at all? Just...missing entirely."

"That's right. They had to amputate all the way back to the knuckle." He was watching her, his eyes alert, his voice quiet with tension. "So you *do* know him."

"I—I'm not sure. There was a man with an amputated finger—the left middle finger—"

"What? Where?"

"The Emergency Room. It was a few weeks ago. I remember he was wearing gloves, and he didn't want to take them off. But I had to check his pulse. So I pulled off the left glove. And I was so startled to see he was missing a finger. He'd stuffed the glove finger with cotton. I think I...I must have stared. I remember I asked him how he lost it. He told me he'd caught it in some machinery."

"Why was he in the ER?"

"It was—I think an accident. Oh, I remember. He was knocked down by a bicycle. He'd cut his arm and needed stitches put in. The strange part about it all was the way he vanished afterward. Right after the cut was sutured, I left the room to get something. When I came back, he was gone. No thank you, nothing. Just—disappeared. I thought he was trying to get away without paying his bill. But I found out later that he did pay the clerk. In cash."

"Do you remember his name?"

"No." She gave a shrug. "I'm terrible with names."

"Describe him for me. Everything you remember."

She was silent for a moment, struggling to conjure up the face of a man she'd seen weeks ago, and only once. "I remember he was fairly tall. When he lay down on the treatment table, his feet hung over the edge." She looked at Sam. "He'd be about your height."

"I'm six feet. Vincent Spectre's five-eleven. What about his face? Hair, eyes?"

"He had dark hair. Almost black. And his eyes..." She sat back, frowning in concentration. Remembered how startled she'd been by the missing finger. That she'd looked up and met the patient's gaze. "I think they were blue."

"The blue eyes would match Spectre's. The black hair doesn't. He could've dyed it."

"But the face was different. It didn't look like this photo."

"Spectre has resources. He could've paid for plastic surgery, completely changed his appearance. For six months we assumed he was dead. During that time he could've remade himself into an entirely different man."

"All right, what if it *was* Spectre I saw in the ER that day?

Why does that make me a target? Why would he want to kill me?"

"You saw his face. You could identify him."

"A lot of people must have seen his face!"

"You're the only one who could connect that face with a man who was missing a finger. You said he was wearing gloves, that he didn't want to remove them."

"Yes, but it was part of his uniform. Maybe the only reason for the gloves was—"

"What uniform?"

"Some sort of long-sleeved jacket with brass buttons. White gloves. Pants with this side stripe. You know, like an elevator operator. Or a bellhop."

"Was there a logo embroidered on the jacket? A building or hotel name?"

"No."

Sam was on his feet now, pacing back and forth with new excitement. "Okay. Okay, he has a minor accident. Cuts his arm, has to go to the ER for stitches. You see that he's missing a finger. You see his face. And you see he's wearing some sort of uniform...."

"It's not enough to make me a threat."

"Maybe it is. Right now, he's operating under a completely new identity. The authorities have no idea what he looks like. But that missing finger is a giveaway. You saw it. And his face. You could identify him for us."

"I didn't know anything about Vincent Spectre. I wouldn't have thought to go to the police."

"We were already raising questions about his so-called death. Wondering if he was still alive and operating. Another bombing, and we might have figured out the truth. All we had to do was tell the public we were looking for a man missing his left middle finger. You would have come forward. Wouldn't you?"

She nodded. "Of course."

"That may be what he was afraid of. That you'd tell us the one thing we didn't know. What he looks like."

For a long moment she was silent. She was staring down at the book of mug shots, thinking about that day in the ER. Trying to remember the patients, the crises. Sore throats and sprained ankles. She'd been a nurse for eight years, had treated so many patients, that the days all seemed to blend together. But she did remember one more detail about that visit from the man with the gloves. A detail that left her suddenly chilled.

"The doctor," she said softly. "The doctor who sutured the cut—"

"Yes? Who was it?"

"Robert. It was Robert."

Sam stared at her. In that instant, he understood. They both did. Robert had been in the same room as well. He'd seen the patient's face, had seen the mutilated left hand. He, like Nina, could have identified Vincent Spectre.

Now Robert was dead.

Sam reached down to take Nina's hand. "Come on." He pulled her to her feet.

They were standing face-to-face now, and she felt her body respond immediately to his nearness, felt her stomach dance that little dance of excitement. Arousal.

"I'm driving you back to Portland," he said.

"Tonight?"

"I want you to meet with our police artist. See if you two can come up with a sketch of Spectre's face."

"I'm not sure I can. If I saw him, I'd recognize him. But just to describe his face—"

"The artist will walk you through it. The important thing is that we have something to work with. Also, I need you to help me go through the ER records. Maybe there's some information you've forgotten."

"We keep a copy of all the encounter forms. I can find his record for you." *I'll do anything you want me to do,* she thought, *if only you'll stop this tough-cop act.*

As they stood gazing at each other, she thought she saw a ripple of longing in his eyes. Too quickly, he turned away to get a jacket from the closet. He draped it over her shoulders. Just the brushing of his fingers against her skin made her quiver.

She shifted around to face him. To confront him.

"Has something happened between us?" she asked softly.

"What do you mean?"

"Last night. I didn't imagine it, Sam. We made love, right here in this room. Now I'm wondering what I did wrong. Why you seem so...indifferent."

He sighed, a sound of weariness. And perhaps regret. "Last night," he began, "shouldn't have happened. It was a mistake."

"I didn't think so."

"Nina, it's always a mistake to fall in love with the investigating cop. You're scared, you're looking for a hero. I happen to fall into the role."

"But you're not playing a role! Neither am I. Sam, I care about you. I think I'm falling in love with you."

He just looked at her without speaking, his silence as cutting as any words.

She turned away, so that she wouldn't have to see that flat, emotionless gaze of his. With a forced laugh she said, "God, I feel like such an idiot. Of course, this must happen to you all the time. Women throwing themselves at you."

"It's not like that."

"Isn't it? The hero cop. Who could resist?" She turned back to him. "So, how do I compare with all the others?"

"There aren't any others! Nina, I'm not trying to shove you away. I just want you to understand that it's the situation that's pulled us together. The danger. The intensity. You look at me and you completely miss all the flaws. All the reasons I'm not the right guy for you. You were engaged to Robert Bledsoe. Ivy League. Medical degree. House on the water. What the hell am I but a civil servant?"

She shook her head, tears suddenly filling her eyes. "Do you really think that's how I see you? As just a civil servant? Just a cop?"

"It's what I am."

"You're so much more." She reached up to touch his face. He flinched, but didn't pull away as her fingers caressed the roughness of his jaw. "Oh, Sam. You're kind. And gentle. And brave. I haven't met any other man like you. Okay, so you're a cop. It's just part of who you are. You've kept me alive. You've watched over me...."

"It was my job."

"Is that all it was?"

He didn't answer right away. He just looked at her, as though reluctant to tell the truth.

"Is it, Sam? Just a part of your job?"

He sighed. "No," he admitted. "It was more than that. You're more than that."

Pure joy made her smile. Last night she'd felt it—his warmth, his caring. For all his denials, there was a living, breathing man under that mask of indifference. She wanted so badly to fall into his arms, to coax the real Sam Navarro out from his hiding place.

He reached up for her hand and gently but firmly lowered it from his face. "Please, Nina," he said. "Don't make this hard for both of us. I have a job to do, and I can't be distracted. It's dangerous. For you and for me."

"But you do care. That's all I need to know. That you care."

He nodded. It was the most she could hope for.

"It's getting late. We should leave," he mumbled. And he turned toward the door. "I'll be waiting for you in the car."

NINA FROWNED at the computer-generated sketch of the suspect's face. "It's not quite right," she said.

"What's not right about it?" asked Sam.

"I don't know. It's not easy to conjure up a man's face. I saw him only that one time. I didn't consciously register the shape of his nose or jaw."

"Does he look anything like this picture?"

She studied the image on the computer screen. For an hour, they'd played with different hairlines, noses, shapes of jaws and chins. What they'd come up with seemed generic, lifeless. Like every other police sketch she'd ever seen.

"To be honest," she admitted with a sigh, "I can't be sure this is what he looks like. If you put the real man in a lineup, I think I'd be able to identify him. But I'm not very good at re-creating what I saw."

Sam, obviously disappointed, turned to the computer technician. "Print it up anyway. Send copies to the news stations and wire services."

"Sure thing, Navarro," the tech replied and he flipped on the printer switch.

As Sam led Nina away, she said miserably, "I'm sorry. I guess I wasn't much help."

"You did fine. And you're right, it's not easy to re-create a face. Especially one you saw only once. You really think you'd know him if you saw him?"

"Yes. I'm pretty sure of it."

He gave her arm a squeeze. "That may be all we'll need from you. Assuming we ever get our hands on him. Which leads to the next item on our agenda."

"What's that?"

"Gillis is already at the hospital, pulling those treatment records. He'll need you to interpret a few things on the encounter form."

She nodded. "*That* I know I can do."

They found Gillis sitting in a back room of the ER, papers piled up on the table in front of him. His face was pasty with fatigue under the fluorescent lights. It was nearly midnight, and he'd been on the job since 7:00 a.m. So had Sam.

For both of them, the night was just beginning.

"I pulled what I think is the right encounter form," said Gillis. "May 29, 5:00 p.m. Sound about right, Miss Cormier?"

"It could be."

Gillis handed her the sheet. It was the one-page record of an ER visit. On top was the name Lawrence Foley, his address, and billing information. On the line Chief Complaint, she recognized her own handwriting: Laceration, left forearm. Below that, she had written: forty-six-year-old white male hit by bicycle in crosswalk. Fell, cut arm on fender. No loss of consciousness."

She nodded. "This is the one. Here's Robert's signature, on the bottom. Treating physician. He sutured the cut—four stitches, according to his notes."

"Have we checked out this name, Lawrence Foley?" Sam asked Gillis.

"No one by that name living at that address," Gillis informed him. "And that's a nonexistent phone number."

"Bingo," said Sam. "False address, false identity. This is our man."

"But we're no closer to catching him," stressed Gillis. "He left no trail, no clues. Where are we supposed to look?"

"We have a sketch of his face circulating. We know he was wearing some sort of uniform, possibly a bellhop's. So we check all the hotels. Try to match the sketch with any of their employees." Sam paused, frowning. "A hotel. Why would he be working at a hotel?"

"He needed a job?" Gillis offered.

"As a bellhop?" Sam shook his head. "If this is really Vincent Spectre, he had a reason to be there. A contract. A target..." He sat back and rubbed his eyes. The late hour, the stress, was showing in his face. All those shadows, all those lines of weariness. Nina longed to reach out to him, to stroke away the worry she saw there, but she didn't dare. Not in front of Gillis. Maybe not ever. He'd made it perfectly clear she was a distraction to him, to his work, and that distractions were dangerous. That much she accepted.

Yet how she ached to touch him.

Sam rose to his feet and began to move about, as though forcing himself to stay awake. "We need to check all the hotels. Set up a lineup of bellhops. And we need to check police reports. Maybe someone called in that bicycle accident."

"Okay, I'll get Cooley on it."

"What we really need to know is—who is he after? Who's the target?"

"We're not going to figure that out tonight," said Gillis. "We need more to go on." He yawned, and added, "And we need some sleep. Both of us."

"He's right," said Nina. "You can't function without rest, Sam. You need to sleep on this."

"In the meantime, Spectre's at work on God knows what catastrophe. So far we've been lucky. Only one bombing casualty. But the next time..." Sam stopped pacing. Stopped because he'd simply run out of steam. He was standing in one spot, his shoulders slumped, his whole body drooping.

Gillis looked at Nina. "Get him home, will ya? Before he keels over and I have to drag him."

Nina rose from her chair. "Come on, Sam," she said softly. "I'll drive you home."

Heading out to the car, he kept insisting he could drive, that he was in perfectly good shape to take the wheel. She, just as insistently, pointed out that he was a menace on the road.

He let her drive.

Scarcely after she'd pulled out of the hospital parking lot, he was sound asleep.

At his house, she roused him just long enough to climb out of the car and walk in the front door. In his bedroom, he shrugged off his gun holster, pulled off his shoes, and collapsed on the bed. His last words were some sort of apology. Then he was fast asleep.

Smiling, she pulled the covers over him and went out to check the windows and doors. Everything was locked tight; the house was secure—as secure as it could be.

Back in Sam's room, she undressed in the dark and climbed into bed beside him. He didn't stir. Gently she stroked her fingers through his hair and thought, *My poor, exhausted Sam. Tonight, I'll watch over you.*

Sighing, he turned toward her, his arm reaching out to hug her against him. Even in his sleep, he was trying to protect her.

Like no other man I've ever known.

Nothing could hurt her. Not tonight, not in his arms.

She'd stake her life on it.

THEY WERE SHOWING his picture on the morning news.

Vincent Spectre took one look at the police sketch on the TV screen and he laughed softly. What a joke. The picture looked nothing like him. The ears were too big, the jaw was too wide, and the eyes looked beady. He did not have beady eyes. How had they gotten it so wrong? What had happened to the quality of law enforcement?

"Can't catch me, I'm the gingerbread man," he murmured.

Sam Navarro was slipping, if that drawing was the best he could come up with. A pity. Navarro had seemed such a clever man, a truly worthy opponent. Now it appeared he was as dumb a cop as all the others. Though he *had* managed to draw one correct conclusion.

Vincent Spectre was alive and back in the game.

"Just wait till you see how alive I am," he said.

That Cormier woman must have described his face to the police artist. Although the sketch wasn't anything for him to worry about, Nina Cormier did concern him. Chances were, she'd recognize him in a room of anonymous strangers. She was the only one who could link his face to his identity, the only one who could ruin his plan. She would have to be disposed of.

Eventually.

He turned off the TV and went into the apartment bedroom, where the woman was still asleep. He'd met Marilyn Dukoff three weeks ago at the Stop Light Club, where he'd gone to watch the topless dance revue. Marilyn had been the blonde in the purple-sequined G-string. Her face was coarse, her IQ a joke, but her figure was a marvel of nature and silicone. Like so many other women on the exotic dance circuit, she was in desperate need of money and affection.

He'd offered her both, in abundance.

She'd accepted his gifts with true gratitude. She was like a puppy who'd been neglected too long, loyal and hungry for approval. Best of all, she asked no questions. She knew enough not to.

He sat down beside her on the bed and nudged her awake. "Marilyn?"

She opened one sleepy eye and smiled at him. "Good morning."

He returned her smile. And followed it with a kiss. As usual, she responded eagerly. Gratefully. He removed his clothes and climbed under the sheets, next to that architecturally astonishing body. It took no coaxing at all to get her into the mood.

When they had finished, and she lay smiling and satisfied beside him, he knew it was the right time to ask.

And he said, "I need another favor from you."

TWO HOURS LATER, a blond woman in a gray suit presented her ID to the prison official. "I'm an attorney with Frick and Darien," she said. "Here to see our client, Billy Binford."

Moments later she was escorted to the visiting room. Billy "The Snowman" took a seat on the other side of the Plexiglas. He regarded her for a moment, then said, "I been watching the news on TV. What the hell's all this other stuff going on?"

"He says it's all necessary," said the blonde.

"Look, I just wanted the job done like he promised."

"It's being taken care of. Everything's on schedule. All you have to do is sit back and wait."

Billy glanced at the prison guard, who was standing off to the side and obviously bored. "I got everything riding on this," he muttered.

"It will happen. But he wants to make sure you keep up your end of the bargain. Payment, by the end of the week."

"Not yet. Not till I'm sure it's done. I got a court date coming up fast—too fast. I'm counting on this."

The blonde merely smiled. "It'll happen," she said. "He guarantees it."

Chapter Ten

Sam woke up to the smell of coffee and the aroma of something cooking, something delicious. It was Saturday. He was alone in the bed, but there was no question that someone else was in the house. He could hear the bustle in the kitchen, the soft clink of dishes. For the first time in months, he found himself smiling as he rose from bed and headed to the shower. There was a woman in the kitchen, a woman who was actually cooking breakfast. Amazing how different that made the whole house feel. Warm. Welcoming.

He came out of the shower and stood in front of the mirror to shave. That's when his smile faded. He suddenly wondered how long he'd been asleep. He'd slept so heavily he hadn't heard Nina get out of bed this morning, hadn't even heard her take a shower. But she'd been in here; the shower curtain had already been damp when he stepped in.

Last night someone could have broken into the house, and he would have slept right through it.

I'm useless to her, he thought. He couldn't track down Spectre and keep Nina safe at the same time. He didn't have the stamina or the objectivity. He was worse than useless; he was endangering her life.

This was exactly what he'd been afraid would happen.

He finished shaving, got dressed, and went into the kitchen.

Just the sight of her standing at the stove was enough to shake his determination. She turned and smiled at him.

"Good morning," she murmured, and wrapped her arms around him in a sweetly scented hug. Lord, this was every man's fantasy. Or, at least, it was *his* fantasy: a gorgeous woman in his kitchen. The good morning smile. Pancakes cooking in the skillet.

A woman in the house.

Not just any woman. Nina. Already he felt his resistance

weakening, felt the masculine urges taking over again. This was what always happened when he got too close to her.

He took her by the shoulders and stepped away. "Nina, we have to talk."

"You mean...about the case?"

"No. I mean about you. And me."

All at once that radiant smile was gone from her face. She'd sensed that a blow was about to fall, a blow that would be delivered by *him.* Mutely she turned, lifted the pancake from the skillet, and slid it onto a plate. Then she just stood there, looking at it lying on the countertop.

He hated himself at that moment. At the same time he knew there was no other way to handle this—not if he really cared about her.

"Last night shouldn't have happened," he said.

"But nothing *did* happen between us. I just brought you home and put you to bed."

"That's exactly what I'm talking about. Nina, I was so exhausted last night, someone could've driven a damn train through my bedroom and I wouldn't have moved a muscle. How am I supposed to keep you safe when I can't even keep my eyes open?"

"Oh, Sam." She stepped toward him, her hands rising to caress his face. "I don't expect you to be my guardian. Last night, I wanted to take care of *you.* I was so happy to do it."

"I'm the cop, Nina. I'm responsible for your safety."

"For once, can't you stop being a cop? Can't you let me take care of *you?* I'm not so helpless. And you're not so tough that you don't need someone. When I was scared, you were there for me. And I want to be here for *you.*"

"I'm not the one who could get killed." He took both her hands and firmly lowered them from his face. "This isn't a good idea, getting involved, and we both know it. I can't watch out for you the way I should. Any other cop could do a better job."

"I don't trust any other cop. I trust you."

"And that could be a fatal mistake." He pulled away, gaining himself some breathing space. Anything to put distance between them. He couldn't think clearly when she was so near; her scent, her touch, were too distracting. He turned and matter-of-factly poured himself a cup of coffee, noting as he did it that his hand wasn't quite steady. Her effect, again. Not looking at her, he said, "It's time to focus on the case, Nina. On finding Spectre. That's the best way to ensure your safety. By doing my job and doing it right."

She said nothing.

He turned and saw that she was gazing listlessly at the table. It had already been set with silverware and napkins, glasses of juice, and a small crock of maple syrup. Again he felt that stab of regret. *I've finally found a woman I care about, a woman I could love, and I'm doing my best to push her away.*

"So," she said softly. "What do you propose, Sam?"

"I think another man should be assigned to protect you. Someone who has no personal involvement with you."

"Is that what we have? A personal involvement?"

"What else would you call it?"

She shook her head. "I'm beginning to think we have no involvement at all."

"For God's sake, Nina. We slept with each other! How can two people get more involved than that?"

"For some people, sex is purely a physical act. And that's all it is." Her chin tilted up in silent inquiry. *For some people. Meaning me?*

Damn it, he refused to get caught up in this hopeless conversation. She was baiting him, trying to get him to admit there was more to that act of lovemaking than just sex. He was not about to admit the truth, not about to let her know how terrified he was of losing her.

He knew what had to be done.

He crossed the kitchen to the telephone. He'd call Coopersmith, ask him to assign a man to pull guard duty. He was about to pick up the receiver when the phone suddenly rang.

He answered it with a curt "Navarro."

"Sam, it's me."

"Morning, Gillis."

"Morning? It's nearly noon. I've already put in a full day here."

"Yeah, I'm hanging my head in shame."

"You should. We've got that lineup scheduled for one o'clock. Bellhops from five different hotels. You think you can bring Nina Cormier down here to take a look? That is, if she's there with you."

"She's here," admitted Sam.

"That's what I figured. Be here at one o'clock, got it?"

"We'll be there." He hung up and ran his hand through his damp hair. God. Nearly noon? He was getting lazy. Careless. All this agonizing over him and Nina, over a relationship that really had nowhere to go, was cutting into his effectiveness as a cop. If he didn't do his job right, *she* was the one who'd suffer.

"What did Gillis say?" he heard her ask.

He turned to her. "They've scheduled a lineup at one o'clock. Want you to look at a few hotel bellhops. You up to it?"

"Of course. I want this over with as much as you do."

"Good."

"And you're right about turning me over to another cop. It's all for the best." She met his gaze with a look of clear-eyed determination. "You have more important things to do than baby-sit me."

He didn't try to argue with her. In fact, he didn't say a thing. But as she walked out of the kitchen, leaving him standing alone by that cozily set breakfast table, he thought, *You're wrong. There's no more important job in the world to me than watching over you.*

EIGHT MEN STOOD on the other side of the one-way mirror. All of them were facing forward. All of them looked a little sheepish about being there.

Nina carefully regarded each man's uniform in turn, searching for any hint of familiarity. Any detail at all that might trip a memory.

She shook her head. "I don't see the right uniform."

"You're absolutely certain?" asked Gillis.

"I'm certain. It wasn't any of those."

She heard an undisguised snort of disappointment. It came from Norm Liddell, the D.A. who was standing next to Gillis. Sam, poker-faced, said nothing.

"Well, this was a big waste of my time," muttered Liddell. "Is this all you've come up with, Navarro? A bellhop roundup?"

"We know Spectre was wearing some sort of uniform similar to a bellhop's," said Sam. "We just wanted her to look over a few."

"We did track down a police report of that bike accident," said Gillis. "The bicyclist himself called it in. I think he was worried about a lawsuit, so he made a point of stating that he hit the man outside a crosswalk. Apparently, Spectre was jay-walking when he was hit on Congress Street."

"Congress?" Liddell frowned.

"Right near the Pioneer Hotel," said Sam. "Which, we've found out, is where the Governor plans to stay day after tomorrow. He's the guest speaker at some small business seminar."

"You think Spectre's target is the Governor?"

"It's a possibility. We're having the Pioneer checked and double-checked. Especially the Governor's room."

"What about the Pioneer's bellhops?"

"We eliminated all of them, just based on height and age. No one's missing any fingers. That one there—number three—is the closest to Spectre's description. But he has all his fingers, too. We just wanted Nina to take a look at the uniform, see if it jogged a memory."

"But no one in that lineup is Spectre."

"No. We've looked at everyone's hands. No missing fingers."

Nina's gaze turned to number three in the lineup. He was dressed in a bellhop's red jacket and black pants. "Is that what all the Pioneer's bellhops wear?" she asked.

"Yeah," said Gillis. "Why?"

"I don't think that's the uniform I saw."

"What's different about it?"

"The man I saw in the ER—I'm just remembering it—his jacket was green. Sort of a forest green. It was definitely not red."

Gillis shook his head. "We got us a problem then. The Holiday Inn's uniform is red, too. Marriott's green, but it's not located anywhere near the bicycle accident."

"Check out their staff anyway," Liddell ordered. "If you have to interview every bellhop in town, I want this guy caught. And I sure as hell want him caught before he blows up some high-muck-a-muck. When's the Governor arriving tomorrow?"

"Sometime in the afternoon," said Gillis.

Liddell glanced at his watch. "We have a full twenty-four hours. If anything comes up, I get called. Got it?"

"Yes, sir, your highness," muttered Gillis.

Liddell glanced sharply at him, but obviously decided to drop it. "My wife and I'll be at the Brant Theater tonight. I'll have my beeper with me, just in case."

"You'll be first on our list to call," said Sam.

"We're in the spotlight on this. So let's not screw up." It was Liddell's parting shot, and the two cops took it in silence.

Only after Liddell had left the room did Gillis growl, "I'm gonna get that guy. I swear, I'm gonna get him."

"Cool it, Gillis. He may be governor someday."

"In which case, I'll help Spectre plant the damn bomb myself."

Sam took Nina's arm and walked her out of the room. "Come on. I have my hands full today. I'll introduce you to your new watchdog."

Passing me off already, she thought. Was she such a nuisance to him?

"For now, we're keeping you in a hotel," he said. "Officer Pressler's been assigned to watch over you. He's a sharp cop. I trust him."

"Meaning I should, too?"

"Absolutely. I'll call you if we turn up any suspects. We'll need you to identify them."

"So I may not be seeing you for a while."

He stopped in the hallway and looked at her. "No. It may be a while."

They faced each other for a moment. The hallway was hardly private; certainly this wasn't the time or the place to confess how she felt about him. *She* wasn't even sure how she felt about him. All she knew was that it hurt to say goodbye. What hurt even worse was to look in his eyes and see no regret, no distress. Just that flat, unemotional gaze.

So it was back to Mr. Civil Servant. She could deal with that. After the trauma of this last week, she could deal with anything, including the realization that she had, once again, gotten involved with the wrong man.

She met his gaze with one just as cool and said, "You find Spectre. I'll identify him. Just do it soon, okay? So I can get on with my life."

"We're working on it round the clock. We'll keep you informed."

"Can I count on that?"

He answered with a curt dip of the head. "It's part of my job."

OFFICER LEON PRESSLER was not a conversationalist. In fact, whether he could converse at all was in question. For the past three hours, the muscular young cop had done a terrific sphinx imitation, saying nary a word as he roamed the hotel room, alternately checking the door and glancing out the third floor window. The most he would say was "Yes, ma'am," or "No, ma'am," and that was only in response to a direct question. Was the strong, silent bit some kind of cop thing? Nina wondered. Or was he under orders not to get too chatty with the witness?

She tried to read a novel she'd picked up in the hotel gift shop, but after a few chapters she gave up. His silence made her too nervous. It was simply not natural to spend a day in a hotel room with another person and not, at the very least, talk to each other. Lord knew, she tried to draw him out.

"Have you been a cop a long time, Leon?" she asked.

"Yes, ma'am."

"Do you enjoy it?"

"Yes, ma'am."

"Does it ever scare you?"

"No, ma'am."

"Never?"

"Sometimes."

Now they were getting somewhere, she thought.

But then Officer Pressler crossed the room and peered out the window, ignoring her.

She put her book aside and launched another attempt at conversation.

"Does this sort of assignment bore you?" she asked.

"No, ma'am."

"It would bore me. Spending all day in a hotel room doing nothing."

"Things could happen."

"And I'm sure you'll be ready for it." Sighing, she reached for the remote and clicked on the TV. Five minutes of channel surfing turned up nothing of interest. She clicked it off again. "Can I make a phone call?" she asked.

"Sorry."

"I just want to call my nursing supervisor at Maine Medical. To tell her I won't be coming in next week."

"Detective Navarro said no phone calls. It's necessary for your safety. He was very specific on that."

"What else did the good detective tell you?"

"I'm to keep a close eye. Not let my guard down for a minute. Because if anything happened to you..." He paused and gave a nervous cough.

"What?"

"He'd, uh, have my hide."

"That's quite an incentive."

"He wanted to make sure I took special care. Not that I'd let anything happen. I owe him that much."

She frowned at him. He was at the window again, peering down at the street. "What do you mean, you owe him?"

Officer Pressler didn't move from the window. He stood looking out, as though unwilling to meet her gaze. "It was a few years back. I was on this domestic call. Husband didn't much like me sticking my nose into his business. So he shot me."

"My god."

"I radioed for help. Navarro was first to respond." Pressler turned and looked at her. "So you see, I do owe him." Calmly he turned back to the window.

"How well do you know him?" she asked softly.

Pressler shrugged. "He's a good cop. But real private. I'm not sure anyone knows him very well."

Including me, she thought. Sighing, she clicked on the boob tube again and channel surfed past a jumble of daytime soaps, a TV court show and a golf tournament. She could almost feel another few brain cells collapse into mush.

What was Sam doing right now? she wondered.

And ruthlessly suppressed the thought. Sam Navarro was his own man. That much was perfectly clear.

She would have to be her own woman.

I WONDER WHAT Nina's doing right now. At once Sam tried to suppress the thought, tried to concentrate instead on what was being said at the meeting, but his mind kept drifting back to the subject of Nina. Specifically, her safety. He had every reason to trust Leon Pressler. The young cop was sharp and reliable, and he owed his life to Sam. If anyone could be trusted to keep Nina out of harm's way, it would be Pressler.

Still, he couldn't shake that lingering sense of uneasiness. And fear. It was one more indication that he'd lost his objectivity, that his feelings were way out of control. To the point of affecting his work...

"...the best we can do? Sam?"

Sam suddenly focused on Abe Coopersmith. "Excuse me?"

Coopersmith sighed. "Where the hell are you, Navarro?"

"I'm sorry. I let my attention drift for a moment."

Gillis said, "Chief asked if we're following any other leads."

"We're following every lead we have," Sam informed him. "The sketch of Spectre is circulating. We've checked all the hotels in Portland. So far, no employees with a missing finger. Problem is, we're operating blind. We don't know Spectre's target, when he plans to strike, or where he plans to strike. All we have is a witness who's seen his face."

"And this bit about the bellhop's uniform."

"That's right."

"Have you shown all those uniforms to Miss Cormier? To help us identify which hotel we're talking about?"

"We're getting together a few more samples for her to look at," said Gillis. "Also, we've interviewed that bicyclist. He doesn't remember much about the man he hit. It happened so fast, he didn't really pay attention to the face. But he does back up Miss Cormier's recollection that the uniform jacket was green. Some shade of it, anyway. And he confirms that it happened on Congress Street, near Franklin Avenue."

"We've combed that whole area," said Sam. "Showed the sketch to every shopkeeper and clerk within a five-block radius. No one recognized the face."

Coopersmith gave a grunt of frustration. "We've got the Governor arriving tomorrow afternoon. And a bomber somewhere in the city."

"We don't know if there's a connection. Spectre could be targeting someone else entirely. It all depends on who hired him."

"He may not even plan a hit at all," suggested Gillis. "Maybe he's finished his job. Maybe he's left town."

"We have to assume he's still here," cautioned Coopersmith. "And up to no good."

Sam nodded in agreement. "We have twenty-four hours before the Governor's meeting. By then, something's bound to turn up."

"God, I hope so," said Coopersmith, and he rose to leave. "If there's one thing we don't need, it's another bomb going off. And a dead Governor."

"LET'S TAKE IT from the top. Measure 36." The conductor raised his baton, brought it down again. Four beats later, the trumpets blared out the opening notes of "Wrong Side of the Track Blues," to be joined seconds later by woodwinds and bass. Then the sax slid in, its plaintive whine picking up the melody.

"Never did understand jazz," complained the Brant Theater manager, watching the rehearsal from the middle aisle. "Lotta sour notes if you ask me. All the instruments fighting with each other."

"I like jazz," said the head usher.

"Yeah, well, you like rap, too. So I don't think much of your taste." The manager glanced around the theater, surveying the empty seats. He noted that everything was clean, that there was no litter in the aisles. The audience tonight would be a discriminating crowd. Bunch of lawyer types. They wouldn't appreciate sticky floors or wadded up programs in the chairs.

Just a year ago, this building had been a porn palace, showing X-rated films to an audience of nameless, faceless men. The new owner had changed all that. Now, with a little private money from a local benefactor, the Brant Theater had been rehabilitated into a live performance center, featuring stage plays and musical artists. Unfortunately, the live performances brought in fewer crowds than the porn had. The manager wasn't surprised.

Tonight, at least, a big audience was assured—five hundred paid and reserved seats, with additional walk-ins expected, to benefit the local Legal Aid office. Imagine that. All those lawyers actually paying to hear jazz. He didn't get it. But he was glad these seats would be filled.

"Looks like we may be short a man tonight," said the head usher.

"Who?"

"That new guy you hired. You know, the one from the

Agency. Showed up for work two days ago. Haven't heard from him since. I tried calling him, but no luck."

The manager cursed. "Can't rely on these agency hires."

"That's for sure."

"You just gotta work the crowd with four men tonight."

"Gonna be a bear. Five hundred reserved seats and all."

"Let some of 'em find their own seats. They're lawyers. They're supposed to have brains." The manager glanced at his watch. It was six-thirty. He'd have just enough time to wolf down that corned beef sandwich in his office. "Doors open in an hour," he said. "Better get your supper now."

"Sure thing," replied the head usher. He swept up the green uniform jacket from the seat where he'd left it. And, whistling, he headed up the aisle for his dinner.

AT SEVEN-THIRTY, Officer Pressler escorted Nina back to police headquarters. The building was quieter than it had been that afternoon, most of the desks deserted, and only an occasional clerk circulating in the halls. Pressler brought Nina upstairs and ushered her into an office.

Sam was there.

He gave her only the most noncommittal of greetings: a nod, a quiet hello. She responded in kind. Pressler was in the room too, as were Gillis and another man in plainclothes, no doubt a cop as well. With an audience watching, she was not about to let her feelings show. Obviously Sam wasn't, either.

"We wanted you to take a look at these uniforms," Sam said, gesturing to the long conference table. Laid out on the table were a half dozen uniform jackets of various colors. "We've got bellhops, an elevator operator, and an usher's uniform from the downtown Cineplex. Do any of them strike you as familiar?"

Nina approached the table. Thoughtfully she eyed each one, examining the fabrics, the buttons. Some of them had embroidered hotel logos. Some were trimmed with gold braid or nametags.

She shook her head. "It wasn't one of these."

"What about that green one, on the end?"

"It has gold braid. The jacket I remember had black braid, sort of coiled up here, on the shoulder."

"Geez," murmured Gillis. "Women remember the weirdest things."

"Okay," Sam said with a sigh. "That's it for this session. Thanks, everyone. Pressler, why don't you take a break and get some supper. I'll bring Miss Cormier back to her hotel. You can meet us there in an hour or so."

The room emptied out. All except Sam and Nina.

For a moment, they didn't speak to each other. They didn't even look at each other. Nina almost wished that the earnest Officer Pressler was back with her again; at least *he* didn't make her feel like turning tail and running.

"I hope your hotel room's all right," he finally said.

"It's fine. But I'll be going stir crazy in another day. I have to get out of there."

"It's not safe yet."

"When will it be safe?"

"When we have Spectre."

"That could be never." She shook her head. "I can't live this way. I have a job. I have a life. I can't stay in a hotel room with some cop who drives me up a wall."

Sam frowned. "What's Pressler done?"

"He won't sit still! He never stops checking the windows. He won't let me touch the phone. And he can't carry on a decent conversation."

"Oh." Sam's frown evaporated. "That's just Leon doing his job. He's good."

"Maybe he is. But he still drives me crazy." Sighing, she took a step toward him. "Sam, I can't stay cooped up. I have to get on with my life."

"You will. But we have to get you through this part alive."

"What if I left town? Went somewhere else for a while—"

"We might need you here, Nina."

"You don't. You have his prints. You know he's missing a finger. You could identify him without any question—"

"But we need to spot him first. And for that, we might need you to pick him out of a crowd. So you have to stay in town. Available. We'll keep you safe, I promise."

"I suppose you'll have to. If you want to catch your man."

He took her by the shoulders. "That's not the only reason, and you know it."

"Do I?"

He leaned closer. For one astonishing moment she thought he

was going to kiss her. Then a rap on the door made them both jerk apart.

Gillis, looking distinctly ill at ease, stood in the doorway. "Uh...I'm heading over to get a burger. You want I should get you something, Sam?"

"No. We'll pick something up at her hotel."

"Okay." Gillis gave an apologetic wave. "I'll be back here in an hour." He departed, leaving Sam and Nina alone once again.

But the moment was gone forever. If he'd intended to kiss her, she saw no hint of it in his face.

He said, simply, "I'll drive you back now."

In Sam's car, she felt as if they'd reverted right back to the very first day they'd met, to the time when he'd been the stone-faced detective and she'd been the bewildered citizen. It was as if all the events of the past week—their nights together, their lovemaking—had never happened. He seemed determined to avoid any talk of feelings tonight, and she was just as determined not to broach the subject.

The only safe topic was the case. And even on that topic, he was not very forthcoming.

"I notice you've circulated the police sketch," she said.

"It's been everywhere. TV, the papers."

"Any response?"

"We've been inundated by calls. We've spent all day chasing them down. So far, nothing's panned out."

"I'm afraid my description wasn't very helpful."

"You did the best you could."

She looked out the window, at the streets of downtown Portland. It was already eight o'clock, the summer dusk just slipping into night. "If I saw him again, I'd know him. I'm sure I would."

"That's all we need from you, Nina."

All you want from me, too, she thought sadly. She asked, "What happens tomorrow?"

"More of the same. Chase down leads. Hope someone recognizes that sketch."

"Do you know if Spectre's even in the city?"

"No. He may be long gone. In which case we're just spinning our wheels. But my instincts are telling me he's still here somewhere. And he's got something planned, something big." He glanced at her. "*You* could be the wrench in the works. The one person who can recognize him. That's why we have to keep you under wraps."

"I can't stand much more of this. I'm not even allowed to make a phone call."

"We don't want people to know your whereabouts."

"I won't tell anyone. I promise. It's just that I feel so cut off from everyone."

"Okay." He sighed. "Who do you want to call?"

"I could start with my sister Wendy."

"I thought you two didn't get along."

"We don't. But she's still my sister. And she can tell the rest of the family I'm okay."

He thought it over for a moment, then said, "All right, go ahead and call her. You can use the car phone. But don't—"

"I know, I know. Don't tell her where I am." She picked up the receiver and dialed Wendy's number. She heard three rings, and then a woman's voice answered—a voice she didn't recognize.

"Hayward residence."

"Hello, this is Nina. I'm Wendy's sister. Is she there?"

"I'm sorry, but Mr. and Mrs. Hayward are out for the evening. I'm the baby-sitter."

That's how worried she is about me, thought Nina with an irrational sense of abandonment.

"Would you like her to call you back?" asked the baby-sitter.

"No, I, uh, won't be available. But maybe I can call her later. Do you know what time she'll be home?"

"They're at the Brant Theater for that Legal Aid benefit. I think it runs till ten-thirty. And then they usually go out for coffee and dessert, so I'd expect them home around midnight."

"Oh. That's too late. I'll call tomorrow, thanks." She hung up and gave a sigh of disappointment.

"Not home?"

"No. I should have guessed they'd be out. In Jake's law firm, the business day doesn't end at five. The evenings are taken up by business affairs, too."

"Your brother-in-law's an attorney?"

"With ambitions of being a judge. And he's only thirty years old."

"Sounds like a fast-tracker."

"He is. Which means he needs a fast-track wife. Wendy's perfect that way. I'll bet you that right at this moment, she's at the theater charming the socks off some judge. And she can do it without even trying. She's the politician in the family." She glanced at Sam and saw that he was frowning. "Is something wrong?" she asked.

"What theater? Where did they go tonight?"

"The Brant Theater. That's where the benefit is."

"Benefit?"

"The baby-sitter said it was for Legal Aid. Why?"

Sam stared ahead at the road. "The Brant Theater. Didn't it just reopen?"

"A month ago. It was a disgrace before. All those porn flicks."

"Damn. Why didn't I think of it?"

Without warning, he made a screeching U-turn and headed the car the way they'd come, back toward the downtown district.

"What are you doing?" she demanded.

"The Brant Theater. A Legal Aid benefit. Who do you suppose'll be there?"

"A bunch of lawyers?"

"Right. As well as our esteemed D.A., Norm Liddell. Now, I'm not particularly fond of lawyers, but I'm not crazy about picking up their dead bodies, either."

She stared at him. "You think that's the target? The Brant Theater?"

"They'll need ushers tonight. Think about it. What does an usher wear?"

"Sometimes it's just black pants and a white shirt."

"But in a grand old theater like the Brant? They just might be dressed in green jackets with black braid...."

"That's where we're going?"

He nodded. "I want you to take a look. Tell me if we're warm. Tell me if that uniform you saw could've been a theater usher's."

By the time they pulled up across the street from the Brant Theater, it was 8:20. Sam didn't waste his time looking for a parking space; he left the car angled against the red-painted curb. As he and Nina climbed out, they heard a doorman yell, "Hey, you can't park there!"

"Police!" Sam answered, waving his badge. "We need to get in the theater."

The doorman stepped aside and waved them in.

The lobby was deserted. Through the closed aisle doors, they could hear the bluesy wail of clarinets, the syncopated beats of a snare drum. No ushers were in sight.

Sam yanked open an aisle door and slipped into the theater. Seconds later, he reemerged with a short and loudly protesting usher in tow. "Look at the uniform," he said to Nina. "Look familiar?"

Nina took one glance at the short green jacket, the black braid and brass buttons, and she nodded. "That's it. That's the one I saw."

"*What's* the one?" demanded the usher, yanking himself free.

"How many ushers working here tonight?" snapped Sam.

"Who are you, anyway?"

Again Sam whipped out his badge. "Police. There's a chance you have a bomb somewhere in there. So tell me quick. How many ushers?"

"A bomb?" The man's gaze darted nervously toward the lobby exit. "Uh, we got four working tonight."

"That's it?"

"Yeah. One didn't show up."

"Did he have a missing finger?"

"Hell, I don't know. We all wear gloves." The usher looked again toward the exit. "You really think there could be a bomb in there?"

"We can't afford to make a wrong guess. I'm evacuating the building." He glanced at Nina. "Get out of here. Wait in the car."

"But you'll need help—"

He was already pushing through the door, into the darkened theater. From the open doorway, she watched him walk swiftly down the aisle. He climbed up to the stage and crossed to the conductor, who regarded him with a look of startled outrage.

The musicians, just as startled, stopped playing.

Sam grabbed the conductor's microphone. "Ladies and gentlemen," he said curtly. "This is the Portland Police. We have had a bomb threat. Calmly, but without delay, will everyone please evacuate the building. I repeat, stay calm, but please evacuate the building."

Almost immediately the exodus began. Nina had to scramble backward out of the doorway to avoid the first rush of people heading up the aisle. In the confusion, she lost sight of Sam, but she could still hear his voice over the speaker system.

"Please remain calm. There is no immediate danger. Exit the building in an orderly fashion."

He's going to be the last one out, she thought. *The one most likely hurt if a bomb does go off.*

The exodus was in full force now, a rush of frightened men and women in evening clothes. The first hint of disaster happened so quickly Nina didn't even see it. Perhaps someone had tripped over a long hem; perhaps there were simply too many feet storming the doorway. Suddenly people were stumbling, falling over each other. A woman screamed. Those still backed up in the aisle instantly panicked.

And rushed for the door.

Chapter Eleven

Nina watched in horror as a woman in a long evening gown fell beneath the stampede. Struggling to reach her, Nina shoved through the crowd, only to be swept along with them and forced out the lobby doors and into the street. To get back inside the building was impossible; she'd be moving against the crowd, against the full force of panic.

Already the street was filling up with evacuees, everyone milling about looking dazed. To her relief, she caught sight of Wendy and Jake among the crowd; at least her sister was safe and out of the building. The flood of people out the doors gradually began to ebb.

But where was Sam? Had he made it out yet?

Then, through the crowd, she spotted him emerging from the lobby door. He had his arm around an elderly man, whom he hauled to the sidewalk and set down against the lamppost.

As Nina started toward him, Sam spotted her and yelled, "This one needs attention. Take care of him!"

"Where are you going?"

"Back inside. There are a few more in there."

"I can help you—"

"Help me by staying *out* of the building. And see to that man."

He has his job to do, she thought, watching Sam head back into the theater. *So do I.*

She turned her attention to the elderly man propped up against the lamppost. Kneeling beside him she asked, "Sir, are you all right?"

"My chest. It hurts..."

Oh, no. A coronary. And no ambulance in sight. At once she lowered his head onto the sidewalk, checked his pulse, and unbuttoned his shirt. She was so busy attending to her patient she scarcely noticed when the first patrol car pulled up in front of the theater. By then the crowd was a mass of confusion, everyone demanding to know what was going on.

She looked up to see Sam push out the lobby door again, this time carrying the woman in the evening dress. He lay the woman down beside Nina.

"One more inside," he said, turning back to the building. "Check the lady out."

"Navarro!" yelled a voice.

Sam glanced back as a man in a tuxedo approached.

"What the hell is going on?"

"Can't talk, Liddell. I've got work to do."

"Was there a bomb call or not?"

"Not a call."

"Then why'd you order an evacuation?"

"The usher's uniform." Again Sam turned toward the building.

"Navarro!" Liddell yelled. "I want an explanation! People have been hurt because of this! Unless you can justify it—"

Sam had vanished through the lobby doors.

Liddell paced the sidewalk, waiting to resume his harangue. At last, in frustration, he shouted, "I'm going to have your ass for this, Navarro!"

Those were the last words out of Liddell's mouth before the bomb exploded.

The force of the blast threw Nina backward, onto the street. She landed hard, her elbows scraping across the pavement, but she felt no pain. The shock of the impact left her too stunned to feel anything at all except a strange sense of unreality. She saw broken glass pelt the cars in the street. Saw smoke curl through the air and scores of people lying on the road, all of them just as stunned as she was. And she saw that the lobby door of the Brant Theater was tilted at a crazy angle and hanging by one hinge.

Through the pall of silence, she heard the first moan. Then another. Then came sobs, cries from the injured. Slowly she struggled to sit up. Only then did she feel the pain. Her elbows were torn and bleeding. Her head ached so badly she had to clutch it just to keep from throwing up. But as the awareness of pain crept into her consciousness, so too did the memory of what had happened just before the blast.

Sam. Sam had gone into the building.

Where was he? She scanned the road, the sidewalk, but her vision was blurry. She saw Liddell, sitting up now and groaning by the lamppost. Next to him was the elderly man whom Sam had dragged out of the theater. He, too, was conscious and moving. But there was no Sam.

She stumbled to her feet. A wave of dizziness almost sent her back down to her knees. Fighting it, she forced herself to move toward that open door and stepped inside.

It was dark, too dark to see anything. The only light was the faint glow from the street, shining through the doorway. She stumbled across debris and landed on her knees. Quickly she rose back to her feet, but she knew it was hopeless. It was impossible to navigate, much less find anyone in this darkness.

"Sam?" she cried, moving deeper into the shadows. *"Sam?"*

Her own voice, thick with despair, echoed back at her.

She remembered that he'd stepped into the lobby a moment before the blast. He could be anywhere in the building, or he could be somewhere nearby. Somewhere she could reach him.

Again she cried out, "Sam!"

This time, faintly, she heard a reply. "Nina?" It didn't come from inside the building. It came from the outside. From the street.

She turned and felt her way back toward the exit, guided by the glow of the doorway. Even before she reached it, she saw him standing there, silhouetted in the light from the street.

"Nina?"

"I'm here. I'm here...." She stumbled through the last stretch of darkness dividing them and was instantly swept into an embrace that was too fierce to be gentle, too terrified to be comforting.

"What the hell were you doing in *there?*" he demanded.

"Looking for you."

"You were supposed to stay outside. Away from the building. When I couldn't find you..." His arms tightened around her, drawing her so close she felt as though it were his heart hammering in her chest. "Next time, you *listen* to me."

"I thought you were inside—"

"I came out the other door."

"I didn't see you!"

"I was dragging the last man out. I'd just got out when the bomb went off. It blew us both out onto the sidewalk." He pulled back and looked at her. Only then did she see the blood trickling down his temple.

"Sam, you need to see a doctor—"

"We have a lot of people here who need a doctor." He glanced around at the street. "I can wait."

Nina, too, focused on the chaos surrounding them. "We've got to get people triaged for the ambulances. I'll get to work."

"You feeling up to it?"

She gave him a nod. And a quick smile. "This is my forte, Detective. Disasters." She waded off into the crowd.

Now that she knew Sam was alive and safe, she could concentrate on what needed to be done. And one glance at the scene told her this was the start of a busy night. Not just here, in the street, but in the ER as well. All the area hospitals would need to call in every ER nurse they had to attend to these people.

Her head was starting to ache worse than ever, her scraped elbows stung every time she bent her arms. But at this moment, as far as she knew, she was the only nurse on the scene.

She focused on the nearest victim, a woman whose leg was cut and bleeding. Nina knelt down, ripped a strip of fabric from the victim's hem, and quickly wrapped a makeshift pressure bandage around the bleeding limb. When she'd finished tying it off, she noted to her satisfaction that the flow of blood had stopped.

That was only the first, she thought, and she looked around for the next patient. There were dozens more to go....

ACROSS THE STREET, his face hidden in the shadows, Vincent Spectre watched the chaos and muttered a curse. Both Judge Stanley Dalton and Norm Liddell were still alive. Spectre could see the young D.A. sitting against the lamppost, clutching his head. The blond woman sitting beside him must be Liddell's wife. They were right in the thick of things, surrounded by dozens of other injured theater patrons. Spectre couldn't just walk right over and dispatch Liddell, not without being seen by a score of witnesses. Sam Navarro was just a few yards from Liddell, and Navarro would certainly be armed.

Another humiliation. This would destroy his reputation, not to mention his back account. The Showman had promised four hundred thousand dollars for the deaths of Dalton and Liddell. Spectre had thought this an elegant solution: to kill both of them at once. With so many other victims, the identity of the targets might never be pinpointed.

But the targets were still alive, and there'd be no payment forthcoming.

The job had become too risky to complete, especially with Navarro on the scent. Thanks to Navarro, Spectre would have to bow out. And kiss his four hundred thousand goodbye.

He shifted his gaze, refocusing on another figure in the crowd. It was that nurse, Nina Cormier, bandaging one of the injured. This fiasco was her fault, too; he was sure of it. She must've given the police just enough info to tip them off to the bomb. The usher's uniform, no doubt, had been the vital clue.

She was another detail he hadn't bothered to clean up, and look at the result. No hit, no money. Plus, she could identify him. Though that police sketch was hopelessly generic, Spectre had a feeling that, if Nina Cormier ever saw his face, she would remember him. That made her a threat he could no longer ignore.

But now was not the opportunity. Not in this crowd, in this street. The ambulances were arriving, siren after siren whooping to a stop. And the police had cordoned off the street from stray vehicles.

Time to leave.

Spectre turned and walked away, his frustration mounting with every step he took. He'd always prided himself on paying attention to the little things. Anyone who worked with explosives had to have a fetish for details, or they didn't last long. Spectre intended to hang around in this business, which meant he would continue to fuss over the details.

And the next detail to attend to was Nina Cormier.

SHE WAS MAGNIFICENT. Sam paused wearily amid the broken glass and shouting voices and he gazed in Nina's direction. It was ten-thirty, and hour and a half since the explosion, and the street was still a scene of confusion. Police cars and ambulances were parked haphazardly up and down the block, their lights flashing like a dozen strobes. Emergency personnel were everywhere, picking through the wreckage, sorting through the victims. The most seriously injured had already been evacuated, but there were dozens more still to be transported to hospitals.

In the midst of all that wreckage, Nina seemed an island of calm efficiency. As Sam watched, she knelt down beside a groaning man and dressed his bleeding arm with a makeshift bandage. Then, with a reassuring pat and a soft word, she moved on to the next patient. As though sensing she was being watched, she suddenly glanced in Sam's direction. Just for a moment their gazes locked across the chaos, and she read the question in his eyes: *Are you holding up okay?*

She gave him a wave, a nod of reassurance. Then she turned back to her patient.

They both had their work cut out for them tonight. He focused his attention, once again, on the bomb scene investigation.

Gillis had arrived forty-five minutes ago with the personal body armor and mask. The rest of the team had straggled in one by one—three techs, Ernie Takeda, Detective Cooley. Even Abe Coopersmith had appeared, his presence more symbolic than practical. This was Sam's show, and everyone knew it. The bomb disposal truck was in place and parked nearby. Everyone was waiting.

It was time to go in the building. Time to search for any second device.

Sam and Gillis, both of them wearing headlamps, entered the theater.

The darkness made the search slow and difficult. Stepping gingerly over debris, Sam headed down the left aisle, Gillis the right. The back rows of seats had sustained damage only to the upholstery—shredded fabric and stuffing. The further they advanced the more severe the damage.

"Dynamite," Gillis noted, sniffing the air.

"Looks like the blast center's near the front."

Sam moved slowly toward the orchestra pit, the beam of his headlamp slicing the darkness left and right as he scanned the area around the stage—or what had once been the stage. A few splintered boards was all that remained.

"Crater's right here," observed Gillis.

Sam joined him. The two men knelt down for a closer inspection. Like the church bomb a week before, this one was shallow—a low-velocity blast. Dynamite.

"Looks like the third row, center stage," said Sam. "Wonder who was sitting here."

"Assigned seating, you figure?"

"If so, then we'll have ourselves a convenient list of potential targets."

"Looks all clear to me," Gillis declared.

"We can call in the searchers." Sam rose to his feet and at once felt a little dizzy. The aftereffects of the blast. He'd been in so many bombs lately, his brain must be getting scrambled. Maybe some fresh air would clear his head.

"You okay?" asked Gillis.

"Yeah. I just need to get out of here for a moment." He stumbled back up the aisle and through the lobby doors. Outside he leaned against a lamppost, breathing gulps of night air. His dizziness faded and he became aware, once again, of the activity in the street. He noticed that the crowds had thinned, and that the injured had all been evacuated. Only one ambulance was still parked in the road.

Where was Nina?

That one thought instantly cleared his head. He glanced up and down the street, but caught no glimpse of her. Had she left the scene? Or was she taken from it?

A young cop manning the police line glanced up as Sam approached. "Yes, sir?"

"There was a woman—a nurse in street clothes—working out here. Where'd she go?"

"You mean the dark-haired lady? The pretty one?"

"That's her."

"She left in one of the ambulances, about twenty minutes ago. I think she was helping with a patient."

"Thanks." Sam went to his car and reached inside for his cellular phone. He was not taking any chances; he had to be sure she was safe. He dialed Maine Med ER.

The line was busy.

In frustration he climbed in the car. "I'm heading to the hospital!" he yelled to Gillis. "Be right back."

Ignoring his partner's look of puzzlement, Sam lurched away from the curb and steered through the obstacle course of police vehicles. Fifteen minutes later, he pulled into a parking stall near the hospital's emergency entrance.

Even before he walked in the doors, he could hear the sounds of frantic activity inside. The waiting area was mobbed. He pushed his way through the crowd until he'd reached the triage desk, manned by a clearly embattled nurse.

"I'm Detective Navarro, Portland Police," he said. "Is Nina Cormier working here?"

"Nina? Not tonight, as far as I know."

"She came in with one of the ambulances."

"I might have missed her. Let me check." She punched the intercom button and said, "There's a policeman out here. Wants to speak to Nina. If she's back there, can you ask her to come out?"

For a good ten minutes, he waited with growing impatience. Nina didn't appear. The crowd in the ER seemed to grow even larger, packing into every available square inch of the waiting area. Even worse, the reporters had shown up, TV cameras and all. The triage nurse had her hands full; she'd forgotten entirely about Sam.

Unable to wait any longer, he pushed past the front desk. The nurse was calming down a hysterical family member; she didn't even notice Sam had crossed into the inner sanctum and was heading up the ER corridor.

Treatment rooms lined both sides of the halls. He glanced in each one as he passed. All were occupied and overflowing with victims from the bombing. He saw stunned faces, bloodied clothes. But no Nina.

He turned, retraced his steps down the hall, and paused outside a closed door. It was the trauma room. From beyond the door came the sound of voices, the clang of cabinets. He knew that a crisis was in full swing, and he was reluctant to intrude, but he had no alternative. He had to confirm that Nina was here, that she'd made it safely to the ER.

He pushed open the door.

A patient—a man—was lying on the table, his body white and flaccid under the lights. Half a dozen medical personnel were laboring over him, one performing CPR, the others scurrying about with IV's and drugs. Sam paused, momentarily stunned by the horror of the scene.

"Sam?"

Only then did he notice Nina moving toward him from the other side of the room. Like all the other nurses, she was dressed in scrub clothes. He hadn't even noticed her in that first glimpse of blue-clad personnel.

She took his arm and quickly tugged him out of the room. "What are you doing here?" she whispered.

"You left the blast site. I wasn't sure what happened to you."

"I rode here in one of the ambulances. I figured they needed me." She glanced back at the door to the trauma room. "I was right."

"Nina, you can't just take off without telling me! I had no idea if you were all right."

She regarded him with an expression of quiet wonder, but didn't say a thing.

"Are you listening to me?" he said.

"Yes," she replied softly. "But I don't believe what I'm hearing. You actually sound scared."

"I wasn't scared. I was just—I mean—" He shook his head in frustration. "Okay, I was worried. I didn't want something to happen to you."

"Because I'm your witness?"

He looked into her eyes, those beautiful, thoughtful eyes. Never in his life had he felt so vulnerable. This was a new feeling for him and he didn't like it. He was not a man who was easily frightened, and the fact that he had experienced such fear at the thought of losing her told him he was far more deeply involved than he'd ever intended to be.

"Sam?" She reached up and touched his face.

He grasped her hand and gently lowered it. "Next time," he instructed, "I want you to tell me where you're going. It's *your* life at stake. If you want to risk it, that's your business. But until Spectre's under arrest, your safety's my concern. Do you understand?"

She withdrew her hand from his. The retreat was more than physical; he could feel her pulling away emotionally as well, and it hurt him. It was a pain of his own choosing, and that made it even worse.

She said, tightly, "I understand perfectly well."

"Good. Now, I think you should go back to the hotel where we can keep an eye on you tonight."

"I can't leave. They need me here."

"I need you, too. Alive."

"Look at this place!" She waved toward the waiting area, crowded with the injured. "These people all have to be examined and treated. I can't walk out now."

"Nina, I have a job to do. And your safety is part of that job."

"I have a job to do, too!" she asserted.

They faced each other for a moment, neither one willing to back down.

Then Nina snapped, "I don't have time for this," and she turned back toward the trauma room.

"Nina!"

"I'll do my job, Sam. You do yours."

"Then I'm sending a man over to keep an eye on you."

"Do whatever you want."

"When will you be finished here?"

She stopped and glanced at the waiting patients. "My guess? Not till morning."

"Then I'll be back to get you at 6:00 a.m."

"Whatever you say, Detective," she retorted and pushed into the trauma room. He caught a fleeting glimpse of her as she rejoined the surgical team, and then the door closed behind her.

I'll do my job. You do yours, she'd told him.

She's right, he thought. *That's exactly what I should be focusing on. My job.*

From his car phone, he put in a call to Officer Pressler and told him to send his relief officer down to Maine Med ER, where he'd be the official baby-sitting service for the night. Then, satisfied that Nina was in good hands, he headed back to the bomb scene.

It was eleven-thirty. The night was just beginning.

NINA MADE IT THROUGH the next seven hours on sheer nerve. Her conversation with Sam had left her hurt and angry, and she had to force herself to concentrate on the work at hand—tending to the dozens of patients who now filled the waiting area. Their injuries, their discomfort, had to take priority. But every so often, when she'd pause to collect her thoughts or catch her breath, she'd find herself thinking about Sam, about what he'd said.

I have a job to do. And your safety is part of that job.

Is that all I am to you? she wondered as she signed her name to yet another patient instruction sheet. A job, a burden? And what had she expected, anyway? From the beginning, he'd been the unflappable public official, Mr. Cool himself. There'd been flashes of warmth, of course, even the occasional glimpse of the man inside, a man of genuine kindness. But every time she thought she'd touched the real Sam Navarro, he'd pull away from her as though scalded by the contact.

What am I to do with you, Sam? she wondered sadly. And what was she to do with all the feelings she had for him?

Work was all that kept her going that night. She never even noticed when the sun came up.

By the time 6:00 a.m. rolled around, she was so tired she could scarcely walk without weaving, but at last the waiting room was empty and the patients all sent home. Most of the ER staff had gathered, shell-shocked, in the employee lounge for a well-deserved coffee break. Nina was about to join them when she heard her name called.

She turned. Sam was standing in the waiting room.

He looked every bit as exhausted as she felt, his eyes bleary, his jaw dark with a day's growth of beard. At her first sight of his face, all the anger she'd felt the night before instantly evaporated.

My poor, poor Sam, she thought. *You give so much of yourself. And what comfort do you have at the end of the day?*

She went to him. He didn't speak; he just looked at her with that expression of weariness. She put her arms around him. For a moment they held each other, their bodies trembling with fatigue. Then she heard him say, softly, "Let's go home."

"I'd like that," she said. And smiled.

She didn't know how he managed to pilot the car to his house. All she knew was that a moment after she dozed off, they were in his driveway, and he was gently prodding her awake. Together they dragged themselves into the house, into his bedroom. No thoughts of lust crossed her mind, even as they undressed and crawled into bed together, even as she felt his lips brush her face, felt his breath warm her hair.

She fell asleep in his arms.

SHE FELT SO WARM, so perfect, lying beside him. As if she belonged here, in his bed.

Sam gazed through drowsy eyes at Nina, who was still sound asleep. It was already afternoon. He should have been up and dressed hours ago, but sheer exhaustion had taken its toll.

He was getting too old for this job. For the past eighteen years, he'd been a cop through and through. Though there were times when he hated the work, when the ugly side of it seemed to overwhelm his love for the job, he'd never once doubted that a cop was exactly what he was meant to be. And so it dismayed him now that, at this moment, being a cop was the furthest thing from his mind.

What he wanted, really wanted, was to spend eternity in this bed, gazing at this woman. Studying her face, enjoying the view. Only when Nina was asleep did he feel it was safe to really look at her. When she was awake, he felt too vulnerable, as though she could read his thoughts, could see past his barriers, straight to his heart. He was afraid to admit, even to himself, the feelings he harbored there.

As he studied her now, he realized there was no point denying it to himself: he couldn't bear the thought of her walking out of his life. Did that mean he loved her? He didn't know.

He did know this was not the turn of events he'd wanted or expected.

But last night he'd watched her at work in the wreckage of the bomb site, and he'd admired a new dimension of Nina, one he saw for the first time. A woman with both compassion and strength.

It would be so easy to fall in love with her. It would be such a mistake.

In a month, a year, she'd come to see him for what he was: no hero with a badge, but an everyday guy doing his job the best way he knew how. And there she'd be in that hospital, working side by side with men like Robert Bledsoe. Men with medical degrees and houses on the water. How long would it take for her to grow weary of the cop who just happened to love her?

He sat up on the side of the bed and ran his hands through his hair, trying to shake off the last vestiges of sleep. His brain wasn't feeling alert yet. He needed coffee, food, anything to snap him back into gear. There were so many details to follow up on, so many leads still to check out.

Then he felt a touch, soft as silk, caress his bare back. All at once, work was the last thing on his mind.

He turned and met her gaze. She was looking drowsily at him, her smile relaxed and contented. "What time is it?" she murmured.

"Almost three."

"We slept that long?"

"We needed it. Both of us. It was okay to let our guard down. Pressler was watching the house."

"You mean he was outside all day?"

"I made the arrangements last night. Before he went off duty. I knew I wanted to bring you home with me."

She opened her arms to him. That gesture of invitation was too tempting to resist. With a groan of surrender, he lay down beside her and met her lips with a kiss. At once his body was responding, and so was she. Their arms were entwined now, their warmth mingling. He couldn't stop, couldn't turn back; he wanted her too badly. He wanted to feel their bodies join, just one last time. If he couldn't have her for the rest of his life, at least he would have her for this moment. And he'd remember, always, her face, her smile, her sweet moans of desire as he thrust, hard and deep, inside her.

They both took. They both gave.

But even as he reached his climax, even as he felt the first glorious release, he thought, *This is not enough. This could never be enough.* He wanted to know more than just her body; he wanted to know her soul.

His passion was temporarily sated, yet he felt both unsatisfied and depressed as he lay beside her afterward. Not at all what the carefree bachelor should expect to feel after a conquest. If anything, he was angry at himself for sliding into this situation. For allowing this woman to become so important to him.

And here she was, smiling, working her way even deeper into his life.

His response was to pull away, to rise from the bed and head into the shower. When he reemerged, clean and still damp, she was sitting up on the side of the bed, watching him with a look of bewilderment.

"I have to get back to work," he said, pulling on a clean shirt. "I'll invite Pressler inside to sit with you."

"The bombing's over and done with. Spectre's probably a thousand miles away by now."

"I can't take that chance."

"There are others who know his face. The theater ushers. They could identify him."

"One of them hit his head on the sidewalk. He's still in and out of consciousness. The other one can't even decide on the color of Spectre's eyes. That's how helpful the ushers are."

"Nevertheless, you've got other witnesses and Spectre knows it." She paused. "I'd say that lets both of us off the hook."

"What do you mean?"

"I can stop worrying about being a target. And you can stop worrying about keeping me alive. And go back to your real job."

"This is part of my job."

"So you've told me." She tilted her chin up, and he saw the brief gleam of tears in her eyes. "I wish I was more than that. God, I wish..."

"Nina, please. This doesn't help either one of us."

Her head drooped. The sight of her, hurt, silent, was almost more than he could stand. He knelt down before her and took her hands in his. "You know I'm attracted to you."

She gave a softly ironic laugh. "That much, I guess, is obvious to us both."

"And you also know that I think you're a terrific woman. If I ever get hauled to the ER in an ambulance, I hope you're the nurse who takes care of me."

"But?"

"But..." He sighed. "I just don't see us together. Not for the long haul."

She looked down again, and he could sense her struggle for composure. He'd hurt her, and he hated himself for it, hated his own cowardice. That's what it was, of course. He didn't believe hard enough in their chances. He didn't believe in *her.*

All he was certain of was that he'd never, ever get over her.

He rose to his feet. She didn't react, but just sat on the bed, staring down. "It's not you, Nina," he said. "It's *me.* It's something that happened to me years ago. It convinced me that this situation we're in—it doesn't last. It's artificial. A scared woman. And a cop. It's a setup for all kinds of unrealistic expectations."

"Don't give me the old psychology lecture, Sam. I don't need to hear about transference and misplaced affections."

"You have to hear it. And understand it. Because the effect goes both ways. How you feel about me, and how I feel about you. My wanting to take care of you, protect you. It's something I can't help, either." He sighed, a sound of both frustration and despair. *It's too late,* he thought. *We both feel things we shouldn't be feeling. And it's impossible to turn back the clock.*

"You were saying something happened to you. Years ago," she said. "Was it...another woman?"

He nodded.

"The same situation? Scared woman, protective cop?"

Again he nodded.

"Oh." She shook her head and murmured in a tone of self-disgust, "I guess I fell right into it."

"We both did."

"So who left whom, Sam? The last time this happened?"

"It was the only time it happened. Except for you." He turned away, began to move around the room. "I was just a rookie patrolman. Twenty-two years old. Assigned to protect a woman being stalked. She was twenty-eight going on forty when it came to sophistication. It's not surprising I got a little infatuated. The surprising part was that she seemed to return the sentiment. At least, until the crisis was over. Then she decided I wasn't so impressive after all. And she was right." He stopped and looked at her. "It's that damn thing called reality. It has a way of stripping us all down to what we really are. And in my case, I'm just a hardworking cop. Honest for the most part. Brighter than some, dumber than others. In short, I'm not anyone's hero. And when she finally saw that, she turned right around and walked out, leaving behind one sadder but wiser rookie."

"And you think that's what I'm going to do."

"It's what you should do. Because you deserve so much, Nina. More than I can ever give you."

She shook her head. "What I really want, Sam, has nothing to do with what a man can *give* me."

"Think about Robert. What you could have had with him."

"Robert was the perfect example! He had it all. Everything except what I wanted from him."

"What did you want, Nina?"

"Love. Loyalty." She met his gaze. "Honesty."

What he saw in her eyes left him shaken. Those were the things he wanted to give her. The very things he was afraid to give her.

"Right now you think it's enough," he remarked. "But maybe you'll find out it's not."

"It's more than I ever got from Robert." *More than I'll ever get from you, too,* was what her eyes said.

He didn't try to convince her otherwise. Instead, he turned toward the door.

"I'm going to call Pressler inside," he told her. "Have him stay with you all day today."

"There's no need."

"You shouldn't be alone, Nina."

"I won't be." She looked up at him. "I can go back to my father's house. He has that fancy security system. Not to mention a few dogs. Now that we know Daniella isn't the one running around planting bombs, I should be perfectly safe there." She glanced around the room. "I shouldn't be staying here, anyway. Not in your house."

"You can. As long as you need to."

"No." She met his gaze. "I don't really see the point, Sam. Since it's so apparent to us both that this is a hopeless relationship."

He didn't argue with her. And that, more than anything else, was what hurt her. He could see it in her face.

He simply said, "I'll drive you there." Then he turned and left the room. He had to.

He couldn't bear to see the look in her eyes.

Chapter Twelve

"We think we know who the target was," reported Sam. "It was our wonderful D.A., Liddell."

Chief Coopersmith stared across the conference table at Sam and Gillis. "Are you certain?"

"Everything points that way. We pinpointed the bomb placement to somewhere in Row Three, Seats G through J. The seating last night was reserved weeks in advance. We've gone over the list of people sitting in that row and section. And Liddell and his wife were right smack in the center. They would've been killed instantly."

"Who else was in that row?"

"Judge Dalton was about six seats away," said Gillis. "Chances are, he would've been killed, too. Or at least seriously maimed."

"And the other people in that row?"

"We've checked them all out. A visiting law professor from California. A few relatives of Judge Dalton's. A pair of law clerks. We doubt any of them would've attracted the interest of a hired killer. Oh, and you may be interested to hear Ernie Takeda's latest report. He called it in from the lab this afternoon. It was dynamite, Dupont label. Prima detonating cord. Green electrical tape."

"Spectre," said Coopersmith. He leaned back and exhaled a loud sigh of weariness. They were all tired. Every one of them had worked straight through the night, caught a few hours of sleep, and then returned to the job. Now it was 5:00 p.m., and another night was just beginning. "God, the man is back with a vengeance."

"Yeah, but he's not having much luck," commented Gillis. "His targets keep surviving. Liddell. Judge Dalton. Nina Cormier. I'd say that the legendary Vincent Spectre must be feeling pretty frustrated about now."

"Embarrassed, too," added Sam. "His reputation's on the

line, if it isn't already shot. After this fiasco, he's washed up as a contract man. Anyone with the money to hire will go elsewhere."

"Do we know who *did* hire him?"

Sam and Gillis glanced at each other. "We can make a wild guess," said Gillis.

"Billy Binford?"

Sam nodded. "The Snowman's trial is coming up in a month. And Liddell was dead set against any plea bargains. Rumor has it, he was going to use a conviction as a jumping-off place for some political campaign. I think The Snowman knows he's in for a long stay in jail. I think he wants Liddell off the prosecution team. Permanently."

"If Sam hadn't cleared that theater," added Gillis, "we could have lost half our prosecutors. The courts would've been backed up for months. In that situation, Binford's lawyers could've written the plea bargain for him."

"Any way we can pin this down with proof?"

"Not yet. Binford's attorney, Albert Darien, denies any knowledge of this. We're not going to be able to shake a word out of him. ATF's going over the videotapes from the prison surveillance cameras, looking over all the visitors that Binford had. We may be able to identify a go-between."

"You think it's someone other than his attorney?"

"Possibly. If we can identify that go-between, we may have a link to Spectre."

"Go for it," said Coopersmith. "I want this guy, and I want him bad."

At five-thirty, the meeting broke up and Sam headed for the coffee machine in search of a caffeine boost that would keep him going for the next eight hours. He was just taking his first sip when Norm Liddell walked into the station. Sam couldn't help feeling a prick of satisfaction at the sight of the bruises and scrapes on Liddell's face. The injuries were minor, but last night, after the bomb, Liddell had been among those screaming the loudest for medical assistance. His own wife, who'd sustained a broken arm, had finally told her husband to shut up and act like a man.

Now here he was, sporting a few nasty scrapes on his face as well as a look of—could it be? Contrition?

"Afternoon, Navarro," said Liddell, his voice subdued.

"Afternoon."

"I, uh..." Liddell cleared his throat and glanced around the hall, as though to check if anyone was listening. No one was.

"How's the wife doing?" asked Sam.

"Fine. She'll be in a cast for a while. Luckily, it was just a closed fracture."

"She handled herself pretty well last night, considering her injury," Sam commented. *Unlike you.*

"Yes, well, my wife's got a spine of steel. In fact, that's sort of why I want to talk to you."

"Oh?"

"Look, Navarro. Last night...I guess I jumped on you prematurely. I mean, I didn't realize you had information about any bomb."

Sam didn't say a word. He didn't want to interrupt this enjoyable performance.

"So when I got on your case last night—about evacuating the building—I should've realized you had your reasons. But damn it, Navarro, all I could see was all those people hurt in the stampede. I thought you'd gotten them panicked for nothing, and I—" He paused, obviously struggling to bite back his words. "Anyway, I apologize."

"Apology accepted."

Liddell gave a curt nod of relief.

"Now you can tell your wife you're off the hook."

The look on Liddell's face was all Sam needed to know that he'd guessed right. This apology had been Mrs. Liddell's idea, bless her steely spine. He couldn't help grinning as he watched the other man turn and walk stiffly toward Chief Coopersmith's office. The good D.A., it appeared, was not the one wearing the pants in the family.

"Hey, Sam!" Gillis was heading toward him, pulling on his jacket. "Let's go."

"Where?"

"Prison's got a surveillance videotape they want us to look at. It's The Snowman and some unknown visitor from a few days ago."

Sam felt a sudden adrenaline rush. "Was it Spectre?"

"No. It was a woman."

"THERE. THE BLONDE," said Detective Cooley.

Sam and Gillis leaned toward the TV screen, their gazes fixed on the black-and-white image of the woman. The view of her face was intermittently blocked by other visitors moving in the foreground, but from what they could see, the woman was indeed a blonde, twenties to thirties, and built like a showgirl.

"Okay, freeze it there," Cooley said to the video tech. "That's a good view of her."

The woman was caught in a still frame, her face turned to the surveillance camera, her figure momentarily visible between two passersby. She was dressed in a skirt suit, and she appeared to be carrying a briefcase. Judging by her attire, she might be an attorney or some other professional. But two details didn't fit.

One was her shoes. The camera's angle, facing downward, captured a view of her right foot, perched atop a sexy spike-heeled sandal with a delicate ankle strap.

"Not the kind of shoes you wear to court," noted Sam.

"Not unless you're out to give the judge a thrill," Gillis said. "And look at that makeup."

It was the second detail that didn't fit. This woman was made up like no lawyer Sam had ever seen. Obviously false eyelashes. Eyeshadow like some tropical fish. Lipstick painted on in bold, broad smears.

"Man, she sure ain't the girl next door," Gillis observed.

"What's the name on the visitor log?" asked Sam.

Cooley glanced at a sheet of paper. "She signed in as Marilyn Dukoff. Identified her purpose for visiting The Snowman as attorney-client consultation."

Gillis laughed. "If she's an attorney, then I'm applying to law school."

"Which law firm did she say she was with?" asked Sam.

"Frick and Darien."

"Not true?"

Cooley shook his head. "She's not on the firm's list of partners, associates or clerks. But..." He leaned forward, a grin on his face. "We think we know where she *did* work."

"Where?"

"The Stop Light."

Gillis shot Sam a look of *Didn't I tell ya?* No one had to explain a thing. They knew all about the Stop Light and its stage shows, pasties optional.

"Let me guess," said Sam. "Exotic dancer."

"You got it," affirmed Cooley.

"Are we sure we're talking about the right Marilyn Dukoff?"

"I think we are," Cooley answered. "See, all visitors to the prison have to present ID, and that's the name she gave, backed up by a Maine driver's license. We've pulled the license file. And here's the photo." Cooley passed a copy of the photo to Sam and Gillis.

"It's her," said Gillis.

"Which means we're talking about the right Marilyn Dukoff," said Cooley. "I think she just waltzed in under her own name and didn't bother with fake IDs. All she faked was her profession."

"Which is obviously not in the legal field," Gillis drawled.

Sam gave a nod to Cooley. "Good work."

"Unfortunately," added the younger detective, "I can't seem to locate the woman herself. We know where she *was* employed, but she left the job two weeks ago. I sent a man to the address listed on her license. She doesn't answer the door. And her phone's just been disconnected." He paused. "I think it's time for a search warrant."

"Let's get it." Sam rose to his feet and glanced at Gillis. "Meet you in the car, ten minutes."

"The blonde's?"

"Unless you've got somewhere better to go."

Gillis looked back at the video screen. At that still shot of a slim ankle, a sexy shoe. "Better than *that?*" He laughed. "I don't think so."

THE POLICE WERE getting too close for comfort.

Spectre slouched in the doorway of an apartment building half a block away and watched the cops come out of Marilyn's old building. Only moments before, Spectre had been inside that apartment, checking to make sure Marilyn hadn't left behind any clues to her current whereabouts. Luckily for him, he'd slipped out just ahead of Navarro's arrival.

They'd been inside almost an hour. They were good, all right—but Spectre was cleverer. Hours after the theater bombing, he'd hustled Marilyn into a different apartment across town. He'd known that his target might become apparent once they'd pinpointed the bomb placement in the theater. And that Marilyn would inevitably come under their scrutiny. Luckily, she'd been cooperative.

Unfortunately, her usefulness was just about over, and the time had come to end their association. But first, he needed her for one more task.

His face tightened as he spotted a familiar figure emerge from the building. Navarro again. The detective had come to represent all the failures that Spectre had suffered over the past week. Navarro was the brains behind the investigation, the one man responsible for Liddell still being alive.

No hit. No fee. Navarro had cost him money—a lot of it.

Spectre watched the cops confer on the sidewalk. There were five of them, three in plain clothes, two in uniform, but it was Navarro on whom he focused his rage. This had turned into a battle of wits between them, a test of determination. In all his years as a "fuse" man, Spectre had never matched skills with such a wily opponent.

The safe thing to do was merely to slip away from this town and seek out contracts elsewhere. Miami or New Orleans. But his reputation had suffered a serious blow here; he wasn't sure he could land a job in Miami. And he had the feeling Navarro wouldn't give up the pursuit, that, wherever Spectre went, the detective would be dogging his trail.

And then, there was the matter of getting even. Spectre wasn't going to walk away without exacting some kind of payback.

The three plainclothes cops climbed into an unmarked car and drove away. A moment later, the uniformed cops were gone as well. They had found nothing in Marilyn's apartment; Spectre had seen to it.

Catch me if you can, Navarro, he thought. *Or will I catch you first?*

He straightened and stamped his feet, feeling the blood return to his legs. Then he left the doorway and walked around the corner, to his car.

Navarro. Once and for all, he had to take care of Navarro. And he had the perfect plan. It would require Marilyn's help. One little phone call—that's all he'd ask. And then he'd ask no more of her.

Ever again.

THE DINNER WAS EXCELLENT. The company was wretched.

Daniella, dressed in an iridescent green leotard and a slinky wraparound skirt, sullenly picked at her salad, ignoring the platter of roast duckling and wild rice. She was not speaking to her husband, and he was not speaking to her, and Nina was too uncomfortable to speak to either one of them.

After all those questions by the police, the matter of Daniella's affair with Robert had come to light. While Nina would never forgive Daniella for that betrayal, at least she could manage to pull off a civil evening with the woman.

Nina's father could not. He was still in a state of shock from the revelation. His showpiece wife, the stunning blonde thirty years his junior, had not been satisfied with marrying mere wealth. She'd wanted a younger man. After four marriages, George Cormier still didn't know how to choose the right wife.

Now it looks like this will be his fourth divorce, Nina thought. She glanced at her father, then at Daniella. Though she loved her father, she couldn't help feeling that he and Daniella deserved each other. In the worst possible way.

Daniella set down her fork. "If you'll excuse me," she said, "I don't really have much of an appetite. I think I'll skip out for a movie."

"What about me?" snapped George. "I know I'm just your husband, but a few evenings a week with your boring old spouse isn't too much to ask, is it? Considering all the benefits you get in exchange."

"Benefits? *Benefits?*" Daniella drew herself to her feet in anger. "All the money in the world can't make up for being married to an old goat like you."

"Goat?"

"An old goat. Do you hear me? *Old.*" She leaned across the table. "In every sense of the word."

He, too, rose to his feet. "Why, you bitch..."

"Go ahead. Call me names. I can think of just as many to call you back." With a whisk of her blond hair, she turned and walked out of the dining room.

George stared after her for a moment. Slowly, he sank back in his chair. "God," he whispered. "What was I thinking when I married her?"

You weren't thinking at all, Nina felt like saying. She touched her father's arm. "Seems like neither one of us is any good at picking spouses. Are we, Dad?"

He regarded his daughter with a look of shared misery. "I sincerely hope you haven't inherited my bad luck with love, sweetheart."

They sat for a moment without speaking. Their supper lay, almost untouched, on the table. In another room, music had started up, the fast and thumping rhythm of an aerobics tape. Daniella was at it again, working off her anger by sculpting a new and better body. Smart girl; she was going to come out of a divorce looking like a million bucks.

Nina sighed and leaned back. "Whether it's bad luck or character flaws, Dad, maybe some people are just meant to be single."

"Not you, Nina. You *need* to love someone. You always have. And that's what makes you so easy to love."

She gave a sad laugh but said nothing. *Easy to love, easy to leave,* she thought.

Once again, she found herself wondering what Sam was doing. What he was thinking. Not about her, surely; he was too much the cop to be bothered by minor distractions.

Yet when the phone rang, she couldn't suppress the sudden hope that he was calling. She sat at the table, heart thumping hard as she listened to Daniella's voice in the next room talking on the phone.

A moment later, Daniella appeared in the doorway and said, "It's for you, Nina. The hospital. They said they've been trying to reach you."

Disappointed, Nina rose to take the call. "Hello?"

"Hi, this is Gladys Power, the night nursing supervisor. Sorry to bother you—we got your phone number from your mother. We have a number of staff out sick tonight, and we were wondering if you could come in to cover for the ER."

"Night shift?"

"Yes. We could really use you."

Nina glanced toward Daniella's exercise room, where the music was playing louder than ever. She had to get out of this house. Away from this emotional battleground.

She said, "Okay, I'll take the shift."

"See you at eleven o'clock."

"Eleven?" Nina frowned. The night shift usually started at midnight. "You want me there an hour early?"

"If you could manage it. We're shorthanded on the evening shift as well."

"Right. I'll be there, eleven o'clock." She hung up and breathed a soft sigh of relief. Work was exactly what she needed. Maybe eight hours of crises, major and minor, would get her mind back on track.

And off the subject of Sam Navarro.

MARILYN HUNG UP THE PHONE. "She said she'd be there."

Spectre gave a nod of approval. "You handled it well."

"Of course." Marilyn favored him with that satisfied smile of hers. A smile that said, *I'm worth every penny you pay me.*

"Did she seem at all suspicious?" he asked.

"Not a bit. I'm telling you, she'll be there. Eleven o'clock, just like you wanted." Marilyn tilted back her head and gave her lips a predatory lick. "Now, do I get what I want?"

He smiled. "What *do* you want?"

"You know." She sidled toward him and unbuckled his belt. His breath caught in an involuntary gasp as that hot little hand slid inside his trousers. Her touch was delicious, expert, her technique designed to reduce a man to begging. Oh yes, he knew exactly what she was asking for.

And it wasn't sex.

Why not enjoy the moment? he thought. She was willing, and he still had the time to spare. Three hours until Nina Cormier showed up for her shift at the hospital. Some quick amusement with Marilyn, and then on to more serious business.

She dropped to her knees before him. "You said you'd pay me what I was worth," she whispered.

He groaned. "I promised..."

"I'm worth a lot. Don't you think?"

"Absolutely."

"I can be worth even more to you."

He gave a jerk of pleasure and grasped her face. Breathing heavily, he stroked down her cheek, her jaw, to her neck. Such a long, slender neck. How easy it should be to finish it. First, though, he'd let *her* finish...

"Oh, yes," she murmured. "You're ready for me."

He pulled her, hard, against him. And he thought, *A pity you won't be ready for me.*

IT WAS TEN-THIRTY by the time a weary Sam stepped through his front door. The first thing he noticed was the silence. The emptiness. It was a house that had somehow lost its soul.

He turned on the lights, but even the glow of all those lamps couldn't seem to dispel the shadows. For the past three years, this was the house he'd called home, the house he'd returned to every evening after work. Now the place felt cold to him, like the house of a stranger. Not a home at all.

He poured himself a glass of milk and drank it in a few thirsty gulps. So much for supper; he didn't have the energy to cook. He poured a second glass and carried it over to the telephone. All evening, he'd been itching to make this call, but something had always interrupted him. Now that he had a few blessed moments of peace, he was going to call Nina. He was going to tell her what he'd been afraid to tell her, what he could no longer deny to her, or to himself.

It had come to him this afternoon, a realization that had struck him, oddly enough, in the midst of searching Marilyn Dukoff's apartment. He'd stood in the woman's bedroom and gazed at the empty bureau drawers, the stripped mattress. And without warning, he'd been struck by a sense of loneliness so intense it made his chest ache. Because that abandoned room had suddenly come to represent his life. It had a purpose, a function, but it was nevertheless empty.

I've been a cop too long, he'd thought. *I've let it take over my life.* Only at that moment, standing in that empty bedroom, did it occur to him how little of his own life he really had. No wife, no kids, no family.

Nina had opened his eyes to the possibilities. Yes, he was scared. Yes, he knew just how much, how deeply, he would be hurt if she ever left him. But the alternative was just as bleak; that he would never even give it a chance.

He'd been a coward. But no longer.

He picked up the phone and dialed Nina's father's house.

A few rings later, the call was answered by a bland "Hello?" Not Nina but Daniella, the fitness freak.

"This is Sam Navarro," he said. "Sorry to call so late. May I speak to Nina?"

"She's not here."

His immediate pang of disappointment was quickly followed by a cop's sense of dismay. How could she not be there? She was supposed to stay in a safe place tonight, not run around unprotected.

"Mind telling me where she went?" he asked.

"The hospital. They called her in to work the night shift."

"The Emergency Room?"

"I guess so."

"Thanks." He hung up, his disappointment so heavy it felt like a physical weight on his shoulders. What the hell. He was not going to hold off any longer. He was going to tell her now. Tonight.

He dialed Maine Medical ER.

"Emergency Room."

"This is Detective Sam Navarro, Portland Police. May I speak with Nina Cormier?"

"Nina's not here tonight."

"Well, when she gets there, could you ask her to call me at home?"

"She's not scheduled to come in."

"Excuse me?"

"I have the time sheet right in front of me. Her name's not down here for tonight."

"I was told someone called her in to work the night shift."

"I don't know anything about that."

"Well, can you find out? This is urgent."

"Let me check with the supervisor. Can you hold?"

In the silence that followed, Sam could hear his own blood rushing through his ears. Something was wrong. That old instinct of his was tingling.

The woman came back on the line. "Detective? I've checked with the supervisor. She says she doesn't know anything about it, either. According to her schedule, Nina isn't listed for any shifts until next week."

"Thank you," said Sam softly.

For a moment he sat thinking about that phone call from the hospital. Someone had known enough to locate Nina at her father's house. Someone had talked her into leaving those protective gates at an hour of night when there'd be few witnesses to see what was about to happen.

Not just someone. Spectre.

It was 10:45.

In a heartbeat, he was out the door and running to his car.

Even as he roared out of his driveway, he knew he might already be too late. Racing for the freeway, he steered with one hand and dialed his car phone with the other.

"Gillis here," answered a weary voice.

"I'm on my way to Maine Med," Sam said. "Spectre's there."

"What?"

"Nina got a bogus call asking her to come in to work. I'm sure it was him. She's already left the house—"

Gillis replied, "I'll meet you there," and hung up.

Sam turned his full attention to the road. The speedometer hit seventy. Eighty.

Don't let me be too late, he prayed.

He floored the accelerator.

THE HOSPITAL PARKING garage was deserted, a fact that scarcely concerned Nina as she drove through the automatic gate. She had often been in this garage late at night, either coming to, or leaving from, her shifts in the ER, and she'd never encountered any problems. Portland, after all, was one of the safest towns in America.

Provided you're not on someone's hit list, she reminded herself.

She pulled into a parking stall and sat there for a moment, trying to calm her nerves. She wanted to start her shift with her mind focused clearly on the job. Not on death threats. Not on Sam Navarro. Once she walked in those doors, she was first and foremost a professional. Peoples' lives depended on it.

She opened the door and stepped out of the car.

It was still an hour before the usual shift change. Come midnight, this garage would be busy with hospital staff coming or going. But at this moment, no one else was around. She quickened her pace. The hospital elevator was just ahead; the way was clear. Only a dozen yards to go.

She never saw the man step out from behind the parked car.

But she felt a hand grasp her arm, felt the bite of a gun barrel pressed against her temple. Her scream was cut off by the first words he uttered.

"Not a sound or you're dead." The gun at her head was all the emphasis needed to keep her silent.

He yanked her away from the elevator, shoved her toward a

row of parked cars. She caught a fleeting glimpse of his face as she was spun around. *Spectre.* They were moving now, Nina sobbing as she stumbled forward, the man gripping her arm with terrifying strength.

He's going to kill me now, here, where no one will see it....

The pounding of her own pulse was so loud at first, she didn't hear the faint squeal of tires across pavement.

But her captor did. Spectre froze, his grip still around her arm.

Now Nina heard it too: car tires, screeching up the garage ramp.

With savage force, Spectre wrenched her sideways, toward the cover of a parked car. *This is my only chance to escape,* she thought.

In an instant she was fighting back, struggling against his grip. He was going to shoot her anyway. Whether it happened in some dark corner or out here, in the open, she would not go down without a fight. She kicked, flailed, clawed at his face.

He swung at her, a swift, ugly blow that slammed against her chin. The pain was blinding. She staggered, felt herself falling. He grasped her arm and began dragging her across the pavement. She was too stunned to fight now, to save herself.

Light suddenly glared in her eyes, a light so bright it seemed to stab straight through her aching head. She heard tires screech and realized she was staring at a pair of headlights.

A voice yelled, *''Freeze!''*

Sam. It was Sam.

''Let her go, Spectre!'' Sam shouted.

The gun barrel was back at Nina's head, pressing harder than ever. ''What superb timing, Navarro,'' Spectre drawled without a trace of panic in his voice.

''I said, *let her go.*''

''Is that a command, Detective? I certainly hope not. Because, considering the young woman's situation—'' Spectre grabbed her by the chin and turned her face toward Sam ''—offending me could prove hazardous to her health.''

''I know your face. So do the ushers at the Brant Theater. You have no reason to kill her now!''

''No reason? Think again.'' Spectre, still holding the gun to Nina's head, nudged her forward. Toward Sam. ''Move out of the way, Navarro.''

''She's worthless to you—''

"But not to you."

Nina caught a glimpse of Sam's face, saw his look of helpless panic. He was gripping his gun in both hands, the barrel aimed, but he didn't dare shoot. Not with her in the line of fire.

She tried to go limp, tried to slump to the ground. No good; Spectre was too strong and he had too firm a grip around her neck. He simply dragged her beside him, his arm like a vise around her throat.

"Back off!" Spectre yelled.

"You don't want her!"

"Back off or it ends here, with her brains all over the ground!"

Sam took a step back, then another. Though his gun was still raised, it was useless to him. In that instant, Nina's gaze locked with his, and she saw more than fear, more than panic in his eyes. She saw despair.

"Nina," he said. "Nina—"

It was her last glimpse of Sam before Spectre pulled her into Sam's car. He slammed the door shut and threw the car in Reverse. Suddenly they were screeching backward down the ramp. She caught a fast-moving view of parked cars and concrete pillars, and then they crashed through the arm of the security gate.

Spectre spun the car around to face forward and hit the accelerator. They roared out of the driveway and onto the road.

Before she could recover her wits, the gun was back at her head. She looked at him, and saw a face that was frighteningly calm. The face of a man who knows he's in complete control.

"I have nothing to lose by killing you," he said.

"Then why don't you?" she whispered.

"I have plans. Plans that happen to include you."

"What plans?"

He gave a low, amused laugh. "Let's just say they involve Detective Navarro, his Bomb Squad, and a rather large amount of dynamite. I like spectacular endings, don't you?" He smiled at her.

That's when she realized whom she was looking at. What she was looking at.

A monster.

Chapter Thirteen

Sam raced down the parking garage ramp, his legs pumping with desperate speed. He emerged from the building just in time to see his car, Spectre at the wheel, careening out of the driveway and taking off down the road.

I've lost her, he thought as the taillights winked into the night. *My God. Nina...*

He sprinted to the sidewalk and ran halfway down the block before he finally came to a stop. The taillights had vanished.

The car was gone.

He gave a shout of rage, of despair, and heard his voice echo in the darkness. Too late. He was too late.

A flash of light made him spin around. A pair of headlights had just rounded the corner. Another car was approaching—one he recognized.

"Gillis!" he shouted.

The car braked to a stop near the curb. Sam dashed to the passenger door and scrambled inside.

"Go. *Go!*" he barked.

A perplexed Gillis stared at him. "What?"

"Spectre's got Nina! Move it!"

Gillis threw the car into gear. They screeched away from the curb. "Which way?"

"Left. Here!"

Gillis swerved around the corner.

Sam caught a glimpse of his own car, two blocks ahead, as it moved into an intersection and turned right.

"There!"

"I see it," Gillis said, and made the same turn.

Spectre must have spotted them, too. A moment later he accelerated and shot through a red light. Cars skidded to a stop in the intersection.

As Gillis steered through the maze of vehicles and pressed his pursuit, Sam picked up the car phone and called for assistance from all available patrol cars. With a little help, they could have Spectre boxed in.

For now, they just had to keep him in sight.

"This guy's a maniac," Gillis muttered.

"Don't lose her."

"He's gonna get us all killed. Look!"

Up ahead, Spectre swerved into the left lane, passed a car, and swerved back to the right just as a truck barreled down on him.

"Stay with them!" Sam ordered.

"I'm trying, I'm trying," Gillis, too, swerved left to pass. Too much traffic was heading toward them; he swerved back.

Seconds were lost. Seconds that Spectre pushed to his advantage.

Gillis tried again, this time managing to scoot back into his lane before colliding head-on with an oncoming van.

Spectre was nowhere in sight.

"What the hell?" muttered Gillis.

They stared at the road, saw stray taillights here and there, but otherwise it was an empty street. They drove on, through intersection after intersection, scanning the side roads. With every block they passed, Sam's panic swelled.

A half mile later, he was forced to accept the obvious. They had lost Spectre.

He had lost Nina.

Gillis was driving in grim silence now. Sam's despair had rubbed off on him as well. Neither one said it, but both of them knew. Nina was as good as dead.

"I'm sorry, Sam," murmured Gillis. "God, I'm sorry."

Sam could only stare ahead, wordless, his view blurring in a haze of tears. Moments passed. An eternity.

Patrol cars reported in. No trace of the car. Or Spectre.

Finally, at midnight, Gillis pulled over and parked at the curb. Both men sat in silence.

Gillis said, "There's still a chance."

Sam dropped his head in his hands. *A chance.* Spectre could be fifty miles away by now. Or he could be right around the corner. *What I would give for one, small chance....*

His gaze fell and he focused on Gillis's car phone.

One small chance.

He picked up the phone and dialed.

"Who're you calling?" asked Gillis.

"Spectre."

"What?"

"I'm calling my car phone." He listened as it rang. Five, six times.

Spectre answered, his voice raised in a bizarre falsetto. "Hello, you have reached the Portland Bomb Squad. No one's available to answer your call, as we seem to have misplaced our damn telephone."

"This is Navarro," growled Sam.

"Why hello, Detective Navarro. How *are* you?"

"Is she all right?"

"Who?"

"Is she all right?"

"Ah, you must be referring to the young lady. Perhaps I'll let her speak for herself."

There was a pause. He heard muffled voices, some sort of scraping sound. A soft, distant whine. Then Nina's voice came on, quiet, frightened. "Sam?"

"Are you hurt?"

"No. No, I'm fine."

"Where are you? Where's he taken you?"

"Oops," cut in Spectre. "Forbidden topic, Detective. Afraid I must abort this phone call."

"Wait. *Wait!*" cried Sam.

"Any parting words?"

"If you hurt her, Spectre—if anything happens to her—I swear I'll kill you."

"Is this a *law* enforcement officer I'm speaking to?"

"I mean it. I'll *kill* you."

"I'm shocked. *Shocked,* I tell you."

"Spectre!"

He was answered by laughter, soft and mocking. And then, abruptly, the line went dead.

Frantically Sam redialed and got a busy signal. He hung up, counted to ten, and dialed once more.

Another busy signal. Spectre had taken the phone off the hook.

Sam slammed the receiver down. "She's still alive."

"Where are they?"

"She never got the chance to tell me."

"It's been an hour. They could be anywhere within a fifty-mile radius."

"I know, I know." Sam sat back, trying to think through his swirl of panic. During his years as a cop, he'd always managed to keep his head cool, his thoughts focused. But tonight, for the first time in his career, he felt paralyzed by fear. By the knowledge that, with every moment that passed, every moment he did nothing, Nina's chances for survival faded.

"Why hasn't he killed her?" murmured Gillis. "Why is she still alive?"

Sam looked at his partner. At least Gillis still had a functioning brain. And he was thinking. Puzzling over a question that should've been obvious to them both.

"He's keeping her alive for a reason," said Gillis.

"A trump card. Insurance in case he's trapped."

"No, he's already home free. Right now, she's more of a liability than a help. Hostages slow you down. Complicate things. But he's allowed her to live."

So far, thought Sam with a wave of helpless rage. *I'm losing it, losing my ability to think straight. Her life depends on me. I can't afford to blow it.*

He looked at the phone again, and a memory echoed in his head. Something he'd heard over the phone during that brief pause between hearing Spectre's voice and Nina's. That distant wail, rising and falling.

A siren.

He reached for the phone again and dialed 911.

"Emergency operator," answered a voice.

"This is Detective Sam Navarro, Portland Police. I need a list of all emergency dispatches made in the last twenty minutes. Anywhere in the Portland-South Portland area."

"Which vehicles, sir?"

"Everything. Ambulance, fire, police. All of them."

There was a brief silence, then another voice came on the line. Sam had his notepad ready.

"This is the supervisor, Detective Navarro," a woman said. "I've checked with the South Portland dispatcher. Combined, we've had three dispatches in the last twenty minutes. At 11:55, an ambulance was sent to 2203 Green Street in Portland. At 12:10, the police were dispatched to a burglar alarm at 751 Bickford Street in South Portland. And at 12:13, a squad car was called to the vicinity of Munjoy Hill for a report of some disturbance of the peace. There were no fire trucks dispatched during that period."

"Okay, thanks." Sam hung up and rifled through the glove compartment for a map. Quickly he circled the three dispatch locations.

"What now?" asked Gillis.

"I heard a siren over the phone, when I was talking to Spectre. Which means he had to be within hearing distance of some emergency vehicle. And these are the only three locations vehicles were dispatched to."

Gillis glanced at the map and shook his head. "We've got dozens of city blocks covered there! From point of dispatch to destination."

"But these are starting points."

"Like a haystack's a starting point."

"It's all we have to go on. Let's start at Munjoy Hill."

"This is crazy. The APB's out on your car. We've got people looking for it already. We'd be running ourselves ragged trying to chase sirens."

"Munjoy Hill, Gillis. Go."

"You're beat. I'm beat. We should go back to HQ and wait for things to develop."

"You want me to drive? Then move the hell over."

"Sam, are you *hearing* me?"

"*Yes, damn you!*" Sam shouted back in a sudden outburst of rage. Then, with a groan, he dropped his head in his hands. Quietly he said, "It's my fault. My fault she's going to die. They were right there in front of me. And I couldn't think of any way to save her. Any way to keep her alive."

Gillis gave a sigh of comprehension. "She means that much to you?"

"And Spectre knows it. Somehow he knows it. That's why he's keeping her alive. To torment me. Manipulate me. He has the winning hand and he's using it." He looked at Gillis. "We have to find her."

"Right now, he has the advantage. He has someone who means a lot to you. And *you're* the cop he seems to be focused on. The cop he wants to get back at." He glanced down at his car phone. It was ringing.

He answered it. "Gillis here." A moment later he hung up

and started the car. "Jackman Avenue," he said, pulling into the road. "It could be our break."

"What's on Jackman Avenue?"

"An apartment, unit 338-D. They just found a body there."

Sam went very still. A sense of dread had clamped down on his chest, making it difficult to breathe. He asked, softly, "Whose body?"

"Marilyn Dukoff's."

HE WAS SINGING "Dixie!" as he worked, stringing out wire in multicolored lengths along the floor. Nina, hands and feet bound to a heavy chair, could only sit and watch helplessly. Next to Spectre was a toolbox, a soldering iron, and two dozen dynamite sticks.

"In Dixieland where I was born, early on a frosty mornin'..."

Spectre finished laying out the wire and turned his attention to the dynamite. With green electrical tape, he neatly bundled the sticks together in groups of three and set the bundles in a cardboard box.

"In Dixieland we'll make our stand, to live and die in Dixie. Away, away, away down south, in DIXIE!" he boomed out, and his voice echoed in the far reaches of the vast and empty warehouse. Then, turning to Nina, he dipped his head in a bow.

"You're crazy," whispered Nina.

"But what is madness? Who's to say?" Spectre wound green tape around the last three dynamite sticks. Then he gazed at the bundles, admiring his work. "What's that saying? 'Don't get mad, get even'? Well, I'm not mad, in any sense of the word. But I *am* going to get even."

He picked up the box of dynamite and was carrying it toward Nina when he seemed to stumble. Nina's heart almost stopped as the box of explosives tilted toward the floor. Toward her.

Spectre gave a loud gasp of horror just before he caught the box. To Nina's astonishment, he suddenly burst out laughing. "Just an old joke," he admitted. "But it never fails to get a reaction."

He really was crazy, she thought, her heart thudding.

Carrying the box of dynamite, he moved about the warehouse, laying bundles of explosives at measured intervals around the perimeter. "It's a shame, really," he said, "to waste so much quality dynamite on one building. But I do want to leave a good impression. A lasting impression. And I've had quite enough of Sam Navarro and his nine lives. This should take care of any extra lives he still has."

"You're laying a trap."

"You're so clever."

"Why? Why do you want to kill him?"

"Because."

"He's just a policeman doing his job."

"*Just* a policeman?" Spectre turned to her, but his expression remained hidden in the shadows of the warehouse. "Navarro is more than that. He's a challenge. My nemesis. To think, after all these years of success in cities like Boston and Miami, I should find my match in a small town like this. Not even Portland, Oregon, but Portland, *Maine.*" He gave a laugh of self-disgust. "It ends here, in this warehouse. Between Navarro and me."

Spectre crossed toward her, carrying the final bundle of dynamite. He knelt beside the rocking chair where Nina sat with hands and ankles bound. "I saved the last blast for you, Miss Cormier," he said. And he taped the bundle under Nina's chair. "You won't feel a thing," he assured her. "It will happen so fast, why, the next thing you know, you'll be sprouting angel's wings. So will Navarro. If he gets his wings at all."

"He's not stupid. He'll know you've set a trap."

Spectre began stringing out more color-coded wire now, yards and yards of it. "Yes, it should be quite obvious this isn't any run-of-the-mill bomb. All this wire, tangled up to confuse him. Circuitry that makes no sense..." He snipped a white wire, then a red one. With his soldering iron, he connected the ends. "And the time ticking away. Minutes, then seconds. Which is the detonator wire? Which wire should he cut? The wrong one, and it all goes up in smoke. The warehouse. You. And him—if he has nerve enough to see it to the end. It's a hopeless dilemma, you see. He stays to disarm it and you could both die. He chickens out and runs, and *you* die, leaving him with guilt he'll never forget. Either way, Sam Navarro suffers. And I win."

"You can't win."

"Spare me the moralistic warnings. I have work to do. And not much time to do it." He strung the wires out to the other dynamite bundles, crisscrossing colors, splicing ends to blasting caps.

Not much time to do it, he had said. How much time was he talking about?

She glanced down at the other items laid out on the floor. A digital timer. A radio transmitter. It was to be a timed device, she realized, the countdown triggered by that transmitter. Spectre would be safely out of the building when he armed the bomb. Out of harm's way when it exploded.

Stay away, Sam, she thought. *Please stay away. And live.*

Spectre rose to his feet and glanced at his watch. "Another hour and I should be ready to make the call." He looked at her and smiled. "Three in the morning, Miss Cormier. That seems as good an hour as any to die, don't you think?"

THE WOMAN WAS NUDE from the waist down, her body crumpled on the wood floor. She had been shot once, in the head.

"The report came in at 10:45," said Yeats from Homicide. "Tenant below us noticed bloodstains seeping across the ceiling and called the landlady. She opened the door, saw the body and called us. We found the victim's ID in her purse. That's why we called you."

"Any witnesses? Anyone see anything, hear anything?" asked Gillis.

"No. He must've used a silencer. Then slipped out without being seen."

Sam gazed around at the sparsely furnished room. The walls were bare, the closets half empty, and there were boxes of clothes on the floor—all signs that Marilyn Dukoff had not yet settled into this apartment.

Yeats confirmed it. "She moved in a day ago, under the name Marilyn Brown. Paid the deposit and first month's rent in cash. That's all the landlady could tell me."

"She have any visitors?" asked Gillis.

"Next-door tenant heard a man's voice in here yesterday. But never saw him."

"Spectre," said Sam. He focused once again on the body. The criminalists were already combing the room, dusting for prints, searching for evidence. They would find none, Sam already knew; Spectre would've seen to it.

There was no point hanging around here; they'd be better off trying to chase sirens. He turned to the door, then paused as he heard one of the detectives say, ''Not much in the purse. Wallet, keys, a few bills—''

''What bills?'' asked Sam.

''Electric, phone. Water. Look like they're to the old apartment. The name Dukoff's on them. Delivered to a PO box.''

''Let me see the phone bill.''

At his first glance at the bill, Sam almost uttered a groan of frustration. It was two sheets long and covered with long distance calls, most of them to Bangor numbers, a few to Massachusetts and Florida. It would take hours to track all those numbers down, and the chances were it would simply lead them to Marilyn Dukoff's bewildered friends or family.

Then he focused on one number, at the bottom of the bill. It was a collect call charge, from a South Portland prefix, dated a week and a half ago at 10:17 p.m. Someone had called collect and Marilyn Dukoff had accepted the charges.

''This could be something,'' Sam noted. ''I need the location of this number.''

''We can call the operator from my car,'' said Gillis. ''but I don't know what it's going to get you.''

''A hunch. That's what I'm going on,'' Sam admitted.

Back in Gillis's car, Sam called the Directory Assistance supervisor.

After checking her computer, she confirmed it was a pay phone. ''It's near the corner of Calderwood and Hardwick, in South Portland.''

''Isn't there a gas station on that corner?'' asked Sam. ''I seem to remember one there.''

''There may be, Detective. I can't tell you for certain.''

Sam hung up and reached for the South Portland map. Under the dome light, he pinpointed the location of the pay phone. ''Here it is,'' he said to Gillis.

''There's just some industrial buildings out there.''

''Yeah, which makes a collect call at 10:17 p.m. all the more interesting.''

''Could've been anyone calling her. Friends, family. For all we know—''

''It was Spectre,'' Sam said. His head jerked up in sudden excitement. ''South Portland. Let's *go.*''

''What?''

Sam thrust the map toward Gillis. ''Here's Bickford Street. A squad car was dispatched there at 12:10. And here's Calderwood and Hardwick. The squad car would've gone right through this area.''

''You think Spectre's holed up around there?''

Sam scrawled a circle on the map, a three-block radius around Calderwood and Hardwick. ''He's here. He's got to be around here.''

Gillis started the car. ''I think our haystack just got a hell of a lot smaller.''

Twenty minutes later, they were at the corner of Hardwick and Calderwood. There was, indeed, a gas station there, but it had been closed down and a For Sale—Commercial Property sign was posted in the scraggly strip of a garden near the road. Sam and Gillis sat in their idling car for a moment, scanning the street. There was no other traffic in sight.

Gillis began to drive up Hardwick. The neighborhood was mostly industrial. Vacant lots, a boating supply outlet. A lumber wholesaler. A furniture maker. Everything was closed for the night, the parking lots empty, the buildings dark. They turned onto Calderwood.

A few hundred yards later, Sam spotted the light. It was faint, no more than a yellowish glow from a small window—the only window in the building. As they pulled closer, Gillis cut his headlights. They stopped half a block away.

''It's the old Stimson warehouse,'' said Sam.

''No cars in the lot,'' Gillis noted. ''But it looks like someone's home.''

''Didn't the Stimson cannery close down last year?''

Sam didn't answer; he was already stepping out of the car.

''Hey!'' whispered Gillis. ''Shouldn't we call for backup?''

''You call. I'm checking it out.''

''Sam!'' Gillis hissed. ''Sam!''

Adrenaline pumping, Sam ignored his partner's warnings and started toward the warehouse. The darkness was in his favor; whoever was inside wouldn't be able to spot his approach. Through the cracks in the truck bay doors, he saw more light, vertical slivers of yellow.

He circled the building, but spotted no ground floor windows, no way to look inside. There was a back door and a front door, but both were locked.

At the front of the building, he met up with Gillis.

"Backup's on the way," Gillis informed him.

"I have to get in there."

"We don't know what we'll find in there—" Gillis suddenly paused and glanced at his car.

The phone was ringing.

Both men scurried back to answer it.

Sam grabbed the receiver. "Navarro here."

"Detective Navarro," said the police operator. "We have an outside phone call for you. The man says it's urgent. I'll put it through."

There was a pause, a few clicks, and then a man's voice said, "I'm so glad to reach you, Detective. This car phone of yours is coming in handy."

"Spectre?"

"I'd like to issue a personal invitation, Detective. To you and you alone. A reunion, with a certain someone who's right here beside me."

"Is she all right?"

"She's perfectly fine." Spectre paused and added with a soft tone of threat. "For the moment."

"What do you want from me?"

"Nothing at all. I'd just like you to come and take Miss Cormier off my hands. She's becoming an inconvenience. And I have other places to go to."

"Where is she?"

"I'll give you a clue. Herring."

"What?"

"Maybe the name *Stimson* rings a bell? You can look up the address. Sorry I won't be here to greet you, but I really *must* be going."

SPECTRE HUNG UP the phone and smiled at Nina. "Time for me to go. Lover boy should be here any minute." He picked up his toolbox and set it in the car, which he'd driven through the loading bay to keep it out of sight.

He's leaving, she thought. *Leaving me as bait for the trap.*

It was cool in the warehouse, but she felt a drop of sweat slide down her temple as she watched Spectre reach down for the radio transmitter. All he had to do was flick one switch on that radio device, and the bomb would be armed, the countdown started.

Ten minutes later, it would explode.

Her heart gave a painful thud as she saw him reach for the radio switch. Then he smiled at her.

"Not yet," he said. "I wouldn't want things to happen prematurely."

Turning, he walked toward the truck bay door. He gave Nina a farewell salute. "Say goodbye to Navarro for me. Tell him I'm so sorry to miss the big kaboom." He unlatched the bay door and gave the handle a yank. It slid up with the sound of grating metal. It was almost open when Spectre suddenly froze.

Right in front of him, a pair of headlights came on.

"Freeze, Spectre!" came a command from somewhere in the darkness. "Hands over your head!"

Sam, thought Nina. *You found me....*

"Hands up!" yelled Sam. "Do it!"

Silhouetted against the headlights, Spectre seemed to hesitate for a few seconds. Then, slowly, he raised his hands over his head.

He was still holding the transmitter.

"Sam!" cried Nina. "There's a bomb! He's got a transmitter!"

"Put it down," Sam ordered. "Put it down or I shoot!"

"Certainly," agreed Spectre. Slowly he dropped to a crouch and lowered the transmitter toward the floor. But as he lay it down, there was a distinct *click* that echoed through the warehouse.

My God, he's armed the bomb, thought Nina.

"Better run," said Spectre. And he dived sideways, toward a stack of crates.

He wasn't fast enough. In the next instant, Sam squeezed off two shots. Both bullets found their target.

Spectre seemed to stumble. He dropped to his knees and began to crawl forward, but his limbs were moving drunkenly, like a swimmer trying to paddle across land. He was making gurgling sounds now, gasping out curses with his last few breaths.

"Dead," wheezed Spectre, and it was almost a laugh. "You're all dead...."

Sam stepped over Spectre's motionless body and started straight toward Nina.

"No!" she cried. "Stay away!"

He stopped dead, staring at her with a look of bewilderment. "What is it?"

"He's wired a bomb to my chair," sobbed Nina. "If you try to cut me loose it'll go off!"

At once Sam's gaze shot to the coils of wire ringing her chair, then followed the trail of wire to the warehouse wall, to the first bundle of dynamite, lying in plain view.

"He has eighteen sticks planted all around the building," she said. "Three are under my chair. It's set to go off in ten minutes. Less, now."

Their gazes met. And in that one glance she saw his look of panic. It was quickly suppressed. He stepped across the wire and crouched by her chair.

"I'm getting you out of here," he vowed.

"There's not enough time!"

"Ten minutes?" He gave a terse laugh. "That's loads of time." He knelt down and peered under the seat. He didn't say a thing, but when he rose again, his expression was grim. He turned and called, "Gillis?"

"Right here," Gillis answered, stepping gingerly over the wires. "I got the toolbox. What do we have?"

"Three sticks under the chair, and a digital timer." Sam gently slid out the timing device, bristling with wires, and set it carefully on the floor. "It looks like a simple series-parallel circuit. I'll need time to analyze it."

"How long do we have?"

"Eight minutes and forty-five seconds and counting."

Gillis cursed. "No time to get the bomb truck."

A wail of a siren suddenly cut through the night. Two police cruisers pulled up outside the bay door.

"Backup's here," Gillis said. He hurried over to the doors, waving at the other cops. "Stay back!" he yelled. "We got a bomb in here! I want a perimeter evac *now!* And get an ambulance here on standby."

I won't need an ambulance, thought Nina. *If this bomb goes off, there'll be nothing left of me to pick up.*

She tried to calm her racing heart, tried to stop her slide toward hysteria, but sheer terror was making it hard for her to breathe. There was nothing she could do to save herself. Her wrists were tightly bound; so were her ankles. If she so much as shifted too far in her chair, the bomb could be triggered.

It was all up to Sam.

Chapter Fourteen

Sam's jaw was taut as he studied the tangle of wires and circuitry. There were so many wires! It would take an hour just to sort them all out. But all they had were minutes. Though he didn't say a word, she could read the urgency in his face, could see the first droplets of sweat forming on his forehead.

Gillis returned to his partner's side. "I checked the perimeter. Spectre's got the building wired with fifteen or more sticks. No other action fuses as far as I can see. The brain to this whole device is right there in your hands."

"It's too easy," muttered Sam, scanning the circuitry. "He *wants* me to cut this wire."

"Could it be a double feint? He knew we'd be suspicious. So he made it simple on purpose—just to throw us?"

Sam swallowed. "This looks like the arming switch right here. But over here, he's got the cover soldered shut. He could have a completely different switch inside. Magnetic reed or a Castle-Robins device. If I pry off that cap, it could fire."

Gillis glanced at the digital timer. "Five minutes left."

"I know, I know." Sam's voice was hoarse with tension, but his hands were absolutely steady as he traced the circuitry. One tug on the wrong wire, and all three of them could be instantly vaporized.

Outside, more sirens whined to a stop. Nina could hear voices, the sounds of confusion.

But inside, there was silence.

Sam took a breath and glanced up at her. "You okay?"

She gave a tense nod. And she saw, in his face, the first glimpse of panic. *He won't figure this out in time, and he knows it.*

This was just what Spectre had planned. The hopeless dilemma. The fatal choice. Which wire to cut? One? None? Does he gamble with his own life? Or does he make the rational choice to abandon the building—and her?

She knew the choice he would make. She could see it in his eyes.

They were both going to die.

"Two and a half minutes," said Gillis.

"Go on, get out of here," Sam ordered.

"You need an extra pair of hands."

"And your kids need a father. Get the hell out."

Gillis didn't budge.

Sam picked up the wire cutters and isolated a white wire.

"You're guessing, Sam. You don't know."

"Instinct, buddy. I've always had good instincts. Better leave. We're down to two minutes. And you're not doing me any good."

Gillis rose to his feet, but lingered there, torn between leaving and staying. "Sam—"

"Move."

Gillis said, softly, "I'll have a bottle of Scotch waiting for you, buddy."

"You do that. Now get out of here."

Without another word, Gillis left the building.

Only Sam and Nina remained. *He doesn't have to stay,* she thought. *He doesn't have to die.*

"Sam," she whispered.

He didn't seem to hear her; he was concentrating too hard on the circuit board, his wire cutters hovering between a life-and-death choice.

"Leave, Sam," she begged.

"This is my job, Nina."

"It's not your job to die!"

"We're not going to die."

"You're right. *We* aren't. *You* aren't. If you leave now—"

"I'm not leaving. You understand? I'm *not.*" His gaze rose to meet hers. And she saw, in those steady eyes, that he had made up his mind. He'd made the choice to live—or die—with her. This was not the cop looking at her, but the man who loved her. The man *she* loved.

She felt tears trickle down her face. Only then did she realize she was crying.

"We're down to a minute. I'm going to make a guess here," he said. "If I'm right, cutting this wire should do the trick. If I'm wrong..." He let out a breath. "We'll know pretty quick one way or the other.'' He slipped the teeth of the cutter around the white wire. ''Okay, I'm going with this one.''

''Wait.''

''What is it?''

''When Spectre was putting it together, he soldered a white wire to a red one, then he covered it all up with green tape. Does that make a difference?''

Sam stared down at the wire he'd been about to cut. ''It does,'' he said softly. ''It makes a hell of a lot of difference.''

''Sam!'' came Gillis's shout through a megaphone. ''You've got ten seconds left!''

Ten seconds to run.

Sam didn't run. He moved the wire cutter to a black wire and positioned the jaws to cut. Then he stopped and looked up at Nina.

They stared at each other one last time.

''I love you,'' he said.

She nodded, the tears streaming down her face. ''I love you too,'' she whispered.

Their gazes remained locked, unwavering, as he slowly closed the cutter over the wire. Even as the jaws came together, even as the teeth bit into the plastic coating, Sam was looking at her, and she at him.

The wire snapped in two.

For a moment neither one of them moved. They were still frozen in place, still paralyzed by the certainty of death.

Then, outside, Gillis yelled, ''Sam? You're past countdown! *Sam!*''

All at once, Sam was cutting the bonds from her hands, her ankles. She was too numb to stand, but she didn't need to. He gathered her up into his arms and carried her out of the warehouse, into the night.

Outside, the street was ablaze with the flashing lights of emergency vehicles: squad cars, ambulances, fire trucks. Sam carried her safely past the yellow police tape and set her down on her feet.

Instantly they were surrounded by a mob of officials, Chief Coopersmith and Liddell among them, all clamoring to know the bomb's status. Sam ignored them all. He just stood there with his arms around Nina, shielding her from the chaos.

''Everyone back!'' shouted Gillis, waving the crowd away.

''Give 'em some breathing space!'' He turned to Sam. ''What about the device?''

''It's disarmed,'' said Sam. ''But be careful. Spectre may have left us one last surprise.''

''I'll take care of it.'' Gillis started toward the warehouse, then turned back. ''Hey, Sam?''

''Yeah?''

''I'd say you just earned your retirement.'' Gillis grinned. And then he walked away.

Nina looked up at Sam. Though the danger was over, she could still feel his heart pounding, could feel her own heart beating just as wildly.

''You didn't leave me,'' she whispered, new tears sliding down her face. ''You could have—''

''No, I couldn't.''

''I told you to go! I *wanted* you to go.''

''And I wanted to stay.'' He took her face in his hands. Firmly, insistently. ''There was no other place I'd be but right there beside you, Nina. There's no other place I ever want to be.''

She knew a dozen pairs of eyes were watching them. Already the news media had arrived with their camera flashbulbs and their shouted questions. The night was alive with voices and multicolored lights. But at that moment, as he held her, as they kissed, there was no one else but Sam.

When dawn broke, he would still be holding her.

Epilogue

The wedding was on. No doubt about it.

Accompanied by a lilting Irish melody played by flute and harp, Nina and her father walked arm in arm into the forest glade. There, beneath the fiery brilliance of autumn foliage, stood Sam. Just as she knew he would be.

He was grinning, as nervous as a rookie cop on his first beat. Beside him stood his best man, Gillis, and Reverend Sullivan, both wearing smiles. A small circle of friends and family stood gathered under the trees: Wendy and her husband. Chief Coopersmith. Nina's colleagues from the hospital. Also among the guests was Lydia, looking quietly resigned to the fact her daughter was marrying a mere cop.

Some things in life, thought Nina, cannot be changed. She had accepted that. Perhaps Lydia, some day, would learn to be as accepting.

The music faded, and the leaves of autumn drifted down in a soft rain of red and orange. Sam reached out to her. His smile told her all she needed to know. This was right; this was meant to be.

She took his hand.

Midnight Rainbow

Linda
HOWARD

Chapter One

He was getting too old for this kind of crap, Grant Sullivan thought irritably. What the hell was he doing crouched here, when he'd promised himself he'd never set foot in a jungle again? He was supposed to rescue a bubble-brained society deb, but from what he'd seen in the two days he'd had this jungle fortress under surveillance, he thought she might not *want* to be rescued. She looked as if she was having the time of her life: laughing, flirting, lying by the pool in the heat of the day. She slept late; she drank champagne on the flagstone patio. Her father was almost out of his mind with worry about her, thinking that she was suffering unspeakable torture at the hands of her captors. Instead, she was lolling around as if she were vacationing on the Riviera. She certainly wasn't being tortured. If anyone was being tortured, Grant thought with growing ire, it was he himself. Mosquitoes were biting him, flies were stinging him, sweat was running off him in rivers, and his legs were aching from sitting still for so long. He'd been eating field rations again, and he'd forgotten how much he hated field rations. The humidity made all of his old wounds ache, and he had plenty of old wounds to ache. No doubt about it: he was definitely too old.

He was thirty-eight, and he'd spent over half his life involved in some war, somewhere. He was tired, tired enough that he'd opted out the year before, wanting nothing more than to wake up in the same bed every morning. He hadn't wanted company or advice or anything, except to be left the hell alone. When he had burned out, he'd burned to the core.

He hadn't quite retreated to the mountains to live in a cave, where he wouldn't have to see or speak to another human being, but he had definitely considered it. Instead, he'd bought a rundown farm in Tennessee, just in the shadow of the mountains, and let the green mists heal him. He'd dropped out, but apparently he hadn't dropped far enough: they had still known how to find him. He supposed wearily that his reputation made it necessary for certain people to know his whereabouts at all times. Whenever a job called for jungle experience and expertise, they called for Grant Sullivan.

A movement on the patio caught his attention, and he cautiously moved a broad leaf a fraction of an inch to clear his line of vision. There she was, dressed to the nines in a frothy sundress and heels, with an enormous pair of sunglasses shading her eyes. She carried a book and a tall glass of something that looked deliciously cool; she arranged herself artfully on one of the poolside deck chairs, and prepared to wile away the muggy afternoon. She waved to the guards who patrolled the plantation grounds and flashed them her dimpled smile.

Damn her pretty, useless little hide! Why couldn't she have stayed under Daddy's wing, instead of sashaying around the world to prove how "independent" she was? All she'd proved was that she had a remarkable talent for landing herself in hot water.

Poor dumb little twit, he thought. She probably didn't even realize that she was one of the central characters in a nasty little espionage caper that had at least three government and several other factions, all hostile, scrambling to find a missing microfilm.The only thing that had saved her life so far was that no one was sure how much she knew, or whether she knew anything at all. Had she been involved in George Persall's espionage activities, he wondered, or had she only been his mistress, his high class "secretary"? Did she know where the microfilm was, or did Luis Marcel, who had disappeared, have it? The only thing anyone knew for certain was that George Persall had had the microfilm in his possession. But he'd died of a heart attack—in *her* bedroom—and the microfilm hadn't been found. Had Persall already passed it to Luis Marcel? Marcel had dropped out of sight two days before Persall died—if he had the microfilm, he certainly wasn't talking about it. The Americans wanted it, the Russians wanted it, the Sandinistas wanted it, and every rebel group in Central and South America wanted it. Hell, Sullivan thought, as far as he knew, even the Eskimos wanted it.

So where was the microfilm? What had George Persall done with it? If he had indeed passed it to Luis Marcel, who was his normal contact, then where was Luis? Had Luis decided to sell the microfilm to the highest bidder? That seemed unlikely. Grant knew Luis personally; they had been in some tight spots together and he trusted Luis at his back, which said a lot.

Government agents had been chasing this particular microfilm for about a month now. A high-level executive of a research firm in California had made a deal to sell the government-classified laser technology his firm had developed, technology that could place laser weaponry in space in the near future. The firm's own security people had become suspicious of the man and alerted the proper government authorities; together they had apprehended the executive in the middle of the sale. But the two buyers had escaped, taking the microfilm with them. Then one of the buyers double-crossed his partner and took himself and the microfilm to South America to strike his own deal. Agents all over Central and South America had been alerted, and an American agent in Costa Rica had made contact with the man, setting up a ''sting'' to buy the microfilm. Things became completely confused at that point. The deal had gone sour, and the agent had been wounded, but he had gotten away with the microfilm. The film should have been destroyed at that point, but it hadn't been. Somehow the agent had gotten it to George Persall, who could come and go freely in Costa Rica because of his business connections. Who would have suspected George Persall of being involved in espionage? He'd always seemed just a tame businessman, albeit with a passion for gorgeous ''secretaries''—a weakness any Latin man would understand. Persall had been known to only a few agents, Luis Marcel among them, and that had made him extraordinarily effective. But in this case, George had been left in the dark; the agent had been feverish from his wound and hadn't told George to destroy the film.

Luis Marcel had been supposed to contact George, but instead Luis had disappeared. Then George, who had always seemed to be disgustingly healthy, had died of a heart attack…and no one knew where the microfilm was. The Americans wanted to be certain that the technology didn't fall into anyone else's hands; the Russians wanted the technology just as badly, and every revolutionary in the hemisphere wanted the microfilm in order to sell it to the highest bidder. An arsenal of weapons could be purchased, revolutions could be staged, with the amount of money that small piece of film would bring on the open market.

Manuel Turego, head of national security in Costa Rica, was a very smart man; he was a bastard, Grant thought, but a smart one. He'd promptly snatched up Ms. Priscilla Jane Hamilton Greer and carried her off to this heavily guarded inland "plantation." He'd probably told her that she was under protective custody, and she was probably stupid enough that she was very grateful to him for "protecting" her. Turego had played it cool; so far he hadn't harmed her. Evidently he knew that her father was a very wealthy, very influential man, and that it wasn't wise to enrage wealthy, influential men unless it was absolutely necessary. Turego was playing a waiting game; he was waiting for Luis Marcel to surface, waiting for the microfilm to surface, as it eventually had to. In the meantime, he had Priscilla; he could afford to wait. Whether she knew anything or not, she was valuable to him as a negotiating tool, if nothing else.

From the moment Priscilla had disappeared, her father had been frantic. He'd been calling in political favors with a heavy hand, but he'd found that none of the favors owed to him could get Priscilla away from Turego. Until Luis was found, the American government wasn't going to lift a hand to free the young woman. The confusion about whether or not she actually knew anything, the tantalizing possibility that she *could* know the location of the microfilm, seemed to have blunted the intensity of the search for Luis. Her captivity could give him the edge he needed by attracting attention away from him.

Finally, desperate with worry and enraged by the lack of response he'd been getting from the government, James Hamilton had decided to take matters into his own hands. He'd spent a small fortune ferreting out his daughter's location, and then had been stymied by the inaccessibility of the well-guarded plantation. If he sent in enough men to take over the plantation, he realized, there was a strong possibility that his daughter would be killed in the fight. Then someone had mentioned Grant Sullivan's name.

A man as wealthy as James Hamilton could find someone who didn't want to be found, even a wary, burnt-out ex-government agent who had buried himself in the Tennessee mountains. Within twenty-four hours, Grant had been sitting across from Hamilton, in the library of a huge estate house that shouted of old money. Hamilton had made an offer that would pay off the mortgage on Grant's farm completely. All the man wanted was to have his daughter back, safe and sound. His face had been lined and taut with worry, and there had been a desperation about him that, even more than the money, made Grant reluctantly accept the job.

The difficulty of rescuing her had seemed enormous, perhaps even insurmountable; if he were able to penetrate the security of the plantation—something he didn't really doubt—getting her out would be something else entirely. Not only that, but Grant had his own personal experiences to remind him that, even if he found her, the odds were greatly against her being alive or recognizably human. He hadn't let himself think about what could have happened to her since the day she'd been kidnapped.

But getting to her had been made ridiculously easy; as soon as he left Hamilton's house, a new wrinkle had developed. Not a mile down the highway from Hamilton's estate, he'd glanced in the rearview mirror and found a plain blue sedan on his tail. He'd lifted one eyebrow sardonically and pulled over to the shoulder of the road.

He lit a cigarette and inhaled leisurely as he waited for the two men to approach his car. "Hiya, Curtis."

Ted Curtis leaned down and peered in the open window, grinning. "Guess who wants to see you?"

"Hell," Grant swore irritably. "All right, lead the way. I don't have to drive all the way to Virginia, do I?"

"Naw, just to the next town. He's waiting in a motel."

The fact that Sabin had felt it necessary to leave headquarters at all told Grant a lot. He knew Kell Sabin from the old days; the man didn't have a nerve in his body, and ice water ran in his veins. He wasn't a comfortable man to be around, but Grant knew that the same had been said about himself. They were both men to whom no rules applied, men who had intimate knowledge of hell, who had lived and hunted in that gray jungle where no laws existed. The difference between them was that Sabin was comfortable in that cold grayness; it was his life—but Grant wanted no more of it. Things had gone too far; he had felt himself becoming less than human. He had begun to lose his sense of who he was and why he was there. Nothing seemed to matter any longer. The only time he'd felt alive was during the chase, when adrenaline pumped through his veins and fired all his senses into acute awareness. The bullet that had almost killed him had instead saved him, because it had stopped him long enough to let him begin thinking again. That was when he'd decided to get out.

Twenty-five minutes later, with his hand curled around a mug of strong, hot coffee, his booted feet propped comfortably on the genuine, wood-grained plastic coffee table that was standard issue for motels, Grant had murmured, "Well, I'm here. Talk."

Kell Sabin was an even six feet tall, an inch shorter than Grant, and the hard musculature of his frame revealed that he made it a point to stay in shape, even though he was no longer in the field. He was dark—black-haired, black-eyed, with an olive complexion—and the cold fire of his energy generated a force field around him. He was impossible to read, and was as canny as a stalking panther, but Grant trusted him. He couldn't say that he liked Sabin; Sabin wasn't a man to be friendly. Yet for twenty years their lives had been intertwined until they were virtually a part of each other. In his mind, Grant saw a red-orange flash of gunfire, and abruptly he felt the thick, moist heat of the jungle, smelled the rotting vegetation, saw the flash of weapons being discharged...and felt, at his back, so close that each had braced his shoulders against the other, the same man who sat across from him now. Things like that stayed in a man's memory.

A dangerous man, Kell Sabin. Hostile governments would gladly have paid a fortune to get to him, but Sabin was nothing more than a shadow slipping away from the sunshine, as he directed his troops from the gray mists.

Without a flicker of expression in his black eyes, Sabin studied the man who sat across from him in a lazy sprawl—a deceptively lazy sprawl, he knew. Grant was, if anything, even leaner and harder than he had been in the field. Hibernating for a year hadn't made him go soft. There was still something wild about Grant Sullivan, something dangerous and untamed. It was in the wary, restless glitter of his amber eyes, eyes that glowed as fierce and golden as an eagle's under the dark, level brows. His dark blond hair was shaggy, curling down over his collar in back, emphasizing that he wasn't quite civilized. He was darkly tanned; the small scar on his chin wasn't very noticeable, but the thin line that slashed across his left cheekbone was silver against his bronzed skin. They weren't disfiguring scars, but reminders of battles.

If Sabin had had to pick anyone to go after Hamilton's daughter, he'd have picked this man. In the jungle Sullivan was as stealthy as a cat; he could become part of the jungle, blending into it, using it. He'd been useful in the concrete jungles, too, but it was in the green hells of the world that no one could equal him.

"Are you going after her?" Sabin finally asked in a quiet tone.

"Yeah."

"Then let me fill you in." Totally disregarding the fact that Grant no longer had security clearance, Sabin told him about the missing microfilm. He told him about George Persall, Luis Marcel, the whole deadly cat-and-mouse game, and dumb little Priscilla sitting in the middle of it. She was being used as a smokescreen for Luis, but Kell was more than a little worried about Luis. It wasn't like the man to disappear, and Costa Rica wasn't the most tranquil place on earth. Anything could have happened to him. Yet, wherever he was, he wasn't in the hands of any government or political faction, because everyone was still searching for him, and everyone except Manuel Turego and the American government was searching for Priscilla. Not even the Costa Rican government knew that Turego had the woman; he was operating on his own.

"Persall was a dark horse," Kell admitted irritably. "He wasn't a professional. I don't even have a file on him."

If Sabin didn't have a file on him, Persall had been more than a dark horse; he'd been totally invisible. "How did this thing blow open?" Grant drawled, closing his eyes until they were little more than slits. He looked as if he were going to fall asleep, but Sabin knew differently.

"Our man was being followed. They were closing in on him. He was out of his mind with fever. He couldn't find Luis, but he remembered how to contact Persall. No one knew Persall's name, until then, or how to find him if they needed him. Our man just barely got the film to Persall before all hell broke loose. Persall got away."

"What about our man?"

"He's alive. We got him out, but not before Turego got his hands on him."

Grant grunted. "So Turego knows our guy didn't tell Persall to destroy the film."

Kell looked completely disgusted. "*Everyone* knows. There's no security down there. Too many people will sell any scrap of information they can find. Turego has a leak in his organization, so by morning it was common knowledge. Also by morning, Persall had died of a heart attack, in Priscilla's room. Before we could move in, Turego took the girl.''

Dark brown lashes veiled the golden glitter of Grant's eyes almost completely. He looked as if he would begin snoring at any minute. ''Well? Does she know anything about the microfilm or not?''

''We don't know. My guess is that she doesn't. Persall had several hours to hide the microfilm before he went to her room.''

''Why the hell couldn't she have stayed with Daddy, where she belongs?'' Grant murmured.

''Hamilton has been raising hell for us to get her out of there, but they aren't really close. She's a party girl. Divorced, more interested in having a good time than in doing anything constructive. In fact, Hamilton cut her out of his will several years ago, and she's been wandering all around the globe since. She'd been with Persall for a couple of years. They weren't shy about their relationship. Persall liked to have a flashy woman on his arm, and he could afford her. He always seemed like an easy-going good time guy, well-suited to her type. I sure as hell never figured him for a courier, especially one sharp enough to fool me.''

''Why don't you go in and get the girl out?'' Grant asked suddenly, and he opened his eyes, staring at Kell, his gaze cold and yellow.

''Two reasons. One, I don't think she knows anything about the film. I have to concentrate on finding the film, and I think that means finding Luis Marcel. Two, you're the best man for the job. I thought so when I...ah...arranged for you to be brought to Hamilton's attention.''

So Kell was working to get the girl out, after all, but going about it in his own circuitous way. Well, staying behind the scenes was the only way he could be effective. ''You won't have any trouble getting into Costa Rica,'' Kell said. ''I've already arranged it. But if you can't get the girl out...''

Grant got to his feet, a tawny, graceful savage, silent and lethal. ''I know,'' he said quietly. Neither of them had to say it, but both knew that a bullet in her head would be a great deal kinder than what would happen to her if Turego decided that she did know the location of the microfilm. She was being held only as a safety measure now, but if that microfilm didn't surface, she would eventually be the only remaining link to it. Then her life wouldn't be worth a plugged nickel.

So now he was in Costa Rica, deep in the rain forest and too damned near the Nicaraguan border for comfort. Roaming bands of rebels, soldiers, revolutionaries and just plain terrorists made life miserable for people who just wanted to live their simple lives in peace, but none of it touched Priscilla. She might have been a tropical princess, sipping daintily at her iced drink, ignoring the jungle that ate continuously at the boundaries of the plantation and had to be cut back regularly.

Well, he'd seen enough. Tonight was the night. He knew her schedule now, knew the routine of the guards, and had already found all the trip lines. He didn't like traveling through the jungle at night, but there wasn't any choice. He had to have several hours to get her away from here before anyone realized she was missing; luckily, she always slept late, until at least ten every morning. No one would really think anything of it if she didn't appear by eleven. By then, they'd be long gone. Pablo would pick them up by helicopter at the designated clearing tomorrow morning, not long after dawn.

Grant backed slowly away from the edge of the jungle, worming himself into the thick greenery until it formed a solid curtain separating him from the house. Only then did he rise to his feet, walking silently and with assurance, because he'd taken care of the trip lines and sensors as he'd found them. He'd been in the jungle for three days, moving cautiously around the perimeter of the plantation, carefully getting the layout of the house. He knew where the girl slept, and he knew how he was going to get in. It couldn't have been better; Turego wasn't in the house. He'd left the day before, and since he wasn't back by now, Grant knew that he wasn't coming. It was already twilight, and it wasn't safe to travel the river in the darkness.

Grant knew exactly how treacherous the river was; that was why he would take the girl through the jungle. Even given its dangers, the river would be the logical route for them to take. If by some chance her departure were discovered before Pablo picked them up, the search would be concentrated along the river, at least for a while. Long enough, he hoped, for them to reach the helicopter.

He'd have to wait several more hours before he could go into the house and get the girl out. That would give everyone time to get tired, bored and sleepy. He made his way to the small clearing where he'd stashed his supplies, and carefully checked it for snakes, especially the velvety brown fer-de-lance, which liked to lie in clearings and wait for its next meal. After satisfying himself that the clearing was safe, he sat down on a fallen tree to smoke a cigarette. He took a drink of water, but he wasn't hungry. He knew that he wouldn't be until sometime tomorrow. Once the action was going down he couldn't eat; he was too keyed up, all his senses enhanced so that even the smallest sound of the jungle crashed against his eardrums like thunder. Adrenaline was already pumping through his veins, making him so high that he could understand why the Vikings had gone berserk during battle. Waiting was almost unbearable, but that was what he had to do. He checked his watch again, the illuminated dial a strange bit of civilization in a jungle that swallowed men alive, and frowned when he saw that only a little over half an hour had passed.

To give himself something to do, to calm his tightly wound nerves, he began packing methodically, arranging everything so he would know exactly where it was. He checked his weapons and his ammunition, hoping he wouldn't have to use them. What he needed more than anything, if he was to get the girl out alive, was a totally silent operation. If he had to use his carbine or the automatic pistol, he'd give away their position. He preferred a knife, which was silent and deadly.

He felt sweat trickle down his spine. God, if only the girl would have sense enough to keep her mouth shut and not start squawking when he hauled her out of there. If he had to, he'd knock her out, but that would make her dead weight to carry through vegetation that reached out to wrap around his legs like living fingers.

He realized that he was fondling his knife, his long, lean fingers sliding over the deadly blade with a lover's touch, and he shoved it into its sheath. Damn her, he thought bitterly. Because of her, he was back in the thick of things, and he could feel it taking hold of him again. The rush of danger was as addictive as any drug, and it was in his veins again, burning him, eating at him like an acid—killing him and intensifying the feeling of life all at once. Damn her, damn her to hell. All this for a spoiled, silly society brat who liked to amuse herself in various beds.

Still, her round heels might have kept her alive, because Turego fancied himself quite a lover.

The night sounds of the jungle began to build around him: the screams of the howler monkeys, the rustles and chirps and coughs of the night denizens as they went about their business. Somewhere down close to the river he heard a jaguar cough, but he never minded the normal jungle sounds. He was at home here. The peculiar combination of his genes and the skills he'd learned as a boy in the swamps of south Georgia made him as much a part of the jungle as the jaguar that prowled the river's edge. Though the thick canopy blocked out all light, he didn't light a lamp or switch on a flashlight; he wanted his eyes to be perfectly adjusted to the dark when he began moving. He relied on his ears and his instincts, knowing that there was no danger close to him. The danger would come from men, not from the shy jungle animals. As long as those reassuring noises surrounded him, he knew that no men were near.

At midnight he rose and began easing along the route he'd marked in his mind, and the animals and insects were so unalarmed by his presence that the din continued without pause. The only caution he felt was that a fer-de-lance or a bushmaster might be hunting along the path he'd chosen, but that was a chance he'd have to take. He carried a long stick that he swept silently across the ground before him. When he reached the edge of the plantation he put the stick aside and crouched down to survey the grounds, making certain everything was as expected, before he moved in.

From where he crouched, he could see that the guards were at their normal posts, probably asleep, except for the one who patrolled the perimeter, and he'd soon settle down for a nap, too. They were sloppy, he thought contemptuously. They obviously didn't expect any visitors in as remote a place as this upriver plantation. During the three days he'd spent observing them, he'd noted that they stood around talking a great deal of the time, smoking cigarettes, not keeping a close watch on anything. But they were still there, and those rifles were loaded with real bullets. One of the reasons Grant had reached the age of thirty-eight was that he had a healthy respect for weapons and what they could do to human flesh. He didn't believe in recklessness, because it cost lives. He waited. At least now he could see, for the night was clear, and the stars hung low and brilliant in the sky. He didn't mind the starlight; there were plenty of shadows that would cover his movements.

The guard at the left corner of the house hadn't moved an inch since Grant had been watching him; he was asleep. The guard walking the grounds had settled down against one of the pillars at the front of the house. The faint red glow near the guard's hand told Grant that he was smoking and if he followed his usual pattern, he'd pull his cap over his eyes after he'd finished the cigarette, and sleep through the night.

As silently as a wraith, Grant left the concealing jungle and moved onto the grounds, slipping from tree to bush, invisible in the black shadows. Soundlessly, he mounted the veranda that ran alongside the house, flattening himself against the wall and checking the scene again. It was silent and peaceful. The guards relied far too heavily on those trip lines, not realizing they could be dismantled.

Priscilla's room was toward the back. It had double sliding glass doors, which might be locked, but that didn't worry him; he had a way with locks. He eased up to the doors, put out his hand and pulled silently. The door moved easily, and his brows rose. Not locked. Thoughtful of her.

Gently, gently, a fraction of an inch at a time, he slid the door open until there was enough room for him to slip through. As soon as he was in the room he paused, waiting for his eyes to adjust again. After the starlight, the room seemed as dark as the jungle. He didn't move a muscle, but waited, poised and listening.

Soon he could see again. The room was big and airy, with cool wooden floors covered with straw mats. The bed was against the wall to his right, ghostly with the folds of mosquito netting draped around it. Through the netting he could see the rumpled covers, the small mound on the far side of the bed. A chair, a small round table and a tall floor lamp were on this side of the bed. The shadows were deeper to his left, but he could see a door that probably opened to the bathroom. An enormous wardrobe stood against the wall. Slowly, as silently as a tiger stalking its prey, he moved around the wall, blending into the darkness near the wardrobe. Now he could see a chair on the far side of the bed, next to where she slept. A long white garment, perhaps her robe or nightgown, lay across the chair. The thought that she might be sleeping naked made his mouth quirk in a sudden grin that held no real amusement. If she did sleep naked, she'd fight like a wildcat when he woke her. Just what he needed. For both their sakes, he hoped she was clothed.

He moved closer to the bed, his eyes on the small figure. She was so still.... The hair prickled on the back of his neck in warning, and without thinking he flung himself to the side, taking the blow on his shoulder instead of his neck. He rolled, and came to his feet expecting to face his assailant, but the room was still and dark again. Nothing moved, not even the woman on the bed. Grant faded back into the shadows, trying to hear the soft whisper of breathing, the rustle of clothing, anything. The silence in the room was deafening. Where was his attacker? Like Grant, he'd moved into the shadows, which were deep enough to shield several men.

Who was his assailant? What was he doing here in the woman's bedroom? Had he been sent to kill her or was he, too, trying to steal her from Turego?

His opponent was probably in the black corner beside the wardrobe. Grant eased the knife out of its sheath, then pushed it in again; his hands would be as silent as the knife.

There...just for a moment, the slightest of movements, but enough to pinpoint the man's position. Grant crouched then moved forward in a blurred rush, catching the man low and flipping him. The stranger rolled as he landed and came to his feet with a lithe twist, a slim dark figure outlined against the white mosquito netting. He kicked out, and Grant dodged the blow, but he felt the breeze of the kick pass his chin. Moving in, he caught the man's arm with a numbing chop. He saw the arm fall uselessly to the man's side. Coldly, without emotion, not even breathing hard, Grant threw the slim figure to the floor and knelt with one knee on the good arm and his other knee pressed to the man's chest. Just as he raised his hand to strike the blow that would end their silent struggle, Grant became aware of something odd, something soft swelling beneath his knee. Then he understood. The too-still form on the bed was so still because it was a mound of covers, not a human being. The girl hadn't been in bed; she'd seen him come through the sliding doors and had hidden herself in the shadows. But why hadn't she screamed? Why had she attacked, knowing that she had no chance of overpowering him? He moved his knee off her breasts and quickly slid his hand to the soft mounds to make certain his weight hadn't cut off her breath. He felt the reassuring rise of her chest, heard the soft, startled gasp as she felt his touch, and he eased a little away from her.

"It's all right," he started to whisper, but she suddenly twisted on the floor, wrenching away from him. Her knee slashed upward; he was unguarded, totally vulnerable, and her knee crashed into his groin with a force that sent agony through his whole body. Red lights danced before his eyes, and he sagged to one side, gagging at the bitter bile that rose in his throat, his hands automatically cupping his agonized flesh as he ground his teeth to contain the groan that fought for release.

She scrambled away from him, and he heard a low sob, perhaps of terror. Through pain-blurred eyes he saw her pick up something dark and bulky; then she slipped through the open glass door and was gone.

Pure fury propelled him to his feet. Damn it, she was escaping on her own. She was going to ruin the whole setup! Ignoring the pain in his loins, he started after her. He had a score to settle.

Chapter Two

Jane had just reached for her bundle of supplies when some instinct left over from her cave-dwelling ancestors told her that someone was near. There hadn't been any sound to alert her, but suddenly she was aware of another presence. The fine hairs on the back of her neck and her forearms stood up, and she had frozen, turning terrified eyes toward the double glass doors. The doors had slid open noiselessly, and she had seen the darker shadow of a man briefly outlined against the night. He was a big man, but one who moved with total silence. It was the eerie soundlessness of his movements that had frightened her more than anything, sending chills of pure terror chasing over her skin. For days now she had lived by her nerves, holding the terror at bay while she walked a tightrope, trying to lull Turego's suspicions, yet always poised for an escape attempt. But nothing had frightened her as much as that dark shadow slipping into her room.

Any faint hope that she would be rescued had died when Turego had installed her here. She had assessed the situation realistically. The only person who would try to get her out would be her father, but it would be beyond his power. She could depend on only herself and her wits. To that end, she had flirted and flattered and downright lied, doing everything she could to convince Turego that she was both brainless and harmless. In that, she thought, she'd succeeded, but time was fast running out. When an aide had brought an urgent message to Turego the day before, Jane had eavesdropped; Luis Marcel's location had been discovered, and Turego wanted Luis, badly.

But by now Turego surely would have discovered that Luis had no knowledge of the missing microfilm, and that would leave her as the sole suspect. She had to escape, tonight, before Turego returned.

She hadn't been idle since she'd been here; she'd carefully memorized the routine of the guards, especially at night, when the terror brought on by the darkness made it impossible for her to sleep. She'd spent the nights standing at the double doors, watching the guards, clocking them, studying their habits. By keeping her mind busy, she'd been able to control the fear. When dawn would begin to lighten the sky, she had slept. She had been preparing since the first day she'd been here for the possibility that she might have to bolt into the jungle. She'd been sneaking food and supplies, hoarding them, and steeling herself for what lay ahead. Even now, only the raw fear of what awaited her at Turego's hands gave her the courage to brave the black jungle, where the night demons were waiting for her.

But none of that had been as sinister, as lethal, as the dark shape moving through her bedroom. She shrank back into the thick shadows, not even breathing in her acute terror. Oh, God, she prayed, what do I do now? Why was he there? To murder her in her bed? Was it one of the guards, tonight of all nights, come to rape her?

As he passed in front of her, moving in a slight crouch toward her bed, an odd rage suddenly filled Jane. After all she had endured, she was damned if she'd allow him to spoil her escape attempt! She'd talked herself into it, despite her horrible fear of the dark, and now he was ruining it!

Her jaw set, she clenched her fists as she'd been taught to do in her self-defense classes. She struck at the back of his neck, but suddenly he was gone, a shadow twisting away from the blow, and her fist struck his shoulder instead. Instantly terrified again, she shrank back into the shelter of the wardrobe, straining her eyes to see him, but he'd disappeared. Had he been a wraith, a figment of her imagination? No, her fist had struck a very solid shoulder, and the faint rippling of the white curtains over the glass doors testified that the doors were indeed open. He was in the room, somewhere, but *where*? How could a man that big disappear so completely?

Then, abruptly, his weight struck her in the side, bowling her over, and she barely bit off the instinctive scream that surged up from her throat. She didn't have a chance. She tried automatically to kick him in the throat, but he moved like lightning, blocking her attack. Then a hard blow to her arm numbed it all the way to her elbow, and a split second later she was thrown to the floor, a knee pressing into her chest and making it impossible to breathe.

The man raised his arm and Jane tensed, willing now to scream, but unable to make a sound. Then, suddenly, the man paused, and for some reason lifted his weight from her chest. Air rushed into her lungs, along with a dizzying sense of relief, then she felt his hand moving boldly over her breasts and realized why he'd shifted position. Both terrified and angry that this should be happening to her, she moved instinctively the split second she realized his vulnerability, and slashed upward with her knee. He sagged to the side, holding himself, and she felt an absurd sense of pity. Then she realized that he hadn't even groaned aloud. The man wasn't human! Choking back a sob of terror, she struggled to her feet and grabbed her supplies, then darted through the open door. At that point she wasn't escaping from Turego so much as from that dark, silent demon in her room.

Heedlessly, she flung herself across the plantation grounds; her heart was pounding so violently that the sound of her blood pumping through her veins made a roar in her ears. Her lungs hurt, and she realized that she was holding her breath. She tried to remind herself to be quiet, but the urge to flee was too strong for caution; she stumbled over a rough section of ground and sprawled on her hands and knees. As she began scrambling to her feet, she was suddenly overwhelmed by something big and warm, smashing her back to the ground. Cold, pure terror froze her blood in her veins, but before even an instinctive scream could find voice, his hand was on the back of her neck and everything went black.

Jane regained consciousness by degrees, confused by her upside down position, the jouncing she was suffering, the discomfort of her arms. Strange noises assailed her ears, noises that she tried and failed to identify. Even when she opened her eyes she saw only blackness. It was one of the worst nightmares she'd ever had. She began kicking and struggling to wake up, to end the dream, and abruptly a sharp slap stung her bottom. ''Settle down,'' an ill-tempered voice said from somewhere above and behind her. The voice was that of a stranger, but there was something in that laconic drawl that made her obey instantly.

Slowly things began to shift into a recognizable pattern, and her senses righted themselves. She was being carried over a man's shoulder through the jungle. Her wrists had been taped behind her, and her ankles were also secured. Another wide band of tape covered her mouth, preventing her from doing anything more than grunting or humming. She didn't feel like humming, so she used her limited voice to grunt out exactly what she thought of him, in language that would have left her elegant mother white with shock. A hard hand again made contact with the seat of her pants. "Would you shut the hell up?" he growled. "You sound like a pig grunting at the trough."

American! she thought, stunned. He was an American! He'd come to rescue her, even though he was being unnecessarily rough about it...or was he a rescuer? Chilled, she thought of all the different factions who would like to get their hands on her. Some of those factions were fully capable of hiring an American mercenary to get her, or of training one of their own to imitate an American accent and win her trust.

She didn't dare trust anyone, she realized. Not anyone. She was alone in this.

The man stopped and lifted her from his shoulder, standing her on her feet. Jane blinked her eyes, then widened them in an effort to see, but the darkness under the thick canopy was total, she couldn't see anything. The night pressed in on her, suffocating her with its thick darkness. Where was he? Had he simply dropped her here in the jungle and left her to be breakfast for a jaguar? She could sense movement around her, but no sounds that she could identify as him; the howls and chittering and squawks and rustles of the jungle filled her ears. A whimper rose in her throat, and she tried to move, to seek a tree or something to protect her back, but she'd forgotten her bound feet and she stumbled to the ground, scratching her face on a bush.

A low obscenity came to her ears, then she was roughly grasped and hauled to her feet. "Damn it, stay put!"

So he was still there. How could he see? What was he doing? No matter who he was or what he was doing, at that moment Jane was grateful for his presence. She could not conquer her fear of darkness but the fact that she wasn't alone held the terror at bay. She gasped as he abruptly lifted her and tossed her over his shoulder again, as effortlessly as if she were a rag doll. She felt the bulk of a backpack, which hadn't been there before, but he showed no sign of strain. He moved through the stygian darkness with a peculiar sure-footedness, a lithe, powerful grace that never faltered.

Her own pack of pilfered supplies was still slung around her shoulders, the straps holding it even though it had slid down and was bumping against the back of her head. A can of something was banging against her skull; she'd probably have concussion if this macho fool didn't ease up. What did he think this was, some sort of jungle marathon? Her ribs were being bruised against his hard shoulder, and she felt various aches all over her body, probably as a result of his roughness in throwing her to the floor. Her arm ached to the bone from his blow. Even if this was a real rescue, she thought, she'd be lucky if she lived through it.

She bounced on his shoulder for what seemed like days, the pain in her cramped limbs increasing with every step he took. Nausea began to rise in her, and she took deep breaths in an effort to stave off throwing up. If she began to vomit, with her mouth taped the way it was, she could suffocate. Desperately she began to struggle, knowing only that she needed to get into an upright position.

"Easy there, Pris." Somehow he seemed to know how she was feeling. He stopped and lifted her off his shoulder, easing her onto her back on the ground. When her weight came down on her bound arms she couldn't suppress a whimper of pain. "All right," the man said. "I'm going to cut you loose now, but if you start acting up, I'll truss you up like a Christmas turkey again and leave you that way. Understand?"

She nodded wildly, wondering if he could see her in the dark. Evidently he could, because he turned her on her side and she felt a knife slicing through the tape that bound her wrists. Tears stung her eyes from the pain as he pulled her arms around and began massaging them roughly to ease her cramped muscles.

"Your daddy sent me to get you out of here," the man drawled calmly as he began easing the tape off of her mouth. Instead of ripping the adhesive away and taking skin with it, he was careful, and Jane was torn between gratitude and indignation, since he'd taped her mouth in the first place.

Jane moved her mouth back and forth, restoring it to working condition. "My daddy?" she asked hoarsely.

"Yeah. Okay, now, Pris, I'm going to free your legs, but if you look like you're even thinking about kicking me again, I won't be as easy with you as I was the last time." Despite his drawl, there was something menacing in his tone, and Jane didn't doubt his word.

"I wouldn't have kicked you the first time if you hadn't started pawing at me like a high school sophomore!" she hissed.

"I was checking to see if you were breathing."

"Sure you were, and taking your time about it, too."

"Gagging you was a damned good idea," he said reflectively, and Jane shut up. She had yet to see him as anything more than a shadow. She couldn't even put a name to him, but she knew enough about him to know that he would bind and gag her again without a moment's compunction.

He cut the tape from around her ankles, and again she was subjected to his rough but effective massage. In only a moment she was being pulled to her feet; she staggered momentarily before regaining her sense of balance.

"We don't have much farther to go; stay right behind me, and don't say a word."

"Wait!" Jane whispered frantically. "How can I follow you when I can't see you?"

He took her hand and carried it to his waist. "Hang on to my belt."

She did better than that. Acutely aware of the vast jungle around her, and with only his presence shielding her from the night terrors, she hooked her fingers inside the waistband of his pants in a death grip. She knotted the material so tightly that he muttered a protest, but she wasn't about to let go of him.

Maybe it didn't seem very far to him, but to Jane, being towed in his wake, stumbling over roots and vines that she couldn't see, it seemed like miles before he halted. "We'll wait here," he whispered. "I don't want to go any closer until I hear the helicopter come in."

"When will that be?" Jane whispered back, figuring that if he could talk, so could she.

"A little after dawn."

"When is dawn?"

"Half an hour."

Still clutching the waistband of his pants, she stood behind him and waited for dawn. The seconds and minutes crawled by, but they gave her the chance to realize for the first time that she'd truly escaped from Turego. She was safe and free...well almost. She was out of his clutches, she was the only one who knew what a close call she'd had. Turego would almost certainly return to the plantation this morning to find that his prisoner had escaped. For a moment she was surprised at her own lack of elation, then she realized that she wasn't out of danger yet. This man said that her father had sent him, but he hadn't given her a name or any proof. All she had was his word, and Jane was more than a little wary. Until she was actually on American soil, until she knew beyond any doubt that she was safe, she was going to follow poor George Persall's ironclad rule: when in doubt, lie.

The man shifted uncomfortably, drawing her attention. "Look, honey, do you think you could loosen up on my pants? Or are you trying to finish the job you started on me with your knee?"

Jane felt the blood rush to her cheeks, and she hastily released her hold. "I'm sorry, I didn't realize," she whispered. She stood stiffly for a moment, her arms at her sides; then panic began to rise in her. She couldn't see him in the darkness, she couldn't hear him breathing, and now that she was no longer touching him, she couldn't be certain that he hadn't left her. Was he still there? What if she was alone? The air became thick and oppressive, and she struggled to breathe, to fight down the fear that she knew was unreasonable but that no amount of reason could conquer. Even knowing its source didn't help. She simply couldn't stand the darkness. She couldn't sleep without a light; she never went into a room without first reaching in and turning on the light switch, and she always left her lights on if she knew she would be late returning home. She, who always took extraordinary precautions against being left in the dark, was standing in the middle of a jungle in darkness so complete that it was like being blind.

Her fragile control broke and she reached out wildly, clawing for him, for reassurance that he was still there. Her outstretched fingers touched fabric, and she threw herself against him, gasping in mingled panic and relief. The next second steely fingers grasped her shirt and she was hurled through the air to land flat on her back in the smelly, rotting vegetation. Before she could move, before she could suck air back into her lungs, her hair was pulled back and she felt the suffocating pressure of his knee on her chest again. His breath was a low rasp above her, his voice little more than a snarl "Don't ever—*ever*—come at me from behind again."

Jane writhed, pushing at his knee. After a moment he lifted

it, and eased the grip on her hair. Even being thrown over his shoulder had been better than being left alone in the darkness, and she grabbed for him again, catching him around the knees. Automatically he tried to step away from her entangling arms but she lunged for him. He uttered a startled curse, tried to regain his balance, then crashed to the ground.

He lay so still that Jane's heart plummeted. What would she do if he were hurt? She couldn't possibly carry him, but neither could she leave him lying there, injured and unable to protect himself. Feeling her way up his body, she scrambled to crouch by his shoulders. "Mister, are you all right?" she whispered, running her hands up his shoulders to his face, then searching his head for any cuts or lumps. There was an elasticized band around his head, and she followed it, her nervous fingers finding an odd type of glasses over his eyes. "Are you hurt?" she demanded again, her voice tight with fear. "Damn it, answer me!"

"Lady," the man said in a low, furious voice, "you're crazier than hell. If I was your daddy, I'd *pay* Turego to keep you!"

She didn't know him, but his words caused an odd little pain in her chest. She sat silently, shocked that he could hurt her feelings. She didn't know him, and he didn't know her—how could his opinion matter? But it did, somehow, and she felt strangely vulnerable.

He eased himself to a sitting position, and when she didn't say anything, he sighed. "Why did you jump me like that?" he asked in resignation.

"I'm afraid of the dark," she said with quiet dignity. "I couldn't hear you breathing, and I can't see a thing. I panicked. I'm sorry."

After a moment he said, "All right," and got to his feet. Bending down, he grasped her wrists and pulled her up to stand beside him. Jane inched a little closer to him.

"You can see because of those glasses you're wearing, can't you?" she asked.

"Yeah. There's not a lot of light, but enough that I can make out where I'm going. Infrared lenses."

A howler monkey suddenly screamed somewhere above their heads, and Jane jumped, bumping into him. "Got another pair?" she asked shakily.

She could feel him hesitate, then his arm went around her shoulders. "Nope, just these. Don't worry, Pris, I'm not going to lose you. In another five minutes or so, it'll start getting light."

"I'm all right now," she said, and she was, as long as she could touch him and know that she wasn't alone. That was the real terror: being alone in the darkness. For years she had fought a battle against the nightmare that had begun when she was nine years old, but at last she had come to accept it, and in the acceptance she'd won peace. She knew it was there, knew when to expect it and what to do to ward it off, and that knowledge gave her the ability to enjoy life again. She hadn't let the nightmare cripple her. Maybe her methods of combating it were a little unorthodox, but she had found the balance within herself and she was happy with it.

Feeling remarkably safe with that steely arm looped over her shoulders, Jane waited beside him, and in a very short time she found that she could indeed see a little better. Deep in the rain forest there was no brilliant sunrise to announce the day—the sunrise could not be seen from beneath the canopy of vegetation. Even during the hottest noon, the light that reached the jungle floor was dim, filtered through layers of greenery. She waited as the faint gray light slowly became stronger, until she could pick out more of the details of the lush foliage that surrounded her. She felt almost swamped by the plant life. She'd never been in the jungle before; her only knowledge of it came from movies and what little she'd been able to see during the trip upriver to the plantation. During her days at the plantation she'd begun to think of the jungle as a living entity, huge and green, surrounding her, waiting. She had known from the first that to escape she would have to plunge into that seemingly impenetrable green barrier, and she had spent hours staring at it.

Now she was deep within it, and it wasn't quite what she'd expected. It wasn't a thick tangle, where paths had to be cut with a machete. The jungle floor was littered with rotting vegetation, and laced with networks of vines and roots, but for all that it was surprisingly clear. Plant life that lingered near the jungle floor was doomed. To compete for the precious light it had to rise and spread out its broad leaves, to gather as much light as it could. She stared at a fern that wasn't quite a fern; it was a tree with a buttressed root system, rising to a height of at least eight feet, only at the top it feathered into a fern.

"You can see now," he muttered suddenly, lifting his arm

from her shoulders and stripping off the night vision goggles. He placed them carefully in a zippered section of his field pack.

Jane stared at him in open curiosity, wishing that the light were better so she could really see him. What she *could* see gave wing to hundreds of tiny butterflies in her stomach. It would take one brave *hombre* to meet this man in a dark alley, she thought with a frightened shiver. She couldn't tell the color of his eyes, but they glittered at her from beneath fierce, level dark brows. His face was blackened, which made those eyes all the brighter. His light colored hair was far too long, and he'd tied a strip of cloth around his head to keep the hair out of his eyes. He was clad in tiger-striped camouflage fatigues, and he wore the trappings of war. A wicked knife was stuck casually in his belt, and a pistol rode his left hip while he carried a carbine slung over his right shoulder. Her startled eyes darted back up to his face, a strong-boned face that revealed no emotion, though he had been aware of her survey.

"Loaded for bear, aren't you?" she quipped, eyeing the knife again. For some reason it looked more deadly than either of the guns.

"I don't walk into anything unprepared," he said flatly.

Well, he certainly looked prepared for anything. She eyed him again, more warily this time; he was about six feet tall, and looked like…looked like… Her mind groped for and found the phrase. It had been bandied about and almost turned into a joke, but with this man, it was deadly serious. He looked like a lean, mean, fighting machine, every hard, muscled inch of him. His shoulders looked to be a yard wide, and he'd carried her dead weight through the jungle without even a hint of strain. He'd knocked her down twice, and she realized the only reason she wasn't badly hurt was that, both times, he'd tempered his strength.

Abruptly his attention left her, and his head lifted with a quick, alert motion, like that of an eagle. His eyes narrowed as he listened. "The helicopter is coming," he told her. "Let's go."

Jane listened, but she couldn't hear anything. "Are you sure?" she asked doubtfully.

"I said let's go," he repeated impatiently, and walked away from her. It took Jane only a few seconds to realize that he was heading out, and in the jungle he would be completely hidden from view before he'd gone ten yards. She hurried to catch up to him.

"Hey, slow down!" she whispered frantically, catching at his belt.

"Move it," he said with a total lack of sympathy. "The helicopter won't wait forever; Pablo's on the quick side anyway."

"Who's Pablo?"

"The pilot."

Just then a faint vibration reached her ears. In only a moment it had intensified to the recognizable beat of a helicopter. How could he have heard it before? She knew that she had good hearing, but his senses must be almost painfully acute.

He moved swiftly, surely, as if he knew exactly where he was going. Jane concentrated on keeping up with him and avoiding the roots that tried to catch her toes, she paid little attention to their surroundings. When he climbed, she climbed; it was simple. She was mildly surprised when he stopped abruptly and she lifted her head to look around. The jungle of Costa Rica was mountainous, and they had climbed to the edge of a small cliff, looking down on a narrow, hidden valley with a natural clearing. The helicopter sat in that clearing, the blades lazily whirling.

"Better than a taxicab," Jane murmured in relief, and started past him.

His hand closed over her shoulder and jerked her back. "Be quiet," he ordered, his narrowed gaze moving restlessly, surveying the area.

"Is something wrong?"

"Shut up!"

Jane glared at him, incensed by his unnecessary rudeness, but his hand was still clamped on her shoulder in a grip that bordered on being painful. It was a warning that if she tried to leave the protective cover of the jungle before he was satisfied that everything was safe, he would stop her with real pain. She stood quietly, staring at the clearing herself, but she couldn't see anything wrong. Everything was quiet. The pilot was leaning against the outside of the helicopter, occupied with cleaning his nails; he certainly wasn't concerned with anything.

Long minutes dragged past. The pilot began to fidget, craning his neck and staring into the jungle, though anyone standing just a few feet behind the trees would be completely hidden from view. He looked at his watch, then scanned the jungle again, his gaze moving nervously from left to right.

Jane felt the tension in the man standing beside her, tension that was echoed in the hand that held her shoulder. What was wrong? What was he looking for, and why was he waiting? He was as motionless as a jaguar lying in wait for its prey to pass beneath its tree limb.

"This sucks," he muttered abruptly, easing deeper into the jungle and dragging her with him.

Jane sputtered at the inelegant expression. "It does? Why? What's wrong?"

"Stay here." He pushed her to the ground, deep in the green-black shadow of the buttressed roots of an enormous tree.

Startled, she took a moment to realize that she'd been abandoned. He had simply melted into the jungle, so silently and swiftly that she wasn't certain which way he'd gone. She twisted around but could see nothing that indicated his direction; no swaying vines or limbs.

She wrapped her arms around her drawn-up legs and propped her chin on her knees, staring thoughtfully at the ground. A green stick with legs was dragging a large spider off to be devoured. What if he didn't come back...whoever he was. Why hadn't she asked him his name? If something happened to him, she'd like to know his name, so she could tell someone—assuming that she could manage to get out of the jungle herself. Well, she wasn't any worse off now than she had been before. She was away from Turego, and that was what counted.

Wait here, he'd said. For how long? Until lunch? Sundown? Her next birthday? Men gave such inexact instructions! Of course, this particular man seemed a little limited in the conversation department. Shut up, Stay here and Stay put seemed to be the highlights of his repertoire.

This was quite a tree he'd parked her by. The bottom of the trunk flared into buttressed roots, forming enormous wings that wrapped around her almost like arms. If she sat back against the tree, the wings would shield her completely from the view of someone approaching at any angle except head on.

The straps of her backpack were irritating her shoulders, so she slid it off and stretched, feeling remarkably lighter. She hauled the pack around and opened it, then began digging for her hairbrush. Finding this backpack had been a stroke of luck, she thought, though Turego's soldiers really should be a little more careful with their belongings. Without it, she'd have had to wrap things up in a blanket, which would have been awkward.

Finally locating the hairbrush, she diligently worked through the mass of tangles that had accumulated in her long hair during the night. A small monkey with an indignant expression hung from a branch overhead. It scolded her throughout the operation, evidently angry that she had intruded on its territory. She waved at it.

Congratulating herself for her foresight, she pinned her hair up and pulled a black baseball cap out of the pack. She jammed the cap on and tugged the bill down low over her eyes, then shoved it back up. There wasn't any sun down here. Staring upward, she could see bright pinpoints of sun high in the trees, but only a muted green light filtered down to the floor. She'd have been better off with some of those fancy goggles that What's-his-name had.

How long had she been sitting there? Was he in trouble?

Her legs were going to sleep, so she stood and stomped around to get her blood flowing again. The longer she waited, the more uneasy she became, and she had the feeling that a time would come when she'd better be able to move fast. Jane was an instinctive creature, as sensitive to atmosphere as any finely tuned barometer. That trait had enabled her to hold Turego at bay for what seemed like an endless succession of days and nights, reading him, sidestepping him, keeping him constantly disarmed, and even charmed. Now the same instinct warned her of danger. There was some slight change in the very air that stroked her bare arms. Warily, she leaned down to pick up her backpack, slipping her arms through the straps and anchoring it this time by fastening the third strap around her middle.

The sudden thunderous burst of automatic weapon fire made her whirl, her heart jumping into her throat. Listening to the staccato blasts, she knew that several weapons were being fired, but at whom? Had her friend been detected or was this something else entirely? Was this the trouble he'd sensed that had made him shy away from the clearing? She wanted to think that he was safe, observing everything from an invisible vantage point in the jungle, but with a chill she realized that she couldn't take that for granted.

Her hands felt cold, and with a distant surprise she realized that she was trembling. What should she do? Wait, or run? What if he needed help? She realized that there was very little she could do, since she was unarmed, but she couldn't just run away if he needed help. He wasn't the most amiable man she'd ever met, and she still didn't exactly trust him, but he was the closest thing to a friend she had here.

Ignoring the unwillingness of her feet and the icy lump of fear in her stomach, Jane left the shelter of the giant tree and began cautiously inching through the forest, back toward the clearing. There were only sporadic bursts of gunfire now, still coming from the same general direction.

Suddenly she froze as the faint sound of voices filtered through the forest. In a cold panic she dove for the shelter of another large tree. What would she do if they were coming in this direction? The rough bark scratched her hands as she cautiously moved her head just enough to peer around the trunk.

A steely hand clamped over her mouth. As a scream rose in her throat, a deep, furious voice growled in her ear, "Damn it, I told you to stay put!"

Chapter Three

Jane glared at him over the hand that still covered her mouth, her fright turning into relieved anger. She didn't like this man. She didn't like him at all, and as soon as they were out of this mess, she was going to tell him about it!

He removed his hand and shoved her to the ground on her hands and knees. "Crawl!" he ordered in a harsh whisper, and pointed to their left.

Jane crawled, ignoring the scratches she incurred as she squirmed through the undergrowth, ignoring even the disgusting squishiness when she accidentally smashed something with her hand. Odd, but now that he was with her again, her panic had faded; it hadn't gone completely, but it wasn't the heart-pounding, nauseating variety, either. Whatever his faults, he knew his way around.

He was on her tail, literally, his hard shoulder against the back of her thighs, pushing her onward whenever he thought she wasn't moving fast enough. Once he halted her by the simple method of grabbing her ankle and jerking her flat, his urgent grip warning her to be quiet. She held her breath, listening to the faint rustle that betrayed the presence of someone, or something, nearby. She didn't dare turn her head, but she could detect movement with her peripheral vision. In a moment the man was close enough that she could see him plainly. He was obviously of Latin ancestry, and he was dressed in camouflage fatigues with a cap covering his head. He held an automatic rifle at the ready before him.

In only a moment she could no longer see or hear him, but they stayed motionless in the thick tangle of ferns for long, agonizing minutes. Then her ankle was released and a hand on her hip urged her forward.

They were moving away from the soldier at a right angle. Perhaps they were going to try to get behind their pursuers, then take off in the helicopter while the soldiers were still deep in the jungle. She wanted to know where they were going, what they would do, who the soldiers were and what they wanted—but the questions had to remain bottled up inside her. Now was definitely not the time for talking, not with this man—what *was* his name?—practically shoving her through the undergrowth.

Abruptly the forest cleared somewhat, allowing small patches of sunlight to filter through. Grasping her arm, he hauled her to her feet. "Run, but be as quiet as you can," he hissed in her ear.

Great. Run, but do it quietly. She threw him a dirty look, then ran, taking off like a startled deer. The most disgusting thing was that he was right behind her, and she couldn't hear him making a sound, while her own feet seemed to pound the earth like a drum. But her body seemed cheered by the small amount of sunlight, because she felt her energy level surge despite her sleepless night. The pack on her shoulders seemed lighter, and her steps became quick and effortless as adrenaline began pumping through her veins.

The brush became thicker, and they had to slow their pace. After about fifteen minutes he stopped her with a hand on her shoulder and pulled her behind the trunk of a tree. "Rest a minute," he whispered. "The humidity will wipe you out if you aren't used to it."

Until that moment Jane hadn't noticed that she was wringing wet with sweat. She'd been too intent on saving her skin to worry about its dampness. Now, she became aware of the intense humidity of the rain forest pressing down on her, making every breath she drew lie heavily in her lungs. She wiped the moisture from her face, the salt of her perspiration stinging the small scratches on her cheeks.

He took a canteen from his pack. "Take a drink; you look like you need it."

She had a very good idea what she looked like, and she smiled wryly. She accepted the canteen and drank a little of the water, then capped it and returned it to him. "Thanks."

He looked at her quizzically. "You can have more if you want."

"I'm okay." She looked at him, seeing now that his eyes were a peculiar golden brown color, like amber. His pupils seemed piercingly black against that tawny background. He was streaked with sweat, too, but he wasn't even breathing hard. Whoever he was, whatever he was, he was damned good at this. ''What's your name?'' she asked him, desperately needing to call him something, as if that would give him more substance, make him more familiar.

He looked a little wary, and she sensed that he disliked giving even that much of himself away. A name was only a small thing, but it was a chink in his armor, a link to another person that he didn't want. ''Sullivan,'' he finally said reluctantly.

''First or last?''

''Last.''

''What's your first name?''

''Grant.''

Grant Sullivan. She liked the name. It wasn't fancy; he wasn't fancy. He was a far cry from the sleekly sophisticated men she usually met, but the difference was exciting. He was hard and dangerous, mean when he had to be, but he wasn't vicious. The contrast between him and Turego, who was a truly vicious man, couldn't have been more clear-cut.

''Let's go,'' he said. ''We need to put a lot more space between the hounds and the foxes.''

Obediently she followed his direction, but found that her burst of adrenaline was already dissipating. She felt more exhausted now than she had before the short rest. She stumbled once, catching her booted foot in a liana vine, but he rescued her with a quick grab. She gave him a tired smile of thanks, but when she tried to step away from him he held her. He stood rigid and it frightened her. She jerked around to look at him, but his face was a cold, blank mask, and he was staring behind her. She whirled again, and looked down the barrel of a rifle.

The sweat congealed on her body. For one moment of frozen terror she expected to be shot; then the moment passed and she was still alive. She was able then to look past the barrel to the hard, dark face of the soldier who held the rifle. His black eyes were narrowed, fastened on Sullivan. He said something, but Jane was too upset to translate the Spanish.

Slowly, deliberately, Sullivan released Jane and raised his arms, clasping his hands on top of his head. ''Step away from me,'' he said quietly.

The soldier barked an order at him. Jane's eyes widened. If she moved an inch this maniac would probably shoot her down. But Sullivan had told her to move, so she moved, her face so white that the small freckles across her nose stood out as bright dots of color. The rifle barrel jerked in her direction, and the soldier said something else. He was nervous, Jane suddenly realized. The tension was obvious in his voice, in his jerky movements. God, if his finger twitched on the trigger...! Then, just as abruptly, he aimed the rifle at Sullivan again.

Sullivan was going to do something. She could sense it. The fool! He'd get himself killed if he tried to jump this guy! She stared at the soldier's shaking hands on the rifle, and suddenly something jumped into her consciousness. He didn't have the rifle on automatic. It took her another moment to realize the implications; then she reacted without thought. Her body, trained to dance, trained in the graceful moves of self-defense, went into fluid motion. He began moving a split second later, swinging the weapon around, but by then she was close enough that her left foot sliced upward under the barrel of the gun, and the shot that he fired went into the canopy over their heads. He never got a chance at another shot.

Grant was on him then, grabbing the gun with one hand and slashing at the man's unprotected neck with the side of the other. The soldier's eyes glazed over, and he sank limply to the ground, his breathing raspy but steady.

Grant grabbed Jane's arm. ''Run! That shot will bring every one of them swarming down on us!''

The urgency of his tone made it possible for her to obey, though she was rapidly depleting her reserves of energy. Her legs were leaden, and her boots weighed fifty pounds each. Burning agony slashed her thighs, but she forced herself to ignore it; sore muscles weren't nearly as permanent as being dead. Urged on by his hand at her back, she stumbled over roots and through bushes, adding to her collection of scratches. It was purely a natural defense mechanism, but her mind shut down and her body operated automatically, her feet moving, her lungs sucking desperately at the heavy, moist air. She was so tired now that she no longer felt the pain in her body.

The ground abruptly sloped out from under her feet. Her senses dulled by both terror and fatigue, she was unable to regain her balance. Grant grabbed for her, but the momentum of her body carried them both over the edge of the hill. His arms wrapped around her, and they rolled down the steep slope. The earth and trees spun crazily, but she saw a rocky, shallow stream at the bottom of the slope and a small, hoarse cry tore from her throat. Some of those rocks were big enough to kill them and the smaller ones could cut them to pieces.

Grant swore, and tightened his grip on her until she thought her ribs would splinter under the pressure. She felt his muscles tighten, felt the desperate twist he made, and somehow he managed to get his feet and legs in front of him. Then they were sliding down in a fairly upright position, rather than rolling. He dug his heels in and their descent slowed, then stopped. ''Pris?'' he asked roughly, cupping her chin in his hand and turning her face so he could see it. ''Are you hurt?''

''No, no,'' she quickly assured him, ignoring the new aches in her body. Her right arm wasn't broken, but it was badly bruised; she winced as she tried to move it. One of the straps on the backpack had broken, and the pack was hanging lopsidedly off her left shoulder. Her cap was missing.

He adjusted the rifle on his shoulder, and Jane wondered how he had managed to hold on to it. Didn't he ever drop anything, or get lost, or tired, or hungry? She hadn't even seen him take a drink of water!

''My cap came off,'' she said, turning to stare up the slope. The top was almost thirty yards above them and the slope steep enough that it was a miracle they hadn't crashed into the rocks at the streambed.

''I see it.'' He swarmed up the slope, lithe and sure-footed. He snatched the cap from a broken branch and in only a moment was back beside her. Jamming the cap on her head, he said, ''Can you make it up the other side?''

There was no way, she thought. Her body refused to function any longer. She looked at him and lifted her chin. ''Of course.''

He didn't smile, but there was a faint softening of his expression, as if he knew how desperately tired she was. ''We have to keep moving,'' he said, taking her arm and urging her across the stream. She didn't care that her boots were getting wet; she just sloshed through the water, moving downstream while he scanned the bank for an easy place to climb up. On this side of the stream, the bank wasn't sloped; it was almost vertical and covered with what looked like an impenetrable tangle of vines and bushes. The stream created a break in the foliage that allowed more sunlight to pour down, letting the plants grow much more thickly.

"Okay, let's go up this way," he finally said, pointing. Jane lifted her head and stared at the bank, but she didn't see any break in the wild tangle.

"Let's talk about this," she hedged.

He gave an exasperated sigh. "Look, Pris, I know you're tired, but—"

Something snapped inside Jane, and she whirled on him, catching him by the shirt front and drawing back her fist. "If you call me 'Pris' just one more time, I'm going to feed you a knuckle sandwich!" she roared, unreasonably angry at his continued use of that hated name. No one, but no one, had ever been allowed to call her Priscilla, Pris, or even Cilla, more than once. This damned commando had been rubbing her face in it from the beginning. She'd kept quiet about it, figuring she owed him for kicking him in the groin, but she was tired and hungry and scared and enough was enough!

He moved so quickly that she didn't even have time to blink. His hand snaked out and caught her drawn back fist, while the fingers of his other hand laced around her wrist, removing her grip from his shirt. "Damn it, can't you keep quiet? *I* didn't name you Priscilla, your parents did, so if you don't like it take it up with them. But until then, climb!"

Jane climbed, even though she was certain at every moment that she was going to collapse on her face. Grabbing vines for hand holds, using roots and rocks and bushes and small trees, she squirmed and wiggled her way through the foliage. It was so thick that it could have been swarming with jaguars and she wouldn't have been able to see one until she stuck her hand in its mouth. She remembered that jaguars liked water, spending most of their time resting comfortably near a river or stream, and she swore vengeance on Grant Sullivan for making her do this.

Finally she scrambled over the top, and after pushing forward several yards found that the foliage had once again thinned, and walking was much easier. She adjusted the pack on her back, wincing as she found new bruises. "Are we heading for the helicopter?"

"No," he said curtly. "The helicopter is being watched."

"Who are those men?"

He shrugged. "Who knows? Sandinistas, maybe; we're only

a few klicks from the Nicaraguan border. They could be any guerrilla faction. That damned Pablo sold us out.''

Jane didn't waste time worrying about Pablo's duplicity; she was too tired to really care. ''Where are we going?''

''South.''

She ground her teeth. Getting information out of this man was like pulling teeth. ''South *where*?''

''Limon, eventually. Right now, we're going due east.''

Jane knew enough about Costa Rica to know what lay due east, and she didn't like what she'd just been told. Due east lay the Caribbean coast, where the rain forest became swamp land. If they were only a few kilometers from the Nicaraguan border, then Limon was roughly a hundred miles away. In her weariness, she felt it might as well have been five hundred miles. How long would it take them to walk a hundred miles? Four or five days? She didn't know if she could stand four or five days with Mr. Sunshine. She'd known him less than twelve hours, and she was already close to death.

''Why can't we just go south and forget about east?''

He jerked his head in the direction from which they'd come. ''Because of them. They weren't Turego's men, but Turego will soon know that you came in this direction, and he'll be after us. He can't afford to have the government find out about his little clandestine operations. So...we go where he can't easily follow.''

It made sense. She didn't like it, but it made sense. She'd never been in the Caribbean coastal region of Costa Rica, so she didn't know what to expect, but it had to be better than being Turego's prisoner. Poisonous snakes, alligators, quicksand, whatever...it was better than Turego. She'd worry about the swamp when they were actually in it. With that settled in her mind, she returned to her most pressing problem.

''When do we get to rest? And eat? And, frankly, Attila, you may have a bladder the size of New Jersey, but I've got to *go*!''

Again she caught that unwilling twitch of his lips, as if he'd almost grinned. ''We can't stop yet, but you can eat while we walk. As for the other, go behind that tree there.'' He pointed, and she turned to see another of those huge, funny trees with the enormous buttressed roots. In the absence of indoor plumbing it would have to do. She plunged for its shelter.

When they started out again he gave her something hard and

dark to chew on; it tasted faintly like meat, but after examining it suspiciously she decided not to question him too closely about it. It eased the empty pains in her stomach, and after washing a few bites down with cautious sips of water, she began to feel better and the rubbery feeling left her legs. He chewed a stick of it, too, which reassured her in regard to his humanity.

Still, after walking steadily for a few hours, Jane began to lose the strength that had come with her second wind. Her legs were moving clumsily, and she felt as if she were wading in knee-deep water. The temperature had risen steadily; it was well over ninety now, even in the thick shelter of the canopy. The humidity was draining her as she continued to sweat, losing water that she wasn't replacing. Just when she was about to tell him that she couldn't take another step, he turned and surveyed her with an impersonal professionalism.

"Stay here while I find some sort of shelter for us. It's going to start raining in a little while, so we might as well sit it out. You look pretty well beat, anyway."

Jane pulled her cap off and wiped her streaming face with her forearm, too tired to comment as he melted from sight. How did he know it was going to start raining? It rained almost every day, of course, so it didn't take a fortune-teller to predict rain, but she hadn't heard the thunder that usually preceded it.

He was back in only a short while, taking her arm and leading her to a small rise, where a scattering of boulders testified to Costa Rica's volcanic origin. After taking his knife from his belt, he cut small limbs and lashed them together with vines, then propped one end of his contraption up by wedging sturdier limbs under the corners. Producing a rolled up tarp from his backpack like a magician, he tied the tarp over the crude lean-to, making it waterproof. "Well, crawl in and get comfortable," he growled when Jane simply stood there, staring in astonishment at the shelter he'd constructed in just a few minutes.

Obediently she crawled in, groaning with relief as she shrugged out of her backpack and relaxed her aching muscles. Her ears caught the first distant rumble of thunder; whatever he did for a living, the man certainly knew his way around the jungle.

Grant ducked under the shelter, too, relieving his shoulders of the weight of his own backpack. He had apparently decided that while they were waiting out the rain they might as well eat, because he dug out a couple of cans of field rations.

Jane sat up straight and leaned closer, staring at the cans. "What's that?"

"Food."

"What kind of food?"

He shrugged. "I've never looked at it long enough to identify it. Take my advice: don't think about it. Just eat it."

She put her hand on his as he started to open the cans. "Wait. Why don't we save those for have-to situations?"

"This *is* a have-to situation," he grunted. "We *have* to eat."

"Yes, but we don't have to eat *that*!"

Exasperation tightened his hard features. "Honey, we either eat this, or two more cans exactly like them!"

"Oh, ye of little faith," she scoffed, dragging her own backpack closer. She began delving around in it, and in a moment produced a small packet wrapped in a purloined towel. With an air of triumph she unwrapped it to expose two badly smashed but still edible sandwiches, then returned to the backpack to dig around again. Her face flushed with success, she pulled out two cans of orange juice. "Here!" she said cheerfully, handing him one of the cans. "A peanut butter and jelly sandwich, and a can of orange juice. Protein, carbohydrates and vitamin C. What more could we ask for?"

Grant took the sandwich and the pop-top can she offered him, staring at them in disbelief. He blinked once, then an amazing thing happened: he laughed. It wasn't much of a laugh. It was rather rusty sounding, but it revealed his straight white teeth and made his amber eyes crinkle at the corners. The rough texture of that laugh gave her a funny little feeling in her chest. It was obvious that he rarely laughed, that life didn't hold much humor for him, and she felt both happy that she'd made him laugh and sad that he'd had so little to laugh about. Without laughter she would never have kept her sanity, so she knew how precious it was.

Chewing on his sandwich, Grant relished the gooiness of the peanut butter and the sweetness of the jelly. So what if the bread was a little stale? The unexpected treat made such a detail unimportant. He leaned back and propped himself against his backpack, stretching his long legs out before him. The first drops of rain began to patter against the upper canopy. It would be impossible for anyone to track them through the downpour that was coming, even if those guerrillas had an Indian tracker with them, which he doubted. For the first time since he'd seen the helicopter that morning, he relaxed, his highly developed sense of danger no longer nagging him.

He finished the sandwich and poured the rest of the orange juice down his throat, then glanced over at Jane to see her daintily licking the last bit of jelly from her fingers. She looked up, caught his gaze, and gave him a cheerful smile that made her dimples flash, then returned to the task of cleaning her fingers.

Against his will, Grant felt his body tighten with a surge of lust that surprised him with its strength. She was a charmer, all right, but not at all what he'd expected. He'd expected a spoiled, helpless, petulant debutante, and instead she had had the spirit, the pure guts, to hurl herself into the jungle with two peanut butter sandwiches and some orange juice as provisions. She'd also dressed in common-sense clothing, with good sturdy boots and green khaki pants, and a short-sleeved black blouse. Not right out of the fashion pages, but he'd had a few distracting moments crawling behind her, seeing those pants molded to her shapely bottom. He hadn't been able to prevent a deep masculine appreciation for the soft roundness of her buttocks.

She was a mass of contradictions. She was a jet-setter, so wild that her father had disinherited her, and she'd been George Persall's mistress, yet he couldn't detect any signs of hard living in her face. If anything, her face was as open and innocent as a child's, with a child's enthusiasm for life shining out of her dark brown eyes. She had a look of perpetual mischievousness on her face, yet it was a face of honest sensuality. Her long hair was so dark a brown that it was almost black, and it hung around her shoulders in snarls and tangles. She had pushed it away from her face with total unconcern. Her dark brown eyes were long and a little narrow, slanting in her high-cheekboned face in a way that made him think she might have a little Indian blood. A smattering of small freckles danced across those elegant cheekbones and the dainty bridge of her nose. Her mouth was soft and full, with the upper lip fuller than the lower one, which gave her an astonishingly sensual look. All in all, she was far from beautiful, but there was a freshness and zest about her that made all the other women he'd known suddenly seem bland.

Certainly he'd never been as intimate with any other woman's knee.

Even now, the thought of it made him angry. Part of it was chagrin that he'd left himself open to the blow; he'd been bested by a lightweight! But another part of it was an instinctive, purely male anger, sexually based. He'd watch her knee now whenever she was within striking distance. Still, the fact that she'd defended herself, and the moves she'd made, told him that she'd had professional training, and that was another contradiction. She wasn't an expert, but she knew what to do. Why would a wild, spoiled playgirl know anything about self-defense? Some of the pieces didn't fit, and Grant was always uneasy when he sensed details that didn't jibe.

He felt pretty grim about the entire operation. Their situation right now was little short of desperate, regardless of the fact that they were, for the moment, rather secure. They had probably managed to shake the soldiers, whoever they worked for, but Turego was a different story. The microfilm wasn't the only issue now. Turego had been operating without the sanction of the government, and if Jane made it back and filed a complaint against him, the repercussions would cost him his position, and possibly his freedom.

It was Grant's responsibility to get her out, but it was no longer the simple in-and-out situation he'd planned. From the moment he'd seen Pablo leaning so negligently against the helicopter, waiting for them, he'd known that the deal had gone sour. Pablo wasn't the type to be waiting for them so casually; in all the time Grant had know him, Pablo had been tense, ready to move, always staying in the helicopter with the rotors turning. The elaborate pose of relaxation had tipped Grant off as clearly as if Pablo had hung a sign around his neck. Perhaps Pablo had been trying to warn him. There was no way he'd ever know for certain.

Now he had to get her through the jungle, out of the mountains, and south through a swamp, with Turego in hot pursuit. With luck, in a day or so, they'd find a village and be able to hitch a ride, but even that depended on how close behind Turego was.

And on top of that, he couldn't trust her. She'd disarmed that soldier far too casually, and hadn't turned a hair at anything that had happened. She was far too matter-of-fact about the whole situation. She wasn't what she seemed, and that made her dangerous.

He was wary of her, but at the same time he found that he was unable to stop watching her. She was too damned sexy, as lush and exotic as a jungle orchid. What would it be like to lie with her? Did she use the rich curves of her body to make a man forget who he was? How many men had been taken in by that fresh, open expression? Had Turego found himself off balance with her, wanting her, knowing that he could force her at any time—but being eaten alive by the challenge of trying to win her, of making her give herself freely? How else had she managed to control him? None of it added up to what she should have been, unless she played with men as some sort of ego trip, where the more dangerous the man, the greater the thrill at controlling him.

Grant didn't want her to have that much influence over him; she wasn't worth it. No matter how beguiling the expression in her dark, slanted eyes, she simply wasn't worth it. He didn't need the sort of complication she offered; he just wanted to get her out, collect his money from her father, and get back to the solitude of the farm. Already he'd felt the jungle pulling at him, the heated, almost sexual excitement of danger. The rifle felt like an extension of his body, and the knife fit his palm as if he'd never put it down. All the old moves, the old instincts, were still there, and blackness rose in him as he wondered bitterly if he'd ever really be able to put this life behind him. The blood lust had been there in him, and perhaps he'd have killed that soldier if she hadn't kicked the rifle up when she had.

Was it part of the intoxication of battle that made him want to pull her beneath him and drive himself into her body, until he was mindless with intolerable pleasure? Part of it was, and yet part of it had been born hours ago, on the floor of her bedroom, when he'd felt the soft, velvety roundness of her breasts in his hands. Remembering that, he wanted to know what her breasts looked like, if they thrust out conically or had a full lower slope, if her nipples were small or large, pink or brown. Desire made him harden, and he reminded himself caustically that it had been a while since he'd had a woman, so it was only natural that he would be turned on. If nothing else, he should be glad of the evidence that he could still function!

She yawned, and blinked her dark eyes at him like a sleepy

cat. "I'm going to take a nap," she announced, and curled up on the ground. She rested her head on her arm, closed her eyes and yawned again. He watched her, his eyes narrowed. This utter adaptability she displayed was another piece of the puzzle that didn't fit. She should have been moaning and bitching about how uncomfortable she was, rather than calmly curling up on the ground for a nap. But a nap sounded pretty damned good right now, he thought.

Grant looked around. The rain had become a full-fledged downpour, pounding through the canopy and turning the jungle floor into a river. The constant, torrential rains leeched the nutrients out of the soil, making the jungle into a contradiction, where the world's greatest variety of animal and plant life existed on some of the poorest soil. Right now the rain also made it almost impossible for them to be found. They were safe for the time being, and for the first time he allowed himself to feel the weariness in his muscles. He might as well take a nap, too; he'd wake when the rain stopped, alerted by the total cessation of noise.

Reaching out, he shook her shoulder, and she roused to stare at him sleepily. "Get against the back of the lean-to," he ordered. "Give me a little room to stretch out, too."

She crawled around as he'd instructed and stretched out full length, sighing in ecstasy. He pushed their backpacks to one side, then lay down beside her, his big body between her and the rain. He lay on his back, one brawny arm thrown behind his head. There was no twitching around, no yawning or sighing, for him. He simply lay down, closed his eyes and went to sleep. Jane watched him sleepily, her gaze lingering on the hawklike line of his profile, noting the scar that ran along his left cheekbone. How had he gotten it? His jaw was blurred with several days' growth of beard, and she noticed that his beard was much darker than his hair. His eyebrows and lashes were dark, too, and that made his amber eyes seem even brighter, almost as yellow as an eagle's.

The rain made her feel a little chilled after the intense heat of the day; instinctively she inched closer to the heat she could feel emanating from his body. He was so warm...and she felt so safe...safer than she'd felt since she was nine years old. With one more little sigh, she slept.

Sometime later the rain ceased abruptly, and Grant woke immediately, like a light switch being flipped on. His senses were instantly alert, wary. He started to surge to his feet, only to realize that she was lying curled against his side, with her head pillowed on his arm and her hand lying on his chest. Disbelief made him rigid. How could she have gotten that close to him without waking him? He'd always slept like a cat, alert to the smallest noise or movement—but this damned woman had practically crawled all over him and he hadn't even stirred. She must've been disappointed, he thought furiously. The fury was directed as much at himself as at her, because the incident told him how slack he had become in the past year. That slackness might cost them their lives.

He lay still, aware of the fullness of her breasts against his side. She was soft and lush, and one of her legs was thrown up over his thigh. All he had to do was roll over and he'd be between her legs. The mental image made moisture break out on his forehead. God! She'd be hot and tight, and he clenched his teeth at the heavy surge in his loins. She was no lady, but she was all woman, and he wanted her naked and writhing beneath him with an intensity that tied his guts into knots.

He had to move, or he'd be taking her right there on the rocky ground. Disgusted at himself for letting her get to him the way she had, he eased his arm from beneath her head, then shook her shoulder. "Let's get moving," he said curtly.

She muttered something, her forehead puckering, but she didn't open her eyes, and in a moment her forehead smoothed as she lapsed back into deep sleep. Impatiently, Grant shook her again. "Hey, wake up."

She rolled over on her stomach and sighed deeply, burrowing her head against her folded arm as she sought a more comfortable position. "Come on, we've got to get going," he said, shaking her more vigorously. "Wake up!"

She aimed a drowsy swat at him, as if he were a pesky fly, brushing his hand aside. Exasperated, Grant caught her shoulders and pulled her to a sitting position, shaking her once again. "Damn it, would you get up? On your feet, honey; we've got some walking to do." Her eyes finally opened, and she blinked at him groggily, but she made no move to get up.

Swearing under his breath, Grant hauled her to her feet. "Just stand over there, out of the way," he said, turning her around and starting her on her way with a swat on her bottom before he turned his attention to taking down their shelter.

Chapter Four

Jane stopped, her hand going to her bottom. Awakened now, and irritated by his light, casual slap, she turned. "You didn't have to do that!"

"Do what?" he asked with total disinterest, already busy removing the tarp from the top of the lean-to and rolling it up to replace it in his backpack.

"Hit me! A simple 'wake-up' would have sufficed!"

Grant looked at her in disbelief. "Well, pardon me all to hell," he drawled in a sarcastic tone that made her want to strangle him. "Let me start over. Excuse me, Priscilla, but nappy time is over, and we really do have to—hey! Damn it!" He ducked in time, throwing his arm up to catch the force of her fist. Swiftly he twisted his arm to lock his fingers around her wrist, then caught her other arm before she could swing at him with it. She'd exploded into fury, hurling herself at him like a cat pouncing. Her fist had hit his arm with enough strength that she might have broken his nose if the blow had landed on target. "Woman, what in *hell* is wrong with you?"

"I told you not to call me that!" Jane raged at him, spitting the words out in her fury. She struggled wildly, trying to free her arm so she could hit him again.

Panting, Grant wrestled her to the ground and sat astride her, holding her hands above her head, and this time making damned certain that her knee wouldn't come anywhere near him. She kept wriggling and heaving, and he felt as if he were trying to hold an octopus, but finally he had her subdued.

Glaring at her, he said, "You told me not to call you Pris."

"Well, don't call me Priscilla, either!" she fumed, glaring right back.

"Look, I'm not a mind reader! What am I supposed to call you?"

"Jane!" she shouted at him. "My name is Jane! *Nobody* has *ever* called me Priscilla!"

"All right! All you had to do was tell me! I'm getting damned tired of you snapping at my ankles, understand? I may hurt you before I can stop myself, so you'd better think twice before you attack again. Now, if I let you up, are you going to behave?"

Jane still glared at him, but the weight of his knees on her bruised arms was excruciating. "All right," she said sullenly, and he slowly got up, then surprised her by offering his hand to help her up. She surprised herself by taking it.

A sudden twinkle lit the dark gold of his eyes. "Jane, huh?" he asked reflectively, looking at the surrounding jungle.

She gave him a threatening look. "No 'Me Tarzan, you Jane' stuff," she warned. "I've heard it since grade school." She paused, then said grudgingly, "But it's still better than Priscilla."

He grunted in agreement and turned away to finish dismantling their shelter, and after a moment Jane began helping. He glanced at her, but said nothing. He wasn't much of a talker, she'd noticed, and he didn't improve any on closer acquaintance. But he'd risked his own life to help her, and he hadn't left her behind, even though Jane knew he could have moved a lot faster, and with a lot less risk to himself, on his own. And there was something in his eyes, an expression that was weary and cynical and a little empty, as if he'd seen far too much to have any faith or trust left. That made Jane want to put her arms around him and shield him. Lowering her head so he wouldn't be able to read her expression, she chided herself for feeling protective of a man who was so obviously capable of handling himself. There had been a time in her own life when she had been afraid to trust anyone except her parents, and it had been a horrible, lonely time. She knew what fear was, and loneliness, and she ached for him.

All signs of their shelter obliterated, he swung his backpack up and buckled it on, then slung the rifle over his shoulder, while Jane stuffed her hair up under her cap. He leaned down to pick up her pack for her, and a look of astonishment crossed his face; then his dark brows snapped together. "What the—" he muttered. "What all do you have in this damned thing? It weighs a good twenty pounds more than my pack!"

"Whatever I thought I'd need," Jane replied, taking the pack from him and hooking her arm through the one good shoulder strap, then buckling the waist strap to secure it as well as she could.

"Like what?"

"Things," she said stubbornly. Maybe her provisions weren't exactly proper by military standards, but she'd take her peanut butter sandwiches over his canned whatever any time. She thought he would order her to dump the pack on the ground for him to sort through and decide what to keep, and she was determined not to allow it. She set her jaw and looked at him.

He put his hands on his hips and surveyed her funny, exotic face, her lower lip pouting out in a mutinous expression, her delicate jaw set. She looked ready to light into him again, and he sighed in resignation. Damned if she wasn't the stubbornest, scrappiest woman he'd ever met. "Take it off," he growled, unbuckling his own pack. "I'll carry yours, and you can carry mine."

If anything, the jaw went higher. "I'm doing okay with my own."

"Stop wasting time arguing. That extra weight will slow you down, and you're already tired. Hand it over, and I'll fix that strap before we start out."

Reluctantly she slipped the straps off and gave him the pack, ready to jump him if he showed any sign of dumping it. But he took a small folder from his own pack, opened it to extract a needle and thread, and deftly began to sew the two ends of the broken strap together.

Astounded, Jane watched his lean, calloused hands wielding the small needle with a dexterity that she had to envy. Reattaching a button was the limit of her sewing skill, and she usually managed to prick her finger doing that. "Do they teach sewing in the military now?" she asked, crowding in to get a better look.

He gave her another one of his glances of dismissal. "I'm not in the military."

"Maybe not now," she conceded. "But you were, weren't you?"

"A long time ago."

"Where did you learn how to sew?"

"I just picked it up. It comes in handy." He bit the thread off, then replaced the needle in its package. "Let's get moving; we've wasted too much time as it is."

Jane took his backpack and fell into step behind him; all she had to do was follow him. Her gaze drifted over the width of his shoulders, then eased downward. Had she ever known anyone as physically strong as this man? She didn't think so. He seemed to be immune to weariness, and he ignored the steamy humidity that drained her strength and drenched her clothes in perspiration. His long, powerful legs moved in an effortless stride, the flexing of his thigh muscles pulling the fabric of his pants tight across them. Jane found herself watching his legs and matching her own stride to his. He took a step, and she took a step automatically. It was easier that way; she could separate her mind from her body, and in doing so ignore her protesting muscles.

He stopped once and took a long drink from the canteen, then passed it to Jane without comment. Also without comment, and without wiping the mouth of the canteen, she tipped it up and drank thirstily. Why worry about drinking after him? Catching cold was the least of her concerns. After capping the canteen, she handed it back to him, and they began walking again.

There was madness to his method, or so it seemed to her. If there was a choice between two paths, he invariably chose the more difficult one. The route he took was through the roughest terrain, the thickest vegetation, up the highest, most rugged slope. Jane tore her pants sliding down a bluff, that looked like pure suicide from the top, and not much better than that from the bottom, but she followed without complaining. It wasn't that she didn't think of plenty of complaints, but that she was too tired to voice them. The benefits of her short nap had long since been dissipated. Her legs ached, her back ached, her bruised arms were so painful she could barely move them, and her eyes felt as if they were burning out of their sockets. But she didn't ask him to stop. Even if the pace killed her, she wasn't going to slow him down any more than she already had, because she had no doubt that he could travel much faster without her. The easy movements of his long legs told her that his stamina was far greater than hers; he could probably walk all night long again without a noticeable slowing of his stride. She felt a quiet awe of that sort of strength and conditioning, something that had been completely outside her experience before she'd met him. He wasn't like other men; it was evident in his superb body, in the awesome competence with which he handled everything, in the piercing gold of his eyes.

As if alerted by her thoughts, he stopped and looked back at her, assessing her condition with that sharp gaze that missed nothing. "Can you make it for another mile or so?"

On her own, she couldn't have, but when she met his eyes she knew there was no way she'd admit to that. Her chin lifted, and she ignored the increasingly heavy ache in her legs as she said, "Yes."

A flicker of expression crossed his face so swiftly that she couldn't read it. "Let me have that pack," he growled, coming back to her and jerking the straps free of the buckles, then slipping the pack from her shoulders.

"I'm handling it okay," she protested fiercely, grabbing for the pack and wrapping both arms around it. "I haven't complained, have I?"

His level dark brows drawing together in a frown, he forcefully removed the pack from her grasp. "Use your head," he snapped. "If you collapse from exhaustion, then I'll have to carry you, too."

The logic of that silenced her. Without another word he turned and started walking again. She was better able to keep up with him without the weight of the pack, but she felt frustrated with herself for not being in better shape, for being a burden to him. Jane had fought fiercely for her independence, knowing that her very life depended on it. She'd never been one to sit and wait for someone else to do things for her. She'd charged at life head-on, relishing the challenges that came her way because they reaffirmed her acute sense of the wonder of life. She'd shared the joys, but handled the problems on her own, and it unsettled her now to have to rely on someone else.

They came to another stream, no wider than the first one they had crossed, but deeper. It might rise to her knees in places. The water rushing over the rocks sounded cool, and she thought of how heavenly it would be to refresh her sweaty body in the stream. Looking longingly at it, she stumbled over a root and reached out to catch her balance. Her palm came down hard against a tree trunk, and something squished beneath her fingers.

"Oh, yuk!" she moaned, trying to wipe the dead insect off with a leaf.

Grant stopped. "What is it?"

"I smashed a bug with my hand." The leaf didn't clean too well; a smear still stained her hand, and she looked at Grant with disgust showing plainly on her face. "Is it all right if I wash my hand in the stream?"

He looked around, his amber eyes examining both sides of the stream. "Okay. Come over here."

"I can get down here," she said. The bank was only a few feet high, and the underbrush wasn't that thick. She carefully picked her way over the roots of an enormous tree, bracing her hand against its trunk to steady herself as she started to descend to the stream.

"Watch out!" Grant said sharply, and Jane froze in her tracks, turning her head to look askance at him.

Suddenly something incredibly heavy dropped onto her shoulders, something long and thick and alive, and she gave a stifled scream as it began to coil around her body. She was more startled than frightened, thinking a big vine had fallen; then she saw the movement of a large triangular head and she gave another gasping cry. "Grant! Grant, *help me*!"

Terror clutched at her throat, choking her, and she began to claw at the snake, trying to get it off. It was a calm monster, working its body around her, slowly tightening the lethal muscles that would crush her bones. It twined around her legs and she fell, rolling on the ground. Dimly she could hear Grant cursing, and she could hear her own cries of terror, but they sounded curiously distant. Everything was tumbling in a mad kaleidoscope of brown earth and green trees, of Grant's taut, furious face. He was shouting something at her, but she couldn't understand him; all she could do was struggle against the living bonds that coiled around her. She had one shoulder and arm free, but the boa was tightening itself around her rib cage, and the big head was coming toward her face, its mouth open. Jane screamed, trying to catch its head with her free hand, but the snake was crushing the breath out of her and the scream was almost soundless. A big hand, not hers, caught the snake's head, and she dimly saw a flash of silver.

The snake's coils loosened about her as it turned to meet this new prey, seeking to draw Grant into its deadly embrace, too. She saw the flash of silver again, and something wet splashed into her face. Vaguely she realized that it was his knife she'd seen. He was swearing viciously as he wrestled with the snake, mostly astride her as she writhed on the ground, struggling to free herself. "Damn it, hold still!" he roared. "You'll make me cut you!"

It was impossible to be still; she was wrapped in the snake, and it was writhing with her in its coils. She was too crazed by fear to realize that the snake was in its death throes, not even when she saw Grant throw something aside and begin forcibly removing the thick coils from around her body. It wasn't until she actually felt herself coming free of the constrictor's horrible grasp that she understood it was over, that Grant had killed the snake. She stopped fighting and lay limply on the ground. Her face was utterly white except for the few freckles across her nose and cheekbones; her eyes were fixed on Grant's face.

"It's over," he said roughly, running his hands over her arms and rib cage. "How do you feel? Anything broken?"

Jane couldn't say anything; her throat was frozen, her voice totally gone. All she could do was lie there and stare at him with the remnants of terror in her dark eyes. Her lips trembled like a child's, and there was something pleading in her gaze. He automatically started to gather her into his arms, the way one would a frightened child, but before he could do more than lift his hand, she dragged her gaze away from his with a visible effort. He could see what it cost her in willpower, but somehow she found the inner strength to still the trembling of her lips, and then her chin lifted in that characteristic gesture.

"I'm all right," she managed to say. Her voice was jerky, but she said the words, and in saying them, believed it. She slowly sat up and pushed her hair away from her face. "I feel a little bruised, but there's nothing bro—"

She stopped abruptly, staring at her bloody hand and arm. "I'm all bloody," she said in a bewildered tone, and her voice shook. She looked back at Grant, as if for confirmation. "I'm all bloody," she said again, extending her wildly trembling hand for him to see. "Grant, there's blood all over me!"

"It's the snake's blood," he said, thinking to reassure her, but she stared at him with uncontrolled revulsion.

"Oh, *God*!" she said in a thin, high voice, scrambling to her feet and staring down at herself. Her black blouse was wet and sticky, and big reddish splotches stained her khaki pants. Both her arms had blood smeared down them. Bile rose in her throat as she remembered the wetness that had splashed her face. She raised exploring fingers and found the horrible stickiness on her cheeks, as well as smeared in her hair.

She began to shake even harder, and tears dripped down her cheeks. "Get it off," she said, still in that high, wavering voice of utter hysteria. "I have to get it off. There's blood all over me, and it isn't mine. It's all over me; it's even in my hair... It's in my *hair*!" she sobbed, plunging for the stream.

Cursing, Grant grabbed for her, but in her mad urgency to wash the blood away she jerked free of him, stumbling over the body of the snake and crashing to the ground. Before she could scramble away again, Grant pounced on her, holding her in an almost painful grip while she fought and sobbed, pleading and swearing at him all at once.

"Jane, stop it!" he said sharply. "I'll get the blood off you. Just hold still and let me get our boots off, okay?"

He had to hold her still with one arm and pull her boots off with his free hand, but by the time he started to remove his own boots she was crying so hard that she lay limply on the ground. His face was grim as he looked at her. She'd stood up to so much without turning a hair that he hadn't expected her to fall apart like this. She'd been pulling herself together until she'd seen the blood on herself, and that had evidently been more than she could bear. He jerked his boots off, then turned to her and roughly undid her pants and pulled them off. Lifting her into his arms as easily as he would have lifted a child, he climbed down the bank and waded out into the stream, disregarding the fact that his own pants were being soaked.

When the water reached the middle of his calves, he stood her in the stream and bent to begin splashing water on her legs, rubbing the blood stains from her flesh. Next, cupping water in his palms, he washed her arms and hands clean, dripping the cooling water over her and soaking her blouse. All the while he tended to her, she stood docile, with silent tears still running down her face and making tracks in the blood smeared across her cheeks.

"Everything's all right, honey," he crooned soothingly to her, coaxing her to sit down in the stream so he could wash the blood from her hair. She let him splash water on her head and face, blinking her eyes to protect them from the stinging water, but otherwise keeping her gaze fixed on his hard, intent features. He took a handkerchief from his back pocket and wet it, then gently cleaned her face. She was calmer now, no longer crying in that silent, gut-wrenching way, and he helped her to her feet.

"There, you're all cleaned up," he started to say, then noticed the pink rivulets of water running down her legs. Her blouse was so bloody that he'd have to take it off to get her clean. Without hesitation, he began to unbutton it. "Let's get this off so we can wash it," he said, keeping his voice calm and soothing. She didn't even glance down as he unbuttoned her blouse and pulled it off her shoulders, then tossed it to the bank. She kept her eyes on his face, as if he were her lifeline to sanity and to look away meant a return to madness.

Grant looked down, and his mouth went dry as he stared at her naked breasts. He'd wondered how she looked and now he knew, and it was like being punched in the stomach. Her breasts were round and a little heavier than he'd expected, tipped by small brown nipples, and he wanted to bend down and put his mouth to them, taste them. She might as well have been naked; all she had on was a pair of gossamer panties that had turned transparent in the water. He could see the dark curls of hair beneath the wisp of fabric, and he felt his loins tighten and swell. She was beautifully made, long-legged and slim-hipped, with the sleek muscles of a dancer. Her shoulders were straight, her arms slim but strong, her breasts rich; he wanted to spread her legs and take her right there, driving deeply into her body until he went out of his mind with pleasure. He couldn't remember ever wanting a woman so badly. He'd wanted sex, but that had been simply a physical pleasure, and any willing female body had been acceptable. Now he wanted Jane, the essence of her; it was her legs he wanted wrapped around him, her breasts in his hands, her mouth under his, her body sheathing him.

He jerked his gaze away from her, bending to dip the handkerchief in the water again. That was even worse; his eyes were level with the top of her thighs, and he straightened abruptly. He washed her breasts with a gentle touch, but every moment of it was torture to him, feeling her silky flesh under his fingers, watching her nipples tighten into reddened little nubs as he touched them.

"You're clean," he said hoarsely, tossing the handkerchief to the bank to join her blouse.

"Thank you," she whispered, then fresh tears glittered in her eyes, and with a little whimper she flung herself against him.

Her arms went around him and clung to his back. She buried her face against his chest, feeling reassured by the steady beat of his heart and the warmth of his body. His very presence drove the fear away; with him, she was safe. She wanted to rest in his arms and forget everything.

His hands moved slowly over her bare back, his calloused palms stroking her skin as if he relished the texture of it. Her eyes slid shut, and she nestled closer to him, inhaling the distinctly male scent of his strong body. She felt oddly drunk, disoriented; she wanted to cling to him as the only steady presence in the world. Her body was awash in strange sensations, from the rushing water swirling about her feet to the faint breeze that fanned her wet, naked skin, while he was so hard and warm. An unfamiliar heat swept along her flesh in the path of his hands as they moved from her back to her shoulders. Then one hand stroked up her throat to cup her jaw, his thumb under her chin and his fingers in her hair, and he turned her face up to him.

Taking his time about it, he bent and fitted his mouth to hers, slanting his head to make the contact deep and firm. His tongue moved leisurely into her mouth, touching hers and demanding a response, and Jane found herself helplessly giving him what he wanted. She'd never been kissed like that before, with such complete confidence and expertise, as if she were his for the taking, as if they had reverted to more primitive times when the dominant male had his pick of the women. Vaguely alarmed, she made a small effort to free herself from his grasp. He subdued her with gentle force and kissed her again, holding her head still for the pressure of his mouth. Once again Jane found herself opening her mouth for him, forgetting why she'd struggled to begin with. Since her divorce a lot of men had kissed her and tried to make her respond. They'd left her cold. Why should this rough...mercenary, or whatever he was, make shivers of pleasure chase over her body, when some of the most sophisticated men in the world had only bored her with their passion? His lips were warm and hard, the taste of his mouth heady, his tongue bold in its exploration, and his kisses caused an unfamiliar ache to tighten within her body.

A mindless little whimper of delight escaped her throat, the soft female sound making his arms tighten around her. Her hands slid up to his shoulders, then locked around his neck, hanging on to him for support. She couldn't get close enough to him, though he was crushing her against him. The buttons of his shirt dug into her bare breasts, but she wasn't aware of any pain. His mouth was wild, hungry with a basic need that had flared out of control, bruising her lips with the force of his kisses, and she didn't care. Instead she gloried in it, clinging to him. Her body was suddenly alive with sensations and needs that she didn't recognize, never having felt them before. Her skin actually ached for his touch, yet every stroke of his hard fingers made the ache intensify.

Boldly cupping her breast in his palm, he rubbed the rough pad of his thumb across her tightly puckered nipple, and Jane almost cried aloud at the surge of heat that washed through her. It had never been like this for her before; the urgency of the pure, brazen sensuality of her own body took her by surprise. She'd long ago decided that she simply wasn't a very physical person, then forgotten about it. Sex hadn't been something that interested her very much. The way Grant was making her feel completely shattered her concept of herself. She was a female animal in his arms, grinding against him, feeling and glorying in the swollen response of his body, and hurting with the emptiness deep inside her.

Time disappeared as they stood in the water, the late afternoon sun dappling them with the shifting patterns of light created by the sheltering trees. His hands freely roamed her body. She never even thought of resisting him. It was as if he had every right to her flesh, as if she were his to touch and taste. He bent her back over his arm, making her breasts jut enticingly, and his lips traveled hotly down her throat to the warm, quivering mounds. He took her nipple into his mouth and sucked strongly, and she surged against him like a wild creature, on fire and dying and wanting more.

His hand swept downward, his fingers curving between her legs to caress her through the silk of her panties. The boldness of his touch shocked her out of her sensual frenzy; automatically she stiffened in his grasp and brought her arms down from around his neck to wedge them between their bodies and push against him. A low, gutteral sound rattled in his throat, and for a brief, terrified moment she thought there wouldn't be any stopping him. Then, with a curse, he thrust her away from him.

Jane staggered a little, and his hand shot out to catch her, hauling her back to face him. "Damn you, is this how you get your kicks?'' he asked, infuriated. ''Do you like seeing how far you can push a man?''

Her chin came up, and she swallowed. ''No, that's not it at all. I'm sorry. I know I shouldn't have thrown myself at you like that—''

''Damned right, you shouldn't,'' he interrupted savagely. He *looked* savage; his eyes were narrowed and bright with rage, his nostrils flared, and his mouth a thin, grim line. ''Next time, you'd better make sure you want what you're asking for, because I'm damned sure going to give it to you. Is that clear?''

He turned and began wading to the bank, leaving her standing in the middle of the stream. Jane crossed her arms over her bare breasts, suddenly and acutely aware of her nakedness. She hadn't meant to tease him, but she'd been so frightened, and he'd been so strong and calm that it had seemed the most natural thing in the world to cling to him. Those frenzied kisses and caresses had taken her by surprise, shaken her off balance. Still, she wasn't about to have sex with a man she barely knew, especially when she didn't quite know if she liked what little she did know about him.

He reached the bank and turned to look at her. ''Are you coming or not?'' he snapped, so Jane waded toward him, still keeping her arms over her breasts.

''Don't bother,'' he advised in a curt voice. ''I've already seen, and touched. Why pretend to be modest?'' He gestured to her blouse lying on the ground. ''You might want to wash the blood out of that, since you're so squeamish about it.''

Jane looked at the blood-stained blouse, and she went a little pale again, but she was under control now. ''Yes, I will,'' she said in a low voice. ''Will you...will you get my pants and boots for me, please?''

He snorted, but climbed up the bank and tossed her pants and boots down to her. Keeping her back turned to him, Jane pulled on her pants, shuddering at the blood that stained them, too, but at least they weren't soaked the way her blouse was. Her panties were wet, but there wasn't anything she could do about that now, so she ignored the clammy discomfort. When she was partially clad again, she squatted on the gravel at the edge of the stream and began trying to wash her blouse. Red clouds drifted out of the fabric, staining the water before being swept downstream. She scrubbed and scrubbed before she was satisfied, then wrung out as much water as possible and shook the blouse. As she started to put the blouse on, he said irritably, ''Here,'' and held his shirt in front of her. ''Wear this until yours gets dry.''

She wanted to refuse, but she knew false pride wouldn't gain her anything. She accepted the shirt silently and put it on. It was far too big, but it was dry and warm and not too dirty, and it smelled of sweat, and the musky odor of his skin. The scent was vaguely comforting. There were rust colored stains on it, too, reminding her that he'd saved her life. She tied the tails in a knot at her waist and sat down on the gravel to put on her boots.

When she turned, she found him standing right behind her, his face still grim and angry. He helped her up the bank, then lifted their packs to his shoulders. ''We're not going much farther. Follow me, and for God's sake don't touch anything that I don't touch, or step anywhere except in my footprints. If another boa wants you, I just may let him have you, so don't push your luck.''

Jane pushed her wet hair behind her ears and followed obediently, walking where he walked. For a while, she stared nervously at every tree limb they passed under, then made herself stop thinking about the snake. It was over; there was no use dwelling on it.

Instead she stared at his broad back, wondering how her father had found a man like Grant Sullivan. They obviously lived in two different worlds, so how had they met?

Then something clicked in her mind, and a chill went down her spine. *Had* they met? She couldn't imagine her father knowing anyone like Sullivan. She also knew what her own position was. Everyone wanted to get their hands on her, and she had no way of knowing whose side Grant Sullivan was on. He'd called her Priscilla, which was her first name. If her father had sent him, wouldn't he have known that she was never called Priscilla, that she'd been called Jane from birth? *He hadn't known her name!*

Before he died, George had warned her not to trust anyone. She didn't want to think that she was alone in the middle of the jungle with a man who would casually cut her throat when he had no further use for her. Still, the fact remained that she had no proof that her father had sent him. He'd simply knocked her out, put her over his shoulder and hauled her off into the jungle.

Then she realized that she had to trust this man; she had no alternative. He was all she had. It was dangerous, trusting him, but not as dangerous as trying to make it out of the jungle on her own. He had shown flashes of kindness. She felt a funny constriction in her chest as she remembered the way he'd cared for her after he'd killed the snake. Not just cared for her, kissed her—she was still shaken by the way he'd kissed her. Mercenary or not, enemy or not, he made her want him. Her mind wasn't certain about him, but her body was.

She would have found it funny, if she hadn't been so frightened.

Chapter Five

They moved directly away from the stream at a forty-five-degree angle, and it wasn't long before he stopped, looked around and unslung the packs from his shoulders. "We'll camp here."

Jane stood in silence, feeling awkward and useless, watching as he opened his pack and took out a small, rolled bundle. Under his skilled hands, the bundle was rapidly transformed into a small tent, complete with a polyethylene floor and a flap that could be zipped shut. When the tent was up he began stripping vines and limbs from the nearby trees to cover it, making it virtually invisible. He hadn't so much as glanced in her direction, but after a moment she moved to help him. He did look at her then, and allowed her to gather more limbs while he positioned them over the tent.

When the job was completed, he said, "We can't risk a fire, so we'll just eat and turn in. After today, I'm ready for some sleep."

Jane was, too, but she dreaded the thought of the night to come. The light was rapidly fading, and she knew that it would soon be completely dark. She remembered the total blackness of the night before and felt a cold finger of fear trace up her backbone. Well, there was nothing she could do about it; she'd have to tough it out.

She crouched beside her pack and dug out two more cans of orange juice, tossing one to him; he caught it deftly, and eyed her pack with growing irritation. "How many more cans of this do you have in that traveling supermarket?" he asked sarcastically.

"That's it. We'll have to drink water from now on. How about a granola bar?" She handed it to him, refusing to let herself respond to the irritation in his voice. She was tired, she ached, and she was faced with a long night in total darkness. Given that, his irritation didn't seem very important. He'd get over it.

She ate her own granola bar, but was still hungry, so she rummaged for something else to eat. "Want some cheese and crackers?" she offered, dragging the items out of the depths of the pack.

She looked up to find him watching her with an expression of raw disbelief on his face. He held out his hand, and she divided the cheese and crackers between them. He looked at her again, shook his head and silently ate his share.

Jane saved a little of her orange juice, and when she finished eating she took a small bottle from the pack. Opening it, she shook a pill into the palm of her hand, glanced at Grant, then shook out another one. "Here," she said.

He looked at it, but made no move to take it. "What the hell's that?"

"It's a yeast pill."

"Why should I want to take a yeast pill?"

"So the mosquitoes and things won't bite you."

"Sure they won't."

"They won't! Look at me. I don't have any insect bites, and it's because I take yeast pills. It does something to your skin chemistry. Come on, take it. It won't hurt you."

He took the pill from her hand and held it with a pained expression on his face while she took her own, washing it down with a sip of the orange juice she'd saved. She passed the can to him, and he muttered something obscene before he tossed the pill into his mouth and slugged down the rest of the juice.

"Okay, bedtime," he said, rising to his feet. He jerked his head toward a tree. "There's your bathroom, if you want to go before we turn in."

Jane stepped behind the tree. He was crude, he was rude, he was a little cruel—and he had saved her life. She didn't know what to expect from him. No matter how rough he was, he would eventually disarm her with an unexpected act of kindness. On the other hand, when things were going smoothly between them, he would say things that stung, as if deliberately trying to start a quarrel.

He was waiting for her by the opening of the tent. "I've already put the blanket down. Crawl in."

She knelt down and crawled into the small tent. He had spread the blanket over the floor, and she sat on it. He shoved their packs inside. "Put these out of the way," he instructed. "I'm going to take a quick look around."

She shoved the packs into the far corners of the tent, then lay down on her back and stared tensely at the thin walls. The light was almost gone; only a glimmer entered through the translucent fabric. It wasn't quite as dark outside yet, but the limbs he'd used as camouflage made it darker inside. The flap parted, and he crawled in, then zipped the opening shut.

"Take your boots off and put them in the corner next to your feet."

Sitting up, she did as he said, then lay down again. Her eyes strained open so widely that they burned. Her body stiff with dread, she listened to him stretch and yawn and make himself comfortable.

Moments later the silence became nearly as unbearable as the darkness. "A collapsible tent comes in handy, doesn't it?" she blurted nervously. "What is it made out of?"

"Nylon," he replied, yawning again. "It's nearly indestructible."

"How much does it weigh?"

"Three pounds and eight ounces."

"Is it waterproof?"

"Yes, it's waterproof."

"And bug proof?"

"Bug proof, too," he muttered.

"Do you think a jaguar could—"

"Look, it's *jaguar* proof, *mildew* proof, *fire* proof and *snake* proof. I personally guarantee you that it's proof against everything except elephants, and I don't think we're going to be stomped on by an elephant in Costa Rica! Is there any other damned thing you're worried about?" he exploded. "If not, why don't you be quiet and let me get some sleep?"

Jane lay tensely, and silence fell again. She clenched her fists in an effort to control her nervousness, listening to the growing cacophony of the jungle night. Monkeys howled and chattered; insects squeaked their calls; underbrush rustled. She was exhausted but she had no real hope of sleeping, at least not until dawn, and at dawn this devil beside her would want to start another day of marathon travel.

He was totally silent in that unnerving way of his. She couldn't even hear him breathe. The old fear began to rise in her chest, making her own breathing difficult. She might as well be alone, and that was the one thing she absolutely couldn't bear.

"Where are you from?"

He heaved a sigh. "Georgia."

That explained his drawl. She swallowed, trying to ease the constriction of her dry throat. If she could just keep him talking, then she wouldn't feel so alone. She'd know he was there.

"What part of Georgia?"

"South. Ever hear of the Okefenokee?"

"Yes. It's a swamp."

"I grew up in it. My folks own a farm just on the edge of it." It had been a normal boyhood, except for the skills he'd learned automatically in the swamp, those skills, which had eventually changed his life by shaping him into something not quite human. He willed the memories away, pulling a mental shade down over them, isolating himself. There was no use in thinking about what had been.

"Are you an only child?"

"Why all the questions?" he snapped, edgy at revealing any information about himself.

"I'm just interested, that's all."

He paused, suddenly alert. There was something in her voice, a tone that he couldn't quite place. It was dark, so he couldn't see her face; he had to go entirely by what his ears told him. If he kept her talking, he might be able to figure it out.

"I've got a sister," he finally said reluctantly.

"I'll bet she's younger. You're so bossy, you must be an older brother."

He let the dig pass and said only, "She's four years younger."

"I'm an only child," she volunteered.

"I know."

She searched frantically for something else to say, but the darkness was making her panic. She felt herself move to grab for him, then remembered what he'd said about startling him, and about not making offers she didn't mean. She ground her teeth together and stilled her reaching hands, the effort so intense that tears actually welled in her eyes. She blinked them away. "Grant," she said in a shaking voice.

"What?" he growled.

"I don't want you to think I'm throwing myself at you again because I'm really not, but would you mind very much if I…just held your hand?" she whispered. "I'm sorry, but I'm afraid of the dark, and it helps if I know I'm not alone."

He was still for a moment; then she heard his clothing rustle as he rolled onto his side. "You're really that afraid of the dark?"

Jane tried for a laugh, but the sound was so shaky that it was close to a sob. "The word 'terrified' only begins to describe how afraid I am. I can't sleep in the dark. All the time I was at that wretched plantation I was awake all night long, never sleeping until dawn. But at least I could use that time to watch the guards and figure out their routine. Besides, it wasn't as totally dark there as it is here."

"If you're so all-fired scared of the dark, why were you getting ready to hit the jungle on your own?"

A dark, handsome, incredibly cruel face swam before her mind's eye. "Because even dying in the jungle would be better than Turego," she said quietly.

Grant grunted. He could understand that choice, but the fact that she had so correctly summed up the situation illustrated once again that she was more than what she seemed. Then again, perhaps she already had reason to know just how vile Turego could be. Had Turego raped her, or would it have been rape? With this woman, who knew? "Did you have sex with him?"

The blunt question made her shudder. "No. I'd been holding him off, but when he left yesterday…it *was* just yesterday, wasn't it? It seems like a year ago. Anyway, I knew that, when he came back, I wouldn't be able to stop him any longer. My time had run out."

"What makes you so certain of that?"

Jane paused, wondering just how much to tell him, wondering how much he already knew. If he was involved, he would be familiar with Luis's name; if he wasn't, the name would mean nothing to him. She wanted to tell him; she didn't want to be alone in this nightmare any longer. But she remembered George telling her once that secrecy was synonymous with security, and she quelled the need to turn into Grant's arms and tell him how afraid and alone she had been. If he wasn't involved already, he was safer not knowing anything about it. On the other hand, if he was involved, *she* might be safer if he didn't realize how deeply she was a part of things. Finally, to answer his question, she said, "I wasn't certain. I was just afraid to stay, afraid of Turego."

He grunted, and that seemed to be the end of the conversation. Jane clenched her jaw against the sudden chattering of her teeth. It was hot and steamy inside the dark tent, but chills were running up and down her body. Why didn't he say something else, anything, rather than lying there so quietly? She might as well have been alone. It was unnatural for anyone to be that soundless, that utterly controlled.

"How was Dad?"

"Why?"

"I just wondered." Was he being deliberately evasive? Why didn't he want to talk about her father? Perhaps he hadn't been hired by her father at all and didn't want to be drawn into a conversation about someone he was supposed to have met, but hadn't.

After a measured silence, as if he had carefully considered his answer, he said, "He was worried sick about you. Surprised?"

"No, of course not," she said, startled. "I'd be surprised if he weren't."

"It doesn't surprise you that he'd pay a small fortune to get you out of Turego's hands, even though you don't get along with him?"

He was confusing her; she felt left out of the conversation, as if he were talking about someone else entirely. "What are you talking about? We get along perfectly, always have."

She couldn't see him, couldn't hear him, but suddenly there was something different about him, as if the very air had become electrically charged. A powerful sense of danger made the fine hairs on her body stand up. The danger was coming from him. Without knowing why, she shrank back from him as far as she could in the confines of the small tent, but there was no escape. With the suddenness of a snake striking, he rolled and pinned her down, forcing her hands over her head and holding them shackled there in a grip that hurt her wrists. "All right, Jane, or Priscilla, or whoever you are, we're going to talk. I'm going to ask the questions and you're going to answer them, and you'd better have the right answers or you're in trouble, sugar. Who are you?"

Had he gone mad? Jane struggled briefly against the grip on her wrists, but there was no breaking it. His weight bore down heavily on her, controlling her completely. His muscled legs clasped hers, preventing her from even kicking. "W—what...?" she stammered. "Grant, you're hurting me!"

"Answer me, damn you! Who are you?"

"Jane Greer!" Desperately, she tried to put some humor in her voice, but it wasn't a very successful effort.

"I don't like being lied to, sugar." His voice was velvety soft, and the sound of it chilled her to her marrow. Not even Turego had affected her like this; Turego was a dangerous, vicious man, but the man who held her now was the most lethal person she'd ever seen. He didn't have to reach for a weapon to kill her; he could kill her with his bare hands. She was totally helpless against him.

"I'm not lying!" she protested desperately. "I'm Priscilla Jane Hamilton Greer."

"If you were, you'd know that James Hamilton cut you out of his will several years ago. So you get along with him just perfectly, do you?"

"Yes, I do!" She strained against him, and he deliberately let her feel more of his weight, making it difficult for her to breathe. "He did it to protect me!"

For a long, silent moment in which she could hear the roaring of her blood in her ears, she waited for his reaction. His silence scraped along her nerves. Why didn't he say something? His warm breath was on her cheek, telling her how close he was to her, but she couldn't see him at all in that suffocating darkness. "That's a good one," he finally responded, and she flinched at the icy sarcasm of his tone. "Too bad I don't buy it. Try again."

"I'm telling you the truth! He did it to make me a less attractive kidnap target. It was my idea, damn it!"

"Sure it was," he crooned, and that low, silky sound made her shudder convulsively. "Come on, you can do better than that."

Jane closed her eyes, searching desperately for some way of convincing him of her identity. None came to mind, and she had no identification with her. Turego had taken her passport, so she didn't have even that. "Well, what about you?" she blurted in sudden fury. She'd taken a lot from him, endured without complaining, and now he'd frightened her half out of her mind. She'd had her back to the wall before, and had learned to strike back. "Who are you? How do I know that Dad hired you? If he did why didn't you know that no one ever calls me Priscilla? You were sloppy with your homework!"

"In case you haven't noticed, honey, I'm the one on top. *You* answer *my* questions."

"I did, and you didn't believe me," she snapped. "Sorry, but I don't have my American Express card with me. For God's sake, do I look like a terrorist? You nearly broke my arm; then you knocked me out. You've bounced me on the ground like a rubber ball, and you've got the utter gall to act like *I'm* dangerous? My goodness, you'd better search me, too, so you'll be able to sleep tonight. Who knows? I might have a bazooka strapped to my leg, since I'm such a dangerous character!" Her voice had risen furiously, and he cut her off by resting all his weight on her ribcage. When she gasped, he eased up again.

"No, you're unarmed. I've already had your clothes off, remember?" Even in the darkness, Jane blushed at the memory, thinking of the way he'd kissed her and touched her, and how his hands on her body had made her feel. He moved slowly against her, stopping her breath this time with the suggestive intimacy of his movements. His warm breath stirred her hair as he dipped his head closer to her. "But I wouldn't want to disappoint a lady. If you want to be searched, I'll oblige you. I wouldn't mind giving you a body search."

Fuming, Jane tried again to free her hands, but finally fell back in disgust at the futile action. Raw frustration finally cleared her mind, giving her an idea, and she said harshly, "Did you go in the house when Dad hired you?"

He was still, and she sensed his sudden increase of interest. "Yes."

"Did you go in the study?"

"Yes."

"Then a hotshot like you would have noticed the portrait over the mantle. You're trained to notice things, aren't you? The portrait is of my grandmother, Dad's mother. She was painted sitting down, with a single rose on her lap. Now, you tell me what color her gown was," she challenged.

"Black," he said slowly. "And the rose was blood red."

Thick silence fell between them; then he released her hands and eased his weight from her. "All right," he said finally. "I'll give you the benefit of the doubt—"

"Well, gee, thanks!" Huffily she rubbed her wrists, trying to keep her anger alive in the face of the enormous relief that filled her. Evidently her father had hired him, for otherwise how could he have seen the portrait in the study? She wanted to remain mad at him, but she knew she would forgive him because it was still dark. In spite of everything she was terribly glad he was there. Besides, she told herself cautiously, it was definitely better to stay on this man's good side.

"Don't thank me," he said tiredly. "Just be quiet and go to sleep."

Sleep! If only she could! Consciously, she knew she wasn't alone, but her subconscious mind required additional affirmation from her senses. She needed to see him, hear him, or touch him. Seeing him was out of the question; she doubted he'd leave a flashlight burning all night, even assuming he had one. Nor would he stay awake all night talking to her. Perhaps, if she just barely touched him, he'd think it was an accident and not make a big deal out of it. Stealthily she moved her right hand until the backs of her fingers just barely brushed his hairy forearm—and immediately her wrist was seized in that bruising grip again.

"Ouch!" she yelped, and his fingers loosened.

"Okay, what is it this time?" His tone showed plainly that he was at the end of his patience.

"I just wanted to touch you," Jane admitted, too tired now to care what he thought, "so I'll know I'm not alone."

He grunted. "All right. It looks like that's the only way I'm going to get any sleep." He moved his hand, sliding his rough palm against hers, and twined their fingers together. "*Now* will you go to sleep?"

"Yes," she whispered. "Thank you."

She lay there, enormously and inexplicably comforted by the touch of that hard hand, so warm and strong. Her eyes slowly closed, and she gradually relaxed. The night terrors didn't come. He kept them firmly at bay with the strong, steady clasp of his hand around hers. Everything was going to be all right. Another wave of exhaustion swept over her, and she was asleep with the suddenness of a light turning off.

Grant woke before dawn, his senses instantly alert. He knew where he was, and he knew what time it was; his uncanny sixth sense could pinpoint the time within a few minutes. The normal night sounds of the jungle told him that they were safe, that there was no other human nearby. He knew immediately the identity of the other person in the tent with him. He knew that he couldn't move, and he even knew why: Jane was asleep on top of him.

He really didn't mind being used as a bed. She was soft and warm, and there was a female smell to her that made his nostrils flare in appreciation. The softness of her breasts against him felt good. That special, unmistakable softness never left a man's mind, hovering forever in his memory once he'd felt the fullness of a woman against him. It had been a long time since he'd slept with a woman, and he'd forgotten how good it could feel. He'd had sex—finding an available woman was no problem—but those encounters had been casual, just for the sake of the physical act. Once it was finished, he hadn't been inclined to linger. This past year, especially, he'd been disinclined to tolerate anyone else's presence. He'd spent a lot of time alone, like an injured animal licking its wounds; his mind and his soul had been filled with death. He'd spent so much time in the shadows that he didn't know if he'd ever find the sunlight again, but he'd been trying. The sweet, hot Tennessee sun had healed his body, but there was still an icy darkness in his mind.

Given that, given his acute awareness of his surroundings, even in sleep, how had Jane gotten on top of him without waking him? This was the second time she'd gotten close to him without disturbing him, and he didn't like it. A year ago, she couldn't have twitched without alerting him.

She moved then, sighing a little in her sleep. One of her arms was around his neck, her face pressed into his chest, her warm breath stirring the curls of hair in the low neckline of his undershirt. She lay on him as bonelessly as a cat, her soft body conforming to the hard contours of his. Her legs were tangled with his, her hair draped across his bare shoulder and arm. His body hardened despite his almost savage irritation with himself, and slowly his arms came up to hold her, his hands sliding over her supple back. He could have her if he wanted her. The highly specialized training he'd received had taught him how to deal excruciating pain to another human being, but a side benefit to that knowledge was that he also knew how to give pleasure. He knew all the tender, sensitive places of her body, knew how to excite nerves that she probably didn't even know she had. Beyond that, he knew how to control his own responses, how to prolong a sensual encounter until his partner had been completely satisfied.

The sure knowledge that he could have her ate at him, filling his mind with images and sensations. Within ten minutes he could have her begging him for it, and he'd be inside her, clasped by those long, sleek, dancer's legs. The only thing that stopped him was the almost childlike trust with which she slept curled on top of him. She slept as if she felt utterly safe, as if he could protect her from anything. Trust. His life had been short on trust for so many years that it startled him to find someone who could trust so easily and completely. He was uncomfortable with it, but at the same time it felt good, almost as good as her body in his arms. So he lay there staring into the darkness, holding her as she slept, the bitter blackness of his thoughts contrasting with the warm, elusive sweetness of two bodies pressed together in quiet rest.

When the first faint light began to filter through the trees, he shifted his hand to her shoulder and shook her lightly. "Jane, wake up."

She muttered something unintelligible and burrowed against him, hiding her face against his neck. He shifted gently to his side, easing her onto the blanket. Her arms still hung around his neck, and she tightened her grip as if afraid of falling. "Wait! Don't go," she said urgently, and the sound of her own voice woke her. She opened her eyes, blinking owlishly at him. "Oh. Is it morning?"

"Yes, it's morning. Do you think you could let me up?"

Confused, she stared at him, then seemed to realize that she was still clinging around his neck. She dropped her arms as if scalded, and though the light was too dim for him to be certain, he thought that her cheeks darkened with a blush. "I'm sorry," she apologized.

He was free, yet oddly reluctant to leave the small enclosure of the tent. His left arm was still under her neck, pillowing her head. The need to touch her was overwhelming, guiding his hand under the fabric of her shirt, which was actually his. He flattened his hand against her bare stomach. His fingers and palm luxuriated in the warm silkiness of her skin, tantalized by the knowledge that even richer tactile pleasures waited both above and below where his hand now rested.

Jane felt her breathing hasten in rhythm, and her heartbeat

lurched from the slow, even tempo of sleep to an almost frantic pace. "Grant?" she asked hesitantly. His hand simply rested on her stomach, but she could feel her breasts tightening in anticipation, her nipples puckering. A restless ache stirred to life inside her. It was the same empty need that she'd felt when she'd stood almost naked in his arms, in the middle of the stream, and let him touch her with a raw sensuality that she'd never before experienced. She was a little afraid of that need, and a little afraid of the man who created it with his touch, who leaned over her so intently.

Her only sexual experience had been with her husband. The lack of success in that area of their marriage had severely limited what she knew, leaving her almost completely unawakened, even disinterested. Chris had given her no useful standard, for there was no comparison at all between her ex-husband—a kind, cheerful man, slender and only a few inches taller than she was—and this big, rough, muscular warrior. Chris was totally civilized; Grant wasn't civilized at all. If he took her, would he control his fearsome strength, or would he dominate her completely? Perhaps that was what frightened her most of all, because the greatest struggle of her life had been for independence: for freedom from fear, and from the overprotectiveness of her parents. She'd fought so hard and so long for control of her life that it was scary now to realize that she was totally at Grant's mercy. None of the training she'd had in self-defense was of any use against him; she had no defense at all. All she could do was trust him.

"Don't be afraid," he said evenly. "I'm not a rapist."

"I know." A killer, perhaps, but not a rapist. "I trust you," she whispered, and laid her hand against his stubbled jaw.

He gave a small, cynical laugh. "Don't trust me too much, honey. I want you pretty badly, and waking up with you in my arms is straining my good intentions to the limit." But he turned his head and pressed a quick kiss into the tender palm of the hand that caressed his cheek. "Come on, let's get moving. I feel like a sitting duck in this tent, now that it's daylight."

He heaved himself into a sitting position and reached for his boots, tugging them on and lacing them up with quick, expert movements. Jane was slower to sit up, her entire body protesting. She yawned and shoved her tangled hair back from her face, then put on her own boots. Grant had already left the tent by the time she finished, and she crawled after him. Once on her feet, she stretched her aching muscles, then touched her toes several times to limber up. While she was doing that, Grant swiftly dismantled the tent. He accomplished that in so short a time that she could only blink at him in amazement. In only a moment the tent was once more folded into an impossibly small bundle and stored in his backpack, with the thin blanket rolled up beside it.

"Any more goodies in that bottomless pack of yours?" he asked. "If not, we eat field rations."

"That yukky stuff you have?"

"That's right."

"Well, let's see. I know I don't have any more orange juice...." She opened the pack and peered into it, then thrust her hand into its depths. "Ah! Two more granola bars. Do you mind if I have the one with coconut? I'm not that crazy about raisins."

"Sure," he agreed lazily. "After all, they're yours."

She gave him an irritated glance. "They're *ours*. Wait—here's a can of..." She pulled the can out and read the label, then grinned triumphantly. "Smoked salmon! And some crackers. Please take a seat, sir, and we'll have breakfast."

He obediently sat, then took his knife from his belt and reached for the can of salmon. Jane drew it back, her brows lifted haughtily. "I'll have you know that this is a high class eating establishment. We do not open our cans with knives!"

"We don't? What do we use, our teeth?"

She lifted her chin at him and searched in the backpack again, finally extracting a can opener. "Listen," she said, giving the opener to him, "when I escape, I do it in style."

Taking the opener, he began to open the can of salmon. "So I see. How did you manage to get all of this stuff? I can just see you putting in an order with Turego, collecting what you wanted for an escape."

Jane chuckled, a rich, husky sound that made him lift his dark gold head from his task. Those piercing yellow eyes lit on her face, watching her as if examining a treasure. She was busy fishing crackers out of the backpack, so she missed the fleeting expression. "It was almost like that. I kept getting these 'cravings,' though I seldom mentioned them to Turego. I'd just have a word with the cook, and he generally came up with what I wanted. I raided the kitchen or the soldiers' quarters for a little something almost every night.''

''Like that pack?'' he queried, eyeing the object in question.

She patted it fondly. ''Nice one, isn't it?''

He didn't reply, but there was a faint crinkling at the corners of his eyes, as if he were thinking of smiling. They ate the salmon and crackers in companionable silence, with the food washed down by water from Grant's canteen. He ate his granola bar, but Jane decided to save hers for later.

Squatting beside the pack, she took her brush and restored order to her tangled mane of hair, then cleaned her face and hands with a premoistened towelette. ''Would you like one?'' she asked Grant politely, offering him one of the small packets.

He had been watching her with a stunned sort of amazement, but he took the packet from her hand and tore it open. The small, wet paper had a crisp smell to it, and he felt fresher, cooler, after cleaning his face with it. To his surprise, some of the face black he'd put on before going in after Jane had remained on his skin; he'd probably looked like a devil out of hell, with those streaks on his face.

A familiar sound caught his attention and he turned to look at Jane. A tube of toothpaste lay on the ground beside her, and she was industriously brushing her teeth. As he watched, she spat out the toothpaste, then took a small bottle and tilted it to her mouth, swishing the liquid around, then spitting it out, too. His stunned gaze identified the bottle. For five whole seconds he could only gape at her; then he sat back and began to laugh helplessly. Jane was rinsing her mouth with Perrier water.

Chapter Six

Jane pouted for a moment, but it was so good to hear him laugh that after a few seconds she sat back on her heels and simply watched him, smiling a little herself. When he laughed that harsh, scarred face became younger, even beautiful, as the shadows left his eyes. Something caught in her chest, something that hurt and made a curious melting feeling. She wanted to go over and hold him, to make sure that the shadows never touched him again. She scoffed at herself for her absurd sense of protectiveness. If anyone could take care of himself, it was Grant Sullivan. Nor would he welcome any gesture of caring; he'd probably take it as a sexual invitation.

To hide the way she felt, she put her things back into her pack, then turned to eye him questioningly. "Unless you want to use the toothpaste?" she offered.

He was still chuckling. "Thanks, honey, but I have tooth powder and I'll use the water in the canteen. God! Perrier water!"

"Well, I had to have water, but I wasn't able to snitch a canteen," she explained reasonably. "Believe me, I'd much rather have had a canteen. I had to wrap all the bottles in cloth so they wouldn't clink against each other or break."

It seemed completely logical to her, but it set him off again. He sat with his shoulders hunched and shaking, holding his head between his hands and laughing until tears streamed down his face. After he had stopped, he brushed his own teeth, but he kept making little choking noises that told Jane he was still finding the situation extremely funny. She was lighthearted, happy that she had made him laugh.

She felt her blouse and found it stiff, but dry. "You can have your shirt back," she told him, turning her back to take it off. "Thanks for the loan."

"Is yours dry?"

"Completely." She pulled his shirt off and dropped it on her backpack, and hurriedly began to put her blouse on. She had one arm in a sleeve when he swore violently. She jumped, startled, and looked over her shoulder at him.

His face was grim as he strode rapidly over to her. His expression had been bright with laughter only a moment before, but now he looked like a thundercloud. ''What happened to your arm?'' he snapped, catching her elbow and holding her bruised arm out for his inspection. ''Why didn't you tell me you'd hurt yourself?''

Jane tried to grab the blouse and hold it over her bare breasts with her free arm, feeling horribly vulnerable and exposed. She had been trying for a nonchalant manner while changing, but her fragile poise was shattered by his closeness and his utter disregard for her modesty. Her cheeks reddened, and in self-defense she looked down at her badly bruised arm.

''Stop being so modest,'' he growled irritably when she fumbled with the blouse. ''I told you, I've already seen you without any clothes.'' That was embarrassingly true, but it didn't help. She stood very still, her face burning, while he gently examined her arm.

''That's a hell of a bruise, honey. How does your arm feel?''

''It hurts, but I can use it,'' she said stiffly.

''How did it happen?''

''In a variety of ways,'' she said, trying to hide her embarrassment behind a bright manner. ''This bruise right here is where you hit me on the arm after sneaking into my bedroom and scaring me half to death. The big, multi-colored one is from falling down that bluff yesterday morning. This little interesting welt is where a limb swung back and caught me—''

''Okay, I get the idea.'' He thrust his fingers through his hair. ''I'm sorry I bruised you, but I didn't know who you were. I'd say we were more than even on that score, anyway, after that kick you gave me.''

Jane's dark chocolate eyes widened with remorse. ''I didn't mean to, not really. It was just a reflex. I'd done it before I thought. Are you okay? I mean, I didn't do any permanent damage, did I?''

A small, unwilling grin tugged at his lips as he remembered the torment of arousal he'd been enduring on her account. ''No, everything's in working order,'' he assured her. His gaze dropped to where she clutched her blouse to her chest, and his clear amber eyes darkened to a color like melted gold. "Couldn't you tell that when we were standing in the stream kissing?"

Jane looked down automatically, then jerked her gaze back up in consternation when she realized where she was looking. "Oh," she said blankly.

Grant slowly shook his head, staring at her. She was a constant paradox, an unpredictable blend of innocence and contrariness, of surprising prudery and amazing boldness. In no way was she what he'd expected. He was beginning to enjoy every moment he spent with her, but acknowledging that made him wary. It was his responsibility to get her out of Costa Rica, but he would compromise his own effectiveness if he allowed himself to become involved with her. Worrying over her could cloud his judgment. But, damn, how much could a man stand? He wanted her, and the wanting increased with every moment. In some curious way he felt lighter, happier. She certainly kept him on his toes! He was either laughing at her or contemplating beating her, but he was never bored or impatient in her company. Funny, but he couldn't remember ever laughing with a woman before. Laughter, especially during the past few years, had been in short supply in his life.

A chattering monkey caught his attention, and he looked up. The spots of sunlight darting through the shifting layers of trees reminded him that they were losing traveling time. "Get your blouse on," he said tersely, swinging away from her to sling his backpack on. He buckled it into place, then swung her pack onto his right shoulder. The rifle was slung over his left shoulder. By that time, Jane had jerked her blouse on and buttoned it up. Rather than stuffing it in her pants, she tied the tails in a knot at her waist as she had with Grant's shirt. He was already starting off through the jungle.

"Grant! Wait!" she called to his back, hurrying after him.

"You'll have to stay with me," he said unfeelingly, not slackening his pace.

Well, did he think she couldn't? Jane fumed, panting along in his path. She'd show him! And he could darn well act macho and carry both packs if he wanted; she wasn't going to offer to help! But he wasn't acting macho, she realized, and that deflated some of her indignation. He actually was that strong and indefatigable.

Compared to the harrowing day before, the hours passed quietly, without sight of another human being. She followed right on his heels, never complaining about the punishing pace he set, though the heat and humidity were even worse than the day before, if that were possible. There wasn't any hint of a breeze under the thick, smothering canopy. The air was still and heavy, steamy with an almost palpable thickness. She perspired freely, soaking her clothes and making her long for a real bath. That dousing in the stream the day before had felt refreshing, but didn't really qualify as bathing. Her nose wrinkled. She probably smelled like a goat.

Well, so what, she told herself. If she did, then so did he. In the jungle it was probably required to sweat.

They stopped about midmorning for a break, and Jane tiredly accepted the canteen from him. "Do you have any salt tablets?" she asked. "I think I need one."

"You don't need salt, honey, you need water. Drink up."

She drank, then passed the canteen back to him. "It's nearly empty. Let's pour the Perrier into it and chuck the empty bottles."

He nodded, and they were able to discard three bottles. As he got ready to start out again, Jane asked, "Why are you in such a hurry? Do you think we're being followed?"

"Not followed," he said tersely. "But they're looking for us, and the slower we move, the better chance they have of finding us."

"In this?" Jane joked, waving her hand to indicate the enclosing forest. It was difficult to see ten feet in any direction.

"We can't stay in here forever. Don't underrate Turego; he can mobilize a small army to search for us. The minute we show our faces, he'll know it."

"Something should be done about him," Jane said strongly. "Surely he's not operating with the sanction of the government?"

"No. Extortion and terrorism are his own little sidelines. We've known about him, of course, and occasionally fed him what we wanted him to know."

"We?" Jane asked casually.

His face was immediately shuttered, as cold and blank as a wall. "A figure of speech." Mentally, he swore at himself for being so careless. She was too sharp to miss anything. Before she could ask any more questions, he began walking again. He didn't want to talk about his past, about what he had been. He wanted to forget it all, even in his dreams.

About noon they stopped to eat, and this time they had to resort to the field rations. After a quick glance at what she was eating, Jane didn't look at it at all, just put it in her mouth and swallowed without allowing herself to taste it too much. It wasn't really that bad; it was just so awfully bland. They each drank a bottle of Perrier, and Jane insisted that they take another yeast pill. A roll of thunder announced the daily downpour, so Grant quickly found them shelter under a rocky outcropping. The opening was partially blocked by bushes, making it a snug little haven.

They sat watching the deluge for a few minutes; then Grant stretched out his long legs, leaning back to prop himself on his elbow. "Explain this business of how your father disinherited you as a form of protection."

Jane watched a small brown spider pick its way across the ground. "It's very simple," she said absently. "I wouldn't live with around-the-clock protection the way he wanted, so the next best thing was to remove the incentive for any kidnappers."

"That sounds a little paranoid, seeing kidnappers behind every tree."

"Yes," she agreed, still watching the spider. It finally minced into a crevice in the rock, out of sight, and she sighed. "He *is* paranoid about it, because he's afraid that next time he wouldn't get me back alive again."

"Again?" Grant asked sharply, seizing on the implication of her words. "You've been kidnapped before?"

She nodded. "When I was nine years old."

She made no other comment and he sensed that she wasn't going to elaborate, if given a choice. He wasn't going to allow her that choice. He wanted to know more about her, learn what went on in that unconventional brain. It was new to him, this overwhelming curiosity about a woman; it was almost a compulsion. Despite his relaxed position, tension had tightened his muscles. She was being very matter-of-fact about it, but instinct told him that the kidnapping had played a large part in the formation of the woman she was now. He was on the verge of discovering the hidden layers of her psyche.

"What happened?" he probed, keeping his voice casual.

"Two men kidnapped me after school, took me to an abandoned house and locked me in a closet until Dad paid the ransom."

The explanation was so brief as to be ridiculous; how could something as traumatic as a kidnapping be condensed into one sentence? She was staring at the rain now, her expression pensive and withdrawn.

Grant knew too much about the tactics of kidnappers, the means they used to force anxious relatives into paying the required ransom. Looking at her delicate profile, with the lush provocativeness of her mouth, he felt something savage well up in him at the thought that she might have been abused.

"Did they rape you?" He was no longer concerned about maintaining a casual pose. The harshness of his tone made her glance at him, vague surprise in her exotically slanted eyes.

"No, they didn't do anything like that," she assured him. "They just left me in that closet…alone. It was dark."

And to this day she was afraid of the dark, of being alone in it. So that was the basis for her fear. "Tell me about it," he urged softly.

She shrugged. "There isn't a lot more to tell. I don't know how long I was in the closet. There were no other houses close by, so no one heard me scream. The two men just left me there and went to some other location to negotiate with my parents. After awhile I became convinced that they were never coming back, that I was going to die there in that dark closet, and that no one would ever know what had happened to me."

"Your father paid the ransom?"

"Yes. Dad's not stupid, though. He knew that he wasn't likely to get me back alive if he just trusted the kidnappers, so he brought the police in on it. It's lucky he did. When the kidnappers came back for me, I overheard them making their plans. They were just going to kill me and dump my body somewhere, because I'd seen them and could identify them." She bent her head, studying the ground with great concentration, as if to somehow divorce herself from what she was telling him. "But there were police sharpshooters surrounding the house. When the two men realized that they were trapped, they decided to use me as a hostage. One of them grabbed my arm and held his pistol to my head, forcing me to walk in front of them when they left the house. They were going to take me with them, until it was safe to kill me.''

Jane shrugged, then took a deep breath. ''I didn't plan it, I swear. I don't remember if I tripped, or just fainted for a second. Anyway, I fell, and the guy had to let go of me or be jerked off balance. For a second the pistol wasn't pointed at me, and the policemen fired. They killed both men. The…the man who had held me was shot in the chest and the head, and he fell over on me. His blood splattered all over me, on my face, my hair….'' Her voice trailed away.

For a moment there was something naked in her face, the stark terror and revulsion she'd felt as a child; then, as he had seen her do when he'd rescued her from the snake, she gathered herself together. He watched as she defeated the fear, pushed the shadows away. She smoothed her expression and even managed a glint of humor in her eyes as she turned to look at him. ''Okay, it's your turn. Tell me something that happened to you.''

Once he'd felt nothing much at all; he'd accepted the chilled, shadowed brutality of his life without thought. He still didn't flinch from the memories. They were part of him, as ingrained in his flesh and blood, in his very being, as the color of his eyes and the shape of his body. But when he looked into the uncommon innocence of Jane's eyes, he knew that he couldn't brutalize her mind with even the mildest tale of the life he'd known. Somehow she had kept a part of herself as pure and crystalline as a mountain stream, a part of childhood forever unsullied. Nothing that had happened to her had touched the inner woman, except to increase the courage and gallantry that he'd seen twice now in her determined efforts to pull herself together and face forward again.

''I don't have anything to tell,'' he said mildly.

''Oh, sure!'' she hooted, shifting herself on the ground until she was sitting facing him, her legs folded in a boneless sort of knot that made him blink. She rested her chin in her palm and surveyed him, so big and controlled and capable. If this man had led a normal life, she'd eat her boots, she told herself, then quickly glanced down at the boots in question. Right now they had something green and squishy on them. Yuk. They'd have to be cleaned before even a goat would eat them. She returned her dark gaze to Grant and studied him with the seriousness of a scientist bent over a microscope. His scarred face was hard, a study of planes and angles, of bronzed skin pulled tautly over the fierce sculpture of his bones. His eyes were those of an eagle, or a lion; she couldn't quite decide which. The clear amber color was brighter, paler, than topaz, almost like a yellow diamond, and like an eagle's, the eyes saw everything. They were guarded, expressionless; they hid an almost unbearable burden of experience and weary cynicism.

"Are you an agent?" she asked, probing curiously. Somehow, in those few moments, she had discarded the idea that he was a mercenary. Same field she thought, but a different division.

His mouth quirked. "No."

"Okay, let's try it from another angle. *Were* you an agent?"

"What sort of agent?"

"Stop evading my questions! The cloak-and-dagger sort of agent. You know, the men in overcoats who have forty sets of identification."

"No. Your imagination is running wild. I'm too easily identifiable to be any good undercover."

That was true. He stood out like a warrior at a tea party. Something went quiet within her, and she knew. "Are you retired?"

He was quiet for so long that she thought he wasn't going to answer her. He seemed to be thinking of something else entirely. Then he said flatly, "Yeah, I'm retired. For a year now."

His set, blank face hurt her, on the inside. "You were a... weapon, weren't you?"

There was a terrible clarity in his eyes as he slowly shifted his gaze to her. "Yes," he said harshly. "I was a weapon."

They had aimed him, fired him, and watched him destroy. He would be matchless, she realized. Before she'd even known him, when she'd seen him gliding into her darkened bedroom like a shadow, she'd realized how lethal he could be. And there was something else, something she could see now. He had retired himself, turned his back and walked away from that grim, shadowed life. Certainly his superiors wouldn't have wanted to lose his talents.

She reached out and placed her hand on his, her fingers slim and soft, curling around the awesome strength of his. Her hand was much smaller made with a delicacy that he could crush with a careless movement of his fingers, but implicit in her touch was the trust that he wouldn't turn that strength against her. A deep breath swelled the muscled planes of his chest. He wanted to take her right then, in the dirt. He wanted to stretch her out and pull her clothes off, bury himself in her. He wanted more of her touch, all of her touch, inside and out. But the need for her satiny female flesh was a compulsion that he couldn't satisfy with a quick possession, and there wasn't time for more. The rain was slowing and would stop entirely at any moment. There was a vague feeling marching up and down his spine that told him they couldn't afford to linger any longer.

But it was time she knew. He removed his hand from hers, lifting it to cup her chin. His thumb rubbed lightly over her lips. "Soon," he said, his voice guttural with need, "you're going to lie down for me. Before I take you back to your daddy, I'm going to have you, and the way I feel now, I figure it's going to take a long time before I'm finished with you."

Jane sat frozen, her eyes those of a startled woodland animal. She couldn't even protest, because the harsh desire in his voice flooded her mind and her skin with memories. The day before, standing in the stream, he'd kissed her and touched her with such raw sexuality that, for the first time in her life, she'd felt the coiling, writhing tension of desire in herself. For the first time she'd wanted a man, and she'd been shocked by the unfamiliarity of her own body. Now he was doing it to her again, but this time he was using words. He'd stated his intentions bluntly, and images began forming in her mind of the two of them lying twined together, of his naked, magnificent body surging against her.

He watched the shifting expressions that flitted across her face. She looked surprised, even a little shocked, but she wasn't angry. He'd have understood anger, or even amusement; that blank astonishment puzzled him. It was as if no man had ever told her that he wanted her. Well, she'd get used to the idea.

The rain had stopped, and he picked up the packs and the rifle, settling them on his shoulders. Jane followed him without a word when he stepped out from beneath the rocky outcropping into the already increasing heat. Steam rose in wavering clouds from the forest floor, immediately wrapping them in a stifling, humid blanket.

She was silent for the rest of the afternoon, lost in her thoughts. He stopped at a stream, much smaller than the one they'd seen the day before, and glanced at her. "Care for a bath? You can't soak, but you can splash."

Her eyes lit up, and for the first time that afternoon a smile danced on her full lips. He didn't need an answer to know how she felt about the idea. Grinning, he searched out a small bar of soap from his pack and held it out to her. "I'll keep watch, then you can do the same for me. I'll be up there."

Jane looked up the steep bank that he'd indicated. That was the best vantage point around; he'd have a clear view of the stream and the surrounding area. She started to ask if he was going to watch her, too, but bit back the question. As he'd already pointed out, it was too late for modesty. Besides, she felt infinitely safer knowing that he'd be close by.

He went up the bank as sure-footedly as a cat, and Jane turned to face the stream. It was only about seven feet wide, and wasn't much more than ankle-deep. Still, it looked like heaven. She hunted her lone change of underwear out of her pack, then sat down to pull off her boots. Glancing nervously over her shoulder to where Grant sat, she saw that he was in profile to her, but she knew that he would keep her in his peripheral vision. She resolutely undid her pants and stepped out of them. Nothing was going to keep her from having her bath...except maybe another snake, or a jaguar, she amended.

Naked, she gingerly picked her way over the stony bottom to a large flat rock and sat down in the few inches of water. It was deliciously cool, having run down from a higher altitude, but even tepid water would have felt good on her over-heated skin. She splashed it on her face and head until her hair was soaked. Gradually she felt the sweaty stickiness leave her hair, until the strands were once more silky beneath her fingers. Then she took the small bar of soap out from under her leg, where she'd put it for safekeeping, and rubbed it over her body. The small luxury made her feel like a new woman, and a sense of peace crept into her. It was only a simple pleasure, to bathe in a clear, cool stream, but added to it was her sense of nakedness, of being totally without restrictions. She knew that he was there, knew that he was watching her, and felt her breasts grow tight.

What would it be like if he came down from that bank and splashed into the water with her? If he took the blanket from his pack and laid her down on it? She closed her eyes, shivering in reaction, thinking of his hard body pressing down on her, thrusting into her. It had been so many years, and the few experiences she'd had with Chris hadn't taught her that she could be a creature of wanting, but with Grant she wasn't the same woman.

Her heart beat heavily in her breast as she rinsed herself by cupping water in her palms and pouring it over her. Standing up, she twisted the water out of her hair, then waded out. She was trembling as she pulled on her clean underwear, then dressed distastefully in her stained pants and shirt. "I'm finished," she called, lacing up her boots.

He appeared soundlessly beside her. "Sit in the same place where I sat," he instructed, placing the rifle in her hands. "Do you know how to use this?"

The weapon was heavy, but her slim hands looked capable as she handled it. "Yes. I'm a fairly good shot." A wry smile curved her lips. "With paper targets and clay pigeons, anyway."

"That's good enough." He began unbuttoning his shirt, and she stood there in a daze, her eyes on his hands. He paused. "Are you going to guard me from down here?"

She blushed. "No. Sorry." Quickly she turned and scrambled up the bank, then took a seat in the exact spot where he'd sat. She could see both banks, but at the same time there was a fair amount of cover that she could use if the need arose. He'd probably picked this out as the best vantage point without even thinking about it, just automatically sifting through the choices and arriving at the correct one. He might be retired, but his training was ingrained.

A movement, a flash of bronze, detected out of the corner of her eye, told her that he was wading into the stream. She shifted her gaze a fraction so she wouldn't be able to see him at all, but just the knowledge that he was as naked as she had been kept her heart pounding erratically. She swallowed, then licked her lips, forcing herself to concentrate on the surrounding jungle, but the compulsion to look at him continued.

She heard splashing and pictured him standing there like a savage, bare and completely at home.

She closed her eyes, but the image remained before her. Slowly, totally unable to control herself, she opened her eyes and turned her head to look at him. It was only a small movement, a fraction of an inch, until she was able to see him, but that wasn't enough. Stolen glances weren't enough. She wanted to study every inch of him, drink in the sight of his powerful body. Shifting around, she looked fully at him, and froze. He was beautiful, so beautiful that she forgot to breathe. Without being handsome, he had the raw power and grace of a predator, all the terrible beauty of a hunter. He was bronzed all over, his tan a deep, even brown. Unlike her, he didn't keep his back turned in case she looked; he had a complete disregard for modesty. He was taking a bath; she could look or not look, as she wished.

His skin was sleek and shiny with water, and the droplets caught in the hair on his chest glittered like captured diamonds. His body hair was dark, despite the sun-streaked blondness of his head. It shadowed his chest, ran in a thin line down his flat, muscled stomach, and bloomed again at the juncture of his legs. His legs were as solid as tree trunks, long and roped with muscle; every movement he made set off ripples beneath his skin. It was like watching a painting by one of the old masters come to life.

He soaped himself all over, then squatted in the water to rinse in the same manner she had, cupping his palms to scoop up the water. When he was rinsed clean, he stood and looked up at her, probably to check on her, and met her gaze head on. Jane couldn't look away, couldn't pretend that she hadn't been staring at him with an almost painful appreciation. He stood very still in the stream, watching her as she watched him, letting her take in every detail of his body. Under her searching gaze, his body began to stir, harden, growing to full, heavy arousal.

"Jane," he said softly, but still she heard him. She was so attuned to him, so painfully sensitive to every move and sound he made, that she would have heard him if he'd whispered. "Do you want to come down here?"

Yes. Oh, God, yes, more than she'd ever wanted anything. But she was still a little afraid of her own feelings, so she held back. This was a part of herself that she didn't know, wasn't certain she could control.

"I can't," she replied, just as softly. "Not yet."

"Then turn around, honey, while you still have a choice."

She quivered, almost unable to make the required movement, but at last her muscles responded and she turned away from him, listening as he waded out of the water. In less than a minute he appeared noiselessly at her side and took the rifle from her hands. He had both packs with him. Typically, he made no further comment on what had just happened. ''We'll get away from the water and set up camp. It'll be night pretty soon.''

Night. Long hours in the dark tent, lying next to him. Jane followed him, and when he stopped she helped him do the work they had done the night before, setting up the tent and hiding it. She didn't protest at the cold field rations, but ate without really tasting anything. Soon she was crawling into the tent and taking off her boots, waiting for him to join her.

When he did, they lay quietly side by side, watching as the remaining light dimmed, then abruptly vanished.

Tension hummed through her, making her muscles tight. The darkness pressed in on her, an unseen monster that sucked her breath away. No list of compulsive questions leaped to her lips tonight; she felt oddly timid, and it had been years since she'd allowed herself to be timid about anything. She no longer knew herself.

''Are you afraid of me?'' he asked, his voice gentle.

Just the sound of his voice enabled her to relax a little. ''No,'' she whispered.

''Then come here and let me keep the dark away from you.''

She felt his hand on her arm, urging her closer, then she was enfolded in arms so strong that nothing could ever make her afraid while they held her. He cradled her against his side, tucking her head into the hollow of his shoulder. With a touch so light that it could have been the brush of a butterfly's wings, he kissed the top of her head. ''Good night, honey,'' he whispered.

''Good night,'' she said in return.

Long after he was asleep, Jane lay in his arms with her eyes open, though she could see nothing. Her heart was pounding in her chest with a slow, heavy rhythm, and her insides felt jittery. It wasn't fear that kept her awake, but a churning emotion that shifted everything inside her. She knew exactly what was wrong with her. For the first time in too many years, everything was right with her.

She'd learned to live her life with a shortage of trust. No matter that she'd learned to enjoy herself and her freedom; there had always been that residual caution that kept her from letting a man get too close. Until now she'd never been strongly enough attracted to a man for the attraction to conquer the caution.... Until now. Until Grant. And now the attraction had become something much stronger. The truth stunned her, yet she had to accept it: she loved him. She hadn't expected it, though for two days she had felt it tugging at her. He was harsh and controlled, badtempered, and his sense of humor was severely underdeveloped, but he had gently washed the snake's blood from her, held her hand during the night, and had gone out of his way to make their trek easier for her. He wanted her, but he hadn't taken her because she wasn't ready. She was afraid of the dark, so he held her in his arms. Loving him was at once the easiest and most difficult thing she'd ever done.

Chapter Seven

Once again he awoke to find her cuddled on top of him, but this time it didn't bother him that he had slept peacefully through the night. Sliding his hands up her back, he accepted that his normally keen instincts weren't alarmed by her because there was absolutely no danger in her except perhaps the danger of her driving him crazy. She managed to do that with every little sway of her behind. Reveling in the touch of her all along his body, he moved his hands down, feeling her slenderness, the small ribs, the delicate spine, the enticing little hollow at the small of her back, then the full, soft mounds of her buttocks. He cupped his palms over them, kneading her with his fingers. She muttered and shifted against him, brushing at a lock of hair that had fallen into her face. Her eyelashes fluttered, then closed completely once more.

He smiled, enjoying the way she woke up. She did it by slow degrees, moaning and grousing while still more asleep than awake, frowning and pouting, and moving against him as if trying to sink herself deeper into him so she wouldn't have to wake up at all. Then her eyes opened, and she blinked several times, and as quickly as that the pout faded from her lips and she gave him a slow smile that would have melted stone.

"Good morning," she said, and yawned. She stretched, then abruptly froze in place. Her head came up, and she stared at him in stupefaction. "I'm on top of you," she said blankly.

"Again," he confirmed.

"Again?"

"You slept on top of me the night before last, too. Evidently my holding you while you sleep isn't enough; you think you have to hold me down."

She slithered off him, sitting up in the tent and straightening her twisted, wrinkled clothing. Color burned in her face. "I'm sorry. I know it can't have been very comfortable for you."

"Don't apologize. I've enjoyed it," he drawled. "If you really want to make it up to me, though, we'll reverse positions to-night.''

Her breath caught and she stared at him in the dim light, her eyes soft and melting. Yes. Everything in her agreed. She wanted to belong to him; she wanted to know everything about his body and let him know everything about hers. She wanted to tell him, but she didn't know how to put it into words. A crooked smile crossed his face; then he sat up and reached for his boots, thrusting his feet into them and lacing them up. Evidently he took her silence for a refusal, because he dropped the subject and began the task of breaking camp.

''We have enough food for one more meal,'' he said as they finished eating. ''Then I'll have to start hunting.''

She didn't like that idea. Hunting meant that he'd leave her alone for long stretches of time. ''I don't mind a vegetarian diet,'' she said hopefully.

''Maybe it won't come to that. We've been gradually working our way out of the mountains, and unless I miss my guess we're close to the edge of the forest. We'll probably see fields and roads today. But we're going to avoid people until I'm certain it's safe, okay?''

She nodded in agreement.

Just as he'd predicted, at midmorning they came abruptly to the end of the jungle. They stood high on a steep cliff, and stretched out below them was a valley with cultivated fields, a small network of roads, and a cozy village situated at the southern end. Jane blinked at the suddenly brilliant sunlight. It was like stepping out of one century into another. The valley looked neat and prosperous, reminding her that Costa Rica was the most highly developed country in Central America, despite the thick tangle of virgin rain forest at her back.

''Oh,'' she breathed. ''Wouldn't it be nice to sleep in a bed again?''

He grunted an absent reply, his narrowed eyes sweeping the valley for any sign of abnormal activity. Jane stood beside him, waiting for him to make his decision.

It was made for them. Abruptly he grabbed her arm and jerked her back into the sheltering foliage, dragging her to the ground behind a huge bush just as a helicopter suddenly roared over their heads. It was flying close to the ground, following the tree line; she had only a glimpse of it before it was gone, hidden by the trees. It was a gunship, and had camouflage paint.

"Did you see any markings?" she asked sharply, her nails digging into his skin.

"No. There weren't any." He rubbed his stubbled jaw. "There's no way of telling who it belonged to, but we can't take any chances. Now we know that we can't just walk across the valley. We'll work our way down, and try to find more cover."

If anything, the terrain was even more difficult now. They were at the edge of a volcanic mountain range, and the land had been carved with a violent hand. It seemed to be either straight up, or straight down. Their pace was agonizingly slow as they worked their way down rocky bluffs and up steep gorges. When they stopped to eat, they had covered less than one-fourth the length of the valley, and Jane's legs ached as they hadn't since the wild run through the jungle the first day.

Right on schedule, just as they finished eating, they heard the boom of thunder. Grant looked around for shelter, considering every outcropping of rock. Then he pointed. "I think that's a cave up there. If it is we'll be in high cotton."

"What?" Jane asked, frowning.

"Sitting pretty," he explained. "Luxurious accommodations, in comparison to what we've had."

"Unless it's already occupied."

"That's why you're going to wait down here while I check it out." He moved up the fern covered wall of the gorge, using bushes and vines and any other toehold he could find. The gorge itself was narrow and steep, enclosing them on all four sides. Its shape gave a curious clarity to the calls of the innumerable birds that flitted among the trees like living Christmas decorations, all decked out in their iridescent plumage. Directly overhead was a streak of sky, but it consisted of rolling black clouds instead of the clear blue that she'd seen only moments before.

Grant reached the cave, then immediately turned and waved to her. "Come on up; it's clear! Can you make it?"

"Have I failed yet?" she quipped, starting the climb, but she'd had to force the humor. The desolation had been growing in her since they'd seen the valley. Knowing that they were so close to civilization made her realize that their time together was limited. While they had been in the forest, the only two people locked in a more primitive time, she'd had no sense of time running out. Now she couldn't ignore the fact that soon, in a few days or less, their time together would end. She felt as if she'd already wasted so much time, as if the golden sand had been trickling through her fingers and she'd only just realized what she held. She felt panic-stricken at the thought of discovering love only to lose it, because there wasn't enough time to let it grow.

He reached his hand down and caught hers, effortlessly lifting her the last few feet. "Make yourself comfortable; we could be here a while. This looks like the granddaddy of all storms."

Jane surveyed their shelter. It wasn't really a cave; it was little more than an indentation in the face of the rock, about eight feet deep. It had a steeply slanting ceiling that soared to ten or eleven feet at the opening of the cave, but was only about five feet high at the back. The floor was rocky, and one big rock, as large as a love seat and shaped like a peanut, lay close to the mouth of the cave. But it was dry, and because of its shallowness it wasn't dark, so Jane wasn't inclined to find fault with it.

Given Grant's eerie sense of timing, she wasn't surprised to hear the first enormous raindrops begin filtering through the trees just as he spread out the tarp at the back of the cave. He placed it behind the big rock, using its bulk to shelter them. She sat down on the tarp and drew her legs up, wrapping her arms around them and resting her chin on her knees, listening to the sound of the rain as it increased in volume.

Soon it was a din and the solid sheets of water that obscured their vision heightened the impression that they were under a waterfall. She could hear the crack of lightning, feel the earth beneath her shake from the enormous claps of thunder. It was dark now, as the rain blotted out what light came through the thick canopy. She could barely see Grant, who was standing just inside the mouth of the cave with his shoulder propped against the wall, occasionally puffing on a cigarette.

Chills raced over her body as the rain cooled the air. Hugging her legs even tighter for warmth, Jane stared through the dimness at the broad, powerful shoulders outlined against the gray curtain of rain. He wasn't an easy man to get to know. His personality was as shadowy as the jungle, yet just the sight of that muscular back made her feel safe and protected. She knew that he stood between her and any danger. He had already risked his life for her on more than one occasion, and was as matter-of-fact about it as if being shot at were an everyday occurrence. Perhaps it was for him, but Jane didn't take it so lightly.

He finished his cigarette and field-stripped it. Jane doubted that anyone would track them here through the rain, but it was second nature to him to be cautious. He went back to his calm perusal of the storm, standing guard while she rested.

Something shifted inside her and coiled painfully in her chest. He was so alone. He was a hard, lonely man, but everything about him drew her like a magnet, pulling at her heart and body.

Her eyes clouded as she watched him. When this was over he'd walk away from her as if these days in the jungle had never existed. This was all routine for him. What she could have of him, all that she could ever have of him, was the present, too few days before this was over. And that just wasn't enough.

She was cold now, chilled to her bones. The unceasing, impenetrable curtain of rain carried a damp coldness with it, and her own spirits chilled her from the inside. Instinctively, like a sinuous cat seeking heat, she uncoiled from the tarp and went up to him, gravitating to his certain warmth and comfort. Silently she slid her arms around his taut waist and pressed her face into the marvelous heat of his chest. Glancing down at her, he lifted an eyebrow in mild inquiry. "I'm cold," she muttered, leaning her head on him and staring pensively at the rain.

He looped his arm around her shoulder, holding her closer to him and sharing his warmth with her. A shiver ran over her; he rubbed his free hand up her bare arm, feeling the coolness of her skin. Of its own accord his hand continued upward, stroking her satiny jaw, smoothing the dark tangle of hair away from her face. She was in a melancholy mood, this funny little cat, staring at the rain as if it would never stop, her eyes shadowed and that full, passionate mouth sad.

Cupping her chin in his hand, he tilted her face up so he could study her quiet expression. A small smile curved the corners of his hard mouth. "What's wrong, honey? Rain making you feel blue?" Before she could answer, he bent his head and kissed her, using his own cure.

Jane's hands went to his shoulders, clinging to him for support. His mouth was hard and demanding and oh so sweet. The taste of him, the feel of him, was just what she wanted. Her teeth parted, allowing the slow probing of his tongue. Deep inside her, fire began to curl, and she curled too, twining against him in an unconscious movement that he read immediately.

Lifting his mouth from hers just a little, he muttered, "Honey, this feels like an offer to me."

Her dark eyes were a little dazed as she looked up at him. "I think it is," she whispered.

He dropped his arms to her waist and wrapped them around her, lifting her off her feet, bringing her level with him. She wound her arms around his neck and kissed him fervently, lost in the taste and feel of his mouth, not even aware he'd moved until he set her down to stand on the tarp. The dimness at the back of the cave hid any expression that was in his eyes, but she could feel his intent amber gaze on her as he began calmly unbuttoning her shirt. Jane's mouth went dry, but her own shaking fingers moved to his chest and began opening his shirt in turn.

When both garments were hanging open, he shrugged out of his and tossed it on the tarp, never taking his eyes from her. Tugging his undershirt free of his pants, he caught the bottom of it and peeled it off over his head. He tossed it aside, too, completely baring his broad, hairy chest. As it had the day before, the sight of his half-naked body mesmerized her. Her chest hurt; breathing was incredibly difficult. Then his hard, hot fingers were inside her shirt, on her breasts, molding them to fit his palms. The contrast of his heated hands on her cool skin made her gasp in shocked pleasure. Closing her eyes, she leaned into his hands, rubbing her nipples against his calloused palms. His chest lifted on a deep, shuddering breath.

She could feel the sexual tension emanating from him in waves. Like no other man she'd known, he made her acutely aware of his sexuality, and equally aware of her own body and its uses. Between her legs, an empty throb began to torment her, and she instinctively pressed her thighs together in an effort to ease the ache.

As slight as it was, he felt her movement. One of his hands left her breast and drifted downward, over her stomach and hips to her tightly clenched thighs. "That won't help," he murmured. "You'll have to open your legs, not close them." His fingers rubbed insistently at her and pleasure exploded along her nerves. A low moan escaped from her lips; then she swayed toward him. She felt her legs parting, allowing him access to her tender body.

He explored her through her pants, creating such shock waves of physical pleasure that her knees finally buckled and she fell against him, her bare breasts flattening against the raspy, hair-covered expanse of his chest.

Quickly he set her down on the tarp and knelt over her, unzipping her pants and pulling them down her legs, his hands rough and urgent. He had to pause to remove her boots, but in only moments she was naked except for the shirt that still hung around her shoulders. The damp air made her shiver, and she reached for him. "I'm cold," she complained softly. "Get me warm."

She offered herself to him so openly and honestly that he wanted to thrust into her immediately, but he also wanted more. He'd had her nearly naked in his arms before. In the stream, that wisp of wet silk had offered no protection, but he hadn't had the time to explore her as he'd wanted. Her body was still a mystery to him; he wanted to touch every inch of her, taste her and enjoy the varying textures of her skin.

Jane's eyes were wide and shadowed as he knelt over her, holding himself away from her outstretched arms. "Not just yet, honey," he said in a low, gravelly voice. "Let me look at you first." Gently he caught her wrists and pressed them down to the tarp above her head, making her round, pretty breasts arch as if they begged for his mouth. Anchoring her wrists with one hand, he slid his free hand to those tempting, gently quivering mounds.

A small, gasping sound escaped from Jane's throat. Why was he holding her hands like that? It made her feel incredibly helpless and exposed, spread out for his delectation, yet she also felt unutterably safe. She could sense him savoring her with his eyes, watching intently as her nipples puckered in response to the rasp of his fingertips. He was so close to her that she could feel the heat of his body, smell the hot, musky maleness of his skin. She arched, trying to turn her body into that warmth and scent, but he forced her flat again.

Then his mouth was on her, sliding up the slope of her breast and closing hotly on her nipple. He sucked strongly at her, making waves of burning pleasure sweep from her breast to her loins. Jane whimpered, then bit her lip to hold back the sound. She hadn't known, had never realized, what a man's mouth on her breasts could do to her. She was on fire, her skin burning with an acute sensitivity that was both ecstatic and unbearable. She squirmed, clenching her legs together, trying to control the ache that threatened to master her.

His mouth went to her other breast, the rasp of his tongue on her nipple intensifying an already unbearable sensation. He swept his hand down to her thighs, his touch demanding that she open herself to him. Her muscles slowly relaxed for him, and he spread her legs gently. His fingers combed through the dark curls that had so enticed him before, making her body jerk in anticipation; then he covered her with his palm and thoroughly explored the soft, vulnerable flesh between her legs. Beneath his touch, Jane began to tremble wildly. "Grant," she moaned, her voice a shaking, helpless plea.

"Easy," he soothed, blowing his warm breath across her flesh. He wanted her so badly that he felt he would explode, but at the same time he couldn't get enough of touching her, of watching her arch higher and higher as he aroused her. He was drunk on her flesh, and still trying to satiate himself. He took her nipple in his mouth and began sucking again, wringing another cry from her.

Between her legs a finger suddenly penetrated, searching out the depths of her readiness, and shock waves battered her body. Something went wild inside her, and she could no longer hold her body still. It writhed and bucked against his hand, and his mouth was turning her breasts into pure flame. Then his thumb brushed insistently over her straining, aching flesh, and she exploded in his arms, blind with the colossal upheaval of her senses, crying out unconsciously. Nothing had ever prepared her for this, for the total, mind-shattering pleasure of her own body.

When it was over, she lay sprawled limply on the tarp. He undid his pants and shoved them off, his eyes glittering and wild. Jane's eyes slowly opened and she stared up at him dazedly. Grasping her legs, he lifted them high and spread them; then he braced himself over her and slowly sank his flesh into hers.

Jane's hands clenched on the tarp, and she bit her lips to keep from crying out as her body was inexorably stretched and filled. He paused, his big body shuddering, allowing her the time to accept him. Then suddenly it was she who couldn't bear any distance at all between them, and she surged upward, taking all of him, reaching up her arms to pull him close.

She never noticed the tears that ran in silvered streaks down her temples, but Grant gently wiped them away with his rough thumbs. Supporting his weight on his arms, sliding his entire body over her in a subtle caress, he began moving with slow, measured strokes. He was so close to the edge that he could feel the feathery sensation along his spine, but he wanted to make it last. He wanted to entice her again to that satisfying explosion, watch her go crazy in his arms.

"Are you all right?" he asked in a raw, husky tone, catching another tear with his tongue as it left the corner of her eye. If he were hurting her, he wouldn't prolong the loving, though he felt it would tear him apart to stop.

"Yes, I'm fine," she breathed, stroking her hands up the moving, surging muscles of his back. Fine... What a word for the wild magnificence of belonging to him. She'd never dreamed it could feel like this. It was as if she'd found a half of herself that she hadn't even known was missing. She'd never dreamed that *she* could feel like this. Her fingers clutched mindlessly at his back as his long, slow movements began to heat her body.

He felt her response and fiercely buried his mouth against the sensitive little hollow between her throat and collarbone, biting her just enough to let her feel his teeth, then licking where he'd bitten. She whimpered, that soft, uncontrollable little sound that drove him crazy, and he lost control. He began driving into her with increasing power, pulling her legs higher around him so he could have more of her, all of her, deeper and harder, hearing her little cries and going still crazier. There was no longer any sense of time, or of danger, only the feel of the woman beneath him and around him. While he was in her arms he could no longer feel the dark, icy edges of the shadows in his mind and soul.

In the aftermath, like that after a storm of unbelievable violence, they lay in exhausted silence, each reluctant to speak for fear it would shatter the fragile peace. His massive shoulders crushed her, making it difficult for her to breathe, but she would gladly have spent the rest of her life lying there. Her fingers slowly stroked the sweat-darkened gold of his hair, threading through the heavy, live silk. Their bodies were reluctant to leave each other, too. He hadn't withdrawn from her; instead, after easing his weight down onto her, he'd nestled closer and now seemed to be lightly dozing.

Perhaps it had happened too quickly between them, but she couldn't regret it. She was fiercely happy that she'd given herself to him. She'd never been in love before, never wanted to explore the physical mysteries of a man and a woman. She'd even convinced herself that she just wasn't a physical person, and had decided to enjoy her solitary life. Now her entire concept of herself had been changed, and it was as if she'd discovered a treasure within herself. After the kidnapping she had withdrawn from people, except for the trusted precious few who she had loved before: her parents, Chris, a couple of other friends. And even though she had married Chris, she had remained essentially alone, emotionally withdrawn. Perhaps that was why their marriage had failed, because she hadn't been willing to let him come close enough to be a real husband. Oh, they had been physically intimate, but she had been unresponsive, and eventually he had stopped bothering her. That was exactly what it had been for her: a bother. Chris had deserved better. He was her best friend, but only a friend, not a lover. He was much better off with the warm, responsive, adoring woman he'd married after their divorce.

She was too honest with herself to even pretend that any blame for their failed marriage belonged to Chris. It had been entirely her fault, and she knew it. She'd thought it was a lack in herself. Now she realized that she did have the warm, passionate instincts of a woman in love—because she was in love for the first time. She hadn't been able to respond to Chris, simply because she hadn't loved him as a woman should love the man she marries.

She was twenty-nine. She wasn't going to pretend to a shyness she didn't feel for the sake of appearance. She loved the man who lay in her arms, and she was going to enjoy to the fullest whatever time she had with him. She hoped to have a lifetime; but if fate weren't that kind, she would not let timidity cheat her out of one minute of the time they did have. Her life had been almost snuffed out twenty years ago, before it had really begun. She knew that life and time were too precious to waste.

Perhaps it didn't mean to Grant what it did to her, to be able to hold and love like this. She knew intuitively that his life had been much harder than hers, that he'd seen things that had changed him, that had stolen the laughter from his eyes. His experiences had hardened him, had left him extraordinarily cautious. But even if he were only taking the shallowest form of comfort from her, that of sexual release, she loved him enough to give him whatever he needed from her, without question. Jane loved as she did everything else, completely and courageously.

He stirred, lifting his weight onto his forearms and staring down at her. His golden eyes were shadowed, but there was something in them that made her heart beat faster, for he was looking at her the way a man looks at the woman who belongs to him. "I've got to be too heavy for you."

"Yes, but I don't care." Jane tightened her arms about his neck and tried to pull him back down, but his strength was so much greater than hers that she couldn't budge him.

He gave her a swift, hard kiss. "It's stopped raining. We have to go."

"Why can't we stay the night here? Aren't we safe?"

He didn't answer, just gently disengaged their bodies and sat up, reaching for his clothes, and that was answer enough. She sighed, but sat up to reach for her own clothes. The sigh became a wince as she became aware of the various aches she'd acquired by making love on the ground.

She could have sworn that he wasn't looking at her, but his awareness of his surroundings was awesome. His head jerked around, and a slight frown pulled his dark brows together. "Did I hurt you?" he asked abruptly.

"No, I'm all right." He didn't look convinced by her reassurance. When they descended the steep slope to the floor of the gorge, he kept himself positioned directly in front of her. He carried her down the last twenty feet, hoisting her over his shoulder despite her startled, then indignant, protests.

It was a waste of time for her to protest, though; he simply ignored her. When he put her down silently and started walking, she had no choice but to follow.

Twice that afternoon they heard a helicopter, and both times he pulled her into the thickest cover, waiting until the sound had completely faded away before emerging. The grim line of his mouth told her that he didn't consider it just a coincidence. They were being hunted, and only the dense cover of the forest kept them from being caught. Jane's nerves twisted at the thought of leaving that cover; she wasn't afraid for just herself now, but for Grant, too. He put himself in jeopardy just by being with her. Turego wanted her alive, but Grant was of no use to him at all.

If it came to a choice between Grant's life and giving Turego what he wanted, Jane knew that she would give in. She'd have to take her chances with Turego, though it would be impossible now to catch him off guard the way she had the first time. He knew now that she wasn't a rich man's flirtatious, charming plaything. She'd made a fool of him, and he wouldn't forget.

Grant stepped over a large fallen tree and turned back to catch her around the waist and lift her over it with that effortless strength of his. Pausing, he pushed her tangled hair back from her face, his touch surprisingly gentle. She knew how lethal those hands could be. "You're too quiet," he muttered. "It makes me think you're up to something, and that makes me nervous."

"I was just thinking," she defended herself.

"That's what I was afraid of."

"If Turego catches us..."

"He won't," Grant said flatly. Staring down at her, he saw more now than just an appealing, sloe-eyed woman. He knew her now, knew her courage and strength, her secret fears and her sunny nature. He also knew her temper, which could flare or fade in an instant. Sabin's advice had been to kill her quickly rather than let Turego get his hands on her; Grant had seen enough death to accept that as a realistic option at the time. But that was before he had known her, tasted her and felt the silky texture of her skin, watched her go wild beneath him. Things had changed now. He had changed—in ways that he neither welcomed nor trusted, but had to acknowledge. Jane had become important to him. He couldn't allow that, but for the time being he had to accept it. Until she was safe, she could be his, but no longer. There wasn't any room in his life for permanency, for roots, because he still wasn't certain that he'd ever live in the sunshine again. Like Sabin, he'd been in the shadows too long. There were still dark spots on his soul that were revealed in the lack of emotion in his eyes. There was still the terrible, calm acceptance of things that were too terrible to be accepted.

If things had gone as originally planned, they would have gotten on that helicopter and she would be safely home by now. He would never have really known her; he would have delivered her to her father and walked away. But instead, they had been forced to spend days with only each other for company. They had slept side by side, eaten together, shared moments of danger and of humor. Perhaps the laughter was the more intimate, to him; he'd known danger many times with many people, but humor was rare in his life. She had made him laugh, and in doing so had captured a part of him.

Damn her for being the woman she was, for being lively and good-natured and desirable, when he'd expected a spoiled, sulky bitch. Damn her for making men want her, for making *him* want her. For the first time in his life he felt a savage jealousy swelling in his heart. He knew that he would have to leave her, but until then he wanted her to be his and only his. Remembering the feel of her body under his, he knew that he would have to have her again. His golden eyes narrowed at the feeling of intense possessiveness that gripped him. An expression of controlled violence crossed his face, an expression that the people who knew him had learned to avoid provoking. Grant Sullivan was dangerous enough in the normal way of things; angered, he was deadly. She was his now, and her life was being threatened. He'd lost too much already; his youth, his laughter, his trust in others, even part of his own humanity. He couldn't afford to lose anything else. He was a desperate man trying to recapture his soul. He needed to find again even a small part of the boy from Georgia who had walked barefoot in the warm dirt of plowed fields, who had learned survival in the mysterious depths of the great swamp. What Vietnam had begun, the years of working in intelligence and operations had almost completed, coming close to destroying him as a man.

Jane and her screwball brand of gallantry were the source of the only warmth he'd felt in years.

He reached out and caught her by the nape of her neck, his strong fingers halting her. Surprised, she turned an inquiring glance at him, and the small smile that had begun forming on her lips faded at the fierce expression he couldn't hide.

"Grant? Is something wrong?"

Without thinking, he used the grip he had on her neck to pull her to him, and kissed her full lips, still faintly swollen from the lovemaking they'd shared in the cave. He took his time about it, kissing her with slow, deep movements of his tongue. With a small sound of pleasure she wound her arms around his neck and lifted herself on tiptoe to press more fully against him. He felt the soft juncture of her thighs and ground himself against her, his body jolting with desire at the way she automatically adjusted herself to his hardness.

She was his, as she'd never belonged to any other man.

Her safety hinged on how swiftly he could get her out of the country, for he sensed Turego closing in on them. That man would never give up, not while the microfilm was still missing. There was no way in hell, Grant vowed, that he would allow Turego ever to touch Jane again. Lifting his mouth from hers, he muttered in a harsh tone, "You're mine now. I'll take care of you."

Jane rested her head against his chest. "I know," she whispered.

Chapter Eight

That night changed forever the way Jane thought of the darkness. The fear of being alone in the dark would probably always remain with her, but when Grant reached out for her, it stopped being an enemy to be held at bay. It became instead a warm blanket of safety that wrapped around them, isolating them from the world. She felt his hands on her and forgot about the night.

He kissed her until she was clinging to him, begging him wordlessly for release from the need he'd created in her. Then he gently stripped her and himself, then rolled to his back, lifting her astride him. "I hurt you this morning," he said, his voice low and rough. "You control it this time; take only as much as you're comfortable with."

Comfort didn't matter; making love with him was a primitive glory, and she couldn't place any limits on it. She lost control, moving wildly on him, and her uninhibited delight snapped the thin thread of control he was trying to maintain. He made a rough sound deep in his throat and clasped her to him, rolling once again until she was beneath him. The wildly soaring pleasure they gave each other wiped her mind clear of everything but him and the love that swelled inside of her. There was no darkness. With his passion, with the driving need of his body, he took her out of the darkness. When she fell asleep in his arms, it was without once having thought of the impenetrable darkness that surrounded them.

The next morning, as always, she awoke slowly, moving and murmuring to herself, snuggling against the wonderfully warm, hard body beneath her, knowing even in her sleep that it was Grant's. His hands moved down her back to cup and knead her buttocks, awakening her fully. Then he shifted gently onto his side, holding her in his arms and depositing her on her back. Her eyes fluttered open, but it was still dark, so she closed them again and turned to press her face against his neck.

"It's almost dawn, honey," he said against her hair, but he

couldn't force himself to stop touching her, to sit up and put on his clothing. His hands slipped over her bare, silky skin, discovering anew all the places he'd touched and kissed during the night. Her response still overwhelmed him. She was so open and generous, wanting him and offering herself with a simplicity that took his breath away.

She groaned, and he eased her into a sitting position, then reached out to unzip the flap of the tent and let in a faint glimmer of light. "Are you awake?"

"No," she grumbled, leaning against him and yawning.

"We have to go."

"I know." Muttering something under her breath, she found what she presumed to be her shirt and began trying to untangle it. There was too much cloth, so she stopped in frustration and handed it to him. "I think this is yours. It's too big to be mine."

He took the shirt, and Jane scrambled around until she found her own under the blanket they'd been lying on. "Can't you steal a truck or something?" she asked, not wanting even to think about another day of walking.

He didn't laugh, but she could almost feel the way the corners of his lips twitched. "That's against the law, you know."

"Stop laughing at me! You've had a lot of specialized training, haven't you? Don't you know how to hot-wire an ignition?"

He sighed. "I guess I can hot-wire anything we'd be likely to find, but stealing a vehicle would be like advertising our position to Turego."

"How far can we be from Limon? Surely we could get there before Turego would be able to search every village between here and there?"

"It'd be too risky, honey. Our safest bet is still to cut across to the east coast swamps, then work our way down the coast. We can't be tracked in the swamp." He paused. "I'll have to go into the village for food but you're going to stay hidden in the trees."

Jane drew back. "Like hell."

"Damn it, don't you realize that it's too dangerous for you to show your face?"

"What about *your* face? At least I have dark hair and eyes like everyone else. Don't forget, that soldier saw you, and your pilot friend no doubt told them all about you, so they know we're together. That long blond mane of yours is pretty unusual around here.''

He ran his hand through his shaggy hair, faintly surprised at how long it was. ''It can't be helped.''

She folded her arms stubbornly. ''You're not going anywhere without me.''

Silence lay between them for a moment. She was beginning to think she'd won a surprisingly easy victory when he spoke, and the even, almost mild tone of his voice made chills go up her spine, because it was the most implacable voice she'd ever heard. ''You'll do what I say, or I'll tie and gag you and leave you here in the tent.''

Now it was her turn to fall silent. The intimacy that had been forged between them had made her forget that he was a warrior first, and her lover second. Despite the gentle passion with which he made love to her, he was still the same man who had knocked her out and thrown her over his shoulder, carrying her away into the jungle. She hadn't held a grudge against him for that, after the reception she'd given him, but this was something else entirely. She felt as if he were forcibly reminding her of the original basis of their relationship, making her acknowledge that their physical intimacy had not made her an equal in his eyes. It was as if he'd used her body, since she had so willingly offered it, but saw no reason to let that give her any influence over him.

Jane turned away from him, fumbling with her shirt and finally getting it straight. She wouldn't let him see any hint of hurt in her eyes; she'd known that the love she felt was completely one-sided.

His hand shot out and pulled the shirt away from her. Startled, she looked at him. ''I have to get dressed. You said we need to—''

''I know what I said,'' he growled, easing her down onto the blanket. The lure of her soft body, the knowledge that he'd hurt her and her characteristic chin-up attempt to keep him from seeing it, all made it impossible for him to remember the importance of moving on. The core of ice deep inside his chest kept him from whispering to her how much she meant to him. The remoteness bred into him by years of living on the edge of death hadn't yet been overcome; perhaps it never would be. It was still vital to him to keep some small significant part of himself sealed away, aloof and cold. Still, he couldn't let her draw away from him with that carefully blank expression on her face. She was his, and it was time she came to terms with the fact.

Putting his hands on her thighs, he spread them apart and mounted her. Jane caught her breath, her hands going up to grab at his back. He slowly pushed into her, filling her with a powerful movement that had her body arching on the blanket.

He went deep inside her, holding her tightly to him. Her inner tightness made him almost groan aloud as wild shivers of pleasure ran up his spine. Shoving his hand into her hair, he turned her head until her mouth was under his, then kissed her with a violence that only hinted at the inferno inside him. She responded to him immediately. Her mouth molded to his and her body rose to meet his thrusts in increasingly ecstatic undulations. He wanted to immerse himself in her, go deeper and deeper until they were bonded together, their flesh fused. He held her beneath him, their bodies locked together in total intimacy. He reveled in the waves of intensifying pleasure that made them clutch at each other, straining together in an effort to reach the peak of their passion. When he was inside her, he no longer felt the need to isolate himself. She was taking a part of him that he hadn't meant to offer, but he couldn't stop it. It was as if he'd gotten on a roller coaster and there was no way to get off until it reached the end of the line. He'd just have to go along for the ride, and he meant to wring every moment of pleasure he could from the short time that he had her all to himself.

Jane clung to his shoulders, driven out of her senses by the pounding of his body. He seemed to have lost all control; he was wild, almost violent, his flesh so heated that his skin burned her palms. She was caught up in the depth of his passion, writhing against him and begging for more. Then, abruptly, her pleasure crested, and he ground his mouth against hers to catch her mindless cries. Her hot flare of ecstasy caught him in its explosion, and he began shuddering as the final shock waves jolted through his body. Now it was she who held him, and when it was over he collapsed on her, his eyes closed and his chest heaving, his body glistening with sweat.

Her fingers gently touched the shaggy, dark gold threads of his hair, pushing them away from his forehead. She didn't know what had triggered his sudden, violent possession, but it didn't matter. What mattered was that, despite everything, he needed her in a basic way that he didn't welcome, but couldn't deny. That wasn't what she wanted, but it was a start. Slowly she trailed her hand down his back, feeling the powerful muscles that lay under his supple bronzed skin. The muscles twitched then relaxed under her touch, and he grew heavier as the tension left him.

"Now we *really* have to go," he murmured against her breast.

"Ummm." She didn't want to stir; her limbs were heavy, totally relaxed. She could happily have lain there for the rest of the day, dozing with him and waking to make love again. She knew that the peace wouldn't last; in a moment he stirred and eased their bodies apart.

They dressed in silence, except for the rustling of their clothing, until she began lacing her boots on her feet. He reached out and tilted her chin then, his thumb rubbing over her bottom lip. "Promise me," he demanded, making her look at him. "Tell me that you're going to do what I say, without an argument. Don't make me tie you up."

Was he asking for obedience, or trust? Jane hesitated, then went with her instincts. "All right," she whispered. "I promise."

His pupils dilated, and his thumb probed at the corner of her lips. "I'll take care of you," he said, and it was more than a promise.

They took down the tent; then Jane got out the meager supply of remaining food. She emptied the last of the Perrier into his canteen, disposed of the bottles, and broke in two the granola bar that she'd been saving. That and a small can of grapefruit was their breakfast, and the last of their food.

The morning was almost gone, and the heat and humidity had risen to almost unbearable levels, when Grant stopped and looked around. He wiped his forehead on his sleeve. "We're almost even with the village. Stay here, and I'll be back in an hour or so."

"How long is 'or so'?" she asked politely, but the sound of her teeth snapping together made him grin.

"Until I get back." He took the pistol out of its holster and extended it to her. "I take it you know how to use this, too?"

Jane took the weapon from his hand, a grim expression on her mouth. "Yes. After I was kidnapped, Dad insisted that I learn how to protect myself. That included a course in firearms, as well as self-defense classes.'' Her slim hand handled the gun with respect, and reluctant expertise. ''I've never seen one quite like this. What is it?''

''A Bren 10 millimeter,'' he grunted.

Her eyebrows lifted. ''Isn't it still considered experimental?''

He shrugged. ''By some people. I've used it for a while; it does what I want.'' He watched her for a moment, then a frown drew his brows together. ''Could you use it, if you had to?''

''I don't know.'' A smile wobbled on her mouth. ''Let's hope it doesn't come to that.''

He touched her hair, hoping fervently that she never had to find the answer to his question. He didn't want anything ever to dim the gaiety of her smile. Bending, he kissed her roughly, thoroughly, then without a word blended into the forest in that silent, unnerving way of his. Jane stared at the gun in her hand for a long moment, then walked over to a fallen tree and carefully inspected it for animal life before sitting down.

She couldn't relax. Her nerves were jumpy, and though she didn't jerk around at every raucous bird call or chattering monkey, or even the alarming rustles in the underbrush, her senses were acutely, painfully attuned to the noises. She had become used to having Grant close by, his mere presence making her feel protected. Without him, she felt vulnerable and more alone than she had ever felt before.

Fear ate at her, but it was fear for Grant, not herself. She had walked into this with her eyes open, accepting the danger as the price to be paid, but Grant was involved solely because of her. If anything happened to him, she knew she wouldn't be able to bear it, and she was afraid. How could he expect to walk calmly into a small village and not be noticed. Everything about him drew attention, from his stature to his shaggy blond hair and those wild, golden eyes. She *knew* how single-mindedly Turego would search for her, and since Grant had been seen with her, his life was on the line now just as much as hers.

By now Turego must know that she had the microfilm. He'd be both furious and desperate; furious because she'd played him for a fool, and desperate because she could destroy his government career. Jane twisted her fingers together, her dark eyes intent. She thought of destroying the microfilm, to ensure that it would never fall into the hands of Turego or any hostile group or government—but she didn't know what was on it, only that it was supremely important. She didn't want to destroy information that her own country might need. Not only that, but she might need it as a negotiating tool. George had taught her well, steeped her in his cautious, quicksilver tactics, the tactics that had made him so shadowy that few people had known of his existence. If she had her back to the wall, she would use every advantage she had, do whatever she had to—but she hoped it wouldn't come to that kind of desperation. The best scenario would be that Grant would be able to smuggle her out of the country. Once she was safe in the States, she'd make contact and turn the microfilm over to the people who should have it. Then she could concentrate on chasing Grant until he realized that he couldn't live without her. The worst scenario she could imagine would be for something to happen to Grant. Everything in her shied away even from the thought.

He'd been hurt too much already. He was a rough, hardened warrior, but he bore scars, invisible ones inside as well as the ones that scored his body. He'd retired, trying to pull himself away, but the wasteland mirrored in his eyes told her that he still lived partially in the shadows, where sunlight and warmth couldn't penetrate.

A fierce protectiveness welled up inside her. She was strong; she'd already lived through so much, overcome a childhood horror that could have crippled her emotionally. She hadn't allowed that to clip her wings, had learned instead to soar even higher, reveling in her freedom. But she wasn't strong enough to survive a world without Grant. She had to know that he was alive and well, or there would be no more sunshine for her. If anyone dared harm him…

Perspiration curled the hair at her temples and trickled between her breasts. Sighing, she wondered how long she had been waiting. She wiped her face and twisted her hair into a knot on top of her head to relieve herself of its hot weight on the back of her neck. It was so hot! The air was steamy, lying on her skin like a wet, warm blanket, making it difficult to breathe. It had to rain soon; it was nearing the time of day when the storms usually came.

She watched a line of ants for a time, then tried to amuse herself by counting the different types of birds that flitted and chirped in the leafy terraces above her head. The jungle teemed with life, and she'd come to learn that, with caution, it was safe to walk through it—not that she wanted to try it without Grant. The knowledge and the experience were his. But she was no longer certain that death awaited her behind every bush. The animal life that flourished in the green depths was generally shy, and skittered away from the approach of man. It was true that the most dangerous animal in the jungle was man himself.

Well over an hour had passed, and a sense of unease was prickling her spine. She sat very still, her green and black clothing mingling well with the surrounding foliage, her senses alert.

She saw nothing, heard nothing out of the ordinary, but the prickling sensation along her spine increased. Jane sat still for a moment longer, then gave in to the screaming of her instincts. Danger was near, very near. Slowly she moved, taking care not to rustle even a leaf, and crawled behind the shelter of the fallen tree's roots. They were draped in vines and bushes that had sprung to life already, feeding off the death of the great plant. The heaviness of the pistol she held reminded her that Grant had had a reason for leaving it with her.

A flash of movement caught her attention, but she turned only her eyes to study it. It was several long seconds before she saw it again, a bit of tanned skin and a green shape that was not plant or animal, but a cap. The man was moving slowly, cautiously, making little noise. He carried a rifle, and he was headed in the general direction of the village.

Jane's heart thudded in her breast. Grant could well meet him face to face, but Grant might be surprised, while this man, this guerrilla, was expecting to find him. Jane didn't doubt that normally Grant would be the victor, but if he were overtaken from behind he could be shot before he had a chance to act.

The distinctive beating of helicopter blades assaulted the air, still distant, but signaling the intensified search. Jane waited while the noise of the helicopter faded, hoping that its presence had alerted Grant. Surely it had; he was far too wary not to be on guard. For that, if nothing else, she was grateful for the presence of the helicopters.

She had to find Grant before he came face to face with one of the guerrillas and before they found her. This lone man wouldn't be the only one searching for her.

She had learned a lot from Grant these past few days, absorbing the silent manner in which he walked, his instinctive use of the best shelter available. She slid into the jungle, moving slowly, keeping low, and always staying behind and to the side of the silent stalker. Terror fluttered in her chest, almost choking her, but she reminded herself that she had no choice.

A thorny vine caught her hair, jerking it painfully, and tears sprang to her eyes as she bit her lip to stifle a reflexive cry of pain. Trembling, she freed her hair from the vine. Oh, God, where was Grant? Had he been caught already?

Her knees trembled so badly that she could no longer walk at a crouch. She sank to her hands and knees and began crawling, as Grant had taught her, keeping the thickest foliage between herself and the man, awkwardly clutching the pistol in her hand as she moved.

Thunder rumbled in the distance, signaling the approach of the daily rains. She both dreaded and prayed for the rain. It would drown out all sound and reduce visibility to a few feet, increasing her chances for escape—but it would also make it almost impossible for Grant to find her.

A faint crackle in the brush behind her alerted her, but she whirled a split second too late. Before she could bring the pistol around, the man was upon her, knocking the gun from her grip and twisting her arm up behind her, then pushing her face into the ground. She gasped, her breath almost cut off by the pressure of his knee on her back. The moist, decaying vegetation that littered the forest floor was ground into her mouth. Twisting her head to one side, Jane spat out the dirt. She tried to wrench her arm free; he cursed and twisted her arm higher behind her back, wringing an involuntary cry of pain from her.

Someone shouted in the distance, and the man answered, but Jane's ears were roaring and she couldn't understand what they said. Then he roughly searched her, slapping his free hand over her body and making her face turn red with fury. When he was satisfied that she carried no other weapons, he released her arm and flipped her onto her back.

She started to surge to her feet, but he swung his rifle around so close that the long, glinting barrel was only a few inches from her face. She glanced at it, then lifted her eyes to glare at her captor. Perhaps she could catch him off guard. "Who are you?" she demanded in a good imitation of a furious, insulted woman, and swatted the barrel away as if it were an insect. His flat, dark eyes briefly registered surprise, then wariness. Jane scrambled to her feet and thrust her face up close to his, letting him see her narrowed, angry eyes. Using all the Spanish she knew, she proceeded to tell him what she thought of him. For good measure she added all the ethnic invective she'd learned in college, silently wondering at the meaning of everything she was calling the soldier, who looked more stunned by the moment.

She poked him repeatedly in the chest with her finger, advancing toward him, and he actually fell back a few paces. Then the other soldier, the one she'd spotted before, joined them, and the man pulled himself together.

"Be quiet!" he shouted.

"I won't be quiet!" Jane shouted in return, but the other soldier grabbed her arms and tied her wrists. Incensed, Jane kicked out behind her, catching him on the shin with her boot. He gave a startled cry of pain, then whirled her around and drew his fist back, but at the last moment stayed his blow. Turego probably had given orders that she wasn't to be hurt, at least until he'd gotten the information he wanted from her.

Shaking her tangled hair away from her eyes, Jane glared at her captors. "What do you want? Who are you?"

They ignored her, and pushed her roughly ahead of them. With her arms tied behind her, her balance was off, and she stumbled over a tangled vine. She couldn't catch herself, and pitched forward with a small cry. Instinctively one of the soldiers grabbed for her. Trying to make it look accidental, she flung out one of her legs and tangled it through his, sending him crashing into a bush. She landed with a jolt on a knotted root, which momentarily stunned her and made her ears ring.

He came out of nowhere. One moment he wasn't there; the next he was in the midst of them. Three quick blows with the side of his hand to the first soldier's face and neck had the man crumpling like a broken doll. The soldier who Jane had tripped yelled and tried to swing his rifle around, but Grant lashed out with his boot, catching the man on the chin. There was a sickening thud; the man's head jerked back, and he went limp.

Grant wasn't even breathing hard, but his face was set and coldly furious as he hauled Jane to her feet and roughly turned her around. His knife sliced easily through the bonds around her wrists. "Why didn't you stay where I left you?" he grated. "If I hadn't heard you yelling—"

She didn't want to think about that. "I did stay," she protested. "Until those two almost walked over me. I was trying to hide, and to find you before you ran straight into them!"

He gave her an impatient glance. "I would've handled them." He grabbed her wrist and began dragging her after him. Jane started to defend herself, then sighed. Since he so obviously *had* handled them, what could she say? She concentrated instead on keeping her feet under her and dodging the limbs and thorny vines that swung at her.

"Where are we going?"

"Be quiet."

There was a loud crack, and Grant knocked her to the ground, covering her with his body. Winded, at first Jane thought that the thunder of the approaching storm had startled him; then her heart convulsed in her chest as she realized what the noise had been. Someone was shooting at them! The two soldiers hadn't been the only ones nearby. Her eyes widened to dark pools; they were shooting at Grant, not at her! They would have orders to take her alive. Panic tightened her throat, and she clutched at him.

"Grant! Are you all right?"

"Yeah," he grunted, slipping his right arm around her and crawling with her behind the shelter of a large mahogany tree, dragging her like a predator carrying off its prey. "What happened to the Bren?"

"He knocked it out of my hand...over there." She waved her hand to indicate the general area where she'd lost the gun. Grant glanced around, measuring the shelter available to him and swearing as he decided it was too much of a risk.

"I'm sorry," Jane said, her dark eyes full of guilt.

"Forget it." He unslung the rifle from his shoulder, his motions sure and swift as he handled the weapon. Jane hugged the ground, watching as he darted a quick look around the huge tree trunk. There was a glitter in his amber eyes that made her feel a little in awe of him; at this moment he was the quintessential warrior, superbly trained and toned, coolly assessing the situation and determining what steps to take.

Another shot zinged through the trees, sending bark flying only inches from Grant's face. He jerked back, then swiped at a thin line of blood that trickled down from his cheekbone, where a splinter had caught him.

"Stay low," he ordered, his tone flat and hard. "Crawl on

your belly through those bushes right behind us, and keep going no matter what. We've got to get out of here."

She'd gone white at the sight of the blood ribboning down his face, but she didn't say anything. Controlling the shaking of her legs and arms, she got down on her stomach and obeyed, snaking her way into the emergent shrubs. She could feel him right behind her, directing her with his hand on her leg. He was deliberately keeping himself between her and the direction from which the shots had come, and the realization made her heart squeeze painfully.

Thunder rumbled, so close now that the earth shuddered from the shock waves. Grant glanced up. "Come on, rain," he muttered. "Come on."

It began a few minutes later, filtering through the leaves with a dripping sound, then rapidly intensifying to the thunderous deluge that she'd come to expect. They were soaked to the skin immediately, as if they'd been tossed into a waterfall. Grant shoved her ahead of him, heedless now of any noise they made, because the roar of the rain obliterated everything else. They covered about a hundred yards on their hands and knees, then he pulled her upright and brought his mouth close to her ear. "Run!" he yelled, barely making himself heard over the din of the pummeling rain.

Jane didn't know how she could run but she did. Her legs were trembling, she was dizzy and disoriented, but somehow her feet moved as Grant pulled her through the forest at breakneck speed. Her vision was blurred; she could see only a confused jumble of green, and the rain, always the rain. She had no idea where they were going, but trusted Grant's instincts to guide them.

Suddenly they broke free of the jungle's edge, where man had cut back the foliage in an attempt to bring civilization to a small part of the tropical rain forest. Staggering across fields turned into a quagmire by the rain, Jane was held upright only by Grant's unbreakable grip on her wrist. She fell to her knees once and he dragged her for a few feet before he noticed. Without a word he scooped her up and tossed her over his shoulder, carrying her as effortlessly as ever, showing no trace of the exhaustion she felt.

She closed her eyes and hung on, already dizzy and now becoming nauseated as her stomach was jolted by his hard shoulder. Their surroundings had become a nightmare of endless gray water slapping at them, wrapping them in a curtain that obliterated sight and sound. Terror lay in her stomach in a cold, soggy lump, triggered by the sight of the blood on Grant's face. She couldn't bear it if anything happened to him, she simply couldn't....

He lifted her from his shoulder, propping her against something hard and cold. Jane's fingers spread against the support, and dimly she recognized the texture of metal. Then he wrenched open the door of the ancient pickup truck and picked her up to thrust her into the shelter of the cab. With a lithe twist of his body he slid under the wheel, then slammed the door.

"Jane," he bit out, grabbing her shoulder in a tight grip and shaking her. "Are you all right? Are you hit?"

She was sobbing, but her eyes were dry. She stretched out a trembling hand to touch the red streak that ran down his rain-wet face. "You're hurt," she whispered; he couldn't hear her over the thunder of the rain pounding on the metal top of the old truck, but he read her lips and gathered her in his arms, pressing hard, swift kisses to her dripping hair.

"It's just a scratch, honey," he reassured her. "What about you? Are you okay?"

She managed a nod, clinging to him, feeling the incredible warmth of his body despite the soggy condition of his clothes. He held her for a moment, then pulled her arms from around his neck and put her on the other side of the truck. "Sit tight while I get this thing going. We've got to get out of here before the rain stops and everyone comes out."

He bent down and reached under the dash of the truck, pulling some wires loose.

"What are you doing?" Jane asked numbly.

"Hot-wiring this old crate," he replied, and gave her a quick grin. "Pay close attention, since you've been so insistent that I do this. You may want to steal a truck someday."

"You can't see to drive in this," she said, still in that helpless, numb tone of voice, so unlike her usual cheerful matter-of-fact manner. A frown drew his brows together, but he couldn't stop to cradle her in his arms and reassure her that everything was going to be all right. He wasn't too sure of that himself; all hell had broken loose, reminding him how much he disliked being shot at—and now Jane was a target as well. He hated this whole set-up so much that a certain deadly look had come into his eyes, the look that had become legend in the jungles and rice paddies of Southeast Asia.

"I can see well enough to get us out of here."

He put two wires together, and the engine coughed and turned over, but didn't start. Swearing under his breath, he tried it again, and the second time the engine caught. He put the old truck in gear and let up on the clutch. They lurched into motion with the old vehicle groaning and protesting. The rain on the windshield was so heavy that the feeble wipers were almost useless, but Grant seemed to know where he was going.

Looking around, Jane saw a surprisingly large number of buildings through the rain, and several streets seemed to branch away from the one they were on. The village was a prosperous one, with most of the trappings of civilization, and it looked somehow incongruous existing so close to the jungle.

"Where are we going?" she asked.

"South, honey. To Limon, or at least as far as this crate will carry us down the road."

Chapter Nine

Limon. The name sounded like heaven, and as she clung to the tattered seat of the old truck, the city seemed just as far away. Her dark eyes were wide and vulnerable as she stared at the streaming windshield, trying to see the road. Grant gave her a quick look, all he could safely spare when driving took so much of his attention. Keeping his voice calm, he said, "Jane, scoot as far into the corner as you can. Get your head away from the back window. Do you understand?"

"Yes." She obeyed, shrinking into the corner. The old truck had a small window in back and smaller windows on each side, leaving deep pockets of protection in the corners. A broken spring dug into the back of her leg, making her shift her weight. The upholstery on this side of the seat was almost nonexistent, consisting mostly of miscellaneous pieces of cloth covering some of the springs. Grant was sitting on a grimy patch of burlap. Looking down, she saw a large hole in the floorboard beside the door.

"This thing has character," she commented, regaining a small portion of her composure.

"Yeah, all of it bad." The truck skewed sideways on a sea of mud, and Grant gave all his attention to steering the thing in a straight line again.

"How can you tell where we're going?"

"I can't. I'm guessing." A devilish grin twisted his lips, a sign of the adrenaline that was racing through his system. It was a physical high, an acute sensitivity brought on by pitting his wits and his skills against the enemy. If it hadn't been for the danger to Jane, he might even have enjoyed this game of cat and mouse. He risked another quick glance at her, relaxing a little as he saw that she was calmer now, gathering herself together and mastering her fear. The fear was still there, but she was in control.

"You'd better be a good guesser," she gasped as the truck

lurched sickeningly to the side. "If you drive us off a cliff, I swear I'll never forgive you!"

He grinned again and shifted his weight uncomfortably. He leaned forward over the wheel. "Can you get these packs off? They're in the way. And keep down!"

She slithered across the seat and unbuckled the backpacks, pulling them away from him so he could lean back. How could she have forgotten her pack? Stricken that she'd been so utterly reckless with it, she drew the buckles through the belt loops of her pants and fastened the straps.

He wasn't paying any attention to her now, but was frowning at the dash. He rapped at a gauge with his knuckle. "Damn it!"

Jane groaned. "Don't tell me. We're almost out of gas!"

"I don't know. The damned gauge doesn't work. We could have a full tank, or it could quit on us at any time."

She looked around. The rain wasn't as torrential as it had been, though it was still heavy. The forest pressed closely on both sides of the road, and the village was out of sight behind them. The road wasn't paved, and the truck kept jouncing over the uneven surface, forcing her to cling to the seat to stay in it—but it was a road and the truck was still running along it. Even if it quit that minute, they were still better off than they had been only a short while before. At least they weren't being shot at now. With any luck Turego would think they were still afoot and continue searching close by, at least for a while. Every moment was precious now, putting distance between them and their pursuers.

Half an hour later the rain stopped, and the temperature immediately began to climb. Jane rolled down the window on her side of the truck, searching for any coolness she could find. "Does this thing have a radio?" she asked.

He snorted. "What do you want to listen to, the top forty? No, it doesn't have a radio."

"There's no need to get snippy," she sniffed.

Grant wondered if he'd ever been accused of being "snippy" before. He'd been called a lot of things, but never that; Jane had a unique way of looking at things. If they *had* met up with a jaguar, she probably would have called it a "nice kitty"! The familiar urge rose in him, making him want to either throttle her or make love to her. His somber expression lightened as he considered which would give him the most pleasure.

The truck brushed against a bush that was encroaching on the narrow road. Jane ducked barely in time to avoid being slapped in the face by the branches that sprang through the open window, showering them with the raindrops that had been clinging to the leaves.

"Roll that window up," he ordered, concern making his voice sharp. Jane obeyed and sat back in the corner again. Already she could feel perspiration beading on her face, and she wiped her sleeve across her forehead. Her hand touched her hair, and she pushed the heavy mass away from her face, appalled at the tangled ringlets she found. What she wouldn't give for a bath! A real bath, with hot water and soap and shampoo, not a rinsing in a rocky stream. And clean clothes! She thought of the hairbrush in her pack, but she didn't have the energy to reach for it right now.

Well, there was no sense in wasting her time wishing for something she couldn't have. There were more important issues at hand. "Did you get any food?"

"In my pack."

She grabbed the pack and opened it, pulling out a towel-wrapped bundle of bread and cheese. That was all there was, but she wasn't in the mood to quibble about the limited menu. Food was food. Right now, even field rations would have been good.

Leaning over, she took his knife from his belt and swiftly sliced the bread and cheese. In less than a minute, she'd made two thick cheese sandwiches and returned the knife to its sheath. "Can you hold the sandwich and drive, or do you want me to feed you?"

"I can manage." It was awkward, wrestling with the steering wheel and holding the sandwich at the same time, but she would have to slide closer to him to feed him, and that would expose her head in the back window. The road behind them was still empty, but he wasn't going to take any chances with her welfare.

"I could lie down with my head in your lap and feed you," she suggested softly, and her dark eyes were sleepy and tender.

He jerked slightly, his entire body tensing. "Honey, if you put your head in my lap, I might drive this crate up a tree. You'd better stay where you are."

Was it only yesterday that he'd taken her so completely in that cave? He'd made her his, possessed her and changed her, until she found it difficult to remember what it had been like before she'd known him. The focus of her entire life had shifted, redirected itself onto him.

What she was feeling was plainly revealed in her eyes, in her expressive face. A quick glance at her had him swallowing to relieve an abruptly dry throat, and his hands clenched on the wheel. He wanted her, immediately; he wanted to stop the truck and pull her astride him, then bury himself in her inner heat. The taste and scent of her lingered in his mind, and his body still felt the silk of her skin beneath his. Perhaps he wouldn't be able to get enough of her to satisfy him in the short time they had remaining, but he was going to try, and the trying would probably drive him crazy with pleasure.

They wolfed down the sandwiches, then Jane passed him the canteen. The Perrier was flat, but it was still wet, and he gulped it thirstily. When he gave the canteen back to her, she found herself gulping, too, in an effort to replenish the moisture her body was losing in perspiration. It was so hot in the truck! Somehow, even trekking through the jungle hadn't seemed this hot, though there hadn't been even a hint of breeze beneath the canopy. The metal shell of the truck made her feel canned, like a boiled shrimp. She forced herself to stop drinking before she emptied the canteen, and capped it again.

Ten minutes later the truck began sputtering and coughing; then the engine stopped altogether, and Grant coasted to a stop, as far to one side of the narrow road as he could get. "It lasted almost two hours," he said, opening the door and getting out.

Jane scrambled across the truck and got out on his side, since he'd parked so close to the edge that her door was blocked by a tree. "How far do you think we got?"

"Thirty miles or so." He wound a lock of her hair around his forefinger and smiled down at her. "Feel up to a walk?"

"A nice afternoon stroll? Sure, why not?"

He lowered his head and took a hard kiss from her mouth. Before she could respond he'd drawn away and pushed her off the road and into the shelter of the forest again. He returned to the truck, and she looked back to see him obliterating their footprints; then he leaped easily up the low bank and came to her side. "There's another village down the road a few more miles; I hoped we'd make it so we could buy more gas, but—" He broke off and shrugged at the change of plans. "We'll follow the road and try to get to the village by nightfall, unless they get too close to us. If they do, we'll have to go back into the interior.''

''We're not going to the swamp?''

''We can't,'' he explained gently. ''There's too much open ground to cover, now that they know we're in the area.''

A bleak expression came and went in her eyes so fast that he wasn't certain he'd seen it. ''It's my fault. If I'd just hidden from them, instead of trying to find you...''

''It's done. Don't worry about it. We just have to adjust our plans, and the plan now is to get to Limon as fast as we can, any way we can.''

''You're going to steal another truck?''

''I'll do whatever has to be done.''

Yes, he would. That knowledge was what made her feel so safe with him; he was infinitely capable, in many different areas. Even wearily following him through the overgrown tangle of greenery made her happy, because she was with him. She didn't let herself think of the fact that they would soon part, that he'd casually kiss her goodbye and walk away, as if she were nothing more than another job finished. She'd deal with that when it happened; she wasn't going to borrow trouble. She had to devote her energies now to getting out of Costa Rica, or at least to some trustworthy authorities, where Grant wouldn't be in danger of being shot while trying to protect her. When she'd seen the blood on his face, some vital part inside of her had frozen knowing that she couldn't survive if anything happened to him. Even though she'd been able to see that he wasn't badly hurt, the realization of his vulnerability had frightened her. As strong as he was, as vital and dangerous, he was a man, and therefore mortal.

They heard only one vehicle on the road, and it was moving toward the village where they'd stolen the truck. The sun edged downward, and the dim light in the forest began to fade. Right before the darkness became total, they came to the edge of a field, and down the road about half a mile they could see the other village spread out. It was really more of a small town than a village; there were bright electric lights, and cars and trucks were parked on the streets. After days spent in the jungle, it looked like a booming metropolis, a cornerstone of civilization.

''We'll stay here until it's completely dark, then go into town,'' Grant decided, dropping to the ground and stretching out flat on his back. Jane stared at the twinkling lights of the town, torn between a vague uneasiness and an eagerness to take advantage of the comforts a town offered. She wanted a bath, and to sleep in a bed, but after so much time spent alone with Grant, the thought of once more being surrounded by other people made her wary. She couldn't relax the way Grant did, so she remained on her feet, her face tense and her hands clenched.

"You might as well rest, instead of twitching like a nervous cat."

"I am nervous. Are we going on to Limon tonight?"

"Depends on what we find when we get into town."

She glared down at him in sudden irritation. He was a master at avoiding straight answers. It was so dark that she couldn't make out his features; he was only a black form on the ground, but she was certain that he was aware of her anger, and that the corner of his mouth was turning up in that almost-smile of his. She was too tired to find much humor in it, though, so she walked away from him a few paces and sat down, leaning her head on her drawn-up knees and closing her eyes.

There wasn't even a whisper of sound to warn her, but suddenly he was behind her, his strong hands massaging the tight muscles of her shoulders and neck. "Would you like to sleep in a real bed tonight?" he murmured in her ear.

"And take a real bath. And eat real food. Yes, I'd like that," she said, unaware of how wistful her tone was.

"A town this size probably has a hotel of some sort, but we can't risk going there, not looking the way we do. I'll try to find someone who takes in boarders and won't ask many questions."

Taking her hand, he pulled her to her feet and draped his arm over her shoulder. "Let's go, then. A bed sounds good to me, too."

Walking across the field, ever closer to the beckoning lights, Jane became more conscious of how she looked, and she pushed her fingers through her tangled hair. She knew that her clothes were filthy, and that her face was probably dirty. "No one is going to let us in," she predicted.

"Money has a way of making people look past the dirt."

She glanced up at him in surprise. "You have money?"

"A good Boy Scout is always prepared."

In the distance, the peculiarly mournful wail of a train whistle floated into the air, reinforcing the fact that they'd left the isolation of the rain forest behind. Oddly, Jane felt almost nakedly vulnerable, and she moved closer to Grant. "This is stupid, but I'm scared," she whispered.

"It's just a mild form of culture shock. You'll feel better when you're in a tub of hot water."

They kept to the fringes of the town, in the shadows. It appeared to be a bustling little community. Some of the streets were paved, and the main thoroughfare was lined with prosperous looking stores. People walked and laughed and chatted, and from somewhere came the unmistakable sound of a jukebox, another element of civilization that jarred her nerves. The universally-known red and white sign of a soft drink swung over a sidewalk, making her feel as if she had emerged from a time warp. This was definitely culture shock.

Keeping her pushed behind him, Grant stopped and carried on a quiet conversation with a rheumy-eyed old man who seemed reluctant to be bothered. Finally Grant thanked him and walked away, still keeping a firm grip on Jane's arm. "His sister-in-law's first cousin's daughter takes in boarders," he told her, and Jane swallowed a gasp of laughter.

"Do you know where his sister-in-law's first cousin's daughter lives?"

"Sure. Down this street, turn left, then right, follow the alley until it dead ends in a courtyard."

"If you say so."

Of course he found the boarding house easily, and Jane leaned against the white adobe wall that surrounded the courtyard while he rang the bell and talked with the small, plump woman who answered the door. She seemed reluctant to admit such exceedingly grimy guests. Grant passed her a wad of bills and explained that he and his wife had been doing field research for an American pharmaceutical company, but their vehicle had broken down, forcing them to walk in from their camp. Whether it was the money or the tale of woe that swayed Señora Trejos, her face softened and she opened the grill, letting them in.

Seeing the tautness of Jane's face, Señora Trejos softened even more. "Poor lamb," she cooed, ignoring Jane's dirty state and putting her plump arm around the young woman's sagging shoulders. "You are exhausted, no? I have a nice cool bedroom with a soft bed for you and the *señor*, and I will bring you something good to eat. You will feel better then?"

Jane couldn't help smiling into the woman's kind dark eyes. "That sounds wonderful, all of it," she managed in her less-than-fluent Spanish. "But most of all, I need a bath. Would that be possible?"

"But of course!" Señora Trejos beamed with pride. "Santos and I, we have the water heated by the tank. He brings the fuel for the heating from San Jose."

Chatting away, she led them inside her comfortable house, with cool tiles on the floors and soothing white walls. "The upstairs rooms are taken," she said apologetically. "I have only the one room below the stairs, but it is nice and cool, and closer to the conveniences."

"Thank you, Señora Trejos," Grant said. "The downstairs room will more than make us happy."

It did. It was small, with bare floors and plain white walls, and there was no furniture except for the wood framed double bed, a cane chair by the lone, gracefully arched window, and a small wooden washstand that held a pitcher and bowl. Jane gazed at the bed with undisguised longing. It looked so cool and comfortable, with fat fluffy pillows.

Grant thanked Señora Trejos again; then she went off to prepare them something to eat, and they were alone. Jane glanced at him and found that he was watching her steadily. Somehow, being alone with him in a bedroom felt different from being alone with him in a jungle. There, their seclusion had been accepted. Here there was the sensation of closing out the world, of coming together in greater intimacy.

"You take the first turn at the bath," he finally said. "Just don't go to sleep in the tub."

Jane didn't waste time protesting. She searched the lower floor, following her nose, until she found Señora Trejos happily puttering about the kitchen. "Pardon, *señora*," she said haltingly. She didn't know all the words needed to explain her shortage of a robe or anything to wear after taking a bath, but Señora Trejos caught on immediately. A few minutes later Jane had a plain white nightgown thrust into her hands and was shown to the *señora's* prized bathroom.

The bathroom had cracked tile and a deep, old-fashioned tub with curved claw feet, but when she turned on the water it gushed out in a hot flood. Sighing in satisfaction, Jane quickly unbuckled the backpack from her belt and set it out of the way, then stripped off her clothes and got into the tub, unwilling to wait until it was full. The heat seeped into her sore muscles and a moan of pleasure escaped her. She would have liked to soak in the tub for hours, but Grant was waiting for his own bath, so she didn't allow herself to lean against the high back and relax. Quickly she washed away the layers of grime, unable to believe how good it felt to be clean again. Then she washed her hair, sighing in relief as the strands came unmatted and once again slipped through her fingers like wet silk.

Hurrying, she wrapped her hair in a towel and got her safety razor out of the backpack. Sitting on the edge of the tub, she shaved her legs and under her arms, then smoothed moisturizer into her skin. A smile kept tugging at her mouth as she thought of spending the night in Grant's arms again. She was going to be clean and sweet-smelling, her skin silky. After all, it wasn't going to be easy to win a warrior's love, and she was going to use all the weapons at her disposal.

She brushed her teeth, then combed out her wet hair and pulled the white nightgown over her head, hoping that she wouldn't meet any of Señora Trejos's other boarders on the short trip back to her room. The *señora* had told her to leave her clothes on the bathroom floor, that she would see that they were washed, so Jane got the backpack and hurried down the hall to the room where Grant waited.

He had closed the shutters over the arched window and was leaning with one shoulder propped against the wall, declining to sit in the single chair. He looked up at her entrance, and the inky pupils at the center of his golden irises expanded until there was only a thin ring of amber circling the black. Jane paused, dropping the pack beside the bed, feeling abruptly shy, despite the tempestuous lovemaking she'd shared with this man. He looked at her as if he were about to pounce on her, and she found herself crossing her arms over her breasts, aware that her nakedness was fully apparent beneath the thin nightgown. She cleared her throat, her mouth suddenly dry. "The bathroom is all yours."

He straightened slowly, not taking his eyes from her. "Why don't you go on to bed?"

"I'd rather wait for you," she whispered.

"I'll wake you up when I come to bed." The intensity of his gaze promised her that she wasn't going to sleep alone that night.

"My hair...I have to dry my hair."

He nodded and left the room, and Jane sat down on the chair weakly, shaking inside from the way he'd looked at her. Bending over, she rubbed her hair briskly, then began to brush it dry. It was so thick and long that it was still damp when Grant came back into the room and stood silently, watching her as she sat bent over, her slender arms curving as she drew the brush through the dark mass. She sat up, tossing her head to fling her hair back over her shoulders, and for a moment they simply stared at each other.

They had made love before, but now sensual awareness was zinging between them like an electric current. Without even touching each other, they were both becoming aroused, their heartbeats quickening, their skin growing hot.

He had shaved, probably using the razor she'd left in the bathroom. It was the first time she'd seen him without several days' growth of beard, and the clean, hard lines of his scarred face made her breath catch. He was naked except for a towel knotted around his lean waist, and as she watched he pulled the towel free and dropped it to the floor. Reaching behind him, he locked the door. "Are you ready for bed?"

"My hair...isn't quite dry."

"Leave it," he said, coming toward her.

The brush dropped to the floor as he caught her hand and pulled her up. Instantly she was in his arms, lifted off her feet by his fierce embrace. Their mouths met hungrily, and her fingers tangled in his water-darkened hair, holding him to her. His mouth was fresh and hot, his tongue thrusting deep into her mouth in a kiss that made her whimper as currents of desire sizzled her nerves.

He was hard against her, his manhood pushing against her softness, his hands kneading her hips and rubbing her over him. Jane pulled her mouth free, gasping, and dropped her head to his broad shoulder. She couldn't contain the wild pleasure he was evoking, as if her body were out of control, already reaching for the peak that his arousal promised. She'd been quite content to live celibately for years, the passion in her unawakened until she met Grant. He was as wild and beautiful and free as the majestic jaguars that melted silently through the tangled green jungle. The wildness in him demanded a response, and she was helpless to restrain it. He didn't have to patiently build her passion; one kiss and she trembled against him, empty and aching and ready for him, her breasts swollen and painful, her body growing wet and soft.

"Let's get this thing off you," he whispered, pulling at the nightgown and easing it up. Reluctantly she released him, and he pulled the gown over her head, dropping it over the chair; then she was back in his arms, and he carried her to the bed.

Their naked bodies moved together, and there was no more waiting. He surged into her, and she cried out a little from the delicious shock of it. Catching the small cry with his mouth, he lifted her legs and placed them around his waist, then began to move more deeply into her.

It was like the night before. She gave no thought to anything but the man with shoulders so broad that they blocked out the light. The bed was soft beneath them, the sheets cool and smooth, and the rhythmic creak of the springs in time with his movements was accompanied by the singing of insects outside the window. Time meant nothing. There was only his mouth on hers, his hands on her body, the slow thrusts that went deep inside her and touched off a wildfire of sensation, until they strained together in frenzied pleasure and the sheets were no longer cool, but warm from their damp, heated flesh.

Then it was quiet again, and he lay heavily on her, drawing in deep breaths while her hands moved over his powerful back. Her lips trembled with the words of love that she wanted to give him, but she held them back. All her instincts told her that he wouldn't want to know, and she didn't want to do anything to spoil their time together.

Perhaps he had given her something anyway, if not his love, something at least as infinitely precious. As her sensitive fingertips explored the deep valley of his spine, she wondered if he had given her his baby. A tremor of pleasure rippled down her body, and she held him closer, hoping that her body would be receptive to his seed.

He stirred, reaching out to turn off the lamp, and in the darkness he moved to lie beside her. She curled against his side, her head on his shoulder, and after a moment he gave a low chuckle.

"Why don't you just save time and get on top of me now?" he suggested, scooping her up and settling her on his chest.

Jane gave a sigh of deep satisfaction, stretching out on him and looping her arm around his neck. With her face pressed against his throat she was comfortable and safe, as if she'd found a sheltering harbor. "I love you," she said silently, moving her lips without sound against his throat.

They woke with the bright early morning sun coming through the slats of the shutters. Leaving Jane stretching and grousing on the bed, Grant got up and opened the shutters, letting the rosy light pour into the room. When he turned, he saw the way the light glowed on her warm-toned skin, turning her nipples to apricot, catching the glossy lights in her dark hair. Her face was flushed, her eyes still heavy with sleep.

Suddenly his body throbbed, and he couldn't bear to be separated from her by even the width of the small room. He went back to the bed and pulled her under him, then watched the way her face changed as he slowly eased into her, watched the radiance that lit her. Something swelled in his chest, making it difficult for him to breathe, and as he lost himself in the soft depths of her body he had one last, glaringly clear thought: she'd gotten too close to him, and letting her go was going to be the hardest thing he'd ever done.

He dressed, pulling on the freshly washed clothes that one of Señora Trejos's daughters had brought, along with a tray of fruit, bread and cheese. Jane flushed wildly when she realized that Señora Trejos must have brought a tray to them the night before, then discreetly left when she heard the sounds they had been making. A quick glance at Grant told her that he'd had the same thought, because the corner of his mouth was twitching in amusement.

The *señora* had also sent along a soft white off-the-shoulder blouse, and Jane donned it with pleasure, more than glad to discard her tattered black shirt. After selecting a piece of orange from the tray, she bit into the juicy fruit as she watched him pull his dark green undershirt over his head.

"You're going to be pretty noticeable in those camouflage fatigues," she said, poking a bit of the orange into his mouth.

"I know." He quickly kissed her orange-sticky lips. "Put the shirt in your pack and be ready to go when I get back."

"Get back? Where are you going?"

"I'm going to try to get some sort of transport. It won't be as easy this time."

"We could take the train," she pointed out.

"The rifle would be a mite conspicuous, honey."

"Why can't I go with you?"

"Because you're safer here."

"The last time you left me, I got into trouble," she felt obliged to remind him.

He didn't appreciate the reminder. He scowled down at her as he reached for a spear of melon. "If you'll just keep your little butt where I tell you to, you'll be fine."

"I'm fine when I'm with you."

"Damn it, stop arguing with me!"

"I'm not arguing. *I'm* pointing out some obvious facts! *You're* the one who's arguing!"

His eyes were yellow fire. He bent down until they were almost nose to nose, his control under severe stress. His teeth were clenched together as he said, evenly spacing the words out, "If you make it home without having the worst spanking of your life, it'll be a miracle."

"I've never had a spanking in my life," she protested.

"It shows!"

She flounced into the chair and pouted. Grant's hands clenched; then he reached for her and pulled her out of the chair, hauling her up to him for a deep, hard kiss. "Be good, for a change," he said, aware that he was almost pleading with her. "I'll be back in an hour—"

"Or so!" she finished in unison with him. "All right, I'll wait! But I don't like it!"

He left before he completely lost his temper with her, and Jane munched on more of the fruit, terribly grateful for something fresh to eat. Deciding that he'd meant only for her to stay in the house, not in the room, she first got everything ready for them to leave, as he'd instructed, then sought out the *señora* and had a pleasant chat with her. The woman was bustling around the kitchen preparing food for her boarders, while two of her daughters diligently cleaned the house and did a mountain of laundry. Jane had her arms deep in a bowl of dough when Grant returned.

He'd gone first to their room, and when he found her in the kitchen there was a flicker of intense relief in his eyes before he masked it. Jane sensed his presence and looked up, smiling. "Is everything arranged?"

"Yes. Are you ready?"

"Just as soon as I wash my hands."

She hugged the *señora* and thanked her, while Grant leaned in the doorway and watched her. Did she charm everyone so effortlessly? The *señora* was beaming at her, wishing her a safe journey and inviting her back. There would always be a room for the lovely young *señora* and her husband in the Trejos house!

They collected their packs, and Grant slung the rifle over his shoulder. They risked attracting attention because of it, but he didn't dare leave it behind. With any luck they would be on a plane out of Costa Rica by nightfall, but until they were actually on their way he couldn't let his guard down. The close call the day before had been proof of that. Turego wasn't giving up; he stood to lose too much.

Out in the alley, Jane glanced up at him. "What exactly did you arrange?"

"A farmer is going into Limon, and he's giving us a ride."

After the adventure of the last several days that seemed almost boringly tame, but Jane was happy to be bored. A nice, quiet ride, that was the ticket. How good it would be not to feel hunted!

As they neared the end of the alley, a man stepped suddenly in front of them. Grant reacted immediately, shoving Jane aside, but before he could swing the rifle around there was a pistol in his face, and several more men stepped into the alley, all of them armed, all of them with their weapons pointed at Grant. Jane stopped breathing, her eyes wide with horror. Then she recognized the man in the middle, and her heart stopped. Was Grant going to die now, because of her?

She couldn't bear it. She had to do something, anything.

"Manuel!" she cried, filling her voice with joy. She ran to him and flung her arms around him. "I'm so glad you found me!"

Chapter Ten

It was a nightmare. Grant hadn't taken his narrowed gaze off her, and the hatred that glittered in his eyes made her stomach knot, but there was no way she could reassure him. She was acting for all she was worth, clinging to Turego and babbling her head off, telling him how frightened she'd been and how this madman had knocked her out and stolen her away from the plantation, all the while clinging to Turego's shirt as if she couldn't bear to release him. She had no clear idea of what she was going to do, only that somehow she had to stay unfettered so she could help Grant, and to do that she had to win Turego's trust and soothe his wounded vanity.

The entire situation was balanced on a knife edge; things could go in either direction. Wariness was in Turego's dark eyes, as well as a certain amount of cruel satisfaction in having cornered his prey. He wanted to make her suffer for having eluded him, she knew, yet for the moment she was safe from any real harm, because he still wanted the microfilm. It was Grant whose life was threatened, and it would take only a word from Turego for those men to kill him where he stood. Grant had to know it, yet there wasn't even a flicker of fear in his expression, only the cold, consuming hatred of his glare as he stared at Jane. Perhaps it was that, in the end, that eased Turego's suspicions somewhat. He would never relax his guard around her again, but Jane could only worry about one thing at a time. Right now, she had to protect Grant in any way she could.

Turego's arm stole around her waist, pulling her tightly against him. He bent his head and kissed her, a deeply intimate kiss that Jane had to steel herself not to resist in any way, even though she shuddered at having to endure the touch and taste of him. She knew what he was doing; he was illustrating his power, his control, and using her as a weapon against Grant. When he lifted his head, a cruel little smile was on his handsome mouth.

"I have you now, *chiquita*," he reassured her in a smooth

tone. "You are quite safe. This…madman, as you called him, will not bother you again, I promise. I am impressed," he continued mockingly, inclining his head toward Grant. "I have heard of you, *señor*. Surely there can be only one with the yellow eyes and scarred face, who melts through jungles like a silent cat. You are a legend, but it was thought that you were dead. It has been a long time since anything was heard of you."

Grant was silent, his attention now on Turego, ignoring Jane as if she no longer existed. Not a muscle moved; it was as if he'd turned to stone. He wasn't even breathing. His utter stillness was unnerving, yet there was also the impression of great strength under control, a wild animal waiting for the perfect moment to pounce. Even though he was only one against many, the others were like jackals surrounding a mighty tiger; the men who held their weapons trained on him were visibly nervous.

"Perhaps it would be interesting to know who now pays you for your services. And there are others who would like very much to have an opportunity to question you, yes? Tie him, and put him in the truck," Turego ordered, still keeping his arm around Jane. She forced herself not to watch as Grant was roughly bound and dragged over to a two ton military-type truck, with a canvas top stretched over the back. Instead she gave Turego her most dazzling smile and leaned her head on his shoulder.

"I've been so frightened," she whispered.

"Of course you have, *chiquita*. Is that why you resisted my men when they found you in the forest yesterday?"

She might have known he was too sharp to simply believe her! She let her eyes widen incredulously. "Those were *your* men? Well, why didn't they say so? They were shoving me around, and I was afraid they wanted to…to attack me. I had managed to slip away from that crazy man; I'd have made it, too, if it hadn't been for all the noise your men made! They led him right to me!" Her voice quivered with indignation.

"It is over; I will take care of you now." He led her to the truck and assisted her into the cab, then climbed in beside her and gave terse instructions to the driver.

That was exactly what she was afraid of, being taken care of by Turego, but for the moment she had to play up to him and somehow convince him that she was totally innocent of her escape from under the noses of his guards. He hadn't gotten where he was by being a gullible idiot; though she'd successfully fooled him the first time, the second time would be much more difficult.

"Where are we going?" she asked innocently, leaning against him. "Back to the plantation? Did you bring any of my clothes with you? *He* brought me this blouse this morning," she said, plucking at the soft white fabric, "but I'd really like to have my own clothes."

"I have been so worried about you that I did not think of your clothes, I confess," Turego lied smoothly. His hard arm was around her shoulders, and Jane smiled up at him. He was unnaturally handsome, with perfect features that would have done better on a statue than a man, though perhaps Turego wasn't quite human. He didn't show his age; he looked to be in his twenties, though Jane knew that he was in his early forties. Emotion hadn't changed his face; he had no wrinkles, no attractive crinkles at the corners of his eyes, no signs that time or life had touched him. His only weakness was his vanity; he knew he could force himself on Jane at any time, but he wanted to seduce her into giving herself willingly to him. She would be another feather in his cap; then, once he had the microfilm, he could dispose of her without regret.

She had only the microfilm to protect her, and only herself to protect Grant. Her mind raced, trying to think of some way she could free him from his bonds, get some sort of weapon to him. All he needed was a small advantage.

"Who *is* he? You seem to know him."

"He hasn't introduced himself? But you have spent several days alone with him, my heart. Surely you know his name."

Again she had to make a split second decision. Was Grant's real name commonly known? Was Grant his real name, anyway? She couldn't take the chance. "He told me that his name is Joe Tyson. Isn't that his real name?" she asked in an incredulous voice, sitting up to turn the full force of her brown eyes on him, blinking as if in astonishment.

Oddly, Turego hesitated. "That may be what he calls himself now. If he is who I think he is, he was once known as the Tiger."

He was uneasy! Grant was tied, and there were ten guns on him, but still Turego was made uneasy by his presence! Did that slight hesitation mean that Turego wasn't certain of Grant's real name and didn't want to reveal his lack of knowledge—or was the uncertainty of a greater scope? Was he not entirely certain that Grant was the Tiger? Turego wouldn't want to make himself look foolish by claiming to have captured the Tiger, only to have his prisoner turn out to be someone much less interesting.

Tiger. She could see how he had gained the name, and the reputation. With his amber eyes and deadly grace, the comparison had been inevitable. But he was a man, too, and she'd slept in his arms. He'd held her during the long hours of darkness, keeping the night demons away from her, and he'd shown her a part of herself that she hadn't known existed. Because of Grant, she felt like a whole person, capable of love and passion, a warm, giving woman. Though she could see what he had been, the way she saw him now was colored by love. He was a man, not a supernatural creature who melted through the dark, tangled jungles of the world. He could bleed, and hurt. He could laugh, that deep, rusty laugh that caught at her heart. After Grant, she felt contaminated just by sitting next to Turego.

She gave a tinkling laugh. "That sounds so cloak-and-daggerish! Do you mean he's a spy?"

"No, of course not. Nothing so romantic. He is really just a mercenary, hiring himself out to anyone for any sort of dirty job."

"Like kidnapping me? Why would he do that? I mean, no one is going to pay any ransom for me! My father doesn't even speak to me, and I certainly don't have any money of my own!"

"Perhaps something else was wanted from you," he suggested.

"But I don't have anything!" She managed to fill her face and voice with bewilderment, and Turego smiled down at her.

"Perhaps you have it and are not aware of it."

"What? Do you know?"

"In time, love, we shall find out."

"No one tells me anything!" she wailed, and lapsed into a pout. She allowed herself to hold the pout for about thirty seconds, then roused to demand of him again, like an impatient child, "Where are we going?"

"Just down this street, love."

They were on the very fringes of the town, and a dilapidated tin warehouse sat at the end of the street. It was in sad shape, its walls sagging, the tin roof curled up in several places, sections of it missing altogether in others. A scarred blue door hung crookedly on its hinges. The warehouse was their destination, and when the truck stopped beside the blue door and Turego helped Jane from the cab, she saw why. There were few people about, and those who were in the vicinity quickly turned their eyes away and scurried off.

Grant was hauled out of the back of the truck and shoved toward the door; he stumbled and barely caught his balance before he would have crashed headlong against the building. Someone chuckled, and when Grant straightened to turn his unnerving stare on his captors, Jane saw that a thin trickle of blood had dried at the corner of his mouth. His lip was split and puffy. Her heart lurched, and her breath caught. Someone had hit him while he had his hands tied behind his back! Right behind her first sick reaction came fury, raw and powerful, surging through her like a tidal wave. She shook with the effort it took to disguise it before she turned to Turego again.

"What are we going to do here?"

"I just want to ask a few questions of our friend. Nothing important."

She was firmly escorted into the building, and she gasped as the heat hit her in the face like a blow. The tin building was a furnace, heating the air until it was almost impossible to breathe. Perspiration immediately beaded on her skin, and she felt dizzy, unable to drag in enough oxygen to satisfy her need.

Evidently Turego had been using the warehouse as a sort of base, because there was equipment scattered around. Leaving Grant under guard, Turego led Jane to the back of the building, where several small rooms connected with each other, probably the former offices. It was just as hot there, but a small window was opened and let in a measure of fresh air. The room he took her to was filthy, piled with musty smelling papers and netted with cobwebs. An old wooden desk, missing a leg, listed drunkenly to one side, and there was the unmistakable stench of rodents. Jane wrinkled her nose fastidiously. "Ugh!" she said in completely honest disgust.

"I apologize for the room," Turego said smoothly, bestowing one of his toothpaste-ad smiles on her. "Hopefully, we won't be here long. Alfonso will stay with you while I question our friend about his activities, and who hired him to abduct you."

What he meant was that she was also under guard. Jane didn't protest, not wanting to arouse his suspicions even more, but her skin crawled. She was very much afraid of the form his "questioning" would take. She had to think of something fast! But nothing came to mind, and Turego tilted her chin up to kiss her again. "I won't be long," he murmured. "Alfonso, watch her carefully. I would be very upset if someone stole her from me again."

Jane thought she recognized Alfonso as one of the guards who had been at the plantation. When Turego had gone, closing the door behind him, Jane gave Alfonso a slow glance from under lowered lashes and essayed a tentative smile. He was fairly young and good-looking. He had probably been warned against her, but still he couldn't help responding to her smile.

"You were a guard at the plantation?" she asked in Spanish.

He gave a reluctant nod.

"I thought I recognized you. I never forget a good-looking man," she said with more enthusiasm than precision, her pronunciation mangled just enough to bring a hint of amusement to Alfonso's face. She wondered if he knew what Turego was up to, or if he had been told some fabrication about protecting her.

Whatever he had been told, he wasn't inclined toward conversation. Jane poked around the room, looking for anything to use as a weapon, but trying not to be obvious about it. She kept straining her ears for any sound from the warehouse, her nerves jumping. What was Turego doing? If he harmed Grant...

How long had it been? Five minutes? Ten? Or less than that? She had no idea, but suddenly she couldn't stand it any longer, and she went to the door. Alfonso stretched his arm in front of her, barring her way.

"I want to see Turego," she said impatiently. "It's too hot to wait in here."

"You must stay here."

"Well, I won't! Don't be such a stuffed shirt, Alfonso; he won't mind. You can come with me, if you can't let me out of your sight."

She ducked under his arm and had the door open before he could stop her. With a muffled oath he came after her, but Jane darted through the door and the connecting offices. Just as she entered the main warehouse she heard the sickening thud of a fist against flesh, and the blood drained from her face.

Two men held Grant between them, holding him up by his bound arms, while another stood before him, rubbing his fist.

Turego stood to the side, a small, inhuman smile on his lips. Grant's head sagged forward on his chest, and drops of blood spotted the floor at his feet.

"This silence will gain you nothing but more pain, my friend," Turego said softly. "Tell me who hired you. That is all I want to know, for now."

Grant said nothing, and one of the men holding him grabbed a fistful of hair, jerking his head up. Just before Alfonso took her arm, Jane saw Grant's face, and she jerked free, driven by a wild strength.

"Turego!" she cried shrilly, drawing everyone's attention to her. Turego's brows snapped together over his nose.

"What are you doing here? Alfonso, take her back!"

"No!" she yelled, pushing Alfonso away. "It's too hot back there, and I won't stay! Really, this is too much! I've had a miserable time in that jungle, and I thought when you rescued me that I'd be comfortable again, but no, you drag me to this miserable dump and leave me in that grungy little room. I insist that you take me to a hotel!"

"Jane, Jane, you don't understand these things," Turego said, coming up to her and taking her arm. "Just a few moments more and he will tell me what I want to know. Aren't you interested in knowing who hired him?" He turned her away, leading her back to the offices again. "Please be patient, love."

Jane subsided, letting herself be led docilely away. She risked a quick glance back at Grant and his captors, and saw that they were waiting for Turego's return before resuming the beating. He was sagging limply in their grasp, unable even to stand erect.

"You are to stay here," Turego said sternly when they reached the office again. "Promise me, yes?"

"I promise," Jane said, turning toward him with a smile on her face; he never saw the blow coming. She caught him under the nose with the bridge of her hand, snapping his head back and making blood spurt. Before he could yell with pain or surprise, she slammed her elbow into his solar plexus and he doubled over with an agonized grunt. As if in a well-choreographed ballet, she brought her knee up under his unprotected chin, and Turego collapsed like a stuffed doll. Jane cast a quick thought of thanks to her father for insisting that she take all of those self-defense classes, then bent down and quickly jerked the pistol from Turego's holster.

Just as she started through the doorway again, a shot reverberated through the tin building, and she froze in horror. "No," she moaned, then launched herself toward the sound.

When Jane had hurled herself into Turego's arms, Grant had been seized by a fury so consuming that a mist of red had fallen over his vision, but he'd been trained to control himself, and that control had held, even though he had been on the edge of madness. Then the mist had cleared, and cold contempt had taken its place. Hell, what had he expected? Jane was a survivor, adept at keeping her feet. First she had charmed Turego, then Grant had stolen her from Turego and she'd charmed him as effortlessly as she had put Turego under her spell. Now Turego was back, and since he had the upper hand, it was a case of So long, Sullivan. He even felt a sort of bitter admiration for the way she had so quickly and accurately summed up the situation, then known exactly the tone to set to begin bringing Turego back to heel.

Still, the sense of betrayal was staggering, and nothing would have pleased him at that moment as much as to get his hands on her. Damn her for being a lying, treacherous little bitch! He should have known, should have suspected that her patented look of wide-eyed innocence was nothing but a well-rehearsed act.

The old instincts, only partially shelved, suddenly returned in full force. Forget about the bitch. He had to look out for himself first, then see to her. She was curling in Turego's arms like a cat, while Grant knew that his own future was nonexistent unless he did some fast thinking.

Part of the thinking was done for him when Turego put two and two together and came up with an accurate guess about Grant's identity. A year had been far too short a time for people in the business to even begin forgetting him. After he'd disappeared, his absence had probably made his reputation grow to legendary proportions. Well, let Turego think that he was after the missing microfilm, too; Grant felt no compunction about using Jane in any way he could. She'd not only used him, she'd had him dancing to her tune like a puppet on a fancy little string. If he hadn't agreed to bring her out of Costa Rica, he would have wished the joy of her on Turego, and gotten himself out any way he could. But he'd taken the job, so he had to finish it—if he came out of this alive. When he got his hands on her again she'd find that there would be no more kid glove treatment.

Turego was curious. With his hands tied behind his back, supported between two of the hired goons, Grant found out just how curious.

"Who hired you? Or are you an independent now?"

"Naw, I'm still a Protestant," Grant said, smiling smoothly. At a nod from Turego, a fist crashed into his face, splitting his lip and filling his mouth with blood. The next blow was into his midsection, and he'd have jacknifed if it hadn't been for the cruel support of his twisted arms.

"Really, I don't have the time for this," Turego murmured. "You are the one known as the Tiger; you aren't a man who works for nothing."

"Sure I am; I'm a walking charity."

The fist landed on his cheekbone, snapping his head back. This guy was a real boxer; he placed his blows with precision. The face a couple of times, then the ribs and kidneys. Pain sliced through Grant until his stomach heaved. He gasped, his vision blurred even though his mind was still clear, and he deliberately let all his weight fall on his two supporters, his knees buckling.

Then he heard Jane's voice, petulant and demanding, as he'd never heard it before, followed by Turego's smooth reassurances. The men's attention wasn't on him; he sensed its absence, like a wild animal acutely sensitive to every nuance. He sagged even more, deliberately putting stress on the bonds around his wrists, and fierce satisfaction welled in him as he felt them slip on his right hand.

He had powerful hands, hands that could destroy. He used that power against the cord that bound him, extending his hand to the fullest and stretching the cord, then relaxing and letting the cord slip even lower. Twice he did that, and the cord dropped around his fingers in loose coils.

Looking about through slitted eyes, he saw that no one was paying much attention to him, not even the boxer, who was absently rubbing his knuckles and waiting for Turego to return from wherever he'd gone. Jane was nowhere in sight, either. Now was the time.

The two men holding him were off guard; he threw them away from him like discarded toys. For a split second everyone was disconcerted, and that split second was all he needed. He grabbed a rifle and kicked its butt up under the chin of the soldier he'd taken it from, sending him staggering backward. He whirled, lashing out with his feet and the stock of the rifle. The soldiers really didn't have much of a chance; they didn't have a fraction of the training he'd had, or the years of experience. They didn't know how to react to an attacker who struck and whirled away before anyone could move. Only one managed to get his rifle up, and he fired wildly, the bullet zinging far over Grant's head. That soldier was the last one standing; Grant took him out with almost contemptuous ease. Then he hesitated only the barest moment as he waited for movement from any of them, but there was none. His gaze moved to the door at the far end of the warehouse, and a cold, twisted smile touched his bruised and bloody lips. He went after Jane.

She'd never known such terror; even her fear of the dark was nothing compared to the way she felt now. She couldn't move fast enough; her feet felt as if they were slogging through syrup. Oh, God, what if they'd killed him? The thought was too horrible to be borne, yet it swelled in her chest until she couldn't breathe. No, she thought, no, no, *no*!

She burst through the door, the pistol in her hand, half-crazed with fear and ready to fight for her man, for her very life. She saw a confused scene of sprawled men and her mind reeled, unable to comprehend why so many were lying there. Hadn't there been only one shot?

Then an arm snaked around her neck, jerking her back and locking under her chin. Another arm reached out, and long fingers clamped around the hand that held the pistol, removing it from her grip.

"Funny thing, sweetheart, but I feel safer when you're unarmed," a low voice hissed in her ear.

At the sound of that voice, Jane's eyes closed, and two tears squeezed out from under the lids. "Grant," she whispered.

"Afraid so. You can tell me how glad you are to see me later; right now we're moving."

He released his arm lock about her neck, but when she tried to turn to face him, he caught her right arm and pulled it up behind her back, not so high that she was in pain, but high enough that she would be if he moved it even a fraction of an inch higher. "Move!" he barked, thrusting her forward, and Jane stumbled under the force of the motion, wrenching her arm and emitting an involuntary cry.

"You're hurting me," she whimpered, still dazed and trying to understand. "Grant, wait!"

"Cut the crap," he advised, kicking open the door and shoving her out into the searing white sunlight. The transport truck was sitting there, and he didn't hesitate. "Get in. We're going for a ride."

He opened the door and half-lifted, half-threw Jane into the truck, sending her sprawling on the seat. She cried out, her soft cry knifing through him, but he told himself not to be a fool; she didn't need anyone to look after her. Like a cat, she always landed on her feet.

Jane scrambled to a sitting position, her dark eyes full of tears as she stared at his battered, bloody face in both pain and horror. She wanted to reassure him, tell him that it had all been an act, a desperate gamble to save both their lives, but he didn't seem inclined to listen. Surely he wouldn't so easily forget everything they'd shared, everything they'd been to each other! Still, she couldn't give up. She'd lifted her hand to reach out for him when a movement in the door beyond them caught her eye, and she screamed a warning.

"Grant!"

He whirled, and as he did Turego lifted the rifle he held and fired. The explosive crack of sound split the air, but still Jane heard, felt, sensed the grunt of pain that Grant gave as he dropped to one knee and lifted the pistol. Turego lunged to one side, looking for cover, but the pistol spat fire, and a small red flower bloomed high on Turego's right shoulder, sending him tumbling back through the door.

Jane heard someone screaming, but the sound was high and far away. She lunged through the open door of the truck, falling to her hands and knees on the hot, rocky ground. Grant was on his knees, leaning against the running board of the truck, his right hand clamped over his upper left arm, and bright red blood was dripping through his fingers. He looked up at her, his golden eyes bright and burning with the fire of battle, fierce even in his swollen and discolored face.

She went a little mad then. She grabbed him by his undershirt and hauled him to his feet, using a strength she'd had no idea she possessed. "Get in the truck!" she screamed, pushing him in the door. "Damn it, get in the truck! Are you trying to get yourself killed?"

He winced as the side of the seat smashed into his bruised ribs; Jane was shoving at him and screaming like a banshee, tears streaming down her face. "Would you shut up!" he yelled, painfully pulling himself inside.

"Don't you tell me to shut up!" she screamed, pushing him until he moved over. She slapped the tears from her cheeks and climbed into the truck herself. "Get out of the way so I can get this thing started! Are there any keys? Where are the keys? Oh, damn!" She dove headfirst under the steering wheel, feeling under the dash and pulling wires out frantically.

"What're you doing?" Grant groaned, his mind reeling with pain.

"I'm hot-wiring the truck!" she sobbed.

"You're tearing the damned wiring out!" If she was trying to disable their only transportation, she was doing a good job of it. He started to yank her out from under the steering wheel when suddenly she bounced out on her own, jamming the clutch in and touching two wires together. The motor roared into life, and Jane slammed the door on her side, shoved the truck into gear and let out on the clutch. The truck lurched forward violently, throwing Grant against the door.

"Put it in low gear!" he yelled, pulling himself into a sitting position and getting a tighter grip on the seat.

"I don't know where the low gear is! I just took what I could find!"

Swearing, he reached for the gear shift, the pain in his wounded arm like a hot knife as he closed his hand over the knob. There was nothing he could do about the pain, so he ignored it. "Put the clutch in," he ordered. "I'll change gears. Jane, put the damned clutch in!"

"Stop yelling at me!" she screamed, jamming in the clutch. Grant put the truck in the proper gear and she let out on the clutch; this time the truck moved more smoothly. She put her foot on the gas pedal, shoving it to the floor, and slung the heavy truck around a corner, sending its rear wheels sliding on the gravel.

"Turn right," Grant directed, and she took the next right.

The truck was lunging under her heavy urging, its transmission groaning as she kept her foot down on the gas pedal.

"Change gears!"

"Change them yourself!"

"Put in the clutch!"

She put in the clutch, and he geared up. "When I tell you, put in the clutch, and I'll change the gears, understand?"

She was still crying, swiping at her face at irregular intervals. Grant said, "Turn left," and she swung the truck in a turn that sent a pickup dodging to the side of the road to avoid them.

The road took them out of town, but they were only a couple of miles out when Grant said tersely, "Pull over." Jane didn't question him; she pulled over to the side of the road and stopped the truck.

"Okay, get out." Again she obeyed without question, jumping out and standing there awkwardly as he eased himself to the ground. His left arm was streaked with blood, but from the look on his face Jane knew that he wasn't about to stop. He shoved the pistol into his belt and slung the rifle over his shoulder. "Let's go."

"Where are we going?"

"Back into town. Your boyfriend won't expect us to double back on him. You can stop crying," he added cruelly. "I didn't kill him."

"He's not my boyfriend!" Jane spat, whirling on him.

"Sure looked like it from where I was."

"I was trying to catch him off guard! One of us had to stay free!"

"Save it," he advised, his tone bored. "I bought your act once, but it won't sell again. Now, are you going to walk?"

She decided that there was no use trying to reason with him now. When he'd calmed down enough to listen, when she'd calmed down enough to make a coherent explanation, then they'd get this settled. As she turned away from him, she looked in the open door of the truck and caught a glimpse of something shoved in the far corner of the floor. Her backpack! She crawled up in the truck and leaned far over to drag the pack out from under the seat; in the excitement, it had been totally overlooked and forgotten.

"Leave the damned thing!" Grant snapped.

"I need it," she snapped in return. She buckled it to her belt-loop again.

He drew the pistol out of his belt and Jane swallowed, her

eyes growing enormous. Calmly he shot out one of the front tires of the truck, then stuck the pistol back into his belt.

"Why did you do that?" she whispered, swallowing again.

"So it'll look as if we were forced to abandon the truck."

He caught her upper arm in a tight grip and pulled her off the road. Whenever he heard an engine he forced her to the ground and they lay still until the sound had faded. Her blouse, so white and pretty only an hour or so before, became streaked with mud and torn in places where the thorns caught it. She gave it a brief glance, then forgot about it.

"When will Turego be after us again?" she panted.

"Soon. Impatient already?"

Grinding her teeth together, she ignored him. In twenty more minutes they approached the edge of the town again, and he circled it widely. She wanted to ask him what he was looking for, but after the way he'd just bitten her head off, she kept silent. She wanted to sit down to wash his bruised face, and bandage the wound in his arm, but she could do none of those things. He didn't want anything from her now.

Still, what else could she have done? There was no way she could have known he was going to be able to escape. She'd had to use the best plan she had at the time.

Finally they slipped into a ramshackle shed behind an equally ramshackle house and collapsed on the ground in the relatively cool interior. Grant winced as he inadvertently strained his left arm, but when Jane started toward him, he gave her a cold glare that stopped her in her tracks. She sank back to the ground and rested her forehead on her drawn up knees. "What are we going to do now?"

"We're getting out of the country, any way we can," he said flatly. "Your daddy hired me to bring you home, and that's what I'm going to do. The sooner I turn you over to him, the better."

Chapter Eleven

After that Jane sat quietly, keeping her forehead down on her knees and closing her eyes. A cold desolation was growing inside her, filling her, thrusting aside anxiety and fear. What if she could never convince him that she hadn't betrayed him? With the life he'd led, it was probably something that he'd had to guard against constantly, so he wasn't even surprised by betrayal. She would try again to reason with him, of course; until he actually left her, she wouldn't stop trying. But...what if he wouldn't listen? What would she do then? Somehow she just couldn't imagine her future without Grant. The emotional distance between them now was agonizing, but she could still lift her head and see him, take comfort in his physical proximity. What would she do if he weren't there at all?

The heat and humidity began building, negating the coolness of the shade offered by the old, open-sided shed, and in the distance thunder rumbled as it announced the approach of the daily rain. A door creaked loudly, and soon a stooped old woman, moving slowly, came around the side of the house to a small pen where pigs had been grunting occasionally as they lay in the mud and tried to escape the heat. Grant watched her, his eyes alert, not a muscle moving. There wasn't any real danger that she would see them; weeds and bushes grew out of control, over waist-high, between the house and the shed, with only a faint little-used path leading to the shed. The pigs squealed in loud enthusiasm when the old woman fed them, and after chatting fondly to them for a moment she laboriously made her way back into the shack.

Jane hadn't moved a muscle, not opening her eyes even when the pigs had begun celebrating the arrival of food. Grant looked at her, a faint puzzlement creeping into the coldness of his eyes. It was unlike her to sit so quietly and not investigate the noise. She knew it was the pigs, of course, but she hadn't looked up to see what was making them squeal so loudly, or even when the old woman had begun talking to them. She was normally as curious as a cat, poking her nose into everything whether it concerned her or not. It was difficult to tell, the way she had her head down, but he thought that she was pale; the few freckles he could see stood out plainly.

An image flashed into his mind of Turego bending his head to press his mouth to Jane's, and the way Jane had stood so quiescently to accept that kiss. Rage curled inside him again, and his fists knotted. Damn her! How could she have let that slime touch her?

The thunder moved closer, cracking loudly, and the air carried the scent of rain. Wind began to swirl, darting through the shed and bringing with it welcome coolness. The air was alive, almost shining with the electrical energy it carried. The small creatures began to take shelter, birds winging back and forth in an effort to find the most secure perch to wait out the storm.

During the rain would be a good time to leave, as everyone else would take shelter until it was over, but his body ached from the beating he'd received, and his left arm was still sullenly oozing blood. They were in no immediate danger here, so he was content to rest. Night would be an even better time to move.

The rain started, going from a sprinkle to a deluge in less than a minute. The ground wasn't able to soak up that enormous amount of water, and a small stream began to trickle through the shed. Grant got up, stifling a groan as his stiff body protested, and found a seat on top of a half-rotten vegetable crate. It gave a little, but held his weight.

Jane still hadn't moved. She didn't look up until the moisture began to dampen the seat of her pants; then her head lifted and she realized that a river was beginning to flow around her. She didn't look at Grant, though she moved away from the water, shifting to the side. She sat with her back to him and resumed her earlier posture, with her knees drawn up, her arms locked around her legs, and her head bent down to rest on her knees.

Grant knew how to wait; patience was second nature to him. He could hold a position all day long, if necessary, ignoring physical discomfort as if it didn't exist. But the silence and lack of motion in the shed began to grate on his nerves, because it wasn't what he'd learned to expect from Jane. Was she planning something?

Eventually the rain stopped, and the steamy heat began to

build again. "Are we going to sit here all day?" Jane finally asked fretfully, breaking her long silence.

"Might as well. I don't have anything better to do. Do you?"

She didn't answer that, or ask any more questions, realizing that he wasn't in the mood to tell her anything. She was so hungry that she was sick, but there wasn't any food in her pack, and she wasn't about to complain to him. She dropped her head back to her knees and tried to seek refuge in a nap; at least then she could forget how miserable she was.

She actually managed to sleep, and he woke her at twilight, shaking her shoulder. "Let's go," he said, pulling her to her feet. Jane's heart stopped because just for that moment his touch was strong but gentle, and she had the crazy hope that he'd cooled down and come to his senses while she was napping. But then he dropped her arm and stepped away from her, his face hard, and the hope died.

She followed him like a toy on a string, right in his footsteps, stopping when he stopped, always the same distance behind him. He went boldly into the center of town, walking down the streets as if no one at all was looking for him, let alone a small army. Several people looked at them oddly, but no one stopped them. Jane supposed they did look strange: a tall blond man with a bruised, swollen face and a rifle carried easily in one hand, followed by a woman with wild tangled hair, dirty clothes and a backpack buckled to her belt and swinging against her legs as she walked. Well, everything seemed strange to her, too. She felt as if they'd gotten lost in a video game, with crazy neon images flashing at her. After a moment she realized that the images were real; a street sign advertising a cantina flashed its message in neon pink and blue.

What was he doing? They were attracting so much notice that Turego would have to hear of it if he asked any questions at all. For all Grant knew, Turego could have the local law enforcement looking for them under trumped-up charges; Turego certainly had enough authority to mobilize any number of people in the search. It was as if Grant *wanted* Turego to find them.

He turned down a side street and paused outside a small, dimly lit cantina. "Stay close to me, and keep your mouth shut," he ordered tersely, and entered.

It was hot and smoky in the small bar, and the strong odor of alcohol mixed with sweat permeated the air. Except for the waitress, a harried looking girl, and two sultry prostitutes, there were no other women there. Several men eyed Jane, speculation in their dark eyes, but then they looked at Grant and turned back to their drinks, evidently deciding that she wasn't worth the trouble.

Grant found them space at a small table at the back, deep in the shadows. After a while the waitress made it over to them, and without asking Jane her preference, Grant ordered two tequilas.

Jane stopped the waitress. "Wait—do you have lime juice?" At the young woman's nod, she heaved a sigh of relief. "A glass of lime juice, instead of the tequila, please."

Grant lit a cigarette, cupping his hands around the flame. "Are you on the wagon or something?"

"I don't drink on an empty stomach."

"We'll get something to eat later. This place doesn't run to food."

She waited until their drinks were in front of them before saying anything else to him. "Isn't it dangerous for us to be here? Any of Turego's men could have seen us walking down the street."

His eyes were narrow slits as he stared at her through the blue smoke of his cigarette. "Why should that worry you? Don't you think he'd welcome you back with open arms?"

Jane leaned forward, her own eyes narrowed. "Listen to me. I had to buy time, and I did it the only way I could think of. I'm sorry I didn't have time to explain it to you beforehand, but I don't think Turego would have let me call 'time out' and huddle with you! If he'd tied me up, too, there would have been no way I could help you!"

"Thanks, honey, but I can do without your sort of help," he drawled, touching his left eye, which was puffy and red.

Anger seared her; she was innocent, and she was tired of being treated like Benedict Arnold. She thought of pouring the lime juice in his lap, but her stomach growled and revenge took a distant second place to putting something in her empty stomach, even if it was just fruit juice. She sat back in her chair and sipped, wanting to make the juice last as long as possible.

The minutes crawled by, and Jane began to feel a twitch between her shoulder blades. Every second they sat there increased the danger, gave Turego a better chance of finding them. The abandoned truck wouldn't fool him for long.

A man slipped into the chair beside her and Jane jumped, her heart flying into her throat. He gave her only a cursory glance before turning his attention to Grant. He was a nondescript character, his clothing worn, his face covered by a couple of days' growth of beard, and his smell of stale alcohol made Jane wrinkle her nose. But then he said a few words to Grant, so quietly that she couldn't understand them, and it all clicked into place.

Grant had advertised their presence not because he wanted Turego to find them, but because he wanted someone else to find them. It had been a gamble, but it had paid off. He was no longer in the business, but he was known, and he'd trusted his reputation to pull in a contact. This man was probably just a peripheral character, but he would have his uses.

"I need transport," Grant said. "Within the hour. Can you manage it?"

"*Sì,*" the man said, slowly nodding his head for emphasis.

"Good. Have it sitting behind the Blue Pelican exactly one hour from now. Put the keys under the right seat, get out, and walk away."

The man nodded again. "Good luck, amigo."

That hard, lopsided smile curved Grant's lips. "Thanks. I could use some about now."

The man blended in with the crowd, then was gone. Jane slowly twirled the glass of juice between her palms, keeping her eyes on the table. "Now that you've made your contact, shouldn't we get out of here?"

Grant lifted the tequila to his mouth, his strong throat working as he swallowed the sharp tasting liquid. "We'll wait a while longer."

No, it wouldn't do to follow the other man too closely. George had always told her how important it was to make contact without seeming to. The man had taken a chance by walking up to them so openly, but then, Grant had taken a chance by making himself so available. It had probably been clear that the situation was desperate, though Grant looked as if he was thinking about nothing more important than going to sleep. He was sprawled in his chair, his eyes half-closed, and if Jane hadn't noticed that he kept his left hand on the rifle she would have thought that he was totally relaxed.

"Do you suppose we could find a bathroom?" she asked, keeping her tone light.

"In here? I doubt it."

"Anywhere."

"Okay. Are you finished with that?" He downed the rest of his tequila, and Jane did the same with her lime juice. Her skin was crawling again; she felt that tingling on the back of her neck, and it intensified as she stood up.

They threaded their way through the tangle of feet and tables and chairs to the door, and as soon as they stepped outside Jane said, "I think we were being watched."

"I know we were. That's why we're going in the opposite direction of the Blue Pelican."

"What on earth is the Blue Pelican? How do you know so much about this town? Have you been here before?"

"No, but I keep my eyes open. The Blue Pelican is the first cantina we passed."

Now she remembered. It was the cantina with the flashing neon sign, the one that had given her such an intense feeling of unreality.

They were walking down the small side street into a yawning cave of darkness. The street wasn't paved, and there were no sidewalks, no street lights, not even one of the incongruous neon signs to lend its garish light. The ground was uneven beneath her boots, and the sour smell of old garbage surrounded her. Jane didn't think; her hand shot out, and she grabbed Grant's belt.

He hesitated, then resumed walking without saying anything. Jane swallowed, belatedly realizing that she could have found herself sailing over his shoulder again, as she had the first time she'd grabbed him from behind. What would she do if she no longer had him to cling to in the dark? Stand around wringing her hands? She'd already come a long way from the child who had sat in a terrified stupor for days, and perhaps it was time for one step more. Slowly, deliberately, Jane released her grip on his belt and let her arm drop to her side.

He stopped and looked around at her, darkness shrouding his features. "I don't mind you holding on to my belt."

She remained silent, feeling his reluctant curiosity, but unable to give him any explanation. All her milestones had been inner ones, attained only by wrenching effort, and this wasn't something she could easily talk about. Not even the frighteningly expensive child psychologist to whom her parents had taken her had been able to draw her out about the kidnapping. Everyone knew about the nightmares she'd had, and her abrupt, unreasonable fear of the dark, but she'd never told anyone the details of her experience. Not her parents, not even Chris, and he'd been her best friend long before he'd been her husband. In all the years since the kidnapping, she'd told only one person, trusted only one person enough. Now there was a distance between them that she'd tried to bridge, but he kept pushing her away. No matter how she wanted to throw herself into his arms, she had to stand alone, because soon she might have no choice in the matter.

The fear of being alone in the dark was nothing compared to the fear that she might be alone for the rest of her life.

He wove a crazy path through the town, crisscrossing, backtracking, changing their route so many times that Jane completely lost her sense of direction. She chugged along doggedly, staying right on his heels. He stopped once, and stood guard while Jane sneaked in the back of the local version of a greasy spoon. The plumbing was pre-World War II, the lighting was a single dim bulb hanging from the ceiling, and the carcass of an enormous cockroach lay on its back in the corner, but she wasn't in the mood to quibble. At least the plumbing worked, and when she turned on the water in the cracked basin a thin, lukewarm stream came out. She washed her hands and, bending over, splashed water on her face. There was no towel, so she wiped her hands on her pants and left her face to dry naturally.

When she tiptoed out of the building, Grant stepped from the shadows where he had concealed himself and took her arm. They weren't far from the Blue Pelican, as it turned out; when they turned the corner, she could see the blue and pink sign flashing. But Grant didn't walk straight to it; he circled the entire area, sometimes standing motionless for long minutes while he waited, and watched.

At last they approached the old Ford station wagon that was parked behind the cantina, but even then he was cautious. He raised the hood and used his cigarette lighter to examine the motor. Jane didn't ask what he was looking for, because she had the chilling idea that she knew. He closed the hood as quietly as possible, evidently reassured.

"Get in, and get the keys out from under the seat."

She opened the door. The dome light didn't come on, but that was to be expected. Doing a little checking on her own, she peered over the back of the seat, holding her breath in case there was actually someone there. But the floorboard was empty, and her breath hissed out of her lungs in relief.

Leaning over, she swept her hand under the seat, searching for the keys. The other door opened, and the car swayed under Grant's weight. "Hurry," he snapped.

"I can't find the keys!" Her scrabbling fingers found a lot of dirt, a few screws, a scrap of paper, but no keys. "Maybe this isn't the right car!"

"It'll have to do. Check again."

She got down on the floor and reached as far under the seat as she could, sweeping her hands back and forth. "Nothing. Try under yours."

He leaned down, extending his arm to search under his seat. Swearing softly, he pulled out a single key wired to a small length of wood. Muttering under his breath about damned people not being able to follow simple instructions, he put the key in the ignition and started the car.

Despite its age, the engine was quiet and smooth. Grant shifted into gear and backed out of the alley. He didn't turn on the headlights until they were well away from the Blue Pelican and the well-lit main street.

Jane leaned back in the musty smelling seat, unable to believe that at last they seemed to be well on their way. So much had happened since that morning that she'd lost her sense of time. It couldn't be late; it was probably about ten o'clock, if that. She watched the road for a while, hypnotized by the way it unwound just ahead of the reach of their headlights, tired but unable to sleep. "Are we still going to Limon?"

"Why? Is that what you told your lover?"

Jane sat very still, clenching her teeth against the anger that shook her. All right, she'd try one more time. "He isn't my lover, and I didn't tell him anything. All I was trying to do was to stay untied until I could catch one of them off guard and get his gun." She spat the words out evenly, but her chest was heaving as she tried to control her anger. "Just how do you think I got the pistol that you took away from me?"

She felt that was a point that he couldn't ignore, but he did, shrugging it away. "Look, you don't have to keep making explanations," he said in a bored tone. "I'm not interested—"

"Stop the car!" she shouted, enraged.

"Don't start pitching one of your fits," he warned, slanting her a hard look.

Jane dived for the steering wheel, too angry to care if she caused them to crash. He pushed her off with one hand, cursing, but Jane ducked under his arm and caught the wheel, wrenching it violently toward her. Grant hit the brake, fighting to keep the car under control with one hand while he held Jane off with the other. She caught the wheel again and pulled it, and the car jolted violently as it hit the shoulder of the road.

Grant let go of her and wrestled with the car as it slewed back and forth on the narrow road. He braked sharply, finally bringing the car to a complete halt so he could give his full attention to Jane, but even before the car had completely stopped she threw the door open and jumped out. "I'll get myself out of Costa Rica!" she yelled, slamming the door.

He got out of the car. "Jane, come back here," he warned as she started walking off.

"I'm not going another mile with you, not another *inch*!"

"You're going if I have to hog-tie you," he said, coming after her, his stride measured.

She didn't stop. "That's your remedy for everything, isn't it?" she sneered.

Without warning, he sprinted. He moved so fast that Jane didn't have time to run. She gave a startled cry, twisting away as he reached her; his outstretched hand caught her blouse and Jane jerked as he stopped her. It was doubly infuriating to find herself so easily caught, and with a fresh burst of rage she threw herself away from him, twisting and doubling her lithe body, trying to break his grip.

He caught her wildly flailing arm and pinned it to her side. "Damn, woman, why do you have to do everything the hard way?" he panted.

"Let...*go*!" she shouted, but he wrapped his arms around her, holding her arms pinned down. She kicked and shrieked, but he was too strong; there was nothing she could do as he carried her back to the car.

But he had to release her with one arm so he could open the car door, and when he did she twisted violently, at the same time lifting her feet. The combination of the twist and the sudden addition of weight broke his grip, and she slid under his arm. He grabbed for her again, his fingers hooking in the low neckline of the blouse. The fabric parted under the strain, tearing away from her shoulders.

Tears spurted from Jane's eyes as she scrambled to cover her breasts, holding the ruined cloth over them. "Now look what you've done!" Turning away from him, she burst into sobs, her shoulders shaking.

The raw, hard sobs that tore from her throat were so violent that he dropped his outstretched arms. Wearily he rubbed his face. Why couldn't she cry with sedate little sniffles, instead of these sobs that sounded as if she had been beaten? Despite everything that had happened, he wanted to take her in his arms and hold her head to his chest, stroke her dark hair and whisper that everything was going to be all right.

She whirled on him, wiping her face with one hand and clutching the ruined blouse to her breasts with the other. "Think about a few things!" she said hoarsely. "Think about how I got that pistol. And think about Turego. Remember when he came up behind you with the rifle, and I warned you? Did you notice, before you shot him, that his face was bloody? Do you remember the way his nose was bleeding? Do you think it was the altitude that made his nose bleed? You big, stupid, boneheaded *jackass*!" she bellowed, so beside herself with fury that she was shaking her fist under his nose. "Damn it, can't you tell that I love you?"

Grant was as still as stone, not a muscle moving in his face, but he felt winded, as if he'd just taken a huge blow in the chest. Everything hit him at once, and he staggered under the weight of it. She was right. Turego's face had been bloody, but he hadn't thought anything about it at the time. He'd been so damned angry and jealous that he hadn't been thinking at all, only reacting to what had looked like betrayal. Not only had she done some quick thinking to avoid being tied up, she'd charged to his rescue as soon as she could, and when he remembered the way she'd looked when she came through that door, so white and wild—Turego's goons were probably lucky that he'd gotten free first. *She loved him!* He stared down at her, at the small fist that was waving dangerously close to his nose. She was utterly magnificent, her hair a wild tangle around her shoulders, her face filled with a temper that burned out of control, yelling at him like some banshee. She clutched that ridiculous scrap of cloth to her breasts with the hand that wasn't threatening his profile. Indomitable. Courageous. Maddening. And so damned desirable that he was suddenly shaking with need.

He caught her fist and jerked her to him, holding her to him so tightly that she gasped, his face buried against her hair.

She was still struggling against him, beating at his back with her fists and crying again. "Let me go! Please, just let me go."

"I can't," he whispered, and caught her chin, turning her face up to him. Fiercely he ground his mouth down on hers and, like a cornered cat, she tried to bite him. He jerked his head back, laughing, a wild joy running through him. The torn blouse had fallen away, and her naked breasts were flattened against him, their soft fullness reminding him of how good it felt when she wasn't fighting him. He kissed her again, roughly, and cupped her breast in his palm, rubbing his thumb over the velvet nipple and making it tighten.

Jane whimpered under the onslaught of his mouth, but her temper had worn itself out, and she softened against him, suddenly aware that she'd gotten through to him. She wanted to hold on to her anger, but she couldn't hold a grudge. All she could do was kiss him back, her arms sliding up to lock around his neck. His hand burned her breast, his thumb exciting her acutely sensitive skin and beginning to tighten the coil of desire deep in her loins. He had no need to hold her still for his kisses now, so he put his other hand on her bottom and urged her against him, demonstrating graphically that she wasn't the only one affected.

He lifted his mouth from hers, pressing his lips to her forehead. "I swear, that temper of yours is something," he whispered. "Do you forgive me?"

That was a silly question; what was she supposed to say, considering that she was hanging around his neck like a Christmas ornament? "No," she said, rubbing her face into the hollow of his throat, seeking his warm, heady male scent. "I'm going to save this to throw up at you the next time we have a fight." She wanted to say "for the rest of our lives," but though his arms were hard around her, he hadn't yet said that he loved her. She wasn't going to dig for the words, knowing that he might not be able to say them and mean it.

"You will, too," he said, and laughed. Reluctantly his arms loosened, and he reached up, removing her arms from his neck. "I'd like to stay like this, but we need to get to Limon." He looked down at her breasts, and a taut look came over his battered face. "When this is over with, I'm going to take you to a hotel and keep you in bed until neither of us can walk."

They got back in the car, and Jane removed the remnants of the blouse, stuffing it in the backpack and pulling on Grant's camouflage shirt that she'd put in the pack that morning. It would have wrapped around her twice, and the shoulder seams hung almost to her elbows. She rolled the sleeves up as far as they would go, then gathered the long tails and tied them at her waist. Definitely not high fashion, she thought, but she was covered.

The Ford rolled into Limon in the early hours of the morning, and though the streets were nearly deserted, it was obvious that the port was a well-populated city of medium size. Jane's hands clenched on the car seat. Were they safe, then? Had Turego been fooled by the abandoned truck?

"What now?"

"Now I try to get in touch with someone who can get us out tonight. I don't want to wait until morning."

So he thought Turego's men were too close for safety. Was it never going to end? She wished they had remained in the jungle, hidden so deeply in the rain forest that no one would ever have found them.

Evidently Grant had been in Limon before; he negotiated the streets with ease. He drove to the train station, and Jane gave him a puzzled look. "Are we going to take the train?"

"No, but there's a telephone here. Come on."

Limon wasn't an isolated jungle village, or even a tiny town at the edge of the forest; it was a city, with all of the rules of a city. He had to leave the rifle in the back of the station wagon, but he stuck the pistol into his boot. Even without his being obviously armed, Jane thought there was no chance at all of them going anywhere without being noticed. They both looked as if they'd come fresh from a battle, which, in effect, they had. The ticket agent eyed them with sharp curiosity, but Grant ignored him, heading straight for a telephone. He called someone named Angel, and his voice was sharp as he demanded a number. Hanging up, he fed more coins into the slot, then dialed another number.

"Who are you calling?" Jane whispered.

"An old friend."

The old friend's name was Vincente, and intense satisfaction was on Grant's face when he hung up. "They're pulling us out of here. In another hour we'll be home free."

"Who's 'they'?" Jane asked.

"Don't ask too many questions."

She scowled at him, then something else took her attention. "While we're here, could we clean up a little? You look awful."

There was a public bathroom—empty, she was thankful to see—and Grant washed his face while Jane brushed her hair out and quickly pulled it back into a loose braid. Then she wet a towel and painstakingly cleaned the wound on Grant's arm; the bullet hadn't penetrated, but the graze was deep and ugly. After washing it with a strong smelling soap, she produced a small first-aid kit from her backpack.

"One of these days I'm going to see what all's in that thing," Grant growled.

Jane uncapped a small bottle of alcohol and poured it on the graze. He caught a sharp breath, and said something extremely explicit. "Don't be such a baby," Jane scolded. "You didn't make this much fuss when you were shot."

She smeared an antibiotic cream on the wound, then wrapped gauze snugly around his arm and tied the ends together. After replacing the kit, she made certain the pack was still securely buckled to her belt-loop.

Grant opened the door, then abruptly stepped back and closed it again. Jane had been right behind him, and the impact of their bodies made her stagger. He caught her arm, keeping her from falling. "Turego and a few of his men just came into the station." He looked around, his eyes narrowed and alert. "We'll go out a window."

Her heart pounding, Jane stared in dismay at the row of small, high windows that lined the restroom. They were well over her head. "I can't get up there."

"Sure you can." Grant bent down and grasped her around the knees, lifting her until she could reach the windows. "Open one, and go through it. Quick! We only have a minute."

"But how will you get up—"

"I'll make it! Jane, get through that window!"

She twisted the handle and shoved the window open. Without giving herself time to think about how high above the ground on the other side it might be, she grasped the bottom edge of the frame and hauled herself through, jumping into the darkness and hoping she didn't kill herself on a railroad tie or something. She landed on her hands and knees in loose gravel, and she had to bite back a cry of pain as the gravel cut her palms. Quickly she scrambled out of the way, and a moment later Grant landed beside her.

"Are you all right?" he asked, hauling her to her feet.

"I think so. No broken bones," she reported breathlessly.

He started running along the side of the building, dragging her behind him. They heard a shot behind them, but didn't slow down or look back. Jane stumbled and was saved from falling only by his grip on her hand. "Can't we go back for the Ford?" she wailed.

"No. We'll have to get there on foot."

"Get where?"

"To the pick up point."

"How far is that?"

"Not too far."

"Give it to me in yards and miles!" she demanded

He dodged down a street and pulled her into the deep shadows of an alley. He was laughing. "Maybe a mile," he said, and kissed her, his mouth hard and hungry, his tongue finding hers. He hugged her fiercely.

"Whatever you did to Turego, honey, he looks like hell."

"I think I broke his nose," she admitted.

He laughed again. "I think you did, too. It's swollen all over his face. He won't forget you for a long time!"

"Never, if I have anything to do with it. We're going to tell the government about that man," she vowed.

"Later, honey. Right now, we're getting out of here."

Chapter Twelve

A helicopter came in low and fast, and settled lightly on its runners, looking like a giant mosquito. Grant and Jane ran across the small field, bent low against the wind whipped up by the rotors, which the pilot hadn't cut. Behind them people were pouring out of their houses to see what the uproar was about. Jane began to giggle, lightheaded with the triumph of the moment; by the time Grant boosted her into the helicopter, she was laughing so hard she was crying. They'd done it! Turego couldn't catch them now. They would be out of the country before he could mobilize his own helicopters to search for them, and he wouldn't dare pursue them across the border.

Grant flashed her a grin, telling her that he understood her idiotic laughter. He shouted, "Buckle up!" at her, then levered himself into the seat beside the pilot and gave him the thumbs-up sign. The pilot nodded, grinned, and the helicopter rose into the night. Grant put on the headset that would allow him to talk to the pilot, but there wasn't one in the back. Jane gave up trying to hear what they were saying and gripped the sides of her seat, staring out through the open sides of the helicopter. The night air swirled around her, and the world stretched out beyond the small craft. It was the first time she'd ever been in a helicopter, and it was a totally different sensation from being in a jet. She felt adrift in the velvet darkness, and she wished that it wasn't night, so she could see the land below.

The flight didn't take long, but when they set down, Jane recognized the airport and reached up to grab Grant's shoulder. "We're in San Jose!" she yelled, anxiety filling her voice. This was where it had all begun. Turego had plenty of men in the capitol!

Grant took off the headset. The pilot cut the rotors, and the noise began to decrease. They shook hands, and the pilot said, "Nice to see you again! Word filtered down that you were in the area, and that we should give you any assistance you asked for. Good luck. You'd better run. You have just enough time to get on that flight.''

They jumped to the asphalt and began running toward the terminal. ''What flight is that?'' Jane panted.

''The flight to Mexico City that's leaving in about five minutes.''

Mexico City! That sounded more like it! The thought lent her strength.

The terminal was almost deserted at that time of night, because the flight for Mexico City had already boarded. The ticket clerk stared at them as they approached, reminding Jane once again of how they looked. ''Grant Sullivan and Jane Greer,'' Grant said tersely. ''You're holding our tickets.''

The clerk had regained his composure. ''Yes, sir, and the plane,'' he returned in perfect English, handing over two ticket folders. ''Ernesto will take you directly aboard.''

Ernesto was an airport guard, and he led the way, running. Grant held Jane's hand to make certain she kept up with them. She had a fleeting thought about the pistol stuck in his boot, but they bypassed all checkpoints. Grant certainly had connections, she thought admiringly.

The jet was indeed waiting, and the smiling stewardess welcomed them aboard as calmly as if there was nothing unusual about them. Jane wanted to giggle again; maybe they didn't look as outlandish as she felt they did. After all, camouflage clothing was all the rage in the States. So what if Grant was sporting an almost black eye, a puffy lip and a bandage on his arm? Maybe they looked like journalists who had had a rough time in the field.

As soon as they were seated, the plane began rolling. As they buckled their seat belts, Grant and Jane exchanged glances. It was well and truly over now, but they still had some time together. The next stop was Mexico City, an enormous international city with shops, restaurants...and hotels. Her body longed for a bed, but even deeper than her weariness ran the tingling awareness that Grant would be in that bed with her. He lifted the armrest between their seats and pulled her over so her head nestled into the hollow of his shoulder. ''Soon,'' he murmured against her temple. ''In a couple of hours we'll be in Mexico. Home free.''

''I'm going to call Dad as soon as we get there, so he and

Mom will stop worrying.'' Jane sighed. ''Do you have anyone to call? Does your family know where you were?''

His eyes took on that remote look. ''No, they don't know anything about what I do. I'm not close to my family, not anymore.''

That was sad, but Jane supposed that when someone was in the business Grant had been in, it was safer for his family not to be close to him. She turned her face into his neck and closed her eyes, holding tightly to him in an effort to let him know that he wasn't alone anymore. Had his nights been spent like hers, lying awake in bed, so achingly alone that every nerve in her body cried out against it?

She slept, and Grant did, too, exhaustion finally sweeping over him as he allowed his bruised body to relax. With her in his arms, it was easy to find the necessary relaxation. She nestled against him as trustingly as a child, but he could never forget that she was a woman, as fierce and elemental as wind or fire. She could have been the spoiled debutante he'd expected. It was what she *should* have been, and no one would have thought the less of her for being the product of her environment—no one expected her to be any more than that. But she'd risen above that, and above the crippling trauma of her childhood, to become a woman of strength and humor and passion.

She was a woman in whose arms a wary, battered, burnt-out warrior could sleep.

The sky was turning pearl pink with dawn when they landed in Mexico City. The terminal was teeming with people scurrying to catch early flights, a multitude of languages and accents assailing the air. Grant hailed a cab, which took them on a hair-raising ride through traffic that made every moment an exercise in survival—or it would have been hair-raising if Jane had had the energy to care. After what she'd been through, the Mexico City traffic looked mundane.

The city was beautiful at dawn, with its wide avenues and fragrant trees; and the white of the buildings glowed rosily in the early morning sun. The sky was already a deep blue bowl overhead, and the air carried that velvet feel that only the warmer climes achieved. Despite the odor of exhaust fumes she could smell the sweetness of orange blossoms, and Grant was warm beside her, his strong leg pressed against hers.

The desk clerk in the pristine white, high-rise hotel was reluctant to give them a room without a reservation. His black eyes kept wandering to Grant's bruised face as he rattled off excuses in rapid-fire Spanish. Grant shrugged, reached into his pocket and peeled off a couple of bills from a roll. The clerk suddenly smiled; that changed everything. Grant signed them in, and the clerk slid a key across the desk. After taking a few steps, Grant turned back. "By the way," he said easily, "I don't want any interruptions. If anyone calls or asks, we aren't here. *¿Comprende?* I'm dead tired, and I get irritable if I'm jerked out of a sound sleep."

His voice was full of silky, lazy menace, and the clerk nodded rapidly.

With Grant's arm draped across her shoulders, they walked over to the bank of elevators. He punched the button for the nineteenth floor, and the doors slid silently shut. Jane said dazedly, "We're safe."

"Having trouble believing it?"

"I'm going to get that man. He's not going to get off scot-free!"

"He won't," Grant drawled. "He'll be taken care of, through channels."

"I don't want 'channels' to take care of him! I want to do it myself!"

He smiled down at her. "You're a bloodthirsty little wench, aren't you? I almost think you enjoyed this."

"Only parts of it," she replied, giving him a slow smile.

Their room was spacious, with a terrace for sunning, a separate sitting area with a dining table and a stunningly modern bath. Jane poked her head into it and withdrew with a beatific smile on her face. "All the modern conveniences," she crowed.

Grant was studying the in-house registry for room service. Picking up the phone, he ordered two enormous breakfasts, and Jane's mouth watered at the thought. It had been almost twenty-four hours since they'd eaten. While they were waiting for their food, she began the process of making a phone call to Connecticut. It took about five minutes for the call to go through, and Jane sat with the receiver gripped tightly in her hand, taut with the need to hear her parents' voices.

"Mom? Mom, it's Jane! I'm all right—don't cry, I can't talk to you if you're crying," Jane said, and wiped away a few tears herself. "Put Dad on the line so I can tell him what's going on.

We'll blubber together just as soon as I get home, I promise." She waited a few moments, smiling mistily at Grant, her dark eyes liquid.

"Jane? Is it really you?" Her father's voice boomed across the line.

"Yes, it really is. I'm in Mexico City. Grant got me out; we just flew in a few minutes ago."

Her father made a choked sound, and Jane realized that he was crying, too, but he controlled himself. "Well, what now?" he demanded. "When are you going to be here? Where are you going from there?"

"I don't know," she said, lifting her brows at Grant and taking the receiver from her ear. "Where are we going next?"

He took the phone from her. "This is Sullivan. We'll probably be here for a couple of days, getting some paperwork straightened out. We came in here without being checked for passports, but I'll have to make some calls before we can get into the States. Yes, we're okay. I'll let you know as soon as I find out something."

When he hung up, he turned to find Jane surveying him with pursed lips. "How *did* we get here without being checked for passports?"

"A few people turned their heads, that's all. They knew we were coming through. I'll report our passports as being lost, and get duplicates from the American Embassy. No big deal."

"How did you manage to set all that up so quickly? I know this wasn't the original plan."

"No, but we had some inside help." Sabin had been as good as his word, Grant reflected. All the old contacts had been there, and they had all been notified to give him whatever he needed.

"Your...former business associates?" Jane hazarded a guess.

"The less you know, the better. You pick up on this too damned quickly. Like hot-wiring that truck. Had you ever done it before?"

"No, but I watched you do it the first time," she explained, her eyes full of innocence.

He grunted. "Don't waste your time giving me that wide-eyed look."

A tap on the door and a singsong voice announced that room service had arrived in record time. Grant checked through the fish-eye viewer, then unbolted the door and let the young boy in. The aroma of hot coffee filled the room, and Jane's mouth started watering. She hovered over the boy as he set the food out on the table.

"Look at this," she crooned. "Fresh oranges and melon. Toast. Apricot Danish. Eggs. Butter. Real coffee!"

"You're drooling," Grant teased, giving the boy a generous tip, but he was just as ravenous, and between them they destroyed the array of food. Every crumb was gone and the pot of coffee was empty before they looked at each other and smiled.

"I feel almost human again," Jane sighed. "Now for a hot shower!"

She began unlacing her boots, pulling them off and sighing in relief as she wiggled her toes. Glancing at him, she saw that he was watching her with that lopsided smile that she loved so much. Her heart kicked into time and a half rhythm. "Aren't you going to shower with me?" she asked innocently, sauntering into the bathroom.

She was already under the deliciously warm spray of water, her head tilted up so it hit her directly in the face, when the shower door slid open and he joined her. She turned, wiping the moisture from her eyes, a smile ready on her lips, but the smile faded when she saw the mottled bruises on his ribcage and abdomen. "Oh, Grant," she whispered, reaching out to run her fingers lightly over the dark, ugly splotches. "I'm so sorry."

He gave her a quizzical look. He was sore and stiff, but nothing was broken and the bruises would fade. He'd suffered much worse than this, many times. Of course, if Turego had been able to carry the beating as far as he'd wanted, Grant knew that he probably would have died of internal injuries. But it hadn't happened, so he didn't worry about it. He caught her chin, turning her face up to him. "We're both covered with bruises, honey, in case you haven't noticed. I'm okay." He covered her mouth with his, tasting her sweetness with his tongue, easing her against him.

Their wet, naked bodies created a marvelous friction against each other, heating them, tightening the coil of desire. The rather boring process of soaping and rinsing became a lingering series of strokes, her hands slipping over the muscles and intriguing hardness of his body, his finding the soft curves and slopes of hers, the enticing depths. He lifted her off her feet and bent her back over his arm, kissing her breasts and sucking at her nipples until they were hard and reddened, tasting the freshness of newly soaped skin and the sweetness of her flesh that no soap could ever disguise. Jane writhed against him, her legs twining with his, and heat fogged his mind as he thrust himself against the juncture of her thighs.

She wanted him, wanted him, wanted him. Her body ached and burned. The bed was suddenly too far away. Her legs parted, lifting to wrap around his waist, and with a hoarse cry he pinned her to the wall. She shuddered as he drove into her, going as deep as he could with a single, powerful thrust, as if any distance at all between them was far too much. Digging his fingers into her hair, he pulled her head back and kissed her, his mouth wild and rough, the kiss deep, his tongue twining with hers, the water beating down on them. The power of his thrusts made her consciousness dim, but she clung to him, whimpering, begging him not to stop. He couldn't have stopped, couldn't even have slowed, his body demanding release inside her. The red mists that clouded his mind blocked out everything but the hot ecstasy of the way her body sheathed him, so softly, so tightly.

She cried out again and again as the almost unbearable waves of pleasure crashed over her. She clung tightly to his shoulders, trembling and shivering, the velvet clasp of her body driving him to the edge. He poured himself into her, heaving against her, feeling that he was dying a little, and yet so intensely alive that he almost screamed from the conflict.

They barely made it to the bed. Drying off had taken all their energy, and Jane was so weak she could barely walk. Grant was shaking in every muscle of his big body. They tumbled onto the bed, not caring that their wet hair soaked the pillows.

Grant reached out for her. "Crawl up here," he rumbled, hauling her on top of him. Blissfully, her eyes closing, she made herself comfortable on the hard expanse of his chest. He adjusted her legs, parting them, and her lashes fluttered open as he eased into her. A purr of pleasure escaped her lips, but she was so sleepy, so tired… "Now we can sleep," he said, his lips moving on her hair.

The room was hot when they awoke, the Mexican sun broiling through the closed curtains. Their skin was stuck together with perspiration and made a wet, sucking noise as Grant lifted her off him. He got up and turned the air-conditioning on full blast, and stood for a moment with the cold air hitting his naked body. Then he came back to the bed and turned her onto her back.

They scarcely left the bed that day. They made love, napped and woke to make love again. She couldn't get enough of him, nor he, it seemed, of her. There was no sense of urgency now to their lovemaking, only a deep reluctance to be parted from each other. He taught her the unlimited reaches of her own sensuality, tasting her all over, making love to her with his mouth until she was shivering and shuddering with pleasure, mindless, helpless. She told him that she loved him. She couldn't keep the words unsaid, not now, when she'd already told him anyway and soon the world would intrude on them again.

Night came, and finally they left the room. Walking hand in hand in the warm Mexican night, they sought out some shops that were open late. Jane bought a pink sundress that made her tanned skin look like honey, a pair of sandals and new underwear. Grant wasn't much on shopping, so she blithely picked out jeans, loafers and a white polo shirt for him. "You might as well change," she instructed, pushing him toward the dressing room. "We're going out to eat tonight."

There wasn't any talking her out of it, either. It wasn't until he was seated across from her in a dimly lit restaurant with a bottle of wine between them that he realized this was the first time in years that he'd been with a woman in a strictly social setting. They had nothing to do but eat and talk, sip the wine, and think about what they were going to do when they got back to the hotel. Even after he'd retired, he'd kept to himself on the farm, sometimes going for weeks without seeing another human being. When the need for supplies had forced him to go into town, he'd gone straight there and back, a lot of times without speaking to anyone. He hadn't been able to stand anyone else around him. But now he was relaxed, not even thinking about the strangers surrounding him, accepting their presence but not noticing them, because his mind and his senses were on Jane.

She was radiant, incandescent with energy. Her dark eyes shone; her tanned skin glowed; her laughter sparkled. Her breasts thrust against the bodice of the sundress, her nipples puckered by the coolness of the restaurant, and desire began to stir inside him again. They didn't have much more time together; soon they would be back in the States, and his job would be finished. It was too soon, far too soon. He hadn't had his fill yet of the taste of her, the wild sweetness of her body beneath him, or the way her laughter somehow eased all the knots of tension inside him.

They went back to the hotel, and back to bed. He made love to her furiously, trying to sate himself, trying to hoard enough memories to hold him during the long, empty years ahead. Being alone was a habit deeply ingrained in him; he wanted her, but couldn't see taking her back to the farm with him, and there was no way he could fit into her world. She liked having people around her, while he was more comfortable with a wall at his back. She was outgoing, while he was controlled, secretive.

She knew, too, that it was almost over. Lying on his chest, with the darkness wrapped around them like a blanket, she talked. It was a gift that she gave him, the tales of her childhood, where she'd gone to school, her food and music preferences, what she liked to read. Because she talked, he found it easier to return the favor, his voice low and rusty as he told her about the white-haired young boy he'd been, his skin burned dark by the hot, south Georgia summers, running wild in the swamp. He'd learned to hunt and fish almost as soon as he'd learned how to walk. He told her about playing football during high school, chasing after the cheerleaders, getting drunk and raising hell, then trying to sneak into the house so his mother wouldn't catch him.

Her fingers played in the hair on his chest, aware that silence had fallen because he'd reached the point in his story where his life had changed. There were no more easy tales of growing up.

"Then what happened?" she whispered.

His chest rose and fell. "Vietnam happened. I was drafted when I was eighteen. I was too damned good at sneaking through jungles, so that's where they put me. I went home, once, for R & R, but the folks were just the same as always, while I was nothing like what I had been. We couldn't even talk to each other. So I went back."

"And stayed?"

"Yeah. I stayed." His voice was flat.

"How did you get into the secret agent business, or whatever you call it?"

"Covert activities. High risk missions. The war ended, and I came home, but there was nothing for me to do. What was I going to do, work in a grocery store, when I'd been trained to such an edge that people would be taking their lives in their hands to walk up to me and ask the price of eggs? I guess I'd have settled down eventually, but I didn't want to hang around to find out. I was embarrassing the folks, and I was a stranger to them anyway. When an old colleague contacted me, I took him up on his offer.''

''But you're retired now. Did you go back to Georgia?''

''Just for a few days, to let them know where I'd be. I couldn't settle there; too many people knew me, and I wanted to be left alone. So I bought a farm close to the mountains in Tennessee, and I've been hibernating there ever since. Until your dad hired me to fetch you home.''

''Have you ever married? Been engaged?''

''No,'' he said, and kissed her. ''That's enough questions. Go to sleep.''

''Grant?''

''Hmmm?''

''Do you think he's really given up?''

''Who?''

''Turego.''

Amusement laced his voice. ''Honey, I promise you, he'll be taken care of. Don't worry about it. Now that you're safe and sound, steps can be taken to neutralize him.''

''You're using some ominous sounding phrases. What do 'taken care of' and 'neutralize' mean?''

''That he's going to be spending some time in those gracious Central American jails that everyone hears so much about. Go to sleep.''

She obeyed, her lips curved in a contented smile, his arms securely around her.

Someone had pulled strings again. It could have been her father, or the mysterious ''friend'' of Grant's who kept arranging things, or possibly Grant had intimidated someone at the embassy. However it happened, the next afternoon they had passports. They could have taken the next flight to Dallas, but instead they spent another night together, making love in that king-size bed, the door securely bolted. She didn't want to leave. As long as they were still in Mexico City, she could pretend that it wasn't over, that the job wasn't finished. But her parents were waiting for her, and Grant had his own life to go back to. She had to find another job, as well as take care of the little chore that had gotten her into so much trouble to begin with. There was no way they could stay in Mexico.

Still, tears burned the back of her eyes when they boarded the jet that would take them to Dallas. She knew that Grant had booked separate flights for them from Dallas; she was going on to New York, and he was flying to Knoxville. Their goodbyes would be said in the vast, busy Dallas-Ft. Worth airport, and she couldn't stand it. If she didn't get a tight hold on herself she'd be squalling like a baby, and he wouldn't want that. If he wanted more of her than what he'd already had, he'd have asked her, because she'd made it more than obvious that she was willing to give him whatever he wanted. But he hadn't asked, so he didn't want her. She'd known that this time would come, and she'd accepted it, taken the risk, grabbed for what happiness she could get. Pay up time had come.

She controlled her tears. She read the airline magazine; and was even able to comprehend what she was reading. For a while she held his hand, but she released it when the in-flight meal was served. She ordered a gin and tonic, gulped it down, then ordered another.

Grant eyed her narrowly, but she gave him a bright, glittering smile, determined not to let him see that she was shattering on the inside.

Too soon, far too soon, they landed at Dallas and filed out of the plane through the portable tunnel. Jane clutched the dirty, battered backpack, for the first time realizing that his boots and fatigues were in it along with her clothing. "I need your address," she chattered brightly, nervously. "To mail your clothes to you. Unless you want to buy a bag in the airport shop, that is. We have plenty of time before our flights."

He checked his watch. "You have twenty-eight minutes, so we'd better find your gate. Do you have your ticket?"

"Yes, it's right here. What about your clothes?"

"I'll be in touch with your father. Don't worry about it."

Yes, of course; there was the matter of payment for dragging her out of Costa Rica. His face was hard and expressionless, his amber eyes cool. She held out her hand, not noticing how it was shaking. "Well, goodbye, then. It's—" She broke off. What could she say? *It's been nice meeting you?* She swallowed. "It's been fun."

He looked down at her extended hand, then back up at her,

disbelief edging into the coolness of his eyes. He said slowly, "The hell you say," caught her hand, and jerked her into his arms. His mouth was hot, covering hers, his tongue curling slowly into her mouth as if they weren't surrounded by curiously gawking people. She clung to him, shaking.

He set her away from him. His jaw was clenched. "Go on. Your folks are waiting for you. I'll be in touch in a few days." The last slipped out; he'd intended this to be the final break, but her dark eyes were so lost and full of pain, and she'd kissed him so hungrily, that he couldn't stop the words. One more time, then. He'd give himself one more time with her.

She nodded, drawing herself up. She wasn't going to break down and cry all over him. He almost wished she would cry, because then he'd have an excuse to hold her again. But she was stronger than that. "Goodbye," she said, then turned and walked away from him.

She barely saw where she was going; people blurred in her vision, and she stubbornly blinked her eyes to keep the tears back. Well, she was alone again. He'd said he'd be in touch, but she knew he wouldn't. It was over. She had to accept that and be grateful for the time she'd had. It had been obvious from the first that Grant Sullivan wasn't a man to be tied down.

Someone touched her arm, the touch warm and strong, a man's touch. She stopped, wild hope springing into her breast, but when she turned she found that it wasn't Grant who had stopped her. The man had dark hair and eyes, and his skin was dark, his features strongly Latin. "Jane Greer?" he asked politely.

She nodded, wondering how he'd known her name and recognized her. His grip tightened on her arm. "Would you please come with me," he said, and though his voice remained polite, it was an order, not a question.

Alarm skittered through her, jerking her out of her misery. She smiled at the man and swung the backpack by its straps, catching him on the side of the head with it and sending him staggering. From the solid 'thunk' it made, she knew Grant's boots had hit him.

"Grant!" she screamed, her voice slicing through the bustle of thousands of people. *"Grant!"*

The man caught himself and lunged for her. Jane began running back in the direction she'd come from, dodging around people. Up ahead she saw Grant coming through the crowd like a running back, shoving people out of his path. The man caught up with her, catching her arm; then Grant was there. People were screaming and scattering, and the airport guards were running toward them. Grant sent the man sprawling, then grabbed Jane's arm and ran for the nearest exit, ducking past the milling crowds and ignoring the shouts to stop.

"What the hell's going on?" he roared, jerking her out into the bright Texas sunlight. The humid heat settled over them.

"I don't know! That man just came up to me and asked if my name was Jane Greer; then he caught my arm and told me to come with him, so I hit him in the head with the backpack and started screaming."

"Makes perfect sense to me," he muttered, flagging a cab and putting her in it, then crawling in beside her.

"Where to, folks?" the cab driver asked.

"Downtown."

"Any particular place downtown?"

"I'll tell you where to stop."

The driver shrugged. As they pulled away from the curb there seemed to be a lot of people spilling out of the terminal, but Jane didn't look back. She was still shaking. "It can't be Turego again, can it?"

Grant shrugged. "It's possible, if he has enough money. I'm going to make a phone call."

She'd thought she was safe, that they were both safe. After the two peaceful days spent in Mexico, the sudden fear seemed that much sharper and more acrid. She couldn't stop trembling.

They didn't go all the way into Dallas. Grant instructed the driver to drop them at a shopping mall. "Why a shopping mall?" Jane asked, looking around.

"There are telephones here, and it's safer than standing in a phone booth on the side of a street." He put his arm around her and hugged her briefly to him. "Don't look so worried, honey."

They went inside and found a bank of pay telephones, but it was a busy day and all the lines were in use. They waited while a teenager argued extensively with her mother about how late she could stay out that night, but at last she hung up and stormed away, evidently having lost the argument. Grant stepped in and commandeered the telephone before anyone else could reach it. Standing close by him, Jane watched as he dropped in the coins, punched in a number, then dropped in more coins. He leaned casually against the fieldstone nook that housed the telephone, listening to the rings on the other end.

"Sullivan," he finally drawled when the phone was answered. "She was nearly grabbed in DFW." He listened a moment; then his eyes flicked to Jane. "Okay, I got it. We'll be there. By the way, that was a dumb move. She could've killed the guy." He hung up, and his lips twitched.

"Well?" Jane demanded.

"You just belted an agent."

"An agent? You mean, one of your friend's men?"

"Yeah. We're taking a little detour. You're going to be debriefed. It was left up to some other people to pick you up, and they decided to pick you up after we'd parted company, since I'm no longer in the business and this doesn't officially concern me. Sabin will pin their ears back."

"Sabin? Is he your friend?"

He was smiling down at her. "He's the one." He stroked her cheekbone very gently with the backs of his fingers. "And that's a name you're going to forget, honey. Why don't you call your parents and let them know that you won't be in tonight? It'll be tomorrow; you can call them again when we know something definite."

"Are you going, too?"

"I wouldn't miss it." He grinned a little wolfishly, already anticipating Kell's reaction to Jane.

"But where are we going?"

"Virginia, but don't tell your parents that. Just tell them that you missed your flight."

She reached for the phone, then stopped. "Your friend must be pretty important."

"He's got some power," Grant understated.

So, they must know about the microfilm. Jane punched in her credit card number. She'd be glad to get the whole thing over with, and at least Grant was going to be with her one more day. Just one more day! It was a reprieve, but she didn't know if she'd have the strength for another good-bye.

Chapter Thirteen

The Virginia countryside around the place was quiet and serene, the trees green, the flowering shrubs well-tended. It looked rather like her father's Connecticut estate. Everyone was polite, and several people greeted Grant, but Jane noticed that even the ones who spoke to him did so hesitantly, as if they were a little wary of him.

Kell's office was right where it had always been, and the door still had no name on it. The agent who had escorted them knocked quietly. "Sullivan is here, sir."

"Send them in."

The first thing Jane noticed was the old-fashioned charm of the room. The ceilings were high; the mantel was surely the original one that had been built with the house over a hundred years before. Tall glass doors behind the big desk let in the late afternoon sun. They also placed the man behind the desk in silhouette, while anyone who came in the door was spotlighted by the blazing sun, something George had told her about. He rose to his feet as they entered, a tall man, maybe not quite as tall as Grant, but lean and hard with a whipcord toughness that wasn't maintained by sitting behind a desk.

He stepped forward to greet them. "You look like hell, Sullivan," he said, and the two men shook hands; then he turned his eyes on her, and for the first time Jane felt his power. His eyes were so black that there was no light in them at all; they absorbed light, drawing it into the depths of the irises. His hair was thick and black, his complexion dark, and there was an intense energy about him that seared her.

"Ms. Greer," he said, holding out his hand.

"Mr. Sabin," she returned, calmly shaking his hand.

"I have a very embarrassed agent in Dallas."

"He shouldn't be," Grant drawled behind her. "She let him off easy."

"Grant's boots were in the pack," Jane explained. "That's what stunned him so badly when I hit him in the head."

There was the first hint in Sabin's eyes that Jane wasn't quite what he'd expected. Grant stood behind her, his arms calmly folded, and waited.

Sabin examined her open expression, the catlike slant of her dark eyes, the light dusting of freckles across her cheekbones. Then he quickly glanced at Grant, who was planted like the Rock of Gibraltar behind her. He could question her, but he had the feeling that Grant wouldn't let her be harrassed in any way. It wasn't like Sullivan to get involved, but he was out of the business now, so the old rules didn't apply. She wasn't a great beauty, but there was a lively charm about her that almost made Sabin want to smile. Maybe she'd gotten close to Sullivan. Sabin didn't trust that openness, however, because he knew more about her now than he had in the beginning.

"Ms. Greer," he began slowly, "did you know that George Persall was—"

"Yes, I did," Jane interrupted cheerfully. "I helped him sometimes, but not often, because he liked to use different methods every time. I believe this is what you want." She opened the backpack and began digging in it. "I know it's in here. There!" She produced the small roll of film, placing it on his desk.

Both men looked thunderstruck. "You've just been carrying it around?" Sabin asked in disbelief.

"Well, I didn't have a chance to hide it. Sometimes I put it in my pocket. That way Turego could search my room all he wanted and he'd never find anything. All of you spy types try to make everything too complicated. George always told me to keep it simple."

Grant began to chuckle. He couldn't help it; it was funny. "Jane, why didn't you tell me you had the microfilm?"

"I thought it would be safer for you if you didn't know about it."

Again Sabin looked thunderstruck, as if he couldn't believe anyone would actually feel the need to protect Grant Sullivan. As Kell was normally the most impassive of men, Grant knew that Jane had tilted him off balance, just as she did everyone she met. Sabin coughed to cover his reaction.

"Ms. Greer," he asked cautiously, "do you know what's on the film?"

"No. Neither did George."

Grant was laughing again. "Go ahead," he told Sabin. "Tell her about the film. Or, better yet, show her. She'll enjoy it."

Sabin shook his head, then picked up the film and pulled it out, unwinding it. Grant produced his cigarette lighter, leaned forward, and set the end of the film on fire. The three watched as the flames slowly ate up the length of celluloid until it burned close to Sabin's fingers and he dropped it into a large ashtray. "The film," Sabin explained, "was a copy of something we don't want anyone else to know. All we wanted was for it to be destroyed before anyone saw it."

With the stench of burning plastic in her nostrils, Jane silently watched the last of the film curl and crumble. All they'd wanted was for it to be destroyed, and she'd hauled it through a jungle and across half a continent—just to hand it over and watch it burn. Her lips twitched; she was afraid of making a scene, so she tried to control the urge. But it was irresistible; it rolled upward, and a giggle escaped. She turned, looking at Grant, and between them flashed the memory of everything they'd been through. She giggled again, then they were both laughing, Jane hanging on to his shirt because she was laughing so hard her knees had gone limp.

"I fell down a cliff," she gasped. "We stole a truck...shot another truck...I broke Turego's nose...all to watch it *burn*!"

Grant went into another spasm of laughter, holding his sore ribs and bending double. Sabin watched them clinging to each other and laughing uproariously. Curiosity seized him. "Why did you shoot a truck?" he asked; then suddenly he was laughing, too.

An agent paused outside the door, his head tilted, listening. No, it was impossible. Sabin never laughed.

They lay in bed in a hotel in the middle of Washington, D.C., pleasantly tired. They had made love as soon as the door was locked behind them, falling on the bed and removing only the necessary clothing. But that had been hours before, and now they were completely nude, slipping gradually into sleep.

Grant's hand moved up and down her back in a lazy pattern. "Just how involved were you in Persall's activities?"

"Not very," she murmured. "Oh, I knew about them. I had to know, so I could cover for him if I had to. And he sometimes used me as a courier, but not very often. Still, he talked to me a lot, telling me things. He was a strange, lonely man."

"Was he your lover?"

She lifted her head from his chest, surprised. "George? Of course not!"

"Why 'of course not'? He was a man, wasn't he? And he was in your bedroom when he died."

She paused. "George had a problem, a medical one. He wasn't capable of being anyone's lover."

"So that part of the report was wrong, too."

"Deliberately. He used me as a sort of shield."

He put his hand in her hair and held her for his kiss. "I'm glad. He was too old for you."

Jane watched him with wise, dark eyes. "Even if he hadn't been, I wasn't interested. You might as well know, you're the only lover I've ever had. Until I met you, I'd never...wanted anyone."

"And when you met me...?" he murmured.

"I wanted." She lowered her head and kissed him, wrapping her arms around him, slithering her body over his until she felt his hardening response.

"I wanted, too," he said, his words a mere breath over her skin.

"I love you." The words were a cry of pain, launched by desperation, because she knew this was definitely the last time unless she took the chance. "Will you marry me?"

"Jane, don't."

"Don't what? Tell you that I love you? Or ask you to marry me?" She sat up, moving her legs astride him, and shook her dark hair back behind her shoulders.

"We can't live together," he explained, his eyes turning dark gold. "I can't give you what you need, and you'd be miserable."

"I'll be miserable anyway," she said reasonably, striving for a light tone. "I'd rather be miserable with you than miserable without you."

"I'm a loner. Marriage is a partnership, and I'd rather go it alone. Face it, honey. We're good together in bed, but that's all there is."

"Maybe for you. I love you." Despite herself, she couldn't keep the echo of pain out of her voice.

"Do you? We were under a lot of stress. It's human nature to turn to each other. I'd have been surprised if we hadn't made love."

"Please, spare me your combat psychology! I'm not a child, or stupid! I know when I love someone, and damn it, I love you! You don't have to like it, but don't try to talk me out of it!"

"All right." He lay on his back, looking up into her angry eyes. "Do you want me to get another room?"

"No. This is our last night together, and we're going to spend it *together*."

"Even if we're fighting?"

"Why not?" she dared.

"I don't want to fight," he said, lunging up and twisting. Jane found herself on her back, blinking up at him in astonishment. Slowly he entered her, pushing her legs high. She closed her eyes, excitement spiraling through her. He was right; the time was far better spent making love.

She didn't try again to convince him that they had a future together. She knew from experience just how hardheaded he was; he'd have to figure it out for himself. So she spent her time loving him, trying to make certain that he never forgot her, that no other woman could begin to give him the pleasure that she did. This would be her goodbye.

Late in the night she leaned over him. "You're afraid," she accused softly. "You've seen so much that you're afraid to let yourself love anyone, because you know how easily a world can be wrecked."

His voice was tired. "Jane, let it be."

"All right. That's my last word, except for this: if you decide to take a chance, come get me."

She crept out of bed early the next morning and left him sleeping. She knew that he was too light a sleeper not to have awakened some time during the shower she took, or while she was dressing, but he didn't roll over or in any way indicate that he was awake, so she preserved the pretence between them. Without even kissing him, she slipped out the door. After all, they'd already said their goodbyes.

At the sound of the door closing Grant rolled over in the bed, his eyes bleak as he stared at the empty room.

* * *

Jane and her parents fell into each other's arms, laughing and crying and hugging each other exuberantly. Her return called for a family celebration that lasted hours, so it was late that night before she and her father had any time alone. Jane had few secrets from her father; he was too shrewd, too realistic. By silent, instinctive agreement, they kept from her mother the things that would upset her, but Jane was like her father in that she had an inner toughness.

She told him how the entire situation in Costa Rica had come about, and even told him about the trek through the rain forest. Because he was shrewd, he picked up on the nuances in her voice when she mentioned Grant.

"You're in love with Sullivan, aren't you?"

She nodded, sipping her glass of wine. "You met him. What did you think about him?" The answer was important to her, because she trusted her father's judgment of character.

"I thought him unusual. There's something in his eyes that's almost scary. But I trusted him with my daughter's life, if that tells you what you want to know, and I'd do so again."

"Would you mind having him in the family?"

"I'd welcome him with open arms. I think he could keep you in one place," James said grumpily.

"Well, I asked him to marry me, but he turned me down. I'm going to give him a while to stew over it; then I'm going to fight dirty."

Her father grinned, the quick, cheerful grin that his daughter had inherited. "What are you planning?"

"I'm going to chase that man like he's never been chased before. I think I'll stay here for a week or two; then I'm going to Europe."

"But he's not in Europe!"

"I know. I'll chase him from a distance. The idea is for him to know how much he misses me, and he'll miss me a lot more when he finds out how far away I am."

"But how is he going to find out?"

"I'll arrange that somehow. And even if it doesn't work, a trip to Europe is never a waste!"

It was odd how much he missed her. She'd never been to the farm, but sometimes it seemed haunted by her. He'd think he heard her say something and turn to find no one there. At night...God, the nights were awful! He couldn't sleep, missing her soft weight sprawled on top of him.

He tried to lose himself in hard physical work. Chores piled up fast on a farm, and he'd been gone for two weeks. With the money he'd been paid for finding Jane, he was able to free the farm from debt and still have plenty left over, so he could have hired someone to do the work for him. But the work had been therapy for him when he'd first come here, still weak from his wounds, and so tightly drawn that a pine cone dropping from a tree in the night had been enough to send him diving from the bed, reaching for his knife.

So he labored in the sun, doing the backbreaking work of digging new holes for the fence posts, putting up new sections of fencing, patching and painting the barn. He reroofed the house, worked on the old tractor that had come with the farm; and thought about doing more planting the next spring. All he'd planted so far was a few vegetables for himself, but if he was going to own a farm, he might as well farm it. A man wouldn't get rich at it, not on this scale, but he knew how to do it. Working the earth gave him a measure of peace, as if it put him in contact with the boy he'd once been, before war had changed his life.

In the distance loomed the mountains, the great, misty mountains where the ghosts of the Cherokee still walked. The vast slopes were uninhabited now, but then, only a few hardy souls other than the Cherokee had ever called the mountains home. Jane would like the mountains. They were older, wreathed in silvery veils, once the mightiest mountain range on earth, but worn down by more years than people could imagine. There were places in those mountains where time stood still.

The mountains, and the earth, had healed him, and the process had been so gradual that he hadn't realized he was healed until now. Perhaps the final healing had come when Jane had shown him how to laugh again.

He had told her to let it be, and she had. She had left in the quiet morning, without a word, because he'd told her to go. She loved him; he knew that. He'd pretended that it was something else, the pressure of stress that had brought them together, but even then he'd known better, and so had she.

Well, hell! He missed her so badly that he hurt, and if this wasn't love, then he hoped he never loved anyone, because he didn't think he could stand it. He couldn't get her out of his mind, and her absence was an empty ache that he couldn't fill, couldn't ease.

She'd been right; he was afraid to take the chance, afraid to leave himself open to more hurt. But he was hurting anyway. He'd be a fool if he let her get away.

But first there were old rifts to try to heal.

He loved his parents, and he knew they loved him, but they were simple people, living close to the earth, and he'd turned into someone they didn't recognize. His sister was a pretty, blond woman, content with her job at the local library, her quiet husband, and her three children. It had been a couple of years since he'd even seen his nephew and two nieces. When he'd stopped by the year before to tell his parents that he'd retired and had bought a farm in Tennessee, they'd all been so uncomfortable that he'd stayed for only a few hours, and had left without seeing Rae, or the kids.

So he drove down to Georgia, and stood on the weathered old porch, knocking on the door of the house where he'd grown up. His mother came to the door, wiping her hands on her apron. It was close to noon; as always, as it had been from the time he could remember, she was cooking lunch for his father. But they didn't call it lunch in this part of the country; the noon meal was dinner, and the evening meal was supper.

Surprise lit her honey-brown eyes, the eyes that were so like his, only darker. "Why, son, this is a surprise. What on earth are you knocking for? Why didn't you just come in?"

"I didn't want to get shot," he said honestly.

"Now, you know I don't let your daddy keep a gun in the house. The only gun is that old shotgun, out in the barn. What makes you say a thing like that?" Turning, she went back to the kitchen, and he followed. Everything in the old frame house was familiar, as familiar to him as his own face.

He settled his weight in one of the straight chairs that were grouped around the kitchen table. This was the table he'd eaten at as a boy. "Mama," he said slowly, "I've been shot at so much that I guess I think that's the normal way of things."

She was still for a moment, her head bent; then she resumed making her biscuits. "I know, son. We've always known. But we didn't know how to reach you, how to bring you back to us again. You was still a boy when you left, but you came back a man, and we didn't know how to talk to you."

"There wasn't any talking to me. I was still too raw, too wild. But the farm that I bought, up in Tennessee...it's helped."

He didn't have to elaborate, and he knew it. Grace Sullivan had the simple wisdom of people who lived close to the land. She was a farm girl, had never pretended to be anything else, and he loved her because of it.

"Will you stay for dinner?"

"I'd like to stay for a couple of days, if I won't be messing up any plans."

"Grant Sullivan, you know your daddy and I don't have any *plans* to go off gallivanting anywhere."

She sounded just like she had when he had been five years old and had managed to get his clothes dirty as fast as she could put them on him. He remembered how she'd looked then, her hair dark, her face smooth and young, her honey-gold eyes sparkling at him.

He laughed, because everything was getting better, and his mother glanced at him in surprise. It had been twenty years since she'd heard her son laugh. "That's good," he said cheerfully. "Because it'll take me at least that long to tell you about the woman I'm going to marry."

"What!" She whirled on him, laughing, too. "You're pulling my leg! Are you really going to get married? Tell me about her!"

"Mama, you'll love her," he said. "She's nuts."

He'd never thought that finding her would be so hard. Somehow he'd thought that it would be as simple as calling her father and getting her address from him, but he should have known. With Jane, nothing was ever as it should be.

To begin with, it took him three days to get in touch with her father. Evidently her parents had been out of town, and the housekeeper either hadn't known where Jane was, or she'd been instructed not to give out any information. Considering Jane's circumstances, he thought it was probably the latter. So he cooled his heels for three days until he was finally able to speak to her father, but that wasn't much better.

"She's in Europe," James explained easily enough. "She stayed here for about a week, then took off again."

Grant felt like cursing. ''Where in Europe?''

''I don't really know. She was vague about it. You know Jane.''

He was afraid that he did. ''Has she called?''

''Yes, a couple of times.''

''Mr. Hamilton, I need to talk to her. When she calls again, would you find out where she is and tell her to stay put until I get in touch?''

''That could be a couple of weeks. Jane doesn't call regularly. But if it's urgent, you may know someone who knows exactly where she is. She did mention that she's talked to a friend of yours...let's see, what was his name?''

''Sabin,'' Grant supplied, grinding his teeth in rage.

''Yes, that's it. Sabin. Why don't you give him a call? It may save you a lot of time.''

Grant didn't want to call Kell; he wanted to see him face to face and strangle him. Damn him! If he'd recruited Jane into that gray network...!

He was wasting time and money chasing over the country after her, and his temper was short when he reached Virginia. He didn't have the clearance to go in, so he called Kell directly. ''Sullivan. Clear me through. I'll be there in five minutes.''

''Grant—''

Grant hung up, not wanting to hear it over the phone.

Ten minutes later he was leaning over Kell's desk. ''Where is she?''

''Monte Carlo.''

''Damn it!'' he yelled, pounding his fist on the desk. ''How could you drag her into this?''

''I didn't drag her,'' Kell said coolly, his dark eyes watchful. ''*She* called *me*. She said she'd noticed something funny and thought I might like to know. She was right; I was highly interested.''

''How could she call you? Your number isn't exactly listed.''

''I asked her the same thing. It seems she was standing beside you when you called me from Dallas.''

Grant swore, rubbing his eyes. ''I should have known. I should have been expecting it after she hot-wired that truck. She watched me do it, just once, then did it herself the next time.''

''If it's any consolation, she didn't get it exactly right. She remembered the numbers, but not the right order. She told me I was the fifth call she'd placed.''

''Oh, hell. What kind of situation is she in?''

''A pretty explosive one. She's stumbled across a high rolling counterfeiter. He has some high quality plates of the pound, the franc and several denominations of our currency. He's setting up the deal now. Some of our comrades are very interested.''

''I can imagine. Just what does she think she can do?''

''She's going to try to steal the plates.''

Grant went white. ''And you were going to let her?''

''Damn it, Grant!'' Kell exploded. ''It's not a matter of letting her and you know it! The problem is stopping her without tipping the guy off and sending him so deep underground we can't find him. I've got agents tiptoeing all around her, but the guy thinks he's in love with her, and his buyer has watchdogs sniffing around, and we simply can't snatch her without blowing the whole thing sky high!''

''All right, all right. I'll get her out of it.''

''How?'' Kell demanded.

''I'll get the plates myself, then jerk her out of there and make damned certain she never calls you again!''

''I would deeply appreciate it,'' Kell said. ''What are you going to do with her?''

''Marry her.''

Something lightened in Kell's dark face, and he leaned back in his chair, looping his hands behind his head. ''Well, I'll be damned. Do you know what you're getting into? That woman doesn't think like most people.''

That was a polite way of saying it, but Kell wasn't telling him anything he didn't already know. Within moments of meeting her, Grant had realized that Jane was just a little unorthodox. But he loved her, and she couldn't get into too much trouble on the farm.

''Yeah, I know. By the way, you're invited to the wedding.''

Jane smiled at Felix, her eyes twinkling at him. He was such a funny little guy; she really liked him, despite the fact that he was a counterfeiter and was planning to do something that could really damage her country. He was slightly built, with shy eyes and a faint stutter. He loved to gamble, but had atrocious luck; that is, he'd had atrocious luck until Jane had started sitting beside him. Since then he'd been winning regularly, and he was now devoted to her.

Despite everything she was having fun in Monte Carlo. Grant was being slow coming around, but she hadn't been bored. If she had trouble sleeping, if she sometimes woke to find her cheeks wet, that was something she had to accept. She missed him. It was as if part of herself were gone. Without him there was no one she could trust, no one in whose arms she could rest.

It was a dangerous tightrope she was walking, and the excitement of it helped keep her from settling into depression. The only thing was, how much longer was it going to last? If she saw that Felix was finally going to make up his mind who to sell to, she would be forced to do something—fast—before the plates got into the wrong hands.

Felix was winning again, as he had every night since he'd met Jane. The elegant casino was buzzing, and the chandeliers rivaled in brilliance the diamonds that were roped about necks and dripping from ears. The men in their formal evening wear, the women in their gowns and jewels, casually wagering fortunes on the roll of the dice or the turn of a card, all created an atmosphere that was unequaled anywhere in the world. Jane fit into it easily, slim and graceful in her black silk gown, her shoulders and back bare. Jet earrings dangled to her shoulders, and her hair was piled on top of her head in a careless, becoming twist. She wore no necklace, no bracelets, only the earrings that touched the glowing gold of her skin.

Across the table Bruno was watching them closely. He was becoming impatient with Felix's dithering, and his impatience was likely to force her hand.

Well, why not? She'd really waited as long as she could. If Grant had been interested, he'd have shown up before now.

She stood and bent down to kiss Felix on the forehead. "I'm going back to the hotel," she said, smiling at him. "I have a headache."

He looked up, dismayed. "Are you really ill?"

"It's just a headache. I was on the beach too long today. You don't have to leave; stay and enjoy your game."

He began to look panicky, and she winked at him. "Why don't you see if you can win now without me? Who knows, it may not be me at all."

He brightened, the poor little man, and turned back to his game with renewed fervor. Jane left the casino and hurried back to the hotel, going straight to her room. She always allowed for being followed, because she sensed that she always was. Bruno was a very suspicious man. Swiftly she stripped off her gown, and she was reaching into the closet for a dark pair of pants and a shirt when a hand closed over her mouth and a a muscular arm clamped around her waist.

"Don't scream," a low, faintly raspy voice said in her ear, and her heart jumped. The hand left her mouth, and Jane turned in his arms, burying her face against his neck, breathing in the delicious, familiar male scent of him.

"What are you doing here?" she breathed.

"What do you think I'm doing here?" he asked irritably, but his hands were sliding over her nearly-naked body, reacquainting himself with her flesh. "When I get you home, I just may give you that spanking I've threatened you with a couple of times. I get you away from Turego, and as soon as my back is turned you plunge right back into trouble."

"I'm not in trouble," she snapped.

"You couldn't prove it by me. Get dressed. We're getting out of here."

"I can't! There are some counterfeit plates that I've got to get. My room is being watched, so I was going to climb out the window and work my way around to Felix's room. I have a pretty good idea where he's hidden them."

"And you say you're not in trouble."

"I'm not! But really, Grant, we've got to get those plates."

"I've already got them."

She blinked, her brown eyes owlish. "You do? But…how? I mean, how did you know—never mind. Kell told you, didn't he? Well, where did Felix have them hidden?"

She was enjoying this. He sighed. "Where do you think he had them?"

"In the ceiling. I think he pushed up a square of the ceiling and hid the plates in there. It's really the only good hiding place in the room, and he isn't the type to put them in a safety deposit box in a bank, which is where I'd have put them."

"No, you wouldn't," he said, annoyed. "You'd have put them in the ceiling, just like he did."

She grinned. "I was right!"

"Yes, you were right." And he probably never should have told her. Turning her around, he gave her a pat on the bottom. "Start packing. Your little friend is probably the nervous sort who checks his hidey-hole every night before he goes to bed, and we want to be long gone before he does."

She dragged down her suitcases and started throwing clothes into them. He watched her, sweat popping out on his brow. She looked even better than he remembered, her breasts ripe and round, her legs long and shapely. He hadn't even kissed her. He caught her arm, swinging her around and catching her close to him. "I've missed you," he said, and lowered his mouth to hers.

Her response was instantaneous. She rose on tiptoe, moving against him, her arms coiled around his neck and her fingers deep in his hair. He'd had a haircut, and the dark blond strands slipped through her fingers to fall back in place, shaped perfectly to his head. "I've missed you, too," she whispered when he released her mouth.

His breathing was ragged as he reluctantly let her go. "We'll finish this when we have more time. Jane, would you please put on some clothes?"

She obeyed without question, pulling on green silk trousers and a matching green tunic. "Where are we going?"

"Right now? We're driving to the beach and turning the plates over to an agent. Then we're going to catch a flight to Paris, London and New York."

"Unless, of course, Bruno is waiting just outside the door, and instead we end up sailing across the Mediterranean."

"Bruno isn't waiting outside the door. Would you hurry?"

"I'm finished."

He picked up the suitcases and they went downstairs, where he checked her out. It all went like clockwork. There was no sign of Bruno, or any of the men she had dubbed "Bruno's goons." They turned the plates over to the promised agent and drove to the airport. Jane's heart was thudding with a slow, strong, powerful beat as Grant slipped into the seat beside her and buckled himself in. "You know, you never did actually tell me what you're doing here. You're retired, remember? You're not supposed to be doing things like this."

"Don't play innocent," he advised, giving her a look from molten gold eyes. "I saw your fine hand in this from the beginning. It worked. I came after you. I love you; I'm taking you to

Tennessee; and we're going to be married. But you'd better remember that I'm on to your tricks now, and I know you're too slick for your own good. Did I leave anything out?''

''No,'' Jane said, settling back in her seat. ''I think you have everything covered.''